The Magic Crystals

Antimagic

by

Stephen Hayes

Antimagic
Book 7 in the Magic Crystals series

Written by Stephen Hayes

Published 2022 by Stephen Hayes, Australia

www.StephenHayesOnline.com

ISBN-13: 978-0-6453093-0-0

Contents

Prologue

It has been said to me that the War of the Crystals was short. Vast, certainly, but it all happened in such an incredibly condensed period of time. I don't know—it all felt quite long to me, but perhaps that's something to do with my age. I was only fourteen throughout the whole thing, and for teenagers, time tends to stretch out more than it does for adults. Or maybe it has nothing to do with that, and it only seemed short because most wars of such magnitude happen over several years. Either way, it wasn't short for those of us who had to fight it. Perhaps the best way to figure out which it was would be to summarise the year as it has been for me, John Playman of 16 Lopher Lane, Chopville.

Highlights for January: the summer holidays ended and I, along with my brother Peter, my sister Nicole, and our friends the Thomases (James, Felicity and Jessica), the Maivises (Harry and Simon), Natalie Fletcher and Lisa Pont, had to return to school at Chopville High. I met several people who would become close friends including Marc Moran, Lucien Moran, Tommy Blue, Serena Forgrey and Erica Tyanon. I would start to become closer friends with a few people I had known from previous years such as Katie Knight (Harry's new girlfriend), Sophie Crow (Simon's new girlfriend), and Kylie Cunkourd (James's crush). Most importantly, though, I would have my first ever conversation with Stella Hammerson, one of the Sorcerers (from the bad family, but not bad herself, as it turned out). Oh, and I found out that my English teacher was none other than Mr. Hall, a man who despised many of us for no good reason.

Highlights for February: well, that was when things kicked up. In the first week, Marc and Lucien's father went nuts, stole the magic from the six Sorcerers and called on Fewul, the Beast of Magic, so that he could take over the world. We were only able to stop him with the help of Marc, the Seventh Sorcerer, and Tommy, who could play a magical musical instrument called the Maahoo. The knowledge of how to do this came to me in a dream which I would later learn was actually magical in nature (from something called the Enlightener, an external source I sometimes connected to when I slept). It was also hinted at in a prophecy written more than two thousand years earlier by the first two Sorcerers, Sien and Leoard. Moran did a fair bit of damage while he had magic; not through his own doing, but because the global climate froze over twice during the week. After it was over, the Woodwards (the good Sorcerers), along with Stella, had to go all over the world, fixing everything that had been damaged. Moran was thrown in jail, but was quickly broken out (during an incident in which Tommy was shot and almost killed).

In the second week we went on a school camp to Rock Haulter, only to be followed by Moran, who was commanded by the evil Hammerson Sorcerers to take possession of the Sien-Leoard Crystal—the most powerful of all the Magic Crystals. We beat him to it with the help of Fewul, who Marc was able to call on using the Hero Crystal; and to top it off, we also stole from Moran the Light Crystal, giving us three out of the five Magic Crystals. During the struggle, one of us was required to sacrifice our lives, a sacrifice which Lisa willingly made; but we were then able to resurrect her with magic after we had claimed the crystal. We also resurrected William Playman (my paternal grandfather) and Carl Thomas (James's paternal grandfather), both of whom were killed during the great Sorcerous War.

In the third week, I was given a strange mental test called the Returnamy, which was designed to test my powers of resistance to temptation. What I didn't know until later was that it was recording all my thoughts as they happened, which were then handed over to none other than Arnold Hammerson for examination. While all that was going on, Stella was to turn sixteen, and she requested that we all attend her birthday party. Measures were taken to protect us, but that wasn't enough to prevent Daniel Dasher—a Sorcerous Seer who had fallen in with our group during the Rock Haulter camp—from being killed later in the night, and all because he looked like Marc, who was the real target. It was also at the party that Dorothy Hammerson, Arnold's mother, and more commonly known as Tankom, put an influential charm on Lucien to turn him against us.

In the last week of the month, Lucien implemented a plan to have us all captured by the Hammersons and all the crystals brought into their possession. It mostly failed thanks to the quick magic of Marc and Stella, but Amelia, Peter and I were still captured and taken into captivity in the Hammersons' Basement—a terrible place of pitch-black cells which were magically enchanted to torture their inhabitants at random moments with things like showers of freezing water. That was when Mr. Hall revealed his true colours as a Hammerheart (soldier of the Hammersons) and used his position to capture several more of our friends at school. We were able to escape thanks to Stella, though it did take her a couple of days to find a way to do it without her family being aware of it. During that time, Arnold Hammerson tried (and curiously failed) to kill me, tried (and unfortunately succeeded) to torture me with an agonator (a handheld device capable of thrusting magical and unbearable agony upon a person), and I was able to steal from him the Darkness Crystal, giving us possession of four of the five Magic Crystals. The others were all tortured as well, and in Amelia's case, raped by Ather Hignat and Ugine Wilwog—two school rivals turned bitter enemies—who we now knew they were mixed up with the Hammersons.

Oh, and the week continued, as all that only happened in the first two days. The following day, the Woodwards executed a plan to strip the Hammersons of their magic, giving it to the Fletchers (Natalie, her father Brian, and his mother Alice). I was sent into the Hammersons' lair under cover to watch for when they lost their magic, and the moment it happened, I used the Sien-Leoard Crystal (which would remain in my possession from then until it was eventually lost to Arnold Hammerson) to take the three Hammersons into captivity. I also captured Lucien, Hank Cornish (Arnold's right-hand man) and a female Hammerheart coded 3K17, who I knew little about, but who seemed to be trusted by the Hammersons. I did this last after overhearing them plotting to attack the high school the following day, and although I'd hoped to head it off, I was unsuccessful.

The attack happened the following day, even without the Hammersons there to lead it. Plenty of Chopville High staff were killed in the attack, and many students were captured (although we were able to free them two days later). Sebastian, another who had fallen in with us during the Rock Haulter camp, was able to lead numerous teachers to safety, though doing so enraged Hall; I only just managed to teleport Sebastian to safety before he would have been attacked from behind. We ultimately succeeded in stopping the attack, but at the very end, Lisa was killed for a second time, as were William and Carl, and we found out from Frederic Woodward (Sorcerer and titular head of the Woodward family) that people could only be expected to live for two weeks after being resurrected.

Following that, Arnold and Dorothy, followed by the other prisoners, somehow escaped from the Woodwards' hold. I was sent back into their lair to recapture them if possible, though I was ordered to go without magic of my own (so that it couldn't be stolen if I got into trouble) and had to magically outfit myself before I went. I chose to take Tulip Naval with me, as she had volunteered to assist me in whatever I needed after I had rescued her during the Chopville High battle. The attack went badly, however, and I was lucky to escape with my life—the main distraction coming from the unexpected reappearance of Moran, who we had left for dead on Rock Haulter but who, it turned out, had revived himself with the aid of the Villain Crystal—the last of the five crystals to be accounted for. Tulip was less fortunate, horribly killed by some twisted monster that literally ate her alive.

What Arnold Hammerson tried to do to me in the brief moment he had me captive, prior to killing me, was to remove an enchantment that had been placed upon Stella and me at some point in the past, which caused us to be able to see into each other's minds when we each slept. I had only become aware of it earlier in the week, while Stella had discovered it a few weeks earlier, which was what had prompted her to approach me in the first place. Strangely, though, I still couldn't understand Stella's mind, and due to that (and the fact that she had chosen to return to the Hammerson base with her family, and quite probably aided them in their escape, having been out of her cell just prior to it happening) had caused me to turn away from her. As a result, Stella was excommunicated by the Woodwards, and would wander alone for a while after that.

But the week was still not over: I was to learn from Stella that the Returnamy had identified me as a wanted person by the Hammersons, one whom Arnold had wanted to kill since I was a child. I had no idea why this was, nor did any of the Woodwards or even my parents, although the mind-link with Stella may have had something to do with it. They were only my adoptive parents, however; I knew nothing about my biological family, and it was assumed that whatever had put me on Hammerson's radar pre-dated my adoption, so my goal going forward was to find the man who had given me to the Playmans in the first place: Rafael Smiley.

That wasn't all that happened in February, either. We were teenagers, after all, and teenagers have a lot of hormones that simply cannot be denied, no matter what else is happening. Quite apart from Stella's party, during which Peter hooked up with Kylie and Marc hooked up with Amelia (the latter devastating Nicole, who had been crushing on him as well), James gave up on Kylie and accepted affections from Erica, who had made it clear since the last weekend of January that she was hot for him. Natalie was my crush, but before my eyes at the party I saw Tommy sweep her away from me, even though I had found out during the Rock Haulter camp (thanks to Sebastian reading her diary) that she was interested in me.

Further complicating matters, at the same time I found out that Lena Tuck—yet another person who had fallen in with us during the camp— had developed a keen and frankly mystifying obsession with me. She was difficult to deny because she was one of the most attractive girls I had ever clapped eyes on, but she didn't have whatever X-factor Natalie had that had always drawn her to me. I would also observe hints that Stella liked me, and slightly more than mere hints that Serena too liked me, but the one I would ultimately lose my virginity to in the last few days of February was Tulip. She hadn't even been on my radar at the time, and maybe that had been a factor—or maybe it had simply been that I had been very vulnerable at that moment in the aftermath of the battle, having failed to save Lisa, and also struggling to deal with the knowledge that Tommy had cheated on Natalie with her sister Rebecca, and Natalie had not yet dumped him.

I think that brings us to the end of February. Phiew, maybe a lot really *did* happen in a short space of time, but you can be the judge. Shall we continue?

Highlights for March: not as many as the previous month, mainly thanks to the state of the war. The Hammersons laid low for a while, having been stripped of their magic and needing to put some further preparations in place before they could implement the next stage of their plan. The Woodwards settled in to wait and watch, and to do what they could to stop them in their tracks. Still, a few things did happen, including a second failed attempt to capture Chopville High (far less dramatic than the first had been) and influential charms starting to be placed on government officials in preparation for the Hammersons' takeover of the world. We also found that there was a spy within the Woodward ranks as someone succeeded in stealing the Darkness Crystal and returning it to the Hammersons, meaning that after we had basically set Stella adrift, she had probably been not guilty of assisting her family to escape after all.

The spy did more than just steal one crystal, however. They also fed quite a lot of information to the Hammersons, some of which resulted in the deaths of our friends. Craig Hardy and David Rockson were killed during an ill-fated attempt to block off the Hammerheart Highway (a global network of underground tunnels, traversed by small carts which rocketed around the world in seconds); and Justin Time was exposed and killed while trying to spy for us.

We also learnt quite a lot while trying to track down the mysterious Rafael Smiley. Smiley possessed a strange power which gave him an understanding of things the rest of us could only imagine, and he had gotten it in a strange plane crash—a crash which had likely been caused by Tankom. Tommy, who possessed a magical quirk of his own—two bodies on opposite sides of the planet, which his consciousness switched between whenever he fell asleep in one location—had also been in the plane crash, and had likely acquired his curse at the same time. Smiley could also play the Maahoo and had been Tommy's tutor for a few years before the war, but unfortunately, Tommy was none the wiser as to Smiley's location.

And then there was me. While Marc and I were scouting out the Moran house, in case he was hiding the Villain Crystal there somewhere, we came across evidence that my biological parents had been none other than Marc and Lucien's parents, meaning that I was, in fact, Marc and Lucien's younger brother. This evidence came in the form of a picture of our mother on Moran's wall—a woman whom Moran had supposedly murdered thirteen years earlier, but whom he had brought back as a ghost during the Rock Haulter camp in his efforts to reach the Sien-Leoard Crystal before us. I had found out earlier from something Hank Cornish had said to me while in captivity that she had been my mother, so once Marc confirmed that she was also my mother, the connection was obvious.

Oh, and the other thing that happened to me in March: almost immediately after losing the girl who had taken my virginity to a horrible fate, I entered into my first relationship. Serena was the girl who had been in the right place at the right time to once again, capitalise on my vulnerability—although in our case, rather than going all the way on the first day, we didn't actually do that for another three weeks. It was good, but it came with a couple of regrets on my part: firstly, Natalie became single just four days later, dumping Tommy after catching him cheating yet again, this time with one of Rebecca's friends; and I began to develop feelings for Amelia, likely as a result of our shared experiences while locked up in the Basement. Of all the girls who may have liked me (Natalie, Stella, Lena, Serena), Amelia was the only one who was absolutely off-limits, being in a steady relationship as she was with Marc.

Highlights for April: it had begun with the Woodwards starting to make inroads into identifying the spy, and each time they did, the Hammersons would retaliate by causing devastating natural disasters with the use of the Darkness Crystal. On the 10th, they demonstrated to the world that they were capable of taking control of whatever they wanted, whenever they chose, by assassinating numerous world leaders within the space of a few hours. This was followed by the Hammersons testing nuclear weapons in the Australian desert, once again to prove to the world that they had the power, although they never needed to do so. It had ended, in the last three days, with a global coup which had, by the 3rd of May, destabilised or entirely taken over every country in Asia, Europe, North America and the Pacific, including Australia. They did this mostly through the use of bogglers—handheld devices capable of putting anyone under a spell to make them loyal to the Hammersons—and although there was fighting, the casualties were remarkably low— considerably lower than the natural disasters had been, anyway.

For most of this time, though, I was either safe inside the Woodward Base, or out in the business of hunting for Smiley—with only a few exceptions. At the start of the month, we were able to track Smiley down to his last known location, eventually finding his only living relative— his grandson, a rather conceited nineteen-year old Englishman named Jacob Underwood. When we approached him, he first tried to crack onto Natalie and Amelia, and when that was unsuccessful and he became aware that we were there for his grandfather, he immediately shut us down and refused to help us.

Observing how he had been with the girls, however, I had hatched a plan to seduce him into giving us what we needed, deciding that Lena Tuck would be the best person to do it—assuming she would be willing. She wasn't, at least not when she found out exactly what we wanted from her, but she was prepared to make a deal: she would do what I asked if I would take her virginity. I hadn't even known that she was a virgin until then, but that was her price for helping me. For most guys, it probably would have taken no thought as well, but I had resisted until over a week later, after I'd had an unpleasant argument with Serena about Amelia, who had been going through a rough time emotionally—her experience at the hands of Hignat and Wilwog finally catching up with her.

I knew what needed to be done by the end of the month thanks to Stella, who had been using my mind link to let me know that she was helping us, and using it the same way to find out what we were up to so that she could do just that. She was able to covertly sneak the Darkness Crystal back into our possession after the first time the spy took it from us, and then she went to England to attempt to seduce Underwood herself. She failed, but she was at least able to find out from him that he used a magical device to communicate with his grandfather. So in the last week of the month, immediately prior to the coup, I went with Lena to England; well, Lena went with me hitchhiking in her body, able to take possession of her at will so that I could actually run the operation against Underwood. This was simpler than trying to explain it all to her and then leaving it to fate, and it had the added bonus that without my body there, Lena wouldn't be able to seduce me into cheating on Serena again. The operation was ultimately successful, and other than kissing and some light petting, we were able to steal the 'Life Assistant' without actually having to have sex with him.

Then, at the same time as the coup, a lot of other stuff started going down. Stella joined forces with Moran and Lucien, the latter of whom had run out on the Hammersons after being too scared to defend them when they were attacked mid-month in an operation aimed at recapturing them. (The said operation was successfully executed by Jane Hammer and Darcy Bolter, but the spy released them within days.) The three of them attacked the Hammerheart Base a couple of times and even the Hammerheart Highway (doing what Craig and David had failed to do), then capturing Natalie and Amelia for additional magical protection. I freed them both, but while Natalie immediately teleported into battle against the Hammerhearts executing the coup, Amelia was too traumatised to follow, so she remained at the base.

This was a great stroke of fortune, for she was able to prevent the spy from capturing me, Marc and Tommy—and if we'd been captured, the spy would have reclaimed all the crystals we had, and through this, we finally identified the spy in our midst: Sebastian Williams. It turned out he had been bitter ever since the first Chopville High battle, believing that he didn't get enough recognition or respect from the Woodwards, while the Hammersons gave him just enough to make him feel good about himself. This was a boy who had betrayed no less than five people to their deaths in March and April (not to mention Tulip, who was also killed as a result of his treachery). One of those deaths was Nicole, killed in an attack that had been targeted at me while we had been sleeping in our house on Lopher Lane, a rare treat to be able to go home to the family. Of course, once the coup started I immediately went out and brought all the families into the protection of the Woodward Base, so nothing like that could happen again.

And it didn't quite end there: we also decided to bring Jacob Underwood into protection, but that proved to be more difficult. He had been sleeping over at the home of his fifteen-year old girlfriend Siobhan Zona at the time, and when Marc and I had tried to go in there to get him, her parents had caught them in bed together. Then, because the morning wasn't bad enough already, Hammerhearts showed up and opened fire on the house, wounding Marc and killing everyone in the family except for Siobhan and Underwood themselves, so we had to take her into protection as well as him.

Highlights for May: the Hammerhearts consolidated their hold on the four continents they had taken over during the coup, while the Woodwards essentially sat back and let them do what they needed to do, only able to hinder them in small ways each time. This was an incredible feat given that the Woodwards and Fletchers were Sorcerers, plus we had possession of the Hero, Light and Sien-Leoard Crystals, while the Hammersons only had the Darkness Crystal (and that only for the first few days of the month, as we succeeded in stealing it from them for good). The main advantage the Hammersons had was the years upon years of preparation for this moment, and especially the work they had done in March in light of losing their own magic. They didn't need to be everywhere at once: they only needed all their Hammerhearts utterly loyal to them, doing their bidding unflinchingly wherever they went, and they seemed unstoppable.

For us, the month began with finally communicating with Smiley through the Life Assistant, a handheld device capable of long-distance telepathy, and discovering that he had been hidden since February on Rock Haulter. The magical portals protecting the island, which only opened four times a year, were due to open on May 11, so the time between was spent preparing for our second trip to the Rock. Smiley's only condition for this information was that we had to bring Jacob Underwood with us, which we reluctantly agreed to do. Underwood was as unpleasant as ever and seemed not to appreciate how we had rescued him from certain death when the Hammerhearts caught up with him, though he did have a little justification: Peter and I were able to convince Siobhan to dump his sorry arse by telling her about what he had done with Stella and tried to do with Lena.

We were then distracted for a few days by our parents and other assorted adults seeking to send us back to school. This turned out to be disastrous, for one of the teachers (a man named Devin Hall, apparently related to Dermott Hall) betrayed us to the Hammerhearts. In the attack that followed, which was run by Ather Hignat's father Tom in conjunction with Dermott Hall himself, who had become the Chief of

Police in Australia (and whose main job seemed to be to make life as unpleasant for me and my friends as possible), I was to be brought in, along with Natalie, Amelia, Marc and Tommy, and any of the crystals we possessed; but since Frederic Woodward had foreseen this possible danger, he hadn't allowed any of us to have our crystals with us at school. It meant that other than the magical weapons in our pockets, including agonators, bludginators (knife-like devices which could strike someone over a small distance without physical contact) and solid-outliners (a device which shot thicky prison, a magical substance which would completely immobilise a person), we had no way to defend ourselves. Most unfortunately, the time taken to get ourselves into a position where we could fight back cost Kylie her life.

More death was to come as Stella, under duress after having been recaptured by her father and quickly abandoned by Moran and Lucien when they realised they had no way to defend her, covertly gave us a note which threatened harm to us if we didn't release Sebastian. Mr. Woodward refused, of course, and quickly put a plan in place to take back the Darkness Crystal. The plan was ultimately successful, but it was executed too late: the Darkness Crystal was used to give Mr. Woodward's wife Rachael a massive heart attack, killing her almost instantly and well before Tommy was able to fight off the dark magic with the Light Crystal. We buried Mrs. Woodward and Kylie in the private Woodward cemetery on the morning of the 11th, immediately before several of us set off for Rock Haulter for our meeting with Smiley.

The meeting was most illuminating in many ways. We firstly learned from him how the Great Sorcerous War of the late '70s and early '80s had truly ended, not the publicly known story but the real thing: a humanoid creature from another dimension known as a Honnie stepped into our world and found himself confronted by magic. Scared, he agreed to assist the Woodwards against the Hammersons. He did this by using his Honnie mind, which was capable of holding human minds inside it and manipulating their every thought and feeling. It didn't go entirely the way the Woodwards had planned, for the Honnie chose to take no less than ten thousand captive Hammerhearts back to his own world where they would be slaughtered, but the Woodwards were able to use it to their advantage by convincing the Hammersons that they were behind the disappearance, and that more would come if they didn't back down. It was enough to stop that war in its tracks, though in hindsight, not destroying the Hammersons outright had only set the scene for the war we were in now.

Smiley had then given us a series of recorded memories that he had prepared for us, or someone like us seeking his knowledge and wisdom, which we spent the remainder of our time on the Rock observing. It showed us the beginning and end of the war; the scenario which had led to Stella's birth and Arnold's dislike for her; the plane crash that had given Smiley his magical abilities (which turned out to be that he was four-dimensional, and could move along a fourth dimension to either side, making him impossible for anyone to find him when he did it—he called this being in his 'shadow'); Smiley's second experience with Honnies, where he found out their true nature; a scene showing Moran making a magical pact with Arnold Hammerson not to use the Villain Crystal against him (death to him if he did); and a spell which Hammerson placed upon himself, Tankom and Cornish, making them almost impossible to kill unless it were done by someone using their bare hands.

I had also found out quite a lot about myself while on the Rock. I knew from my first trip there that I could see and communicate with ghosts, but now I found out that the magical quirk had been hereditary and I had gotten it from Moran, though it had skipped Marc and Lucien. It gave me an ability to perceive people in their shadows, and to send my mind along the fourth dimension and even along the time axis to perceive things from the past in that exact location. In this way, I learnt of a prophecy that had identified me as the one with the ability to defeat Arnold Hammerson, and right when he had been about to prevent it from coming true by killing me (what else?), Stella got in the way just enough to cause the magic to spill over onto her. She was a Sorcerer and so couldn't be killed, and her magic had protected me with the side-effect of fusing our minds together. Before Hammerson could undo the damage, however, Moran snatched me up and fled from Rock Haulter, taking his family into hiding.

Moran tracked down Smiley in England and handed me over to him, and it was through him that I was passed to Frederic Woodward and then on to the Playmans—and all this was observed by Charlie Thomas, who had known my origin all along but chosen not to tell anyone in case it tainted my parents' love for me. Months after the handover, however, Moran and his family were captured, and Hammerson took the opportunity to punish them for what they had done. Our mother was executed horribly, and a curse was put on Lucien which would be triggered at some unknown point in the future—the nature of the curse unknown to all except Hammerson himself.

Then, on the day we were due to leave the Rock, I had gone into Stella's mind and observed that Tankom had captured Tommy in Germany, and was threatening him that his other body—the one that was with us—had to come to her. Sure enough, the Australian Tommy wouldn't wake up, as Tankom kept him awake for long hours in Germany, and so we hurried back to the Woodwards to arrange a rescue mission. Strangely, to us anyway, Frederic Woodward decided that as teenagers, we had done quite enough, and a mission of such danger should be handled by adults with more experience.

So instead of rescuing Tommy, I was given the job to go into the prison yard I had constructed using the Sien-Leoard Crystal and make sure all was well with the prisoners. There, I was overpowered and wrested of the crystal in a plot put together by Ather Hignat, who had been captured weeks earlier at school. The crystal was given to Sebastian, who used it to escape with the Hammerhearts from the prison and then from the Woodward Base, and all that while I was magically bound on the floor of someone's bedroom for hours, unable to tell anyone what had happened. By the time Marc came looking for me, the Sien-Leoard Crystal was already on its way to Arnold Hammerson and it was too late to stop it.

While I had been stuck in the prison, the rest of the 'Young Army', as we called ourselves, had put together a plan to defy the adults and rescue Tommy on our own. We did enough to get into the Berlin Base where he was being held, but it all went downhill from there thanks to all the spells put on the place to pick up possible intruders. Jane and Serena were both killed by Tankom, while Natalie and Rebecca were both tortured. A number of us were then locked in cells in yet another Basement, though only for a short time before Marc rescued us. At that point, the operation looked like being a success, as Marc had indeed managed to rescue Tommy, but while I had been in my cell, I'd felt a growing wrath towards Tankom, and I wasn't about to leave the base without doing something about it.

So on the way out, I made a dash away from the others, found Tankom, and killed her. It was a bit more complicated than that, and I did use my bare hands, but there was also magic involved—I'll spare you the gruesome details. Along with several others who had followed me, I was chased and prevented from leaving the base by Hammerhearts. In the struggle that followed, Tommy committed suicide in his German body, breaking the curse upon him and allowing him to live a normal life in a single body. Moran was also killed after following us to the base for reasons only known to himself, betrayed by the Villain Crystal he dared to use against the Hammerhearts. The only good thing that could be said was that I was able to hit Lucien with an unboggler—a magical device I had created to undo the effects of the influential charm—thereby bringing him back to our side.

Then we were briefly prevented from leaving the base by Arnold Hammerson himself, who had turned up with the Sien-Leoard Crystal with murder on his mind. Marc, with some assistance from Natalie and Fewul, was able to get us out without any further loss of life, but it came at a cost: we were unable to recapture either the Sien-Leoard Crystal from Hammerson, or the Villain Crystal from Moran. The latter had been inside Moran's stomach, and Hammerson had extracted it by barbecuing the body, after which it was given to Hall as a reward for his good work.

Highlights for June: the Hammerhearts incorporated all the territory they controlled into a single nation state known as Hammersonia. Arnold Hammerson was the Head of State, naturally, while Cornish was his regent in Australia, and Hall the Police Commissioner of Australia. They wasted no time in tearing the old customs to shreds as they installed their rule-by-magic utopia. The Woodwards were able to stall them in some places and even recapture a few smaller territories, but Arnold Hammerson was no longer concerned with us, having driven us so effectively underground that we could do little to slow him down.

For us teenagers, the end of May through to the end of June was desperately dull. As a result of disobeying the adults on the daring mission to rescue Tommy, our parents had finally snapped and insisted that the Woodwards use their magic to keep us safely locked up inside the base. Many of us were moved into family suites where our parents could keep an eye on us, and for most of that month, were forced into a sort of home schooling program. I sank into a depression during this time, anxious to find out more about the prophecy I had found out about on the Rock and to learn if I really *could* defeat Arnold Hammerson in some way, but having no outlet for any of it.

With nothing else to do, we teenagers quickly went back to doing what teenagers did best: hooking up. After losing Kylie a month earlier, Peter had started a tentative relationship with Siobhan. Tommy and Jessica had also gotten into a new relationship, after Tommy had finally given up on Natalie. This was after he had used the Darkness Crystal in an attempt to seduce her while we had been on Rock Haulter, and then out of pure jealousy, had abandoned me while the two of us had been hiding the Darkness Crystal on the Rock, leaving me in a perilous position. I too was single, having decided to break up with Serena while on the Rock, though not actually getting a chance to do so before she was killed by Tankom. I wasn't in any psychological state to go after Natalie, though, and wouldn't have been able to anyway, as she and Amelia were busy fighting the war and had been prevented from spending any time with the rest of us through that entire time.

Then there was Marc. He and Amelia had broken up in early May, and weeks later, he started dating Lena. Ironically, Lena was the only girl I had left that I could date, but I had come to realise that the main feelings I had for her were lust, and so I had told her to move on from me, which she had done without too much trouble—or so I thought, anyway. And then there was Stella, who I still kept track of through our mind connection. She had managed to split from her father again and was, during this time, on the run. I would have liked nothing more than to get her back on our side, as I knew she wanted nothing more than to be with us, but I had no way to make it happen.

Everything changed in the last few days of June. Hall was able to infiltrate the base in spectral form and take possession of people whose minds weren't protected. Jessica and Rebecca were his first two targets before we figured out a way to stop him, but he had more tricks up his sleeves. In one particularly horrible incident, he reanimated the dead and buried bodies of Kylie, Serena and Mrs. Woodward, getting them out of the ground and getting them to come into Peter and my bedrooms, and the Woodwards' living quarters respectively. In the last assault, he weakened the magical protection of the base so that Arnold Hammerson could sneak in and plant bombs, destroying the base from the inside, killing several people, trying (and failing once again) to kill me, and forcing us all to evacuate in a hurry.

It was the chance we teenagers needed to give the over-protective adults the slip, which we did. We quickly set up our own base, having the magic of Marc, Natalie, Amelia and the Light Crystal at our disposal. By the time the adults realised we were gone, there was nothing they could do about it, and although they weren't happy about it, they at least recognised that we had made this choice and they had to let us do what we were going to do. It was a good move on their part, because we were quickly able to learn more about the Enlightener and the prophecy, and even recapture Stella—though once she knew what was happening, she was a more-than-willing captive. What I learnt for myself was that the prophecy identified that I *could* defeat Hammerson, but not necessarily that I *would*. James convinced me that this meant that I was more capable than anyone else, and if I really cared about winning the war, I had an obligation to do what I could.

Highlights for July: on the face of it, right up until mid-August in fact, nothing much changed in the war. The Woodwards and Fletchers had set up a new, mobile base and had gone back to stopping Hammerheart progress wherever they could. Arnold Hammerson, and even Hall, so far as we knew, had turned their attention away from us, apparently preferring to focus on their own business and wait for us to cause trouble, satisfied that as long as we stayed out of their way, they need not bother with us. The Young Army did indeed use this time to prepare for an assault, this time aimed at wresting the Villain Crystal from Hall, but no serious action was taken for the next six weeks.

This was because another plan was running parallel to that one, and it involved preparing for the aftermath of the war. It had been James's idea to use what we had learnt from Smiley to get assistance from a Honnie, and six of us—me, Peter, Tommy, Natalie, Rebecca and Candice —agreed to go into their world, armed with as much protective magic as we could dream up, to give this a go. (In case I hadn't mentioned it earlier, Candice was the girl who had shot Tommy in February, killed Lisa, been captured twice, released once by Sebastian, and finally brought to our side as the very first person to have an unboggler used on her.)

The venture into the Honnie world was a trial. The first two Honnies we met were May and her daughter Ingi, and May was so strong that she was able to shatter our magical protection using her mind alone. On the plus side, though, May could speak our language, and her mind strength alone made her the perfect candidate to help us. The problem was that for a long time, she was utterly unwilling to do so; to her mind, she had six free humans that she and her daughter could feed on to strengthen themselves mentally and physically. We were fortunate that no feasting was to happen until they returned to their hometown, and that gave us the time we needed to try to convince May to change her mind.

During our time in the Honnie world, I had been almost killed by Ingi when she ripped my arm off, and Candice and Tommy had both been hit by love beams. (The love beam was something a Honnie could do to make all humans of the opposite sex close enough fall desperately in love with them.) Candice had been hit accidentally by a stranger, and that stranger had killed her when he realised what he had done; while Tommy had been hit by Ingi, who had taken a liking to him and wished to keep him with her. It meant that although Tommy went on living, his mental faculties were pretty much shot to pieces, and there was no prospect of him ever returning to our world.

As for our world, while we had been away, a few new relationships had popped up while two dozen teenagers were in an enclosed space together with no adult supervision. Siobhan, having given up on Peter for dead when he went into the Honnie world, started dating Liam Stammerus; while Amelia, after initially being devastated when confronted with Marc and Lena's new relationship, had begun dating Darcy. Then there was Stella and Lucien; Lucien had been taken with Stella for a while but had never had the courage to do anything about it. Stella, of course, was far more taken with me, and she told him as much, but she was prepared to date him if she couldn't have what she really wanted. It would have been an unsatisfying relationship for both of them, but if I had never returned from the Honnie world, maybe it could have grown into something more. And then there was Jessica: at some point while we were away, she discovered that she had become pregnant with Tommy's child.

Highlights of August: if you thought a lot happened in February, you ain't seen nothin' yet. For me, there was time travel involved in August, so my month probably went for about forty days. In my own mind, August can be split into two sub-months: pre-Hammerson's death and post-Hammerson's death. And in case you can't tell, the main highlight in August was, of course, the defeat of Arnold Hammerson.

The events leading up to Hammerson's death began with our escape from the Honnie world, bringing May with us but leaving Tommy in the hopefully capable hands of Ingi. May agreed to come with us after an event which almost killed her, and which I was able to use to our advantage to make her understand that it would be worth her while helping us. When we returned to our base, and after Marc had magically restored my missing arm, we rapidly put into play a plan which Marc, Lucien, James, Amelia and Stella had put together in our absence. It involved attacking Chopville High, which the Hammerhearts had turned into an on-ground base, where we would find Hall and wrest the Villain Crystal from him. August 23 was the day we put this plan into action, and when we did, it caused a chain of events which would, in a few hours, net us the Villain and Sien-Leoard Crystals, and end with the defeat of Hammerson himself.

I won't go into a blow-by-blow of all that happened in those few hours, so I'll strip it down to the highlights: we had found a way to sneak through the magical protections around the school, only to set off an alarm somewhere and send Hammerhearts running. Among them had been Ather Hignat, who had recognised us and quickly called for backup. We had ultimately escaped from them by setting fire to some playground equipment which they were unable to escape (that had been my doing, and it had been an act of desperation). We had then assailed the administration building where Hall had been doing battle with Amelia, enclosed in an anti-teleportation ring so that he couldn't escape.

Hall won that battle by hitting Amelia with a curse which completely wiped her brain of all memories, leaving her with only the most basic of instincts with which she could operate her body. If we hadn't had a Honnie with us Amelia would have been lost forever, but when the dust had settled, May was able to put her back together using memories scraped out of all our minds. The Amelia who emerged wasn't exactly the same as the old Amelia, but it was close enough, and Amelia herself knew no different.

After Amelia had been knocked out of the fight, we had done battle with Hall, and had come close to beating him, but he ultimately overpowered us, captured Natalie and me, and escaped with us to the Hammerheart Base where we were promptly thrown in a cell. There, we were interrogated and tortured by Ather Hignat and Ugine Wilwog, and Natalie was very nearly raped, but by covertly freeing Natalie from an earlier attack which had blocked her magic, we were able to overpower them and escape from the cell. We then met up with the rest of our group in the Hammerson living quarters, empty for now, and prepared for our final assault. We knew that Hall had gone to fetch Hammerson, and that it would only be a matter of time before the two of them arrived to, in their minds, subdue us with ease. To prepare, May had taken the minds of every Hammerheart in the base and turned them to our side, though in such a way that it wouldn't be noticeable to Hall or Hammerson until we had them surrounded.

When the attack came, we had the initiative all the way through, mainly thanks to Fewul. Marc ordered the Beast of Magic to capture

Hall, wrest the Villain Crystal from him and knock him out the moment he came close enough, and that was just how it played out. Then came Hammerson: amazingly, he was able to do battle with the Beast of Magic and remain standing, though it took all of his concentration to do so. We got the upper hand on him thanks to May using her mind to confuse him for only a moment, but it was enough for him to drop the Sien-Leoard Crystal, which Lucien was able to pick up as we chased Hammerson through the base, finally cornering him in his own Execution Chamber.

A brief standoff ensued, but Hammerson was out of magic and out of options by this point. When he realised that we knew about the bare-hands protection spell, he knew there was nothing he could do to stop us killing him, and the only thing he could do was remind us that even with his death, the fight wouldn't be over. He had looked at Lucien as he said this, and those of us who knew about the time bomb curse he had placed on the oldest of the Moran boys knew that it would be triggered by his death. Marc knew all this, but in the time he had, he reasoned that keeping Hammerson alive would be worse than whatever consequences may follow his death. The death blow was then dealt, and that part of the battle was over.

We all had enough time to think that maybe it really *would* be all over. May and Amelia went with the rest of the Woodwards on a global mission to restore the world to how it had been before the global coups, May using her mind to undo the mental damage done to so many people. The rest of us celebrated into the night, with the exception of Stella, who was hit by a strange melancholy now that she was the last of the Hammersons. Lucien used the Sien-Leoard Crystal to assist her to visit the graveyard where her father's body would have teleported itself to, and there, something had happened to Lucien. The time bomb curse triggered when he got close to the grave, and he was possessed by the soul of Arnold Hammerson. He was still Lucien, but now he had a cold intelligence, a knowledge of magic greater than any of ours, and an ambition to take over the world. I had seen all of this in Stella's mind as I had been sleeping at the time, and it was confirmed when Stella returned to the base. We had made the mistake of letting Lucien keep the Sien-Leoard Crystal, and now we would have another enemy to fight.

For a few days, nothing happened, and then Lucien sprang into action. Within a period of just over twenty-four hours, he somehow stole the Hero Crystal; changed the properties of five of the six Sorcerous Crystals (leaving Natalie as the only Sorcerer); invaded the Woodward Base; captured and enslaved everyone within it in his newly-created Honnie mind, inspired by what he knew from May (though May herself was able to escape with an unconscious Amelia); announce to the world that he was their new ruler; take Natalie's magic the moment the other Sorcerers came around; invade our base; and capture almost everyone in it in the same way. Marc, Peter and James had seen the invasion from the control room, and realising that they were outmatched, they had managed to escape before Lucien had found them. I had eventually escaped as well, though I had taken a much more interesting route along the way.

I had been with Natalie when she had passed out, the two of us having begun a relationship days earlier when, trapped in a Basement cell together, we had finally confessed our feelings for one another. Stella had come to find me in the hopes of the two of us escaping together, but while we had been doing so, something had happened to her. We had then been stopped by Lucien, who got down on one knee in front of Stella in a proposal of marriage. This in the middle of a battlefield was one of the stranger things I had seen, but Stella still had feelings for me and she didn't accept. What she did do, though, when Lucien ordered her, was bind me in ropes and take me into Lucien's bedroom to wait for further instructions.

That was when I finally understood what Lucien must have done: he had put a time bomb curse on Stella, and he had triggered it while we had been trying to escape from the base. Up until that point, Stella *had* been on our side, but now she was firmly on his, and he was even in the process of transferring Natalie's crystal chip to her to boot. I argued with her and dared her to let me go, and maybe she would have done (she certainly considered it), but it came at a cost: I was forced to sit there and listen to her confess her own feelings for me, something I had already known but never spoken of so openly with her. Stella was perhaps my second preference, as Lucien was her second preference, but after she had allowed Natalie's unconscious body to fall into Lucien's hands, I could never consider dating her.

Then Sebastian showed up, unwelcome by both of us, tied us together and activated a device which Lucien had designed to break the mental connection between us. I would have been happy about that while Stella certainly wouldn't have been, but true to form, he had messed up and made the connection stronger rather than weaker. When Lucien arrived to see how we were going, he was forced to destroy the device before it could do any further damage. His shock and dismay had been the opportunity I'd needed to make a break for it; I had run the gauntlet with Lucien giving chase, just managing to escape through the control room before he could catch me. I found out later that in that moment, he exploded with rage, decimating the buildings in our base and killing eleven people, including six of our number: Dean and Joanne Abbodi, Della Rockson, Robyn Lloyd, Belinda Pensinger and George Tuck, Lena's younger brother.

I had met up with Marc, Peter and James, and after a brief rest (during which I learnt of just how much stronger my connection with Stella had become—I practically became her when I slept), we snuck into the Chopville Hammerheart Base to stock up on magical weapons, as we had none with us. We had then escape to Melbourne through the

Hammerheart Highway and hidden in a shelter for homeless people, fully aware that Lucien could trace us and capture us at any time, but knowing from my observations of him through Stella that he wasn't going to do so just yet. His plan was to make us suffer so that we would go to him willingly, wanting it to all be over. His intention was to have us as his advisors, not for us to end up dead or tortured, so he permitted us to dangle on the string, so to speak, for the time being.

This changed when May and Amelia finally joined us a little over twenty-four hours after the escape, having spent most of that time on a plane from the UK. May being back with us meant that we had a greater ability to resist Lucien, so he was forced to increase his pressure on us. He put a spell on Marc and me to make us so sexually aroused that we could barely control ourselves, the aim being to force us to hit on May and Amelia and cause problems within our group. Marc and I had almost come to blows when we had both gone to Amelia in desperation, but May had used her mind to settle the problem down. When he saw this, Lucien only became more enraged and he put another plan in motion, this one to threaten the life of Ingi if May didn't return to her own world.

I had been in Stella's mind at the time and had gone to tell May about this almost as soon as I woke up. She had almost gone to her world then and there to protect her daughter, but I had convinced her to stay on the grounds that Ingi was way too far from our current location, and she would never be able to reach her in time anyway. This turned out to be very good for us, because May had several more tricks up her sleeves. The first of these was an idea James had to communicate with each other without needing to speak aloud, by thinking thoughts and having May place them in the others' heads as if they had been spoken aloud. This meant that we could plan things without Lucien being able to eavesdrop, and that was the final straw for him.

A small army was sent to capture us and bring us in at last, and it might have succeeded if not for May. It transpired that like Smiley, she had the ability (as did all Honnies) to move along the fourth dimension. It was how she had escaped with Amelia when the Woodward Base had been invaded, and it was how she helped us to escape now. Being in our shadows was extremely weird for all of us, but I was at least able to perceive where I was. The others only had three-dimensional senses, so they could neither see nor hear nothing. May had to use her mind once again to make it possible for us to perceive our surroundings, so it was very good that she had the mental capacity to concentrate on so many things simultaneously.

It also turned out that May had the ability to move along the time axis, something she herself hadn't known until Peter—of all people—came up with the brilliant idea. What we needed to fight Lucien was more magic, and the only place we could get it was Rock Haulter. The portals had most recently opened three weeks earlier, and wouldn't be opening again until November, so the six of us went back in time a few weeks so that we could slip through the portals. We had needed to go into the Hammerheart Base again first, though, so that Amelia could find out from her father where we would need to go to get on board the ship that would be going through, as we didn't have the magic to make our own vessel as we had last time.

While Amelia had gone to speak to her father, I had gone on a rampage, leaving an unimaginable trail of destruction in my wake. While I had been under Lucien's sexual curse, I had hooked up with both Amelia and May—Amelia when I went to get my clothes out of her room and apologise for what Marc and I had tried to do to her the night before, and May when she had agreed to stay and help us, admitting that she was curious about recreational sex with a human. Amelia had used the Light Crystal to lift the curse from us, but in fury, Lucien had placed it back on me, apparently judging that I was more persuadable to do damage than Marc had been—an opinion which was probably justified in hindsight.

So when we went back into the Hammerheart Base, I had gone with Amelia so that I could track Natalie down and confess what I had done, sure that she would find out from Stella eventually, and wanting to get out in front of that possibility. Stella had been in my mind during the whole incident between me, Marc and Amelia, and since she desired me for herself, it would be in her interest to tell Natalie about what had happened, and not just her either: Lena was back in the frame after breaking up with Marc and letting both Natalie and Stella know that she wanted me and was going to fight them for me if necessary. Before I could find Natalie, though, I had been found by Lena, who had been far too titillating for me to resist. Of course, Natalie saw me, understood what had happened and promptly broke up with me, and then to top it all off, Stella had collared me on my way out, and I'd had sex with her as well.

By the time Amelia lifted the curse from me a second time, my self-worth was through the floor and I would have liked to crawl into a hole and die. The curse wouldn't be put back on me, but during the week or so that we spent on Rock Haulter, I would end up having sex with both May and Amelia on a few occasions. Each time I did, I would think to myself that Natalie was already lost to me and it wouldn't make a difference, and then afterwards, I would immediately regret having done it. May didn't mind, as it was all a bit of harmless fun for her, but it was more damaging for Amelia. Darcy had broken up with her after he had been captured by Lucien, while Marc had found that he still had feelings for her. Amelia herself was torn between me and Marc, and in the end, I had practically begged May to use her mind to settle it, wanting Marc and Amelia to be together as I didn't feel that I really deserved Amelia as my girlfriend.

While all this had been going on, I had been dealing with something new from the Enlightener. Lisa kept appearing to me in my dreams, telling me that she had something important that she needed to tell me, and the answer could be found in her diary. The only part of her diary I had seen was the part where she had written about the in-between, so I assumed that it had something to do with that. After talking it over with the others, it was decided that I would use my mind to go back to Lisa's death to see if I could speak to her spectral form there; and if that didn't work, it may be necessary for one of us to die and be brought back so that we too would be in the in-between, where we could find out what needed to be known and pass it onto those who still lived.

By the time we were ready to leave the Rock, we were in a brand new magical base, armed with brand new magical weapons, and some of it was magic that Lucien wouldn't know about and couldn't anticipate. When we got back, though, we found that Lucien had learnt some of our doings by pressing Frederic Woodward, who had to confess that he had told Amelia about the Rock Haulter portals that had opened three weeks earlier. Lucien had no idea how we could have gone back in time—that shouldn't have been possible, in his opinion—but he wasn't foolish enough to disregard the idea on that basis.

Not knowing what else to do, Lucien had pulled the trigger on his Ingi plan. She, along with her two half-human brothers and even Tommy, were captured and brought to Lucien. Natalie and Lena were also brought before Lucien as an attempt to lure me to him if I thought they were in danger. With Ingi bound, there was no question of us not going to him—May took control of all our minds and gave us no say in the matter. As it was, though, Lucien was slowly sucking the life out of Ingi, and though we tried with our new magical weapons, we weren't able to stop him. May was forced to surrender herself to him, and his response was to wipe her and Ingi's minds of all memories of us. They were sent back to their own world with no idea that they had ever been in ours, and I would never see them again or find out what had happened to them, or if they would ever find out that something strange had happened to them. (If they had ever passed near to the place in their capital city where May had become a collector, she may have been questioned.)

Tommy remained with Lucien, repaired to the best of Lucien's magical abilities, but Lucien wasn't quite done with us. He then threatened Natalie with death if I didn't give myself up, but I was able to buy us twenty-four hours of reprieve there. We slunk away from that encounter, still in the game but feeling pretty hopeless and desperate. The last thing we had done that night was activate a spell which James claimed would bring the will of Sien and Leoard to our side so long as we kept a promise to them. The promise was that one of us would allow ourselves to be brought back to life if we died so that we could learn what needed to be learnt from Lisa.

And that brings us to the present. Admittedly I skipped a lot of stuff along the way—minor details that seemed important at the time but probably don't matter in the scheme of things. If we survive this war, maybe I'll tell you more about it sometime, but we'll just have to see. I think I only really left out one majorly important thing.

Highlights for September: the end of the world as we had always known it....

Part 1: The Beginning of Forever

Chapter 1: The Situation, as It Stands

Everything around us was created by magic—that was one thing. Quite a lot of said magic had been performed by me—that was another thing. It wasn't just the base which sheltered us with several layers of magical protection (invisibility, sound-proofing, the ability to shrink to microscopic size, and a couple of others which were totally new and which Lucien, my older brother who had turned disturbingly evil lately, didn't yet know about). It wasn't even the enchantments we had placed upon our very bodies to give us a small amount of magical power (in my case, a fair bit more, because I had been more adventurous).

The most obvious sign of the magic lay in the numerous devices and gadgets that were scattered over the various seats within the control room, which provided the most readily available magic for us to use. Most of them didn't look magical at all, but perhaps as a sign of our ages and the times, looked more like smallish electronic devices. Some of them were old Hammerheart devices that we had stolen, like the solid-outliners and bludginators which we had happily turned on the henchmen of their creators throughout this war. Others were a range of things we had recently created specifically to help us take down Lucien.

James had been minding the control room as Marc and I returned from our bedrooms, each carrying armfuls of devices which we had just dropped into the empty seats around the room. We had to act fast; Lucien was presently asleep, after seemingly staying up most of the night with Lena, who he had just claimed as his—well, I'm not sure if 'girlfriend' would be the right word for what he wanted her for. While he had been sleeping, we had used our new forms of magic to sneak into Lucien's lair without setting off any alarms, and had used a couple more of our newly created magical devices to free the minds of many of our friends and families from Lucien's grasp so that they could return to our side. Peter and Amelia were presently helping them find rooms and settle into this brand-spanking new base, leaving the three of us to decide what to do next.

"Okay, so I think these are our options," James said, holding up a hand, palm out, and lowering each finger one-by-one. "One: force Fewul away before Lucien knows what's happening, so that we'll have a clearer shot at what comes next. Two: track down the location of the Sorcerous Crystals so that we can figure out how much protection we'll have to bust through. Three: recapture Stella before we do anything else, so that she can use her magic to help us do whatever we need to do next. Four: go back out there"—he gestured at the display screens, which showed the

Big Room—Lucien's accommodation for our friends and families—"and collect anyone we missed. Five: I shut up, and check to see if you two have any ideas that I missed."

Marc and I smirked at each other, James's words letting some of the tension out of the room, then he said, "Sounds to me like getting rid of Fewul is the smart thing to do, because he'll probably come teleporting straight to us the moment we do something big."

"I thought that too," James said, "but remember what we agreed last night: we have to make sure that if we do that, Lucien will have no way of calling Fewul back again. He could wake up at any time, perhaps less time than we have to get the Sorcerous Crystals and knock him out for twenty-four hours."

"There's also a chance he'll think to give himself a magical alert to let him know if we recall Fewul," I pointed out. When they only raised their eyebrows at me, I added, "Well, recalling Fewul is exactly what he did before stealing the Hero Crystal, so he might think of it—just in case."

"Good point," James said heavily, "so are we all agreed that option one is out?"

We both nodded reluctantly.

"In that case, what about option two?" he asked.

"It can't hurt to at least have a look at the tracker," Marc said, leaning over and picking up one of the many magical devices from on top of a nearby chair. This device, created by Amelia in the creations cave on Rock Haulter, simultaneously a few days ago and a few weeks ago thanks to a quirk of time travel, was capable of tracking down the exact location of all of the Magic Crystals anywhere on Earth, capable of zooming from a full map of the world, right down to a very specific black-and-white view of where it was.

The device was large and flat, reminding me of a laptop screen without the rest of the laptop, and Marc laid it across his knees so that we could all see it (in my case, upside-down). According to the map, all the crystals in the world were, in fact, in the vicinity of Chopville (not counting the Darkness Crystal, which didn't show up on the map thanks to its current location on Rock Haulter). Marc had to zoom in several times before they started to disperse, but even then, what we saw was not what we wanted. Two crystals were almost taking up the same space, while another was almost in the same place, though a little off at a slight angle. That was the Sien-Leoard Crystal, and it appeared to be on Lucien's person—not a surprise. The other two crystals were the Light and Villain Crystals, and they were right here in this base (the former of these being in James's pocket). As for the Sorcerous Crystals, they were nowhere to be found.

The three of us stared at this for almost half a minute before James slowly said, "Could he be shielding them from us somehow?"

"Maybe," Marc said slowly, "maybe. This isn't the first crystal-tracking device that's ever existed, so I suppose he could have thought of something that would stop us from using them to work out where he's hidden them. Amelia probably wasn't thinking too deeply about how the magic worked when she created this, so this thing,"—he tapped the screen on his knees—"is probably no different from the rest of it, apart from the zooming feature."

"But then wouldn't he have hidden that one as well?" I asked, indicating the Sien-Leoard Crystal.

"Not necessarily," James said, and now he indicated another magical device, this one resting against one of the control panels, though not pushing any buttons. "Lucien's smart, but he does have a bit of over-confidence going on. This thing shows that he doesn't even think he needs to be untraceable anymore, so he could easily think that as long as he has the crystal with him, he'll be able to protect himself."

The device he had indicated was one of those which I had created in that same creations cave, alongside Amelia on the same day that she had created the crystal tracker. That day was one I tried not to think about—that whole time in the creations cave with Amelia was something I tried not to think about—although doing so was just about impossible given the things we had done in there, things that these two had no business knowing. But what was I talking about? Oh yeah, the device: it was a spyer, one of a few we had set up in here, and it continued to show Lucien asleep in bed with Lena. It was capable of using magic to spy on a number of identities pre-programmed into it, giving us a view of where they were as well as providing an audio feed.

"Okay," Marc said, wrenching my thoughts quickly back to the here and now, "so if we can't use the tracker to locate the crystals, and we can't get rid of Fewul until we're ready to take on Lucien, and we can't take on Lucien until we have the crystals…is this starting to sound circular to you guys too?"

A silence followed this before James said, "Well, that's only two options. What about Stella? Could she help us come up with something? Maybe she knows where he hid them."

A stroke of inspiration hit me then, and I almost tripped over my tongue in my rush to tell them what I'd just thought of. "I don't think she knows anything—at least she didn't the last time I entered her mind—but if the crystals are together, then she might be able to lead us straight to them. Remember when your dad was hunting for the crystals on the Hammersons' orders earlier in the year?" I said to Marc, "Well, they were somehow able to use their own magic to track the location of their own crystals. If Stella did that then, she can do it now for us."

A stunned silence followed, but there was excitement in James's eyes. "That could work, John," he said, enthusiasm building. "That could really work. I mean," he faltered, and I saw the effort he was making to get himself back under control, "there's a chance it might not work. We don't know exactly how that kind of tracking works, or whether or not it's affected by what Lucien's done, but it definitely can't hurt to find out."

"Great," Marc said, "so what now? We capture Stella?"

I opened my mouth, not sure what I was going to say exactly, but before I could, the main door of the control room opened, the one which led to the elevator and the rest of the base, and three people came in: Amelia, Peter, and Mr. Woodward.

"Aren't you guys supposed to be helping our guests?" James asked, surveying the two teenagers.

"It's done already," Peter said. "It's really not that hard to figure out the rooms, and they were all excited to learn. So what have you guys figured out for what comes next?"

The three of us swapped uncomfortable looks. It wasn't Peter or Amelia, nor was it the next job we were about to undertake. It was the presence of Mr. Woodward in the control room. Here was a man who had been on the frontline of the war against Arnold Hammerson, and who had not only failed to hold the line and prevent the establishment of Hammersonia (a single state, ruled by a Hammerheart government with Arnold Hammerson as its head of state), containing almost the whole world except for the continents of Africa and South America, but had failed almost completely to do anything to bring about Arnold's downfall. Yes, he had orchestrated the transfer of magic from the Hammersons to the Fletchers, but that was many months ago now, and he had spectacularly failed to follow it up.

And that wasn't even the worst of it. He had left it to us to figure out how to actually end the war, preferring to play politics and military jostling rather than dealing with the Hammersons directly. When we had finally done it for him, he had entirely failed to take us seriously when we warned him about Lucien, a mistake for which he paid with his (and everyone else's) magic. When he had woken up, Lucien had his mind in his grasp, and during that time, Mr. Woodward had (under duress) given Lucien the information he needed to deduce that we had somehow gone back in time to magically outfit ourselves on Rock Haulter, blowing a cover we had really needed to keep as long as possible.

"Well, we've decided to capture Stella next, Pete," James said, but it was Mr. Woodward at whom he was looking. "We would be open to suggestions, but time is too precious for that now."

Mr. Woodward may not have been able to read minds anymore, but he had been doing it for his whole life save the last few days, so naturally he knew exactly what the facial expressions he was getting meant. Smiling slightly, he said, "Whatever you think is best, James. You've proven beyond any doubt that you're best at drilling down to the heart of the matter. I'm just here to help out however you think is best, even if it just means not telling Charlie and Marge what goes on down here."

We all laughed a little at that, some more of the tension leaking out of the room. One good thing that could be said about Mr. Woodward was that for all but a couple of months of the war, he had been prepared to step back and let us do our own thing, so long as whatever it was didn't interfere with what he and the other Sorcerers were doing. In May, though, after the night we had disobeyed his orders and gone to rescue Tommy from a Hammerheart base in Germany (resulting in the deaths of two of our number), our parents (Mum and Dad, Marge and Charlie, Harry and Simon's grandparents, and the parents of several other teenagers who had been involved) had formed a coalition to demand that the Sorcerers take steps to make sure it would be impossible for us to do anything so reckless again. In the six or seven weeks that we had been practically imprisoned in the old Woodward base, Arnold Hammerson had stabilised most of his territory and taken great strides in setting up the foundations of his rule-by-magic utopia. Who knew how long it might have gone on for if the Hammerhearts hadn't invaded and ultimately destroyed the old Woodward base, forcing us all to flee and giving us the opportunity we needed to give the over-protective adults the slip.

"Great," James said, clapping his hands. "So basically, the crystal tracker you made can't seem to find the Sorcerous Crystals, Amelia, and we don't wanna get rid of Fewul too early before we're ready to take on Lucien in case he just calls it back to him. So we're gonna go for Stella so that once we've got her, she can use whatever it is she's got to track her own Sorcerous Crystal. Do you know anything about how that works?" he asked Mr. Woodward.

"I've never done it myself," he admitted, "but every time we use our magic—*used* our magic," he amended a little sadly, "we had a sense of where it was coming from, and if we concentrated, it would be possible to follow that sense back to its source just by continuing to use small amounts of magic."

"I don't remember noticing anything like that," Amelia shrugged.

"You would if you'd known about it," her father told her. "It's one of those things that's hard to notice if you don't know about it, but once you do notice it, it's just about impossible to un-notice."

"And Stella does know about it," Marc said, "because like John said, she had to do that at the start of the year before my dad decided to go nuts, so she'll be able to do it for us now."

"Only if we go now," James said crisply, turning back to the control panel and picking up one of the other spyers, this one having been set the night before to keep track of Stella. "Looks like she's still in her lounge room, and still pretty upset, and—oh."

"Oh what?" Peter asked.

"Tommy's with her," James said simply.

We all started to gather around the spyer so that we could get a look at Stella, but James grunted at us. "Seriously," he said, leaning around Peter and snagging another device off one of the seats. This was another one that had been created that afternoon in the creation cave, this time by Amelia, and which was capable of duplicating anything at which it pointed (other than people). James pointed it at the spyers still focused on Stella and began clicking it, handing the duplicates around to each of us so that we could all watch without getting in each other's way.

I felt yet another stab of guilt as I watched Stella on the display screen of the duplicate spyer I had taken, where she sat in the living room of what had once been the Hammerson living quarters, but which was now effectively Lucien's loft. It was my fault that she was upset—apparently, she had been waiting for me to appear so that she could confront me and—well I still didn't actually know what she had planned to say to me, or even if she'd had a plan. But when she had hurried into the Big Room, it was in time to see me leading a tearfully apologetic Natalie forward. Stella hadn't known that we were re-converting our friends back to our side—she wouldn't have known that we had the power to do that—so she had naturally assumed that Natalie had somehow found it in herself to forgive me and take me back for the horrible things I'd done to her over the past few days.

That piled on top of the horrible things I had also done to Stella in that same time period. In fact, it was very much fair to say that since Lucien had risen to power, I had been a horrible person altogether. When Stella had told me a few days ago that she loved me (which seemed like much longer to me, thanks to the whole time traveling thing), I had minimised her feelings and essentially told her that it didn't matter how she felt, because I was in love with Natalie, and I wouldn't be about to turn my back on her in favour of someone who had, minutes earlier, allowed Natalie's unconscious body to fall into Lucien's clutches.

Then roughly forty hours later, I had gone and cheated on Natalie with four different females in less than twenty-four hours (and a fifth when you took the time traveling thing into account). To make matters worse, I had, at least briefly, led three of those females on into thinking that maybe what we did could be something more—and Stella had been one of them. Then as soon as I'd finished doing what I'd done with her, I had turned my back on her and left her sitting partially clothed on the floor in tears. And yes, there were some extenuating circumstances that had caused me to act like such an unspeakable douchebag, such as Lucien having put a spell on me to make me unbearably horny, but if I'd been a better person, I would have found the strength within myself to resist—at least the first few times, if not all those other times.

The only good thing that could be said was at least now they all knew what a total scumbag I was, and had adjusted accordingly. Lena, after having had the hots for me most of the year for reasons I never really understood anyway, and who had even maintained those feelings during her almost-three-month relationship with Marc, had showed signs of having finally given up on me the night before Lucien had worked his magic on her and made absolutely sure of it. Amelia's mind had been altered by our former ally May, effectively removing her romantic feelings for me so that she could be happy with Marc again (at my request). May herself had been forced by Lucien to return to her own world, with all her memories of me and this whole business wiped clean. Natalie knew I had cheated on her with Amelia and Lena, and that had been enough to put me outside the possibility of her taking me back. And Stella—well, she was now just coming to terms with the truth that I could never be hers, even though I actually *could* be hers now that no one else wanted me.

"You don't have to worry about me," she now said to Tommy. "I'll find a way to be okay."

"Will you?" he asked. "Will you really? I'm missing her like a hole in my heart; I don't think I'll ever really be okay until I find a way to get back to her."

Stella, who was sitting opposite him on the other couch, gave a sad little smile. I thought I knew what she was probably thinking: the chances of Tommy ever finding Ingi again were next to zero. Lucien had done his best to make Tommy forget the young Honnie, but whatever Ingi had done to Tommy's mind to make him fall so desperately in love with her had been beyond anything Lucien's magic, or his magically-created Honnie mind, could reach. Lucien wouldn't let Tommy go back to the Honnie world, and even if Tommy did somehow get back there, the chances of him actually finding Ingi before another Honnie found him and ate him for dinner were, again, next to zero.

And even if they did meet again, it wouldn't mean a thing. The Honnies would be able to read Tommy's mind and they would know that he was totally serious, and that Ingi had done that to him, but Ingi herself would have no memory of it. Like her mother, her mind had been wiped clean of everything to do with us. Stella had been there when Lucien had said he was going to do that, but Tommy had been unconscious at the time. I saw the exact moment when Stella decided that it would be a bad idea to tell Tommy the truth about his situation.

"Well, maybe we can find something else to make of our lives," she said, looking down at her knees, "even if I have been replaced in practically every way possible, by everyone possible."

My heart lurched again. It wasn't just my rejection of her with which she was struggling, but also the knowledge that Lucien had quickly and easily moved on from her rejection of him. There was probably a part of her, and no small part, that regretted having chosen me over him, when if she had just given him a chance, Lucien could have given her true love.

He had certainly cared more for her as a person than he now cared for Lena, but the fact that he had chosen to take Lena put any possibility of a future with Stella to bed—excuse the pun. Of course, I was only speculating, but it did make sense; and given the newly-strengthened mental connection I still shared with Stella, it was possible that I had a subconscious link to her emotions, even when I was awake.

Tommy, meanwhile, was shaking his head. "You still have a major advantage, you know. You can still fight for what you want. You have everything you need to get it, if you can bring yourself to do what you need to do to make it happen. I've got no way of getting over there without magical help; for all I know, she's hooking up with some super-hot Honnie dude even as we stew."

"What's the point?" Stella shrugged. "He's made it pretty clear where we stand, and I'm not going to use magic to force him into something."

"Even if you know it would make him very happy?" Tommy asked. "That would seem like a kindness to me. I'll never stop appreciating what Ingi did for me; showing me how deeply it's possible to love someone, even if it is causing me agony now."

The expression on Stella's face chilled me a bit, and for a moment, it looked like she was seriously considering Tommy's words. Up until now, Stella could have taken me by force several times over, but she had refused to do so, not wanting anything we had to be based on dishonesty. Things would be extremely different right now if she had changed her mind about that when I'd been with her in the Big Room the day before, but apparently she was ready to consider changing her mind now.

Before I could give it any more thought, though, I was distracted by the look on Peter's face. His expression was one I hadn't seen on his face for quite some time; it looked like he was fighting back tears. "Wow, she really did a number on him, didn't she?" he said, sounding a little choked. "He can barely string a sentence together without it coming back around to Ingi, even now."

"Okay," James said loudly, clapping his hands again; he was all business. "It looks like those two are going to keep talking, so what's the plan for Tommy? Should we bring him in as well?"

"Can't hurt," Amelia said. I glanced at her and saw that like Peter, she looked close to tears.

"Actually, maybe it can," Marc said heavily. "None of us really understand the damage that's been done to Tommy's mind. He could need regular maintenance to stop him going off the rails. It could actually be better for him to stay with Lucien. Let's face it; we can't do anything to make it better for him. If mind control doesn't work, no other magic we have will do either."

"There is a chance that Lucien will grow tired of him," Mr. Woodward pointed out. "If he intends to be everything Arnold

Hammerson was and more, he's going to have a lot of work ahead of him, and Tommy could become a nuisance. I'm assuming his reason for trying to save Tommy now is out of loyalty because of their prior friendship, but Lucien's on a slippery slope now, and those loyalties are apt to become much less important as he grows into his new role."

"And if he does grow tired of him," James said slowly, "then there's really only two things that could happen. Either he'll palm him off on someone else, someone who won't have any chance of keeping him under control, or he'll just put him out of his misery, whether by killing him outright, letting him try his luck in the Honnie world after all, or maybe just—"

"Stop, James, just stop," Amelia snapped at him. "We get the idea."

"Sorry," he shrugged, looking sheepish.

"But then what would we do with him in here?" Marc asked. "Sure we can keep him safe, but at what cost? What's he going to try to do once he's in here? What if he does something that puts us in danger somehow?"

"There are a lot of people here who would be happy to look after him," Mr. Woodward reminded us. "Remember, not everyone you rescued is the fighting type; some, like your mothers," he said to me, Peter and James, "are more domesticated. Keeping tabs on a wayward teenager is exactly what they're about."

Peter and James both seemed satisfied with that, but I had a stirring of unease. Tommy was at least half a foot taller than both Mum and Marge, and outweighed them significantly. If he got out of control and threw a desperate tantrum, he could really hurt them. Then the rest of my mind caught up with what I was thinking: they would be fine if we taught them how to use stunners and a couple of other magical devices good for subduing a person.

"Okay, so how will we do this?" James said, checking his watch and then glancing at the spyer on the control panel. "Good, he's still asleep; we need to capitalise on this opportunity."

"I think we need to do it in a way that she knows isn't aggressive," I contributed. "If we sneak up on her, she may react with her magic before we have a chance to unboggle her. Her magical reflexes are very quick; remember how she fought Tankom in that memory of Smiley's?" I reminded them, and Marc, Peter and James nodded in agreement while the two Woodwards just looked puzzled.

"Well, in that case, John, you're the best person for it," James said, and my heart sank—I had walked right into that one. "She'd be suspicious if she saw any of us, but if she saw you, she could just think that you've come to explain yourself, or to apologise, or to forgive her, or whatever you think will work best."

I hesitated for a couple of reasons: the very real fact that I could be putting myself in danger, whether from Stella or from Lucien, who would be within earshot if something loud enough happened to wake him up, and also because the idea of actually having another frank conversation with Stella about whatever was going on between us caused my stomach to knot.

"We'll have your back," Peter reassured me. "We'll have someone in here, ready to drag you back in a moment if it looks like something might happen."

"It might be a good idea for a couple of us to go out there with him," James said, "just in case we're forced to fight our way out. John shouldn't have to do it alone."

"I don't mind going," Marc offered, "so long as I can stay safely in my shadow."

"I will too," Amelia added.

"Okay then," James said, "and the three of us will stay here and keep watch, and be ready if anything unexpected happens. Now, before we let you out, what magic should you take with you?"

"This one, and this one," Marc said, getting off his seat and walking around the room, picking up various devices. "This one, of course, and definitely this one for us, and this one for John, just in case—"

"Hey, hold up," I said, a little alarmed—I couldn't possibly carry all those devices. "I don't need a lot of that stuff, remember?"

I looked pointedly at them, and three of them looked a little annoyed and glanced back at me—Amelia, James and Marc hadn't been all that pleased when I had gone back to the enchantments cave and given myself the ability to perform a lot of those specific spells with my mind, rather than needing to hold a device. I knew that if it came down to a fight with Stella, I would be no match for her—not just because she actually had magic of her own, but because she was so much more magically experienced than me; and although my reflexes had gotten pretty good during the two-and-a-half months I'd had custody of the Sien-Leoard Crystal, they had never reached Stella's level.

"Well, you're still going to need some of it," Marc said, holding two devices out to me, but I didn't take them. These two devices were what I would need to free Stella from Lucien's clutches, if I hadn't already programmed them into myself. One of them was a duplicate of the unboggler I had created four months earlier, while the other would extract Stella from Lucien's Honnie mind without either of them noticing anything—Marc had created that one in the creations cave, though not on the same day that I'd been in there having sex with his girlfriend.

"You're going to need some of this, though," Peter said, taking the other two devices Marc had picked up, pointing one of them at me and clicking it. A moment later, though, it showed no outward sign of its power. I would be completely untraceable—even to Lucien's ability to detect untraceable people and objects. Marc had created this in the creations cave too, and aside from being able to skip to another point along the fourth dimension, it was the best protection we had.

"And a shield would be a good idea too," James said, glancing around for the appropriate device, locating it and handing it to me; I turned it on myself agreeably enough. That was one of my devices from that day; if Stella cast a spell at me now, it would either deflect off the shield or just dissolve against it, depending on the type of magic used - either way, leaving me untouched. "And—er—anything else?"

There was a pause, before I said, "I don't think I should take anything else, but you two," I said to Marc and Amelia, "make sure you've got everything we might need to fight, especially including that thing that'll imprison Lucien's magic, and those things that'll knock someone out from the fourth dimension if you intend to stay there."

Those were a couple of particularly nifty devices. Amelia had created one that would put a shield around a Sorcerer, trapping their magic within so that if they tried to perform a spell, it would rebound upon its caster. The knock-out device that worked from within the fourth dimension was another one of mine, and would be a way for Marc or Amelia to possibly knock an attacker out without having to expose themselves.

"And don't forget to make yourselves untraceable," James reminded Marc and Amelia, who quickly did so.

"You should probably take this one too, even if it is a bit simple by comparison," Mr. Woodward said, handing a device to Amelia. I looked more closely and saw that it was a standard invisibility toggle, the sort that Mr. Woodward himself had created six long months earlier.

At last, though, we were ready to go. James took the controls of the base and began steering us out of the Big Room, through the Hammerheart base, and up to the top level, where we saw on the display screen that Stella and Tommy were still talking together in the living room and thankfully, Stella appeared to have stopped crying. Even more thankfully, there was no sign of Lucien. Finally, James edged us along the fourth dimension so that when he dropped us out of the base, we would be in our shadow.

"Good luck, you guys," James said, "but do remember that if something goes wrong, John's the one we'll be pulling in first, so you have to be prepared to fight for at least a little bit."

Marc and Amelia nodded stiffly, their faces set. One by one, we stepped into the corner of the control room; James pushed a button on the control panel, and the person standing there would disappear from the base altogether, appearing a moment later just beneath it and outside of its protection.

Chapter 2: Succumbing to Evil

Being in one's shadow was not an easy feeling to get used to. It hadn't felt like anything when it had been the base moving along the fourth dimension, and us going along inside it, but here in the Hammerheart base the world was only three-dimensional. Marc, Amelia and I were basically standing on nothing, able to see each other quite clearly, but only able to look at the rest of the world as though we were viewing it from a short way inside a dark tunnel. It was possible to move around without freezing on the spot or falling down towards whatever, though, just by making yourself perceive that there ought to be something beneath you on which to stand. This wasn't too difficult, given that when we looked down, we could still see the living room floor beneath our feet.

Stella and Tommy were still talking, but none of us were really listening to them now. They were completely oblivious to our presence here, neither of them having the ability to see ghosts (that's how we would have appeared to either of them if they had been imprinterals, as I was). They also couldn't hear us at all, but that didn't stop us from quietly scampering to the door into the hallway outside and conversing in whispers.

"So how are we gonna do this?" Marc asked us.

"Well I guess I'm the one who has to go out there," I gestured vaguely at nothing, but they both knew I meant leaving my shadow, "and I suppose you two could either stay in here, or one of you could stay and the other could follow me—you'll be fine as long as you're invisible and untraceable," I added, seeing the looks on their faces.

They both considered the options for a few seconds, and then Amelia said, "I think we're better off staying here. Remember, James will be covering you in the base, and we can cover you with these," she indicated her inter-dimensional knock-out device.

"I think the most useful thing we can do is keep a watch," Marc said. "I'll go down there," he indicated the hallway leading to the bedrooms, "and yell out to you if I see Lucien coming—or anyone else for that matter. You will hear me when you're out there, won't you?"

"Yep," I said, remembering back to the first of my now three trips to Rock Haulter, and how easily I had been able to hear the voices of the ghosts which we and Moran had summoned.

"And I guess I'll stand here," Amelia said, looking through the door into the hallway leading to the rest of the base, "and do the same, but I'll also be ready to help you out if Stella tries anything. Is that okay?"

"Yeah, that'll be fine," I said uneasily. My unease had little to do with safety now, and a lot to do with the fact that I had no idea what I would even say to Stella; that the conversation was apt to be pretty awkward, and the whole thing was going to be watched by Marc, Amelia, Peter, James, Mr. Woodward, and anyone else who happened to walk into the control room while we were out here.

"You ready?" Marc asked, patting me on the shoulder.

I shrugged and smiled a little weakly. "No time like the present. I'm just gonna go out there and come in that way so that I don't startle her more than necessary."

I turned away from them and followed the outside hallway, down the stairs and to the wall which secured this part of the base from the rest of it. I took a moment to gather my composure—whatever was going to happen here was apt to be humbling for me, and even if getting Stella to forgive me was something I wanted to do anyway, I had to remind myself that it wasn't the main job here today. Wherever this discussion went, I had to be ready to unboggle her and extract her from Lucien's Honnie mind, preferably not in that order, and then do the same to Tommy.

I took a deep breath and shifted myself along the fourth dimension, leaving that dark tunnel and emerging completely into the light—or at least, what little light there was here. This had been one of those few magical abilities that we had all given ourselves back in the enchantment cave, not just one I'd claimed for myself, as it would be seriously useful when escaping from an enemy who didn't know that sort of magic was possible.

I began to climb the stairs, making no effort to be quiet or especially loud. The voices of Tommy and Stella were dim from here, but just loud enough for me to hear the exact moment when they heard me coming and conversation abruptly ceased. My heart was pounding in my chest now, because I could imagine the two of them looking towards the door, exactly at where Amelia stood invisibly, and where I would appear just moments later.

I reached the top of the stairs, walked down the hallway to the right, and turned left into the living room. Amelia had been standing there with her back to me, semi-transparent to my vision and invisible to everyone else's, but just far enough to the side that I wouldn't have to walk through her to enter the room. I had raised my fist as though to knock on the side of the door to let them know I was there just in case, but that hadn't been necessary; as I had imagined, they were watching the door, but while Tommy's reaction to the sight of me was barely a reaction at all, Stella's expression was a mask of horror.

"John!" she squeaked, bounding up off her couch and sending a spell almost directly at where Marc stood with his back to the action. Whatever it was, it plastered itself invisibly against the doorway to the hallway to the bedrooms. "That'll dull our voices but we still have to be quiet," she told me. "What the hell are you doing here? You have to stop doing this; it's not safe for you here, especially after what you pulled last night."

"Hello to you too," I said, smiling at her, and this smile was real. Despite the circumstances, it was difficult not to be amused by such a reaction.

Stella didn't share my amusement. "You need to leave, now," she said. "I mean it."

I shook my head, shaking off the amusement. "No, not this time. You and I need to talk."

She also shook her head. "No, we really don't, not anymore—"

"I'm not leaving here until we do," I insisted, but actually I had no idea what I needed to say to her. Now that I was here, it was even harder than I had expected it to be.

"I saw you just before," she snapped at me, and now I could see the pain plainly on her face, "with her. Is that how it is with you now? You've come to reiterate that I'm nothing to you? It wouldn't surprise me, since you didn't even notice I was there."

I ignored that last part; it was more true than I wanted to admit. "That's not how it is, and before you get any ideas in your head, I'm pretty sure Natalie has no intention of ever forgiving me—and I really don't blame her, I hardly deserve it. And that's not what I want to talk about either."

She opened her mouth, looking like she was about to scream something at me, and then with a glance at the hallway, remembered that she still needed to keep her voice down, lest Lucien bust in and take the matter out of her hands. "Then what," she snapped in almost a whisper.

I still didn't know exactly what, and my mind flicked over possibilities—everything from asking for her forgiveness to asking if she would take me back herself. Before I could give voice to any of these bad ideas, though, I was distracted by Amelia's ghostly voice behind me. "Better move this along a little quicker, John," she said, reminding me of the true reason why we were here. Whatever did or didn't exist between me and Stella now, it could be sorted out later on when she was firmly on our side.

Trying not to show that I'd heard a voice that no one else had, I said simply, "I want you to come with me."

Whatever she'd expected me to say, it wasn't that—even though I'd said the same thing to her just yesterday. It took her a few seconds to regain her composure, and then she said, "Go with you where?"

"Out of here," I said, indicating the living room around us, "away from Lucien. We all think things are gonna get pretty bad around here soon, and whatever you may think of me, I do still care about you and I'd prefer you be out of the way when it happens."

It was a hopeless request, as I had expected. I could tell by the look on her face that she had no intention at all of turning her back on Lucien, even though he had moved on from her. He had done a good enough job on her mind that she would rather stay here with him than come away with me, even though staying here meant that Lena would be an every-day presence in her life. After the two of them had been in competition for me before, even though neither of them had ultimately ended up with me, I could imagine that Lena would still feel as though she had come out well ahead of Stella—and if Stella didn't feel that way yet, she probably would very soon.

"Is that what you were doing in the Big Room then?" she asked me. "Getting the others out of the way of something you think is going to happen?"

Something that she didn't believe would happen; the subtext was clear.

I shrugged. "Come with me, and I'll tell you everything. Stay here, and feel free to guess away."

Once again, she didn't take the bait. "Look, I know you're still clinging to the old fight," she said, "and you seem to be doing pretty well —I really have no idea how you did what you did last night without Lucien or even Fewul being able to find you. But there isn't a fight anymore, and the sooner you realise that the happier you'll be, which is why I know you'll be pissed at me even if you know deep in your heart that it's the right thing to do."

I knew what was coming a split-second before it happened, thankfully, I had anticipated that it might when I'd seen that look on Stella's face back in the control room. Even more thankfully, the magical shield I'd put around myself was strong and designed with this spell, among others, in mind. I don't know whether the influential charm had been meant to make me loyal to Lucien, or loyal to Stella, or perhaps both; whatever it had been, it dissolved harmlessly against my shield, leaving me untouched.

Stella's eyes widened as she realiied that her trick hadn't worked, and I felt her cast another spell at me. This one was a little more difficult for my shield to handle, partially because it was specifically designed to neutralise magical shields, and partially because the magic Stella could call on from her crystal chip was greater than the magic we could encapsulate in magical devices. Fortunately, I had seen this coming as well, and had made it so that the shield could only be removed by the device which had first created it. If she'd had more time, Stella might have found a creative way to get through it—undoubtedly such ways existed for those smart enough to find them—but I had no intention of giving her that time.

"How are you doing that?" Stella whispered, looking panicky as I moved slowly forward towards her, moving sideways around the couch that sat between us; and then, "I'm sorry," she whispered.

Of course, now that the influential charm hadn't worked, I was free to resent her for attempting to boggle me in the first place. I didn't, though, because I understood why she'd done it; and also because I knew exactly what to do about it. I walked right up to her where she stood and put my hands on her shoulders, having to look up slightly to meet her eyes as she was still a little taller than me. The height differential wasn't as great as it had been six months earlier—I must have grown more than her in that time. Her eyes were filling with tears again, apparently this time in apprehension of me lashing out at her, but she seemed too shocked and puzzled by what had just happened to step back from me or perform any more magic.

"I'm sure you thought you were doing the right thing," I told her. "I imagine you resented Lucien a little when he put an influential charm on you, but then realised that you were happier with it than without. But if that had never happened, you would have been even more happy, and a more independent thinker, without an influential charm."

As I spoke, without removing my hands from her shoulders (giving no sign that I was doing anything than talking to her, in other words), my mind felt for Stella's and carefully extracted it from Lucien's Honnie mind. Stella noticed nothing as I did this, and since he hadn't come barrelling down the hallway yet, Lucien hadn't noticed anything either.

"I don't want you to make me happy by doing that, though, because it would only be an illusion of happiness," I told her, then seeing the look on her face added, "and yeah, I know it would seem no less real to me if I didn't know any better; but the thing is, Stella, I do know better. What I would much prefer is for you to come back to my side, rather than me come over to yours. We can talk about other stuff later, when we're safely away from here and it's just the two of us."

Only part of my mind had been on my words; the rest had been on the unboggler, or more specifically my inner unboggler, which I was readying to use at just the right moment. That moment came on my last word and I sent the spell straight at her face, causing her to stagger as her mind went blank for just a moment. She didn't fall, though; my hands on her shoulders made sure she stayed balanced. Her expression cleared a moment later, and grew puzzled all over again as she tried to figure out what had just happened to her.

"Okay then," she said softly, and then froze as comprehension finally hit her. Only when she had found herself agreeing to come with me had she noticed that something significant had changed, and her expression grew more horrified as she realised what it was. I had seen that expression before; it was the same way that Candice Young had looked when I had first tested the unboggler on her, and it was also very similar to how Natalie had looked this morning right before she had burst into tears and apologised over and over again for being on Lucien's side.

"*No!*" Tommy's loud voice almost made both of us jump out of our skins. I had all but forgotten he was even in the room all this time—he had stayed so silent throughout—but now he came hurtling at me, knocking hard into me and pushing me sideways away from Stella. I lost my balance and hit the floor, turning my body mid-fall so that I wouldn't hurt myself, and then rolling and springing back to my feet. Stella cried out something in alarm, and Tommy's angry voice clearly said, "You can't do that—Lucien won't let you take her awa—"

Then Tommy collapsed in a heap where he stood in front of Stella, taking both of us by surprise. I glanced around and was in time to see Amelia pocketing one of her magical devices—I didn't have to wonder what had just happened.

"Did you do that?" Stella asked, her eyes huge in her face.

"It doesn't matter," I said, taking a breath and then faltering. How was I supposed to deal with Tommy while he was unconscious? I couldn't unboggle him until he came around, and I didn't think I'd be able to reach his mind either.

"You have to go now!" Stella hissed at me. "He just made a lot of noise."

"Good point," I said, taking a step towards her and taking hold of one of her wrists. There was no time to prepare her for what was about to happen; I moved myself back along the fourth dimension, back into my shadow, and dragged the three-dimensional Stella along with me. She didn't resist, but let out a terrified scream of fright when the world around her suddenly dimmed and the floor seemed to vanish from beneath her feet, leaving her standing upright and balanced on nothing.

We were just in time; a bang echoed from down the hallway in the direction of the bedrooms, and then Marc said, "No time to take Tommy, we'll have to leave him."

I heard his words and the sound of running footsteps, but my attention was still on Stella. All the colour had drained from her face and she was turning her head from side-to-side, her eyes staring blankly ahead, looking on the verge of fainting. She was making little noises of fright, the occasional word mixed in with the babble. I had forgotten that since she was a three-dimensional being, she couldn't perceive anything here; just as none of the others had been able to do without May's assistance (until we had come back from Rock Haulter, anyway).

Fortunately, we had foreseen that we would need to do this for other people when we got back, and I'd given myself the ability to do it without needing to use a device. I concentrated hard for a moment and then sent the magic at her, causing her to stagger a second time, but when she looked around at me, she was now seeing me again. Then her eyes widened in horror as she took in the person who had run right through Marc seconds earlier, before coming to such a sudden stop at the sight of Tommy on the floor that he had almost fallen over.

"Lucien," she gasped, her expression desperate, "it's not what it—it
—looks like."

She faltered as she realised that he could neither see nor hear her.
She glanced with some confusion at me, and I said, "This is the fourth
dimension. This is where Smiley could go to get his memories, and this
is where we're hiding. Lucien can't see us or hear anything we say."

While I had been speaking, Lucien had gone to Tommy and used his
magic to revive him. Without giving Tommy a chance to stand up,
Lucien had levitated him into a sitting position and placed him on the
couch, almost exactly where he'd been sitting when he'd been talking to
Stella earlier. Now he said, "What happened to you? Did you faint, or
were you attacked?"

Tommy didn't answer, but his expression flickered. Though I
couldn't be completely sure, it appeared that Lucien had taken Tommy's
mind in an iron grip and was forcing it to recount what had just
happened.

"The same thing," Lucien breathed, his face darkening, "and it
happened because—"

He faltered, then his face darkened even more. "No, she wouldn't
have done. They don't have that kind of power—"

He faltered again, his face screwing up in concentration. Then he
stood up, and when Tommy's expression cleared, I knew he'd let his
mind go. "I believe that *you* believe Stella's gone," Lucien said, "but I
don't believe she would have done that. I guess I'd better make sure,
though."

"Oh shit," Amelia said, and before any of us could ask what she was
cussing about, she withdrew another magical device, pointed it at Stella,
and gave it a click. I recognised it as she put it away: the untraceability
2.0 device. Good thinking, Amelia. I then glanced back at Stella; she was
just standing there, watching the proceedings, tears falling silently down
her face. I had an urge to give her a hug but fought it off; even if Stella
would accept a hug from me now, it was still an awful time to be getting
emotional.

Lucien's face had darkened even more as he stood there, seeming to
be casting his mind around. "What do you know?" Tommy asked him.

"Well, this is very interesting," Lucien said slowly. "It appears you
may be right, Tommy; I can't find Stella anywhere. She's not in my mind
anymore, I can't trace her at all, and there's definitely no one untraceable
anywhere around here."

"What does that mean?" Tommy asked, looking simultaneously
angry and scared.

"I don't know," Lucien said softly, but the expression on his face said
he had suspicions. "I'd better check something else."

Another silence followed, but it only lasted for about fifteen seconds
before Lucien snarled, "I don't fucking believe this."

"What?" Tommy asked, now looking more scared than angry.

"Other people have left us too," he said, his voice beginning to rise in fury. "Frederic Woodward is nowhere to be found. Lillian Woodward, Natalie Fletcher, Rebecca Fletcher, the Playmans, the Thomases, the Maivises—they've all just vanished. I wouldn't have thought it possible, but they have found a way to both unboggle people and actually free them from my Honnie mind—and all without me noticing anything, and all without having a Honnie of their own, now that May is gone. How? How? *How*!"

His voice had been gradually rising so that on the last word it was a roar of outrage. Tommy cowered back in his couch as Lucien teetered on the edge of an explosion, but this time, thankfully, he managed to stay in control of his emotions—just.

"I have to see what's happened down there," he said distractedly, "see who's missing, if they're really gone or just undetectable—yeah."

He turned his back on Tommy and hurried back down the hallway to his bedroom; to do what, I wasn't sure. I took a moment to follow him in my mind and saw that he had returned to his bedroom, apparently to make sure that Lena was still there. She was, sitting up in bed, having been woken up at the same time as Lucien, and apparently naked in there —at least, her chest was completely bare. I could have forgotten myself and stayed there looking at her, but when Amelia spoke quite close to me I wrenched myself back to the here and now.

"What do we do now?" she was asking. "We didn't get everyone earlier; he might take it out on them."

"And he'll know exactly who's missing and who isn't," Marc agreed, coming over to us. "We should at least try to stop him before he can get down there. I'll put that magical prison around him and you try to knock him out from in here," he said to Amelia, taking a couple of devices from his pockets. He then made himself invisible so that he could safely leave his shadow to begin the attack.

"Er—there's a gaping flaw in that plan," I told Amelia. "How will we know when Marc's done his bit if we can't see what he's doing, and if Lucien doesn't notice anything?"

Amelia smiled slightly and said, "If my thing works, it won't matter whether his does or not."

"He'll have a shield around him," Stella said flatly.

If there had been time, I would have told Stella exactly why that didn't matter in this case; that Marc's spell would wrap around the outside of his shield and be just as effective that way, while Amelia's spell, if she could be close enough when she cast it, would leave its shadow within Lucien's entirely three-dimensional shield. But loud footsteps announced the return of Lucien. A moment later he hurtled back into the living room, swinging hard to the right so that he could leave the living quarters.

The attack only took about a second, but a lot happened in that time. Marc must have hit Lucien with his magical prison first after all, though none of us were sure of it until a little later, but Amelia's knock-out spell hit its mark just as Lucien was about to pass through the doorway and out into the hallway. Unfortunately, she hadn't been close enough and Stella had been right; his shield deflected the spell, causing him to stagger to a halt. And as if that wasn't bad enough, apparently following some sort of order from whenever, Fewul appeared beside him a split-second later.

"Oh crap," Marc said. A moment later, he re-appeared, pocketing the two devices. "Now what? We can't overpower him—I mean her," he added, blushing slightly. Fewul itself was genderless, but we called it 'he' most of the time because most of the previous forms it had taken had been male; but right now, the Beast of Magic was still using the form of May.

"I was attacked, wasn't I?" Lucien asked, and Fewul nodded. "Is there anyone here?"

"No, Master," Fewul said in May's voice, and it felt so weird and wrong that he (I mean she) could imitate her stance and her thick accent with such ease. The only thing that really gave it away was the look on her face; where May's expression had usually been quite indifferent, depending on what was happening, the look her face wore now was much more subservient than a Honnie would ever wear when addressing a human.

"Then how?" he whispered, screwing up his face. "How are they doing this? Are you sure there are no signs of untraceability anywhere around here?"

"No, Master."

"What about in the wider area? Chopville? Hell, anywhere in the country?"

"No, there is nothing, Master."

Lucien sighed. "This is staggering. By all the laws of magic that I know of, they shouldn't be able to do this. What about Stella? Can you sense her anywhere?"

"No, Master. She seems to have disappeared."

"Is she dead?"

"I did not sense her death, Master. I only sensed her disappear."

"The same as the others, in other words," Lucien said, and Fewul nodded. "So it's true, then. She really has left me and joined them, and is now under their protection. She wouldn't have done so on her own, I made sure of that—I made sure of it with all of them—which can only mean they truly have found a way to extract minds from within my own. Could that be possible to do with magic?"

"Perhaps, if they understand Honnie minds fully," Fewul said, "or if they detected a weakness in your simulation of your Honnie mind."

Lucien shook his head. "My mind is not weak—it is strong, stronger than a standard Honnie mind because I have even more power over it. No, May must have helped them do this before I forced her to leave. Even now, even with all of my power and position, they continue to defy me at every turn."

His face was black with rage, and he was trembling to hold it in. Unperturbed, Fewul said, "Yes, Master, but it does not explain where they acquired the magic to do such a thing. The Light Crystal would not perform such magic under any circumstances, and they needed magic they didn't have in order to access the Villain Crystal."

Lucien wasn't listening; he was losing control of his rage. He was fighting, but he was losing. "Fewul, help me!" he snarled at the beast, and Fewul responded.

Exactly how it happened, or even exactly what happened, I was never quite sure. From where the four of us stood, watching in trepidation, it looked as though Fewul cast some sort of spell on Lucien that caused his rage—whatever it was that needed to explode before he could be himself again—to become a tangible thing. Whatever it was, it was big and poisonous, and it appeared to be stuck inside Lucien's body. He gagged as whatever it was lodged somewhere between his neck and his chest, causing part of his neck to bulge and his face to start turning black for real.

"No," Marc whispered in horror. "No, it can't end like this."

"No," Lucien gasped, eerily echoing his younger brother. "I said—I said—help me."

"You need to spit it out, Master," Fewul said earnestly. "I cannot help you with this; you need to let it exit your body, and then you will be well."

My heart leapt in sudden hope. Could this actually work? If my hunch about Fewul's words was correct, Lucien had just been given a golden opportunity to shake Arnold Hammerson's influence on him free for good, if he could only find the strength to spit it out. The trouble was, Lucien appeared to be losing this battle; he collapsed to his knees, his hands pressed against his chest. A series of desperate coughs wracked his body and that appeared to be the last straw for Tommy, who I'd completely forgotten about for the second time that morning. He jumped off the couch, hurried over to Lucien, and began pounding him on the back.

Later, I would think back to that moment, and understand that this was where everything went irreversibly wrong. Who knows how many millions of lives might have been saved if Tommy had given Lucien the Heimlich manoeuvre instead, or even if he'd just left him alone and allowed nature to take its course, even if it had cost Lucien his life. Instead, Tommy's actions caused whatever it was inside Lucien to slide further into his body, seeming to lodge somewhere in his chest and then disperse. I was making assumptions here, but they were based on what I was seeing. The bulge in Lucien's neck had disappeared, his airways cleared, and he was able to breathe again. He was still shuddering, though, and I knew it had to be because the thing that Fewul had meant to come out of him was now very much inside him—very much a part of him.

After about fifteen seconds the shuddering stopped, and Lucien was able to raise his head. All four of us gasped in horror when we saw his face; it was still Lucien's face, at least in a physical sense, but something about it had changed. It was darker, less human, and much more terrible. I knew what must have happened; again, I was making assumptions, but it just fit together like a perfect and awful puzzle, and once you saw the truth of it, it couldn't be unseen. The terrible thing that had been Arnold Hammerson's influence, instead of leaving Lucien's body, had been completely absorbed into it, taking it over at the basest of levels. Perhaps Lucien's personality was still alive in there somewhere, screaming in a tiny prison of agony; but for all intents and purposes, the Lucien who had helped us so much in the past was gone for good.

This was perfectly demonstrated a moment later when he snapped at Tommy, who had been pounding him on the back all this time. "That is very annoying," he said flatly, almost expressionlessly. He stood up, took one of Tommy's arms, and hurled him back into the living room with more force than should have been possible for a human; Tommy hit the back of the nearest couch, toppled over the top of it, and collapsed onto the cushions.

"We have to go now," Amelia whispered, tugging on Marc's arm. "We can't do anything here now."

"But—but," Marc stammered, watching Lucien, his face tortured.

Amelia's voice and face were more tender than I'd ever seen as she said, "It's too late, honey. He's gone."

She was right, too. It was quite a lot like having just watched a love one die; only this was worse because the loved one in question was still walking around, even if they were now essentially an entirely different person. The thought of leaving now felt awful to me too, especially with Tommy, Lena, and all those left in the Big Room still in the path of whatever magical cyclone was heading their way, but there was no denying Amelia's words - it really was too late. There was nothing we could do, and moreover, if we tried to take on Lucien at this very moment, with Fewul standing right there ready to take his orders, there was no way we could win. Up until now, Lucien had been prepared to let us enjoy an illusion of freedom; now, he would hurt, or even kill, anyone who got in his way. Because it wasn't Lucien who was in charge anymore.

Amelia and I raised our hands to either side of our faces, the signal on which we had agreed the night before. A moment later, I felt myself being sucked in no particular direction; and then another moment later I was back in the corner of the control room, locked in place by the enchantment I'd put there to make sure that people we let into the base wouldn't have the freedom to do any damage unless we authorised them. James quickly released me from the enchantment so that I could get out of the way and let the other three in.

"What was that, John?" Peter asked me as I took a seat near the control panel. I was joined shortly by Stella who had been pulled in second, and was looking around herself with a somewhat dazed expression.

"If you mean what just happened to Lucien," I said heavily, "what it was, was a whole lot of evil. I don't think we can rely on his unwillingness to kill deliberately anymore."

"Definitely right," Amelia said, having just appeared in the room in time to hear the last sentence of what I'd just said.

"I suggest we abandon the rest of this mission for now," said James, tapping his thumb on one of the displays—one which was showing the Beast of Magic, still standing beside Lucien. "With her around, we're not going to be able to retrieve Tommy without possibly giving ourselves away."

"Shush," Amelia said, "listen, he's talking."

The room fell silent then, everyone going still all at once (leaving Marc trapped against the wall, as James had just let him in but hadn't freed him from the captive enchantment yet). Watched by Fewul and a confused-and-still-scared-looking Tommy, Lucien was speaking to people whom he wasn't entirely sure were present. We missed the start of it, but we did catch most of it.

"—As I imagine you couldn't help yourself but to stay around and see if anything interesting happened—any opportunity worth taking advantage of," he was saying, looking around himself as he spoke, as though attempting to address every corner of the room rather than because he actually expected to see someone. "And of course, it doesn't hurt me one way or the other to assume that you're still here, so I'm going to assume that you are, and I'm going to tell you this: I'm extremely pissed at you, John. You've pissed me off several times over the last few days, for a few different reasons, but daring to persuade Stella to abandon me, after I gave her the most valuable gift in the world when she joined me, is beyond anything I can forgive. You've forced my hand and left me with no alternative. I hope you understand, John, that what happens next is your fault. If you are still here, I suggest you follow me; then you'll know what I'm talking about."

Chapter 3: The Value of Life

"Should we follow him?" Peter asked even as James began doing just that, though not before finally releasing Marc so that he could come and take a seat.

"I think it would be a good idea if we at least knew what he's capable of now," Mr. Woodward said, looking uneasy. "It doesn't appear that he or Fewul can sense us where we are, so it should be safe enough to watch."

"Which we could have done on the spyers, but whatever," Peter shrugged.

We floated along behind Lucien as he and Fewul descended through the base in the elevator, stopping on the level of the dining hall, Worship Hall, and of course, the Big Room. Lucien went into the Big Room but then stopped just inside it to one side of the small door. He stood there long enough for me to get a little bored watching—at least five minutes, maybe longer. Finally, though, he snapped out of whatever trance he'd been in and proceeded further into the room, walking down aisles and turning corners as though he knew exactly where he was going or who he was looking for. Several people called out to him and bowed respectfully as he passed, but he ignored them all until…

"Ah, here we are," he said, stopping in front of four older men, all of whom I instantly recognised: Rob, Bob, Grillion and Graham. They had all been soldiers for the Woodwards in the old war, and had returned to the fray in this war, though from what I understood they were in a more advisory role than actually going out there and putting their boots on the ground. Rob and Bob I had known all my life as friends of Dad and Charlie who were the number-one repairmen in Chopville, while Grillion had always run the little canteen outside Hamster's Stretch Reserve. Only Graham I had met recently; suffering post-traumatic stress disorder and with barely a dollar to his name after the war, he had never really left Mr. Woodward's side, spending most of his days reading and drinking his life away.

"Lucien, sir," all four of them said now, snapping him a crisp salute which made the younger man smile.

"That's pretty cool. Have you been practicing that in case I came down here again?" he asked, and they all shuffled their feet, looking a little chagrined. "You, Graham," Lucien said now, picking him out from the others for something, and an awful feeling of premonition swept me, "how would you like to do something special for me? Something that very few people in this room could do as well as you?"

"I'd be honoured," Graham said at once. "Whataya need me to do?"

For a few seconds all of them just stood there, waiting for Lucien to speak; while Lucien himself stood there, appearing to be concentrating on something, judging by the look on his face—perhaps he was reading their minds to figure something out? Then he grunted in surprise. Turning to Fewul, who was still behind him (and had now taken on the appearance of a non-descript middle-aged man, perhaps so as not to alarm anyone in the Big Room), he asked, "Am I missing something here? Why is it happening to me instead of him?"

Comprehension smacked us all the instant Fewul opened his mouth to answer, and I had a moment—just a moment—in which I hoped that maybe, just maybe, we had succeeded in significantly hindering him. But then Fewul said, "Someone seems to have put a shield around you that traps any magic you perform within in, whether performed by your Sorcerous powers or the Sien-Leoard Crystal."

Lucien scowled. "Can you remove it for me?"

"Of course, Master," Fewul said at once, and Lucien smiled. He turned back to the four men, and a moment later all four of their shirts had changed colour.

"Perfect; I'm back in business," he said, "now where were we—ah, yes. You three; please take a couple of steps back from Graham here," he said, and they obliged without question. None of them, not even Graham, looked worried about what was coming; either Lucien was suppressing their emotions with his Honnie mind, or they genuinely believed he wouldn't actually hurt them.

Lucien lapsed back into concentration, his eyes fixed on Graham, who froze in place, his expression changing to one of surprise and perhaps slight alarm before it too froze in place. It took a few seconds to understand exactly what was happening; Graham was frozen in place because Lucien was actually freezing him, lowering and lowering his body temperature more and more as we watched. All the colour disappeared from his face and the light went out of his eyes; he was probably unconscious now, and maybe even already dead, before Lucien suddenly pivoted on one ankle and kicked out, his shoe connecting squarely with the centre of Graham's torso.

Rob, Bob and Grillion cried out in horror and shrank away from Lucien, but I barely heard them over the equally horrified gasps and exclamations filling the control room. Upon contact Graham's body had practically exploded, shattering into more little pieces of frozen flesh and tissue than anyone would ever be able to count. Beside me, Stella's eyes were huge in her face again; she had never really believed Lucien would deliberately do something so awful. Amelia was rocking back and forth in her seat, looking close to tears, but Mr. Woodward appeared more distressed than anyone. I thought I understood why: he had known Graham for more than thirty years, had stood by the soldier when no one else had, and they had probably been good mates for a lot of that time.

Lucien, meanwhile, had cast a disdainful look at Rob, Bob and Grillion where they stood before turning his back dismissively on the whole scene and walking away, back towards the entrance of the Big Room. The spyers tracked his progress, but we didn't; the shock was too great for any of us to think of watching him, or to move the base from its view of the terrible scene. Rob, Bob and Grillion had crept forward again with awful fascination, to do what I had no idea—there was nothing left to do for poor Graham except clean him up off the floor.

"He—he," Peter finally stammered, wiping sweat off his forehead. "He really has gone evil now, hasn't he? He wouldn't have done that before."

"No, he wouldn't have," Mr. Woodward said, his voice gruff. "What we just saw is out of the Hammerson playbook. Tankom had enjoyed finding creative ways to end people's lives, preferably making them suffer as much along the way as she could, and Arnold grew up believing that was okay if the people being killed were serving a greater purpose, or if they deserved to suffer."

"And that's what Lucien thought just now," James said softly, looking at me. "He did that because it served the purpose of showing John that he's done mucking around, and that he'll just keep on killing if he has to—if we don't give him what he wants."

"What can we do?" Amelia sobbed. "He wants us all to hand ourselves in, and we can't do that now, especially not now that he's gone so dark—he might not settle for putting influential charms on us anymore."

"And we can't walk away from the fight either," James said flatly, "at least, not in good conscience. It would be a mistake to think that Lucien will stop killing people, even if he gets what he wants this time, because there will always be a next time, and I imagine that killing would get easier each time you do it."

"Everything I've seen in my life backs up that hypothesis," Mr. Woodward agreed.

"So—we have to stop him then," Marc said decisively. With what looked like a great effort, he sat up ramrod-straight in his seat and said, "You're right, Amelia. My big brother really *is* gone, and it would be foolish for us to treat Lucien like anything other than an enemy who must be destroyed, just like Arnold Hammerson."

Amelia patted Marc's shoulder sympathetically.

"Okay then," James said, once again business-like, "so what's the next thing we—"

He broke off very suddenly when another voice spoke from outside the control room. It wasn't very loud, but it was loud enough for all of us to hear. A little distorted, it came through in unison from every spyer that was still following Lucien, who was now back in the elevator and ascending with Fewul to the top floor of the Hammerheart base.

"You may or may not have followed me down there, and you may not be following me now; but if you are, then I'm sure you understand the point I made. And if you really weren't there and I'm presently talking to myself, I'm confident that you'll hear about it soon enough—perhaps the next time you sneak in here and try to pull something right under my nose. All I want from you is to turn yourself and all the others in; I can no longer promise that I'll be lenient, as I would have been a couple of days ago, but it would still be the best alternative compared to what you'll have to watch me do to anyone and everyone you care about—that is, everyone I can reach."

He may have wanted to say more, to expand perhaps on exactly what horrors he was considering committing, but that was when the elevator doors opened onto the long corridor beneath the living quarters. He shook his head, smiling a little, and set off towards the far end, Fewul following along as usual.

When it became clear that Lucien was done speaking to us, James said, "Well, nothing we didn't already know. So as I was saying before that interruption, what's the next thing we should do?"

"*Now* can we recall Fewul?" Peter asked. "I suggested we do that while you guys were out there," he told me, Marc and Amelia, "but JSandwich here shot me down—something about not giving Lucien time to react or something."

"What I said," James said, a little irritably, "is that we couldn't afford for Lucien to know that we're capable of recalling Fewul, and that's assuming it even works. We can't let him know that we can do that until he has no chance at all of calling Fewul back to him. But maybe we will be able to recall it now, or at least as soon as Lucien orders it to go and do something else, if we can now figure out where the Sorcerous Crystals are."

"That actually makes sense when you explain it like that," Marc said, and then he turned to Stella. "Well firstly, welcome back to the good guys. How are you doing?"

"Awful," she said, her voice a little choked, and when I looked more closely at her, I could see her fighting to hold back tears again. "I dunno if I'm up for this."

"You can go upstairs and have a rest, if you like," Amelia said gently, "but we really *do* need you to help us with something first—it shouldn't take too long. Does that sound okay?"

"I suppose," she conceded, gazing curiously at Amelia. "Er—you're—you—how are you?"

I had forgotten until that moment that this would have been the first time Stella had come face-to-face with Amelia in person (excluding any magical spying she may have done, or any watching from my eyes through our mind connection) since her mind had been wiped clean by my former English teacher, now police commissioner, Mr. Dermott Hall, during the battle that had culminated in Arnold Hammerson's death. The Amelia who existed now resided in the same body as the former Amelia, and was similar in just about every noticeable way; but the copy which May had made for us based on all the memories of Amelia's she had collected prior to the wipe, as well as all our existing memories of times with Amelia, was imperfect. Amelia was similar enough that much of the time it was easy to forget that she wasn't quite the same person she had been for most of the time I had known her; but occasionally, the differences would become more obvious.

In response to Stella's question, Amelia shrugged, guessing what she was referring to. "I'm fine, really. I'm just me."

"And she's mostly the same as she was before," Peter added, "but you probably know that already, if you've kept an eye on us since Saturday."

Stella flushed and looked down at her lap, but didn't have any response.

"Firstly, do you happen to know where Lucien hid the Sorcerous Crystals?" Mr. Woodward asked her. "My guess is 'no', but we have to check."

"Yeah, you're right," she said, still not looking up from the tops of her knees. "Lucien didn't tell me anything that he didn't want any of you guys to know, because John could have been in my mind at the time and picked up on it."

"Damn," Marc whistled through his teeth. "Even now, people keep secrets from you because of your mind. That's gotta suck."

"Never mind," James said, giving her what he probably hoped was a comforting smile, but I could see a note of impatience there. "There is something else you can do for us - would you be able to try to use your magic to track your crystal's location?"

She did look up then, her expression startled, but not in a bad way. It looked as though the idea hadn't even occurred to her until that moment. "I—I can try that," she said, "but the odds of him putting all six of them together are pretty slim."

"Doesn't matter, it'd still be enough to knock him out for—" Marc broke off, raising his eyebrows at the expressions we were all giving him.

"You mean it would knock Stella out, leaving Lucien completely unharmed," James said pointedly, and Marc blushed in embarrassment. "If it turns out that they're not together, then it won't be a total loss. We can at least see what sort of protection Lucien has put around it, and look for signs of that same protection elsewhere. Do you know what to do, Stella?"

"Yeah," she said, and then lapsed into concentration. Whatever magic she was performing wasn't visible, but judging by her slowly shifting expression, it was working. The seconds lengthened as Stella focused harder and harder on what she was doing and the rest of us watched her, careful not to break her concentration. The longer it went on, the less hopeful I became that she would be able to do this; and even less when her expression grew more and more puzzled.

Finally, she seemed to stop what she was doing and look around at us. "Okay, I don't really understand what I'm sensing here."

"Just try to describe what you felt," Mr. Woodward told her. "don't try to make sense of it yet—we can help you with that."

"Okay," she took a deep breath. "So I've only done this once before, and back then I didn't even know that I was tracking a Sorcerous Crystal. My father just told me what to do and promised me a reward afterwards —which he never gave me, but then maybe he'd intended to give it to me after we'd taken you guys' magic—I don't know. Anyway, it supposed to make me feel a pull from a certain direction—you know, north, south, east, west, northwest, sou-southwest—whatever it is. But that's not happening this time; I can feel the pull coming from somewhere, so I know the crystal is there and not being magically concealed, but I can't figure out which direction."

A confused silence followed this little speech before, then in a much smaller voice than before, Stella said, "Did I mess up?"

"I don't think so," James said, his brow furrowing. "I can think of a couple of possibilities that might fit what you just described. For instance, if he somehow hid it deep enough in the Earth that it's practically in the core, the direction you would need to go would be down, regardless of where you are on the planet. The other possibility is that he's put it somewhere in space."

"That's good thinking, James," Mr. Woodward said, smiling at him, "but if it *is* in space, then chances are it's in motion. Could you sense any subtle movement in the direction, Stella?"

James's face lit up. "That's an excellent point - that would differentiate between those two possibilities - whether or not it's in motion relative to Stella's position."

"Let me see if I can figure that out," Stella said, and lapsed into another period of deep concentration—this one lasting at least five minutes. We were all starting to get a bit impatient when she finally came out of it. "You're right," she said to Mr. Woodward, "I think it may be in orbit around the Earth."

"That would make the moon the top suspect," Peter said, looking excited, "but I suppose it could be attached to the International Space Station or some other satellite—or maybe it's floating loose in some sort of magical container."

"Then we need to get up there and find out," James said, and he turned his attention to me. "Please tell me that this base is capable of going into space; this thing's gonna be so much harder if it isn't."

My stomach fell. "Er—I never made any specific enchantments to make it fly in space, but since it is gravity resistant, and contains its own atmosphere, it should be fine—shouldn't it?"

"Geez, we're gonna be taking a risk," James said. "It sounds like it'll handle the vacuum okay, but what about the freezing temperatures? Or impacts with tiny flying objects at thousands of kilometres an hour?"

"Yes, and yes," I said at once. "It's temperature resistant on the outside as well as the inside, just in case we had to fly through a Worship Hall at some point, and it can't be damaged by anything that hit it from the outside, regardless of how hard it hits. I even made sure no vibrations would pass through the structure so that we would all be safe."

"Sounds like the thing that hits us will come off worse," Peter smirked. "It might be a good idea to move along the fourth dimension a step if it looks like we're gonna make impact with something, though, just so we don't demolish any satellites beaming the Internet down or anything."

"Guys, this is all great and all," Amelia said, "but what are we gonna do when we actually find the thing? We still don't know how it's protected, and more than likely at least one of us will have to leave the base to go and get it. How's that gonna work if we're floating around in outer space?"

Mr. Woodward smiled indulgently at his daughter. "don't forget that we do have a Sorcerer with us now."

"And that's not the only thing," Peter said, patting his pocket. "I know it's not great to rely on it, but we have the Villain Crystal as well, and that probably does have the power to help us get the Sorcerous Crystals if we can just figure out a way to harness it."

A brief silence followed this before I chipped in, "That isn't the worst idea. We may not think we're villains, but from where Lucien's standing, he would probably think of himself as the good guy and us as the villains. If villains think they're doing the right thing then theoretically, that crystal wouldn't work for anyone, except we know that's not true. So maybe there is a way to convince it that Lucien's in the right and we aren't."

"Wouldn't that only work if the person using it also believed—" James began, but I cut him off.

"Come on, not everyone who's ever used that thing would believe they're the bad guys, right? Moran could use it pretty well even when he wasn't harming us—"

"That's not quite how it works either," Mr. Woodward jumped in. "So far as anyone knows, the Villain Crystal responds only to a person's intent in that moment, not whether or not they believe they're doing the right thing for all—because John is right about that. Even the Hammersons thought they were ultimately doing the best thing for the world by creating a magical empire. In this case, if we were to focus on stealing the Sorcerous Crystals so that we can strip Lucien of his power and not focus on whatever comes after that, the Villain Crystal would likely be very obliging."

"Er—guys," Stella said softly, and we all looked at her. "Can I go now? I don't think I can deal with this right now."

James appeared to be struggling with himself. "I get that, but we might need something still, if—"

"Let her go," Amelia interrupted, giving Stella a warm smile. "She's been through enough, and she probably needs a little time to figure out where her head's at. We can bring her back down here if we need her for something else."

"Wait," Marc said quickly, "we still need some way of tracking the direction of her crystal. Stella, do you think you can create some sort of device that we can use to do that so that you don't have to stay here the whole time?"

"A three-dimensional one, so that it isn't limited in the same way as the other tracker," I added.

"Fair enough," she said, and lapsed into concentration a third time, though this was much shorter than the previous two.

A few seconds later, she was holding something that resembled a model of a windmill—it didn't actually look anything like a windmill, but that was merely the first thing I thought of. It sat on a small board about the size of a person's hand, stretching up about a foot into the air, the top third of the appendage able to rotate independently of the rest of the device. Stella demonstrated by tilting the board to one side and then the other; the thing at the top, which now resembled an arrow when I saw it in those terms, remained pointing in the same direction. It effectively functioned as a three-dimensional compass. And right now, it was pointing upward, though by no means straight up; the actual direction was up, forward, and a little to the left.

"Perfect," James said, taking the new tracker from her and placing it on the control panel. "We may ask you to try to modify it if it turns out that the crystals aren't all together, if that's even possible, but for now this'll do. Who wants to help Stella get a room?"

Of course everyone looked at me, even Stella. I sighed. "Okay, I'll do it. Er—I'm not sure how long I'll—"

"Take all the time you need," Marc said, grinning at me. "You've done the biggest job of the day so far, so leave the next little bit to us."

"But we will come and find you if we need either of you for something," James said, turning his attention to the display screens. "Oh shit—"

We had all forgotten that the base was still in the Big Room, had been there this whole time, overlooking the scene of a grisly murder. He began working the controls, turning us quickly around and speeding in the direction of the door, flying straight through people's compartments as we went. Most were empty, but someone was asleep in one. While he did that, the rest of us took a look at the spyers which were focused on Lucien, ignoring the ones which had gone dark ever since Stella became untraceable. He was back in the living room, now accompanied by Tommy and Lena (who had gotten dressed since the last time I'd seen her); and, of course, the Beast of Magic, who had shifted form yet again.

"Oh lovely," Stella said drily, gazing at herself on the screens. "I guess he's going to make it look like I never left him."

"Does that mean we still can't recall Fewul?" Peter asked.

"No," James sighed, "and I'm starting to wonder if he's going to send Fewul away at all. After this morning, he may want to be more certain of his security before going it alone again."

"Then let's hurry up and get those crystals," Marc said.

"There's one thing we need to decide before we leave Earth," Mr. Woodward said, looking around at us all, "bearing in mind that we won't have any way of letting people back down here once we're in the sky—"

"Come on," I said quietly to Stella, getting up and beckoning for her to follow me, which she did with a grateful but tentative smile.

As I ushered Stella through the door, I looked back over my shoulder at the control panel—or rather, one specific screen on the panel, which was illuminated with the number '3'. I tried to do a quick calculation in my head, but couldn't remember the exact number of people we had rescued from the Big Room that morning—but surely it was less than thirty. That meant with three floors with twelve bedrooms each, there would almost certainly be somewhere to put Stella.

And if there wasn't, it wouldn't be a big deal. When I had first constructed this base, I had only given it one level of bedrooms, but I had also given it the ability to magically create new identical levels on top of them if we needed them. Only create—it couldn't un-create them once they were there. Amelia had already used the controls beside that number '3' to create two new levels that very morning, which meant that if I needed to, I could create a fourth one if there weren't any spare bedrooms left.

I pushed the button to call the elevator, and then while we waited, said, "Er—do you want me to show you around the base a bit, or would you rather just get a room?"

"I'd rather just get a room," she said, a little shortly I thought, and that made me remember that there were still a whole load of things between us which needed to be dealt with. I didn't really feel like dealing with them now, but I supposed if it could be done sooner rather than later, it would be ultimately better for both of us. That was assuming it would even be possible for us to return to a healthy friendship after all that had passed between us. And with these thoughts racing around in my head, I was very glad when the doors before us opened, revealing the empty lift.

I took Stella up to level one and got out of the elevator there, having a quick look around. The foyer was deserted and all twelve bedroom doors were closed, but that didn't mean some of them weren't empty.

Each door had a little digital display set into it, which showed the name of the person to whom that room belonged, if it had been claimed by someone. A quick look around told me that almost all the rooms here had been claimed: me, Marc, Amelia, Peter and James first; and then Jessica, Felicity, Natalie, Rebecca and Erica this morning. One of the other two doors had a note taped over the display, which I saw read 'Reserved for Darcy' when I took a closer look. Darcy was one who hadn't been rescued that morning; he was Jessica's boyfriend, and his reserved room was right next to hers, so it was no mystery as to who had written that note.

The last room happened to be right next to mine. It was in the front-left corner of the level (front and left if you were facing the control panel two levels below, which was how I preferred to orientate myself). I led Stella inside, gave her a chance to look around and recognise that these rooms were an almost perfect duplication of our bedrooms from the old base which Lucien had destroyed, and then went over to one of the differences between this room and those ones: the control panel near the door.

"You need to tell the room that it's yours before you can relax," I told her, opening the panel and beckoning her over to me; until then, she had been just standing a short way inside the door, looking around with a strangely vacant expression. "Just put your hand on this handle and think at it that it's yours."

She came over and did as she was told, while I stepped back outside to watch the door. I knew it had worked when the display changed to show her full name, and I gave her a reassuring smile that she didn't see as she was too busy staring at nothing in particular, so far as I could tell.

"Are you—are you okay?" I asked her, starting to get a little worried about this almost total lack of anything from her.

"I—I'm not sure," she said, not looking at me but continuing to look at the wall in front of her.

Trying to hide my own nerves, I closed her bedroom door, took her by the shoulder and guided her to the side of her bed. I then sat down a couple of feet from her—not too close, in other words. Part of me hoped she would tell me to leave her alone, that we could talk about things later on, even though the sensible part of me knew that wouldn't necessarily be the best thing to do. And that was assuming there would be time for talking later; we had been given an unexpected reprieve from the action, but moments like this may be harder to come by if things with Lucien really got going.

Before I could think of some way to break the ice, she asked me in a somewhat choked voice, "How come you don't hate me?"

"Erm," I said brilliantly, "should I?"

She covered her face with her hands and spoke, her voice a little muffled but still coherent. "I've been such an awful person. I turned on all you guys. I let all of this happen. And I messed up your life so badly. I can barely live with myself, so how come you can stand to be in the same room as me?"

I took a second to process all of this, then said, "Okay, first of all, I don't actually agree with any of that, except maybe the turning-on-us part, but you're not alone there—just about everyone did the same thing, because they had no choice. You know how the influential charm works —"

"Yeah, the spell I tried to use on you back there."

I sighed. "Okay, maybe I should be madder about *that* part of it, but for some reason, I'm not. It's like you said at the time—I would have thanked you if it had worked, because I wouldn't have known any better."

She shook her head, lowering her hands so that I could see her pain-filled eyes. "It's worse than that. I found ways to justify everything that was happening—everything Lucien was doing. I probably would have been okay with him killing that man back there if I'd thought it was for some bigger purpose, and that's just a sick way to think."

"Okay," I said slowly, my heart having sunk a little at her words. "Yeah, that *is* pretty bad, but those few days are just something you'll have to find a way to live with from now on, otherwise you'll go crazy. Maybe you should focus on your actions in that time, rather than your thoughts. You didn't do anything really bad while you were with him— not that I know of anyway."

"I didn't kill anyone," she admitted reluctantly, "but I never really tried to talk Lucien out of the things he was doing either, I only made perfunctory efforts which always ended with me deciding that he would know what he was doing and it would be for the best—"

"Which sounds a lot like the influential charm working," I said, "or maybe he was using that weird Honnie mind he has going to actually make you stop questioning him, so you can hardly blame yourself for that either."

She bit her lower lip, looking like she wanted to say something else. "What? What is it?" I asked.

"It doesn't change the fact that I messed everything up for you," she said in a small voice.

It was my turn to shake my head. "Stella, you didn't do anything wrong there. That was Lucien's doing, and I know for a fact that you weren't happy with him for it—"

"And why do you think Lucien chose to do that particular thing to you?" she shot back. "Because he wanted you to drive all those other girls away by your own actions so that you would end up choosing me. And actually, I did mess it up for you: if I hadn't told Lena about you and Amelia, it never would have got back to Natalie."

Which meant that Lena might not have tried to seduce me in the exact way that she did, which would have meant that Natalie wouldn't have caught us together. The whole thing could have happened differently if not for that one thing that Stella had let slip to Lena during a strange interlude between the two of them. But then my reason caught up with my jabbering thoughts: "If all you say is true, Lucien would have arranged for everyone to find out anyway, so your actions didn't make any difference. And for what it's worth, I don't blame you for any of that: I blame Lucien, but mostly I just blame myself, because I still did that stuff."

"You don't have to tell me, I was in your mind when you were with Amelia," she said, and I felt my face redden. "No, I mean, I know how bad it was and I don't see how you could have resisted, so you're the one who needs to stop beating yourself up."

I pondered these words, surprised to find some comfort in them. It wouldn't stop me from beating myself up, of course, but it made me realise that there actually was some value in our strange mind connection after all: Stella was the only girl who could possibly understand what being cursed in that way had been like, because she had gone through some of it with me. Then I remembered something else to make this whole situation more awkward: being in my mind with Amelia wasn't the only contact Stella had had with that curse. Less than twenty-four hours ago in Stella's world (over a week ago in mine, thanks to time travel), shortly after she had been in my mind, I had been in her body.

"That actually does make me feel a little better," I said truthfully, "and well—since we're on the topic, I really owe you a huge apology for —er—yesterday," I faltered, reminding myself again that it was so much more recent for her than it was for me. "I really, really shouldn't have— well—you know—"

She shook her head more violently this time. "I don't want to hear your apology. I don't want to hear that you think it was all a huge big mistake and it was all down to the curse and that it meant nothing. Do you know how much that would hurt me?"

Why did this road have to be so full of potholes? There was so much anguish on Stella's face that it was almost unbearable to look at. I couldn't think of a single thing to say that would make this situation any better. The truth, so far as I could figure it, was that I cared greatly about Stella, that I cared enough that I could have her as a girlfriend, and that our sexual interlude had meant something (although I wasn't exactly sure what)—but that those feelings still paled into insignificance next to my feelings for Natalie. Telling her that it had just been the curse would be a lie, and it would probably hurt her more than anything else I could say, but it was also the only thing I could think of that would dash her hopes. But I couldn't bring myself to do that.

After a silence that felt a lot longer than it actually was, I said, "Okay, so you know that's not true—you have to know it wasn't completely meaningless, otherwise I would have been able to resist. But it was still a mistake to do that to you under those circumstances because —well—"

I hesitated again, not wanting to mention Natalie's name again, but before I could think how to continue, Stella said, "Because I'm not your preference. I never was. Okay."

I looked away, unable to take her sadness any longer. My instincts were urging me to scoot over to her and give her a hug, but that would definitely send the wrong message in this situation, assuming she would even let me touch her now. I wished that I'd given myself the ability to magically cheer a person up while I'd been on Rock Haulter, even if only temporarily; but of course, the only thing even close that I'd thought of was the ability to seduce a person. The exact nature of the charm I'd given myself was that it would cause a girl to be horny for a certain amount of time, however long I wanted to keep it going, but it wouldn't make them desire me specifically—even at the time, doing more than that felt like abusing power.

I knew it was a terrible idea, but because I was desperate for a way out of this mess that wouldn't involve hurting Stella any more, I turned back to her and began subtly working that charm on her—not enough to make her notice anything, not enough that it would cause her to do anything, but hopefully just enough to make her think a few less-dark thoughts.

"Okay," I said as I worked my magic, "that may be true, but I'm not going to apologise for how I feel about Natalie—I've felt like that since forever. But what you need to understand is that I've had a lot of time to think since yesterday—more time than you realise," I suppressed a smirk, "and although I'm definitely not over her, I think I am coming to terms with the thought that I won't be able to get her back. And that was the only reason why you weren't my preference."

"So," she hesitated, her eyes becoming intent on my face as she looked at me. Seeing that some of the sadness had indeed leaked out of her, I felt a little more confident laying the charm on just a little thicker. "So, you're saying that you and I—maybe—"

I shook my head. The word 'misfire' was screaming in my head. "Stella, I really can't think about the future now—it's still too soon for me to do that."

"Yeah, of course," she said quickly, blushing a little. "I only—I just thought—sorry," she finished in a whisper.

I gave into my instinct and wriggled closer to her so that I could give her a hug, still half-expecting her to pull roughly away from me. Thankfully, she returned it gratefully, resting her chin on one of my shoulders so that I had to do the same to her. We were both sitting on the side of her bed, our legs hanging down, so the angle was a little weird, but it was still enough for me to feel a stirring of desire for her. I could feel her breasts pressing against my chest, and I could smell her scent—it was a clean smell, but without perfume, and yet it drew me. I could only suppress the feeling with difficulty.

"Don't be sorry," I said finally.

"Okay," she said, sounding like she may have been smiling a little. "Can I ask you something?"

"Yeah, sure."

"What were you thinking about when we were—you know—yesterday—"

"Oh," I said, taken aback, and when she stiffened in my arms as though expecting a sharp retort, I rubbed her back a little to hopefully settle her down. "To be honest, I'm not sure. I—I don't think I was really thinking at all until it was over."

"Okay," she said, "fair enough, I suppose. But not counting the curse, did you at least—er—enjoy it?"

Smiling reluctantly, I gently pulled back from her so that I could see her face—she looked rather nervous and shy, her face a little flushed. Not letting go of her, and with her arms still loosely around me, I said, "If that's your way of asking if I thought you were any good, the answer is yes. It wouldn't have mattered a whole lot if you weren't, but you were."

She smiled a slow and rather sexy smile. "Well, I liked it; even though it was a bit rough, and it did hurt a little. I still liked it."

That was when I kissed her. I didn't think about it. I didn't decide to do it, and I didn't decide not to do it; I just did it. Our faces had been quite close together, so leaning forward those few inches and putting my lips on hers was a very easy thing to do. She had frozen in my arms for a moment, almost long enough for me to pull back thinking I'd made a dreadful mistake, but before I could do so, she kissed me back. A lot of things happened when she did that; the kiss deepened, we tightened our arms around each other, and I was no longer able to stop myself from desiring her.

"I thought—I thought you said—" Stella said between kisses.

"I know what I said," I replied, before continuing to kiss her.

"Is this a mistake?"

"Maybe."

"Do you regret it?"

"No."

"Good."

I probably would regret it later, but right now I was all desire and hormones, and Stella was all I wanted. Even the shadow that was the absence of Natalie lifted from my heart for a while; while I was here with her, it was hard to believe there had ever been a time when I didn't want Stella. She and I continued to kiss, running our hands over the accessible parts of each other's bodies with a kind of desperate intensity before we both needed more.

And so it was more that we did.

Chapter 4: The Moon Base

Well that was really something, I thought as I slunk out of Stella's room sometime later. That certainly hadn't been how I'd intended for that encounter to go, and I still didn't know if it was a good thing or not. In my case, my main regret was Natalie, and what this would do to my chances of getting her back if she found out (which she probably would eventually, given that everyone was now confined to such a small area); but then, I'd already screwed up so badly with Natalie that I had probably already lost her, and this bit of extra confirmation wouldn't make a whole lot of difference. So for me, the real question now was: did I want Stella as my girlfriend after all?

She had asked me if I regretted kissing her and I had told her 'no', which certainly had been true at the time. In a way it was still true for me, but now that it was over, it left me with more questions than answers. Ironically, it was Stella who seemed to regret the way it had gone; she had been fully into it for a good while, but eventually (sooner than I would have liked), she asked me to leave so that she could get some rest. I wasn't fooled—she wanted me to leave so that she could think, and I suspected I knew what she was thinking: giving herself to me would have been a mistake if I wasn't ready to give myself back to her, and neither of us really knew if I was.

And there was another reason: Stella had made it clear that she would like to be my girlfriend, but she wasn't so desperate that she was prepared to be my last resort—the girlfriend I went to because I couldn't have anyone else who I preferred over her. Up until this point, and perhaps still, that hadn't been the case—I had always wanted Natalie more than I had wanted Stella. But even if that were still true, Stella was now firmly my second preference, now that I had really, truly come to terms with Amelia being unavailable to me; and now that Lena had, by force, become unavailable to me.

I had been in Stella's room for almost two hours, and in another hour or so it would be lunch time. That made me feel like a real slacker, so I took the lift straight back down to the control room to find out what I had missed. Marc, James and Mr. Woodward were all still there, but they had been joined at some point since I'd been gone by Natalie and Erica. My heart sank a little at the sight of Natalie, especially when the cool, calm look she gave me told me that she'd been told where I'd gone (and with whom), but other than a look, she didn't acknowledge my arrival.

"Everything okay, John?" Marc asked me, turning his attention back to the screens as he spoke.

"Yeah, it's all good. What's been—where are we?" I asked, catching sight of the display screens and the unearthly scene they revealed.

"Just teleported to the moon's surface," Mr. Woodward told me, and I gaped at him—I hadn't even noticed the suspension of animation that usually came with teleportation. "We figured out the crystal was there when we flew right beneath it. And now, as you can see, Lucien is about to lead us straight to it."

"What?" I said again, my brain jamming, unable to process the true meaning of his words.

Marc rolled his eyes and looked back at me. "After you left, Lucien called a meeting of his closest Hammerhearts and told them that he had decided to transfer Stella's chip to someone else, and that Stella had agreed to this—and with Fewul sitting there doing a disturbingly good imitation of her, she confirmed it. They all squabbled over who should get the chip until Lucien decided they were all a bunch of immature children and he was going to take the last chip for himself, making him the one and only Sorcerer, and saying he would use the Sien-Leoard Crystal to make sure the weather didn't go funny."

"Oh," I said, and a second later, comprehension hit me. "Wait, so we're not going to stop him from doing that?"

"If we can see how he gets to the crystal, the payoff will be enormous," James said absently, his focus mostly on steering the base after Lucien, who surprisingly wasn't alone: he had a woman with him, a woman I vaguely recognised as a nurse from the old Woodward base. Neither of them were having any trouble breathing on the surface of the moon, so there was obviously magic involved.

"Don't you think we should try a little harder to stop him from taking Stella's magic?" I asked, alarm growing. "That's an invaluable asset we really should be protecting."

Natalie made a sniffing noise then, causing me to glance sideways at her. Her expression was set, and there was something else in it I couldn't recall seeing before: she looked a little mean in that moment. I had the distinct idea that sacrificing Stella's magic in order to see where the crystal was and how it was protected had originally been her idea, and the others had agreed, seeing the logic in it. Sadly, I could see some of the logic too: if we were able to get the crystal back, even after Lucien had messed with it, we would eventually be able to undo the damage and return Stella's magic—or perhaps return it to Natalie, depending on how the base as a whole voted.

Confirming some of this, Marc said, "Getting that crystal would be an even more invaluable asset, especially if it leads us to the other five."

That was another good point: if we got all six crystals, Marc would have the magic of the Hero Crystal back in his possession. I still felt uneasy about this, and a little sad about what was going to happen to Stella very shortly, so I cast around for something else to say, uncomfortably aware of Natalie's presence just a few feet from me. "Hey, where are Peter and Amelia?"

"We left them behind," Erica told me, "on Earth, so that they could try to stop anything bad that might happen. Apparently they're bringing more people from the Big Room back now."

"We're keeping in touch with them," Marc told me, seeing the look on my face, "telepathically, I mean, which gives me an idea...."

He went silent then, and I looked more closely at him. Only then did I notice what he was holding in one hand: a white device which I recognised as a telepathic communicator. All of us had one of those, and by holding them and placing a finger on a pad on the device, we could send thoughts to someone else, or everyone else, who had an identical device in their possession (if they didn't have their finger on their corresponding pad at the same time, they would be taken by an urge to touch it). I had also create red and blue communicators, but they weren't for the army as a whole. The red ones were to communicate with Jacob Underwood back on Rock Haulter, just in case we needed him to put the magic of the Rock to use for our benefit, and the blue ones were mine, and nobody else in the base knew about them.

"What are you doing?" I asked him.

"Advising Amelia to have a go at capturing Tommy and Lena while the cat's away."

"Good thinking," Mr. Woodward agreed, not taking his eyes from the display screens.

A silence fell then as, having run out of things to say, we all watched James carefully steering the base along, keeping so close to Lucien's shoulder that we were always in danger of hitting it, though we never actually did. He was leading the woman down into a crater, but they didn't go all the way to the bottom; instead, they squeezed into a gap between a couple of rocks that I wouldn't have even noticed otherwise. Lucien used his magic to light up the interior of this new cave, except it wasn't really much of a cave; just a little nook, barely big enough for the two of them to squeeze into.

The woman looked nervous, but not scared, as she watched Lucien roving his hand over some of the rocks, shifting them around in such a way that looked very deliberate. I would have been a lot more frightened if I'd been in her position, because I had a terrible feeling about what her presence beside Lucien at this point meant: he needed to use her somehow to access the crystals, and the only thing I could think of that she could do which he couldn't do himself was to sacrifice her life. I felt sick as I watched the screens, but knew what Marc and James and possibly Mr. Woodward would say if I objected to trying to save her life —we could save a lot more lives if we could see how the crystals were protected.

Of course, if getting them required human sacrifice, then we would be in a world of trouble anyway.

Lucien had opened a small hole between the rocks. He reached down, seemed to feel around for something, and then came up holding something invisible in his fist. He made it visible, revealing it to be some sort of cable (appearing to be metallic, but flexible and bendy) and then proceeded to move it around in what looked like very deliberate patterns. After about fifteen seconds of this, an audible click sounded through the cave, probably coming from the floor from where that cable protruded, but it was impossible to be sure from inside the base. Lucien pulled on the length, dragging something larger up from beneath the rocks.

It was a door, floating in the air slightly off the floor of the cave, apparently hanging from the cable in Lucien's hand. It was pretty small —both of them would have to duck to fit through it. Lucien began tying the cable behind the door into a knot large enough so that it would prevent the whole thing from sliding back into the rocks, taking the door with it—that was what it looked like, anyway. He then stepped back in front of the door and took the nurse's arm again as, with his other hand, he opened the door, needing not to use any magic for this layer of the protection.

Beyond was a long tunnel, very different from the cave. It was made of solid, unblemished stone, and obviously crafted by Lucien's magic specifically for the purpose of containing the crystals, rather than this cave which had most likely already existed, but been taken over by Lucien for his own usage. It was dark in there too, no magical light to speak of, and the dim light from this cave shone only a short way inside. Even as I thought this Lucien extinguished the light in the cave, plunging all of us into total darkness. The nurse let out a tiny squeak, but Lucien was quick to hush her.

James was ready. He darted straight through the door in the darkness, already having been pointed at it prior to the light going out, and then shooting up to the ceiling so fast that the base bounced off it—harming none of us in any way, of course. We heard Lucien and the nurse pass beneath us just before he created another magical light, properly showing us the tunnel for the first time. The doorway behind us remained open, but I wasn't born last night: I was sure Lucien had done something to make sure no one else could get through it, and now I understood why James had gone through ahead of him.

We returned to our position just over Lucien's shoulder as we followed him down the tunnel, which ended with another doorway, this one containing no door. Beyond was a room, in the centre of which sat a table or bench of no real description. Far more interesting was what sat atop the table or bench of no real description: six individual shields, all of them a semi-transparent, bluish colour, and each containing one of the six Sorcerous Crystals. Finally, we had reached our destination, but with those shields in place there was still something else to be done.

"Stay there," Lucien said to the nurse, leaving her by the entryway and proceeding to walk in slow circles around the table, one hand in his pocket as he eyed each of the crystals in turn. My guess was that he was using the Sien-Leoard Crystal to determine which of the Sorcerous Crystals contained Stella's magic, and sure enough, he stopped in front of one of them, observing it for several seconds before seeming to snap out of a trance.

He then beckoned to the nurse to join him, and she did so obediently, though not with any enthusiasm, and kept a safe distance from the shields around the crystals. When she joined him, he opened his mouth and then shut it just as quickly, his expression suddenly startled. He opened his mouth again, said, "Stella, I need you," and a moment later, Fewul teleported straight to his other side, still in Stella's form.

"You called?" she said, and now it was my turn to be startled. If I didn't know that was Fewul, I wouldn't have believed it wasn't Stella there with him. Marc had been right: this imitation of Stella was eerily perfect.

"Yes," he said, "but this won't take long. You know more about this than I do. Do I need to recall Fewul in order to change the properties of this crystal here?"

Stella (Fewul) shook her head. "Nope, you called Fewul with the Sien-Leoard Crystal, remember? So the rule about the Beast of Magic preventing the movement of the crystal chips doesn't apply. You had Fewul helping Cornish while I was receiving my chip, remember?"

Holy crap—this was creepier than I could ever have imagined.

"Oh yeah, that's true, and I'm real glad to hear it," he said. "And what about the weather? Will that be affected by what I'm about to do?"

"Yes, but you can balance that using the Sien-Leoard Crystal, so no probs."

"Great, even better," he grinned. "Thanks, you can get back to what you were doing now."

"Sure thing," she said, and teleported out of there a moment later.

"Okay, now we can continue," Lucien said to the nurse. "don't worry, this is straightforward, and it won't hurt you. At most it'll give you a little shock, but that's all. You see that crystal there?"

He indicated the one in front of them and the nurse nodded.

"I just need you to reach in there and pull it out for me," he said. "don't worry, that bluish thing is just light; your hand will pass right through it, and it'll only give you a little shock, like I said."

A lie, of course, for if that were all it did, he could just reach in and get it himself—or better yet, use his magic to vanish those shields altogether. I supposed he had created those shields so that they couldn't be vanished by magic—even his own—for that would weaken them against a possible future attack by the likes of us. None of these thoughts occurred to the nurse, of course; and if they had, Lucien would have immediately swept them away with his Honnie mind. She therefore obeyed him without question, reaching her hand forward towards the blueish shield.

The moment her hand made contact with it, two things happened very quickly. The shield changed colour, lightening to a pale-blue colour around that one crystal while remaining the same around the other five. At the same time, the nurse fell backward away from the table, falling to the floor and not moving. Natalie and Mr. Woodward both let out despairing groans, while James let out a similar noise of frustration and regret. She was dead, of course, as I had feared would happen. Lucien hadn't been lying about the shock part, though; her slightly widened eyes suggested that whatever had happened to her hadn't really hurt her, only given her a bit of a shock.

Lucien didn't even spare her a glance. The moment the shield changed colour, he reached into it with his own hand, gripped the crystal, held it for about ten seconds and then stepped away. A few seconds later, the shield changed colour again, returning to the same bluish colour as the rest of them. Lucien observed this with satisfaction before starting to leave the room, coming back only when he realised that he'd forgotten about the dead woman. He levitated her body into the air and made it follow him from the room, back along the tunnel and toward that weird door.

James didn't go after him.

A long, long silence followed Lucien's exit. I had no idea how long it went for, but we didn't speak until Marc broke everyone out of whatever thoughts were occupying them by snapping up his telepathic communicator. "Just letting Amelia know he's coming back," he said to several pairs of raised eyebrows.

"I can't believe we just sat back and let that happen," Erica said tearfully.

"I'd known her for more than twenty-five years," Mr. Woodward said in a choked voice.

Another silence followed before James said, "I don't think we could necessarily have saved her even if we had tried, not with Lucien so close, and even less so while Fewul was there. The most we can do is to make sure her sacrifice wasn't in vain, and we can do that because we now know how to get the crystals out of those shields."

"Oh really," I snapped, mockingly counting around the room. "Well there are six of us here, so yeah, we can open those shields at the very least. You did notice that it only opened when she died, right?"

"Yeah," James sighed. "I'm guessing Lucien got the idea for human sacrifice from the obstacles around the Sien-Leoard Crystal on Rock Haulter. The best way to protect something is to put a price on it that the vast majority of people won't be willing to pay. That's why I think the best way for us to handle this, and feel free to disagree with me if you have a better idea, is to capture six people we know for sure are Hammerhearts, not under an influential charm, and use them to lower those shields for us."

"I dunno how I feel about that," Erica admitted nervously.

Neither did I. Yes, it would work, but actually killing people? Even those we knew were Hammerhearts? I'd been in this position before, or one very like it, forced to kill people in order to save my own life. I didn't like it, and I didn't want to have that on my conscience again, but I couldn't deny the logic in what James was saying. How many more lives could we save if we could get those crystals? More than six was my best guess.

"It may be the best way," Mr. Woodward agreed. "War makes us do things we would rather not have to do but which we have to in order to save more lives, and I think this is one of those things."

"You said disagree if we had a better idea," I said to James. "Does anyone have a better idea before we go rounding up Hammerhearts and feeding them to the shield monster?"

Another silence followed, in which I examined the faces of everyone else in the room. James looked determined while Mr. Woodward looked —well, his expression was more difficult to define. Resigned, perhaps, except that didn't quite fit because there was a certain toughness in it as well, as though he understood that while it would be difficult, it would still be the right thing to do. Natalie and Erica both looked unhappy, and in Natalie's case, I thought perhaps there was some guilt there as well. She had been okay with Stella losing her magical powers, but not so much with sacrificing a woman's life in the process. As for Marc, his face was so carefully controlled that I had no idea what he could be thinking.

"Okay then," James eventually said, fixing one of his most stern expressions on his face. "I know you guys aren't comfortable with this, but you have to understand that it's the only way. Lucien undoubtedly created this obstacle specifically because he knew that if we found the crystals, we would struggle to find a way to negotiate this part of it—we would be unwilling to do what needed to be done. Let's not prove him right. Let's do what needs to be done, only let's make sure it's them, rather than us, who has to pay the price."

"Amelia's not up for it either," Marc said, his expression clearing. "Neither is Peter or Rebecca, for that matter."

James let out an exasperated sigh. "It doesn't matter whether they're up for it or not; unless they have a better idea, it has to be done. We can't afford to sit around here arguing about this while Lucien could be using every second of this time to make himself even stronger."

"Actually, according to Amelia, he's gone straight back to his room to spend more time with Lena," Marc said, his lip curling a little. "Also, there's another reason why they're not up for it: Fewul is there too, and they're worried that he—er, I mean she—would notice if we captured six Hammerhearts so soon after Lucien visited that cave."

Damn it. Not again. Between Lucien and Fewul, just about everything we thought of was no good. Tentatively, James asked, "Do they think trying to get rid of Fewul now would be a good idea? Would Lucien notice?"

Marc used his telepathic communicator again, not speaking for almost a full minute while the rest of us watched him, waiting not-so-patiently. Finally he said, "That could work, but Amelia thinks it's pretty risky. We still don't know if Lucien has set up an alarm to alert him if Fewul vanishes, and if he has, even having sex with Lena might not be enough to distract him—and that's saying something," he added, smiling a little.

"Something about this amuses you?" James asked testily.

Marc shrugged. "There actually *is* a better way to do this. Peter just told me—it's actually so obvious that we all just skipped right over the top of it."

"What?" several people said, including myself. My heart rose with hope.

"Someone four-dimensional just needs to go out there," he gestured at the display screens, which were still showing the crystal chamber, now completely dark except for the six glowing blue shields, "stand in their shadow, and reach through it to get the crystals. As long as the only part of them that reaches through is inside the shield and doesn't touch it, it should be easy."

My heart was sinking again. There was nothing easy about that plan. The shields weren't very big; in fact, they were so small that whoever did that job would have to have fairly small hands just so that they wouldn't accidentally touch the inside of the shield. Even then, even a person with small hands could have an accident. It would only take a single fingernail to ruin everything, costing one of our lives. Then Mr. Woodward thought of something else to concern me.

"Those shields could activate without being touched. They may only need to sense a life form, or part of a life form, within their boundaries to activate. Lucien would have considered that we might try to teleport in or something like that, so I wouldn't put it past him to set up a spell like that."

Marc shook his head. "The space is too small—nobody would consider teleportation an option in this case, and I think Lucien would know that. He probably would have considered that we might try to use magic to levitate the crystals out, or teleport them out, and I imagine the shields would repel that stuff, but he doesn't know about the fourth dimension—at least not yet—so I think this could really work. If you guys aren't brave enough to do it, I volunteer."

"What?" I gasped. "Marc, what if you're wrong?"

"What if I'm right?" he retorted.

"Well, if Marc's right, then we get the Sorcerous Crystals without having to kill anyone," Erica said. "If he's wrong, then we'll have to go back and sacrifice six Hammerhearts - only we would have also lost the Seventh Sorcerer and a dear friend at the same time."

"Well—yeah," Marc admitted, shifting comfortably in his seat, "but guys, I really think it'll work. I think the chances of this working are better than not working. I'm willing to take the chance, so how about backing me up?"

James nodded stiffly. "Well, okay then, if that's how you wanna do it. It would be much better for us if it works, that's for sure. Make yourself invisible and untraceable before you step out there so that your hands won't be traced when you stick them in the shields. I'm just going to put us in our shadow now so that you don't suffocate as soon as you step out there."

"Come to think of it, if he's untraceable, the shields might not even know he's there," I said, hope beginning to rise again in my heart. James was right: it would be so much better for us if this plan worked.

Marc went to stand in the corner where James could let him out of the base. Both Natalie and I got up, in my case intending to give him a hug (just in case something bad actually did happen to him out there), but he waved us back to our seats, saying, "Stop that. Nothing bad's going to happen, okay."

"Of course not," James agreed, "but Marc?"

"Yeah?"

"Remember what we talked about last night, just in case."

A chill swept the room—one which only Marc, James and I could feel—which I guess meant it only swept half the room. James was referring to the promise we had made in blood the previous evening: the first one of Marc, James, Peter, Amelia or me to die gave the others permission to resurrect them. It was necessary for someone to eventually do this so that one of us would have access to the in-between, where we could find out some valuable information from the remains of Lisa Pont's soul which would supposedly help us end this war once and for all. It sounded far-fetched, but according to the Enlightener (that external source of magic that provided me with information as I slept sometimes), it was so.

We had needed to make it a promise for two reasons. Firstly, whoever had the misfortune of being the one would be forced to leave part of their soul forever in the in-between, meaning that when they died a second time (always two weeks after their resurrection), they would be trapped there eternally, never able to move onto whatever was supposed to come after death. Nobody would knowingly volunteer for such a thing, but we needed the information badly, so the promise had been necessary. The other reason was because James had found a way to tap into the magic of Sien and Leoard themselves, the creators of the Magic Crystals, but a sacrifice had been needed to show them that we were serious in our goal - the promise in blood had been our sacrifice.

I remembered all of this in an instant, while Erica, Natalie and Mr. Woodward eyed the three of us with considerable curiosity. Only James looked composed. All the colour had drained out of Marc's face, and he could only bring himself to nod in agreement (or maybe just understanding) before James pushed the button, dropping him beside the table supporting the crystals, though in his shadow so that he wouldn't accidentally touch them—and so that he could breathe, of course.

"What was that all about?" Erica asked, beating the other two to the punch. She was eyeing James suspiciously, while Natalie was giving me a piercing look (which I did my best to ignore) and Mr. Woodward's eyes kept moving between us.

"Not now," James snapped, his eyes fixed on the display screens. They showed Marc now standing right beside the table, close enough that if he so much as leaned over, he could come into contact with one of the shields. He was still in his shadow, of course, but that was an easy fact to forget when an image of that nurse tumbling backward kept springing to mind.

A silence fell in the room then as everyone watched the screens, unable to say or do anything to help. We were mere spectators now, resigned to waiting and hoping that everything worked out. If worse came to worst, I supposed someone would have to go out there and retrieve Marc's lifeless body. I immediately flinched away from that thought and attempted to channel my mind into something more pleasant. If he succeeded, then we would have the crystals, and Lucien wouldn't know a thing—oh wait, but Fewul might. Even if the Beast of Magic couldn't trace Marc, she might still know immediately that the crystals had been moved, and what was the first thing she would do? Tell Lucien, most likely, which would actually be better than taking matters into her own hands because it would give Marc just enough time to finish up and get out of there—hopefully.

I looked around the room at the various magical devices still littering the place, spotted the one I wanted and went over to snatch it up, totally unnoticed by everyone else in the room. I put my finger on the pad of the white device, visualised Amelia's face, and sent a thought in her direction: Marc is getting the crystals now. Be ready in case Fewul reacts. I then waited as I sat down, but I didn't have to wait long for Amelia's response: Lucien was still with Lena and Stella was still nearby, neither of them having noticed anything as yet. That was the content of her thoughts, but the note of anxiety accompanying them made a much greater impression on me. She understood the risk Marc was taking, and that it could result in his death.

I turned my attention back on the screen just in time to see Marc poking his hand through one of the shields, still in the fourth dimension. Slowly, very slowly, he edged his hand along the fourth dimension so that he was able to snag the crystal with just two fingers; then he pulled it in and stuffed it in his pocket. I let out a great sigh of relief and looked around at the others in the room; they were all smiling, though still looking tense.

"Two down, four to go," James breathed.

What? I snapped my eyes back to the screens in time to see Marc standing over the shield next to the one he had just breached; it was one of two that no longer contained a crystal. Apparently, while I had been communicating with Amelia, Marc had already stolen the first crystal. And speaking of Amelia: I hurriedly put my finger on the pad, preparing to tell her that Marc had stolen two already, but her thought came quicker than I could send mine. Fewul was on the move; she had just interrupted Lucien, although so far he was ignoring her, preferring to continue hammering Lena on his bed.

Oh hurry up, Marc, I thought desperately as I turned my attention back to the display screens. Marc had just taken the third crystal and was moving around to the other side of the table to access the other three. Not taking my eyes from him, I sent a thought to Amelia: let me know the instant it looks like either of them is about to teleport out of there. Then aloud, I said, "It looks like Fewul knows that something's up. She told Lucien—or tried to tell him—but we're not sure if either of them is coming yet. Be ready to snatch Marc out of there at any moment, James."

"Sure," James said, taking the controls and manoeuvring them so that it would only take a single push of the button to drag Marc back inside, continuing to stick close to him every time he moved.

Then another thought came through from Amelia: Lucien was shouting at Fewul to leave them alone, and she sent me a mental picture of the scene. It was one I could have done without: Lena on her back on Lucien's bed, completely naked and spread wide open, with Lucien straddling her (also naked), looking over his shoulder in fury at Stella standing in the doorway, looking utterly unperturbed by what she was seeing. It seemed that Lucien still wasn't prepared to listen to what she was saying, and even less likely to stop what he was doing to do something about it—and seeing Lena there like that, I couldn't really blame him. It meant that we still had time—X amount of seconds, anyway.

Marc had four crystals and was moving onto the fifth, thankfully moving a little quicker now that he knew how to get them out of the shields without hurting (or killing) himself. I sat there, more tense than I'd probably ever been in my life, crossing my fingers in my lap as I watched him stretch his fingers into the fifth shield, take hold of a small part of the crystal, and drag it back through the fourth dimension and into his pocket. Five down, one to go. As Marc turned his attention to it and put his hand in place, another thought came through from Amelia: Lucien just shouted at Stella to take care of it herself, before dismissing her and turning his full attention back to Lena.

I opened my mouth, about to tell James to recall Marc immediately even without the final crystal (Marc wouldn't be happy about that), but before I could, yet another thought came through from Amelia, this one taking me by surprise: Fewul had just wasted a few precious seconds by asking Lucien if she should kill or capture the person responsible for this, and Lucien had gruffly told her that she could kill them. Thankful for Fewul's nature to take orders rather than initiative, I forced myself to hold my breath for a few moments, just until Marc had retrieved the sixth and last crystal, then I said loudly, making everyone in the room jump, "Call him back now!"

James obeyed so quickly that when Marc reappeared in the corner of the control room, he hadn't even had a chance to put the last crystal in his pocket. He staggered and opened his mouth, about to say something, but before he could, we were all distracted by the sight of Fewul teleporting into the chamber and sending a wave of magic out in all directions. It passed through us without effect, given that we were in our shadow, but it was still terrifying to watch.

"Let's get the hell out of here," James said shakily, turning us around and rocketing down the tunnel and through the strange door at the end - the door had been dropped back into the rocks, but we just flew through said rocks and then up and out onto the moon's surface.

"Teleport to the Big Room," Erica suggested and James did so a moment later, causing us all to be suspended in action for an unknowable amount of time before we materialised in the Big Room, still in our shadow. After a bit of resizing of the base, James's shoulders finally relaxed.

"We got 'em," he sighed, slumping back in his seat.

"You mind letting me out of here?" Marc asked, and James had to sit back up so that he could push the button to release Marc from his invisible binds.

"Fewul's probably going to go back there and tell Lucien that the crystals are gone," Mr. Woodward reminded us.

"And hopefully, he tells her to bugger off again," I said, grinning at Marc. "Well done, man; the risk paid off."

It certainly had. There was still so much to be done, of course, but at least this time, the good guys had gotten a much-needed win.

Chapter 5: Topping Up

"Okay," James checked his watch, "it's just about lunch time now, but we should make sure everything's wrapped up here before we call it. Firstly, Marc, have you got that thing sorted out?"

"Er—not really," Marc said, perplexed. He had taken all the crystals out of his pockets and had them piled in his lap, but where normally they would reform into the Hero Crystal in the Seventh Sorcerer's hands, nothing seemed to be happening today. "Maybe 'cause we're still in our shadow."

James nodded and moved the base back along the fourth dimension until we were properly in the Big Room, invisible, microscopic and untraceable, hanging high over the heads of anyone who might walk beneath us. Marc tried to pile the crystals into his palms again and this time, they reformed properly. His face broke into a huge grin as he clutched the Hero Crystal in his fist once again.

"Ah, I missed this," he sighed.

"Anything else we need to do?" James asked.

"Take at least one of Lucien's crystal chips as quickly as we can, now that we can," Natalie said at once, "before he has a chance to do any —what?"

She broke off at the look James was giving her. "Er, hate to burst your bubble, Nat, but we can't change any of the crystals' properties while Lucien is receiving Stella's chip. In twenty-four hours, sure, but not right now."

"So we have to hold him at bay for that long," Erica nodded, "but at least we have some magic on our side now, so that might be possible. We should take the Sien-Leoard Crystal from him next so that we have even more power and he doesn't have any after we've taken his chips."

"That won't happen while Fewul's around," James said, "so maybe that should be the next thing we do. Anyone got one of those devices that'll get rid of Fewul?"

"Here," Marc said, snagging one off a nearby chair and handing it to James. "John, let Amelia know what we're doing, and tell her to let us know if Fewul vanishes."

"That's assuming Fewul's back there," I said, putting my finger back on the pad of the communicator.

The moment I did, several thoughts came through from Amelia. Fewul just teleported away! What's going on? Is Marc okay? Why aren't you answering me? I hurriedly sent a response back to let her know that we had succeeded, and asking her where Fewul was now. She responded that Fewul hadn't returned, and I relayed this message back to James.

"So we have no way of knowing for certain that it worked," he said disappointedly. "Well, I guess the best we can do is wait and see. In any case, let Amelia know that we're gonna come and pick her and the others up now so that we can all have lunch."

"What about the Sien-Leoard Crystal?" Natalie asked.

"We'll come back for that," James said. "don't worry about it. I think it's best to get everyone out of there before we try to attack Lucien again, because we're going to have to attack him to get it. Remember, there's a whole bunch of newly converted people out there. I assume Amelia wasn't able to convert Lena but she might have got Tommy, not to mention so many others. John, find out where they all are so we can get them."

"I already know Amelia's in Lucien's bedroom," I said distastefully.

So I focused instead on Peter, and asked him where he was. Peter wasn't very good at this telepathic communication, not having a lot of experience with it, but he eventually managed to tell me that he, Rebecca, and a whole bunch of others were huddled in the fourth dimension close to the entrance of the Big Room—which wasn't far from where we were now, actually, though we were facing the wrong way. I told James all this and he began manoeuvring us into the right position where we could begin bringing them all in, while I focused on Amelia, telling her to come down and meet up with everyone in the Big Room. She responded that Fewul still hadn't returned but that she (Amelia) would come right away, but she might take a few minutes because she would be dragging an unconscious Tommy along behind her.

"In the meantime," Marc said, looking around at us, "could you help them find rooms when we start bringing them in?"

He was speaking to Erica, who nodded a little reluctantly, but James spoke up then. "I'd rather she stay here with me. I was hoping Natalie and Mr. Woodward would take care of that—and Rebecca too, if she doesn't have anything to tell us that Pete can't do."

"Wow, okay, boss," Marc muttered, looking surprised by James's controlling tone.

"I guess I don't mind," Natalie said, and Mr. Woodward nodded.

"Actually, I'm thinking that we—that is, me and Erica—should stay here through lunch and keep an eye on Lucien, just in case," James said, now hovering over the heads of Peter, Rebecca and their group. "Everyone else can probably help you guys—once we've heard anything Amelia and Peter have to tell us, anyway."

James let Rebecca into the base first, and then one-by-one picked up the people who they had converted. Darcy was among them, as were Harry and Simon's sisters and grandparents. Natalie's parents were there, along with Lisa's parents and younger brother. Liam and Siobhan were there. Rob, Bob and Grillion were there, all still looking considerably shell-shocked by what they had seen happen to an old friend of theirs that morning. There were more besides, some of whom I knew, and some of whom I only vaguely recognised from the old Woodward base; and by the time James had brought them all in, including Peter, Amelia and the unconscious Tommy, there was barely enough room to swing a grasshopper in the control room—even though I had deliberately made it bigger than the control room from the old base.

"Darcy, there's a room reserved for you on level one," I called over the hubbub. "Er—I'm not sure where the spare rooms are on the other two levels, but we're definitely going to need at least one more floor, and maybe more than that. James, can you do that?"

"I'm on it," he shouted back, rapidly pushing buttons. "Guys, start showing this crowd to their rooms. Amelia, Peter, you two hang back with me, Marc and John. Everyone else, scram already!"

The room slowly filtered out, the two Fletcher sisters doing their best to hurry things along and Mr. Woodward bringing up the rear—a little reluctantly, I thought, as though he regretted no longer being part of the inner most circle of control in this new army. Finally, only the five of us remained—the initial resistance group, as it were. Oh, and Tommy, of course, since we hadn't quite figured out what we were going to do with him.

"There's still no sign of Fewul," James said, observing the spyers still mounted on the control panel. Several of them still showed Lucien, who incredibly was still busy with Lena—he was quite the horny man, by the look of it. "That could mean that we succeeded, or that she's still up on the moon trying to flush us out. I don't really believe she'd stay there this long, but it would be safest to assume—at least for a while—that she's still around."

"She really is good at acting like Stella," Amelia shivered.

"Okay, so you already know all the important stuff about what happened up there," Marc told her, "and I'm sorry we couldn't save that woman. You knew her, right?"

Amelia nodded, closing her eyes as though holding in tears.

Marc patted her shoulder. "We still need a quick rundown of what happened out there. Peter, what about you?"

Peter shrugged. "Not a lot, actually. Rebecca and I just waited in there till Amelia told us Lucien was preoccupied with his meeting. When we got the signal, we just went around converting as many people as we could, making them four-dimensional and bringing them into their shadows and telling them to stay the hell put—thank God they all did. We hunkered down when Lucien came down—to get that woman, I suppose, although we didn't realise that at the time—and then when he left, we just got back to work."

"What about you, Amelia?" James asked.

Amelia took a moment to regain her composure. "Well, I spied on Lucien's meeting, which I already told you guys about. Cornish and Hall were there, and Hignat's father and some other pretty prominent Hammerhearts, and they were all trying to make a case for why they should get Stella's magic. Even Lena tried to make a case, but everyone pretty much ignored her like she was just Lucien's piece of arse or something, only there to be seen and not heard—that really pissed her off. None of them even cared that Stella was sitting right there, so far as they all knew. Lucien told them that she agreed to transfer her chip and they all just bought it—I suppose they would, with all the mind control Lucien's got going on.

"Anyway, he eventually decided they were all too immature to have magic and that he would take the last chip for himself, making him the one and only Sorcerer. 'The best way to make sure a job is done right is to do it yourself,' he said—or something to that effect. I dunno if that was his plan all along and that meeting was for show, or if he really did consider giving the magic to someone else—"

"I was thinking about that earlier," James interrupted, "and I reckon he probably did consider it. He clearly is power-hungry, but he seems to understand that spreading magic around can get jobs done more quickly —if they're done right, anyway. I guess he doesn't really trust any of those Hammerhearts enough to give them magic, and none more than Stella."

"Well, yeah," Amelia shrugged. "After the meeting, he sent them all away and went to get—get her," she faltered, took a deep breath, and then continued. "I stayed back to try to capture Tommy and Lena, and as you know, I half succeeded. I tried for Lena first, but Lucien did something to her to make her stay put. She wasn't frozen, like a block of ice, but she was put into stasis—and I couldn't do a damn thing to move her or wake her up or anything."

"That's pretty disturbing," I shuddered.

"Agreed," Peter said. "It sounds like he only sees her as a piece of arse as well—like she shouldn't be able to do anything in life except have sex with him whenever he wants her. We've known Lena for six months and there's so much more to her than that—even Lucien knows that."

"Maybe," Amelia hesitated, "but I'm not convinced that was his motivation for doing that to her. I think his greater concern may have been that we would try to convert her while he was gone, and he only did it so that we wouldn't be able to. I could be wrong, but he did let her come to that meeting and that must say something too. He may not love her like he probably did Stella, but I think maybe he has plans for her."

"Yeah, to be his arm candy," I told them, remembering the thoughts I'd had the previous night when I'd watched him charming her. "Not only does he have a hot girlfriend now, but he's a public figure, so now the world can see that he has a hot girlfriend. Now that you mention it, Amelia, it makes sense that he'd work harder to stop us doing anything to her than he would to stop us doing anything to anyone else."

"What can we do then?" Marc asked, looking around the group and then looking down at his lap where he still clutched the Hero Crystal. "We do have some magic now, but we might not be able to find a way through whatever he does to protect her from us. Lena's one of us, so shouldn't we at least try to get her back?"

Amelia gave him a suspicious look and said, "You're not just saying that because she's your ex, right?"

Marc shook his head hard. "No, definitely not. You guys agree with me, right?"

Peter and James both nodded, and James said, "We'll have to wait till he stops doing her before we can convert her, though. So after you gave up on Lena, you went after Tommy, right?"

"Yeah," she looked down at his prone figure on the floor. "I was able to extract him from Lucien's mind, but the unboggler didn't do anything so I suppose Lucien didn't even bother using an influential charm on him. He tried twice to attack me and I was forced to knock him out just so that he couldn't hurt me. I dunno what we'll do with him."

"Magical restraint, I suppose," James shrugged sadly. "There are plenty of people in here capable of doing that. I don't like it either, but there must be a way to keep Tommy both comfortable and safe. He deserves that after all he's been through with us. So go on, after that?"

"After that, Lucien came back, unfroze Lena, and has been doing all kinds of disgusting things with her ever since—she seems to love every bit of it, by the way. I had to watch the whole thing to make sure he didn't stop. I think Fewul must have been watching from outside the room because she came in quickly when you guys started taking the crystals, but Lucien shouted at her to leave and Lena just wanted him to keep going. And…that's pretty much everything. Next thing was you guys telling me you were picking us up."

"I guess that brings us back to Fewul," James said, glancing at the spyers still showing Lucien and then quickly away again. "So, here's what I think should happen now: I'll stay in here and keep an eye on him, after I've gotten myself something to eat, and I'll ask Erica if she wants to keep me company—surely he'll run out of mojo soon," he added, his face twisting in disgust. "The rest of you guys go and have some food, because we're going to need more energy this afternoon. First thing we'll do when we meet up here at half past one is try to take that crystal from him."

"Sounds good to me," I said, checking my watch—it was almost half past twelve, so we had an hour. As James began to speak into the public address system, telling everyone it was now lunch time, I leaned over to Marc and said, "Would you mind coming upstairs with me for a few minutes first? There's something I wanna do and I think I'll need your help."

"Er—okay," he said warily.

The five of us got in the lift together, but while the other three got off on the ground level, Marc and I went up to the first. Only when the other three were out and the doors had closed again did I tell him, "This won't take long. I know Stella's been unconscious for like an hour already, but I just wanna make sure she's—you know—resting comfortably."

It was hard to explain it in a way that didn't sound silly. She was unconscious—even she wouldn't care if she were comfortable until she woke up. A few of the spyers downstairs were still set to follow Stella, but they had gone dark when she had been made untraceable (thank heavens, or everyone would have seen all that had happened between me and her earlier); but that also meant that I had no idea where she had been or what she had been doing when she had fainted. If she really had been lying down then great, but if she had been on her feet, or in the shower perhaps, then it just didn't feel right to leave her where she had fallen for twenty-four hours. Thankfully, I didn't need to illustrate this to Marc; he merely nodded, and together we approached Stella's bedroom door.

The only part I really needed his help for was the first part: the opening of the door. Sadly, we ran into a little hitch at this point: the Hero Crystal refused to operate, and it took us a few minutes to remember that James had moved us back in our shadows when we had picked up Amelia and Peter's group. Marc had to take the elevator back down to the control room to move us back out, then back up again to use magic to open the bedroom door, and then back down again to move the base back into its shadow (where we would be safer). Before he left this time, I told him not to bother coming back up again but to just go and get some lunch—he'd done enough elevator riding for one day, and he'd done what I'd needed him to do.

In the end, the whole thing hadn't been needed anyway. Stella was lying on her back on her bed, looking as peaceful as if she were asleep. For all I knew, she had been asleep when the whole thing had happened; if so, she would be in for a surprise when she woke up tomorrow, but at least she had been spared the knowledge of what was about to happen to her. I hovered over her for a minute, trying to decide if there was anything I ought to do for her, and then left her alone there, shutting the door behind me. It felt best to just let her rest, but I would make sure that I was there when she woke up tomorrow.

At least I would have done, if fate hadn't intervened.

* * *

It seemed that almost everyone in the base was in the dining room by the time I got down there. It was a large room, very reminiscent of the dining room from the old Woodward base, though with a couple of differences. Instead of rectangular tables which seated six, these tables were circular and seated five. The other difference, much more important in terms of how we ate, was that this dining room didn't have a conveyer belt. The dining rooms in the old Woodward base and the old Young Army base provided food from a conveyer belt - a person would stand in front of it and imagine what they wanted to eat. The amount of magical power required to create such a device wasn't available to me when I had created this base, so I had settled for a device not unlike a vending machine, except that it created the programmed foods and drinks on command—and didn't require payment.

I got myself a sandwich from the food creator and then looked around for somewhere to sit. Marc, Amelia, Peter and Rebecca were sitting at one table with an empty seat, so I made for that one. It wasn't the only empty seat I noticed (Natalie was sitting with Felicity, Jessica, Darcy and an empty seat at another table) but it was the one that looked the most inviting, even if it meant being the fifth wheel with two happy couples.

"I don't see James anywhere," I observed as I sat down between Marc and Peter.

"He took Erica downstairs," Peter said, "but not before that."

I followed the direction of his fork…and my mouth fell open in surprise. A couple of tables away, Harry and Simon were sitting with Katie, Sophie, and Tommy. "Er—okay," I said slowly, watching the group. "Actually, he seems relatively okay."

"He's sort of okay," Amelia said quietly. "James and Erica woke him up when they went back down there and I think they must have talked him down. He does look a bit lost, but his need for Ingi seems to be overwhelming any loyalty to Lucien he might still have."

"Except Ingi's not here, obviously, so how long can we expect that to work?" I asked.

"And that's why he's surrounded by four heavily armed teenagers, two of whom are probably stronger than him—hopefully," Peter added.

A silence fell for a little while as we ate, and then Rebecca said, "Okay, so now that everyone's here and you all have a moment, can I ask how you guys managed to do everything you did without magic?"

She spoke in a normal volume, only really loud enough for all five of us to hear, but her voice carried just far enough to reach her father, Brian Fletcher, former Sorcerer, who was sitting at the next table with his wife, his mother, and Frederic and Lillian Woodward. He turned to us and said, "I think that's a great idea. Do tell us how the five of you managed to pull all this off the way you did."

Unlike Rebecca he did speak in a loud voice, loud enough to bring almost every other conversation in the room to a standstill. He didn't look angry or pissed or anything, but he did look very curious, and his look was shared by everyone else at his table—and beyond, by the looks of it. Before any of us could say anything, Katie called, "Yeah, we've all been talking in the lounge room all morning and we really wanna know how you did all this."

Now the room was completely silent as Peter, Marc, Amelia and I all shared startled looks, and Rebecca gave us a sheepish grin. "Sorry," she whispered.

"You know we're just gonna keep asking till you tell us," Felicity added.

"Fine," Marc said irritably, "but do forgive us if we wanna take a mouthful of food between each sentence. We've worked real hard, you know."

"Fair enough," Mr. Woodward said. "Start with what happened when we left your old base last Monday. What exactly happened then?"

"We can tell you that part," Harry said, getting to his feet and bowing so low that his nose almost ended up in his lunch. "As you will no doubt be aware, Lucien was in possession of the Sien-Leoard Crystal after we ghosted Arnold Hammerson, and for reasons best known to himself, he decided that instead of staying with us and helping fix up the mess of the Hammerhearts, he would rather take over and be the next ruler of the universe. Now this is where things get a bit sketchy—"

"Why don't you let me take it from here," Marc said loudly, and Harry made a screeching noise like a car braking hard. "So basically, Arnold Hammerson did something to Lucien as a child, the same day he killed our mother, where it would make Lucien take over from him if he —Hammerson, that is—ever died. Smiley told us about the time bomb curse, but we didn't know what it would do until it was too late. It activated when Lucien accompanied Stella to visit her father's grave, and when it did, he put an influential charm on her so that he would have a mole inside our base—not that she knew that's what she was doing."

"The time bomb curse?" Mr. Woodward repeated, his face having gone very pale. "Are you serious?"

"Yep, he was the first one since Sien who could do it, apparently," said Peter. "And according to John, now Lucien can do it too. That's how he was able to send Stella back to us without us figuring out that anything was wrong."

I shrugged. "He mentioned it just after he made Stella tie me up."

Immediately after he got on one knee in front of her, I reminded myself, a proposal that Stella had rejected a few hours later because she still had feelings for me.

"I still don't understand how Lucien busted into both of our bases," Jessica said.

"We don't really know that part either," Marc said, "except that apparently he used the Sien-Leoard Crystal to send Fewul away, somehow managed to steal the Hero Crystal from me, then changed the properties and then busted into the Woodward base. He didn't do anything to us until twenty-four hours later. Maybe Stella helped him with some of it and just doesn't remember, but if Lucien didn't tell any of you guys how he did it, then there's no way we would know."

"And then you guys somehow went on the run," Simon said—it wasn't a question.

"Me, Marc and James were in the control room when they teleported in," Peter said, "and James said we should run because there was nothing we could do to save you guys. I felt awful about that, but in hindsight, I think he was probably right. John only came later after he got away from Lucien and Stella—you guys all saw that part."

I still got chills thinking about how lucky I had been that day. There were any number of ways that things could have gone differently, and all of them would have seen me under Lucien's influential charm. Firstly, I had been held hostage by Stella on Lucien's orders, bound by magical ropes in his bedroom. Then Sebastian Williams, a jerkoff who had once been part of the Young Army but had betrayed us to the Hammersons— had turned up and bound both me and Stella up to a magical device called an 'undoer', which was designed to break the mental connection she and I shared. Sebastian had messed up and made the connection stronger instead of weaker, and Lucien had been forced to destroy it before it could blend us together into a single mind inhabiting two bodies.

If Lucien hadn't been so distracted by Sebastian's monumental screw-up, I wouldn't have had any opportunity to bolt, but bolt I did. Lucien had given chase and thrown everything at me in order to slow me down—exploding windows, rushing water, moving bushes, a fireball and even a fissure in the ground—but the door of the control room had been left open by Marc, Peter and James, and I'd been able to dash through it just in the nick of time.

"But what about after that?" Mr. Woodward asked. "How did you stay safe? You hardly had any magic to work with—did you?"

"We had bugger all, really," Marc said, "except the Light Crystal, but that could only do so much. Fortunately, Lucien didn't try too hard to capture us—at least at first. He was hoping that we would see the sense in voluntarily coming to him, and he was planning to make us his top advisers. John found this out by entering Stella's mind when he slept, and we were sort of able to use that to our advantage. After we slept a bit, we snuck into the Hammerheart base here in Chopville and stole as many weapons as we could that we knew how to use, and then went to Melbourne where we stayed in a homeless shelter for a couple of nights."

"You stayed in a *homeless shelter*?" Mum almost screamed, her eyes bulging as she stared at me and Peter.

"Calm down," Peter said quickly and loudly before she could get up and rush at us. "John and I are fine; we didn't do drugs or anything. James is fine too," he added, seeing the horrified look on Marge's face.

"And what about you?" Mr. Woodward sternly asked his daughter.

"Well actually, May and I were still in England at first," she said. "May didn't go anywhere until I regained consciousness, and since we didn't have any magic or know how to get into the Hammerheart Highway from there—we had to take a plane, which really slowed us down. We didn't get to Melbourne until Sunday morning, but yeah— after that, we did go to the homeless shelter for about twenty-four hours or so."

"I'm sorry about that, by the way," Rebecca said in a small voice. When we all looked at her, she cleared her throat and said, "Lucien used me to gather intel on Honnies so that he could get rid of her. Part of me knew it wouldn't be doing you guys any favours if I did it, but a greater part of me thought it was for the best—that it would really help."

Peter patted her on the shoulder. "don't beat yourself up. Most people in this room can be ashamed of the same thing, but no one here is responsible for what Lucien did to their minds."

A muttering followed, with many people flushing or looking away briefly, before Amelia spoke again. "Lucien was really determined to get rid of May. At first it was just because he recognised that she could probably help us, but by the next day it was also because she had pissed him off by undermining his plans. He did a few things that were designed to break us up and get us fighting with each other so that we would be even easier targets and we would be more likely to give up and go to him, but May was able to use her mind to override a lot of what he was doing—most of the time, anyway," she added, shivering a little.

I thought I knew what she was thinking about. Lucien's main method of getting us fighting was to make me and Marc irresistibly horny. It had begun not long after May had joined us, and by that evening, we had both been unable to hold it in. I had gone to Amelia first, and feeling lonely and vulnerable after finding out that Darcy (previously her boyfriend) had abandoned her, she had given herself to me. Marc had walked in on us, both naked, while we had been having sex, though before either of us had climaxed, and he had been hoping to do the very same thing. That situation could have turned violent if I hadn't realised, just in time, that something was amiss and that there might be magic involved. May had then settled that particular matter down, but it had still caused a lot of friction between me and Marc from that time forward.

And then there was the following morning. Before we had used the Light Crystal to remove both of our respective curses, I had gone to Amelia to retrieve the clothes I'd left in her room the previous evening and had ended up having sex with her anyway. I had then gone to tell May that Lucien was planning to capture Ingi to motivate her to go back to her own world, and had ended up having sex with her as well. And that was to say nothing of what I had done with Lena and Stella later that day, but I wasn't going to say any of this aloud, for several reasons.

Amelia didn't need Marc to know all the details of what we had done—as far as he knew, she and I hadn't actually done any more than he had interrupted. Natalie also didn't need to know that I'd had sex with May, though she seemed to already know of the rest. Then, of course, there were my parents just over there—they would be much happier kept in ignorance.

"Well, I'm glad that part of his plan didn't work," Mr. Fletcher said, utterly unaware of the untruth of that statement. He didn't see the look of pain on Natalie's face at that point, but I sure did, and it hurt my heart—she understood just how well that part of Lucien's plan had worked.

"What I wanna know is why you came in on Sunday," Rebecca said. "Was it just to see us? If so, I'm really glad you did."

She gave Peter a sickeningly adoring look as she said this.

"Well that was certainly part of it," Amelia said, "but we needed an excuse to come and see you guys, since our main priority was to push back against Lucien somehow. So Marc and May went looking for the crystals on the top level of the base while the rest of us went in the Big Room."

"But then what?" Harry asked. He had re-seated himself at the table after having remained on his feet for about a minute, looking a bit foolish. "How did you go from a homeless shelter yesterday to all of *this* today?"

"Does this have anything at all to do with Rock Haulter?" Mr. Woodward asked. "You did ask me about it yesterday, and Lucien seemed to believe you may have found a way to go back in time to get through the portals. I can't think of any way you could have done that, but I also can't think of any other way you could have done all of this."

Marc, Peter, Amelia and I all swapped looks before Marc said, "Yes, that is what we did, or something very similar to it, but I can't say exactly how we did it—it's not safe for people to know. I'm sure James would say the same thing if he were here. We really can't afford for Lucien to learn what we did, and let's face it, if he manages to break into this place as well, the fewer minds know the secret, the less chance that he will find out about it."

A silence followed this little speech, many people looking disappointed, before Mr. Woodward said, "Well, if you think that's best. I do understand the logic in what you're saying, and I agree that any secret you may need to use again ought to be kept as far from Lucien as possible. For my part, I wish I hadn't divulged our conversation to Lucien, but I think in my defence he would have forced it out of me if I'd refused to speak."

"I'm sure he would have," Marc frowned, but didn't add anything else.

We wouldn't be able to use the secret of time travel again, though, not without a Honnie here, because we had recognised the danger of it and deliberately not given ourselves the ability to do it again. But it still had to be kept away from Lucien: if he figured out how to go back in time now, he would be an unstoppable force of nature. We couldn't rely on him not wanting to open that can of worms, because after what had happened to him earlier this morning, he would stop at nothing to bring us down.

"So what about this morning, then?" Katie asked. "And what comes next?"

"This morning we got all you guys back, as well as Stella," Marc said, "and then we stole the Sorcerous Crystals. The bad news is Lucien's taking Stella's magic for himself, so he'll be the only Sorcerer. As for what comes next, we're going to try to hold him at bay and take the Sien-Leoard Crystal from him as well, and then when Stella wakes up we're going to take his magic from him. Hopefully then, we can finish this thing once and for all."

"Does anyone have any more questions?" Peter asked, looking around the room.

"Is there anything we can do to help?" Felicity asked.

"Probably, we'll let you know," said Amelia, and returned to her lunch.

Chapter 6: Bedroom Ambush

We were all back in the control room immediately after lunch: me, Peter, Marc, Amelia, Mr. Woodward, Lillian Woodward, the Fletcher sisters, and several other former Woodward Army soldiers who felt so terrible about what they had let happen that they were determined to redeem themselves. This included Dad and Charlie, and I didn't at all mind having them there. For the first time since all of this started, even though I was still only fourteen years old (my birthday was in less than three weeks, but that still felt like a long way away), I was feeling as though we teenagers were truly equal to the adults who had been running the show for so long.

"Well, we have been keeping an eye on things," James told us from where he still sat with Erica before the controls, "and as you can see, if you really care to look, is that nothing has happened. Lucien's still busy with Lena, even after all this time, and Fewul hasn't returned. I think it's now safe to assume that the beast is gone."

"I wouldn't say it's safe," Mr. Woodward contradicted, "but I think we have to assume it nevertheless. The time appears to have come for us to take the risk that Fewul is no longer with Lucien."

James nodded. "Yeah, you're right; perhaps 'safe' was the wrong word. So anyway, we've been talking while you guys have been relaxing upstairs, and we still think stealing the Sien-Leoard Crystal is the next logical thing to do. We can't steal his crystal chips since he's still receiving Stella's, but there are two major benefits to taking the Sien-Leoard Crystal: it would prevent him from recalling Fewul, whenever he figures out that she's gone, and—well—it has to be done anyway."

"Have you come up with any bright ideas about how we do that?" Peter asked.

"A few," James said, smiling reluctantly, "but I wouldn't call any of them 'bright'—not in this case, anyway. To be honest, I'm not really confident about doing this; Lucien's bound to have protected it, and without knowing what that protection is or how many layers of it there are, it's hard to come up with any plan that we can really be confident in. But with all that said, I will say one thing: I think the best time to take it would be now, because as you can see he's naked at the moment, so it's probably not on his person."

"Unless he swallowed it, like Hall and my dad did," Marc shuddered.

"Yeah, so the first thing we need to do," James went on, "is to go out there and use one of Amelia's trackers to figure out its exact location. Once we know that, it'll be easier to figure out what comes next. A few people will need to be ready to fight again because I'm sure that even if it's not on his body Lucien will have set up some sort of magical alert to let him know if someone else touches it."

"And someone very quick on the controls needs to be back in here, ready to pull us back in at the first sign of trouble," Marc added. "And if you couldn't tell by my wording, I'm volunteering to go out there."

James nodded. "I would have asked you anyway; if you leave your shadow, you can use the Hero Crystal to help you out. I think I should go out with you guys to help you figure out the next part of the plan, if you think you need it—"

"Okay, but you should stay in your shadow the whole time," I said. "don't worry, we'll be able to hear you; I just don't think you'll be fast enough if it comes to a full-on fight—no offense," I added.

It had probably been a bit unfair of me to say that outright, especially given that James had been in more than one fight over the duration and was still here to talk about them. James did look a little stricken, but he nodded. "And you, John, since you've done this more times than probably anyone here, other than you guys," he added to the various grown-ups.

"I guess that puts me on the controls," Amelia said, looking at James's seat. "don't worry; I know how to use them."

"What about the rest of us?" Peter asked, looking a little left out.

James considered, and then said, "I guess you can come out with us, if you like. You've done this a fair bit yourself."

"No more than that, though," Mr. Woodward cut in, and I saw him glance at Dad and Charlie as he spoke; those two looked very worried, and I found myself wondering if it was such a good idea to have parents in the room for this after all. "I think the four of you will be enough, and the rest of you can keep an eye on things from in here."

"Okay," James agreed, "so we need to figure out how all you guys should be armed. I guess I'd better take some arms too. Untraceability, a soundproof barrier, an invisibility veil—"

"Hold on," Marc cut in, "I'm thinking we go about things a little differently. Untraceability, sure, but I don't think we need to have a soundproof barrier or an invisibility veil."

Amelia nodded. "We can do what we did this morning when we grabbed Stella; all the communicating can be done in our shadow, and neither Lucien nor Lena will hear or see a thing. We'll need some sort of invisibility when we leave our shadow, but maybe only one or two people will need to do that a time unless we get into trouble."

"And the person out of their shadow will still hear and see people in their shadow," I added, glancing at Amelia. "I could both hear and see Amelia as a sort of ghostly form while I was dealing with Stella."

"Okay, so first we make sure every person who leaves is untraceable," Peter said. "Each person carries their own invisibility toggle, and of course Marc will have the Hero Crystal. What other weapons should the rest of us have?"

"That thing to trap Lucien's magic," I said at once, "and the thing that can knock people out from inside our shadows. Perhaps a good solid-outliner will help too; Lucien might not be prepared for thicky prison."

"And the one that can recall Fewul," Mr. Woodward added, "just in case you need it after all."

"Good idea, Dad," Amelia agreed. "We'll also need at least one crystal tracker, but one would probably be enough. Shield devices for everyone, in case Lucien gets a chance to fire on us; a vanisher; the thing that'll make us immune to thicky prison, thanks John for reminding me of that; and definitely a telepathic communicator."

"And you can talk to us through that as well," Natalie said, grinning. "I guess Mr. Woodward and I will be the messengers, since we're the best at telepathy."

"I think I'm pretty good at it—"

"You'll be busy on the controls," Natalie cut an indignant-looking Amelia off, "and we should probably only have one job each."

"Yes, that is a far more efficient use of resources," Mr. Woodward agreed.

While all this had been going on, Peter had been going around the room, picking up the various devices as they were spoken of and handing them out to me, Marc and James, and pocketing some for himself. By the time I had pocketed all of mine, my pockets were bulging and I knew that when I stood up, my pants would feel a bit heavier than usual.

"There is one thing I want to do before we go out there," Marc said, getting to his feet and taking the Hero Crystal from his pocket. "James, can you take us out of our shadow so that I can use this?"

"Sure," James said, taking the controls and obliging. "What are you doing with it?"

"I'm gonna have a go at calling Fewul," Marc told us all, and several people looked alarmed. "don't worry; I've spent a lot of time controlling it and I know I can do it."

"You can try," James said, "but don't be surprised if it doesn't work. I thought Fewul couldn't be called or recalled while the chips were in motion."

"Er—" Marc faltered, "is that a definite rule? I know we couldn't change the chips while Fewul was out, but does it go the other way as well?"

"Also, don't you have to be outside to do that?" Peter added.

Marc shrugged. "It'll only take a couple of minutes. Just teleport me to Main Street or something so that I can try it."

James did teleport us, but we ended up in what looked like a paddock rather than on a busy street. A moment later, I realised where we were: the same paddock where we had spent a lot of time hovering our old base.

"Is it safe to be here?" Peter asked as Marc went to stand in the corner so that James could let him out of the base. "I mean, Lucien does know of this place? He might be keeping a magical eye on it."

"He won't see nothing," Marc said, and a moment later he vanished, apparently using the Hero Crystal to make himself invisible. "Go on, when you're ready, James."

James pushed the button, and as far as any of us could tell, nothing happened. Marc didn't say anything, which meant that he had probably been dropped somewhere out there.

"Er, how are we gonna know when he's ready to come back in?" Natalie asked.

"And how are we gonna find him?" Amelia added.

"I was going to say that he could let us know telepathically," I said, "but I guess we still won't know exactly where he's standing."

"He'll have to make himself visible, briefly," James told us. "We can both go into the fourth dimension to manage it. Geez, I hope he thinks to put a finger on his communicator."

Marc stayed out there for more than a minute before Natalie received a telepathic message from him. "It didn't work," she told us, "I just told him to go into his shadow and make himself visible so that I could find him and pick him up."

He did this, and James also took the base back along the fourth dimension. Less than a minute later Marc was back in the control room, looking thoroughly disappointed.

"It had to be because of the crystal chips," he said, plonking down in his vacated seat. "It's the only reason I could think of why it wouldn't work; I was outside, I wasn't shrunken—"

"You were untraceable," Peter suggested. "Could that have had anything to do with it?"

Marc shook his head. "I don't see how. I mean, the crystal responds to every other bit of magic I do, so long as I'm out of my shadow; I don't see why this would be any different."

"Me neither," James agreed, "but the good news is, we'll be able to call Fewul when we have the Sien-Leoard Crystal, just like Lucien did. Which brings us back to the task at hand. I am now going to teleport us into Lucien's bedroom, okay? If you don't want to see what he's doing, I suggest you find another direction to look in."

A few moments later, after a brief period of everything being frozen in place, we were in Lucien's bedroom, watching the scene through all the displays, though thankfully we were still, for now, safely in our shadow.

"Okay," James said, and got to his feet, indicating that Amelia should take the seat beside Erica. "You guys, are we ready to do this?"

"Ready as we'll ever be," I said, also getting to my feet. Marc and Peter joined us and the four of us made our way to the corner where we could be let out of the base.

"Good luck, you guys," Mr. Woodward said, smiling at us. "You're all very brave. And remember—we'll be ready to rescue you the moment things start going pear-shaped."

"Wait for one of us to be hit with something first," Marc suggested, "just in case we can still take advantage of the situation, even after he's aware of us."

Amelia and her father exchanged a long look before Mr. Woodward said, "Okay, fine, but we'll use our best judgement on that one."

One by one, Amelia let us out of the base and into Lucien's bedroom. We huddled by the closed door, trying to ignore what was happening on the bed, which was much harder now that we could hear it as well as see it—I supposed either James or Erica had turned the volume on the spyers down at some point, unable to stand listening to it. I turned my back on it, feeling strangely jealous of Lucien; I knew that Lena had enjoyed what we had done, but the noises she was making now suggested that although she was exhausted, she was receiving more pleasure than she had ever known. Surely, he had to be using magic (or possibly his Honnie mind) to make that happen...

"So how do you wanna do this?" Peter whispered.

"For starters, we don't have to whisper," James said, screwing up his face as he turned to look at what Lucien was doing. "I guess we start by checking the crystal tracker."

Peter had it. He took it from his pocket and we all gathered around to look. We knew our position immediately because of the six crystals all on top of each other; that was the Hero Crystal, which the tracker could identify even though it was in its shadow. The Light, Villain and Sien-Leoard Crystals were all on top of us as well, and Peter had to zoom in over and over again to put any space between any of them. Finally, we were able to see that the Sien-Leoard Crystal was close, probably somewhere in this room, and definitely roughly in the direction of Lucien himself, but that was the best we could do with this particular device.

"Okay, so what now?" I asked, glancing in Lucien's direction and then back at the three boys. I thought maybe Lucien was getting ready to wrap things up, which had to be good given that he'd been ravaging her nonstop for two hours now, give or take.

"Let me go out there and see if I can determine where it is with this," Marc said, and before any of us could stop him, he made himself invisible and left his shadow.

"Geez, Marc, be careful," Peter hissed at him. "Come back through the moment Lucien does anything suspicious."

Lucien didn't do anything suspicious though; he showed no sign that he had sensed anything happening in front of him. (His current position meant that he would actually have a clear view of Marc if he were visible, especially when Lena lurched forward, but that's all I'll say on the matter.) Marc was only gone for roughly twenty seconds, though, before he became visible to us again, already back in his shadow.

"No good?"

He shrugged. "I don't think it's untraceable, since enchantments like that aren't supposed to bind the Magic Crystals, so maybe it has its own protection of sorts. I don't get it, since the tracker could pick it up, but…" he shrugged again.

"Okay," James sighed, "that means we have to look for it ourselves, and that means we need to put Lucien out of action before he can put us out of action. You guys got any ideas on how we should do this?"

"Ideally, an enormous steel pole," Peter said, and when we all looked at him with raised eyebrows, he smirked. "Well, he might have a magical shield around him, but he obviously doesn't have a physical one. Whacking him in the head hard enough to knock him out is probably not something he's expecting."

Marc and I swapped amused looks, but James took the idea seriously. "Well, that's actually not a bad idea, on the grounds that Lucien almost certainly isn't expecting it. We can't do it this time though, for two reasons: we don't have a heavy steel pole to swing at him, and even if we did, we could seriously hurt Lena if we did that to him now."

Good point. In their current position, a swing to the back of Lucien's head could just as easily miss and hit Lena, most likely on the back or shoulder but quite possibly on her head. Any damage would be temporary, of course—Lucien would make sure she looked as good as ever so long as he had the power—but it would be a huge amount of pain that she didn't deserve.

Peter shrugged. "Okay, so I guess that means we'll be using our weapons. That one that can knock him out from here would be the best, except you know he's almost certainly put up a shield to protect him from that—especially after what happened earlier."

"I'm sure you're right," James said, "which is why I suggest that Marc use his crystal to attack him, after someone has put a shield around him so that he can't attack back, and if whatever Marc does doesn't work, someone should be ready to shoot him with a solid-outliner."

"If Marc's invisible, how will we know when he's attacked?" I asked.

James considered then said, "Marc, could you give us a countdown with the telepathic communicator?"

"Maybe, but I've only got two hands," Marc replied. "Maybe one of you should do the shield thing first, then I'll use the crystal, and if it doesn't work, I'll use a solid-outliner on him. Should we do anything to Lena?"

"Knock her out, preferably at the same time as Lucien," James said. "She's nowhere near as dangerous, obviously, but even though she's—er—not wearing anything, she could be able to fight and cause trouble for us."

It was definitely time to go now. They appeared to have stopped, Lucien lying back against the pillows and Lena relaxing back against him, both of them panting. Surely he would consider it enough and get back to the work of running the world anytime now. After a little discussion, I was selected to use the shield device on Lucien after using a different shield device to protect myself and Marc, just in case; while Peter would attack Lena using an inter-dimensional knockout from in his shadow, and James would direct things, also from in his shadow.

We all positioned ourselves; me to one side of the bed, in line with the head, about a foot from it; Marc directly across the bed from me, right up against the bedside drawers; Peter standing against the far wall, directly opposite the bed where he would have a good shot at Lena; and James, remaining safely by the door. He took his invisibility toggle from his pocket, shot me and Marc with it, and then said, "Okay, you two, out of your shadows now."

Marc and I obliged, and then a few seconds later, James said, "Okay, John, shoot him on three…two…one…"

I fired my shield device at Lucien, knowing that I'd hit by virtue of the fact that he was a stationary target, and then quickly withdrew back into my shadow, as part of the plan, but James was already talking. "Now your turn, Marc, as we discussed, on three…two…one…"

The first countdown had been more for Marc's benefit than my own, so that he would know exactly when I had fired so that he would be prepared for his turn. The second countdown was for Peter's benefit so that he could coordinate with Marc, since while Marc could see Peter in a ghost form, Peter couldn't see Marc at all. What we had discussed was that Marc should firstly try to knock Lucien unconscious, and if that didn't work, he should try any other piece of magic he could think of in the limited time he had before Lucien reacted, before resorting to his solid-outliner and then withdrawing into his shadow.

I saw Peter fire his device a fraction of a second after Marc would have attacked, but thanks to Lucien's reflexes, it looked as though they hit at the same time. Lena was already slack, but the way she went almost completely still and her eyes rolled up made it clear that Peter, at least, had been successful; and unlike Lucien, she hadn't been protected. He wasn't knocked out, and he was quickly aware that someone had attacked him; he pushed Lena off him and rolled the other way, right towards Marc who had to spring out of the way; and, almost making me burst out laughing, tumbled right off the side of the bed, landing hard on his naked butt.

"Hey!" he shouted, jumping to his feet and attempting to perform some piece of magic that appeared to do nothing. "Untraceable again, hey? I—"

Marc hit him again, and this time, strangely, the magic worked; Lucien was thrown into the air, whacking his shoulder hard on the roof before coming back down again. Roaring with outrage, he surged to his feet again and tried something else, and then screamed in agony as his own chest opened up and blood began issuing forth. He then froze as comprehension seemed to hit him. "That shield thing again!" he bellowed.

He rounded on Lena, only then seeing that she was unconscious, unmoved from where he had left her. He woke her up, and Peter and I (and probably Marc and James, although I couldn't see their faces) gaped. How had he done that without using magic? Then I remembered his Honnie mind, and scowled; of course he would have a work-around. She sat up just in time to see Lucien get hit with a jet of pure-white light: thicky prison. Marc had decided that since he couldn't knock Lucien out but was still able to do some magic on him, trapping him in thicky prison would be the best option.

As Marc withdrew back into his shadow, however, the situation rapidly slipped out of our control—after we had come so close to succeeding, too. Lucien allowed the thicky prison to take his body, but he took complete control of Lena's mind and made her act in his place— such complete control that her face actually twisted to look like his, somehow. It was creepy, but it turned very quickly to horrifying as she reached over and scooped something invisible off the top of the bedside drawers, possibly only inches from where Marc had been standing earlier —a few inches that could have made all the difference if we had only realised. Too late, I understood that Lucien had thought of a way to fight us even after we had supposedly beaten him.

Peter took another shot at Lena, but Lucien had already made her put a shield around herself. She leaned back over, opened one of the bedside drawers, withdrew a solid-outliner and shot Lucien with it. Finally, she performed one other piece of magic that I didn't see, but knew had to be her removing the shield I put around him before obediently handing the crystal to him. Only then did he let her go, and her face became her own.

She looked around herself, puzzled. "What just happened?"

"We were attacked," Lucien growled, casting magic around the room in an attempt to flush us out, but naturally, we remained safe where we were. He then cast magic on the two of them so that at last, thankfully, they became fully clothed.

"Shit," James swore under his breath. "If only we'd thought of trying to deal with his Honnie mind as well." The three of us hushed him so that we could hear the rest of their conversation.

"Attacked by what? By who?" Lena was asking.

"You were knocked out somehow," he said, watching her closely but continuing to perform magic in a futile attempt to flush us out, "but I wasn't, because I put a spell on me that would block that kind of magic. They almost got me anyway, but I took your mind and got you to use the crystal to rescue me."

Lena's expression looked a little pissed for a moment before it smoothed over, and I knew that Lucien had used his Honnie mind to suppress any ill feelings she had on the subject. Instead of whatever she had been thinking before, she now said, "So I guess I do okay with magic after all, huh?"

Lucien smiled a little. "Hardly; it was my doing, not yours. And in answer to your second question, I strongly suspect my brothers to be behind this, and any number of their disciples. I wonder what they must have been thinking as they watched me giving you more pleasure than they ever could…"

He let his voice trail off, and Lena's face flushed, but not as though she was embarrassed—more as if she were reliving it in her mind. Then she pulled herself together and said, "How come you didn't sense them? I thought we figured out how to track untraceable things now?"

"Yeah, we did," Lucien said, his temper flaring for a moment, but he quickly got it under control. It appeared that he had a lot more control of his dark side now, perhaps because he now *was* his dark side. "I have no idea how they're doing what they're doing, how they're able to hide from me like this. Tell me, how much do you remember of last night?"

She considered. "You mean what happened in the living room, right? Not what happened after that?"

"No, I mean what happened in the living room," he said. "I know you were knocked out at one point, by one of those same spells that hit you today, only that one had been meant for me; Fewul merely deflected it to you."

"And where is Fewul, anyway?" she asked, frowning. "How come he didn't detect anything?"

"I can only assume that Fewul is bound in the same way I am—"

"But why didn't he teleport straight to you when you were attacked? Didn't you order him to do that?"

Lucien frowned, and my heartbeat quickened. He seemed to clench one of his fists, the one still holding the Sien-Leoard Crystal. "Well, this is certainly interesting. They have found a way to recall Fewul."

Lena also frowned. "How?"

Lucien shrugged. "I don't know, but apparently I am unable to call it back, because of the transfer of the chip. It would have been fine if Fewul had just stayed here, but not so now." He sighed. "Never mind; it is what it is. They are no doubt thinking they had a huge victory by doing that, and I admit it will slow me down, but they have only bought themselves a little extra time—nothing more."

Lena's frown deepened. "You're not going to kill them, are you?"

Lucien didn't answer for a moment—and then Lena smiled, having forgotten that she'd ever asked the question or been worried about such a thing.

"As I was saying, you were knocked out for some of what happened last night," Lucien went on smoothly, and Lena was totally unaware that anything strange had just happened, "but you would have seen the beginning, when May seemed to appear from nowhere. Prior to her appearance, there was no sign of her whatsoever; no sense of her mind, and no magical trace of any kind—and yes, I know I can trace Honnies in that way," he added in response to a thought she'd had, "because I was able to trace her yesterday morning, and on Sunday when she re-joined their group."

"So whatever they're doing to hide themselves, they only started sometime between yesterday morning and last night," Lena summarised.

"Yeah, I already figured that part out," Lucien said, "and I'm also working on the assumption that it has something to do with going back in time so that they can go to Rock Haulter through the Atlantic portal. That shouldn't even be possible, but the evidence I have points in that direction."

"Rock Haulter," Lena repeated, looking dubious. "Well, I suppose there is magic there, but how much could they have actually done without a fresh source of it, like one of the crystals or a crystal chip?"

"That is only limited by the magic on the Rock, and I know that there is almost enough there for them to do—well—anything they can think of."

"But—" Lena said, and then stopped, almost choking on whatever words had been about to come out of her mouth. Her face registered astonishment and then comprehension —and then more comprehension. My head began to swim and I feared I was about to faint, before I got hold of myself. That feeling was brought on by terrible dread, because Lena's expression was almost exactly the same as ours had been when we had first understood that May could access the time axis through the fourth dimension.

"But they didn't have any magic before they went back in time, making the whole thing moot?" Lucien said. "Is that what you were going to say, my dear?"

Lena couldn't bring herself to speak. Her expression had relaxed, but it looked too deliberate.

"All they had at the time was the Light Crystal, which can't really do very much of this sort of thing; the Villain Crystal, which Marc put in a magical box so that nobody could get to it; and whatever devices they were able to steal from us here," Lucien listed off. "Oh and a Honnie, of course, who was able to smooth their passage through the world around them by touching the minds of the nearby humans."

"Yeah, isn't that why you wanted her gone?" Lena asked.

Lucien shook his head. "No, I wanted her gone because she was mucking up the good work I was doing in causing rifts between Marc, John and Amelia. Then when she found a way of using her mind to allow non-magical telepathy between all of them that I couldn't spy on—well, that was the final straw."

"Wow, that *is* pretty clever, actually," Lena said admirably.

Lucien ignored this remark and went on. "Of course, May wasn't the first Honnie you saw, right? I never got to see those memories of Smiley's, but you were lucky enough to have been present for them— even though we both know that you were only brought along because you were John's sex toy, a toy which he was too limp-dick to play with."

He smirked, and Lena flushed again—first in what looked like embarrassment, but then her expression quickly shifted again to something that looked more like shame. Of course Lucien wanted her to feel ashamed of how much she had liked me, and it was clear that while she may not want me and Marc dead, any other feelings she'd once had for us had been cleanly cut out of her mind, as if by a knife, by Lucien's influence.

"Never mind that, I forgive you," he said, reaching out and stroking her neck, making her shiver. "We all have things in our past of which we are ashamed, but what matters is that we're here now, together. My point was that you were there with them when they saw those memories, and you got to see the Honnie who helped end the war back in 1981."

"Yeah, that's right," Lena said, a little breathlessly.

Lucien was silent for several seconds, and then he began to smile—it was the scariest thing I'd seen in a long time. "Thank you, Lena," he said, turning his smile on her, and she shivered again.

"What for?" she asked, her eyes widening.

"You have done so much for me today," he said, getting up off the bed and standing over her. She looked up at him, looking somehow smaller than usual in that position, but no less beautiful. "I think it's only fair that you be rewarded."

He reached down and touched his fingertip to her naval. Instantaneously, Lena cried out and clenched herself; she looked like someone under the influence of an agonator, and for almost a full second I actually believed that was what he was doing. Then I understood what was actually happening, but didn't feel any less tense for it; Lena was experiencing one almighty orgasm, one that just went on and on and on. How long did it go for? I couldn't tell, but Lucien ended it with nothing more than a look. Lena uncurled and collapsed, panting and gasping and looking thoroughly exhausted, but also blissfully happy.

"I'm afraid I must get back to work now," Lucien said, pocketing the Sien-Leoard Crystal at last, and then reaching down to touch her in a way I wished I didn't have to see. "don't worry; I will spend more time with you later on tonight, but there's a big wide world out there that needs someone to run it, and that duty has now fallen to me. I'm sure you understand, right?"

"Yeah," she gasped, "of course."

"While you're here, you can do and have anything you want," he told her. "I've already told the Hammerhearts that they are to answer to your every call, so long as you don't ask for anything political. They may not think a lot of you yet, but they will do as they're told; they know that I will have more than a few words with any who disrespect you."

"Thank you," she replied breathlessly.

He smiled and straightened up, letting her go. "Before I go, I have to do one quick thing."

"What's that?"

He waved his hand at her, making nothing happen that we could see. "I'm not sure where I'll need to go today; I could be far from here, which means that I can't protect you. Our old friends might take it into their heads to take you hostage, perhaps to even attempt to convert you back to their side. You wouldn't want that, right?"

"No way," she said indignantly. "I wish they'd just stop this nonsense."

"Me too," he agreed. "I just placed a little spell on you that will make sure they can't do anything to hurt you, so you'll be totally safe while I'm gone. Do you feel safe, my dear?"

"I trust your judgement," she said, "so if you think I'm safe then I probably am. Will it protect me from thicky prison as well?"

"Oh yes; I wouldn't want a repeat of this little incident."

"What if they try to attack me physically, then?" she asked, and Lucien frowned. "Well, if I was in their position, and I couldn't think of a magical way to do it, I'd resort to non-magic stuff like ropes or whatever."

Lucien hesitated for a moment, then said, "You make a good point. Normally the solution to that would be a physical shield, but if I put something like that around you, you would be trapped in a bubble, unable to do a thing all day."

"Maybe I should just go with you wherever you go," she said, looking hopeful. "I could take notes, or just stand there and look good for you."

"If I were only doing business stuff, then that would be all well and good," he said, "but today's business could possibly be dangerous—I'm not sure. I don't want to risk anything happening to you. I think I know how to handle this."

"How?"

He cast another spell on her, and in the brief silence of this moment, Marc asked, "Should we attack him again before he can do anything else?"

Lucien and James spoke at the same time then, but I instinctively tuned James out so that I could hear Lucien say, "That will defend you from anything they try. Just trust me on this; it won't protect you from everything, period, but it will protect you from them. I would explain exactly how it works but it's a bit complex. Also, there's still a chance that they're listening to all of this, somehow, and they don't need to know the details; they only need know that you are outside their ability to capture."

"Jesus Christ," Peter swore.

I inferred from that, that we weren't going to try anything now. Lucien was fully armed, fully alert, and quite possibly aware of the fourth dimension now. I wasn't sure, but Lena knew everything that Smiley had told us and had seen all his memories. If she recalled the one in which the Honnie from 1981 had taken humans back to his world, seeming to vanish as he went into his shadow and then reappear as he returned, then she would naturally link it to May suddenly appearing out of nowhere in the Hammersons' living room the night before.

And if she had thought it, then Lucien had seen it and understood its meaning.

Chapter 7: Retaliation

Lucien left Lena alone in his bedroom. I suppose she got up and had a shower, or perhaps took a nap, but as there was no question of staying to watch her when the man we really needed to follow had left the room, I could only assume. Followed by the four of us, still in our shadows, Lucien went into the living room, sat himself down on one of the couches, and began performing magic.

"Looks like he's creating something," James observed.

"Something to find us in our shadow?" Marc said, looking pale.

"Should we try to disrupt him?" I asked them.

James considered. "Well, he's probably expecting that we'll try, but I don't think we have anything to lose at this point. Can one of you get in touch with Amelia and make sure she's ready on the button, just in case?"

"Wouldn't the base be in trouble as well?" Peter asked.

"No, the base is still untraceable, and Lucien still doesn't know about that new spell of mine," Marc said.

While they were talking, I had been in contact with Mr. Woodward; I had chosen to communicate with him rather than Natalie. The idea of us touching each other's thoughts, all things considered, was a little more than I could handle at this time—and I imagined she would agree. They had been watching the whole scene in the bedroom and according to Mr. Woodward, Natalie herself, along with Erica, had immediately understood that Lucien had probably gathered, from Lena's mind, that we were using the fourth dimension, and perhaps even that May herself had accessed the time axis. More importantly for the four of us, though, Amelia was well and truly ready on the buttons, and we would be out of there the moment it looked like Lucien was about to hit us with his magic.

The time that we took to decide to act had cost us. By the time I let go of the communicator it was already too late; Marc was making himself visible again, realising that he had missed his chance to attack, and Peter was uttering a string of swear words under his breath that would have made Mum want to hit him across the head. Lucien had created three things that looked a bit like toy aeroplanes; they were bright red, and with no decorations except for a strange, shimmering quality around the edges which I understood only too well. These things were four dimensional, and whatever their purpose, they would be able to find us…or would they?

Lucien touched his finger to one of the planes and said, "Find John Playman. Capture, don't revive, return."

He spoke in such a careful way that it was clear he hadn't taken the time to give this thing a true understanding of the English language, but only the ability to take certain commands. He would probably improve upon these devices later on but for now, his priority seemed to be to test his theory, and to capture me as quickly as possible. The plane lifted into the air and began turning in slow circles which would have caused it to stall and fall to the floor if it hadn't been magical. It then landed carefully on Lucien's knee and stopped.

Lucien frowned and touched his finger to the plane again, repeating his earlier command. The plane repeated its earlier action and then landed back on his knee and coming to rest. Frustrated, he touched it again and commanded, "Error report."

"Cannot trace in any location," the plane spoke in a typically computerised voice—something else Lucien may take the time to improve upon later.

"Seek hole," Lucien commanded. For the third time the plane lifted off and took flight, this time flying in wider circles around the living room. While it was in the air, Lucien touched a finger to one of the other planes and commanded, "Find John Playman. Use Visual Vector, report location only, return, lights off."

None of that meant anything to me, but it meant plenty to Marc; he whirled on me with the Hero Crystal and a moment later, I had become invisible. Another moment later, the second plane took off, and a third moment later it too had become invisible. Another couple of seconds later, the first plane landed back on Lucien's knee.

"Report," Lucien commanded.

"Person, Dermott Hall, location thirty-seven-point—"

"Cycle," Lucien interrupted, and the plane began speaking another name, followed by what I guessed was supposed to be the latitude and longitude coordinates of that person, but Lucien kept interrupting it with the word "cycle" almost as soon as he heard the name.

This was beginning to make sense to me. The plane he was dealing with now had been commanded to look for the holes in reality that corresponded to anything untraceable—the old untraceable, the only one Lucien knew of. The plane had traced as much as it could through this world and probably along the fourth dimension as well, and now was listing everything it had found—and Lucien was becoming more and more frustrated as it seemed to return nothing but Hammerhearts.

As for the other plane, I thought I now understood what that was doing as well. Lucien had commanded it to look for me, but as it was unable to magically trace me it was doing a visual check instead. Thank heavens Marc had understood what Lucien's command had meant and had made me invisible just in the nick of time. As for the plane being invisible as well, that had to be so that I didn't know it was spying on me. It would have worked perfectly if we hadn't just watched the whole thing.

Lucien had had enough. He commanded to the first plane, "End report," and then sat there motionless for about half a minute, his face screwed up in concentration. In that period of silence, I whispered, "Am I going to have to stay invisible forever now?"

"No, we'll find a way to manage this," Marc hissed back, "I promise. Right now, though, we can't let Lucien know that you're in your shadow. He can just as easily order that plane to capture you."

Lucien swept the two remaining planes onto the seat next to him and then stood up, looking around the room, his expression growing blacker and blacker by the second. "Is anyone there?" he asked the room at large, and the four of us froze, waiting. "Anyone at all?"

There was no answer, of course—at least, none that Lucien could hear. Peter answered, though, "What should we do? Should we say something? Do something?"

"Hell no!" James hissed back.

"I think there is," Lucien answered himself. "I think you're here, John, and I think maybe, just maybe, some others are here with you. I can feel eyes on me. You probably think you're doing so well for yourselves right about now, don't you? You probably think you've put me on the mat, so to speak."

The four of us exchanged worried looks. Lucien was utterly furious; he was in control of it now, but he would still have to let it out somehow. What would he do? Would he make us pay again by finding someone we cared about, and then find a particularly horrible way of killing them? It sounded about right, but at least it wouldn't be so bad this time; Peter and Rebecca had all but emptied the Big Room earlier, so unless he took it into his head to search the rest of the big, wide world...

"Why not take it further then, hey? Why not attack me right now. Knock me out like you did to Lena, or try to hit me with thicky prison again. You probably could, you know; I may be protected from some things, but you're creative so maybe you can find a way to hit me which I'm not expecting. I challenge you—nay, dare you—to take your best shot."

Peter actually raised his inter-dimensional knock-out then, but James caught his wrist. "don't even think about it, young man," he said sternly.

"Maybe I should try something," Marc began.

James shook his head. "That's what he wants, Marc. Most likely you won't be able to hurt him, and all you'll do is confirm his suspicions and maybe give away our position in the process."

Lucien had waited through all of this, turning in slow circles so that he could observe every part of the room. Now he smiled, and I also shivered at the sight of it. "Well, either you're not here now, or you're choosing to ignore me. I tend to believe it is the latter. I'm not surprised, but I am disappointed—*severely* disappointed. I think you need me to teach you a lesson, oh dear brother of mine. Whether you're here or not, you still need to be taught a lesson after daring to attack me in my own bedroom. If you follow me now, you will understand; if you don't, then it will all make sense to you later."

"Oh crap," Peter moaned, "not this again."

But at first, Lucien didn't do anything. He merely stood there, either waiting for us to do something or considering his next move. He appeared to come to a decision but before he could do anything, one of the red planes appeared overhead and came down to land beside the other two.

"Report?" Lucien commanded.

"No sighting," the plane responded robotically, and Lucien smiled.

"Of course," he muttered, and then taking us all by some surprise, he teleported away.

"What the hell!" Marc exclaimed. "Where's he going?"

"Amelia, now would be a good time to bring us back—" James started to say, and then he vanished, Amelia having taken care of him.

"How am I gonna get in?" I asked Marc. "She can't see me."

"don't worry, I already thought of that," he said as Peter also disappeared.

A moment later, Marc too was pulled into the base, leaving me standing alone there, still invisible and with no idea what to do. The plane had landed now; surely that meant it would be safe to be visible again? And even if it weren't, the plane would then have to find Lucien and report my location, telling him nothing that he didn't already suspect. I put my hand in my pocket, feeling for my invisibility toggle, but before I could find it, I disappeared from there, appearing a moment later in the corner of the control room within the base.

"How'd you do that?" I asked, looking towards the control panel where Marc was now standing beside a seated Amelia.

"I just put a spell on it to make sure that it could see invisible people," Marc told me, "as ghosts, the same way that we could through those old ghost goggles I made. I'm a little surprised you didn't think to do that yourself."

"Nobody's perfect," I muttered, scooting over to my seat from earlier and sitting down. "So he's—oh no!"

"Yep, we all came to the same conclusion," said Rebecca bitterly.

"Teleporting us now," Amelia told us. A second later, we went through that nothing feeling again, but it didn't last anywhere near as long as it did when we'd been coming back from the moon. We reappeared in the open, just over Lucien's left shoulder.

"Okay, so it's obvious that he's gone to a public place and is probably planning on killing someone, or at least taking a hostage," James said, "but where exactly are we?"

"Let me check," Amelia said, taking the controls and lifting us high into the air. When we had an overhead look at the scene, we could only see the roof of a large, but only single-storey building, surrounded by a large carpark and a few smaller appendages which looked like window shops. Lucien was taking cover beside the building, down a narrow passageway which ended in a door, and presently he was just standing there. Perhaps he was doing what we were doing and simply observing the scene through his mind's eye; or more likely he was working some sort of dark magic.

"That looks like a supermarket," Lillian observed.

"I don't like this," Mr. Woodward said slowly, his face pale. "I don't know what he's planning but I've got a very bad feeling about it. Stay very close to him, Amelia; and Marc, be prepared to jump in with any magic at any moment. I'm fairly sure you can perform it from in here if you're focused on those screens."

"Sure," Marc muttered, his eyes glued to the screens as Amelia lowered us back down to Lucien, who remained motionless.

Minutes passed, and then more minutes. Lucien didn't do a damn thing as far as we could tell, and out of frustration, James turned the sound on all the spyers back up in case they could provide a clue about what was happening here. Eventually, this move paid off: it happened gradually, but it became clear that there was some sort of commotion taking place in the carpark. When Lucien began to smile ominously, Amelia gave up watching him directly and, without waiting for our opinion, took the base back into the air so that we could see what was really happening, and out of our shadow so that we would have a clearer view of it.

And we could only gape in astonishment. The carpark was now jam-packed with vehicles—not just the parking spots, but everything else as well. A few people were trying to leave, honking their horns and shouting at other motorists to get out of the way so that they could get out, but most seemed desperate to get inside and do some shopping. People were scrambling between cars, squeezing through gaps that looked uncomfortably small, and several came very close to getting squashed by a car trying to move closer to a spot. Others were giving up and turning their cars off where they had ended up, getting out and scrambling for the doors.

Mr. Woodward let out a groan. "This is bad...this is *very* bad."

"You can figure this out?" Natalie asked.

"I think I get it too," James said slowly, his face paling. "He wants to pack this place as tight as possible. Either he wants a greater choice of people to hurt, or he's going to find a way to make them all suffer."

"A riot," Mr. Woodward breathed. "That's what this is looking like. People will be crushed and possibly killed in there."

"Can we stop this before it gets going?" Marc asked desperately.

"I don't see how," James said. "I mean, he must have all their minds inside his own, so we can't do anything to change their behaviour. Our only hope is to put Lucien out of action, but does anyone still think we can do that?"

"Probably not now; Lucien will be expecting us to try," I heard myself say, but my head was light and dizzy with anxiety. He was doing this to punish us—particularly me, for some reason—most likely because I had dared to take Stella from him. All these innocent people were about to suffer horribly because of me, and all I could do was watch. And even if we were somehow able to prevent this spiralling into a full-on riot, Lucien could instantly change his plan to something else—perhaps something worse. He would only be limited by his imagination, and unfortunately, his imagination was immense.

"We need to keep an eye on him and watch his every movement," Mr. Woodward said, "and maybe we'll see an opening to do something. Go back down to him, Amelia."

Amelia descended, but not to Lucien; he had disappeared. Had he made himself invisible or had he teleported? Amelia took a chance on the latter and teleported the base back to Lucien's current location. It took a second to figure out where we were, and it was a bit of a shock when we did: Lucien had teleported himself into the supermarket, but rather than subject himself to the throng (which we could hear making an almighty racket not too far away), he had taken shelter in one of the bathrooms. Judging by the lack of a urinal, it seemed to be the ladies' bathroom.

"This must be where he's going to coordinate it from," Peter said.

"Yeah, maybe," James said slowly, "but he could have done that outside, or pretty much from anywhere. If he wanted to go where no one would see him or know he was there, why pick a public bathroom? And why isn't he making himself invisible?"

"He wouldn't need to be invisible if he can prevent people coming in here just by using his mind," Peter pointed out. "Also, he's probably hoping that we're still following him. Maybe he's daring us to try to attack him again."

Yeah, I thought that sounded plausible, which meant...what? Were we supposed to avoid his bait and let him do all kinds of damage here? What if we took the bait? Would we be running the risk of saving those people now, only to expose ourselves and kill the last resistance against him? My head swam again and I had to grip the sides of my seat to steady myself. I'd faced some dilemmas during this war—the one the previous night in which Natalie had very nearly died had been a particularly nasty one—but this was quite likely the worst one yet.

"John, does this base have any weapons that we can use from in here?" Marc asked suddenly.

"No," I said, taken aback, "but you can use your crystal from in here."

"Not when we're in our shadow, I can't."

"But we're not in our shadow—"

He broke off when a noise came through the spyers. We looked sharply up at the display screens, and were astonished all over again by what we saw. A woman had just staggered into the bathroom carrying a shopping bag, red-faced and out-of-breath. She was youngish (probably in her 20s) and quite attractive, even taking into account her obviously harried state. She turned around with her back to the door, and then froze in horror at the sight of Lucien standing there just a couple of metres in front of her.

"Hey! You can't be in here! This is a…"

She trailed off, her expression shifting from major indignation to dawning comprehension. My first thought was that Lucien had used his Honnie mind to deal with her, but then doubt seeped in as she spoke again.

"You're him," she said slowly. "You're—you're the new ruler—are you?"

Lucien smiled. "No, you're right. I am Lucien. Shhh," he put his finger to his lips and winked conspiratorially at her.

"I—" she began, her face turning red as, I assumed, she became star-struck. "I've seen you on TV. You're a lot better than the Hammersons."

"Why, thank you," Lucien smiled charmingly at her.

She gulped and then looked down at the shopping bag swinging loosely from one hand. Then she looked back up at Lucien, her expression settling. "You have magic, right? I know this is probably small by your standards, but there's a real mess out there and some people are already getting hurt—"

He put a hand up to still her speech before it could get going. "I know about that. That's why I'm here; I sensed a disturbance bigger than something the police could manage on their own. Obviously I can't be everywhere at once, but until I have found a magical way to prevent these things without me being on the spot, I can only sort them out on a case-by-case basis."

"Wow," she breathed, her face going red again. "You really *are* gonna be a great ruler. So—so can you help us here today?"

"Well," Lucien said, taking a step towards her—I expected her to take a step backward, but she didn't. "I can tell from your mind that you approve of my policies, even if you weren't enraptured with my predecessors. Sorry, not snooping deliberately," he added quickly. "The mind-reading thing is involuntary, Shana. That is your name, isn't it?"

"Yeah," she said, and swallowed.

"How would you like to help me help them?" he asked her.

"Me?" she gulped. "Well—sure, I'd love to. I mean, you'll remember that I did, right?"

He considered, his smile turning into a grin of amusement. "Sure I will. If you're looking to use this as an opportunity to get ahead, I'm cool with that. I find myself trusting you, Shana, and don't worry; I can mind your shopping while you do what I need you to do."

"What the hell is this?" Peter spoke over the conversation, causing several people to make shushing gestures at him.

After a brief silence, Shana asked, "What do you need from me?"

Lucien took another step towards her so that they were within arms' reach of each other. He reached out and put his hands on her body, causing her to drop the shopping bag and gasp in surprise. For a moment I thought he was going to molest her, but it was over before it had even begun. He had placed his hands on each of her sides at chest height; for a moment, it looked as though her breasts rippled, but when he removed his hands, she looked no different.

"What was that?" she asked curiously, apparently not at all affronted that he'd got into her personal space.

"Something which will send out a magical pulse," he told her, "which will settle the crowd down and make it possible for them to disperse. But in order for it to work, I need you to get to the centre of the supermarket—or as close as you can using your best judgement. Can you do that?"

That made her a little nervous. "Er—I can try," she hesitated, "although it might take a little while, and I might get hurt before I can get there."

He just smiled at that. "You're under my protection now—you won't get hurt by the people out there. Trust me on that. All you need to do is get as close to the centre as you can, and then wait. I'll sense when you're there, and then I'll activate the pulse. You'll know immediately when it's done its job."

"Okay, that doesn't sound too hard," she said. She hesitated then, seeming to be on the verge of saying something else. When he continued to watch her, she blushed and finally took a step back from him, hitting the closed door behind her and letting out a little squeak. What was all that about?

"Go on," he told her, "oh—and don't leave when it's over. I need to remove the pulse from your—er—your chest, and I'd like to give you another reward as well, for helping me."

"A reward? What reward?"

He shook his head. "You'll find out later, but trust me—it will definitely help you in your aspirations."

She beamed at that, and without waiting for any more turned, opened the door, and hurried back out into the throng. When the door had closed, Lucien picked up the shopping bag she had left behind, set it down under one of the basins where it would be out of the way, and then turned his back on the closed door. For a moment I thought he was about to teleport away, but instead, making us all cringe and several faces fall, he began to speak to us.

"I'm sure you're here, watching me. I could be wrong; and if I am, well, it hardly matters. If not, then allow me to explain what this is all about, although it wouldn't surprise me if you've already guessed much of it. I have crammed this place with hundreds of people from the area, making them believe they must do their shopping here and now. It is impossible for any of them to rationalise their way through this and realise that there's no point in coming in here, because I am preventing that line of thinking from occurring to any of them. Some people are already hurt out there, and a few ambulances have been called already, as have the police. I don't mind if paramedics try to get in here, but when the police turn up, they will determine that it is too dangerous for them to enter and so they won't do anything.

"Now, as for Shana, that lovely young woman you just saw me talking to: she is going to help me with my ultimate goal here today, and you must understand, John, that what is about to happen here is directly your fault. I have attached a bomb to her—not a small one, either, but one large enough and explosive enough that when it goes off, it will demolish the entire building and everyone with it."

Marc swore loudly while several other people were making gasping sounds, but nobody could move; we were all paralysed by Lucien's speech.

"I'm sure you will consider it your duty to try to defuse her, but there are a couple of problems with that. Firstly, in case you didn't figure it out, I attached the bomb to her bra, right between her breasts, so it won't be easy for you to walk up to her and take it out. Secondly, and more importantly, I have enchanted the bomb to explode immediately if anyone tries to move or remove it from her bra, or if her bra is removed from her body. So trust me when I say this: you have no hope at all of stopping this from happening…except, perhaps, for one thing.

"Come to me. Reveal yourselves to me. You, John, Marc, Amelia, Stella, James, Natalie, and all the rest of you who have turned your backs on me. Come to me now and allow me to take you back to the Hammerheart base; if you do that, I will defuse her myself, as I have enchanted it to work only if I use my own magic, from my own crystal chips. I am going to teleport outside now, where I will have a good view of the destruction; you can come to me there if you decide that these people's lives aren't worth sacrificing just so that you can continue to resist me. don't take too long to decide; it may take her a few minutes to push her way to the centre of the supermarket, but when she does, your time will have run out."

He vanished from the screens, leaving us alone in the ladies' bathroom. Marc began swearing at the top of his voice, and only when Amelia put a gentle hand on his shoulder did he quiet. She, meanwhile, had tears streaming down her face, and she was most definitely not the only one.

"What do we do?" Peter whispered, just loud enough for most people to hear.

Everyone looked at Mr. Woodward and his mother, the only two people who were qualified to make such a call. It was strange how we had been so ready to take the lead when things were going well, but as soon as we found ourselves in a position where hundreds of innocent lives hung on our decision, we once again reverted back to taking direction from the adults. If the situation hadn't been so dire, I might have taken a few seconds to appreciate this observation.

"We can't do it," Mr. Woodward said quietly, making several people cringe. "I'm sorry, but we just can't. For one thing, I'm not convinced that Lucien will defuse her even if we do what he says; he's determined to punish us, and his evil has taken control of him. For another thing, making deals with terrorists is always a bad move, without exception, because it teaches them that this kind of tactic will work again in the future, and so Lucien may use it again the next time he wants something. We need to make him realise that no matter what he does, we will always fight him."

"So what, we're just gonna watch it all happen?" Amelia sobbed.

"Either way, we're going to suffer and Lucien's going to get something out of it," James said bitterly.

"No," I said, standing up suddenly. An idea had just occurred to me —a possible way to save all those people out there, without revealing ourselves in the process. That woman couldn't be saved—her death certificate had already been signed—but everyone else out there…

"What are you doing, John?" Peter asked.

"Let me out here," I told Amelia, walking around and between the chairs so that I could stand in the corner of the control room. "Let me out here and then teleport after Lucien. See if you can distract him from setting off the bomb for as long as possible."

"What are you going to do?" she asked warily.

"I have an idea," I told her. "It'll take too long to explain. Just trust me on this and let me out while there's still a chance."

Amelia didn't take another second to think about it but quickly pushed the button to drop me into the ladies' room. I heard the beginnings of a loud protest before I vanished—Peter, James, and my father's voices had been among them—but then it all disappeared and was replaced by what I supposed was probably the first ladies' bathroom I had ever set foot in.

I tore out of the bathroom without a second thought, except for an understanding of the danger I was putting myself in. There was the obvious one of the bomb going off before I could get to the woman, in which case I would probably be killed, but there was also the possibility of Lucien detecting me with his Honnie mind and capturing me that way. I didn't think that would happen, not with Marc's untraceability around me, but it was still a remote possibility. Then there was the possibility of being seen and recognised—perhaps by one of these people, or perhaps by the plane which Lucien had ordered to keep an eye out for me, if it were still in the air doing its job. It was a chance I had to take—too many lives would be lost if we did nothing.

As soon as I was out of the bathroom, I was surrounded by desperate shoppers, trying to get to the aisles where the things they needed were, and fighting each other over some of the stock. I pushed violently past the ones around me, actually knocking a man down and causing several people to yell after me—there was so much noise in the place that it was easy to pretend I hadn't heard them. I wished I could take a moment to make myself invisible, but not only could I not afford to waste a second, but people might get suspicious if they felt an invisible force pushing through them.

Heart beating wildly, I pushed relentlessly onward, trying desperately not to be knocked down by the people around me, many of whom were bigger than me. My relatively small size made it possible to squeeze between them some of the time, but it also made it more difficult to get past them if they were determined not to move—as some of them were, while they were trying to access the nearby shelves. In one instance, I almost went over when my foot caught one of the wheels of somebody's shopping trolley, and it was only by grabbing onto a tall man and using him to push onward that I was able to keep going.

I was at the back of the supermarket, pushing along the ends of the aisles, looking down each one, trying to see the woman from the bathroom down any of them. I had a rough idea of where she must be, if she was heading for the centre of the supermarket, but what if her idea of what was 'the centre' was different to mine? I could only keep an eye out for her, but this plan was *not* going well; not only was it hard for me to see over the heads of the people in front of me, given that at least half of them were taller than me, including some of the women, but the woman herself had probably been about my height too.

I could almost hear a ticking in my head now. The woman had left the bathroom probably about three minutes ago already; if she hadn't reached the centre yet, she couldn't be too far from it. Surely, I had to be pretty close myself now—I had pushed, shoved, and in one case fought my way past several aisles now, looking up at the roof every so often, because it was the only hope I had of judging roughly how far I was from each wall. It was too low to see them, unfortunately, but if I couldn't see either wall, then that had to mean that I was far enough from them both that I had to be close to the centre.

Then finally, I caught a lucky break: I'd just come to the head of an aisle, and through a gap between a man and a woman who appeared to be fighting over a bag of potato chips, I saw the woman I was searching for. At least, the little I saw looked like her; same colour top, same colour hair, probably about the same height. I couldn't afford to wait any longer —she was getting very close to the halfway point along the aisle.

I scrambled around the two people in front of me and began pushing my way along. This aisle was so packed, more than any other place I'd been so far, and it hit me that that was probably intentional—Lucien had known she was close, so he had surrounded her with people—the first ones to die. I had to fight very hard against the throng, and when it was clear that this was far too slow, I bellowed at the top of my voice, "Hey! Stop!"

I couldn't even see the woman anymore, but did it matter? Even if she had somehow heard me, she didn't necessarily know, or even suspect, that I was talking to her. I could only fight even harder, ducking my head down and attempting to charge forward amongst a sea of legs. It actually worked at first until I tripped over someone's foot, lost my balance and accidentally head-butted a man squarely in the arse. I fell to the floor and managed to get my back stepped on briefly by someone (who thankfully didn't put their entire weight on me), before pushing myself up and hurtling onward.

Then I saw her again, and this time I knew for sure that it was her because she was side-on to me and I could see her face. She had come to a stop with her back to the shelf behind her, a clear space in front of her, and her expression looked relieved. My stomach lurched in horror as I understood why she looked relieved: she had determined that she was now in the centre of the supermarket, and the hardest part of her job had been completed.

"Hey! You!" I shouted, projecting my voice at her as much as I could as I fought through the last of the throng between us. We were only maybe four or five metres apart now. This time, she *did* hear me; she looked around, saw me fighting my way towards her, and surprise shone on her face. Then she must have gotten a better look at me, and I actually saw the moment of realisation—the exact moment when she understood that she had been played. I couldn't say how I knew that she'd come to that understanding, rather than thinking that I was the danger she ought to be afraid of; I only knew that she knew the truth.

Then she vanished, replaced by a blindingly white light. I only saw it for a moment, though, before an irresistible force crashed into me and shoved me backward. After that, I only knew a fiery light, a roaring sound, and exquisite pain. I registered myself spinning and turning and falling, and not until I was on the rumbling floor was I able to perceive any of it. It was hot, dark and smoky. There was also light as things around me burned. There were screams, but not very many could be heard over the crashing of collapsing shelves and the roaring of the building's structure giving way.

My body had gone into shock, and when I rolled my eyes around in their sockets, I saw why: my left leg was missing. I couldn't remember losing it, but somehow I had. I couldn't see where it had gone; there was another bleeding body part next to me, but it looked like it belonged to someone else. Somewhere in my mind, I wondered where that person was, and if they knew that they were missing something. Then my view of it was cut off as a shelf came crashing down on top of me; I saw it land squarely on my left wrist and cut through it, so that I was now missing two body parts.

The rest of the structure landed on me, but I barely felt it now. I could feel my body draining out, and knew what must be coming. All their faces flashed through my mind: Mum, Dad, Nicole, Peter, James, Felicity, Jessica, Natalie, Amelia, Stella, Serena, Lena, Marc, Tommy, May, Lucien…Lucien. The one who had made this happen. if he didn't know what had happened here, the full extent of it, he soon would. Damn, I had come so close to succeeding too: if I'd had just ten more seconds, I could have reached her, yanked her along the fourth dimension, and then she could have died in there, all alone but taking no one else with her.

I couldn't see the flickering lights of the fires anymore; either there was too much smoke, or it was too dark under all this wreckage. The rumbling seemed to have stopped too—or almost; the roar was very dull now. In seconds, it dimmed even more until I could see nothing, hear nothing, and even feel nothing, as the shock had obviously done its business. There, where I lay, I went to sleep.

First Interlude: The Place

I was in a place. That was all that could be said; nothing else could describe it, because there was nothing else to describe. It was a place. I wasn't lying down, sitting, or standing up; I was just there. I wasn't alarmed by this at all, but I was a little curious. I cast my senses around, and as I did, things began to get a little clearer. Wherever I was, I wasn't alone; others were here in this place, not lying or sitting or standing either, but here all the same, and if I wanted to, I could reach out to them.

Where was I? When was I? Who was I? That last question was the easiest to answer: I was John Playman. I had always been John Playman, so far as I could remember, but what was I doing here? Was I dreaming? I cast my mind back, and vague memories trickled into my awareness. I'd had a body, but I had now left it behind somewhere. Why had I done that? That body had been good to me, and if I had it now, maybe I could lie down, or sit, or stand up, or just about anything.

Another memory came trickling back, a brief moment of being aware of leaving my body before I had come here. The body had been covered in stuff—squashed beneath it, really. That explained it then: I'd left it because it had been damaged beyond repair, and that now meant that I was dead. I waited for a rush of sadness to engulf me, but it didn't come. Actually, I felt nothing. Death had supposedly been so scary, and yet I had been there and done it, and I was okay...wasn't I?

I still didn't know where I was. This couldn't be heaven, or hell for that matter; either of those would surely have more feeling to them than this place. I couldn't be in an eternal dream either, because if I was, surely I would dream of something other than nothingness. Now I was having a feeling, and it was growing: curiosity. I could go on like this forever if I wanted and I didn't think it would bother me at all, but my curiosity was making it hard to settle to anything.

I could think of only one move I could make: I had to reach out to the others around me, and maybe then, I could figure out where I was. This 'reaching out' thing was difficult to explain, even to myself, because I didn't have to move to do it; I simply went to them, or drew them to me. Each time I did this, the other in question would seem to wake up, or be disturbed, as if they had been eternally pondering, as I probably would have been if my curiosity hadn't gotten the better of me.

Only when I finally recognised another, did things begin to change, and my sense of awareness grew even further. I had found one other who I recognised, not by sight or anything, but because we had met sometime previously. The other became aware of me at much the same time, and it was then that I sensed a feeling about this other—they were plagued with eternal sadness. That was the first thing I noticed, but the second thing was even worse—this other was only partially here. It was as though part of them had been torn away somehow, which explained the sadness; they were probably forever wondering what had happened to the rest of them.

Then the other recognised me; I felt the recognition as they too reached out. We linked together somehow, and then everything changed. The place of no description shifted, took on a new form. It was still dark, but the fact that I knew it was dark meant that rather than nothingness, there was instead an absence of light. The feel of the place had changed too; it was dank, wet and empty, but it was still something. Most importantly though, the change meant that the two of us were able to perceive each other in a way other than just sensing each other's presence.

I saw who it was and my curiosity vanished, replaced with understanding. It didn't come all at once, because those pre-death memories were somehow more difficult to access, and some of them were probably untouchable altogether, but the important ones were there. The in-between, the place where souls were trapped if they ever came back from the dead, either as ghosts or through a temporary resurrection. The tearing of the soul if they were resurrected, so that part of them would be forever trapped in the in-between while the rest of them died forever. A fate that had befallen William Playman, Carl Thomas, Lisa Pont, and my mother.

And it was Lisa Pont who I had just encountered here in the in-between.

"John Playman," she observed, and her speech was strange. I could hear it, except it wasn't really sound at all; just like I could see her through the darkness, even though she didn't really have a body to see.

"Lisa," I observed in return.

"You're here too," she said sadly. "I'm sorry."

"Me too," I said, and for the first time, I meant it. I actually *was* sorry that I was here, now that I understood how bad it was.

She paused a moment that wasn't really a moment at all but could have been any length of time, before saying, "You are whole, unlike me."

"What do you mean?"

"I guess you haven't been resurrected," she said. "Have you gone back as a ghost?"

I tried to remember if I had, but nothing came to me. "No."

"So then, you can go back at any time," she said, "if you want to."

I considered this, probing every sense I had available to me. Yes, Lisa was right. There was no time here so I could stay as long as I wanted, but in order for me to be here at all, I would have to go eventually. Also since there was no time here, it wouldn't matter how long I stayed, because I would always end up back in life—whether resurrected or as a ghost—at the same time. It was confusing, and yet it made sense.

"I would have hoped that you learnt your lesson, though," Lisa said sadly.

More understanding trickled through then. Lisa didn't know how much we knew about the in-between, because she had died before Smiley had told us about it. She didn't realise that such a decision would have been deliberate—and, of course, it was, because we had promised that the first one of us to die would agree to do exactly this. Why had we done that? The final piece of understanding trickled through then: we had done it so that I could learn, from Lisa, the important thing we needed to know in order to fight this war.

I could go back at any time, but I wasn't going anywhere just yet.

"Lisa, what do you know about this place?" I asked her.

"I know that we're stuck here for eternity," she said sadly.

I considered. How exactly was I to get her to tell me what I needed to know?

"Do you know about the Enlightener?" I asked her.

She registered surprise then but it quickly disappeared, replaced by her eternal aura of sadness. "Yes, I remember researching that."

"Well, I connect to it," I told her, "and it told me that you needed to tell me something very important."

"I don't remember you ever connecting to the Enlightener," she said.

"Well, I do," I insisted. "We only found out about it after you—after you died. You don't know of anything that's happened after you died, do you?"

"No," she said sadly. "How long ago did I die? How old are you?"

"Er—I outlived you by about six months, that's all. Lisa, what can you tell me that's important? Anything at all that might help us win the war?"

She took a long time to answer, but thanks to there being no time in this place, it made no impression on me. "There was a prophecy," she said, "in the same place as the one about the Seventh Sorcerer. I can't remember how it went, but I remember thinking that it would someday be important if things came to a head."

"Is it about the one who can take down the greatest Sorcerer who ever lived?"

"No, I don't think so. It was something about the last Sorcerer, the one who would bring about the end of the world, or the end of all magic. I forget which, because I wasn't really paying attention."

If I'd had a stomach, it would have done a great big somersault at this point. That sounded an awful lot like Lucien—or rather, what Lucien would become as soon as he received that final crystal chip.

"Thank you," I told her. "I need to go now; I'm not sure what's waiting for me, but I know that for my own sake, I'd better face it now."

Part 2: The Last Sorcerer

Chapter 8: Second Chance

Pain! So much more pain than I had ever known, including that caused by the agonator itself. A spinning sensation. And then, still stunned halfway out of my mind, I fell and hit the floor, landing hard on my left shoulder and jarring it rather nastily. The pain had vanished as quickly as it had come, but the spinning sensation seemed to continue, even as I lay there on a cold, stone floor, rolling onto my back to ease the pain in my shoulder.

"Well, welcome back, John," a voice said, and it took me completely aback. Of all the voices I might have expected, I hadn't expected this one.

"Er—thanks?" I said incredulously, raising my hand in the general direction of the voice.

Jacob Underwood reached down and pulled me to my feet. The world spun and I had to steady myself against the wall of the cave. The wall of the cave? What was I doing back in a cave? Come to think of it, what was I doing back on Rock Haulter, if that was indeed where I was?

"What's going on?" I asked him, looking at him, and then down at myself. I was wearing the same clothes I'd died in, except that they, along with the rest of my body, had repaired themselves.

"You died, mate," he told me, as if I hadn't figured that part out for myself, "and I just brought you back—at Marc's request, that is. He said you agreed to it before you died."

He studied me closely as he said this, and I nodded. "Yeah, I did, but I thought he would have brought me back with his own magic."

"Phiew," Underwood looked extremely relieved. "You know, I didn't agree to it right away. My grandfather told me all about what happened when people were brought back from the dead; I didn't wanna do that to you, and I had a hard time believing that Marc was volunteering you for it. As for why he didn't do it himself, I assume it's because he doesn't have his own magic anymore—does he?"

"Er—I dunno. What day is it? How long was I dead for?"

It felt very strange to say those words, and even more strange that I was okay with them.

"It's Wednesday morning, the first of September," he told me, "on Rock Haulter. In your time, it's probably sometime in the early afternoon, so—"

"So I've been dead for about twenty-four hours, give or take," I finished the thought, quickly doing the calculation. "How much do you know about what happened?"

He shrugged. "Very little. Marc contacted me after lunch yesterday and asked me to bring you back, but I shut off the communication before he could explain because—well—I was appropriately horrified by what he was asking me to do. I tried to contact him again last night to tell him that I'd decided to do it, but I think he must have been asleep. That's all I know. So—how did you die, anyway?"

"Lucien blew up a supermarket," I told him. "I tried to stop it but I wasn't quick enough, and—that's basically what happened. Marc does have his magic now—we stole the crystals from Lucien yesterday morning, before all the shit went down—well, after some of it, but—never mind. Maybe he just thought it could be done better here. What is this cave anyway?"

"A resurrection cave," he told me. "I've never been here before, but when I got up this morning, I searched it out. I've got a way of finding the caves I want if they exist," he added in response to my questioning look.

"Okay. Well, thank you," I said earnestly, "but I've only got two weeks from now. I've gotta get moving."

My stomach fell as I realised this. Two weeks from now, I would be like Lisa—forever sad and searching for the part of myself which I'd lost.

"Right," he said, clapping his hands. "Come see what I did to my hover car."

A little bemused by this seeming change of topic, I followed him into the cave's antechamber where he had left his big, shiny-black hover car. It was the same as I remembered it, with the major exception of the sidecar now attached to it.

"Nice job," I said, grinning and making to get in the hover car, but he grabbed me and yanked me back.

"You sit in the sidecar, boy; I'm the legal driver here."

The resurrection cave, it turned out, was very high up the mountain on the south side of the island—not too far below the protective mote which encircled it near the top. Underwood took me out, down, and around to the east side where his home was, and where I had been a number of times before. He left me sitting in what I thought of as 'the foyer' of his home while he went inside to get breakfast for both of us. I had never been beyond that door; on the few times I had visited him here, as well as the few times I had visited Smiley in this same location months earlier, we had always met in this room, with the comfortable seats and grassy carpet.

While we ate in silence, I examined myself and all my senses. My body felt totally normal, exactly as it had done before it was blasted apart by the explosion I had failed to prevent. Now that my mind was free and out of danger, I could think of a number of other ways it could have been prevented. I could have reached her by running in my shadow, instead of pushing through the masses. We could have sucked her into the base and then dropped her somewhere safe to explode on her own; or better yet, Marc could have just teleported her away from other people. Lucien probably wouldn't have thought to prevent something like that happening, if he didn't know that we could do that—mind you, that was a big assumption to make. By now, he had probably decided that since he didn't know the full extent of our capabilities, he ought to treat us as if we had full magical powers. And that was assuming he didn't yet know about the Sorcerous Crystals being stolen.

I also reached out with my other sense—the one I hadn't been aware of until now. That sense that I had only gained after I'd died and gone to the in-between was still with me, and using it, I had a strange perception of the in-between even now. I wasn't moving around or doing anything in there; as there was no time in there, it was a very simple thing to just do nothing and have nothing happen. But I also knew that if I wanted to converse with Lisa again, or perhaps one of the others, that would be easy too. I made a mental note to check if my biological mother was in there when I had a free moment to concentrate, and then—my stomach fell as the thought hit me—I probably ought to see if Mary Sien really *was* in there as well, because if she was, then perhaps she could tell me something useful about the crystals—like, where they *really* came from or how they were *really* made.

I was very hungry, perhaps because my new body had been created completely empty of any sustenance. When Underwood had finished eating, he went to get seconds for me, but not for himself. While I began eating again, he began using his telepathic communicator (the red one) to let the others know that it was done, and that I had returned. He told me that it was Marc he was speaking to, and that it was almost lunchtime for them. That meant it was half past twelve for them, or thereabouts, which made it half past six in the morning here. This made me appreciate Jacob Underwood even more—he'd gotten up very early to make this happen, much earlier than he'd needed to.

"Ask him if anyone else has died over there," I told him, "or if anyone's hurt."

After a little telepathy between them, he said, "No one's died or been hurt from your group. More than four hundred people died in the supermarket, though, and he set up another terrorist attack just a few hours ago that killed hundreds more. They also failed in something else massive but I didn't ask what that was."

Another terrorist attack? Why was Lucien doing this? Hadn't he got what he wanted with my death? Did he even know I had died? Before I could say anything else, Underwood added, "Oh, and he's saying that you caused the supermarket bombing—that you were a suicide bomber and that all of Hammersonia must unite against these terrorists."

Of course he knew, and he was using it to further his own agenda. It shouldn't have pissed me off, but it did. Seriously, me, a suicide bomber?

"Ask him what else they failed at," I said, tucking into my breakfast, desperate to finish so that I could get to work. While all this had been going on, I had tested my own magic—the spells I had placed upon my body—only to find that they were no longer there. Apparently, this new body had been created without those enchantments. I would need to go and put them back on before I could leave Rock Haulter, something else I needed to do fairly quickly. I only had two weeks—I couldn't afford to waste any of it.

"Taking his magic," Underwood responded a few seconds later. "Apparently, when Stella came around, Marc immediately tried to take one of his chips, but it didn't work. It would appear that he's put an enchantment on his body and all the chips in it so that even if someone has the crystals, they can't transfer the chips out. And on top of that, he called Fewul again. I tell you what, I don't understand a lot of this stuff but I'm getting a clear feeling of walls closing in from Marc's mind."

If nobody could take his magic, and he had all six Sorcerous Crystals representing him, then that really *did* make him the last Sorcerer. If Lisa was right, his arrival would bring about either the end of all magic, or the end of the world. Which was it? Did the prophecy say which it was, and Lisa had just not read it properly, or was the prophecy itself ambiguous? Damn, I would need to track it down to find the wording, because if there was any chance that it was ambiguous, we needed to make sure that it was magic that came to an end, rather than the entire world—that would certainly be the lesser of two calamities.

When I had finished eating, Underwood took my plate and handed me the communicator so that I could speak to Marc directly. His first thought that hit my mind was one of relief, followed immediately by one of frustration that things were going so badly for them. A stream of thoughts followed, during which he gave me a rundown of all that had happened in the last twenty-four hours.

Chaos had ensued in the control room after Amelia had dropped me out of the base, with more than half the people in it thinking she'd made a huge mistake and that she should grab me up before I went and got myself killed out there. Before anyone could actually do anything, though, I had disappeared into the crowd, so the next best idea had been for Marc to attempt to distract Lucien from setting off the bomb in the first place. They had teleported after him again, finding him a safe distance from the supermarket, but still with a good view of it.

Amelia had dropped Marc out and he had engaged Lucien in magical battle, out of his shadow, but still untraceable and invisible so that Lucien couldn't pinpoint his location. Fortunately, Marc himself had more magical experience than Lucien, even if Lucien had more magical power, so he was able to keep his older brother occupied while not succumbing in the battle. What Marc hadn't banked on was the increased powers of concentration Lucien had acquired since creating his own Honnie mind; powers which enabled him to keep track of Shana while not missing a beat against Marc. When the time came, and accepting that he wouldn't be able to flush his brother out, Lucien had set off the bomb and then teleported away, leaving them to clean up the mess.

Unable to just leave, Marc telepathically told Natalie and Mr. Woodward back in the control room that he had to try to save any survivors; and apparently too stunned and horrified by what had just happened, nobody objected, in spite of the risk of exposure. He was then able to save thirty-three people, but everyone else (more than four hundred, as Underwood had said) had perished. He continued looking for me the whole time, including in the fourth dimension in case I had gone there, but hadn't been able to find me. It seemed that my body had eventually been found later on by the official investigators, enabling Lucien to set up the narrative that I had committed the atrocity.

Things had been strange in the base that evening, because there were three different stories circulating about what had happened to me, and what would be happening to me, depending on how much that person ought to know. Only Marc, Amelia, Peter and James were supposed to know about the promise, but they had also told Natalie and Mr. Woodward just prior to dinner that night—and Stella just a short time ago, thinking that she deserved to know the truth about me. Others, such as Erica, Rebecca and Lillian Woodward, knew about my death but not the impending resurrection, so they were believing that I was actually dead and not coming back.

The rest of the base, including my parents who had been in the control room at the time, had been told that I'd survived the explosion, but that I couldn't return to the base at this time because I had another important job to do on the outside, but that I would be returning shortly. This would be a kindness to those people, who would get to see me again very soon and not know that I'd been through death and back, but I would be allowed to tell them the truth myself later on if I chose, giving me a chance to say goodbye to those people before the two weeks was up.

Then came this morning. James had been in the control room while Lucien had been talking to Lena, after having failed to track him (James), Marc and Amelia with those plane things. He heard Lucien tell her that in retribution he would blow up three passenger jets, one for each of them, and then find a way to let it be known to them why he was doing it. James had hurried to gather Marc, Amelia, Peter, Natalie and Mr. Woodward, all of whom were having breakfast, but when they had returned to the control room, they hadn't seen Lucien doing anything interesting or alarming. Only when a frantic Hammerheart had informed

Lucien of the attack did they realise that he'd done the whole thing with his minds-eye, without even leaving the Hammerheart base.

When the Hammerheart had left the living room where Lucien had been at the time, he had been left alone. He had then spoken to the empty living room, once again suspecting that they had been watching, stating for a fact that the attacks had been for them—one each for Marc, James and Amelia—and more would die in increasing numbers if they didn't stop this nonsense and turn themselves and all their magic over to him. He had then left, leaving a shocked control room in silence, and all of them frantically trying to think of anything at all they could do to stop him.

The three planes—Marc hadn't recalled the airlines involved, but one had been flying from Melbourne to Canberra and had been carrying 114 people. Another had been flying from Perth to Sydney and had been carrying 225 people. The third had been a jumbo flying from Hong Kong to Melbourne and carrying 410 people. All had been over Australia when bombs had supposedly gone off in the cargo holds, killing all 749 people plus another six on the ground (debris from the Melbourne–Canberra plane had landed in and around a small town in New South Wales).

I hadn't been blamed for these attacks, but rebels aligned with me supposedly were, as well as some possible anti-Lucien factions within the Hammerheart army who remained loyal to the Hammersons— whether or not such factions actually existed, I had no idea. The idea of many in the base was that he was going to use these attacks as an excuse to impose even harsher magical controls on the people. He was currently calling for unity, and for everyone to not be afraid of these rebels and to stand up to them, but we had all seen this line from politicians before—it was only a matter of time before he started using it to further his own agenda of full control over everyone and everything. That had certainly been Arnold Hammerson's goal, so surely it would be Lucien's too.

As for what had happened later this morning, well really only in the last hour-and-a-half or so: Natalie and Amelia had been left in charge of the control room, neither of them being particularly interested in supporting Stella as she came back to consciousness. Marc, James and Peter had sat beside her bed, waiting for her to come around, Marc ready at any moment with the Sorcerous Crystals to transfer one of the chips away from Lucien and over to Amelia, while Peter held a spyer, keeping an eye on Lucien so that they would know if it worked.

Sadly, Lucien must have set up some sort of magical alert to let him know exactly when it had finished, and the lag time in Stella regaining consciousness gave Lucien the advantage he needed—even if it was only a couple of seconds. By the time Marc tried to transfer the chip, Lucien had locked the last one inside his body; and then before Marc had a chance to reform the Hero Crystal, Lucien had already called Fewul back to himself. So in short, the whole thing had been a bust, and once again, Lucien had found a way to make things extremely hard for us.

This whole story took a lot longer for me to tell in words than it did for Marc to tell it to me in thoughts. In fact, the whole thing came through in about two seconds before I had a chance to cut him off. I told him that I'd spoken briefly to Lisa already, and she had told me of a prophecy that could be very important to us, and I would explain it to all of them when I got back to them. I then asked him if there was anything he needed me to do while I was here on the Rock—anything else we might need. His response came through more slowly now, telling me to just create as many new things as I could that might help us. It wasn't as important now as it had been before, since Marc still had the Hero Crystal, but it might as well be done. More importantly, though, I had to get back to them as quickly as possible, so that we could get on with stopping Lucien once and for all—or failing to stop Lucien once and for all.

When I had finished eating, and now felt properly full and energised for the day, I once again thanked Underwood for his hospitality (and for bringing me back from the dead), and then we got in his hover car again so that he could take me down the mountain—I told him that once I was on the ground, I would be able to take care of myself. This was a half-truth: once I was in our campsite, I would be able to take care of myself. He left me at the foot of the Rock, and I walked for some time until I reached the cave containing one of the entrances to our campsite, and after a few attempts (because I had forgotten the password, not having used it for a while), I was able to let myself in.

While I walked I had time to think about things, my mind going in all sorts of different directions as I considered all sorts of things. The first of these directions was a contemplation of my own mental state: I had just died and been brought back, after having experienced a timeless period of nothingness. Thinking about that made me feel cold, knowing that an eternity of that was waiting for me not too far down the track. In fact, that thought was far more frightening and saddening than the dying part of all this. Compared to that, thinking about my death—the one that had been and the one that was coming—didn't cause me much grief at all. Hopefully, that would make it easier for me to bring comfort and closure to those who would be distressed by it.

My mind then turned to Lucien, and the trouble he was causing us. Yes, he did have a lot of power, but how was he doing so well? He had the six crystal chips, the Sien-Leoard Crystal, and the Beast of Magic; but we had the Hero Crystal, the Light Crystal, and the Villain Crystal— not to mention Marc's untraceability, which was now the only reason why we were still in the game at all. The scales shouldn't have leaned so far to one side, so why were they? This was a question I pondered a lot, and in the end, the only thing I could think of was Arnold Hammerson.

Lucien had been dangerous when he had still been in control, but now that Arnold Hammerson was pulling the strings, using all his acquired magical skill along with Lucien's knowledge of us, and both of their combined imaginations—that was a formidable opponent.

The prophecy Lisa had told me about seemed to suggest that Lucien was too powerful to be matched by any magic we threw at him - and that we would have to destroy magic altogether, or he would destroy the world. How exactly were we to destroy magic? James had been thinking for some time now that the crystals ought to be neutralised, but we were no closer to figuring out how that could be done. Could the crystals self-destruct, perhaps? If the person using them told them to destroy themselves, would they? If we could do that…then my rationality caught up with my hopeful thoughts: if we destroyed the crystals we had, that would leave Lucien with all the magic, and us with no way to get it from him.

And yet, doing that to the Hero Crystal still seemed like a good idea: Marc probably wouldn't be happy about giving it up, but theoretically it would make the crystal chips worthless, which would take away some of Lucien's power—assuming the destruction of the Sorcerous Crystals didn't destroy him as well. If it did then our problem would be solved, and all we would need to do was steal the Sien-Leoard Crystal and destroy that too. But what if it didn't work? Or, what if Fewul continued following Lucien's orders even afterwards? An untamed Beast of Magic was the worst possible outcome, because once we started messing with the balance of magic, there was no telling which, if any, of our magical devices would still work, and that included the one that would send the beast away using the power of the Maahoo.

But what if self-destruction wasn't even possible? Then what ought we to do? We couldn't afford to put all our eggs in one basket; we needed backup plans upon backup plans, and that meant stretching our imaginations as far as they could go. That was why I was still here on Rock Haulter: I needed to utilise this time as much as I could, as quickly as I could, so that we would have a better chance when I returned. Apart from putting those enchantments back on myself, though, I still couldn't think of anything I could do here that Marc couldn't just as easily do with the Hero Crystal…or could I?

My mind ticked over all kinds of possibilities, including some that were very wacky indeed. Could we create our own Honnie mind that would be more powerful than Lucien's? Was it worth me giving myself access to the time axis after all? Were there yet more dimensions we could use to give ourselves an advantage? Could I create a way to use more magic from within the fourth dimension? Could I find a way to cause Fewul to defect to our team? All these ideas were worth considering, but most of them wouldn't work for one simple reason: the magic I had available to create these devices was less powerful than the Hero Crystal, let alone Lucien or Fewul.

Still, I thought that perhaps I could achieve something here, now that I'd seen how the battle against Lucien was going to go with the weapons we had—a foresight we hadn't had when we'd been here a few weeks earlier. So when I got into the Group F campsite, I firstly retrieved a pair of keys from the control panel, and then went through to the carpark, got in my beloved red hover car, and headed straight for the creation cave.

When I got there, after going through the procedure of letting myself into the highly secure chamber, the first thing I did was recreate some of the devices we had made here last time. This was merely for my own use. The invisibility toggle, for example, which hadn't even been created here anyway, was just to make sure that I wasn't spotted by anyone else while I was working here. I wasn't worried about Underwood, but rather the Brazilians who had been here weeks earlier, and who may not have left yet. There had been about thirty teenage students in that group, as well as their teachers, and they would have questions to ask about a young boy suddenly appearing out of nowhere—for May had removed all their memories of us before we had left, in case Lucien ever got hold of them and figured out what we'd been doing.

At least, she had removed *almost* all of their memories. Only one person had been spared the mental assault: Larissa was a girl, a little older than me, who I'd been briefly intimate with during my time here a few weeks ago. At least, for her it would have been a few weeks ago; for me, it was only a few days ago. Unable to bear the thought of her not remembering what we had done, I had asked May to spare her, and after some effort on my part, she had eventually obliged. It was ironic, now, that the same fate had since befallen May herself; she remembered nothing of the good times we'd had together, many of them right here on this island.

More to the point, though, I hadn't decided if it would be a good idea for Larissa herself to see me again here. I'd created telepathic devices for me to keep in touch with her—once again not having the courage to cut her off completely—and had only sent her one message so far, on the night before I had died. In no part of her understanding would I suddenly end up here on the Rock again, and telling her that I'd died and come back didn't seem like such a good idea. Finally, the matter of time itself meant that it really would be best if I kept my distance from her. Ergo, invisibility.

There was another reason for it too: I needed to be able to get back to the others without getting caught by Lucien along the way. That meant being invisible, as well as being untraceable, and not the old untraceability either—I needed to be Marc's version of untraceable, and that meant thinking very carefully of the devices Marc had created and getting the magic in the cave to duplicate them, including the magic they contained. If my new body had not carried with it the enchantments I had given myself last time, then it was practically guaranteed that I would need to make myself untraceable again.

After using these devices on myself I had left that cave, for now, and gone further up the mountain to where I recalled the enchantments cave had been. After getting into the similarly secure chamber, I had proceeded to reinstate all those enchantments I had put on myself, plus some more that had since occurred to me. When I had been here last time, I'd had concerns about the sort of person I was becoming by giving myself so much power, comparing myself to the Hammersons and their desire for more and more power. I had sworn to myself that I wouldn't abuse it, and apart from that incident in Stella's bedroom, I had stuck pretty closely to that goal. Today, I had no such concerns: I only had two weeks left to live, so I felt within my right to give myself as much as I could handle.

By the time I was done, I could stun people or knock them out just with my eyes. I could levitate and manipulate objects, including people, also with my eyes. I could distribute thicky prison at will, while the substance itself couldn't touch me. I could shrink and enlarge myself just by using my mind. I could raise and lower shields around myself. I could fly. I could teleport merely by concentrating on where I wanted to go. I could lift very heavy objects (while not appearing any stronger), and my body would now be strong enough to withstand objects of any weight— with a bit of luck, protecting me from the sort of thing that had killed me before. On top of that, I had given myself regeneration—the ability for my body to heal from any injury almost instantly—just in case something did manage to hurt me.

I had also reinstated the ability to arouse people, as I had done to Stella in an attempt to cheer her up; only now I also gave myself the ability to *only* cheer them up, as I'd wanted to do in the first place. On a stroke of inspiration, I also gave myself the ability to make someone thoroughly confused as well, in the hope that a tactic like that might work on Lucien, rendering him at a disadvantage. I could also communicate telepathically with anyone without needing to hold a communicator; it would work on the same frequency as the communicators we had, except I could use it to send thoughts to anyone I wanted in real time, even if those people couldn't necessarily send thoughts back without telepathic communicators of their own. Finally, I could separate my minds-eye from my body, as I'd done often while in possession of the Sien-Leoard Crystal, so that I could observe things happening in other places.

And it didn't stop there. I had made myself four-dimensional again, as I had been before, but now I gave myself access to the time axis as well, giving into temptation and figuring that the risk didn't really matter anymore since I was already doomed to die in two weeks. I couldn't think of how I could use the time axis as yet, but if something came up, at least the option would be there. When it was done, I put a spell on myself to remove the access restrictions—meaning, I could go back and forth in time beyond my own time, something that Smiley had said was against the rules of magic. I didn't know if it had worked, though, and would only find out if a time came to test it.

I had stayed there for a short time after that, trying to think of more things to do to myself, and had thought of some smaller stuff along the way, such as the ability to recall Fewul mentally with the power of the Maahoo, the ability to normalise anything that had been enchanted, or to vanish anything; but in the end, I had thought of only one more really important thing. I had put a magical shield around my body, making it impossible for anyone—be it Lucien, Fewul, or anyone else—to remove the enchantments I had put on myself. I had locked the enchantments within my body, and after testing a couple of them there in the cave to make sure I hadn't just interfered with my ability to use them, I had gotten in my hover car and headed back to the creation cave.

The first thing I had created in there, because I had lost track of time in the other cave, was a wristwatch—so magical, huh? I had then created a seat for myself to sit in while I contemplated more things to create. I had stayed in there for the rest of the morning and much of the afternoon, using the creator to give myself lunch at around one o'clock and then pushing on. I had created four-dimensional stunners and solid-outliners for the others to use, as well as a type of partial invisibility that would make us invisible to those plane things, but not invisible in any other way. I wasn't all that happy about that device, though; those planes might have been able to do more than what I'd seen, so we couldn't bank on those working. An invisibility veil of the kind Natalie had originally created would probably be more effective.

Running out of good ideas and feeling mental exhaustion creeping up, I had created a device that, when used on myself, would give me a short time (about an hour) of clear, rapid thought. For that time, my brain would be able to work at a hundred percent efficiency, with perfect recall and an ability to make rapid connections and decisions that would take much longer, and a lot more effort, to make under normal circumstances. In this state I was able to come up with about a dozen more creations, all of which I thought could be useful; and the last of them could perhaps be the most useful magical creation yet. Before I could take it back to the others, though, I needed to test it, and so after half past three, I decided to have a bit of recreational fun.

One of the other devices I had created was a map of Rock Haulter, identical to one which James had created the last time we had been here, and which had made it possible to locate the enchantments cave in the first place. Using it now, I had located a number of caves that I could use to entertain myself on this night, and then had given myself a device that would allow me to take control of the magic within those caves, mixing elements of them so that I could take full advantage of them in ways for which they hadn't been intended. Such a device wouldn't have been possible to create with this level of power available to me under normal circumstances, but thanks to my creativity that day, these circumstances had been anything but normal. Later on, exhausted and happy with myself, I had returned to the campsite and gone to bed, falling asleep very quickly so that I could be well rested for the return trip the next morning.

Chapter 9: Deterioration

I woke early the next morning, when my new watch said it was just after four o'clock. I had a moment when I reckoned that I'd woken nice and early and could probably afford to rise slowly, and then remembered that it was six hours later in Chopville and immediately sprang out of bed. I took only a few minutes to have a quick shower in the base before re-dressing myself, putting the bag with all my new creations on my back, and then running out of the campsite. But running wasn't fast enough for my liking, so I launched myself into the air and flew down the path towards the jetty, loving the feeling of being airborne and at great speed —until the path turned and I flew straight into a clump of bushes in the darkness.

I rose again and carefully set myself on my feet, thinking that while I'd done well to put a flying enchantment on myself, I hadn't been quite as specific as I ought to have been—as I surely would have been if I'd had experience flying like that before. I quickly debated with myself, then decided that what I'd given myself would probably be enough—I could learn how to control it in the two weeks I had, rather than wasting more time by making something that mightn't be any better anyway.

But the time I'd stood there had caused another thought to occur to me. I no longer had a telepathic communicator with which to contact the others to let me into the base, or to let Underwood know that I was leaving—but of course, I didn't need one for either of those things. I set my mind on Jacob Underwood, as I had focused it when using the Sien-Leoard Crystal to communicate telepathically so many months ago now, and sent the thought to him: that I greatly appreciated what he had done for me, but now I was leaving to re-join the war effort. I felt him stir and awaken as the thought hit him, and respond with a sleepy affirmative before dropping back off to sleep, and I smiled to myself: it was good for some.

Satisfied, I took a few running steps and launched myself into the air, now heading straight for the jetty. Less than half a minute later I was flying over it, passing by the ship that had brought us here to Rock Haulter along with the Brazilians not so long ago, and then zooming out over the dark water below. As I continued straight, due north, another thought occurred to me: how on earth was I to know when I had left the portal? It was still very dark; dawn would come soon but most likely not for at least an hour, and I hadn't given myself any particular ability to magically know when I passed through it. The only thing I could think of was that I knew roughly how far it was from the portal to the island, having done it a full three times now (six if you counted going both ways), so I reckoned I could estimate the distance, and then go several kilometres further just to be safe.

Flying dead straight and level didn't seem to require a whole lot of concentration, leaving my mind free to notice that I was indeed going pretty fast (perhaps as fast as a car would drive on a highway), and that doing so made me feel pretty damn cold—something else I hadn't taken into consideration when I'd done this. I still enjoyed the feeling and I didn't want to slow down, so in order to take my mind off the wind chill, I set the remainder of my mind back on telepathy and got back in contact with Marc, letting him know that I had just left the Rock and would be back in Australia shortly.

The first thought I'd gotten from him was a question: was I invisible, untraceable, and every other form of protected I could think of? That caused me to start and almost fall out of the air: Yes, I was untraceable, but I'd forgotten to make myself invisible since I had taken the charm off myself during my recreational time the previous evening. I quickly reinstated it now, then cast my mind around to think of anything else I could do to protect myself. Ought I to go into my shadow? I considered it, but I had a warning feeling somewhere in the back of my mind—or perhaps in my soul—telling me that going into my shadow now would be a bad idea. I could think of one reason why that might be so: if the portals were only three dimensional, then going into my shadow might make it impossible to leave.

I sent a message to Marc to let him know that I was as protected as I could be, as I resumed my literal flight from Rock Haulter. His reply came back quickly, and it was another question: what the hell are you doing? He had felt from my mind that I was thinking in a strange way, and I told him that I'd had to replace the enchantments I'd put on my body since they hadn't carried over from my old body, and I'd placed some new ones on myself, one of which was the ability to fly. Marc had initially been jealous of what I'd done—jealous because I hadn't told him about it in time for him to do the same thing—but that feeling had apparently worn off since he had reacquired the Hero Crystal. I was glad to note that in the almost two days since we had stolen the Sorcerous Crystals from Lucien's lunar hideout, we hadn't lost them again.

The next message I got from Marc wasn't a question, but a directive: contact me again when you have reached Chopville and we'll arrange a place where I can bring you back in the base; or contact me if you are unable to get back to Chopville yourself and I'll help you out. I responded by telling him that I would be able to get there on my own and that I would do as he said, after which the telepathy between us ceased for a while. I was left to resume flying away from the Rock, and to remember how damn cold I was. I tried to speed up even more, but even as I arrowed my body to make it as aerodynamic as I could, this seemed to be as fast as my body was able to go.

How far had I gone anyway? Not far enough, I thought. At the speed I was going, if I had my math right, I would need to fly straight from the

Rock for at least twenty minutes, and probably thirty just to be safe. I had been out for no more than five minutes so far, so I resigned myself to having to keep doing this for a long while yet, wondering how long it would take me to tire doing this. So far, it seemed to be straining my body barely at all; it was the effort of keeping my body as straight and narrow as I could in order to make myself as aerodynamic as I could that was having an impact, whereas the act of flying itself seemed to take nothing out of me at all.

With nothing else to do, I began counting in my head as I watched the ocean unfolding beneath me. This was after I'd tried to check my watch, only to find that I would need to slow down just to be able to move my arms away from my sides. Slowly but surely, the seconds turned into minutes, and the minutes ticked away. As I approached one thousand seconds (sixteen minutes to be sure), I began wondering how much further I ought to go, and whether or not I should attempt to teleport from here. I was torn between the worry of what (if anything) might happen to me if I tried to teleport while still inside the portals; and a feeling that time was really passing by while I did this, and that somewhere out there, Lucien was using these precious minutes to do who knew what unspeakable things.

I resisted the temptation and held out a little longer, which turned out to be the right decision. I passed through the portal a few minutes later, and I knew exactly when it happened because there was one almighty storm on the other side of it. While I had been really cold before, now I became freezing as an icy wind and rain lashed at me. I saw what was immediately in front of me and turned my body, shooting higher into the air, narrowly avoiding a swell that looked mean enough to drown me if it could. This was a miserable place to be, and I wasted no time in focusing my mind on Chopville—specifically, the front of Grillion's canteen. A second later, I activated the magic, and the nothingness took me as I teleported away.

The weather in Chopville was considerably better—that is to say, it wasn't rainy and stormy. It was overcast, though, and there was just enough of a breeze that I couldn't stop myself from shivering as I stood there. Sadly, even with of all the magic I'd given myself, and all the devices I had created, none of them could dry me and my clothes after flying through a wild sea storm and almost getting wiped out by a rogue wave. I would have to wait till I was in the base and then Marc could take care of it with the Hero Crystal.

Speaking of which: I contacted Marc again telepathically and let him know that I was back in Chopville, outside Grillion's canteen—which hadn't been taken over by the Hammerhearts and appeared to have fallen into disrepair. It was a sorry sight. His response came back quickly, and it was tinged with excitement: go around to the small space at the back of the canteen; do not make yourself visible or traceable in the meantime.

He visualised the position for me (not that he needed to; I knew this place of old), and I wasted no time in going around there and waiting for him.

It didn't take long. There was no warning, nothing to let me know that it was about to happen; I just felt that familiar sensation of being dragged, and a moment later I was standing in the control room, imprisoned within the binds of the magic I'd designed to make sure no captures could get loose within the base. Marc was in the control room, but he wasn't at the controls; James had been doing the button pushing. Everyone in the room (Marc, Peter, James, Amelia, Stella, Rebecca, Erica, Mr. Woodward and Lillian) was watching the corner expectantly where I now stood invisible.

I understood why they were all there, of course (most of them had been present for my death, and now they all knew the full story about me —apparently, Lillian, Erica and Rebecca had been brought up to speed), but I couldn't help noticing that Natalie was missing. Did she still resent me so much that she didn't want to see me, even knowing that I had less than two weeks left to live? Or worse, did she feel guilty for not having given me a chance to explain myself before, causing her to resent me even more for making her feel this way? I didn't know, but I had a bad feeling about it. Strangely, though, the bad feeling was different from how it might have been in the past; where before I would have been hurt by such a reaction, now I felt more worry for her than anything for me. Yeah, it was still very soon for her, but she didn't have a lot of time left to get closure on all of this and the best way for her to move on with her life after I was gone for good would be to sort all this out while there was still a chance.

I didn't spend any more time on these thoughts but made myself visible, and then took a moment to enjoy the reactions of everyone in the room—all a mixture of gladness and sadness, but all emotional. James quickly released me from my invisible binds and I hurried forward, running into Marc first, who gave me a great big bear hug. Peter and Amelia jumped on me the moment he let go, and then it was Stella's turn; only when she burst into tears and wouldn't let go, did the rest of the group sigh and re-take their seats.

"It is good to have you back, mate," James said, but his expression was sad. "So—er—how much time do we have?"

A lot of people flinched, including me, though in my case it wasn't because of my death, but rather the memory of what would be waiting for me after I died, which had been stirred by James's words. I checked my watch, saw that it was a little after six o'clock (which made it a little after mid-day here), and said, "Well—thirteen days, I think. I guess it will be sometime on the fifteenth of September, although I guess we don't know exactly when—do we?" I added, looking at Mr. Woodward.

"I don't think so," he said heavily, "and the fact that there are time zones involved makes it even more difficult to predict what might happen, and when."

Peter's face was twisting with emotions as he watched me, but he seemed to be struggling to articulate them. Finally he managed to say, "But your birthday's on the seventeenth. You can't die two days before your birthday; that's not fair."

Strangely, paradoxically, that made me smile a little. "Well, a lot's happened to me while I've been fourteen; I guess I will be forever."

The emotion was running very high in the room right then, with everyone affected by it to some degree, and most to a greater degree. Only Frederic and Lillian looked like they weren't about to burst into tears at the slightest provocation, and it was they who were, bit by bit, able to calm everyone down and get all our minds back in the game. Finally, Marc recovered enough to let me know a small portion of what was going on.

"We're the only ones who know the full story," he told me. "Well, almost the only ones. Everyone else has been told that after the supermarket incident, we sent you on a top-secret job that we couldn't tell them about, and we wouldn't be able to tell them of it even after you got back. That should make it a little easier for you, to begin with anyway. We figured you could tell the truth to anyone you wanted to when you wanted to, in case you wanna—well—say goodbye, and all that, but that'll be up to you."

I swallowed, noticing that my throat had become very dry. "Well, thanks, but what do you mean, 'almost the only ones'?"

Uncomfortable looks were swapped between several people. Rebecca looked on the verge of breaking down, perhaps as badly as Stella had already done, and Peter quickly hugged her. I had a bad feeling what this could be about, and sure enough...

"Natalie also knows," Marc said, "and she would be here now, except...well, she was captured yesterday by Lucien."

"What? How?" I gasped. Okay, that was worse than what I had imagined—quite a lot worse.

More looks were swapped between people, a lot of them involving Rebecca, who shook her head minutely. Finally, Amelia said, "Not right now. We'll tell you later, but not now. It's—it's not good."

"Right now," Marc said, checking his own watch, "it's just about lunch time. John, perhaps you wanna go and change your clothes, maybe have a shower or something—"

"I had a shower this morning," I said indignantly, "but yeah, I probably should change these clothes."

"You've got just enough time to go around and catch up with anyone you've missed before lunch—"

"Wait," I said quickly, cutting Marc off. "I need to tell you guys something about—about why we did this, about what I was supposed to find out from going to the in-between."

That roused a lot of their curiosity, but Marc shook his head. "We'll have a meeting back here after lunch and you can tell us then, and we'll catch you up on everything you missed then too. Go on, skedaddle."

And with that, I was dismissed. I left the control room alone, still with my pack of newly created devices on my shoulders, not having been given an opportunity to even tell them about them, let alone show them. Stella had wanted to follow me, but Marc and Amelia had made her stay back. What was going on here? Why were they all of a sudden so desperate to send me away? Obviously they needed to talk about something without me being there, but what? The only guess I could make was that they didn't want to speak about Natalie's plight in front of Rebecca, even though she obviously knew about it already. I could only accept it, however nervous it made me feel.

In the meantime, I went up to my room on the first floor, was relieved to find that I could still get in there even with this new body, and proceeded to change into some new clothes. When that was done, I still had a little over ten minutes before lunch was due to start, and I didn't really feel like going downstairs to the lounge room to socialise with folks like Harry and Simon (assuming that was where they were). Whatever Marc said, I felt sure that they would ask loads of questions about where I'd been the last two days and what I'd been doing, and unless I got very inventive and likely tripped over myself in an attempt to come up with some sort of explanation, I would have no way to answer them.

Then I had an idea for something else I could do with this time: I could send a telepathic message to Larissa, and see if she had sent any to me in the last two days. I hesitated a moment, brought up short by a surprising thought: wasn't this a waste of my precious time? Given that Larissa was in the past, no matter how you looked at it, and I probably wouldn't see her again anyway, wouldn't using my time on her be considered a waste? Maybe, I supposed, but it was less wasteful than hanging around here, trying to figure out what to do with the next few minutes. If I didn't do something soon, it would be lunchtime and I would have spent this entire time doing nothing.

Like the only other time I had communicated with Larissa in this way, she wasn't there to receive my messages. There were some new ones from her, though, initially pleased and thrilled to hear from me at all (part of her had apparently doubted that I would bother with her, even after providing her with a magical device). She stated that she was sorry that things hadn't worked out with me and my girlfriend, although she was unable to conceal her own pleasure at the thought that I was indeed single now. I smiled as I took this in, not hurt by it because I understood where that enjoyment came from, then I sent her a quick 'hello', and 'are you up?', but didn't get a response from her so put the communicator back in my drawer.

There was nothing else to do but go downstairs and start on my lunch. The way it went, I only got to the dining room a few minutes before half past twelve, so I actually wasn't alone in there for much more than a minute before people started coming in. A lot of them came over to me and said hello, asking me how I was doing and if my mission had gone well. Several of them called me a hero for what I'd done back in the supermarket, even if I had failed to stop the explosion. Soon enough, though, they had all settled down to eat, and Stella, Marc and Amelia had joined me at my table, leaving one empty seat that no one ended up taking.

I didn't talk much over lunch to the people around me, except when it came to working out what would come next. We arranged for the ten of us to have another meeting in the control room, a proper one this time, as soon as we had all finished our lunches. I excused myself from the table, telling them that I had to get something and that I would join them in the control room. The thing in question was, of course, the backpack containing all the cool new devices I had brought along to show them. Before I could get upstairs, however, I was waylaid in front of the lift by none other than Mum and Dad themselves.

"We have a bone to pick with you, young man," Dad said sternly. It wasn't the first time he'd said such a thing to me, although usually it was met with a warm smile or twinkling eyes to let me know that I wasn't really in any serious trouble. Today, though, he looked very serious indeed, and Mum looked beyond serious.

"Yes, I know I should have let you know that I would be disappearing for a couple of days," I said warily, hoping to head them off, "and I would have if I could have, but it was top-secret and we weren't sure how long I would be gone for."

Dad shook his head. "I thought you were a smart kid. Certainly most of the things you've done up to this point have been smart. The fact that we're here is a testament to that. But what you did on Tuesday was foolish beyond all description."

My stomach fell. Not only had I failed to head them off, but I now understood completely why they were so upset with me and I couldn't blame them in the slightest. They thought I'd done something incredibly stupid and almost gotten myself killed in the process. What they didn't know was that I *had* done something incredibly stupid and *had* gotten myself killed in the process, only to be brought back, damning my soul to an eternity of being cut apart. As I looked at their faces I knew I would never be able to tell them the full truth, even though they really did deserve to know.

"I'm sorry," I said quietly, abashed and feeling appropriately chastised.

"You're sorry?" Mum repeated, looking ready to blow up, an explosion that would be almost as big as the one that had killed me in the first place. "You're sorry that you almost got yourself killed and then disappeared for two days, leaving us to wonder if you really *were* on a job or you hadn't been killed for real and they weren't trying to cover it up?"

"Er—can we do this in private?" I asked, uncomfortably aware that a few people had crept out of the dining room and were now observing this little scene before the lift.

"This looks like it would be a lot more fun in public," Simon called from the dining room doorway.

That broke a little of the tension with Dad; not so much with Mum. "Sure," he said, pressing the button so that the elevator doors opened before us. "Come on in here."

We went up to the first floor, where I would be able to go straight into my bedroom when we were done with this little interlude, but Mum got started on me as soon as the doors shut and we were rising.

"Did you think, even for a moment?" she fumed. "I mean seriously, did you actually believe you could stop that from happening? Did you even consider how it would make the rest of us feel if you had been killed back there while trying to be a hero? I don't know how you survived, and if Marc did some magic that he isn't telling the rest of us about, but that doesn't make this okay. You can't be so reckless with your life, John; if that had been anyone else, anyone who didn't have friends with magic, they would have died, as most of the people there did."

"I know, Mum," I said, now more weary than wary. "I didn't really think of what would happen if I failed—I didn't have time to think of that. I just wanted to stop it from happening, and I knew how I could have stopped it if I'd just gotten to that woman before the bomb went off."

"Really? How?" Dad asked curiously.

I tried to think how I could answer him—explaining about the fourth dimension felt like it would be too complicated for this discussion—but Mum was too worked up to give me a chance. "You didn't have time to think of it? Oh really? That's the lamest excuse I've ever thought of. Even if I were to try to look at things from your perspective, I imagine I would think something along the lines of, 'I'm sure I can do more good in this war by keeping myself alive a bit longer and living to fight another day, rather than throw it all away on a dash that wasn't going to hurt Lucien one way or the other.'"

That made me blush. "Er—I guess I didn't think of it like that either. I just got an idea in my head and thought I had to try it, or hundreds of people would die. I guess I didn't really look at in terms of the bigger picture."

And I really should have done too. In a way, Mum was right: if we hadn't already agreed to bring someone back from the dead, I would be dead right now because of what had happened in the supermarket two days ago. If I had failed, I would have died along with hundreds of other people, and Lucien would have had one less enemy to worry about. If I had succeeded, only one person would have died, and even if Lucien didn't guess how I had prevented the explosion (as it would have looked to him), it wouldn't have stopped him from trying something else. In hindsight, it would have been much smarter not to have taken the chance on trying to get to that woman, however hard it would have been to doom all those people to death and then watch it all unfold before us.

Of course, the one benefit out of all of this was that I now knew what Lisa had meant to tell me from those dreams I'd had on Rock Haulter, something that we wouldn't have had any way of knowing if I hadn't died. It was supposedly very important, and from what I'd already heard, it certainly was important; and there could be more yet that she needed to tell me, for all I knew. But I couldn't tell my parents any of this without telling them the truth about my death, and none of us were ready for that conversation today.

Dad, meanwhile, rested a hand on my shoulder. "I know how it was. I was in the room when all that stuff was happening, remember? It was hard for all of us, but your mother is right. You're not immortal, John, and you can't afford to let your proximity to magic make you lose sight of that fact. Quite a few of Freddy's men and women were lost in the first war because they made that mistake, and I don't want you—or anyone else here—doing the same thing."

I nodded. "It won't happen again, Dad. Trust me, after what happened in there, I won't be making a mistake like that a second time."

Except that wasn't entirely true. I had no way of knowing how I was going to die in thirteen days' time, but I knew that something was going to happen to cause my death, even if I did nothing to go looking for it. For all I knew, if I kept my head down and tried to stay out of trouble that day, Lucien would somehow invade the base on that day and take care of me (and everyone else)—or if not that, I could choke on a piece of apple at lunchtime. With those two possible scenarios in mind, going out and doing something foolish and potentially making a difference in the war was much more preferable.

"You had better not," Dad said. "We weren't the only ones upset, you know; Marge and Charlie were too, and your grandmother was beside herself with worry. And so soon after you rescued us all from that place too."

I shrugged. "That was Peter's doing as well—"

Mum gave me a hug then, cutting off my words. When she let go, she said, "Promise me you won't do anything so silly again. I may be coming to terms with you doing far more in this war than you should be doing, but I can't handle losing you—none of us can handle that."

I could only nod, knowing that it was a promise I couldn't keep.

"So when are you going to spend some time with us, anyway?" Dad asked, taking me by surprise.

"Er—time?" I repeated, and then pulled myself together. "Oh—well, when there is time, I suppose. Actually—yeah, we should do that sometime soon. I don't know what's gonna happen in the next few days, or weeks, or months, or however long we have to do this—but yeah, we'll have to take some time to enjoy ourselves, otherwise we may never get another chance to."

Which was all well and good for them. In my case, I wanted their most recent memories of me, before my final death, to be good ones. For my part, it wouldn't matter all that much—I didn't know how much of my memory would carry over into the in-between after my death. Based on what I'd seen of Lisa, some of her memories had gone with her soul, but she had left quite a lot of herself behind as well, and I had no idea what parts of me would go with me and what parts would disappear forever when the time came. Most likely, though, memories of Mum and Dad would go with me, since even though they were only my adoptive parents, they had been there for as long as I could remember.

* * *

I was as flat as a pancake by the time I made it back to the control room, the words of my parents, and the promise I wouldn't be able to keep, still ringing in my ears. Rebecca and Lillian were the only ones missing when I got there, and I had time to wonder what could have held them up so long that they would be even later than me, before Peter informed me that for separate reasons, they had both chosen not to participate in this meeting.

"Okay, let's get into this," Marc said. "We don't have a lot of time to spend talking about stuff while Lucien's out there causing more trouble."

He glanced at the spyer sitting on the control panel. Where before there had been several spyers up there, now there was only one, and it was set to keep track of Lucien. I also glanced at it and saw that Lucien appeared to be in a meeting with several official-looking people, with Stella sitting there beside him, smiling at everyone. I glanced over at the real Stella and saw that she was grimacing as she too observed this.

"Well, I'm glad you mentioned that," I said, leaning over my backpack, opening it and beginning to rummage through it. "It just so happens that I've got something here that might help with that."

"Er—might help with what, exactly?" Mr. Woodward asked warily.

It took a couple of minutes to find what I was looking for, so as I looked, I talked. "Marc asked me to go back to the cave where we could create stuff while I was on the Rock, just to see if I could think of anything new to make, now that we could see how the battle with Lucien was likely to look—not that I would be able to do any more than he could do with the Hero Crystal, but that's beside the point. One of the things I made was a box, a bit like the one we used to hide from Hall back in the old base—you know, the one with the ghost walls around the outside?"

That had actually been four-dimensional, although we hadn't really thought of it in those terms at the time. Those boxes had been big enough for several people to sit in, and they had walls around them in its shadow as well, so that as long as we were in there, we could talk without being spied on by ghosts or bodiless forms using magic to watch us from afar. The girls had never seen that box, but Peter, James, Marc and Mr. Woodward all nodded their understanding.

"Well, this one distorts time on the inside," I continued. "When it's closed up, time slows down to a tenth of its normal speed, so that if we were to stay in there for ten minutes, only one minute would have passed on the outside. I even tested it while I was on the Rock to make sure that it worked, by going in there and leaving my watch on the outside—it works perfectly, and it's big enough for all of us."

A stunned silence followed this before James said, "Wow, that's actually quite smart. So we could theoretically do an hour's worth of planning and only have six minutes pass in real time?"

"Exactly right," I said, "although it only works when the box is closed. If it's open, time would still run normally, so we would have to cut ourselves off from everyone while we're doing our six minutes of planning. Ah—here it is."

"That gives us a huge advantage," Peter said excitedly. "Whenever we need more time, we can just go in there and get it, and all Lucien will know is that we seem to be making better use of our time."

"I dunno if it would be such a good idea to use that thing too much," Marc said, watching me as I pulled the hand-sized box from the bag, and then began clearing a space of seats so that there would be room to enlarge it. "I imagine that spending more than a couple of hours a day in there—and I mean a couple of box-hours—would really muck up our body clocks."

"I think that's a lesser concern than getting captured by Lucien and losing the war," I pointed out, "although in my case, I worry that spending more than twenty-four box-hours in there would shorten my life. I mightn't be able to count on thirteen more days if I let that happen, so I should probably spend as much time on the outside as I can. It'll still be an option for you guys, though."

I enlarged the box then, and it fell to the floor in the control room with a loud thump. I then proceeded to show its various features to the others, including the button that would shrink and enlarge it from the outside (only if nobody was in there), an automatically expanding interior which would resize itself depending on how many people tried to get inside it, a one-way window which would allow the people on the inside to see if there was anyone in the room on the outside, and a display screen showing the people on the inside how much time had passed on the outside, since they were apt to lose track of time in there, and taking our watches in with us wasn't such a good idea. I hadn't thought of all that to begin with, but as I had tested it, the ideas had come to me, and I had used the magic of the creations cave to create devices which would make the magical modifications for me—the same way I had gone about building this base, in other words.

"We're gonna need someone to stay out here and keep an eye on Lucien, though," Amelia said as everyone tried to get in the box. "Who wants to sit the meeting out?"

Everyone went very still, not wanting to be singled out by the slightest movement. Nobody wanted to miss the meeting, and after several seconds like this, Peter said, "Maybe I should call Rebecca back after all."

"Not necessary," I said, not wanting to waste any more time. "Someone grab that spyer; it should still work in the Time Box, I hope."

Fortunately, it did work in the Time Box. It took about a minute to be sure, because once we closed the box up with all of us inside, Lucien and those around him began moving and speaking very slowly indeed, but it was clear that they were still moving.

"Okay, so this'll give us a bit more time," Marc said. "Now, back to what I was saying before John brought this whole thing up: we don't have a lot of time to spend doing this while Lucien's out there causing trouble. We may have more of it than we did before, but we still need to get some action happening, so how should we go about this?"

"I do wanna know what happened to Natalie," I said, "but maybe we had better start with my stuff. We might be able to make plans off what I found out, and you can update me on all that stuff while we're doing them. Also, I should probably show you guys the rest of this stuff I made as well."

"Yeah, let's start with what you found out," James said. "You speak as though you did find something out, right?"

I nodded. "This thing, the in-between, it's impossible to really describe it because it's—well—nothing. I don't wanna think about it too much, because it's more frightening than anything I've ever experienced in life, but part of me is there—even now. I can feel it there, resting timelessly, because there's no time there, you understand. I can wake it up whenever I want and try to talk to Lisa again, because I did find her there, but I hope it doesn't come to that. Lisa's not the same as she was in life; it's like part of her has been cut away and doesn't really exist anymore."

The expressions of all the others were growing progressively more horrified as I spoke, and Amelia and Stella both had tears in their eyes. After a short silence, a pale Peter said, "Cut away? You mean the part of her that we brought back to life was cut away? That is what you mean, right?"

I nodded again. "I'm pretty sure that's how it was. That part of her either went where dead people are supposed to go, or it was destroyed. I don't know which, but Smiley did say that part of the soul has to remain trapped in that place for someone to come back in any form, and that's the part of her that's there now—and I guess, the part of me that's there now too. The thing is, though, I don't think she has all her memories in there; some of them seem to have died with her, which I suppose makes sense, since memories are stored in the brain. But at least some of them got carried over by the soul, and when I made her really think— something she was reluctant to do at first because she seemed to be aware that she was missing something important—anyway, when I made her really think, she was able to tap some other memories that she'd forgotten she had."

Another stunned silence, and this one was followed by a few minutes of several people asking me questions about the in-between that were really impossible to answer, such as 'how did it feel' and 'what did it look like'. Finally, though, Marc said, "So what about Lisa, then? What did she tell you? Did she have any idea what you wanted to know?"

"Not at first," I said, ready to get to the important stuff. "She had no idea what I was talking about when I mentioned the Enlightener, so that theory is out the window. I guess it wasn't so much that she wanted to talk to me but that she knew something that we needed to know, and the Enlightener was trying to prod me in that direction. She did tell me something, and it is important, but I have a feeling that there may be even more that I need to get from her, because this information would have been possible to get even without Lisa, if we had known to look for it."

"And what is this information?" James asked.

"Another prophecy," I told them, taking a moment to enjoy the dismayed looks on their faces before continuing. "She found this one on the same CD as the one about the Seventh Sorcerer, and from what she told me, she committed it to memory because even back then, she thought it could be important in the future. Apparently, it foretold the last Sorcerer, the one who would bring about either the end of all magic or the end of the world."

I paused for a few seconds here, allowing these words to sink in. Everyone in the box was smart enough to understand who that prophecy was likely talking about, especially now that he had locked all the crystal chips inside his body. The purely horrified looks on all their faces was how I imagine I must have felt when I first found out, if I'd had a body to feel with. Then I continued, "But Lisa could only remember that much. She didn't remember the wording, whether it was a definite thing, if it had to be one or the other, or if it was specifically one of them and she just couldn't remember which one."

"And if you're right about some of her memories being lost, then there's probably no point going back and trying to lecture her about it, right?" James asked croakily.

I shook my head. "Not for this purpose, no. Also, I really don't want to torment her like that—she's already so sad."

"Then we need to see this prophecy for ourselves, as soon as possible," Mr. Woodward stated. "In fact, I would recommend that we make that our top priority. None of us should doubt the importance of Sien and Leoard's prophecies at this point. It is one of theirs, right? Not someone else's?"

"Yeah, it's theirs," I said. "It was in the same document as the prophecy about Marc being the Seventh Sorcerer, and that was one of theirs."

"Great, so we just have to find those CDs again? Like we did a couple of months ago?" Erica asked.

"If we don't have them now," James said heavily, "then they were most likely destroyed when Lucien busted up our old base. We'll have to find some other way to get the information."

"They came from the magic display we had earlier in the year at school," Amelia told her father, "the one where Stella and I lost our chips that first time. There were some computers that had electronic encyclopedias, and these guys downloaded a whole load of documents onto burnt CDs so that they could continue their research at home. Do you know anything about those encyclopedias?"

"My mother and grandfather are responsible for compiling them," he told us, "and I have added quite a bit to them myself. I only had them digitised about ten years ago, thinking that it would make them easier to search and index—and take up a lot less space," he added, smiling a little.

"So where are they now?" Marc asked. "Please don't tell me they were also destroyed along with one of your bases."

Mr. Woodward shrugged. "No, fortunately we stored them—or should I say 'it', because it's really all one program—on a remote server. Of course, the fact that such valuable information is on the Internet is a big secret, and very few people know how to find it or have credentials to access it if they do."

"And what are the chances of hackers getting hold of it?" James asked warily.

That made the former Sorcerer hesitate for a moment. "Well, I won't say that it's impossible, because when it comes to hacking, there really is no such thing as a fool-proof system. I will say that it is as close to impossible as it could get, and we've even put a little magic in the server itself so that it's even harder."

"And what about Lucien? Could he have gotten it?" Amelia asked.

"Again, not impossible," Mr. Woodward said, but he looked a bit more confident now. "I will say that he never enquired about it, not to me or anyone else that I know of. There were a handful of people in the Big Room who had credentials to access it, so he could have gotten hold of it if he knew about it, or if he thought to ask us all how he could learn more about magic, but so far as I know, it never came up. I don't think he knows, yet, that there is such a treasure trove of magical knowledge out there."

"And you still have the credentials, right?" Marc asked him. "You could go online and access it anytime you wanted?"

"Yeah, I could," Mr. Woodward agreed, "but we do need a computer for that. Do we actually have any computers with Internet access in this base?"

"Nope," I said. "It took a huge amount of work to safely get online back in the old base, and I didn't have time to do that with this one. Besides, the Internet doesn't work in our shadow—we found that out before we went back to Rock Haulter."

"So how are we supposed to go online and get the stuff?" Peter asked. "Do we just walk into the Chopville Public Library and say, 'hey, where are your computers at? I'd like to download a top-secret magical encyclopedia from the Internet, if you don't mind'."

A brief silence, and then James said, "That actually sounds like the best way to do it."

A longer silence this time, with just about everyone gaping at him as though he had just turned into an antelope. Finally Marc said, "Okay, James, just one question for you: how does a person use a computer while they're invisible without it looking super weird for anyone who happens to see it?"

"Also, what if those computers are monitored somehow?" I added.

"I know the risks," James said cautiously, "but hear me out. We're going to have to take a risk to get that information, and this seems like the best one. Someone can go out there and use one of the computers in the public library to download the encyclopedia—you can download it, right?" he asked Mr. Woodward, who nodded. "Okay, so they download it to a USB stick, so that we can search it back here later on. Whoever it is will have to be visible, though, so it shouldn't be someone who Lucien wouldn't think to try to search for with his weird tracker things."

"So, none of us, then," Amelia said, but that wasn't what was worrying Marc.

"James, that still sounds so dangerous. What if Lucien *does* think to search for that person, even if it's—I dunno—your grandmother or something?"

James smiled a little at that. "Well, obviously the person in question —and it certainly won't be the utterly computer-illiterate Violet—will have to be armed and ready to fight at all times, but they should be accompanied by someone invisible as well, who can stand over them and be alert for any sign of trouble. And finally, although we won't be able to watch them on the spyers, because they'll both be untraceable, we can still watch him"—he indicated the spyer in the room with us, which was still showing Lucien in a meeting—"so we'll know right away if he's up to anything, and we can come to the defence."

"I don't mind doing it," Erica said suddenly, taking everyone by surprise and causing James to glare at her.

"You?"

"I'm the only one here who isn't an obvious target for Lucien," she said, looking around at us all, "I'm good with computers, I can fight if I have to, and I already know everything I need to know about why we're doing this. You just need to explain how I would get to the encyclopedia and the credentials I'll need," she said to Mr. Woodward, "and then I'll be good to go."

"She's right," Amelia said, smiling at Erica. "She *is* the only one here that Lucien mightn't think to search for, and it'd be a lot quicker than finding someone else in the base to do it and explaining everything to them."

James hesitated a moment longer, and then nodded. "Well, it was my idea, so I'd be a hypocrite to object to it now."

"And as far as who guards her, I nominate myself," said Marc. "She'll need to be out of her shadow while she's doing it, which gives me an excuse for me to do the same, which means I can use the crystal if there's any trouble."

"And you can use my USB stick," James said, taking it from his pocket and handing it to her. "I've backed everything up already, so if you have to delete the stuff that's on there, it'll be okay. Eight gigs will be enough for the whole thing, right?" he asked Mr. Woodward.

"Yeah, I'm pretty sure it's not that big," he said, "since it's all compressed, and the majority of it is purely text-based with only some pictures—no audio or video to speak of."

"Good, that would take ages to download, and I don't wanna be out there too long," Erica said.

Chapter 10: The Descent of Our Mr. Lucien

With the plan made for that afternoon, we left the Time Box, only a few minutes having passed on the outside, and steered the base towards the Chopville Public Library. By the time we got there, Marc and Erica were both ready to be let out, having both been armed and Erica having been instructed how to access the encyclopedia by Mr. Woodward. We let them out of the base around the corner, making sure that no one was watching as they appeared out of nowhere, and then followed close behind Erica and the now-invisible Marc as they entered the library. We also kept an eye on Lucien through the spyer, but he and Fewul were both still busy in a meeting, and so far, no trouble was forthcoming.

As Erica sat herself down at one of the computers in the library, those of us left in the control room began talking. It was finally time for me to be caught up on what had been happening around here, and most particularly what had happened to Natalie. Peter, James, Amelia and Mr. Woodward ended up telling me everything, even though some of it was very hard to hear, and I now understood why Rebecca hadn't wanted to be around for the retelling. Stella was still there too, but she didn't have much to add to the conversation. I made a mental note of the fact that the entire time I'd been back, she'd said hardly a word to anyone, but I would return to that later; I had more important things to deal with.

It all began after lunch the previous day. This must have been shortly after Marc and I had communicated telepathically and he had caught me up on the terrible things that had happened since I had been killed. James had seen, most likely on the spyers, that Lucien had discovered what Mr. Woodward referred to as Arnold Hammerson's 'store of apocalyptic events'. By the sound of it, these were weapons so dangerous and deadly that they would either destroy the world, or destroy all living things in it. James had hurriedly called the most important people to the control room to discuss this, but they had been unable to come up with anything to stop him from using them if he chose to do so.

"Those weapons were only ever meant to be a deterrent, or for blackmail," Stella spoke up then, "and I told them that yesterday, but if Lucien doesn't realise that, he could go ahead and use one of them, doing all kinds of horrible damage. And the worst thing is we can't destroy them. Well—we could destroy the ones Lucien found, because we saw where they were, but there are many copies of them scattered around the world, and I have no idea where they are—that certainly wasn't something my family entrusted to me. I didn't even know about that location until yesterday."

They had been forced to stay in the control room and watch Lucien throughout the afternoon. Confident in his position, he had instructed Fewul, still in Stella's form, to assist Cornish in stabilising all of

Hammersonia's existing territory within twelve hours; and then incredibly, called together a taskforce of Hammerhearts from around the world to begin planning invasions of Egypt and Colombia, two countries bordering Hammersonia but not yet controlled by the Hammerhearts themselves, so that he could begin to take control of the remaining two continents. He seemed to have decided not to pursue the Young Army any further for the time being, believing that they would expose themselves in good time out of sheer frustration at how much 'good work' he was getting done.

His belief was spot-on, and sadly for her, it was Natalie who was first to snap. Nobody came out and said it, but it sounded as though Natalie had changed somewhat since my death, or perhaps since finding out that I was damned for eternity—whatever it was. Unable to handle watching Lucien getting away with everything, she proposed a head-on confrontation with him—their magical devices and three of the Magic Crystals against him and his magic, the Sien-Leoard Crystal, and even Fewul if necessary. She ranted that such a confrontation was probably inevitable anyway, that Lucien wasn't going to be stopped without a fight, and it was better it happened sooner rather than later. The fact that they had bugger all chance of winning, a fact which just about everyone tried to explain to her, didn't even slow her down. She said that she would do it herself if she had to, with or without their help, and only then did they finally concede to her demands—on the one condition that she be prepared to fall back the moment they looked like being overwhelmed.

It had been a great mistake, and a second great mistake had been committed when, seeing how angry she was with Lucien, they had given her the Villain Crystal in the hope that she could use it to channel her anger into a form that could attack him. My blood went cold as I heard this, a horrible possibility occurring to me, but it would turn out that the Villain Crystal itself hadn't actually betrayed Natalie. On the contrary, it had worked quite well for her, even better than the Hero Crystal had worked for Marc, judging by the description of the battle provided to me.

It had started out with just five of them: Natalie, Marc and James with the Villain, Hero and Light Crystals respectively; and Peter and Amelia with their magical devices. Mr. Woodward had stayed at the controls, while Stella, not feeling up to the fight herself, had gone to tell other people throughout the base what was going on, so that before too long, Rebecca, Erica, Harry, Simon, Katie, Sophie, Felicity, and even Tommy, believe it or not, had joined them, gathering up magical devices of their own. I had interrupted the story briefly at this point to ask how Tommy was doing, and how they managed to get him to take part in a battle like that.

"Actually, Tommy's been a bit better lately," Amelia said. "He's not how he used to be, not even close, but he's definitely on our side now, and you can put that down to Marc. He sat him down for a talk on Tuesday night and basically told him that it may be impossible that he'll ever see Ingi again, and that Lucien had made it that way because he didn't want the Honnies interfering in his business—the truth, in other words. He did say, though, and I wasn't so sure this was a good idea at the time, but he said that if this ever calmed down, Marc would use his magic to try to find a way for Tommy to get back to Ingi again. I dunno if it's possible, but Marc actually thinks that if he could just find those Honnies again, maybe it would be possible to restore their memories. Well anyway, the point is it got Tommy's hopes up, and he's sworn vengeance against Lucien for putting him through this pain."

The story continued. The group had followed Lucien in the base for a short time, launching their attack against him as he was leaving a television station where he had been doing an interview regarding the recent terrorist acts (the supermarket and the three plane crashes). They had chosen that spot because it was fairly open, but the street at that particular time was mostly deserted. They were all under an invisibility veil, of course (along with being untraceable and under a soundproof barrier), and they knew that cops could surround them fairly easily if they showed up in time, but the hope of the attack was to do it so quickly and with such surprise that Lucien never had a chance to call in backup, or to teleport to a location that would be more difficult to fight him at.

Lucien had surrounded himself with a shield that none of them had been able to penetrate. It seemed that it had been in place the entire time, as though Lucien had anticipated that such an attack could hit him at any moment and he was pre-empting it. Although he had been unable to use his own magic to flush any of them out, as they had been impossible to pinpoint and they had all been under those spells which would cause most enchantments to pass right through them, he had still been able to think his way through the battle, and whether beforehand or on the spot, he had come up with a couple of strategies that they hadn't been able to prepare for or prevent.

The first of them had been to teleport himself and everyone else involved in the battle to Hamster's Stretch Reserve, where they were completely alone and in much less danger of being surrounded by backup. If they'd had time to think about it, they would have considered that in isolation, this would have been a good thing for them; as it was, they had no choice but to continue the battle as Lucien didn't miss a beat in his defence. When analysing the battle later on, Marc and the former Sorcerers had supposed that Lucien had somehow measured the distance the magic being used against him had travelled, and then estimated the distance between himself and all of his attackers, and then teleported all matter within that radius along with him. It was the only way he could have teleported them with him while they had been untraceable.

Yet that hadn't been the worst of it—his next strategy had been much worse for them. Perhaps due to the intensity of the attacks against him, he quickly deduced that at least one of the Magic Crystals was being used against him. By spying on him later on, they had learned that he actually thought it had been Marc using the Hero Crystal; and indeed Marc *had* been using the Hero Crystal, but Marc had been further back in the pack, taking on a more defensive and protective role in the fight, making sure that the rest of the group were safe. The person Lucien thought was Marc had actually been Natalie, furiously leading the attack with the Villain Crystal, and so the strategy Lucien had designed to capture his brother and reclaim the Sorcerous Crystals had instead netted Natalie and the Villain Crystal.

Not that Lucien had realised that right away. He had used the Sien-Leoard Crystal to overpower the closest of the Magic Crystals and drag it, along with the person holding it, to himself. When he made physical contact with that person, he quickly subdued them with magic—not by putting a spell *on* them but by putting a spell *around* them, a way of getting around our shield design that none of us had thought of. He had then teleported them both away to the Hammerheart base, leaving the rest of the attack group isolated and confused. They knew what had happened (being under an invisibility veil, they had seen what had happened to Natalie; she had been put into stasis right before being teleported away). Additionally, when Lucien had teleported them to the Stretch, they had left their own base far behind, and it had taken Mr. Woodward at the controls quite some time to get back to them and bring them back in.

"Why wouldn't Marc just teleport after Lucien?" I asked, dumbfounded. "We know *he's* not untraceable."

"He almost did," James said, "but if he had, he would have been all on his own and would have been very vulnerable, so we had to call him back. Losing Natalie was bad enough; we couldn't afford to lose them both."

Most frustratingly, particularly for me, nobody knew what had happened next. By the time they were all back in the base and had teleported to Lucien's location to see what was happening, he was already having his dinner in the Hammerheart Dining Hall, and there was no sign of Natalie anywhere. They had eventually deduced some of what had happened, though: Lucien had discovered his blunder by patting down his captive and finding out, by touching her in certain places that made me feel angry, that she was a girl. He had divested her of the Villain Crystal, put her in four-dimensional binds and then brought her out of stasis, where he had proceeded to interrogate her to firstly find out who she was, and then when he had figured that out, anything else he could get out of her. Fortunately, Natalie hadn't been carrying any devices on her save the Villain Crystal, and Natalie herself didn't know the details of our new untraceability, so those secrets remained ours.

But since Natalie remained untraceable, even to us, the group had no way of knowing where he had put her. They had tried to locate her through tracing the Villain Crystal, which Lucien had put in a shield on his bedside table, and Marc had been able to go in there and retrieve it fairly easily while Lucien had still been at dinner. He took the opportunity to look around the living quarters to see if Natalie was there, but he had no luck there. The next obvious place to look was the Basement, but while Marc was able to find many other prisoners in there, Natalie turned out not to be there either.

I wanted them to skip ahead to the part of the story where they found out where Natalie was, but before that, they told me of the operation that had come next: the rescue of all those prisoners from the Hammerheart Basement. Amelia and Peter had been in favour of said operation, while James and Mr. Woodward had regretfully said that it would expose them to anyone watching the security cameras, something they couldn't afford to happen. Amelia had won the argument by pointing out that even if someone saw what was happening, unless Lucien intervened himself, the Hammerhearts wouldn't be able to do a damn thing to stop them. That turned out not to be a problem; Lucien was quickly informed of what was happening in the Basement, as the folks in the control room observed through the spyers, but he seemed to decide that those prisoners, who had all been captured before his time at the helm, weren't worth trying to keep locked up anyway.

"And they're in here now, right?" I asked, remembering something I had vaguely noticed earlier. "I thought I saw more people at lunch who I didn't recognise, but I just assumed they had come from the Big Room."

"Yes," said Mr. Woodward. "There are plenty of people in here who don't have a lot to do. We basically put them in charge of looking after the former prisoners, making sure they're all okay and healthy and not too traumatised. Sadly, some of them will have permanent psychological damage from their long stints in there; some of them were taken prisoner for dissent against the Hammerhearts months ago, and a few of them are even younger than you kids."

Then the story returned to Natalie, and this was where it started to get *really* bad. After he had finished dinner, Lucien had returned to his living quarters and by way of his watch, called Ather Hignat, Ugine Wilwog, Sebastian Williams and Mr. Hall to join him, apparently telling them that they would be rewarded if they came—so naturally, all four of them did. He seemed to want to know how loyal they were to him, and asked them point-blank if he could count on them to do his bidding no matter what. The three younger boys had emphatically agreed, though everyone present (including me) thought they were probably just saying that because it was the right thing to say in those circumstances. Hall hadn't been so easy, though, telling Lucien that he would do his job but that he was sceptical of Lucien's leadership, and that he still needed to prove himself, in Hall's wise and worldly opinion. Perhaps Hall was part of one of these so-called 'anti-Lucien factions'.

I had a very bad feeling about where this was going, and this time, my feeling was accurate. Lucien had told Hall that he respected his opinion, and had then led the four of them into his bedroom and through a door off the side of it. The bedroom that had once belonged to Arnold Hammerson had three rooms branching off it; a private bathroom, a walk-in wardrobe, and a door that Stella, at least, had never seen open until now. Natalie had been within, and that was where she remained up to this very hour, locked in invisible binds which kept her on the floor against one wall in such a way that she could move around, but not off the floor or away from the wall. Worse, though, was that the magic only touched her; anyone else could pass through it as if it weren't there, which left her horribly exposed. Later on, when Marc had gone in there, he had been unable to remove these binds no matter what magic he tried. It was during that time that Natalie tearfully filled in the gaps in their knowledge to Marc, apologising over and over again for allowing their invisibility veil to fall away and then telling Lucien, under torture, the things that she did.

"I didn't know such a place existed," Stella told me of the room, "but when I saw it, I was pretty sure I knew what it was. I think it was my father's private torture chamber, and now I think maybe he kept a few prisoners in there at any given time. There were…things in there, torture things, and things specifically for him to do things to—to women. I think maybe he even kept my mother in there when she was pregnant with me, if it existed back then."

When Lucien had led Hignat, Wilwog, Sebastian and Hall into the room, there had been two people in there: Natalie on one side of the room, and a tall, muscular male Hammerheart against the opposite wall. He was unbound, but he seemed to have no interest in Natalie at all. That confused me for maybe twenty seconds, or for however long it took James, who was telling this part of the story, to explain his purpose in the room. Lucien shut the door behind them, bound Hall to the wall beside the large man before he knew what was happening (with the same invisible binds that were holding Natalie), and then let the male Hammerheart have his way with our former English teacher. The price of Hall's honesty earlier, and his lack of faith in Lucien, was that he got to have his first homosexual experience, and it was one he would never forget.

Which of course left the other three boys to have their way with Natalie, as I had expected and dreaded. Lucien gave them leave to do whatever they wanted to her, stopping short of putting her through any serious physical pain (though there were no limits on how much psychological pain they could put her through). None of them described exactly what the boys had done to her, except for Amelia to say that it had been somewhat worse than what Hignat and Wilwog had done to her six months earlier. Lucien hadn't joined in the raping of Natalie, at least not then, although he had interrupted them briefly to degrade her in his own way. Nobody told me exactly what this was, and I didn't ask; I was feeling sick to my stomach by this point.

Those who had been in the control room at the time were horrified by what they were being forced to watch, and with Lucien standing right there, they didn't see how they could stop it. When nobody could think of anything else to do, they had taken out some of their frustration by finally capturing Lena, who had been elsewhere in the living quarters at the time, apparently with no idea what was happening not far away. Quite a few people had been all in favour of making Lena suffer when they brought her in out of sheer frustration at not being able to do anything to save Natalie, but the rational heads had prevailed in this case; Lena had only been unboggled and then set free in the base as part of the Young Army.

"But I haven't seen her," I said, feeling confused. "Surely if she had been at lunch, I would have at least noticed her around somewhere."

The five of them swapped a look, and then Peter said, "Well, she's not here anymore, but we'll get to that bit."

When Marc finally returned to base after saving all those prisoners, he hadn't been content with only recapturing Lena. He had snuck into the rape room by way of teleportation, invisible and untraceable and all the rest, put himself as far from Lucien as he could within the confined space, and used the Hero Crystal to knock the three boys assaulting Natalie unconscious. Lucien had responded almost immediately by trying to do to Marc what he had earlier done to Natalie, but Marc had taken magical precautions to make sure he didn't suffer the same fate. He had then attempted to free Natalie from her binds, but he had been unable to do so.

A short battle between the two Morans had begun; Marc getting off the opening shot, not by attacking Lucien directly but by making the floor extremely slippery so that Lucien fell over on his arse. Natalie was forced to watch this (looking very frightened as well as traumatised, according to Amelia), while on the other side of the room, Hall and the man 'taking care of him' went on doing what they were doing without paying any attention to the fight. Even though he had started so well, though, Marc hadn't been able to touch his older brother, and as it slowly turned in Lucien's favour, James, who had been at the controls at the time, had been forced to rescue Marc before he could be disarmed. He had tried to do the same to Natalie, but had once again been unsuccessful.

The good thing to come from the attack, apart from Lucien falling on his arse (how I wish I could have witnessed that delicious moment), was that it ended the torture, at least for then. Lucien revived the three boys and sent them on their way, telling them that they would receive more rewards like that one if they were loyal to him, and more rewards like the one Hall got if they weren't. When it was only him and Natalie left in there, he told her that he would be leaving her there for the time being until he had figured out what he would do with her; or even if she was worth keeping alive.

Only after he had locked her in there, all alone, did he finally realise that Lena had been taken from him, and as he had done before, he spoke to the empty room as though we were there and could hear him—which, in this case, we were and could. To those who had taken his woman, he said something to the effect that they could keep her for a short time now, but they would pay dearly for having defied him so. Three more terrorist acts would take place that night as a result of what they had done, both by having the nerve to steal Lena away from him, and by getting all up in his business just before.

It was at this point that Marc was finally able to go back and make sure that Natalie was okay. She wasn't, of course, but even without the pressure of Lucien being right there, he was still unable to do a damn thing to free her. I wished that Marc were here to recount exactly what she'd said to him because the others could only give me an approximation. It seemed to be something like, 'there's nothing left of the real Lucien inside him now, and you must put all your efforts into bringing him down, even if it means leaving me here to suffer under his thumb.' Marc reluctantly agreed, but promised to come back as soon as he thought of something new to try to free her.

Shortly after this, Natalie's mother demanded to be let out of the base to see Natalie and to take some food and drink to her. While she did that, and attempted to comfort her daughter, those left in the control room (only Peter, James, Rebecca, Brian and Alice Fletcher by this point, everyone else having gone to bed or for some private time) kept an eye on Lucien, waiting to see what he would do—if he would follow up on his threat to commit more acts of terrorism. By this point, I'd given up on the hope that any of Lucien's threats were empty; he seemed ready to deliver on every single one of them. Sure enough, this time was no different, and like he had that morning, he did the whole thing with his mind, never physically leaving the living quarters at all, and supposedly only learning of the horrors when frantic Hammerhearts began reporting them to him.

The horrors this time were even worse than the plane crashes that morning. The worst had been a massive fire in a large apartment building in Sydney, which had spread so rapidly that more than five hundred people were killed and hundreds more were injured. That seemed like a strangely high death toll to me, making me wonder if Lucien had made sure it was unnaturally packed with people as the supermarket had been when the bomb had gone off—or perhaps that the building itself was unnaturally packed with highly flammable materials. Almost as bad had been a similarly large fire in a large hotel on the Gold Coast, which had killed more than four hundred and subjected many more to major burns and smoke inhalation. To top the night off, a series of bombs had been set off on buses in Adelaide, killing 162 people and injuring more than three hundred.

"It didn't take long for that news to spread through the base," Amelia said. "We all came back here as soon as we heard, and everyone else watched it all unfolding on TV in the lounge room. They had live footage of the fire fighters in Sydney trying to deal with it, and something similar on the Gold Coast."

"And then Lucien came on TV," James went on. "We were all in here so we didn't see the broadcast, but we were still tracing him at the time. He basically called for calm, for everyone not to be afraid, and said that they would use all methods at their disposal to catch the terrorists responsible for this and that everyone should be united behind him and not to cower in fear of the opposition. He also said something about introducing new processes to make sure that things like this can't happen in the future, which would be announced in the coming days."

"Which is politician speak for tighter government control, of course," Mr. Woodward said, smiling grimly, "which in this case gives Lucien further justification—as if he needs it—to get even more invasive with his magic. People are really scared of how much 'the opposition', as he's calling us now, will do to undermine him, and how many innocents they'll kill. They don't even need influential charms anymore; most people are coming to hate us and everything we stand for as a result of these last couple of days."

"'Announced in the coming days,'" I repeated James's words. "That makes it sound like he's going to drag his feet on something he could probably implement in about ten seconds if he wanted to. Does that mean what I think it means?"

"That he wants an excuse to torment us with more terrorism before he gets too good at his job and stamps it all out? Yep," said Peter. "The only good thing—well, it's actually not a good thing for anyone, but as it's a bad thing for Lucien then I guess we can claim it as a good thing: there have been other acts of terrorism around the world, apparently inspired by what Lucien's done and not committed by Lucien himself. He's pretty mad about that."

"He made Fewul take the form of a large squadron of police officers," James said, "his 'personal enforcers', as he's calling them. They've been going around the world, scanning people's brains and rounding up anyone who has actively resisted the Hammerhearts or is somehow involved in organised resistance, and has locked them up in the Basements of various Hammerheart bases around the world. He hasn't come out and said it, but I'm betting that he's going to set up a show trial for them so that he can show people that he's truly serious about defending them from bad people. By the time he's done, nobody will have any sympathy for them."

The story continued then, and now things got even worse. At a time when Marc ought to have left the base and done what he could to save lives in at least one of the locations, they were all distracted by what Lucien did next. After he had finished his announcement, he went back into the torture chamber (Natalie's mother had left by then), and told Natalie the story of what he'd done and why, telling her that more would come, worsening each time, until Marc and James handed themselves over to him, along with all the outstanding Magic Crystals. He even went as far as taunting her about my death as a way to break her spirit even more, apparently not knowing that I would be coming back. And then, of course, he put on the final touch by raping her himself—'badly', to use Peter's word. When I asked him what he meant by that, as if there were any other kind of rape, he said, "I mean roughly—*really* roughly, like what he did to Lena, but at least she had wanted that."

Remembering what Lucien had been doing to Lena for well over an hour on Tuesday, in the hours before my death, I shuddered to think how it would have been for Natalie, with him doing that to her against her will. Supposedly, while he was doing that to her, he told her that he didn't care about her at all and he was only doing it for his own pleasure, because the woman he would have preferred to be doing it with had been taken from him, so Natalie would have to fill in. He had also threatened her with other things, such as using his magic to turn her into his personal sex slave and other things besides, as he continued to degrade and humiliate her worse than anything I could ever have imagined. And the worst thing about it for me was that I knew that they were deliberately withholding the worst details of it all, knowing that I could barely handle what I was hearing.

It made me wonder how it would have been for Natalie's family—Rebecca, Brian (her father), Minny (her mother), and Alice (her grandmother). Surely, none of them would have left the control room between Minny visiting Natalie and Lucien going in there, and sure enough, they had witnessed the very worst of it. Her parents, in particular, had been so badly tortured watching such things happening to their daughter that abandoning all rationality, they had demanded to be let out of the base. Naturally, everyone present, including Frederic and Lillian Woodward, refused to budge on such a demand, pointing out that they had no chance of stopping Lucien from doing what he wanted and that things would likely be worse for everyone if they interfered.

It might have ended there, and there was about a second when I thought maybe it had, but unlike the rest of the Fletchers, Rebecca had seen how the control panel worked and before anyone quite knew what was happening, she had forced her way to it and was able to drop her parents out of the base. She would have followed them herself if Peter and Amelia hadn't frantically grabbed her and forced her to the floor in a kicking, screaming pile. By this stage of the story, James was the only one able to speak in anything more than a croak, and Amelia had dissolved completely into sobs. I thought I understood what must have come next, though I dreaded to think it could be that bad; yet for the second time, my feeling was accurate.

Brian and Minny had dropped straight into the room behind Lucien, and he had been so focused on what he was doing, and in such a compromising position, that they had actually succeeded in getting a hit on him—something that we certainly hadn't been able to do. Of course, it was the only thing they had been able to do; they had no shields to speak of, and no invisibility, neither of them having taken the time to prepare themselves in any way for a fight that they had no chance of winning anyway. Lucien had murdered Brian with a wave of his hand and had eventually done the same to Minny, but only after raping her just as he had done to Natalie, and forcing Natalie to watch it all. He had then left to go and have a shower, leaving Natalie alone in the room with the bodies of her dead parents.

"Holy crap," I said, feeling sicker than ever.

"Marc wanted to try to save her while we still could," Amelia whispered.

James smiled bitterly. "If only that were possible. It would have been nice if we could have pulled Natalie's mum back into the base before Lucien—well—ended it, but if we had pulled Lucien in instead, it would have been a disaster for us. And there was a good chance of that happening, because he was really—really all over her."

The story continued. While Lucien had been in the shower, Marc had dropped back into the room to attempt to console Natalie, but she had been distressed beyond adequate description, apparently, and had scolded him for allowing her parents to interfere in the first place. Marc had explained what had happened in the control room, apologised over and over again, and then had taken the bodies of her parents with him back into the base so that they could be treated with dignity. They had had a funeral for the two Fletchers that very night, which everyone in the base had attended, and they had buried the two bodies in the ground just outside the building.

Which brought us almost to the present as nothing else had happened that night, and very little had happened today before I had returned to the base. Lucien would have discovered by now that the bodies of the Fletchers had been removed, which he knew meant that the Young Army must have done it, but so far as anyone knew, he hadn't taken revenge in the form of another terrorist act—not yet, anyway. They hadn't been able to watch Natalie all day as she was untraceable, but by keeping an eye on Lucien, they had been able to make sure that he hadn't done any more harm to Natalie himself, nor had he authorised anyone else to go into the room where she was being held.

They had been taken by surprise by one thing that had happened this morning, though. Mid-morning, probably around the time I had left Rock Haulter and set off across the ocean, Sebastian had come to Lucien and he had brought Lena with him. Incredibly, she had found a way to slip out of the base without anyone knowing—something that should have been impossible. I had specifically designed it with people like Sebastian in mind: On the off-chance that someone we thought we could trust turned out to be a traitor, they would be unable to leave the base unless their intentions were good, or unless we deliberately let them out. Lucien had taken Lena and grilled her on the base, but she hadn't been able to reveal much more than he already knew, other than inconsequential things about the base such as how it was structured.

After some asking around, they had eventually figured out how Lena had gotten free. Although she had been unboggled, whatever other influences Lucien had put on her using his Honnie mind had remained in place so that she was still intent on getting back to him, for her own personal reasons if not because she supported him in the war. She had therefore sat in the lounge room and asked those who were present about the base, and had learned that her only way out in a non-emergency was through the control room, and that there was a scanner in place to make sure that she couldn't enter the control room unless she were going in there for the right reasons.

She had gotten up very early this morning and attempted to enter while the room had been empty, but had been denied by the scanner. Fortunately for her, though, Tommy was also awake at that hour, tormented by dreams of Ingi, and with very little idea of what Lena was really doing. It had been very easy for her to persuade him that she had been told to leave the base, and that she didn't understand why the control room wasn't letting her in. Tommy, not suspecting anything amiss, and probably with only a third of his mind in the game anyway, had helped her enter the control room by walking in ahead of her and dragging her with him, as if she were a prisoner and he were authorising her to enter. Tommy himself had no trouble entering because as far as the scanner went, his mind was totally innocent; he honestly thought he was doing the right thing. After that, it had been easy to instruct Tommy to let her out of the base, dropping her straight into the Jade River below (as that was where the base had been located at the time), and thinking he had done well, Tommy had gone off to wander some more with his tortured thoughts.

"Well," I said, trying to get my head around this and feeling my stomach sink with a dreadful realisation, "I hate to say it, but I think we have no choice but to let Lena go now. If she still wants to be with him even after being unboggled, what choice do we have?"

"Even though we know for a fact that she wouldn't choose to do that if she was in her right mind?" James asked. "I mean, I agree that we have no choice, but only because there's literally nothing we can do to get her back, not without a Honnie to help us anymore."

I shrugged. "I know you're right, but the thing is, if she thinks she's doing what's best for her even after Lucien's interference, who are we to tell her otherwise? How do I explain this…" I hesitated. I knew what I wanted to say, but couldn't figure out, off the top of my head, what words would convey the message. "You guys know that May seemed to trust me more than anyone else here; mainly because I was the one who persuaded her to come here in the first place. The time I spent with her made me wonder a lot about what we can really consider reality, because she could alter what we thought was reality in ways we may never have thought of. In Lena's reality now, she wants to be with Lucien, no matter what he does and no matter how he treats her. Does that—does that fly?"

"Not with me it doesn't," Peter said doubtfully. "I mean, we used to say that about the influential charm as well, and yet you managed to find a magical solution for that. Maybe there is some magical solution to fixing someone whose mind's been screwed with by a Honnie."

James nodded. "I think you may be right about that, Pete, especially considering Lucien used magic to create his Honnie mind—we know that it's not outside the ability of magic to touch. The thing is, Marc's the only one in a position to do anything about that at the moment, and with everything else going on, I don't think we can spare him to save Lena. I think we may have to hope that she'll be okay in Lucien's care, and in this case, I tend to think she probably will be."

"What about the future, then?" Amelia asked. "What if we somehow win this thing? What would we do for Lena then? Would she be able to cope? Would she be traumatised by what he put her through, or would she go to the other extreme and pine for him?"

"Not for us to worry about right now," James said, not unkindly. "I know Lena didn't choose for this to happen, but she did choose to go back to Lucien. However you look at her, even if she wasn't in her right mind, she still made that choice. We have to focus on the bigger picture, and right now, the most we can do for Lena is keep an eye on her and hope that Lucien values her enough, even if it's only for his own gratification, to keep her alive and well."

Chapter 11: Hope and Hopelessness

Marc and Erica finished their mission without event a little over an hour before dinner. They were both able to leave the library and go back to where they had first dropped out of the base without being stopped. Once we had scooped them safely off the seat, we immediately got talking about what came next. Erica had been free to do a lot of thinking while waiting for the encyclopedia to download, and she proposed that she be allowed to recruit a group of smart people from around the base, who didn't have anything better to do, to search through the encyclopedia until they found what we needed regarding the prophecy; leaving the rest of us free to continue dealing directly with Lucien as best we could.

As for Lucien, he had spent most of the afternoon in meetings. We had kept an eye on him with the spyer but we hadn't stopped to listen to what he was actually doing—that may or may not have been a mistake, but we had so much talking to do ourselves. What seemed clear, though, was that he was going to do as he did the day before—continue with his mad plans, not worrying too much about us for the time being, knowing that we were basically powerless to stop him and would only expose ourselves if we tried. That may have been the truth up to this point, but I had a feeling that the new magic I had brought to the table would turn things in our favour, at least a little.

After Erica left the control room, the time had come to show the others the rest of the devices in my backpack.

"None of these are things you couldn't have created with the Hero Crystal," I said to Marc as I lifted the bag containing the new devices onto my lap, "and I don't have as many here as we created the first time, but I was free to get real creative while I was in there so hopefully it makes a difference. I guess it's also possible that you guys might think of something I missed when you see them, and again, Marc can help sort that out.

"So these ones aren't that important—I just created them for myself while I was there," I said, removing the duplicate devices I'd created, including the map of Rock Haulter and another invisibility toggle from the bag and dropping them on the floor. "These ones are a little better, though; when I saw how well the four-dimensional knock-out worked against anyone other than Lucien, I figured some other 4D devices would be useful as well, so I've got a 4D stunner, 4D solid-outliner and 4D bludginator. There's only one of each, but we can just duplicate them as we need them."

"No 4D agonator," Peter observed.

I shrugged. "Not my style, but I suppose Marc can create one of those if you wanna get really mean. Now this one here is a partial invisibility toggle; it works just like a normal invisibility toggle, except that we ourselves won't notice any difference when we use it. I was thinking of those tracking plane things that Lucien was using the other day; if the magic works the way I meant it to, it'll hide us from those things without hiding us from each other."

"An invisibility veil would have accomplished that," James said, "but yeah, this one might be simpler. I can see one flaw in its design, though: how do we know if we're partially invisible or not? If we really won't notice any difference, then we could easily lose track of whose hidden and who isn't, right up until one of those trackers lands on top of someone."

I gaped at him for a few seconds, and then swore. "How on earth did I miss that? Okay, you're right. If a person forgets whether they used it or not, or if they forget if they reversed the toggle on themselves…yeah, we won't be able to use these the way they are at the moment. We'll have to come back to them.

"Now this is a crystal blocker. It uses the same magic as the crystal trackers, except in reverse. It can be used to put a magical shield around any of the Magic Crystals, and theoretically—again, I haven't tested it—but theoretically, it would prevent Lucien from being able to magically track the location of any of the crystals we have. I suppose it would also prevent him doing what he did to capture Natalie, although I guess we can't be sure of that. What I am fairly sure of, though, is that it'll work even against Lucien trying to sense out the source of his magic, if he even thinks to try that."

"Good one," Marc said, "and that one can be tested easily enough right here in the base, so we can try that later on."

"Now this one is a thinking cap simulator," I went on, withdrawing another device from the bag—a thumb-sized thing with only one button on it. "Can anyone guess what that does?"

"My guess is that it would simulate those thinking caps you guys had on your heads when you went into the Honnie world," James said, "only with a single spell rather than a big, clunky thing on your head."

"Those things which turned out to be about as useful as an air conditioner in a blizzard," Peter muttered.

"Both correct," I said, "which is why I specifically thought of both May and Lucien—that is, the artificial Honnie mind he created—when I made this thing. I really think I have enough experience with Honnies now that I was able to make these things in a way that'll work. If we're close enough to Lucien that he would normally be able to snatch our minds on his own, these things ought to hide us from him so that he can't. I don't see them as being especially useful, though; if being untraceable also protects us, then that alone would be enough, but this is a good backup to have just in case something goes wrong.

"Now these two," I pulled two more devices from the bag, "sort of go hand-in-hand. One is an energy booster, which can be used every now and then to keep us operating when we really should be sleeping. I remember when the Hammersons first took over the Australian government and I had to use the Sien-Leoard Crystal to keep myself going for something like thirty hours straight; this device will make it possible for us to do that, if necessary, without needing crystals of our own. The other one is pretty much the opposite; we can use it to give ourselves a good night of deep, dreamless sleep so that we'll be well-rested when we wake up. I even made it so that we can specify how many hours we want, just in case we need to wake up at a certain time."

This earned approving looks from several people, especially Mr. Woodward. "That is definitely a good idea," he said. "I strongly suggest we hand these out to everyone, especially the kids, who really could use it."

That made me smile a little, but I pushed on. "These two also go hand-in-hand. The one thing I spent the most time thinking about in that cave was ways that we could sneak under Lucien's magical shields and hit him with a spell, and I only came up with two good ideas—and for all I know, they mightn't be any good at all. One operates like a bullet, and I think because it's much more concentrated than normal magic, albeit no more powerful, it might be able to slice through a standard shield. All you have to do to use it is fire a bit of magic into the back end of it—say, thicky prison from a solid-outliner—and then fire it at Lucien. Of course, he may just strengthen his shields if he knows about it, so we have to make sure that when we use it we make it a good one, and that Fewul is nowhere near.

"The other one works the same, but instead of being a magic bullet, it's basically magic encoded into light signals. Theoretically this means that it will pass through anything and everything invisible, so again, unless Lucien knows about it, the only way he'd be able to protect himself from it is with an actual visible barrier around himself. The encoding and decoding happens instantly, so as soon as the light hits him the spell will be enacted, so he won't have a chance to do anything about it."

"Unless he sees the light coming, of course," James pointed out.

I shrugged. "Well yeah, that is the limitation. I know it is possible to make invisible light, but in this case, if the light is invisible, then the whole thing doesn't work—at least, that's how it seemed to me when I was trying to think of all this stuff. I guess we just have to make sure Lucien's not looking straight at us when we use it; so then again, he won't have time to react."

James shook his head. "No, I think it may be doable. There are forms of light that aren't visible to humans that are totally non-magical, like infrared or X-rays. If we modified those devices to use one of those kinds of light, Lucien wouldn't see it coming, and they would just as easily pass through any invisible shield he's using. I'll have to do some research before we decide how to do that, though; it seems pretty scientific, and I don't wanna be responsible for buggering it up."

"Wow. Well—that actually sounds pretty good," I said, impressed and taking a moment to enjoy that feeling before pushing on. "Now this one—it's shrunken now, but we can enlarge it later on so that you can see how it works—it's basically another flying capsule, like the ones we've used in the past for missions, except these ones are for two people. I made them that way because I decided, in my infinite wisdom," I grinned at James as I said this, "that if we go on missions, like we had to do the other day when we went up to the moon and a few people stayed back down here, that two people should always go together. In these flying capsules, one person does all the flying while the other person does all the other magic. It doesn't have any other magic built into the thing, besides being able to be invisible and untraceable, but it does let you shoot magic through the glass as if it weren't there, so whoever's using it can just use normal devices from there."

"And that glass only goes one-way, right?" Amelia asked.

"Yeah, of course," I said, "but there's just about zero chance of that theory being tested anyway. One other enchantment it has on it is that spells pass right through it without being deflected, like those other devices we have."

I looked around on the floor for the device in question, couldn't see it anywhere, shrugged, and pushed on. There were only six devices left, not counting the Time Box which I'd already shown them, and I was saving the best ones for last.

"Now this one, if it works, will toggle mind protection for a person. What we would normally have to do by putting someone under a domination charm and then hoping they can beat it, we should be able to do with the push of a button. Similarly, we should be able to remove that protection on someone if, for whatever reason, we need to be able to read their mind for something."

Marc looked a little dubious at this. "I gave this a bunch of thought months ago and I honestly couldn't think of any way to do that, other than using the domination charm. Are you sure that'll work?"

"Nope, not sure at all," I said, looking at each of them in turn, "but it shouldn't be too hard to test it right here in the base, since most of us already have protected minds. It just means that someone—namely you, Marc—will have the uncomfortable job of trying to read people's minds to see if they're still protected or not.

"Now these two also go hand-in-hand. This one," I showed them yet another thumb-sized device with a single button on it, "can capture a person's mind and store it for later. It doesn't take control of them or anything; it just copies the contents of their brain. Everything in there—every memory, in varying levels of clarity, along with everything else that ultimately comprises their personality—will be stored so that we can go back later and browse them, or whatever parts of them we need to see.

"And we do that using this," I showed them a small cube with a single button on it, almost identical to the Time Box in its shrunken form but for the colour; that had been green, whereas this one was navy blue. "I call this the 'mind box', and its interior is very similar to the Time Box. It operates much the same as that cave on Rock Haulter where we viewed Smiley's memories, only with a lot more control during the viewing, so that we can quickly find the parts of the mind that we want to see. All we have to do is transfer the mind from the catcher to the box and we'll be good to go."

"Can we use that thing inside the Time Box?" Peter asked.

"I see no reason why not," I shrugged. "Space won't be an issue, since they both expand internally so that we can fit as many people as we need."

"Good, because I suppose it would take a long time to really get into a person's entire mind," he said. "Incidentally, when would we actually need to use something like that?"

"Maybe never," James said, "but it's good to have it. If the controls are as good as John says they are, it may be a good way to get information out of Hammerhearts whose minds aren't protected—or whose minds are no longer protected," he added. "And if the controls aren't as good as John hopes, well, Marc might be able to do something about that with the crystal."

I nodded and withdrew the third to last device from the bag. "This is an unduplicator. What it basically does is puts a spell on something that prevents any magic from being able to duplicate it. It's a permanent thing too; once this thing is used on something, it can't be reversed. I know you're thinking that it can't possibly have a use case," I added, seeing the sceptical looks on all their faces, "but I have it because I actually used it on the last two devices I have in the bag. I had to do so because I really think these last two devices could be dangerous, and I wanted to make sure that only one of each of them could exist. I really think they should stay in the control room at all times, and only be used for planning stuff or directly in the war effort."

I was glad that I had their complete attention now, and with a small grin, took the opportunity to glance at the spyer on the control panel. Lucien hadn't moved, but he was now in a meeting with Sebastian, of all people, and watched by a bunch of other Hammerhearts.

"This one," I withdrew the first of the devices, along with its companion, "is a brain booster. I actually used it on myself when I was in that cave; if I hadn't done, I may not have been able to come up with half the stuff I did. It basically forced my brain to operate at one hundred percent for a couple of hours so that I was able to get the most out of myself; and let me tell you, it really works. Being able to quickly think your way through something, using everything you've ever known or seen or heard, opens up a whole load of possibilities for strategising against Lucien.

"And that's exactly why it's so dangerous. If Lucien were capable of boosting his mind to full capacity, or even if he thought of doing that, we would be in all sorts of strife. Even worse than that would be if other Hammerhearts were able to do that, which is why I made it impossible to duplicate. Moreover, this thing," I held up the companion device, "is a self-destruct button. If a person pushes it three times in quick succession, the brain booster will vanish. That's to make sure that it can't be used if it falls into the wrong hands."

"Wow," James said, his eyes gleaming. "Yes, you definitely made the right decision with that one, John. I tend to think that Lucien probably is using magic like that, or that Fewul is providing him with the ability to think at full capacity; at least, it would explain why he's had such a sharp edge on us for the last week. Maybe that thing will give us a fair chance to catch up to him."

I nodded and said, "I should point out, though, that it takes a hell of a lot out of you when you use it. I only used it once and it gave me a couple of hours of high-energy thought, but when it wore off, I was bloody exhausted, as if I'd spent all that time wringing every last drop of thought out of my brain. I don't think you could use it twice in a row and not sleep in between without possibly doing some real damage to yourself. I suppose you could use the energy booster if you needed to keep yourself going afterwards, but I wouldn't advise taking it any further than that. Those sleeping devices are here for a reason, after all."

"It'll be nice to be almost as smart as JSandwich, for a change," Peter said, grinning at James.

"So was that it? The last two devices?" Marc asked, looking from the brain booster to its self-destruct device and back again.

"No, there's one more," I said, reaching into the bag and pulling the last two devices out. Like the brain booster, this one too came with a self-destruct component. "This one also can't be duplicated, and it really should be self-destructed if anyone gets hold of it who shouldn't have it. I think of it as the 'magic enhancer', except that's not really an accurate name. I was really trying to think of a way that we could get access to stronger magical power—more than we would be able to put into magical devices—and perhaps even more than Marc could get out of the Hero Crystal. There was no way to do that directly with the magic in that cave, but this device is the next best thing; and I know it works, because I tested it before I left the Rock.

"What it does is it transfers your fingerprint to the Sien-Leoard Crystal, wherever it is at the time. So long as that crystal can be magically traced, then this device will work. It's totally undetectable, so even if Lucien's using the crystal right then, or if Fewul's around, they won't have any idea that it's happening. All you have to do is put your finger on the pad on this device and think, just like you normally do when you're using magic," I looked between Amelia, Stella, Marc and Mr. Woodward, "and by transferring your fingerprint to the Sien-Leoard Crystal, it will enable you to use the magic from that crystal without needing to be anywhere near it."

"Holy crap," James breathed. "And you're absolutely sure that it works?"

"Definitely," I said, grinning and thinking back to how I had used it to manipulate the caves on Rock Haulter to suit my ends. Not only had that required powerful magic to do in the first place, but I had actually recognised the Sien-Leoard Crystal as I used its magic. I wouldn't have thought such a thing was possible, but it was. I wasn't going to tell them any of this, though; I fully planned to take my adventures of the previous evening, unspoken, to the grave. Then I remembered that I only had thirteen days left to do that, and all the pride I'd been feeling since I'd started showing off the devices vanished in a stroke.

The rest of the time before dinner was spent in the control room testing these new devices—except for the brain booster, which nobody was as yet brave enough to have a go at. I declined because even though I knew how well it would work, I also knew it would drain the hell out of me, and I didn't want that when we could still enact some sort of plan later tonight. Marc also attempted to fix the main flaw in the partial invisibility toggle; the best he could come up with was a flash, not unlike flash photography, when partial invisibility was toggled off, but no flash when it was turned on.

I didn't really join in with the enthusiastic testing, though, because I had a couple of other things on my mind. Firstly, not long after Marc and Erica were back in the base, James had taken the controls and steered us back to the Hammerheart base. As the testing got underway, he took us through Lucien's bedroom and into the small chamber beyond where Natalie was being held so that we could check on her and make sure she was okay. She was, for now: She was sitting on the floor against the wall on the left-hand side of the room, but seeing her like that was both better and worse than I had imagined. On one hand, she appeared not to be physically hurt—no bleeding or bruising that I could see—although she did look somewhat dishevelled. On the other hand, I had never seen someone looking so dispirited and defeated in my entire life. Her expression and body language told me plainly that she had given up on all hope of rescue, and probably expected that she would eventually die in that room, though not before Lucien put her through more unpleasantness than she had already faced.

The other distraction for me, once I had gotten over seeing Natalie in that state, was Stella. I hadn't forgotten how little she had contributed to the discussion all afternoon, that she hadn't said a word while I had explained the devices, and wasn't participating in the testing in any way. All she was doing was sitting in a seat and watching the proceedings, looking deep in thought, and her expression suggested that the things she was thinking about weren't particularly good things. I couldn't really talk to her here, though, and I didn't really want to pull her aside from the rest of the group, not after what had ended up happening between us a couple of days ago. All the same, I resolved that if we weren't required here in the control room after dinner, I would collar her and see if I could find out what was troubling her so much.

As luck would have it, we wouldn't be required in the control room that night—not until much later, anyway. Just before we went off to dinner, Marc and Amelia volunteered to remain in the control room and keep an eye on Lucien so that the rest of us could go and eat. I made sure I sat at the same table as Stella over dinner, along with Peter and James, and eventually Rebecca when she finally rocked up; and when everyone dispersed after the meal was done, I followed her out of the dining room and to the doors of the elevator. I wasn't sure if she had figured out that I was trying to get her alone, or if she had put herself in a position where I could get her alone if I chose to do so; either way, she didn't look surprised that I had followed her.

"I wanna talk with you," I told her, pushing the button to call the lift. "Can we go to one of our rooms?"

"Okay," she agreed, but didn't say anything else until I spoke again. Even when we were alone in the lift and rising towards the first floor and I was finally able to give her a proper hug, she merely reciprocated it, and not in a way that suggested she was really into it. She was clearly still distracted by something, and I was going to find out what.

I led her to my bedroom this time, shut the door behind us, and sat down on a seat at the table in the middle of the room (as opposed to the bed, this time). After glancing at the bed, Stella pulled a seat out beside me and sat down.

"What's on your mind?" I asked her without preamble. "I couldn't help noticing that you barely said a word all afternoon."

She opened her mouth and then hesitated, her face twitching as though she had been suddenly stirred by emotions she was trying to keep inside. After a few seconds she said, "Well yeah, I—I dunno how to explain it. I'm—" she gulped, and I could see the beginnings of tears in her eyes, "I'm just—so lost."

I reached out and grasped one of her hands in mine. I would have preferred to hug her again, and I probably would end up doing that if she really got crying, but that would mean getting up again. I wanted to comfort her, but I also wanted her to keep talking because I didn't understand what she meant. How could she be feeling lost when she was finally away from her family and surrounded by people who actually liked and respected her? I didn't want to say this, though, so I waited and watched her. After taking a few seconds to try to get herself back in control, she continued.

"You already know some of it, what I told you the other day before —well, you know. But it's—it's worse than that. I know how important all this is, that we have to do it for the good of everyone, but—but it's difficult to get myself up for it when I think—think that no matter what happens, I'll have nothing."

I took a moment to get my head around that. Finally, I squeezed her hand and said, "Well that's not exactly true. If we succeed, you'll have something you've never had before: a chance to make your own life. Now don't you think that's worth fighting for?"

She hesitated again and then said, "If it were that simple, then yeah, but what kind of life can you really expect a Hammerson to have? Even if I changed my name, I'll always be Arnold Hammerson's daughter to the rest of the world. I don't know if I can overcome that—and especially not—not without you."

Of course, just what I was afraid of. Whatever Stella was going through had been made worse by the knowledge that very soon, I would be dead and gone. That on its own was something I couldn't change, so I said, "Yeah, I know, but you've still got me for the next thirteen days, and even after that, you've still got plenty of people in here who'll support you. I'm sure Amelia and Marc, and even Peter, would have your back."

She smiled sadly. "I know, but it's not the same thing. I've had you for so much longer—I don't know if I can handle losing that. You know, I think our connection might be broken now too. I slept normally last night and I didn't think that was supposed to happen."

That took me by surprise, but only for a moment. With shock, I remembered that I had slept fully and dreamlessly the night before, something that I'd forgotten about until now. "Was the base in its shadow last night? Do you know?"

She shrugged. "I don't think so, but I guess I can't be sure."

But the more I thought about it, the more I thought she was probably right. The connection had been between our minds rather than our bodies, but while I had been dead, I had no mind for her to be connected to for that time. Did that mean this mind in this new body of mine would suddenly reconnect to her as it had been before? It seemed like a stretch to me, and the fact that I'd lost those magical enchantments I'd put on myself after my death seemed to back that up. Still, what existed between me and Stella was something very unique, so there was no way to be sure if it were still there.

"Then, maybe we'll find out tonight," I said reasonably. "I mean, we'll both be in the same dimension when we sleep, even if we don't sleep at the same time, so by tomorrow morning, we ought to know."

"I'm quite sure I already know," she said sadly. "I don't feel the same anymore. I can feel a spot of emptiness inside me where you were— where you had been since Lucien stuffed us up in his bedroom last week. It's there constantly, and very hard to ignore—I don't know if I'll ever be able to function with it there, and I suppose that only magic can put it right. don't you—don't you have it too?"

I tried to examine my mind to see if I did have anything like what she was talking about. What I found was worse. If I looked too hard, I would bring my attention back to that extra sense I'd had since I'd died —the one which connected me to the in-between. As far as my connection with Stella went, though, I felt a spot of sadness and loss, but no more than that. There was no empty feeling like she had described.

"Sorry," I said, "but I don't think I have anything like that. I guess when I was resurrected, I came back as though my mind were fully my own. That does seem to back up your theory that we're no longer connected, though, and maybe that's a good thing. How would it have felt for you if you'd been conscious the moment I'd died? At least this way, we don't have to find out."

That was when she started to cry and I got up and went to her, leaning down so that I could hug her. She hugged me back and cried against me, forcing me into a bit of a stoop over her which wasn't at all comfortable. I endured it for as long as I could, but not without taking action of my own: the time had come to use that enchantment I'd put on myself, the one that would cheer her up, only I didn't hit her with it all at once. Instead I very slowly and carefully poured it into her, allowing her to cry some of the bad feelings out of her before a more positive outlook began dawning in her mind. At least, that was the plan, and it eventually worked out that way.

"Thank you," she finally said, letting me go so that I could straighten up. "I think I needed that, but—but I think I need something else as well."

"Sure, anything," I said without thinking, only realising my mistake a second later when the words were already out of my mouth.

She looked shyly up at me, but also with a little determination, as though I had unintentionally given her a bit of extra courage as well. "Let me be your number one," she said, "just for a little while, while we still can."

My heart sank, not because I wanted to say no to her, but because I didn't really think that would be the best thing for her—right? "Er—I dunno if that's such a good idea."

The stricken expression on her face almost broke my heart, and I quickly added, "It's not that I don't want to. Look, if you're asking what I think you're asking, are you sure it would be a good thing for you? Wouldn't make it hurt more when it's over?"

She only looked pleadingly up at me, still sitting in her seat while I stood beside her. I was uncomfortably aware of our positions, and I had a feeling that Stella had deliberately stayed seated, though hugging would have been easier if she had stood, knowing that unless I also sat down, I would have to look down at her for this part of the conversation. Finally, she said, "It would be a good thing for me, and only I can really decide that. I need it, John, and maybe you do too. At the very least, you shouldn't have to be alone for the rest of your life."

Interesting choice of words, I thought, but didn't say that. I understood her point, though, and perhaps if I was exactly the same now as I had always been, it would have been a valid one, but I had changed a bit since my resurrection. My own loneliness didn't really matter anymore, knowing that there was an end in sight, and it really wasn't very far away. On the flipside, though, for my own sake, there wouldn't be any harm in taking some enjoyment for myself while I still could. Because Stella had successfully refuted my main point: I really didn't have a right to decide what would be best for her in the long-term.

"It's hard to argue with that logic," I said, smiling unwillingly.

She also smiled, her face a little flushed and her eyes bright. "I love you, John."

That knocked me for a loop. I had a pretty good idea that she felt that way, not only from her mind, but because she had actually mentioned that she'd fallen in love with me when she had told me of her 'real imaginary friend' on the day when Lucien had infiltrated our old base. But to hear her come out and say it so boldly was really something; only Natalie had ever been able to have such an effect on me, and she had done it in much the same way—by declaring her love for me while the two of us had been locked in a pitch-black prison cell together. No other girl had actually said those words to me, not even Serena in the two-and-a-half months of our relationship.

"I love you too, Stella," I told her after only a small hesitation, hoping that she was right, and that I wouldn't be making things worse for her in the long run by letting her have this. I wasn't being entirely dishonest: I probably *did* love Stella, even now that our connection had probably broken, but it somehow didn't sound very fair to say it. For one thing, I probably didn't love her as much as she loved me. For another thing, my feelings for her weren't at all like my feelings for Natalie; and yet they were strong enough in their own right to be no less real. There was never a question of not saying the words, though. Not only would that have been like a slap in the face, one which she didn't deserve, but there was still enough truth in the words to make them justifiable. Not for the first time, I found myself thinking that if it weren't for Natalie, things with Stella would be so much less complicated.

She beamed, stood up and threw her arms around me. I embraced her in return, and we stood like that for about a minute, pressed against each other, neither one willing to let go. I had become a little aroused while I'd been standing there, but I had chosen not to try to do anything about it, even though I could have used the magic—the same magic I'd used just a couple of days ago—to help progress things along with her a bit. Eventually, she pulled back from me a bit so that we could look into each other's faces.

Before she could say anything, or I could splutter something embarrassing, I kissed her. It was intense and somehow deeper than the ones we had shared two days ago, but as I led her to my bed, wanting to sit with her but also not wanting to let her go, it had ended up taking us to the same place. We had spent the rest of the evening together and we had ended up sleeping together as well, but something else had happened in between those two things. At a little before eleven o'clock, after we had been on my bed for more than three hours, someone knocked on my bedroom door, making both of us start.

"Hey John, are you in there? Sorry if I woke you, but you gotta come quick. We're having a meeting in the control room—a really important one. Get up and come down as quick as you can, and don't worry about getting dressed if you're in your PJs."

Chapter 12: Mission Confirmed

Stella and I were frozen in place as we listened to Peter's voice outside my bedroom door, neither of us really wanting him to know what was happening in here. We waited until we heard his footsteps move away, and then a little more distantly, but still clear enough to hear, we heard him knocking on Stella's bedroom door and calling to her to wake up and come down to the control room as quickly as she could. A minute later, and even more distantly, we heard the sound of the lift doors opening and closing, but both of us were already in motion by then.

"Oh God, something's happened," she moaned, gazing at me. The two of us had slowly collapsed from where we had been before into a side-by-side position on the bed.

"It'd have to be the worst thing yet for them to call on us this late," I agreed, not wanting to get up, but knowing that I had no choice. Someone else would no doubt come up here if I didn't show my face in the control room very soon, and the last thing Stella needed was to still be in my room if that happened.

I gave her one last hug and a quick kiss, wanting to do more but knowing that I wouldn't want to stop if I started again. I then scrambled off the bed and scrambled back into the clothes I had been wearing that day. Stella watched me for a bit before she too got up and re-dressed herself. I thought I probably looked okay, but Stella looked a bit messed up, as if she'd spent the last few hours rolling around in a bed that may or may not have been her own. I hoped that she could pass it off as having been asleep when Peter knocked; and nothing more than that. I ought not to care what people thought of me and Stella doing this, but for some reason, I really didn't want anyone else to know.

"Give me a couple of minutes' head-start," I told her, going to the door and pausing with my hand on the doorknob, looking back at her. "Take a moment to—I dunno, wash your face or something, just so that it's not obvious we were together."

She shrugged. "I think you're over-thinking it a bit. We could feasibly take the lift down together without having been in the same place beforehand, but okay. I'll wash my face or something. Actually I wouldn't mind a drink of water while I'm at it."

That made me aware of how thirsty I was too. In fact, now that I noticed it, I was utterly parched. It was no mystery why, of course. I decided to get a drink later on, though; whatever was going on in the control room was probably more urgent, and I wanted to take a moment to think about something else in my brief moment of privacy as I took the lift down.

I had done something with Stella that I hadn't consciously done with any other girl I'd been with up until this point. Yes, I had foolishly had unprotected sex with Lena and Stella in the Big Room that day, but that had been carelessness, not a conscious decision. Even when I had been with May, I had only not worn a condom because according to her, it wouldn't have mattered if I did or didn't. Tonight, though, I had very consciously decided not to use protection, and for whatever reason (perhaps I would ask her later), she hadn't objected, or even noticed so far as I was aware.

And the reason I had made that decision? Well, it was a strange one, and even now I wasn't sure if it had been a good one. It had certainly been a selfish one, because at its core it was based on my animalistic drive to spread my seed as far and wide as possible. I supposed I could have tried to justify it, to say that I had been trying to give Stella a gift, but that would have felt like a cop-out, even if there were a small nugget of truth to it. The greater truth was that I wanted to leave part of myself behind after I died, and although I couldn't know if I had actually gotten Stella pregnant tonight, I had certainly given it my best shot, and even now, whatever it might mean for her down the track, I hoped it had worked.

When I entered the control room, I found all the same people who had been there to greet me when I had returned to the base that day (minus Stella) along with a few others: Katie, Sophie, Siobhan and Felicity. It transpired that those four had been Erica's research group, and the fact that they were here meant that they must have found something significant.

"Do you know if Stella's coming, John?" Peter asked, and I started guiltily. "I knocked on her door but didn't hear anything from her room. Did you see her up there?"

I shrugged as indifferently as I could. "I didn't see her, but give her a bit longer. If she was asleep then she would probably wanna get dressed again before coming down here. What's been happening tonight? Has Lucien been up to much?"

The change of subject was very deliberate, and thankfully, it was successful in directing their attention away from Stella.

"Well, James was right in his guess earlier," Amelia said. "It looks like he's going to put all his prisoners on trial. Anyone who repents for their opposition to Lucien will get a long prison sentence, while those who don't will be put to death. He said it was harsh, but necessary, to show the world that he was serious."

"And by now, of course, the public is clamouring for blood," said Mr. Woodward, "after all the propaganda of the last two days. They might actually think he's a bit soft for sparing the repentant ones, but Lucien plans to say that it's mercy, and that it's fair to give people a second chance if they're truly sorry and mean to do better."

I rolled my eyes. "But the whole thing would be a show. He could put them all on his side with magic if he wanted. Would he actually sacrifice their lives just to set an example to the rest of the world?"

"Don't look so shocked, John," said Lillian. "It doesn't take pure evil to condemn countless strangers to death with what might seem to us like a trivial justification. That sort of thing has been happening all throughout the world since time out of mind, and it always comes back to one thing: power. Lucien is intent on consolidating his, so he'll be more than ready to sacrifice any random number of nameless, faceless individuals for his cause."

"I guess," I said, not liking her words but knowing they were true. They were certainly an explanation for the atrocities he had already committed so far—the hundreds upon hundreds of bodies paving his path to power—and him being possessed by evil was just too much of an over-simplification to cover it. Acts of terrorism, mass slaughters, and false flag operations had all been happening before our generation; what Lucien was doing was really not a lot different from a typical tyrant anywhere in the world, the only difference being that he had so much more power than any tyrant before him.

That conversation was put to rest at that point by Stella finally arriving in the control room, and if I didn't know better, I would swear that she had been woken up and hurried to dress herself and get down here as quickly as possible.

"Sorry," Peter told her, "but this is important."

"Yeah, I figure," she said, taking a seat not far from me, but not close enough to surreptitiously touch each other. "How's she doing?"

She had just asked the question I had been ready to ask before she had turned up. The display screen showed that we were still parked in the room where Lucien was holding Natalie. On the outside, her condition hadn't changed at all; she looked as hopeless as ever.

A few looks were swapped before Marc said, "She's refusing to eat now. She's—she's lost her will to fight on, and wouldn't eat anything when I tried to give her something earlier. I practically had to force water down her throat with the crystal—it's bad."

He was leaving something out, I felt sure of it, but I didn't know if they were protecting my feelings or Rebecca's by not sharing the full extent of Natalie's misery. Before I could ask any questions, before I could even think of a follow-up question, James changed the subject.

"This won't take long," he said. "In fact, we probably could have waited till morning, as we're not going to act on anything tonight, but I thought that maybe it would be beneficial for you all to know what Erica and her team found so that you can think about it through the night, or morning, or whatever."

"In other words, he thinks you should hear the prophecy and get the wording in your heads now so that when we meet to talk about it tomorrow, we've all had a chance to think it over," Erica said. "We found a lot of really interesting stuff, and maybe some of it is worth spending time over later, but it was Katie who found the prophecy we're pretty sure is the one Lisa was talking about. At least, it matches what you described, John."

"Well, when it comes to prophecies, it's usually pretty obvious if it's the right one once you read it," I said. "At least, that's how it's been for the other two important ones I know of. The rest of their meaning may not be obvious, but that one fact usually is."

"Well, let's find out," Katie said, lifting her phone out of her lap (I hadn't even seen it sitting there), and beginning to tap the screen. "I copied it down so that we wouldn't have to bring the whole encyclopedia down here. Hang on…"

It took about half a minute for her to get to it, during which James said, "It sounds a bit different from the other two. It's not rhyming like they are, but it's written in such a way that it really does sound prophetic. You'll see what I mean."

"Here," Katie said, and then she began to read the words off the screen. As she did so, I felt my blood run cold. Just as I had said, it was very obvious that this was the right prophecy;

When end times come, the world fades to black.
He rises above, as the world around him falls.
Chaos unrivalled, he revels, he cares not his folly.
The box is open, there is no turning back.
And magic reigning, raining, changing, arranging, pouring, roaring,
searing, disappearing.
The last Sorcerer will take it all.

A long silence followed this. Pale faces looked around at other pale faces as we all digested what we had just heard. It was very cryptic, but it painted a horrible picture. While it did sound like it meant the world would end, rather than just magic ending, I supposed there was wriggle room to interpret it some other way; and given that it was a prophecy, we needed to hold onto that hope. But above all of that, my main thought was that it sounded like Lucien was going to make things a whole lot worse before we could stop him, and that he would be so reckless with his powers that yes, the world really was in danger of coming to an end by his hand.

Finally, Marc spoke up. "Okay. Okay, so the way I heard that, it sounds like Lucien will bring about chaos that will end the world as we know it. At least, I think that's what it said, which means it could be that he ends the world or that he transforms it in such a way that it won't be recognisable."

"But the last part said the last Sorcerer will take it all," Peter said. "What does that mean? Does it just mean that he'll possess all the magic in the world and never let it go?"

"It could," James agreed, "but it could also mean that Lucien will have all the magic when the world comes to an end, so no one else gets to have it. That doesn't sound promising either. Katie, can you read it again?"

She did so, and as I heard the words a second time, I tried to think how Lisa could have interpreted it to mean that magic itself would come to an end rather than the whole world. As Katie read the last part, I thought maybe I understood. It did say that magic would be 'disappearing', but only after it roars and changes and causes all sorts of chaos. As for the last Sorcerer 'taking it all', it could just mean that he ruins it for everyone—that he brings about the end of magic by his actions. Except Lucien wouldn't knowingly do that, which meant that it would have to be our actions that made that happen. Would the prophecy still fit if we were responsible for that part?

"Okay," Mr. Woodward said, "so when I hear that, I think that almost all of it is nothing we ourselves couldn't have predicted. In fact, you could even say that it's already happening, although the words used in the prophecy make it sound like it's going to get a lot worse before it gets better—*if* it gets better. I think the most important part of the prophecy is the line about magic; raining and arranging and all that. Can I see your phone, Katie?"

Taken aback, she handed it to him without protest, and he read the words silently for himself. Then he said, "It's two different spellings of 'rain', not the one word repeated for emphasis." He spelt them out for us as he handed the phone back to Katie, then said, "What I'm not sure about is how important each of those words is, or if they're only there to paint a picture."

I spoke up then, telling them what I had just gathered from those words, then added, "I dunno about the rest of it though, except that it sounds like Lucien will throw magic around all over the place, and it will touch everything in some way. Maybe it's as if magic needs to go through some sort of explosion before it can end, like a supernova or something."

"Good theory, John," James said approvingly. "One thing that the prophecy doesn't specifically say is that Lucien himself has to be the one to bring magic to an end. It does say that he'll rise above, and that he commits some sort of folly, but like Mr. Woodward said, that could easily apply to what's going on right now. Maybe the thing that brings magic to an end could be in response to the last Sorcerer, rather than the last Sorcerer himself. When you're looking at it from a distance, they could mean the same thing—that it's because of Lucien that all this is happening, not just what he's doing but what we're doing as well. Does that—does that make any sense?"

"If you're saying what I think you're saying," Amelia said slowly, "then we need to be the ones to destroy magic. I guess it doesn't say that Lucien will definitely destroy the world—"

"Actually, it kinda does," James pointed out. "It calls this period 'end times', and it calls him 'the last Sorcerer'. If we don't end magic, then something else will happen to ensure that he is the last Sorcerer. It could be that Lucien makes himself immortal and hogs all the power for eternity, which would be bad enough; but it could be that he ends all of us, including himself."

"There is another possibility," Siobhan spoke up suddenly. She blushed when we all looked at her, but she managed to say, "Well—what if the prophecy isn't talking about Lucien at all, but someone else way down the line? What if there's some other way?"

I didn't believe that for a second, but I didn't say so. Judging by the looks on most of the faces in the room, nobody else really believed it either, but to their credit, they didn't speak up; and a few people, like James and Mr. Woodward, actually considered her alternative. Finally, though, James said, "That seems unlikely to me, but even if it's not Lucien, we have to assume the worst possibility. Lucien's actions suggest that he intends to be the last Sorcerer, at least for now, so we have to fight him on that level."

"Which means what for us?" Rebecca asked.

A few looks were swapped, and then James said what I had been expecting him to say almost since I had heard the prophecy. "It means we have to destroy the Magic Crystals ourselves. I'm still not sure how, but that's something we can figure out while we're here. Maybe they can self-destruct if the person using them knows what they're doing."

"Wait, hang on," Marc protested, and I noticed that he looked alarmed. I couldn't blame him for becoming protective of the Hero Crystal, but I couldn't deny James's logic as per usual. "Surely there's another way to do this. Do we really need to actually destroy them? Can't we just destroy the crystal chips so that there are no Sorcerers anymore?"

That actually sounded like a better idea to me, but James was quick to put a wet blanket over it. "Even if that were possible to do without wrecking the Hero Crystal, Marc, it wouldn't actually solve the problem. We mightn't have the six normal Sorcerers any more, but we would still have people with magic. Anyone in possession of a crystal would have magic, which would technically make them a Sorcerer. Lucien still has the Sien-Leoard Crystal, so even without his crystal chips, he might be a little less dangerous but he could still be the last Sorcerer. All he would need to do is make sure he's the one and only person to possess the crystals, and that would be it. We can't afford to take that chance."

Marc was frowning and he looked like he wanted to continue arguing, but he couldn't seem to think of anything to say. I supposed he would fight James on this one, and I really couldn't blame him for wanting to—it would have to hurt to give up the Hero Crystal again—but unfortunately, James was right. It needed to be done and we would have to make Marc understand that, or force him to comply if he didn't. Then I remembered that out of everyone here, Marc was the only one with an independent source of magic. He was the most powerful person in the Young Army, which would make it just about impossible to wrest the Hero Crystal from him if he fought to protect it. That was a very nasty thought, and I forced my mind to scoot away from it in a hurry.

"Okay," Amelia said after a brief silence, resting a hand on Marc's shoulder, seeming to have noticed how worked up he was. "Okay, so we need to try to figure out if there's a way to destroy the Magic Crystals, but in the meantime, we need to get them all. We have three of them now, which is a good start, but unless we can figure out a way to get the Sien-Leoard Crystal off Lucien, the plan's gonna fail anyway. Also, we need to get the Darkness Crystal so that we can destroy that too."

"Damn it," I said, and swore under my breath. "If only we had figured this out twenty-four hours ago, I could have gone and got it. Tommy and I are the only ones who know where we hid it, and he might have forgotten by now."

And Rock Haulter was sealed off from us until November, of course. Then again, we had gotten around that once before. In fact, if you counted me being resurrected there, we had gotten around it twice before. I had given myself access to the time axis this time for a purpose exactly like this one, but before I could say any of this to the others, who didn't know about that extra ability of mine, Peter came up with another idea.

"Underwood is still on Rock Haulter. Do you think he would consent to retrieve it if you told him how?"

"Er—well, it's worth a shot," I said, trying to think of everything as quickly as I could. "We designed it so that only a person who knew it was there, and who had their own source of magic, could get it, but I suppose Underwood could get around that last restriction if he created devices specifically designed to get it out—or if he put those enchantments on himself. I guess the main question is, would he want to? It would mean leaving Rock Haulter, and he seemed pretty reluctant to do that when we left."

"That was more than two weeks ago, as far as he's concerned," James said. "He certainly wasn't enthusiastic then, but he may have opened up a bit more since he's found out more about what's going on out here. He must understand that while he may be safe in there for now, he's also pretty much defenceless, and certainly alone. We may talk about him like he's an idiot, but I think Smiley may have educated him pretty well in the brief time they were together. Maybe he'll understand how important it is and do his bit."

"I'll ask him when we're done here," I told them. "I'll contact him telepathically. Better to do it tonight, since he's six hours behind us where he is, but even in the best case scenario, we can't expect to see him until tomorrow."

The conversation continued for a while after that, but no new ideas were forthcoming. Katie, Sophie, Siobhan and Felicity were the first to leave, and Lillian Woodward wasn't too far behind them. Only at this point did James remind us of something else that I had totally forgotten about until now: When it came time to destroy the crystals, we would have the backing of Sien and Leoard themselves, as we had kept our promise to them by me sacrificing my soul to come back from the dead. I wasn't sure if that necessarily applied, given what we would be trying to do with that power, but I hoped that he was right.

Mr. Woodward had been selected, or had selected himself, to keep an eye on things during the night in the control room—a boring job if Lucien slept through the night, but an important one in case he didn't. I had glanced once at the spyer still following Lucien while we had been talking; he had finished his work for the day and was now in bed with Lena, and they were definitely not asleep. Natalie, on the contrary, had fallen asleep, curled up on the floor in a foetal position in the torture chamber where she had now been kept for more than twenty-four hours. I felt sad as I watched her, but what could we do to help? If Marc really couldn't free her, and everything we tried to do to make her more comfortable would result in escalating retaliations from Lucien, there was basically nothing.

The rest of us had trickled off to bed between midnight and half-past-twelve. Marc and Amelia had gone first, and the last I saw of them was what looked like a quiet but intense argument. I felt a deep sense of unease as the elevator doors closed on them: what if Marc couldn't let go? What if he really *did* fight us on what could be our only chance to save the world? Wanting to take my mind off this thought, I had gone up to my bedroom alone a few minutes later, giving Stella a look that I hope she understood to mean 'don't follow me too quickly'; where I had then settled myself on my bed so that I could mentally converse with Jacob Underwood. It wasn't easy, because sleepiness was creeping up on me in a hurry—I had used the sleep inducer before leaving the control room to give myself six hours of deep sleep, and the magic would take hold quite soon.

I had interrupted him during his dinner, but he seemed in a good enough mood and was glad to know that I had made it back safely. He asked how things were going, and I told him that they weren't great but that we had a plan for making them better. I then asked him if he would be willing to help us with something and his response took me by surprise. He was ready and willing to help, although it would depend somewhat on what it was we wanted him to do. I was glad to know that, but I didn't get my hopes up yet—I needed to know if he would be willing to leave the Rock and join us as part of the mission, something I still felt he would probably be reluctant to do, but I asked the question just the same.

His response was cautious, but that wasn't necessarily a bad sign. He wanted to know why, and I told him that we needed him to retrieve something for us that we had left there—something very powerful that needed to be kept away from anyone who might use it for bad deeds. He asked why we wanted it, and I told him that we intended to destroy it. He asked if it would be possible for him to teleport it to us rather than him have to carry it himself, and I paused long enough to give it some thought, but my belief was that while it might be worth a try, it probably wouldn't work. Even if the portals didn't resist such things, the crystal itself might resist it. In my experience, the crystals only liked to teleport when the operator of the magic was going with them.

He asked me a question that was only really a half-question, and a half-statement: it was obviously very important that this job be done, and we needed him to do it. I could tell that he understood, but I answered in the affirmative anyway. The telepathic communicator went silent then, and remained so for a short time, during which I was interrupted by a soft knock upon my door. I got up to let Stella in, seeing that the hall behind her was empty before I shut the door; and when I returned to the communicator, Underwood had given me his answer.

We made a few more arrangements, agreeing that he would let us know when he was out of the portal, and we would pick him up in or around his old apartment back in London. He wouldn't be untraceable, unfortunately, but hopefully Lucien wouldn't think to look for him; and if he did, well we would have to fight him, if not for Underwood's wellbeing then certainly for the valuable cargo. I had also visualised the hiding place, how we had made it and how we had gotten there, and included that horrible monster that had almost done us in while we had been hiding the crystal—he would need to know that in case it was still there, and so that nothing else would surprise him. Finally, I advised him to wait until daylight to make the journey, even if it meant we wouldn't get the crystal until sometime tomorrow afternoon or evening. Given that we still didn't know how to destroy the crystals we had, let alone that one, it wouldn't matter if we got it a little late, just so long as Lucien didn't get it.

At last, we signed off, and I stowed the communicator back in my top bedside drawer before turning to Stella. She had settled herself on the bed beside me while I had finished with Underwood, watching me earnestly but not making any physical contact, probably not wanting to distract me. It also served the purpose of not letting him know that she was right there beside me, which was good; given their own brief history, during which Stella had tried to seduce the life assistant out of his possession, and had performed a sexual act on him along the way (though refusing to go all the way, and so ultimately failing in her mission). I didn't need him to know that she was now, for all intents and purposes, my girlfriend.

"How did it go?" she asked me, snuggling in close.

"He's on board," I yawned, putting my arms around her. "Sometime tomorrow, probably later in the day, he'll be back in here. I guess a few people won't be happy about that, but they'll have to deal with it."

"I'm one of them," she said, "but I'll deal with it, especially now."

"Especially now?" I repeated, not sure what she meant, a little slow on the uptake, but I got it when she responded by kissing me on the lips.

We continued to snuggle, and I continued to get drowsier. And yet, we both remained in a sitting position for now; in my case, it was because I knew that if I lay down I would fall asleep very quickly, and I didn't really want to sleep just yet. I was enjoying this feeling with Stella too much, and what was more, even though I was tired, I was also becoming more and more aroused by how close her body was to mine. Even after the three plus hours we had spent locked in each other's arms and bodies, I still wanted more of her; and though I couldn't be sure until she said it outright, I had a feeling she wanted the same.

"We really should sleep," I said, yawning and not wanting to follow my own advice.

"Yeah, but can we do something first?" she asked.

"Sure," I said, my hopes rising. I was up to it if she was.

"Make love to me," she said, taking me by surprise, but only for a moment. "Not like how it was earlier, but more—I dunno how to describe it—"

"I know what you mean," I told her, and I did. What we had done earlier, both on Tuesday and earlier this evening, had been letting off a whole load of sexual steam that had been building up for a while—a *long* while, in her case. What she wanted now was more of an emotional connection, and even though I was fourteen going on fifteen (though I would die just shy of my fifteenth birthday now), I understood the difference after my brief but highly active sex life. While I had now had sex with eight different females, I had only really made love to Natalie, and possibly Amelia, though I hadn't thought of it in those terms at the time. I hadn't felt anything close to real love when I'd been with Tulip, Lena, May or Larissa; and even in my time with Serena, I didn't think we'd actually had a connection quite that deep.

None of this actually flashed through my mind as I sat beside Stella though. Well, no, a small part of it did—I was reminded of my time with Natalie, my regretfully short time with her, and how deep that connection had got in just the three full days we had gotten together before the shit had hit the fan. I had a moment to feel deeply sorry for Natalie where she was right now; she didn't deserve whatever was coming her way if we couldn't get her out of there, but I quickly turned my thoughts away from that. Quite apart from being depressing, it was also disrespectful to think about Natalie when I was about to make love to Stella.

And make love we did. It felt very good and made me feel very close to her, even though we were about to find out for absolute certain that our connection was probably broken. Strangely, far from what I would have expected before I got with her, I wouldn't have resented the connection being there—at least some of the time—if it meant that we could have another one of those mental orgasms that we'd accidentally had together after Lucien had strengthened our connection. And the rest of the time, if one of us entered the other's body, if we knew it was happening, we could use that time to give the other some enjoyment.

After that we both fell asleep very quickly, both of us waking up together exactly six hours later, where it was after seven o'clock in the morning and breakfast had already started. We didn't go straight down, though, because Stella decided to join me in my own shower rather than go back to her own room to use hers, and of course, that had resulted in us spending more time than was strictly necessary in the bathroom; and that had been followed by both of us taking much longer than was necessary to get ourselves ready for the day. Well actually, that last part is a lie; we weren't really getting anything ready in most of that time.

Only after half past eight, when breakfast would really be winding down, did we finally snap out of it and seriously get ready. Stella had snuck back to her room then, the hall outside being thankfully empty, while I had gotten dressed and gone straight down to breakfast alone as I was. Only when I got down there did I realise how much we had missed while we had been preoccupied with each other, and how big this Friday, September 3, was likely to be.

Chapter 13: All Out Attack

The dining room was mostly empty when I got down there, but the atmosphere given off by the small number of people in there, none of whom I knew really well save a few adults, was very tense. When I had stepped out of the elevator and walked over to the dining room, I had also heard the sounds coming from the lounge room where most of the teenagers seemed to be hanging out, and it sounded tense in there too. Worried, I quickly ate a piece of toast and then hurried down to the control room with a second piece. In there, I found Marc, Amelia, Peter, James, Mr. Woodward and Lillian Woodward, and they were as tense as anyone.

"Morning, sleepyhead," Peter said to me as I joined them. "What possessed you to take so long getting up today, of all days?"

"I felt like I needed an extra hour," I lied. "What's going on?"

"She's still refusing to eat," Marc said in a low voice, seeing where I was looking. On the display screen, Natalie was curled up in a ball on the floor of her prison; she looked ragged and utterly defeated.

Not wanting to look at that any longer, I switched my gaze to the spyer following Lucien. He appeared to be in a conference room of some sort and was speaking to reporters; either it was live television or some sort of footage for later. He looked very serious indeed, and remembering the tension I'd sensed all around the base since I'd gotten up, I knew it must have been another terrorist incident, no doubt worse than all the others…

But I turned out to be wrong—or rather, half-wrong.

"He's escalating big-time now," James said quietly, also seeing where I was looking. "He hasn't done it yet, but he plans to use a nuclear weapon in the very near future if we don't all hand ourselves over to him."

I froze, gagged and spluttered, "*What?*"

"There's a video floating around on the Internet," Amelia told me, "of about half a dozen men, all Asian and Pakistani, talking in another language and wearing radiation suits. It said they had stolen four nuclear weapons earlier in the year after the Pakistani government fell to the Hammerhearts, but before the Hammerhearts had full control of the region. It even showed the weapons on the screen. They said they'll set the nukes off in strategic locations if their demands aren't met, and they're already working on plans to transport the bombs to those locations. Lucien told his Hammerhearts that the threat looked credible, because four nukes really *have* gone missing from Pakistan, but in public he's downplaying it, saying that they could have been fakes."

"So—so these are the terrorists Lucien's really worried about?" I asked, my blood going cold. This was a whole different kind of enemy than we were used to dealing with. I glanced at the spyer again, and yes —Lucien *did* look worried; I didn't think it was fake. Except…that didn't add up. With Fewul on his side, Lucien would have the power to strip those people of the bombs in an instant.

When I spoke this thought, Marc said, "Well, his public explanation for that is that the men seem to be using magic to make themselves impossible to trace, and we all know what that means, but that's not the real reason. None of us were awake early enough to see it, but Lucien created the whole thing himself; made sure it leaked, first to the police and then on the Internet, and then acted all surprised when he was informed about it. We only know the truth because Amelia, James and I came down here in time to see him telling Natalie about it. He told her that the time to be treated well had now passed, and he has been forced into this position by our unwillingness to roll over and accept him as our ruler. Like James said, he's planning on using one if we don't hand ourselves over to him tonight."

"Tonight?" I choked. No wonder everyone around here looked so serious.

"We're not going to let that happen," Mr. Woodward said firmly. "At least, we're going to do our level best to make sure that doesn't happen."

"But how?" I asked, my mind racing. "Even if we find the nukes and vanish them, he can just get more from somewhere else—or create his own. We can't stop him by being reactive."

Which meant that there were only two ways to stop this: take Lucien out sometime today, before he had a chance to do this evil deed, or hand ourselves over to him as he planned, and end the final resistance against him. The former would certainly be preferable if it were possible, but *was* it possible?

"Agreed," James said, "which means we have to attack him as much as possible today. We have the Light, Villain and Hero Crystals, as well as all our devices, including all those new ones you created, John. We have a lot of things to try, but I fear that no matter what we do, Fewul will find a way to keep Lucien safe. That's why we need to prioritise our own safety first; we can't afford to let ourselves fall victim to the sort of thing that's happened to Natalie."

"I suggest we all get in the Time Box and start planning what to do first," Peter said, "because whatever we do, if it fails, there's gonna be a retaliation. He might end up setting all four of those things off instead of just one."

It was a good idea, so that was what the six of us did. Stella came into the room just as we were getting in the box; James told her to get in as well, then we explained the whole thing to her before we settled down to our planning. We were in an interesting dilemma, where we had so many things we wanted to try and yet there was a strange sense among all of us that whatever we did probably wouldn't work. At one point, I was asked about Underwood and the Darkness Crystal; I told them that we could expect him to turn up here later in the day, but that we probably shouldn't try to use the Darkness Crystal to attack Lucien—it was just too evil to be relied upon.

We spent a good long while in the Time Box; long enough that all of us were starving by the time we came out, even though only a little over twenty minutes had passed on the outside. We went upstairs to eat a quick very-early lunch before going into the lounge room and recruiting Erica, Rebecca, Harry, Simon, Katie, Sophie, Liam, Darcy, Felicity, Jessica, Siobhan and even Tommy; and then returning to the control room to get started. A little while longer was spent bringing the recruits up to speed—though not long enough to fully explain the abilities of all the various devices we would be using—and by ten o'clock, we were ready to go.

The first part of the plan was to trap Lucien within a small area where we could attack him. Marc would create an anti-teleportation ring around the area—like what we had once done in an attempt to trap Hall so that we could wrest the Villain Crystal from him—only this one would have to be even stronger, since Lucien was now able to teleport through the Hammersons' anti-teleportation spells at will. Of course, we couldn't know if Marc's spell would work, but we knew that he was capable of coming up with something that would work, based on his untraceability 2.0 spell which was still resisting all of Lucien's attempts to figure it out.

A few people would be remaining in the control room, all of them agreeing to do so. Lillian Woodward, being by far the oldest of us, was chosen to stay back in the base and work the control panel to keep up with the battle, and draw us back in if necessary. Harry and Simon would also remain behind, ready to lock any Hammerhearts up if we happened to capture them throughout the battle. Jessica would also remain behind, in possession of the Light Crystal and using it throughout the battle to try to keep light and luck on our side. She felt confident enough doing this once James had shown her how to use it and she had felt it go warm in her hand. Siobhan would be responsible for dealing with Fewul at every possible opportunity, by continually pressing the button to recall the Beast of Magic the moment it looked like it was interfering. We knew that Lucien could call it back just about instantly, and probably in the middle of a battle without missing a step, thanks to his Honnie powers of concentration; but we still needed to try it, if only to make it as difficult as possible for him. Marc had even modified the device to make it more effective; it had originally been set so that the person would need to hold the button down for five seconds before the magic was activated, for reasons that had made sense at the time, but such things would only get in the way now.

The shape of the attack would be similar to how it had been on Wednesday, but with a few crucial differences. One was the anti-teleportation ring, which ought to prevent Lucien escaping with a prisoner. Another was the device I had created to shield the crystals from magical tracing, which ought to protect them from what had happened to Natalie. Finally, we had yet more weapons that Lucien didn't know about, which would hopefully give us a fighting chance against him. After what had happened to Natalie, nobody initially wanted to take the Villain Crystal, but Stella had eventually agreed, saying she had a lot of resentment towards Lucien after all he'd done in the last three days, and she could probably harness it through the crystal. She would be leading the attack, while Marc would play the same role he had on Wednesday— holding the outside and protecting the rest of us from Lucien's inevitable retaliations.

We even had a plan for luring him to our chosen battlefield, which was the deserted courtyard in Chopville High. Doing it there would be better than trying to take him out wherever he happened to be at the time, where it would probably be easy for him to call in reinforcements. Of course, he would probably recognise that we were baiting him—he wasn't an idiot—but he would have to, at the very least, send someone to investigate what we were doing. If the someone who came to investigate wasn't Lucien himself, Lillian would capture them in the base, and Harry and Simon would force them into our prison. Given the enchantments in the control room, it wouldn't be a difficult job for them.

Lillian got her practice operating the controls as she took us from the Hammerheart Base to Chopville High, regrettably leaving Natalie behind with no way to keep an eye over her, but there was nothing we could do about that except hope that she would be okay. Marc told me, at one point while we had been in the Time Box, that the previous night (while I'd been with Stella), Hignat and Wilwog had approached Lucien and asked for permission to rape Natalie but he had turned them down, saying they hadn't done anything to earn that reward. That most likely meant that only Lucien was capable of getting into the room where she was held, and when I expressed this view it was more or less confirmed, although Marc and James did swap an uneasy look, making me sure that once again, they weren't telling me something. With all that was about to go down, I let it go—for now.

One by one, the fighting force were let out of the base. I was let out third, right behind Marc and Stella, and right before James. We were already under an invisibility veil, a soundproof barrier, thinking cap simulators, and protected by spells that would cause other spells to pass right through us. Marc had even put an enchantment on the invisibility veil and soundproof barrier to cause revealing spells to pass right through it, theoretically making it impossible for Lucien, or even Fewul, to expose us. Some people, when they got out of the base, immediately moved along the fourth dimension at a pace to one side or the other, where the rest of us could see them as though they were ghosts. That was all part of the plan, increasing the angles from which we could attack Lucien, and hopefully increasing protection for some of us as well.

Marc had already set to work, walking in a wide circle around the courtyard, performing a spell on the boundary so that he could activate magic upon the area without needing to walk around us every time, and so that he could only activate the anti-teleportation portion of the spell after Lucien had teleported inside it. To top it off, the ring itself was untraceable, so that even if Lucien figured out what was happening he wouldn't be able to use his own magic to affect the spells surrounding him. His only way out would be to physically get outside the area, and while it would be possible to prevent that by turning the circle into a four-dimensional physical barrier, we had decided against that just in case we ourselves got into trouble and needed to escape.

At last, we were truly ready to go. Marc walked to the centre of the circle where Stella and I were waiting and prepared to set the bait. It would be my job to set the trigger, along with James; in my case because I could communicate telepathically without needing to hold a communications device. I let Jessica, who was holding a communicator along with the Light Crystal back in the control room, know that we were ready; and she in turn let me know that Lucien had just returned to the Hammerheart base. The time couldn't have been more perfect, and I let her know that it was about to begin.

"Go for it, James," I told him.

James was standing further back in the circle, hopefully well away from where Lucien would teleport in. Sadly, that was one variable we couldn't control, and we would have to quickly regroup once he came down in the circle somewhere. The hope was that he would teleport close to Marc in the centre; that way he would be closest to those most dangerous to him, even though once he was in, Marc would be getting out of his way as quickly as he could. James was further back because even though he had some fighting experience, he wouldn't be as agile if Lucien was able to land spells on us. Katie, Sophie, Erica and Rebecca were further back in the circle as well, though in their case, it was because they were the most petite in the group and not really built for fighting.

James pointed his untraceability 2.0 device at Marc and gave it a single click, making Marc fully traceable for the first time since we had returned from Rock Haulter. The trigger had been activated, and if Lucien was on his game, he would teleport in any second. That didn't happen, but what did happen was something totally out of the plan. Apparently, Jessica had come up with quite a good idea of her own since we had left the control room, and now she put it into effect. I didn't lose sight of what was going on around me, but in a separate area of my brain, I was given a look at what Jessica could see and hear—and her attention, for now, was focused on the spyer which was following Lucien.

As expected and hoped for, he had detected Marc's presence straight away, and had quickly traced him to the school grounds. He had paused for a moment in confusion, wondering what that could all be about, but quickly decided that it was irrelevant compared to the huge opportunity that had been granted him. If the thought of it being a trap occurred to him, he didn't voice it aloud to Fewul who was with him; he simply ordered the beast to go there and capture Marc, and anyone else who was there but impossible to detect from here, and magically bind them somewhere until he had time to deal with them, as he had a lot to do at this time.

Fewul vanished from the spyer but did not appear in the courtyard, and thanks to Jessica's accompanying thought, I knew it was because Siobhan had just then activated the device that would banish the beast. So confident was he in Fewul's ability that Lucien hadn't bothered to follow the impending battle with his minds-eye, but had instead turned his attention to three Hammerhearts who had just entered the room with whom he was due to start a meeting.

"Fewul was supposed to come," I told them, "but Siobhan just banished it, and Lucien hasn't picked up on it yet. Just wait and be ready."

Sadly, it didn't occur to me, or anyone else apparently, that Marc should take the opportunity to call the beast himself. The idea occurred to all of us later, and we would dearly regret it, but for the time being, we were too focused on the battle at hand.

It took about a minute for Lucien to figure out that his order hadn't been completed. He had just gotten started on a meeting that seemed to be about waging war on those parts of the world still not under Hammerheart control, but he had to interrupt it when some magical check of his, which he didn't speak of to the people with him, didn't go the way he had expected. He quickly figured out that Fewul had been recalled, called it back himself, and asked the beast, in Stella's form, if there was anything she could do to prevent it from happening again. She told him that the only way to stop it would be to remove the devices we were using to do it; but otherwise, she remained at the mercy of the magic of the Maahoo. He sighed and called off the meeting, saying that he had more important business to deal with, and then vanished the most recent memories of the Hammerhearts so that they wouldn't know the truth about Stella not really being Stella.

"Now!" I called to the group, no more than three seconds before Lucien appeared just a few feet away from Marc, already in a battle posture and ready to go.

Lucien had to know where Marc was, but he still sent a wave of seriously powerful magic bursting out in all directions. It passed right through me, along with the rest of us, and pummelled into the buildings around us, demolishing all of them in a thunderous roar which left only small sections of classrooms and hallways standing in places. Nobody was hurt, although Marc had been forced to pour all his magical power into a shield specifically directed at Lucien. It was necessary because in order for the trap to work, James's untraceability magic had to be allowed to hit him; and it was necessary for James to do it rather than Marc himself because none of us were sure how much reaction time Marc would have the moment Lucien detected him.

Marc backed hurriedly away from Lucien as James sent more magic at him, this time to make him untraceable again—it missed. Tracing Marc's location, Lucien sent another wave of magic after him—this one seeming to be more concentrated on disabling him rather than blasting him into the middle of next week; but while it still passed through me, and those nearest me, it completely missed Marc thanks to the actions of Stella. Taking a leaf out of Marc's book, she made the ground beneath Lucien's feet ultra-slippery so that once again, he fell over on his arse.

"*How dare you!*" he roared, clearly audible even over the continuing tumult of the collapsing school buildings. His eyes looked black and utterly inhuman in that moment, his face twisted in fury and hatred—it was scary to look at. He made to scramble up, but the next round of attacks was already upon him.

Jets of light came flying at him from every direction, and I contributed to the battle with my newly created ability to make a person confused. Many of the spells dissolved harmlessly against his shield, but he was certainly aware of their presence. One of them, the magic bullet I'd created, fired in this case by Felicity and infused by a solid-outliner, seemed to explode against his shield in such a way that although the magic didn't penetrate it, the explosion itself burnt him. That wasn't the expected result but it was apparently good enough to land a hit on him, and so Felicity didn't switch it for another device.

Meanwhile, Stella made the ground beneath Lucien shift all around him whenever he tried to push himself to his feet—a way to magically affect him without his shield being a factor, and for a while, it worked so well that he was unable to regain his feet. Every time he tried to push up, the ground would shift and he would lose his balance. It made it very difficult for him to fight back, especially the times when he was face-down on the ground. It gave Marc and James the opportunity they needed to make Marc properly untraceable, and for Marc to trigger the anti-teleportation ring.

It was a bit of a stalemate for maybe ten seconds as Stella kept Lucien down, and the rest of us bar Felicity failed to land a hit on him thanks to his shield, but that all changed when both James and Peter, the latter of whom had been using an agonator, both switched to the magic light device. Peter's magic light had been infused by a solid-outliner, but Marc had put a special spell in James's which, if it hit, would remove Lucien's shield from the inside. Both of them fired at the same time;

Peter's hit first because he was closer, but it was very obvious that unlike the magic bullet, this one worked exactly as it was meant to.

Lucien let out a cry of surprise and rage as thicky prison hit his chest and began spreading rapidly, not even noticing right away that his shield had vanished. "I don't know how you're doing this but you will pay!" he threatened at the top of his voice, dipping his hand to his pocket before the thicky prison could render him immobile. So far, he had only used the magic from his crystal chips in battle, but now he was bringing the Sien-Leoard Crystal into service; although in the time it took him to withdraw it from his pocket, the thicky prison covered his whole chest and began spreading around his neck and shoulders; and Amelia was able to land a bludginator swipe on his legs, ripping his perfectly-creased trousers and revealing a trickle of blood.

I saw an opportunity then and I did my level best to take it. Lucien's fingers were gripped around the invisible Sien-Leoard Crystal, and now that I knew its exact location, I attempted to use one of those minor enchantments I had placed upon myself, one which could draw distant objects into my hand if I knew where they were, to steal the crystal from him. It came close to working, but even though more spells were landed on him in the meantime (mostly bludginators), he detected the magic and was able to counter it with his own, causing the crystal to cling to his fingertips and for my less powerful magic to fail to overpower it.

His focus through all of this, meanwhile, in spite of the repeated bludginator swipes tearing into his skin and clothing and the thicky prison now beginning to cover his face, was to call in a powerful reinforcement. I supposed Siobhan had banished Fewul again since Lucien had arrived here, but now the beast reappeared with a mighty roar. The attack halted for a moment as everyone bar Lucien looked around in automatic fear of that sound. Fewul was no longer in Stella's form but had resumed its original form; that of a big, black, brutal-looking teddy bear. It had appeared just outside Marc's anti-teleportation ring, making me marvel at the fact that it couldn't automatically pass through Marc's magic.

Fewul's presence on the battlefield was brief, thanks to Siobhan, but very effective nonetheless. It sent magic at Lucien before it disappeared with a loud bang and a flash of golden light, magic which simultaneously removed the thicky prison and repaired the bludginator cuts to his body (though not the rips in his clothes). Everyone reacted very quickly, resuming the attack on him, but Lucien reacted even quicker. Instead of trying to push off the ground, he used magic to quickly levitate himself into the air, dodging several jets of light that came his way and causing several of those jets to pass through people on the other side of the circle, and when his feet landed on the ground, he was back in control of things. The next spells to hit him once again dissolved against his reinstated shield, and Stella's attempt to shift the ground beneath him failed to make him lose his balance—he had come up with a spell to neutralise it.

Marc and Lucien spoke at the same time then, the latter having no idea of the former. Marc was further away, so I didn't catch all the words, except that it had something to do with strengthening the circle so that no magic could pass through it from the outside to the inside. Lucien, meanwhile, spoke more calmly, but still loudly. "I have no idea how you're doing this, Marc and friends, but it stops now. You can't beat me —"

As if someone like Peter was going to stand around listening to Lucien's little speech. He had levelled his magic lighter again and fired another jet of thicky prison. As before, it passed through the shield; but unlike before, it failed to grip the Sorcerer. Apparently, in the time he had been in the air, he had also placed upon himself an enchantment which would make him immune to thicky prison.

"I told you, you can't beat—"

Felicity struck again, and the explosion knocked him back a step. A moment later, James struck, successfully removing the shield for a second time; and another moment later, Amelia capitalised on it with another bludginator swipe. Lucien grunted in surprise and reinstated the shield himself this time, so that the next spell—another jet of golden light from an agonator, this one operated by Tommy—dissolved against it. It looked as though Lucien was now gauging our abilities a little better, even if he hadn't yet figured out that we were using X-rays to pass through his shields. It was time for a new approach, and after I gave Stella a significant look, she and the Villain Crystal launched a more aggressive attack against him.

It took him completely off-guard, and I saw a momentary look of surprise and even fear on his face before it dissolved into concentration as he fought back. Everyone else took a step back in alarm as it became clear that this battle was beyond any of us, except for perhaps Marc. There was no guarantee that this kind of magic would pass right through us either, given how powerful it obviously was and how focused. I had seen Stella fight with magic once before, in one of Smiley's memories, and this looked like an even higher level than that had been. Lucien didn't have anywhere near the same skill, but he did have enough to stay in the game, and enough raw power from the Sien-Leoard Crystal that any hits she might have landed on him could be overpowered.

"You're not Marc," he growled as he fired spell after spell. "You're using the Villain Crystal. Are you Amelia? I think you must be. I'll make you pay for this. There's a spot on the floor next to Natalie with your name on it."

That was the cue for the rest of us to re-join the attack. Even through the battle, Stella had been unable to remove his shield, but James now did so for the third time, and kept his device levelled in readiness to do it again if Lucien put it back in place. Lucien's powers of concentration, lent to him by his Honnie mind, made it possible for him to reinstate the shield without missing a step in battle, though not before someone was able to land a hit on him in between each time it happened. One of those times, it was me and my confusion spell, though it seemed not to have an effect on him, perhaps again because of his Honnie mind. That was a shame—it made that particular spell almost useless—but I still had enough magic to fall back on that I didn't let it get me down.

The attack on Lucien became more organised as we all took up tactical positions around him and he continued to fire back, mostly on Stella but occasionally in other directions in response to the spells that hit him from others—these spells always passed harmlessly through us, and as he couldn't see us, he had no idea how ineffective they were. Marc took up a position behind Lucien, while Felicity took a side-on position, backed up by me and a few others. The rest of the group took positions on his other side, except for James, who had remained in place almost directly opposite Lucien at about a fifteen-degree angle.

The attack was relentless, all of us sensing that this was our best opportunity yet and we really needed to take it. When Marc began attacking from behind, Lucien found himself outflanked and he was forced to divide his concentration between his brother and his ex-girlfriend. The rest of us were having minimal impact by comparison, especially given that several people were using solid-outliners, believing they were the most effective, meaning that they were quite often cancelling each other out. Also, although Tommy was still using an agonator, he hadn't yet been able to land a hit on Lucien—one jet had missed completely, while the others had all hit the shield.

Lucien was stretched to his limit, but he was still holding his own. What could we do to overpower him once and for all? Marc and Stella were giving it everything they had—we couldn't count on them to finish it on their own at this rate. The rest of us needed to be the difference, but how? If someone landed an agonator on him, that might be enough of a distraction—but then again, given that he now had a Honnie mind, the agonator may be just as ineffective as my confusion spell had been. Knocking him off-balance might work, but Felicity was already doing her best to do that and so far it wasn't working: even though it was hurting him, and one side of his body was looking rather badly burnt, it was as though he had come to expect those explosions, and they were no longer distracting him.

I hesitated for a moment, trying to think of anything I could do to make a difference in this struggle—anything that Lucien wouldn't expect. Right now, he would expect any kind of spell if it came from Marc or Stella, but if I could land something surprising on him from another direction, it might be enough. Flying above his head and firing something on him from directly overhead would be a good start, but what ought I to fire? I rattled through all the magic I had given myself but couldn't think of anything that would really surprise him. He would be expecting someone to try to knock him out, or any of the Hammerheart spells that he himself would have used, so it would need to be something that we had invented ourselves...

Then it hit me. The best one to use was one that we had already tried once, but even though he knew of its existence, he couldn't seem to get rid of it without either Fewul on hand, or an ally he could physically hand the Sien-Leoard Crystal to who could perform the magic for him.

"Does anyone have one of those devices that'll trap his magic inside a shield?" I called over the fighting. "Throw it to me."

"Here, John," Erica called from a distance to my left, and she hurled a device at me, thankfully not asking any questions about why I wanted it or trying to use it herself. I once again used my drawing magic to make sure the device came straight to me and I didn't waste time dropping it and having to go and pick it up.

But I had run out of time, because that was when something happened to turn the battle, and not in our favour this time. Who knows what might have happened if it hadn't been for James missing his target and hitting Stella in the back instead of Lucien. She had been using a shield during the battle as well, and wasn't immediately aware that it had been removed, but it became very clear when Lucien managed to land a hit on her. She was thrown backward a huge distance in an explosion of blood, but I never saw what part of her had been torn away—only that something obviously had been, because there were chunks of flesh and fragments of bone in that explosion. She was hurled into the wreckage of what had formerly been the administration building and didn't re-emerge.

That was a huge distraction for all of us, including Marc. My overriding thought was that if Stella had dropped the Villain Crystal through all of that, she could be in serious danger of actually dying if someone didn't attend to her quickly. Even if she hadn't dropped the crystal, the act of healing herself mightn't be evil enough to work—although surely it had to be close, because after all, villains too needed to heal themselves so that they could continue their villainy. I glanced over in the direction of the building, wanting to run to her, but knowing that while I had given myself the power or physical regeneration, I hadn't given myself the ability to pass it onto someone else.

The only one who could help her was Marc, but he had his hands full with Lucien, who unlike the rest of us, didn't miss a beat after what he had done. He seemed to be aware that he had virtually halved his major opposition, but perhaps not just how effectively he had done so, or that it had been Stella who was blasted out of the fight. With half his attention now free to do other things, he could perhaps have knocked Marc out altogether—or at least levelled more power at him so that he would be in danger of being overwhelmed. Whether Lucien could actually have won the battle from here or not, I had no idea, as the rest of us were already beginning to recover our poise and return to the attack; but as it was, he had another idea in mind.

With an almighty roar, Fewul returned to the battlefield. Once again, its appearance was brief, but also once again no less effective. It performed a single spell before Siobhan sent it packing for the third or fourth time, and it wasn't immediately obvious what that spell was—not until Lucien sent a wave of magic at Marc, which he had to put all his power into dissolving, and in the time it took him to do that, Lucien was able to teleport out of our midst, escaping from the worst jam he'd been in during his brief time as a Sorcerer. He must have attempted an escape at some point during the battle and found that he couldn't teleport, so his top priority, once he had called on Fewul, was that the beast would remove the anti-teleportation ring from the outside. Given that it wasn't a spell that would pass through the ring, Marc's attempted protection hadn't worked.

The battle was over; it had only lasted a few minutes, though a lot sure had happened in those few minutes. But in the end, we had failed. Lucien had escaped, and he had taken with him an even greater estimation of how dangerous we could be to him. There was very little chance we could stop him setting off those nukes now. All the standing around here in stunned horror, and the continual swearing coming out of a few people, couldn't change that.

"We need to get out of here before he comes back with reinforcements," Mr. Woodward called to everyone.

"Marc, go get Stella," I told him, and then lapsed into telepathic communication with Jessica, letting her know to tell Lillian to bring us back into the base. I knew the message had gone through when people around me—those who weren't in their shadows—started disappearing. Those who were in their shadows began coming out so that they too could be brought back in.

I didn't wait for my turn but hurried after Marc to check on Stella, practically diving into the rubble after Marc and following the blood trail until we found her. She didn't have the Villain Crystal with her—it had been tossed out of her hand when she had been blasted backward, and we would need to manually hunt around the school for it at some point, since it couldn't be traced with magic. She was alive, though, thank heavens, although she wouldn't have lived more than a minute or two longer if Marc hadn't patched her up; her legs had been cut off below the knees, and we would later find parts of them on the ground in the court yard while we were searching for the crystal. After she was put back together again, we led her out of the wreckage so that the three of us could return to base.

Chapter 14: Dilemma

"Well, we certainly feel useless right now," Harry was saying as I appeared in the control room, but he was shushed by several people, their attention focused on the spyer following Lucien. From where I stood, I could see that he was back in the living room of his living quarters with Fewul at his side, now back in Stella's form, and the room was otherwise deserted. He was pacing around and alternately asking her questions and muttering under his breath; he didn't look physically hurt, but he did look somewhat rattled. The volume on the spyer had now been turned up all the way.

"I don't understand this," he finally said. "I know that they've got the Hero and Villain Crystals, and they've probably got the Light Crystal too, but how are they able to do this much damage? I made sure they couldn't do this to me, so how are they?"

"They are being creative now, Master," Fewul said, and Stella's voice sounding that expressionless was rather creepy—he seemed to have forgotten to re-instate the order to make it behave more like Stella, "not unlike you have been."

"Great, so I'm going to have to up my game now," he grunted. "How did they do all of that, anyway? What magic were they using?"

"Lots of different magic, Master," Fewul said—rather helpfully, I thought.

He gritted his teeth and said, "Be specific. How did they stop me from hitting them with my spells? Even being untraceable, that shouldn't have happened, and my magic ought to have blasted through any shields they might have put up."

"I do not know, Master," Fewul said, surprising me. "Because they were untraceable, it wasn't possible for me to get a look at what magic they were using during my time on the battlefield. I only know of the magic they were using to encircle you in that one spot; that is why I was able to remove it to enable your escape."

"And what magic was that?"

"An anti-teleportation ring, similar to what the Seventh Sorcerer used during a previous battle."

Lucien let out a sigh. "The one we tried to catch Hall in that time. Of course; how could I have forgotten that. Hmm…" he trailed off, looking deep in concentration, then said, "Well, if I can figure out how to teleport through the protections here, then surely I can do it the next time they try something like that on me. I guess this means you also can't tell me how they were able to get through my shield all those times?"

Fewul shook her head. "No, Master. The amount of magic required to remove a shield must always be greater than the amount of magic used to create that shield. You created yours with the Sien-Leoard Crystal, correct?"

Lucien hesitated then said, "Well, most of them were created that way. I did have to do it once with my own magic, so I suppose Marc could have removed that one by force, but I got the impression that they did it the same way each time. Are there any creative ways you can think they might have done something like that?"

I held my breath, waiting to see if Fewul was smart enough to think of the things I'd thought of back in the cave on Rock Haulter, but she surprised me. "No, Master, I can't think of anything they could do, and yet they have obviously done something."

"Well," Lucien said, finally stopping his pacing and looking around to see that Lena had just entered the room from the corridor leading to the bedrooms. With a dismissive wave, he sent her back from whence she had come, hardly breaking his own train of thought. "Well, in that case, can you think of anything I can do in the meantime to prevent something like that from happening again?"

"Would you like suggestions regarding magic, strategy, or both, Master?"

"Both. Surprise me, why don't you."

"If one of them suddenly becomes traceable again, it probably isn't by accident," Fewul said, "which means they intended for you to detect them and try to capture them. It would make much more sense to not take the bait next time."

"If you'll recall, I sent you over there first," he pointed out.

"Either send someone else entirely," Fewul continued, "or don't go at all. You may work on ways to capture them, but you would be much better served doing it on your own terms rather than waiting for them to show themselves, because as you now know, when they do, it is likely for a good reason."

Lucien scowled. "I've been trying since Tuesday to do that and it's got me bugger all except for John's death, and that was totally unintentional. Anything else?"

"One more thing, Master. It seems that leading into today's battle, and even somewhat on Wednesday, they had an idea of what sort of magic you would likely use against them and how they would be best attacking you. Even though they couldn't capture you or wrest the Sien-Leoard Crystal from you, as I believe was probably their goal, they were still able to occupy your full attention, while eluding capture themselves. I would suggest that the only way they could have been this prepared is if they had spent much time spying on you, and if this is the case, you could simply remove that advantage by making yourself untraceable."

My heart sank to somewhere below my naval. Damn that Beast of Magic.

"Maybe, yeah," he said slowly, "and here was me thinking I didn't need to take those measures anymore. Will you be able to locate me if I'm untraceable, though?"

"By default, no," she said, "but I will be able to come to you at any time if you summon me."

"Could I create some sort of magic that would make it possible for you and only you to trace me?"

"Possibly, Master, but a measure like that may be open to abuse—for instance, if they are able to use magic to impersonate me. If they are able to do it with a Maahoo, then we must assume that it is possible."

Lucien swore under his breath. "Fine, but we really need to think of a way to get those crystals off them. I'll be forever looking over my shoulder until I know that they are safely out of the way."

"Isn't that what the bombs are for, Master?"

He began to smile then—it was an evil thing. "Yes, you're quite right, and that is an advantage of being traceable: I can make sure they understand that I will do what I say I'm going to do, if they don't hand themselves—and all of their magic—over to me by tonight. And I mean all of them must hand themselves over—Marc, James, Stella and the Woodwards most importantly, but the rest as well. Now, recall that meeting I was supposed to have; I have a lot of work to do today."

As Fewul began to carry out his order, the spyer suddenly went dark and silent as, at last, Lucien made himself untraceable. A silence followed in the control room before Peter said, "Great, how do we go about watching him now?"

"I can probably come up with something that can watch untraceable people," Marc said. "At least, it will locate those empty spots where they are and then allow us to watch visually, but in the meantime, we should get this base back down there so we can keep an eye on him ourselves."

"So how come we couldn't stop him out there?" Rebecca asked. "It felt like we could have done that for hours and only held the line."

"If I were to guess, I'd say it was his Honnie mind that gave him the critical advantage," Marc said. "When we were fighting him, it felt like he always had enough focus to keep up with me. It took everything I had just to stop him from over-running me, and I'm almost certain that if Stella hadn't kept him busy from the other end, and if you guys weren't helping out, he would have found a way to capture me and the crystal."

"It did feel like that," Stella agreed.

"Which means that we probably couldn't have won today," James said gloomily. "Our best chance to get him would have been at the very beginning; if we could have just stopped him getting a hand on the Sien-Leoard Crystal and calling Fewul, we probably could have got him. That doesn't make up for me fucking the whole thing up royally, I know, but it's something."

"And we're unlikely to get that opportunity again," Mr. Woodward said, "which means that if we are to try something like that again, we will need to think of a new way to go about it."

Another silence fell before James said, "Well, if his Honnie mind is what gave him the crucial advantage, then we need to find a way to either strip him of it, or neutralise it somehow. We're also going to have to think of a new way to lure him into a trap, because it doesn't look like he's going to fall for that trick again."

* * *

The rest of the day following our failed capture attempt was long and not very fruitful. Lillian took us back to the Hammerheart base, only to find that Lucien had decided to have meetings elsewhere from now on— perhaps he would use the vast network at his disposal to mix the locations up all the time so that we would have an impossible time tracking him. All we saw in the living quarters was a very bored Lena, who eventually left to try to find interesting things to do elsewhere, and Natalie, still bound and dozing on the floor of her room.

With nothing else to do, Marc had set to work on the spyers, vanishing all but one of the ones we had in the control room (I knew that there would be others around the base, but they didn't matter for now), and then modifying the one remaining one so that it could detect those little holes in the fabric of the universe that were the existence of untraceable people and things, and put a perfectly normal sound and visual sensor alongside them, wherever they were. It was even able to lock onto that person or object if they moved around, though that part of the magic fell down if the untraceable person teleported to somewhere else.

The magic itself didn't take very long to perform. What did take a while was using it to find Lucien. Although magic was used to detect where those holes in reality were, it had to be done in such a way that it scanned close locations first, going out in a widening radius; and because the object we were tracing was small (shrunken by the magic of the Hammerheart Network), it had to be done slowly. Ultimately, it was impractical when it came to tracing the untraceable, but just when it seemed hopeless, Marc came up with another good idea. By concentrating on one of the three men Lucien had been meeting with just prior to the battle, he teleported us to his location—and there was Lucien, just wrapping up his meeting with them.

"So what exactly were they talking about before we interrupted them the first time?" I asked Lillian Woodward, the only person who had remained in the control room during the battle who was still in there now.

"It sounded as though they were finalising plans to invade Africa and South America," she said.

"Which would explain why we appear to be in the Hammerheart base in Tel Aviv right now," Mr. Woodward added.

"And because we missed it, we don't know what strategy to use to stop him, or even slow him down," Marc lamented as we followed Lucien down through the base towards the Hammerheart Highway, watching him tapping his watch as he went, most likely setting up the next meeting about whatever. I was glad that for now, he would use the Hammerheart Highway instead of teleporting; that would make it possible for us to trace him at least as far as the next stop.

In fact, what Lucien ultimately did that day was like a tour of the world. His next stop was Hong Kong, where he was briefed on the progress of the rounding up of anti-Hammerheart dissidents as well as the establishment of the trial, which he had already ordered to take place in Hong Kong and scheduled to begin the following Monday. Although those going on trial were currently imprisoned in Basements all around the world, a register of them was being kept here so that they would know what they were doing when the trials began.

From there it was back to Canberra, where he met with Cornish and a few others to discuss local matters, then back up to Tokyo, then across to London, and so on and so on. There was no sign of Fewul through any of this, but we found out the reason for that a little after one o'clock in the afternoon, when most people were in the dining room having lunch but Marc and a few others were in the control room. The invasions of Africa and South America had begun, springing up in different countries across different regions at the same time, performed mostly with the use of the Influential Charm and only a little violence, and with the whole operation being overseen by Fewul, who was taking on a similar role that it had during the school battle in which Hammerson had ultimately died, only a much more active role rather than observing as it had that day.

From that point on, the group became splintered as we tried to keep up with everything that was going on. Marc and Amelia, the latter of whom had now taken possession of the Light Crystal, sat in the control room and attempted to slow the advance of Lucien's armies using their combined magic—not unlike Marc, Tommy and I had tried to do when the Hammersons had launched their global coup back in April. Just as in April, they were having very limited effect—even less than we had, thanks to Fewul. As people passed through the control room throughout the day they would invariably activate the device which would recall the beast, but Lucien always seemed to know when that was happening, and was able to magically call Fewul back into action without seeming to miss a beat during his various meetings.

Feeling that the situation had become even more urgent than before, and with the looming threat of a nuclear attack in an unknown location, James had taken the magical encyclopedia into the Time Box along with Erica, Katie and Sophie and they had gotten down to business, researching anything and everything they could about the Magic Crystals, trying to trace their history and come up with any ideas about how they could be destroyed. Katie and Sophie had emerged after almost an hour (which would have been about nine hours for them), looking thoroughly exhausted and claiming that after all the fruitless work they had done, they needed to go and claim massages from their boyfriends; they both looked like they would fall asleep within an hour. James and Erica, however, simply re-energised themselves with the device I had created for that purpose, and pushed on.

I would have liked to be in there with them—it really seemed like the most useful place to be—but after having spent three hours already in there today (three hours of Time Box time, that was), I didn't dare spend any more time in the Time Box today, in case it ultimately shortened my life even more. I rationalised that there was probably nothing I could add to the process that James and Erica, both of whom were probably smarter and more studious than me, could have done between them. I ended up roving from place to place within the base, checking on progress here and there, including spending some time in the lounge room with the people in there. They were keeping an eye on the news media and reporting that there was very little news coming out of Africa or South America (it was somehow being very effectively suppressed).

From there, it was back to the control room to check in with Marc and Amelia and whoever else was in the room at the time. I would get a bit of an update on what was going on, watch Lucien for a little while, and then go into the Time Box for a few minutes to see how James and Erica were doing (always leaving the door open for the duration, so that time wouldn't warp again until I left). I even picked up the magic enhancer—the device I had created to use the power of the Sien-Leoard Crystal—and attempted to use that to assist Marc and Amelia, but although I was able to do bits and pieces of good, I ended up making no greater difference than they were. Using the Villain Crystal for this job was, of course, out of the question; there was no way this job could be considered evil enough on any scale, even if we tried to do it in a way that would annoy Lucien, because Lucien wasn't even paying attention to the minor details of the advance.

Stella was just as unproductive as me that day, because she pretty much followed me everywhere I went. After she had lifted in a big way for the battle against Lucien, her spirits had since dropped to somewhere around her ankles. I wasn't exactly clear on why, but I assumed it was related, in some way, to the things we had talked about the night before. More than once I considered pulling her aside, taking her upstairs to one of our bedrooms and talking about it with her, but I resisted the temptation to do so. If last night was any indication, this would lead to the two of us doing delicious things together, and I just didn't feel right about doing that while all this chaos was going on. Also, there was the minor matter of Jacob Underwood, who would contact me sometime soon to let me know that he was ready, and I needed to be ready to leap into action myself when that time came.

What came first, at a little after half past five in the evening, was James calling a meeting in the control room, to be attended by me, Stella, Marc, Amelia, Peter and Mr. Woodward. Erica had intended to remain in the Time Box, continuing the research alone, but when the rest of us got a look at James, we had gone in and practically dragged her out. I was unable to calculate in my head how long those two had gone without sleep (more than forty-eight hours was my best guess), but they both looked more exhausted than I had ever seen and the bags under their eyes didn't look healthy at all. Erica had protested against being sent away, but I had turned the sleep-inducing device on her before she could stop me, and thereafter, she was incapable of stopping Harry and Simon from picking her up and carrying her off to bed. James would go to bed himself after this meeting, but for now, he needed to stay here.

"Okay, so you all know that no matter how hard we tried, we couldn't find anything useful in there," James said, swaying a little in his seat. "We found a lot of not-so-useful stuff, but nothing that we could use to destroy the crystals—no direct knowledge, or anything that we were able to form a theory from using our best intellect. I even used your brain thing, John, the one that gave me quicker intelligence for a while, but even with that, we couldn't come up with anything."

"Did you search the entire encyclopedia?" Mr. Woodward asked.

"Not the whole thing," James admitted. "That would take years to do, so we had to be selective, but we did search a lot of stuff. While I suppose it is possible that we missed something that could have been useful, I tend to think that the knowledge we need is probably not in there. Maybe we can use magic to come up with something in the coming days—I mean, we might be able to use it to give ourselves ideas for things we could try—but that isn't going to help us tonight.

"Which leads me to the point of this meeting. If Lucien's serious, and I've got no reason to suspect he isn't, he may be mere hours away from setting off a nuclear bomb somewhere in the world. That is, of course, if we don't hand ourselves and everything we have over to him. Do any of us believe there is anything we can do to prevent him setting off a nuke tonight?"

We all shook our heads, and I reiterated what I had said in this very room that morning. "Even if we vanish the nukes, he can just use his magic to create new ones. The same problem exists that we had this morning: if we don't steal his magic, there is nothing we can do to stop him from using it."

"And after what happened this morning, does anyone believe we can steal his magic in the next few hours?" James asked, and once again, we all shook our heads. "That's what I thought, which leads me to a very painful conclusion. We have only two options here: do what he says, and hand ourselves and everything we have over to him; or do nothing, and live with whatever consequences arise from that decision."

A horrified silence followed this pronouncement, but I wasn't surprised. I had known deep down that if we couldn't find some way to stop Lucien, it would ultimately come to this. Not wanting to admit it to myself didn't change what was.

"You mean like we're still doing after the supermarket and the plane crashes and those fires?" Peter said gloomily. "Well, we only lost a couple of thousand all up from those attacks, so surely a few more thousand won't make a difference, right?"

He was being sarcastic, of course, but Mr. Woodward still replied, "It will be considerably more than a few more thousand. In fact, depending on where he strikes, it could well be in the millions—and that's just the immediate death toll."

"My point exactly," James agreed. "I get that it's important not to negotiate with terrorists, but seriously, in this case, we may not have a choice. Just think of the scale of destruction he may unleash here: even if we're fighting for their freedom, we can't just sit back and let him kill that many people, can we?"

"You're seriously ready to give up, James?" Marc asked. "I mean, that's basically what you're suggesting here. It's not like we can survive to fight another day; if we hand ourselves over to him, it's over. The whole world will lose, and some of us will probably die. I'd be okay with dying if it saved millions of people, but not if it doomed them to an even worse life."

James shrugged. "I know how it sounds, Marc, but today's been a major waste. None of us have done anything to seriously slow him down, let alone stop him."

Another silence followed, then I said, "I know it's bad, but giving up doesn't really feel like an option to me. Maybe it's just because of what I had to do to get here—"

"He makes a fair point," Peter agreed. "Remember what we did the other night; we kept our promise to Sien and Leoard, so if we have faith, we have to stick at it, and then we'll have their support on our side. That is how it works, isn't it?"

James shrugged again. "I think so, but I'm really too tired to think my way through that at the moment."

"There's another reason why we can't give up," Amelia said, and we all looked at her. "If Lucien really *is* the last Sorcerer, then he is going to be the end of either the world, or the end of magic. That's according to the prophecy, and after all our previous experiences with Sien and Leoard's prophecies, we ought to take this one seriously. I think we can all agree that he is unlikely to destroy magic on his own, which means so many more will ultimately die if we let him walk his path without intervening. That means we would be saving more lives if we stayed put and accept whatever it is he does."

Silence for a few seconds, and then Marc said, "She's right. I mean, there's still a chance that Lucien's not the one the prophecy was referring to, but that seems really unlikely to me."

We all looked at James, who appeared so disheartened that it was almost painful to look at. "You all agree then? We need to stay put?"

One by one, we all agreed, and only when we all had, including Mr. Woodward, did James too agree. He looked like a weight had been lifted off his shoulders, and to be honest, that was how I felt. If Lucien really did kill millions of people tonight, it would be painful to watch, but it wasn't as painful as being torn between those two horrible pathways.

* * *

I had just sat down to dinner when a foreign thought slid into my mind: Jacob Underwood was about to exit the portals. I immediately jumped up and tore out of the dining room, catching a few odd looks from people as I left my almost completely untouched dinner behind.

"John, what—" Stella called after me.

"Save my dinner, I won't be long," I called over my shoulder as I punched the button to call the elevator.

Dad and Charlie were minding the fort in the control room when I burst in thirty seconds later, both of them watching the displays with gloomy expressions as Lucien continued to stride forward with his agenda. They both looked around at me in surprise.

"Aren't you supposed to be having dinner, young man?" Dad asked.

"Yeah, but need to do something here," I told them, then hesitated. All of a sudden, I'd been thrown a problem that none of us had thought of. I weighed it up as quickly as I could, then made my decision. "I need to pick someone up from outside—it's extremely important. I need to go out there."

Both of them didn't look happy about that, and Charlie said, "This isn't another stop-the-bomb scenario, is it?"

"No," I said quickly, "and I don't really have time to explain it. He's going to be in a certain place any minute now, and since we can't teleport the base, I have to go out there and get him myself. Trust me on this."

"Why can't we teleport the base?" Dad asked, brow furrowed.

"Because if we do, we'll lose track of Lucien," I told him. "He's untraceable now so we have to stick with him, otherwise we mightn't be able to find him again. Here—"

I had been hunting around on the floor for a telepathic communicator; when I spotted one I snatched it up and gave it to Charlie, who was nearest. "We can keep in touch while I'm out there. I'm going to need you to let us back in, and I guess we're going to have to do that right in front of him."

That would make this a little dangerous, even though I would obviously be invisible and untraceable. Being heard or otherwise sensed —or worse, accidentally bumping into someone or tripping over something—were always possibilities. As for the telepathy, that would certainly be necessary if Lucien moved to another location, necessitating Dad and Charlie to follow.

"Okay, if you're sure of what you're doing," Dad said, but he didn't look very happy about it. "I suggest we don't mention this to your mother, though."

I nodded absent-mindedly and then contacted Underwood telepathically again, asking where he was. He told me that thanks to devices he had created in the creations cave that morning, he was now invisible and had teleported into the apartment we had agreed on the previous evening. However, people were now living in there, so he had teleported to the corridor outside it and would meet me there. I told him to sit tight and be ready for anything, and that I would be there very soon. I then used my own telepathic communication to send a picture of the old Playman and Thomas residences on Lopher Lane, sitting side-by-side and connected by an underground tunnel hidden in the cupboards under each set of stairs, to Dad and Charlie.

Without looking around at them, I said, "Did you get that?"

"Yes," Charlie said slowly, sounding quite awed, and I looked over my shoulder at him. "That was quite remarkable. We never communicated like that under Freddy's watch. Fascinating."

"Well, that's how I'll let you know when I'm ready to be let back in," I said, "and how you can let me know if you have to move somewhere else."

"Okay, good," Dad said, turning to the controls. "So—er—which button to let you out?"

"That one," I said, pointing at it. "Just wait till I get in the corner."

Which I had done about five seconds later. I made myself invisible, and then Dad let me out of the base at last. I dropped into a conference room, took a moment to make sure that nobody had noticed me (they hadn't), and then attempted to teleport away. Nothing happened, and I realised yet another oversight on my part: I was in the Hammerheart Network, and surrounded by anti-teleportation protections. Lucien may have mastered how to get around those protections but I hadn't, and without magic of my own (I hadn't thought to bring the magic enhancer —you could never think of everything), it wouldn't be possible anyway.

Panic threatened to engulf me, but I held it off as best I could. I backed away from the people in the room until I hit the wall behind me, then looked around the door. It was closed (typical, I thought), so I edged into my shadow and walked through it, letting out a sigh of relief when I was on the other side. That had been close; I'd been very close to Lucien just then, and if he'd been on his game, he would have set up spells that would have detected my presence that close to him, untraceable or not. I was a little surprised that he hadn't—or maybe he had, and they just hadn't worked. Either way, I considered myself lucky.

So where was I anyway? I had no idea where I was in the world, let alone this Hammerheart base. I was in a wide, foyer-type area with several doors branching off it, most of which were closed, except for the wide double-doors at the far end of the room. They stood open, and through them, I could see a corridor beyond. I went that way, still tip-toeing even though nobody could hear me while I was in my shadow—it was an automatic reflex.

This base was massive. In fact, this part of the base was massive, but I eventually found my way to another set of double doors, this one with a bright red line across them and two heavily armed guards on the other side. I took a deep breath of nothing and stepped between them, hoping and praying that whatever magic that line contained wouldn't be triggered by a person in his shadow—and once again, I got lucky. In the chamber beyond contained a set of elevators and a stairwell, and I walked through the closed door into the latter. Down I went, looking through the windows in each door until I saw the familiar sight of the Hammerheart Highway, and through that closed door I went. Only when I had located the hidden guest entrance did I finally come out of my shadow, though that was the only protection I lifted off myself.

I had no idea where I came out, except that it was pitch-black and warm, and that it was probably in a park because the ground felt soft beneath my shoes. I thought of Jacob Underwood and without wasting another moment, teleported straight to him, the teleportation feeling like it took quite a while as if it were over a great distance. Soon enough, though, I was standing in a very familiar corridor in a run-down apartment building somewhere in London, and apparently alone. Underwood was here somewhere, but for now, both of us were invisible and unaware of the other's location.

I sent a message to him, asking him if he was still in the corridor, and he responded that he was. After taking a quick look around to make sure that nobody else was around (nobody was), I made myself visible and waited for him to tap me on the shoulder. When he did, I took hold of his arm, made myself invisible again, and teleported us both back to the pitch-black park. I was about to guide him through the guest entrance when I remembered that he wasn't four-dimensional, and had almost certainly never experienced anything like that in his life. He would probably adjust to it okay, thanks to Smiley, but I would need to give him a heads-up.

"We're going to have to go into our shadows to get through this, like your grandfather used to do," I told him as I quietly used my magic to place an enchantment on him to make him four-dimensional, as I had done to Stella a few days earlier. "Did he ever talk to you about that?"

"Yeah," he said, sounding unsettled. "He made it sound easy, but I imagine it's probably not. Is it?"

"It's not that hard, but it is a little strange," I told him. "You'll see when we get in there. Come on."

I led him through the guest entrance and, ignoring his gasp of surprise as the Hammerheart Highway materialised around him, guided him along the fourth dimension. His body stiffened for a moment, but then he relaxed and hissed, "Is this it?"

"Yeah, this is it," I whispered back. "We technically don't have to be quiet now, but it might be a good habit to keep up. Come on, I wanna get back into our base as quickly as possible."

As I had thought, Underwood adjusted to being in his shadow pretty quickly. I was able to lead him, both of us still invisible, across the bridge over the Hammerheart Highway tracks, up the stairs, through the double doors and along the corridor until we were once again outside the room where Lucien was having his meeting. I stuck my head through the door to make sure it was still happening, saw that it was just wrapping up, and hurriedly led Underwood through the door. We needed to do this before Lucien got moving, so I backed us both against one of the walls so that we could come out of our shadow, hopefully well out of the way of everyone in the room as they got up and began moving around.

There, and out of our shadow and potentially vulnerable, I got in touch with Charlie, telling him that we had returned and that it was time to let us back into the base. A moment later, the room vanished as I was drawn back into the control room.

"Thank goodness," Dad said as I made myself visible. "I've been doubting myself for letting you go out there all this time."

"Well I'm glad you did it; it was really important," I said as Dad let me go from the corner and began manoeuvring the controls to bring Underwood in next. "And just in time too; I was worried we would lose you if Lucien finished up here and went somewhere else."

"We talked about that too," Charlie said, "but we think we probably could have remained here so long as we didn't touch the spyer. According to Marc, it should stay locked onto him no matter where we are."

I had forgotten about that, actually, and could have kicked myself. Maybe I hadn't needed to go out there after all. A moment later, Underwood revealed himself to us and Dad released him from the corner as well.

"You look familiar," Charlie said, appraising him. "Where have I seen you before?"

Underwood shrugged. "I was with the Woodwards for a couple of weeks earlier in the year. You may have seen me there, although to be honest, I don't remember either of you.

"Anyway," he turned to me, "I guess you'll be wanting this."

He put his hand in his pocket and withdrew the small box which contained the Darkness Crystal. I took it from him, noticing his relieved expression—he looked happy to be rid of it.

"Thanks," I said, putting it in my pocket. "I'll hold onto it for now, until we figure out what to do with it."

"It's not fun to hold on to it, trust me," he said, shuddering.

"What is it?" Dad asked me.

"Er—the Darkness Crystal," I said, unable to think of any good reason for them not to know. "Don't worry, we're not going to use it," I added, noticing the shocked expressions on their faces. "We just need to hold it for now, that's all. Anyway, did you bring any stuff with you?"

Underwood shrugged. "Quite a lot, actually."

"Okay," I said, taken aback. If he had all his stuff, I had no idea where he was keeping it. If he'd been wearing a backpack it could have been internally expanding, and that would have held all his things; but other than being dressed in thick clothes, he appeared not to be carrying anything except for whatever could fit in his pockets. I could only assume that he had created some sort of magical device small enough to fit in his pocket that could store everything he had wanted to bring with him.

"Anyway, I'll take you upstairs and help you find a room, then leave you because it's dinner time here, and I'm bloody starving. If you're hungry, you can come down and find something to eat on the first floor —it'll be pretty obvious where the dining room is once you get looking around."

Chapter 15: The Welcoming Arms of Danger

Stella had saved my dinner and my seat for me, I found when I returned to the dining room, at a table with Marc and Amelia. My food had gone cold though, so I had ended up vanishing it anyway and getting a fresh dinner. I answered their first couple of questions about what I had just been doing, telling them that Jacob Underwood had been safely retrieved and yes, he had handed over the Darkness Crystal; but thereafter, I focused almost exclusively on eating my dinner. That little mission outside the base had been nerve-wracking enough to make me feel pretty hungry now.

Marc and Amelia settled into conversation, which sounded companionable enough, although I could tell that they were both worried about what might happen tonight. Stella was silently watching me; she had almost finished her dinner when I had sat down, but even after she was done and had gotten rid of her plate, she continued to sit there watching me in a way that made me feel distinctly uncomfortable. Whether she just liked to watch me eat I wasn't sure, but my guess was that she was waiting for me to finish for some reason.

Sure enough, when I had finally finished my dinner and was standing up, she stood up with me and caught my arm. "Can I talk to you about something upstairs?"

"Sure," I said automatically, and we left Marc and Amelia there at the table, both of them already having finished their dinners and now looking after us in some curiosity. I was curious too because Stella looked pretty serious, so I didn't think she had fun stuff on her mind. In truth, neither did I; it had been a long and mostly depressing day, and although I supposed getting naked with Stella might take my mind off the bad stuff for a little while, it wouldn't change the predicament we were all in.

When the two of us were alone in the lift, I asked her, "What's this about?"

"I have something I need to tell you," she said, "and—er—you're not gonna like it."

She said no more until we were shut away in her bedroom, which although was maybe fifteen–twenty seconds later, still gave me enough time to think of all sorts of awful possibilities. Was she about to break my heart in some way? Had she been seeing someone else? Had I gotten her pregnant the other day? I thought I could probably deal with that last one, although it would certainly be a game-changer, and really not something I wanted to have to deal with at this time. Jessica was doing pretty well despite being pregnant with Tommy's child, all things considered, but I didn't at all want to be in her position—or more accurately, to have gotten Stella into her position. That wasn't supposed to happen until after I was gone…

Only when the door had closed did I think of something else she could be about to tell me, something that would be a lot easier for me to deal with, and I quickly seized upon it. "Does this have something to do with Underwood being here? I know you had to get a little—er—close to him—"

She held up a hand to stall me. "No, nothing to do with him. I'm way past caring about that now. This is worse: I've been thinking about this since we had that meeting before dinner, and I've got an idea for something that might—maybe—make Lucien change his mind about going nuclear tonight."

That got my hopes up for a split-second before I remembered that whatever she was about to tell me was probably going to be bad, so staying as calm as I could, said, "What's that?"

"Well," she swallowed, "I know he was bad before, but he's only been this bad—like, killing hundreds of people at a time bad—since I left him and joined you guys. I think maybe he might mellow out a bit if I went back to him—just me, not the rest of you. That way, you'll be free to keep on fighting and maybe he'll think he's scared you badly enough that he won't set off any bombs for a couple of days."

My brain had totally jammed with panic as she spoke. When she finished, I forced myself to say the only coherent thought I had. "That—er—that feels like a really, really, really, *really* bad idea. I can't emphasise enough how bad that idea feels to me."

The sad smile she gave me in response to my reaction scared me worse than anything she had said. "I thought you'd say something like that."

"Okay, okay," I said, beginning to pace as I tried to think my way through this. "First of all, I think you're wrong to think that he'll back down if we only give him you. He was very clear that he wanted all of us, and if he knows he has the advantage, I think he'll push the bargain even harder. Secondly, he's going to get all he can out of you; you know a lot about what's going on in here that I'm sure he'd love to know. Then when he's done with you, if you're lucky he'll only put an influential charm on you; and if you're unlucky—well, I don't even wanna think about that."

She just stood there as I ranted, following my pacing with her eyes, still smiling sadly as if she had come to some deeper understanding than I had yet to grasp.

"Thirdly," I went on, "we need you here—you're too valuable to us. None of us could have done what you did with the Villain Crystal this morning. And—and—I need you, Stella. I don't wanna lose you now, not when I've only got twelve days to live—eleven in a few hours."

I felt a little guilty playing that last card, but I was desperate. I would have said just about anything to make her change her mind on this one; as I had said before, it felt like a really, really, really, *really* bad idea.

"If I may," she said, reaching out and taking me by the shoulder. I could have pulled away and kept pacing, but I chose to let her bring me to a halt so that we could look at each other. "I know there's a chance Lucien won't do as we hope, but at this point, even a small chance is worth taking if it saves all those lives. I'm sure you're right that he'll try to get all he can out of me, but he won't be able to if we protect my mind before I leave here. That device you created to shield us from his mind is exactly suited for this sort of thing."

"Maybe," I conceded, "but then he'll just torture you for it. You know he will, because that's what he did to Natalie."

"You're right, he might," she said, "but he may not go as hard on me. I don't expect him to try to take me back now, not now that he's got Lena"—she looked rather distasteful as she said this—"but it might be just enough to make it bearable. It's nothing I haven't gone through before, and I'm pretty confident in my ability to get through it without giving anything up."

It was hard to argue with her on that point. She'd gotten pretty good at holding up under torture over the years—her father having given her plenty of hands-on experience. I doubted Lucien would go easier on her because of her history, but even if he didn't she might still be able to cope with it, especially if he couldn't access her mind. I still didn't like this—I didn't want to let her go and allow her to walk into the welcoming arms of danger—but her logic was beginning to get the better of my own. I was reminded of how I had felt about the prophecy that had foretold my defeat of Arnold Hammerson: If there was the smallest chance that I could finish it, wasn't I obliged to try, even if it resulted in my own death? And the worst of it, from my perspective, was that I didn't really believe Stella would be risking her own life. It felt far more likely to me that Lucien would put an influential charm on her and force her to be his magical adviser.

"As for the Villain Crystal," she went on, "it would probably be better if we don't use that thing anyway. I didn't feel good using it—it was as though it brought out the worst in me. I would suggest sticking with Marc and his crystal, and that thing you created to take power from the Sien-Leoard Crystal. I can't see you achieving any more than that with the Villain Crystal."

I sighed; I was left with only one option. "And me, Stella?"

She kissed me gently and said quietly, "I think you know what's best here. You were selfless enough to sacrifice your soul for this, after all."

We held each other close then. I wanted to cry, but annoyingly, the tears wouldn't come. Sometimes, I hated being a guy; I had emotions and they were trapped inside me, and I couldn't seem to do anything about them. Stella was going to leave tonight, probably very soon, and I couldn't do a damn thing to stop her, because I understood too well why she was doing it. My only hope now was that one of the others would be able to talk her out of it, but my hopes of that were pretty low; she was no more likely to listen to them than to me.

"When will you go?" I asked quietly.

"Very soon," she said. "What time is it now, half past seven or something? We can't afford to wait too long; Lucien never gave a time for his deadline."

"I know, but—can we spend a little time together first?"

She smiled again, and this one looked considerably happier. "Not too long, but I would like that."

So that was what we did, and it turned out that now that I knew I would be about to lose Stella, most likely for the rest of my life (what little remained of it), I was in the mood for fun stuff after all. It went far too quickly for my liking, though; before long, before I'd had enough, she was telling me it was time to stop. She didn't want to either, I could tell, and I really did try to take advantage of that, but she was so firm in her decision that she resisted. I even stooped to using my own magic to arouse her in the hope that her natural instincts would override her logic, but she resisted that too. She had made up her mind, and was pushing against every temptation to turn back. The only move I didn't stoop to was actually physically restraining her, which I could have done using the magic I had given myself. I knew I would regret that later, but I couldn't bring myself to do that to her.

All I could do, after we had put our clothes back on, was go with her down to the control room and break this dreadful news. The three Woodwards were the only people in the room, which took me a bit by surprise. They were monitoring the displays, which showed that Marc had left the base and appeared to be forcing Natalie to eat—it was awful to watch as she did all she could to refuse, but he had the crystal and he wasn't taking no for an answer. As bad as it looked, I was on Marc's side; I couldn't bear the thought of Natalie starving herself to death. I switched my gaze to the spyer, which was still locked onto Lucien, and showed him sitting in the very familiar den in the Hammerheart base; he appeared to be deep in concentration.

"Hey, you two," Amelia said to us, taking a moment to see who had walked in and then looking back at Marc on the screen. "You done talking?"

"Yes," Stella said, sitting in a seat near the Woodwards, "and we've made a decision."

I said nothing to her use of the word 'we'; this didn't feel like my decision at all. I was just going along with it because I had no choice. I took another moment to watch Marc, and an idea occurred to me—not about Stella, but about Natalie, and about something that we could try to get her out of that prison. It might have been tried before I'd gotten here, I didn't know, but on the off chance that it hadn't been…

"What's that?" Mr. Woodward asked absently.

All three of them were paying very close attention in short order, though, as Stella began to explain the decision she had made. Amelia threw me a few dirty looks throughout, but all I did was sit there, feeling downcast and hoping that one of these three would talk her out of it. I was thankful that James wasn't here; if he had been, he probably would have agreed with her logic. I only interrupted the discussion, which was becoming tearful from both Amelia and Stella, when I noticed that Marc was waving on the display screen, ready to be let back in. When he was updated on the deal, he was at first stunned and then angry, sure that Stella had lost her mind.

It was Mr. Woodward who tried hardest to talk Stella out of what she was doing, using all the same logical points as I had, but with no more success. Stella reiterated over and over again that she knew what she was doing, that she understood the danger she was putting herself in, and that she would almost certainly be put back under an influential charm. I saw the point when first Lillian, and then Mr. Woodward, accepted that there was no changing her mind, and they began trying to think of all they could do to ensure her safety while she was out there.

"Protecting your mind will be most important," Lillian said, "as we need that to protect us. There's no point being invisible or untraceable if you want him to find you, but perhaps some sort of spell that will shield you from his magic should he choose to turn it on you would be good."

I shook my head. "Lucien will have enough raw magic to break through any shield we put around her—that's what Fewul said earlier. Maybe the one that'll make spells pass right through her?"

Mr. Woodward looked uneasy. "That will make it impossible for him to keep her in line, and although that will be fine for us, it may not be fine for Stella. It's likely to send him into a rage, and that could be dangerous for her."

Stella nodded. "You're right, I should go unprotected—physically, anyway," she added, seeing the look on my face. "don't worry about me —I'll suffer a bit, but ultimately I'll be fine."

"Hold up," Marc said loudly, putting his hand up. "Now just hold up a second. We're actually doing this mad plan?"

"She's made up her mind, Marc," Mr. Woodward said gently as he drew his daughter into a hug—Amelia had tears streaming down her face. "I don't want to lose her either, but it's like she said: if there's any small chance it could prevent Lucien from setting off bombs tonight, it's worth trying."

"Not if he kills her and nukes whatever anyway," Marc muttered darkly, but it appeared that the very last of the resistance to Stella's plan had been overcome. My emotions were back, and as I watched her and

Mr. Woodward get up and begin looking around for the appropriate devices to set her up, I felt that this time, I might actually cry. I had to force myself not to—that might have been okay upstairs when it had been just the two of us, but it wasn't now.

Within minutes, Stella was standing there, entirely traceable and with no shields of any kind around her body. They had even removed her access to the fourth dimension, so that Lucien wouldn't have any easy access to it—that is, he would have to create it himself if he was going to follow us that way. Only her mind was protected, shielded from Lucien's Honnie mind so that he wouldn't be able to take control of her that way and access all her memories from the time she had spent in this base— including the intimate times she had spent with me. Lucien possibly finding out about those was very low on my list of concerns, but it was still there. We had also used the device I'd created to protect one's mind from ordinary magical penetration, just in case Lucien thought to resort to his own magical powers to read her mind, and I was relieved when Marc, who was testing it with the Hero Crystal, reported that her mind had become opaque to him. If that hadn't worked, Marc would have used magic to stop her from leaving—something he looked like he wanted to do anyway.

Mr. Woodward had reluctantly steered the base out of Natalie's room and taken it into Stella's old bedroom, which remained as Stella had left it just a few days earlier. As he did, we looked at what Lucien was doing on the spyer; he hadn't moved from the den, and appeared to be in the process of shooing a disgruntled Lena away.

"He's been doing that on and off all evening," Mr. Woodward told me and Stella. "She's desperate for attention from him, and he's intent on doing—well—whatever it is he's doing."

"You're sure he hasn't already set the bomb off?" Stella asked anxiously.

Mr. Woodward hesitated just long enough for me to get my hopes up; if Stella leaving here became pointless, even if it meant that the worst had happened somewhere else, I would be silently thankful. I would never say so, but I would feel it. "I'm fairly sure he hasn't. While we're keeping an eye on things here, we've got other people throughout the base watching the news; someone will let us know if anything big happens."

"Okay, then," she took a deep breath, "then let's do this."

We all got a chance to hug her goodbye then. Mine was the longest, but it still wasn't enough for me. I wanted to kiss her as well, but held myself back. When I let her go and she went to stand in the corner to be let out of the base, I felt horribly empty inside. The sense of loss was heavy on my chest, and I would have been so grateful if someone could have been there for me in that moment to give me a hug and make me feel better. Marc and Amelia were in each other's arms, and Frederic and Lillian were standing close together, but I sat in a seat on my own.

"Good luck, Stella," Mr. Woodward said, leaning around Marc and then pressing the button. Stella vanished from the control room and appeared a moment later in her bedroom—the place where she had spent the best part of her childhood, and which she always seemed to keep coming back to.

"What do we do now?" Amelia asked tearfully.

"We watch her," Mr. Woodward said sadly. "This is going to be difficult, but we need to see what he does to her, and how much he's able to get out of her. John, you don't have to stay if this is too difficult for you to watch—"

"No, I'll stay," I said quickly. I couldn't bear the thought of leaving, because as difficult as this was going to be, not knowing what became of her would haunt me. If I left, I would be running back down here every few minutes to see how things were going—I wouldn't be able to stop myself. I had no choice but to see this through.

Stella had taken a few moments to adjust to her new surroundings, glancing at her wardrobe as though deciding whether or not to change her clothes. Apparently, she felt she didn't have the time, for she turned away from it and headed straight for the bedroom door. She opened it a little and looked out into the hallway; Marc followed her with the controls, but we couldn't see what she could see until she opened the door all the way to reveal that the hallway beyond was empty. She stepped out and shut the door behind her, glancing once to her right, in the direction of Lucien's bedroom, before turning the other way and heading towards the living room.

I quickly glanced at the screen on which Lucien was still being shone; he had straightened up in his seat, a dark smile on his face. He had clearly traced Stella already and judging by the absent look in his eyes, was presently watching her from afar to see what she would do. He made no move to get up, though, nor did he appear to use any magic against her—at least thus far, she seemed to be unaffected by anything. I assumed that for now, he was going to wait to see what she would do, as he would have already determined that he couldn't get into her mind.

Stella got as far as the living room, and was about to turn into the corridor outside the living quarters (heading towards the den, in other words), but that was where she was brought up short by Lena coming in the opposite direction. Unaware of each other due to the blind corner, they almost collided in the entrance to the living quarters. Registering Stella's presence, Lena took a quick step backward, her eyes widening and her face showing raw fear.

"Sorry," she said, taking another step back so that Stella had plenty of room to walk past her.

We couldn't see Stella's face, as we were situated behind her and looking over her shoulder, but she sounded only a little startled and a little amused as she said, "Lena, it's only me—the *real* Stella, not Fewul."

Lena's face remained frozen as she looked more closely at Stella; a few seconds later, she slowly relaxed, but her expression became confused. "Stella? What are you doing here?"

"Looking for Lucien, and I don't have a lot of time," Stella said, taking a step forward, but before she could pass Lena, the latter stepped in front of her.

"You left," she said fiercely, and now she looked pissed going on seriously angry. "You walked out on Lucien, and he's moved on without you. You can't just waltz back in here and expect him to take you back."

"That's not why I'm here," Stella said quickly, "and if you don't mind, I really am in a hurry."

Lena didn't move, but she did do something none of us, including Stella by the look of it, were expecting. She bitch-slapped Stella clean across the face. Stella staggered back a step as Lena advanced on her; we still couldn't see Stella's expression, but Lena's eyes were blazing. She looked mad, beyond anything I could have imagined of her, and I felt pretty sure that this new change had been brought on by whatever tinkering Lucien had done inside her head.

"That was for last week," she hissed, backing Stella against the wall beside the door into the living quarters and getting very close to her. "I know you don't have any magic now, but you were awful when you had it. If I had anything magical on me now, I'd make you pay for that invasion, but I don't, so a slap will have to do."

"Okay," Stella said in a small voice. "I can't argue with you on that one, but it doesn't change the fact that I need to see—"

Lena wasn't done. Cutting off Stella's words she punched her squarely in the ribs, just below her left breast. It was a hard enough punch that Stella was briefly winded, and would have fallen down if the wall behind her hadn't propped her up.

"And that one was for me, and all the trouble you've caused me this year," Lena spat at her. "I did not like the feeling of wanting someone I couldn't have, and don't think I don't know you had a big hand in that. I got the last laugh in the end, though: I've got Lucien, because you didn't appreciate him when you had the chance, so now as far as I'm concerned, you can have John as much as you want. I was so foolish to waste all that time on him when all along, Lucien was so, so much better —in every way you can imagine."

"Good for you," Stella snapped. By the sound of it, her shock had worn off and she was getting pretty pissed herself. "If you don't mind him using magic to make you enjoy it more, then you've got a sweet deal. Now if you don't mind, I need to see him—right now."

Lena hesitated for a moment, and then began to smile. "Okay, then, if you're sure that's what you want," she said sweetly, and the tone along with the malicious expression on her face made me wonder why I'd ever been attracted to Lena. She was pretty and very sexy, and had been a good person not too long ago, but in the process of making her all his, Lucien had put something pretty rotten inside her.

She turned and walked back along the hallway towards the den with Stella following close behind her. They turned the corner and came to the first door on the right, which stood open and revealed Lucien deep in concentration. He'd been pretending to be working so that it would appear he hadn't known a thing when Stella first saw him, even though we all knew better—not only had we seen him following Stella with his minds-eye, but there was no way he couldn't have heard the two girls talking from where he was. He looked up and registered an expression of surprise that looked genuine enough—so he was probably using magic to make it so.

"Stella," he observed. "Is that really you?"

"Yes, it is," she said bravely, taking a step into the den ahead of Lena. Now both of their backs were to us, and the only person whose face we could see was Lucien.

He surveyed her for a few seconds before quickly getting to his feet. "Well, this is just wonderful."

"It is?" Lena said, sounding irritable.

"Of course," he smiled at the two girls, but the smile didn't reach his eyes—they were full of a dark anticipation. "Now that she's here, she can fill the gaps in our knowledge. You know, the things about their base and their working that you yourself weren't able to figure out while you were there."

"You mean you're gonna stop working for her but not for me?" Lena said sulkily.

Lucien turned his smile on her, and there was a touch more warmth in it now. "Oh, I am gonna spank you so hard for that one later; but yes, I am going to postpone my business for Stella—she could have important information for me. I'd like you to leave the top level of the base for a little while, Lena, so that I can deal with her without interruption."

"When can I come back?" she asked, still sounding sulky.

"I'll retrieve you myself, wherever you are," he said, his eyes glinting at her, "and when I do, I'll give you a big reward for being so patient today. Just—don't leave the Hammerheart Network, wherever you decide to go, as I don't know if you'll be safe on the outside."

"Fine, but you really need to help me find things to do while you're spending all this time working," she said, and walked away towards the stairs.

"You'll keep," Lucien called after her, but his attention had already returned to Stella.

Ropes shot from one of his fingers, wrapped tightly around Stella's wrists, ankles and waist, bound her wrists to her sides and raised her ankles up so that they pressed against her butt, and then flipped her upside-down in the air. He raised her up so that their faces were almost level, hers only a little below his, so that he could observe her as the blood rushed to her head. To her credit, Stella bore all of this without complaint, having already resigned herself to this kind of treatment before she had left our base. It was much more difficult for those of us in the control room to cope: Amelia covered her eyes, perhaps reminded of the time when Arnold Hammerson had done the same thing to her—though unlike Amelia had that day, at least Stella wasn't wearing a skirt that would fall down around her when she was hanging upside-down.

As for me, it was painful to watch as Lucien left the den, magically dragging an upside-down Stella along with him, but I forced myself to see it through—I owed that much to Stella. In the end, Lucien took her back to her bedroom where she had begun this ridiculous mission. He bound her against a wall bare of furniture or shelves, twisting the ropes around so that her limbs were at forty-five degree angles to her body. What it meant in practical terms, as I couldn't help noticing, was that it left every part of her body, not counting those pressed against the wall, horribly exposed to whatever Lucien might choose to do to her.

"I find this oddly suspicious behaviour, Stella," he said conversationally as he proceeded to perform spells around them. I couldn't see what they did, but I had a pretty good idea: He was making sure that if we were watching this, we wouldn't be able to intervene to save Stella.

"Why is that?" she asked, doing well to keep her voice level.

"Well, I can't think of a single reason why you would return to me," he said. Having finished his magic he placed himself a few feet in front of her, close enough that he could reach out and touch her, but so far, he didn't. "I mean, I certainly couldn't make you come back. Your *friends* wouldn't make you come back, and I highly doubt you have returned in hopes of getting me back—that doesn't seem like your style. Unless, of course, you have decided that there is no point being with *them* anymore, now that your 'real imaginary friend' is dead."

He was referring to me, of course, using the name Stella had given to me before she had known who I was—when I had just been the person with whom she sometimes connected when she slept. He looked cruelly satisfied as he said this, his intent to hurt her with his words as much as possible. I wished Stella had reacted more strongly; a person who had just lost the love of their life would appear to be in more pain than Stella presently appeared.

"I did choose to come back," she said firmly, "but not because I want to get you back for myself. I can't be with someone who reminds me so much of my father."

Rage flashed across Lucien's face, before it was replaced by an icy coldness. A moment later, Stella screamed as he thrust unendurable agony upon her. He wasn't holding an agonator, but he was clearly using the same magic which those devices employed. Stella couldn't move, obviously, but all her muscles rapidly clenched and unclenched as the torture went on for another ten seconds. When it was over, Stella was panting and shaking in her binds, and Lucien was watching her coldly.

"Then why are you here, Stella? Do tell me, because I cannot figure it out."

"I want back on your team," she gasped through the lingering pain. "It was a mistake to go back to them. It's obvious now that you're going to defeat them. They tried all their best tricks earlier and you still won. You're gonna be great, and I don't wanna go down with them."

It was a good speech—so good, in fact, that Marc and Amelia swapped startled looks, apparently wondering if this was the real reason why she had wanted so badly to leave the base. I wasn't fooled, though, and I didn't think Mr. Woodward was either. Unfortunately, Lucien didn't look convinced either.

"Perhaps," he said slowly. "That would explain why you have come to me without a shield around you, but it also seems that you have not brought me any of their strange magical devices, have you?"

"Er—no. Sorry, I didn't think of it."

"And yet, your mind is hidden from me," he went on, as though talking to himself now. "You know of my Honnie mind, of course, and yet I am unable to take, or even sense your mind. Now why is that, Stella?"

"They have a device that can do that," she admitted, "as you probably guessed. I had to have that protection, though; it was the only way I could get out."

"In other words, for their own protection," Lucien agreed. "Yes, I can understand that. But you see, Stella, it doesn't really matter, because in case you've forgotten, I am a Sorcerer, and your mind is forever open to the observation of Sorcerers thanks to your father. I am reading your mind right now."

Stella looked stricken by that, as did everyone else in the control room. The bottom had fallen out of my stomach: How could that have happened? We had specifically tried to prevent exactly this from happening, and while Marc and Mr. Woodward looked accusingly at me, I looked to where the device we had used to 'attempt' to protect her mind lay on a nearby seat.

"I thought you said it was opaque," Amelia whispered, her terrified voice nevertheless carrying through the room.

"Oh, yes," Lucien said, smiling darkly at Stella. "Your father made arrangements to prevent your mind from ever being truly protected from someone seriously determined to get in, even if you tried the usual tricks to defend yourself. Your thoughts betrayed you just then, Stella; they revealed that you do not wish me to know any more about what your friends are doing than I already do. I could torture you for that, but I have a better idea…"

"Bring her back in," Mr. Woodward said sharply to Marc, who was at the controls. "We can't risk him scraping her mind—it'll put us all in too much danger."

I agreed with that. This mission had misfired and it was time to abort. Marc tried to do just that, but the magic Lucien had performed when he'd first come into Stella's room got in the way; it prevented us from getting close enough to Stella to draw her back into the base. He went for the Hero Crystal and tried desperately to break through the shield, but as it had been created with the Sien-Leoard Crystal, he didn't have enough power. Realising this, I scrambled for the magic enhancer and tried to break through whatever spells Lucien had placed between himself and us, but I only had enough power to equal whatever Lucien had done—and whatever he had done was proving to be resistant to our attempts to break through. By the time Lucien was done doing whatever it was he was doing, we were no closer to them.

"So," Lucien said quietly, watching a fearful Stella closely, "you turned yourself over to me in the hope that it would be enough to stop me from setting off one of my bombs? Ah, Stella, if only it were true, but I made my conditions very clear, and they have not been obeyed. If I am to take your presence here as proof that the rest of your friends will not be coming, then I'm afraid I'll have to—"

"No!" Stella said quickly. "don't do it! They might come. They might, if they know there's no other way."

"I believe there was a meeting earlier today," Lucien said, "in which James suggested they do just that, but everyone in the room rejected the idea. Let's see, who was there besides James? Well there was you, Marc, Amelia, Peter, Frederic, and—who is that last one—well! Well, well, well."

Stella didn't say anything to this. No one needed to point out that Lucien had finally learnt that I was still alive after all.

"That's…disturbing," he said, gazing at her. "Now why would they knowingly do such a terrible thing to him? Even I wouldn't have put him through something like that."

Again, Stella said nothing. Lucien watched her for a few more seconds then said, "Well, that's okay. I've got all I can out of you, Stella, including the fact that you were ready to die tonight. You actually believe that there is nothing left for you, and you were ready to sacrifice yourself —if it came to that—in the hope that it might save others. Well, if that is the case, then there actually *is* something else I want from you."

"You're gonna kill me?" she asked casually, not looking at all scared of the prospect.

"I loved you, you know," he told her. "I would have given you the world, and I thought I was very understanding—very patient with you—for the entire time that I've known you. It hurt when you told me I wasn't your first preference, but I stayed with you because I loved you. It hurt when you told me that you didn't want to fully give yourself to me until you were sure that you couldn't get what you really wanted, but I took it like a man. Or rather, I took it like a pussy, because a real man wouldn't have put up with that kind of crap. Instead, I offered you the world and you turned me down. I accepted it because I loved you, only to have you use me and then run away at the first opportunity.

"So what do you think, Stella? What do you think is the one thing I might want from you now?"

Wow. When Lucien explained it like that, I could actually understand how much pain she had put him through. I would even have sympathised with him if he had delivered a speech like that two weeks ago, before Arnold Hammerson had invaded his soul and he'd gone all psychopathic on us. Stella, too, looked rocked by all he had just said, and there were tears in her eyes as she said, "If you want me to love you back, I don't think I can—not now. I'm damaged goods, Lucien."

He laughed, and any sympathy I might have had for him vanished at the sound of it. "Love, Stella? Really? Why would I want you to love me when I could use my magic to force you to love me? Why would I when I could force every single woman in the world to desire me beyond anything or anyone else, if I so chose? No, Stella, because you see, when you have that kind of power, the things that you can do with it become a lot less valuable. Now, Lena loves me and it doesn't matter if I influenced her mind, because it's just as real as every other kind of love in the world."

"Agree to disagree on that one," Stella muttered.

Lucien raised his hand and Stella was lifted away from the wall, though her arms and legs remained held in place. "No, the only thing I want from you now, Stella, is the only thing of any value you have left to give me. Since I know you won't give it to me willingly, as you refused to do all the time we were dating, I will take it from you. And guess what, Stella? You are going to enjoy it very much. I will be the best you ever had."

He lay her down on the bed and began ravaging her, ripping at her clothes and throwing them aside. He then proceeded to rape her as we were forced to watch, unable to do anything to stop it. Marc and I were back to trying desperately to make some sort of difference with our magic, but even combined, everything we tried failed. Amelia had turned away from the display screens and Mr. Woodward had taken her in his arms and buried her head in his chest, covering her eyes and ears. Lillian too put her head down, unable to watch. I wanted to look away too, but that would have meant giving up trying to rescue her—and through the whole ordeal, I never stopped trying things. Unfortunately, the ordeal itself worked against me, for I was so filled with horror and despair that I probably missed a few ideas that may have worked.

Stella was still bound and unable to do anything to stop him, but at least in the beginning, she was able to lie there without making a sound or showing any sign that she was enjoying it. But Lucien wasn't lying when he said she would enjoy it. He worked his magic on her so that soon enough, she was unable to stop herself from moaning with pleasure, then gasping with it, and eventually crying out for more. This was somehow worse than before, because not only was she being physically raped, but it was as though it were happening to her on a mental level as well. Also—let's not tell a lie, John—it hurt to know that he was forcing more pleasure on her than I would have been able to give, unless I'd given myself that magical ability as well.

It didn't last as long as I'd thought it would. Lucien pulled out of her, causing her to moan and beg him to keep going (that also hurt), but it looked as though he was forcing himself to stop, as though there was something else he wanted to do to her. And so there was: As she lay there, fully naked except for the ropes still holding her in place, he put his hands on her breasts and squeezed. She screamed in agony as blood began pouring from them, and it was only when he raised his hands that I saw what he'd done: His fingers had turned into claws.

A new kind of ravaging began. Over and over again, Lucien dug his claws into her body, ripping through her flesh and splintering her bones in places. He methodically worked over her arms, legs and torso, though not touching anything above her collarbones. Blood soaked through her bed sheets, and when they could absorb no more, began dripping down the side of her bed. Not even in my worst imaginings had I thought of Lucien doing such an awful thing to her. She screamed until she lost her voice, and even then she gasped and whimpered and begged for it to end —for it to just be over.

The whole thing probably only lasted five–ten minutes. Who knew how long it could have gone on for, though (probably until Stella's life gave out), if it hadn't been for a beeping sound that was barely audible to Lucien, let alone those of us in the control room. He began tapping his watch, one of his claws turning back into a finger for the process, before looking down at the pitiful Stella.

"You're lucky; it looks like I'm needed elsewhere, but it was fun while it lasted."

He got to his feet, vanished all the blood on his clothes with a wave of his hand, and then waved the same hand in Stella's direction. She hadn't been moving before, but now she became completely limp and silent. She was dead; I knew it as surely as I knew that I wanted nothing more than to murder Lucien in that moment. He turned and hurried out of the bedroom, passing directly beneath our base on his way out. Now we were left alone in the room with what had been Stella's body, but what now looked like her head next to a bloody pile of meat and bone.

A horrified silence filled the control room for what felt like a very long time. It was Marc who recovered first, gingerly touching the controls, and then informing us that he could now pass through whatever shield Lucien had put in place to keep us from intervening.

"I'm going out there," he told us firmly. "don't anyone try to talk me out of it. I'm going and getting her body, because she doesn't deserve to be left like this."

"Okay," Lillian said, taking his seat as he went to stand in the corner.

She let him out of the base, and the first thing he did was restore Stella's body to what it had been when she'd been alive. With all her flesh and bone repaired and her blood back inside her body where it belonged, she looked like she could have been sleeping. Except that she wasn't: She was dead, and a big part of the reason why was because she had been suicidal. I'd known that she was depressed, but I had totally under-estimated the depth of it. If I'd known, I really would have physically restrained her and not let her leave. In that moment, I resented the dead girl out there, even as Marc put her clothes back together and magically put them back on her body.

I was interrupted from these sad and bitter thoughts by the control room door opening and several people rushing in. Peter was in the lead, and he was followed by Rebecca, Harry, Simon and Felicity. All of them were white-faced with shock, their eyes wide and horrified, and I couldn't blame them in the slightest. That only lasted for a couple of seconds, though, before my mind caught up with my senses, and I realised that none of them had so much as noticed what had happened to Stella. My heart sank even further in the instant before Peter spoke, because I knew what was coming...

"He did it. He actually did it. He nuked Melbourne."

Chapter 16: The Little Garden

Mr. Woodward was out of his seat in an instant. "What? How do you know this?"

"We didn't know for sure at first," Felicity said shakily. "A lot of us were in the lounge room watching the football when the station seemed to lose its feed. Most of us thought it was just a technical glitch except my dad and Peter's dads. They told us to check on other channels, and it was confirmed pretty quickly."

"It looks like he actually targeted the MCG," Peter said—unlike Felicity, his voice was deadly calm, "as if he wanted to get as many people as possible with it. He even waited until early in the third quarter to do it, when everybody would be in and probably no one had left."

"And they said on the TV that there were probably more than sixty thousand people in the stadium alone, to say nothing of the surrounding area," Felicity went on.

"The last thing we saw before we came down here was a video on the ABC," Rebecca added. "It was taken from a helicopter flying towards the city from the southeast, and you can see where it all happened—the mushroom cloud and everything."

This was as bad as anything I could have imagined, and worse. I swapped a look with Amelia, and the wide-eyed expression of horror on her face pretty well reflected how I was feeling inside. Lillian remained in her seat, but she looked as though she had aged about ten years since Stella and I had entered the control room not so long ago, and in spite of everything else that was going on, I was forced to recognise that she really was an old woman, and now that she no longer had magic to keep her alive, this war could actually end up killing her before too long—and not in the same way that it had already killed me and Stella.

Only Frederic Woodward looked resilient enough to deal with this new disaster. When Rebecca finished speaking, he said, "We can't save those who have already been lost, but we must try to save as many who are still living as we can. As soon as Marc is ready, we'll have to go there."

"What happened?" Harry asked in a hushed voice, all his usual bravado gone. He and Simon had been silent this whole time because apparently, unlike the other three who had just entered the room, they had looked at the display screens and seen that Marc and Stella were out there. I too glanced at the display and saw that Marc was standing beside Stella's body, now lying peacefully on her childhood bed, and waving to be let back into the base.

"Lucien killed Stella," I said flatly, and Peter and Rebecca both gasped in horror as they finally realised what else was going on. "She tried to change his mind about the bomb, but he worked out what she was doing, and he raped and tortured her before—before finishing it. I guess he left when someone told him the explosion had happened."

My voice sounded dead in my own ears. My shock over what had transpired in the last five minutes was too huge too allow any real emotions through. I could sense that there were emotions beneath it, though: a great sadness, and beneath that, a terrible rage. I would examine those emotions more closely later, but there was still too much going on for me to even touch them at the moment.

Lillian was too distracted by her own turmoil to notice that Marc was finished, so Frederic leaned around her and pushed the button to let Marc back into the base. He appeared in the corner of the control room a moment later, and because she was no longer a living person, Stella's body was pulled into the base along with him; it crumpled to the floor beside him in a way that was awful to look at.

"Hey," he said as he took in the new arrivals, "I guess they told you what happened?"

"Marc, we need to go now," Frederic said without any preamble. "Lucien has set off a nuclear bomb in Melbourne; we must do what we can."

"What?" Marc said, apparently not taking this in for a few seconds, but as the gravity of Frederic's words sank in, his composure slipped entirely.

"I don't think we should take the base to Melbourne," I said into the silence which followed. "Whoever goes, should go alone so that those of us who stay here won't be in any danger."

Another silence followed before Frederic nodded. "Marc, I know you're in shock, but you are the Seventh Sorcerer. We need you to find all the inner strength you possess to push through this. Can you do that?"

Marc was motionless for a couple of seconds before he nodded stiffly.

"Someone should take the magic enhancer you created, John, to help him. This job is too big for one person to do alone. Are either of you up for it?" Frederic asked, directing the question to Amelia and me.

She shook her head at once, tears still on her face, and I followed her lead. If Stella hadn't just died, I would still be in enormous shock, but I would probably have the strength to push through it and do what I could to help other people. Now, though, no such strength could be found.

"Very well, I'll do it," Frederic said, and I gratefully passed the magic enhancer over to him. "Come now, Marc; there's no time to waste."

He strode quickly to the corner where Marc stood, and Lillian gathered herself enough to push the button to let them out of the base— Marc first, followed quickly by Frederic. The two of them stood in Stella's bedroom a moment later, and after they exchanged a few words, Frederic gripped Marc's arm and the two of them teleported away—

apparently, Frederic was sufficiently accomplished with magic that he too could find a way through anti-teleportation spells. The room outside was now empty, and the control room was silent and still. Now there was just me, Amelia, Lillian, Peter, Rebecca, Harry, Simon and Felicity—and of course Stella's body, lying in the corner where she had fallen.

That wouldn't do at all.

"We need to do something for Stella," I told the room at last. "We need to have a funeral or something, and we need to bury her."

"We can do that," Rebecca said tearfully. "She can go next to my parents."

"I guess we'll have to do it by hand too, since we don't have any magic except for evil stuff now," Peter said shakily.

"We can do that," Simon said at once, swapping a look with his twin. "We'll carry her up to the yard and one of you guys go get a sheet or something—"

But Amelia was already on her feet, the Light Crystal in her hand, lighting up her face and casting the rest of the room into shadow by comparison. I had a moment to think that as good as the Light Crystal was, it wouldn't be very useful in a situation like this; not when there was actual magic we needed to perform for a specific purpose right now. As Amelia walked over to where Stella lay, however, the crystal seemed to glow even more brightly in her hand; and as it did so, a stretcher appeared beneath Stella and raised her slowly into the air. An invisible force rearranged her lifeless body so that it would look as though she were lying peacefully, as if asleep, instead of looking like she'd been disregarded where she had fallen.

Then I understood: Of course the Light Crystal could perform this kind of magic. The Light Crystal was good, and everything about what we were going to do for Stella was good. I remembered back to when we had first taken possession of the Light Crystal, and how I had accidentally used it to get out of a detention with Hall. Hall may have been unusually cruel for a teacher, but it didn't change the fact that how I had used the Light Crystal on that occasion had been pretty selfish, especially compared to a lot of the things we had tried to do with it since then. I wondered why that was, but now was hardly the time to think about such things.

"I'll take her out to the yard," Amelia was telling us, and it appeared that having something to do had given her some new strength. "You guys can come with me if you want, but I think some of you should go around the base and let everyone know what's just happened to Stella—and about the bomb if they don't already know. Just, not James and Erica; let those two sleep and they can wait till morning."

The rest of us got up and left the control room. Only when I looked back and saw it completely empty did I realise that this was probably the first time it had ever been so —except for periods in the middle of the night, I supposed. Lillian realised this at the same time I did, and remembering that her son was out there somewhere, went back to mind the fort. I gave her a grateful smile—which didn't feel like a smile on my lips at all—before skirting the pack and standing close to Peter as we piled into the lift. Most of us got out on the ground floor, except for Felicity, who had decided to go upstairs and check the bedrooms for anyone not in the loop with all that had gone down this evening.

Although I had created this base, in its short lifetime of just five days I had never actually set foot in the outside part. Everything I'd ever needed to do was indoors. In fact, I'd only created the outside part for recreation during off times, or if we were to come under attack. But we hadn't come directly under attack yet, thanks to Marc's untraceability, and we certainly hadn't had any off-time except for sleeping. It was rather colder than I had expected, and I had to wrap my arms around myself to keep them warm. It wasn't as dark as I would have expected though, thanks to the stars overhead, and even more thanks to the Light Crystal closer at hand.

A little garden had been created beside the main building, to the left of the front door as you came out. (By front, I meant front-facing, where the control room always faced front—that was just how I thought of directions within the base.) I hadn't created this garden, which meant that Marc probably had, and it was immediately clear why: This was where Brian and Minny Fletcher had been laid to rest. Two small stone plaques sat side-by-side close to the centre of the garden, shining brightly in the light cast by the crystal in Amelia's hand, looking very pretty surrounded by budding vegetation (which had obviously been enchanted to grow more quickly than usual so that we wouldn't have to wait for months for it to look nice). This would be a nice place for Stella to rest too, I thought...

...or *would* it? Cold as it was out here, I shuddered as a dark thought crossed my mind. The Hammersons had their own private cemetery somewhere within their network; Stella had visited it on the night her father had died, accompanied by Lucien, and it was right there and then that he began to lose his way. I had been in her mind when this had happened, and one thought that had crossed her mind in that time was that an enchantment existed that would teleport the Hammersons' bodies to that cemetery shortly after death, wherever and however it happened, so that they would always be buried together.

I absolutely did *not* want Stella to be teleported away to that awful place—she deserved so much better than that. I doubted very much that she would want to spend the rest of eternity there either. The question was, if it was going to happen, what could we do to stop it? I could think of only one thing that *might* work, and as the group began to disperse a little, giving Amelia a bit of space with Stella, I went up to her and tapped her on the shoulder, making her start.

"What?" she snapped at me.

I reminded her about the cemetery and asked if she thought she could put a block on that enchantment using the Light Crystal. She understood at once what I was talking about—her dread wasn't as strong as mine, probably because she hadn't seen that graveyard at night time—and immediately had a go at the magic. She told me she thought it had worked (at least, the crystal had gone warm in her hand, which usually meant that it had worked), but that we ought to get on with the funeral quickly, just in case it didn't work. I understood the point she was making without her actually saying it outright: even if Stella were to be teleported away to that cemetery, none of us would be bothered by it if we didn't know it had happened, and Stella herself had gone to a place where it didn't matter one bit what happened to her body. Of course, I would always wonder all the same....

More people were joining us in the yard now. At first, Peter and Rebecca had been the only two people to follow Amelia and me (and Stella) outside, the others choosing to go into the lounge room to break the news to the already-stunned people in there. Those people were coming out here now, gathering a short distance away from where Amelia stood beside a table on which Stella now lay. I went to join them, giving a pale-faced Jessica a hug and then being wrapped up by my parents. Mum and Dad didn't know how close I had been to Stella, especially in the last few days of her life, but they obviously knew that there was something there, and they may have even known about the connection (if Frederic had ever mentioned it to them). I felt a little bad for not confiding more in them, but mostly I just felt grateful that they were there.

I also felt that the dam wall holding my emotions back was beginning to crack.

At the edge of the garden, Amelia had laid Stella down on a waist-high table. She was lying face-up with her arms folded across her chest. Amelia had (magically, I assumed) wrapped a sheet around her so that only above her armpits was visible to us. She had even put a pillow beneath Stella's head so that it truly looked as though she were sleeping peacefully there. I supposed that Amelia would soon put her body in a coffin so that she could be buried along with the Fletchers.

I was so intent on watching Stella and trying to contain my emotions that I didn't see Amelia until she was standing right in front of me. This time, it was my turn to start.

"Sorry," she said quickly. "I was just gonna say, since my dad isn't here this time, I'll have to do this funeral. I'll say a few words and then I'll ask if anyone else wants to say something, and I think pretty much everyone is going to expect you to say something, so you should think fast about what you'll say."

"Okay, sure," I nodded, forcing my mind into this new channel. How ought I to eulogise Stella? Amelia was right—everyone would expect me to say a few words—but even if they didn't, I had to do so. Apart from Amelia herself, I had known Stella better than anyone else out here—and in fact, I had probably known her better than even Amelia had. It didn't have to be long, but Stella definitely deserved something.

It looked like everyone who was going to come was now here. The small crowd were gathered in a straggly semi-circle around the garden, everyone on their feet as no seats had been created. The murmuring was low and sad, but it cut off completely as Amelia began waving for everyone's attention. I positioned myself beside Peter at the front of the crowd as Amelia began to speak.

"Hi, everyone. Thanks for coming out here. I know that not many of you really knew Stella very well—she wasn't really in any of our lives until this year—so I appreciate that you all care enough to be here, and I'm sure she would too. Given what else has happened this evening, we won't take too long over this. I would like to say a few words about how *I* knew Stella, but before I do, I think it's important you all know why she died tonight. Even though it didn't go the way she had hoped, you should all know why she did what she did.

"Like all of us, she was terrified by the idea that Lucien might kill tens of thousands of people tonight—and as we all know now, she was right to be. She rationalised that if she handed herself over to him, he might consider it a great enough concession that he would hold off on any more terrorism, even though it would have, at best, meant that she would be put under an influential charm. In hindsight, I believe she knew all too well how much she was risking, and it illustrates perfectly how selfless she was until the very end.

"Of course, her risk didn't pay off. In spite of all the protection we put around her, Lucien figured out what she was really doing, and—well —maybe it was that which caused him to do what he did at that time. He also retaliated against Stella, and I won't describe what that included, except to say that it ended with—well—all of this here. Ultimately, things worked out far worse for us as a result of what she did, because as well as what Lucien did tonight, we lost her as well."

Amelia had held it together pretty well through most of that, but her voice began hitching through the last two sentences. She took a moment to compose herself before continuing, lowering her head and wiping tears out of her eyes. I had to swallow hard as I watched this; I was going to cry at some stage, whether out here or later on when I was alone, there was no doubt about it. And although I was closer to Stella than anyone else in this crowd, I could tell that others were deeply touched by what Amelia was saying. Beside me, Peter's face was scrunched up as he attempted to control his emotions, and on my other side, Liam had sunk to his knees and appeared to be praying.

"But this isn't about us—not right now. This is about Stella, and all that she was willing to give for us." She paused a moment, then went on. "In the time I've known Stella, she's always been like that—trying to help us out, in the full knowledge that her family—particularly her father—would punish her if he found out. She worked with us directly against her family when we captured the Sien-Leoard Crystal from Rock Haulter, and took an even bigger risk by rescuing a bunch of us from their Basement, right under their noses.

"Even when we shafted her and treated her with nothing but suspicion, she never turned on us. If she couldn't help us directly, she tried to do it quietly and without notice, such as when she stole the Darkness Crystal from her family and discretely gave it to us, or resisting them as much as she could when they gave her orders to carry out. This was the case when she was ordered to find a way to recapture the traitor, Sebastian Williams, from our custody; but was more important when she was ordered to use the Darkness Crystal to kill my mother. I wasn't sure for a long time, but I found out from her later that when she received that order, she flat-out refused to comply, causing someone else to do it for her, and resulting in a lot of pain for her."

I gulped as this previously unknown piece of knowledge hit me. I had known that Stella had been given such an order, but I must have assumed that she had carried it out—that she'd been forced to and there hadn't been any other option. I must have even forgiven her for doing so, if I'd made the assumption, and I'd never bothered to ask any follow-up questions about it. I supposed the question must have been broached during the weeks I had been in the Honnie world; that was the longest time since that Amelia and Stella would have spent a lot of time in close proximity. I was relieved that the issue had finally been set at ease for Amelia; if she was comfortable that Stella had done all she could, at her own cost, then the rest of us could be too.

"As a lot of you know, when we were able to bring her back into our army a couple of months ago, she was overjoyed to finally be able to help us directly, and she threw herself into it with unfaltering dedication. She told us everything she knew about what we were up against, which was something she'd been doing for my father even earlier than that—before we had turned her away, anyway. Who knows how many lives were ultimately saved as a result of the intel she gave us—at least hundreds would be my guess.

"Not that Stella ever thought about that. I was always able to read her mind, thanks to a curse her father had put on her long ago that made it impossible to shield her mind, and I can tell you that Stella never thought directly about the people she could be saving with what she knew. She knew it would save lives, of course, but her main thought all the time she was trying to help us was that nobody should have to suffer any portion of the life she had always known. The life she'd had with her family had been utterly miserable, and she knew that it would be somewhat like that for the whole world if the Hammersons were to have their way."

She paused again here, considering, then said, "I could probably ramble on even more about this—about how much she went through and how it made her into the person she was—but I *did* say I would keep this quick, so I'll leave it here. Before we lay her to rest, does anyone have anything they would like to say about Stella? Now's the time."

That was my cue, I knew. Amelia's eyes were directly on me, and as she had predicted, she wasn't the only one: Peter, and Rebecca on his other side, were both looking expectantly at me, and I could feel the gazes of other people as well. I took a deep breath and stepped away from the crowd, moving up to stand beside Amelia. I glanced down and a little to my left to where Stella lay, her sleeping face looking almost directly at me. Her eyes were closed, of course, ruining the effect a little, but then it would have been considerably worse if they had been open. I looked away from her and back to the small sea of waiting faces, most of them impossible to make out in the darkness over there.

"I know everyone was expecting me to say something, so here I am, but I think I would have done so anyway, because I did know Stella well and it wouldn't have been right for me to sit this out. I forget who knows what around here nowadays, but for those who don't, Stella and I had a strange mental connection where we could see into each other's minds when we slept. It came about from when her father failed to kill me as a baby, and was with us all our lives—not that we understood exactly what it was until more recently. It was the reason why she wound up trusting me as much as she did, because she knew what sort of person I was—and apparently she didn't have a problem with it. It was also the reason why I was one of the first to trust her, even when most people still thought she was as evil as the other Hammersons."

I paused here, needing a moment to think what to say next. My mind was flicking over all the memories I had of Stella, most of them taking place either way back in February or in the last few days. Sadly, we had been estranged for most of the time in between, connected only by our minds, so there weren't nearly as many memories as I would have liked; and many of the ones I had, I had no intention of sharing with the world. Additionally, I didn't want to just repeat a bunch of the stuff Amelia had said, which left me with very few options. But the seconds were lengthening, and not wanting everyone to think I was getting emotional (when in actual fact, my emotions were surprisingly controlled for the moment), I landed on the only thing I could think of.

"I hate that we got to spend so little time with her over the period when we—most of us—knew her. She deserved so much better than the hand she was dealt, but although she would occasionally speak of it, mostly she just got on with the present. She was really good to be around like that; I can remember very few times when she would feel negative enough that she would bring the rest of us down, and she certainly never had a mean word to say about any of us."

I was really struggling to find the right words to explain what I was feeling here, and I marvelled at how well Amelia had spoken earlier by comparison. I took another moment to straighten it out in my head, and now felt pretty sure I knew how to wrap this up.

"I regret that we didn't help her sooner, the way she helped us all along. Even when we knew she was on our side, it took months before we finally took action to bring her back into our group. She deserved way better than that, but so far as I know, she never felt any resentment towards us for the actions we took—at least, she had never thought anything along those lines while I was sharing her thoughts. I think that's a pretty good illustration of the sort of person I knew Stella to be."

That was all I could manage, and I lowered my head as I trudged back to stand between Peter and Liam. I couldn't shake the feeling that I hadn't really done Stella justice with that little speech—that I'd really known her better than that—but like Amelia, I didn't want to ramble on out here either. I would just have to reflect on the months I'd had with Stella privately, and find some way to come to terms with the loss. Now that I'd finished speaking, my emotions were bubbling to the surface again and it took everything I had to keep them in check. Soon, very soon, I would be able to let loose whatever was going on in there.

The funeral didn't last much longer after that. Amelia asked if anyone else wanted to speak, and to my surprise, Felicity got up and said a few words. I hadn't realised that she too had been quite fond of Stella, getting to know her a bit during the time I had been in the Honnie world, and the way she spoke brought an interesting thought to mind. So far as I knew, Felicity had never had a boyfriend. Furthermore, so far as I knew, she had never shown interest, not even so much as a crush, on any of the guys we knew. And now she was speaking of Stella in tones which suggested more than a little affection, quite likely more than Stella herself had understood at the time. Felicity's sexuality didn't really matter in the grand scheme of things, especially now, but it was an interesting thought to entertain.

After that, Amelia used the Light Crystal to create a coffin around Stella, cutting the sight of her off for the last time. The garden behind the little table opened up, and the coffin floated down into the hole before it closed up again. The hole had been just in front of the Fletchers' tomb stones, so Stella must have been laid to rest very close to them after all. The table on which Stella had lain disappeared, and a tombstone appeared in the garden, next to those of the Fletchers', with her name, birthdate and date of death on it. Amelia announced that she would be happy to use magic to etch messages into the stone the following day if anyone was interested, but for now, it was time to go inside. Once again,

Stella deserved better, but the truth was, matters in the world were far too pressing for us to spend any more time out here.

Most people went straight back into the lounge room to check for updates on what was going on in stricken Melbourne, while some got in the elevator and probably headed off to bed. When the doors had shut on them, Amelia stopped in front of the doors and waited for it to return.

"I'm going back to the control room," she told me as Peter and I joined her. "You guys can come with me, or go in there and see what info the public is being fed."

"I think I'm gonna go to bed," I told them, "but I'll come down with you so I can use the sleep inducer first, and to see how Marc's going."

"I guess I'll go in there," Peter said, glancing towards the lounge room, "but I probably won't be too far behind you—I'm feeling pretty drained."

"We all are," Amelia said sympathetically.

We stood in silence, watching the display over the elevator doors as people were dropped off on the upper levels, and it began descending towards our level. Before it reached us, however, a shout from the lounge room reached our ears, "Oi, all you guys shut up; you have to hear this."

Silence descended for a moment before being replaced by a fainter voice, only made audible by the fact that someone had turned the television up. We couldn't hear the words, but I was sure I recognised the voice, and disregarding the elevator, I hurried away from the others and towards the lounge room. I stopped in the doorway and watched the screen over a bunch of heads, now clearly able to hear the voice of Police Commissioner Hall as he, along with Hank Cornish and several other official-looking Hammerhearts, delivered a press conference.

"Once again, we reiterate that the situation is quickly being brought under control," Hall was saying. "This is a dark day for Australia, and more importantly for Hammersonia and the world as a whole, but it will be treated as a much-needed wake-up call. We have dangerous enemies, and they do not care how many lives are lost in their quest to overturn the new regime. Our master Lucien Moran has been working throughout the week on new and improved methods of catching these dangerous people, in response to the repeated acts of terrorism against the people of Hammersonia, and although he failed to enact these methods in time to prevent this attack, he is confident that he will be able to stop anything like this from happening again. He will explain these methods, and their rollout across Hammersonia, sometime tomorrow.

"Now I'm going to pass it over to Lucien's left-hand man, Hank Cornish, who will update you on the situation in Melbourne at present."

The camera focus shifted to Cornish, who had only been in the periphery before, and he began to speak.

"Thank you, Commissioner. I would like to begin by reading a short, prepared statement from Lucien. He would have liked to be able to address you himself, but upon learning what had happened, he judged—correctly in our opinion—that a better use of his time would be to go straight to the blast sight and use his magic to prevent any further deaths. His words are as follows: 'I deeply regret what has happened, and my thoughts and prayers go out to all those who have been affected by this great tragedy. Be assured that we will not let this defeat us, and I urge you to remain strong through these desperate times. Our enemies are trying to undermine your faith in the ability of magic to improve your lives—do not let them succeed. I promise that magic will be the answer to the great issues we face, and I will demonstrate this to you very soon.'

"'Very soon' is, as the Commissioner said, sometime tomorrow. I won't pre-empt what he will do except to say that it should be welcomed by anyone and everyone who condemns, as we do, the actions of those who have attacked Melbourne tonight. With that, let's turn our attention to the scene itself. Although we do have footage on the ground and some of it can be seen online, we have decided not to show it to you as it will be quite traumatic for anyone who sees it, and we prefer the decision to see it to be yours rather than ours.

"What I can tell you is that Lucien has brought the situation under control for the present. He has set a magical barrier around the damaged area to prevent anything getting in or out, isolating the area to prevent anyone coming in and getting hurt, or any radioactive fallout from escaping. He has actually used his magic to vanish all the radioactive fallout—before any of it reached the ground, in fact—and he has also put out all the fires that were caused by the explosion. His top priority since then has been to find all those in the area who were injured but not killed, and heal them. Fixing the damaged infrastructure—and sadly, there is a lot of it—will be a job for another day, but I can assure you that it will be done much more quickly than any non-magical authority could do.

"Finally, it is with great sadness that I must tell you of the death toll. The truth is that it will be some time before we can give you an accurate count but once again, thanks to magic, it will be possible to provide one eventually. The estimations we have at the moment, however, surpass two hundred thousand deaths, with thousands more injured. More than sixty-thousand of those deaths were at the Melbourne Cricket Ground, where an AFL match was taking place, and given that the stadium appears to be the direct target of the explosion, it is highly unlikely that any of those attending the match have survived.

"With that, I will now pass you over to General Thorne, who will tell you what we know so far about how this whole situation came about."

The camera then switched to a man on Hall's other side, dressed in military uniform, who began to speak about the bomb itself, and how they believed it came to explode in a place where its presence ought to have been detected much earlier. I knew for a fact that this was all bogus, so I turned and left, heading back to the control room; followed by Peter, who had followed me to the lounge room without me evening noticing his presence. We called the elevator and descended to the control room, where only Amelia and her grandmother sat before the controls.

"They're still out there," Amelia told us as we entered, looking over her shoulder to see who we were. "They're basically looking for injured people and fixing them up, because Lucien's already made sure no one else will be killed by it. He's out there too, and Marc's pretty sure he knows they're there, but for some reason, he's choosing not to try to capture them."

"I think he feels a bit guilty about the damage he has done," Lillian said. "Bad as he may be, he knows that the people who died tonight were entirely innocent."

Somehow, I doubted Lucien felt any remorse for his actions tonight. He may have done a week ago, but not since that lump had slid back into his chest and turned him all-the-way-dark. No, whatever Lucien's reason for not taking advantage of the moment to attack Marc and Frederic, it wasn't guilt. Perhaps he simply felt so supremely confident that he would eventually win that he didn't need to try to attack them.

"Well anyway, he wouldn't be able to even if he tried," Amelia went on. "Dad's put a whole bunch of protection around them specifically so that he can't. I dunno how much longer they'll be out there but they're both flagging pretty bad, so probably not much longer. Lucien's basically doing the same thing they are, so maybe it won't be so bad if they call it a night."

"We know," Peter said, and began to tell the two of them what we had just seen on the television.

I listened for as long as it took me to find the sleep inducer, set it to give myself seven hours of sleep, wished the three of them a good night, and then went upstairs to my bedroom. The hall on the first level was deserted, all the bedroom doors shut, people sleeping behind some of them (James and Erica certainly, plus maybe a few others). There was no one to see me pause and look at the closed door of the room which had been Stella's—the room in which I had been alone with her for the last time that night. It took some effort to tear my gaze away from it and go into my own bedroom.

Weariness was sweeping through me now, but I fought it off for the time being. I wasn't yet ready to sleep. There was stuff going on in my head and I wanted to sort through at least some of it before I got into bed. I stood beside my closed door, looking around my silent, sterile room, warring with myself. I thought I should be sad—I thought I should be crying over my loss—I even thought I should feel guilty for not doing more to stop Stella from taking such a suicidal action. Those feelings were all there, of course, but there was far more going on in my mind— far bigger things that I knew were going to catch up with me sooner or later.

Stella was dead. Two hundred thousand people, give or take a few, were dead. I would be dead in ten days or so. Others would probably be dead between now and then—Marc, Amelia, Peter, James, my parents, etc. Natalie would almost certainly be dead very soon if we couldn't find a way to get her out of that room where Lucien was keeping her. Meanwhile, Lucien was pushing ahead with his agenda at top-speed, using mass murder and terrorism as an excuse to implement more and more draconian policies against the people over whom he ruled.

I stepped over to the control panel and pressed the button to raise the soundproof barrier around my room. I didn't want anyone to interrupt me from outside the room, nor did I want anyone to hear me. There, I clenched my fists, opened my mouth, and yelled as loudly as I could. My head spun and my throat throbbed as I let loose all my pent-up frustration, because that was what it was: anger. I was angry that Stella's death had been for nought. I was frustrated that in spite of everything, we were still losing this war, and losing badly. Most of all, I was enraged that I had apparently sacrificed my own soul for nothing, because let's tell the truth here: We hadn't gained a damn thing from the information I had gotten from Lisa—nothing that we could really use, anyway.

Yelling wasn't enough. I strode to the table in the centre of the room, heaved a chair up over my head, and hurled it at the back wall—it made a satisfying crash as it tumbled onto the floor in the circle of couches. I repeated the process with another chair, and then a third, and may well have done it to a fourth, except that my back was suddenly feeling achy. Still, I was glad I'd had that little tantrum, because the worst of the anger had been burnt away. It left me feeling very small, like the fourteen-year-old boy I should have been—the boy I would have been if the war had never started. I couldn't remember ever feeling as alone and scared in my life as I was right now.

I slowly changed into my pyjamas and climbed achingly into bed, now full of despair. I rolled onto my side and, unable to prevent it any longer, cried into my pillow. I wasn't sure if I was crying out of sadness or frustration, though it was probably both. It took a little while for the tears to subside, and when I felt a little more in control, I rolled back onto my back and stared up at the ceiling. I was very tired now—sleep would probably take me in minutes. In fact, it would have already taken me, most likely, if my brain weren't still running at almost top speed.

Tomorrow would be another day. We would have to put the loss of Stella behind us very quickly and focus on what came next, but after the thoroughly fruitless day we'd had, I had no idea what that would be. This just wasn't good enough; we ought to be in a much better position than this. We now had four of the five Magic Crystals, the Seventh Sorcerer, a way to access the magic of the Sien-Leoard Crystal, and supposedly the power of Sien and Leoard themselves, since we had held up our end of our deal by bringing me back to life after I had died.

This last thought led me to another, and then another. As sleep began to take me, I knew what I had to do. It was time to return to the in-between and find out what else Lisa knew, because there was no way I had gotten all I could out of her. It was just as well I could have my entire exchange with her in a single moment of real time, before I even had a chance to fall asleep....

Second Interlude: Magic Theory

I was back in the place again—that place of nothingness. I wasn't standing, sitting or lying; I was only existing. I wasn't alone in the place, for I could sense the presence of others around me and I could reach out to them if I chose. But there was a major difference this time: I was fully aware of where I was and why I was here. This time, I had a working brain to call on—something that wouldn't be true in less than two weeks, of course—but as it was the case now, I had no curiosity about the nothingness. I was here on business, and while I could continue having these thoughts for as long as I wanted, as there was no time here, I had no desire to do anything except get down to business.

I began reaching out for Lisa, and found her immediately—perhaps because I knew who I was looking for and how to find her, having done it before. She recognised me immediately, and at the same time not quite immediately; and as she did, the place of no description once again took on a new form. It was the same place as last time, and unbidden, I felt a note of curiosity. Unless I was mistaken, this image had been projected by Lisa rather than me, and if that was the case, I had a feeling I knew what it was: the cave in which she had described meeting Mary Sien in her diary entries.

"John Playman," she observed, just as she had done last time.

"Hi, Lisa," I said.

"You're here too," she said sadly. "I'm sorry."

"Me too," I said, taking a moment that was no time at all, to feel bad for myself and the fate that awaited me.

She paused a moment that wasn't really a moment at all but could have been any length of time, before saying, "You are whole, unlike me."

"Yeah, I—er," I faltered, a thought occurring to me. "Do you remember meeting me here before?"

"I don't understand your meaning," she replied.

"I mean here, in the in-between," I said. "When I first died and I had no idea what was going on, we had a talk before I was resurrected. Do you remember?"

"No," she said sadly. "You are resurrected? How long ago?"

"Three days—three and a half," I amended. "I've probably got ten or eleven left. So—so you don't remember telling me about the last Sorcerer?"

This time, I actually felt Lisa's confusion. If I had a body here, I would have let out a long sigh. I even considered doing just that with my actual body before it occurred to me that doing so might break my connection with Lisa (and cause her to forget this whole exchange, bringing us back to the start).

"Never mind that. I came here for a reason. I need to pick your brain about something; it's very important."

"I don't really have a brain worth picking anymore," she said, her sadness overwhelming. I thought I understood why; Lisa had prided herself on her intelligence, and a lot of that had been cut away by her second death. Not all of it, though, and I reckoned there was probably still enough there to work with.

"You have more than you realise. You may not recall, but you told me about a prophecy you read once, that foretold the last Sorcerer."

She registered surprise at this, and then comprehension .,"I still don't remember that, but I know what you're talking about. I did read a prophecy that talked about the last Sorcerer. I wonder how it is that I remember some things from my life, but nothing from here?"

"I have no idea."

"I must have something that can hold memories, otherwise I wouldn't even have the part of my personality capable of asking the question," she said, seeming to forget her sadness for the time being, and I was pleased to see it—she was becoming the inquisitive girl I had known in life. "Perhaps it can only hold memories from life, or perhaps it can only hold sufficiently important memories, and nothing that happens here could possibly be important enough."

"Maybe," I said, wanting to get down to business. "Lisa, do you mind if I ask you some questions?"

"Go ahead," she said, and there was eagerness there now—I had *really* woken her up this time.

I paused then, trying to think how to approach this. It was difficult to know what to ask without knowing what I wanted to find out. Other than the prophecy, which I already knew about, what useful knowledge could Lisa possess? Now that I was here I had doubts that there was anything worth learning at all, but I pushed them aside. After all that had happened since my resurrection, I couldn't accept that this was all I had sacrificed my soul for. I decided to start by giving her some context—perhaps her inquisitive nature would end up leading me to where I needed to go.

"Things are really bad in the world now," I told her, "worse than you can probably imagine. James—do you remember James? James Thomas?"

"Yes, of course," she said at once, and she pictured his face. Exactly how I knew that she pictured his face, I had no idea, but I did.

"He has told us that the only thing we can do to make things better is destroy the Magic Crystals," I told her. "That's how bad it is."

She took a moment (which was once again no time at all) to process this. The mention of the Magic Crystals hadn't made as big an impact on her as the mention of James—perhaps because she'd known James most of her life, and had only really known about the crystals in the final few weeks prior to her death. Eventually, though, she understood the magnitude of what I had said.

"Are you saying the struggle over magic is on the point of destroying the world?"

"Very close, yes," I confirmed, "so here's my question; in anything you ever read, did you ever come across any ideas about how the crystals could be destroyed?"

She was about to say no, and then held herself back, preferring to give the question the thought it really required. I even had a mental image of her open her mouth and almost blurting it out before quickly shutting it again—that was how it would have undoubtedly looked if she'd had a body with which to do that. I waited patiently for her to come back with something (patience was very easy in a place with no time), and eventually, she did.

"I don't know anything," she said, "but I did a lot of reading only a few days before my death, in an evening, I think it was. As far as I know, there is no definite way to destroy them, but it may be possible if any of the theories of magic itself are true. The one that struck me as sounding the most plausible was the one which said that magic and the crystals were two different things; that magic clings to the crystals, and without magic, they would be no different from any other crystals in the world. If it's true, all you would need to do is find a way to separate the two and the crystals would be neutralised."

"That would be great," I said, feeling optimistic, already seeing a few flaws in the idea but feeling that those could probably be overcome, "but how do we know if it *is* true?"

This time, I felt her do something remarkably like a shrug. "Experiment. If you still have magic to use, find ways to test it to disprove the theory. Get James to help you; he would probably be good at that stuff."

And if it wasn't true, it wouldn't be hard to find other theories to test now that we had the magic encyclopedia in our possession. James was going to love this; remembering the project he'd been working on for months now, I wouldn't have been at all surprised if he already had ideas for testing such a theory, without ever knowing if he would get to perform them. Once again, I felt like Lisa had gifted me with gold—and if it turned out to be rubble, I could just come back and see if she had any more.

Part 3: Antimagic

Chapter 17: Checkmark

I woke up a little after six o'clock in the morning, when the faintest of light was coming through my window. This was the light over Chopville, the roof of the base enchanted (by me) to reflect the sky outside so as to give us a feeling of being free while we remained enclosed in this protective environment. It wasn't the light that had woken me, but the dream I'd had shortly before waking. I supposed the sleep inducer had made most of my sleep dreamless, as I'd made it all the way through the seven hours I'd selected, but apparently my brain had been ready to dream something on its way back to waking up.

It hadn't been a good dream. Stella had been there, bleeding and ripped apart as she had been prior to her death, only now she had been on her feet and staring sharply at me in a way that seemed accusatory. It left me with a hollow feeling, and I didn't have to wonder what it meant: I still felt guilty for what had happened to her—for failing to prevent that from happening to her. I sat up in bed and gave my head a little shake; I couldn't afford to let that feeling consume me, knowing that Stella had made up her mind and would have found a way to do her bit no matter what I said or did to stop her.

I got out of bed, noticing as I did so that my back was still sore from the violent episode I'd had last night. The three chairs I'd thrown were still over by the couches, and I went and put them back where they belonged. One of them was actually broken, and I made a mental note to fix it with the magic enhancer when I got a chance, but it was hardly a priority. I then had a shower (a nice, long one felt like a good idea this morning), got dressed, and headed downstairs to see what was happening in the base and beyond.

The dining room turned out to be completely empty (too early for most, I supposed—perhaps they had stayed up really late, keeping track of events on the outside), but I wasn't the only one out of bed. On my way to the dining room, I heard sound coming from the lounge room, and upon having a peek through the doorway, I saw Katie and Sophie sitting together on one of the couches, watching the television with the volume turned down low—watching a news program, by the look of it, and I didn't have to wonder what news they were catching up on.

I didn't disturb them, but went to have a quick breakfast. I ate one slice of toast alone in the dining room before, unable to wait any longer, I took a second slice with me down to the control room. There, I found James and Erica minding the fort, and the first thing I noticed when I went through the door (apart from their presence) was a major change that had taken place in this room between now and last night. No longer were there numerous magical devices littering the floor and seats as there had been before, but a large cabinet had been set up against the wall to my left, opposite the door to our prison and the emergency escape.

"Morning, John," James said, looking around at me. "There's really nothing going on here. How are—how are you doing?"

I shrugged—nobody really wanted to hear what I'd been up to before I'd gone to bed last night. "Well enough, all things considered. I take it you know what happened last night, then?"

They both nodded, looking sad. "Katie and Sophie were keeping watch in here when we got up, and they filled us in on everything," Erica said. "They're supposed to be watching the TV to see if there's any more news if they haven't fallen asleep, but apart from the international response, it doesn't look like much else has happened."

"How did Katie and Sophie know?" I asked. "Weren't they still asleep when it happened too?"

"Some people were still up when they got up," James said. "They took over from Amelia in here and kept watch until we came down here."

"I see," I said, glad that they already knew all there was to know (about the events of last night anyway), which meant that I wouldn't have to go over any of it with them. I instead turned my attention back to the changes that had taken place here, noticing more of them all the time.

A bunch of spyers had been set up along the top of the control panel, apparently permanently attached there and set to follow a different person each. The one in the very centre was focused on Lucien, who was having an early breakfast in the Hammerheart Dining Hall. Other spyers were focused on people like Hall, Cornish, Hignat (both senior and junior), both Wilwogs, Sebastian, Lena, and other familiar Hammerhearts besides. One of them had even been set to track Natalie, for some reason, although right now it showed nothing more interesting than her curled up in a foetal position against the wall of her little prison, apparently asleep. It wasn't the only display on her either: the main display also showed Natalie, meaning that the base was presently located in her chamber.

"What's all this?" I asked the two of them, gesturing to the spyers, and particularly the one following Natalie. "When did this happen?"

"Our doing," James said at once. "I dunno about everyone else, but I couldn't stand how messy and disorganised this place had become, so as long as there was nothing else happening, I decided to do something about it. I used that device you created, John—the one that uses the magic of the Sien-Leoard Crystal—to make all that happen."

"How'd you get that one to follow Natalie?" I asked. "And—er—why?"

"Why, so that we can make sure she's okay if we have to leave her alone for a while," Erica said. "And how—well, it was similar to what Marc did yesterday to keep track of Lucien—"

"That one is exactly the same as what Marc did," James interrupted, "but that one"—he indicated the spyer showing Lucien—"is a little different. Because he's the regular type of untraceable, I put a spell on it to keep track of that particular hole in reality. It seemed like it would be more reliable than using a magical connection to a non-magical type of surveillance."

"I guess so," I said, "and it means we can keep up with him if he teleports now, right?"

"Exactly. We were lucky yesterday that he only used the Hammerheart Highway to get around, but now it won't matter."

"So I assume that means you did all that as well?" I said, looking back at the cabinet.

I looked more closely at it. Along the very top row were five glass-covered cupboards, three of them containing the Light, Darkness and Villain Crystals. The other two were empty, and I assumed they were meant for the Hero and Sien-Leoard Crystals, assuming we would ever have a need to put them in there. I felt sure that Marc, for one, would rather hold onto the Hero Crystal than store it in that cabinet. On either side of the cabinet was an opaque door; the left had the word 'time' written on it, and the right had the word 'mind'. I assumed that meant James had incorporated the Time and Mind Boxes into his design, meaning that they wouldn't be taking up lots of space on the floor. The rest of the structure was made up of small drawers, each with the name and picture of the device stored inside.

"Yep," he said. "I suppose you can figure out how it all works, but just so you know, those drawers will duplicate the devices as you take them out and then vanish the duplicates when you put them back in, so there'll always be one of each device in the drawers at a time."

"And what about those devices I created that have anti-duplication spells on them?" I asked.

He grinned. "Those two are in the very top drawers, and they have different spells on them. They don't duplicate, but they do refuse to open unless it's you, me, Erica, Marc, Amelia, Natalie, Peter, Mr. Woodward, or Lillian Woodward trying to open them. If anyone else wants them, I see no reason why they can't come through us; and if they can't, well, someone with magic can add them to the whitelist."

"Okay, terrific," I said, checking my watch—it was now a quarter to seven. No time like the present, I thought. "Listen, before I went to sleep last night, I talked to Lisa again. I just felt like there had to be more to— well—me being here—than finding out about that prophecy. She may have pointed me in the right direction regarding how we can stop Lucien."

That got their attention. Both of them sat up straighter in their seats, looking very sharp, though James's expression remained wary. "Okay," he said slowly. "What did she say?"

"Magic theory," I told them. "She was doing some research on it before she died—probably not like you did," I added, "but more out of curiosity, and perhaps for her history of magic project for school. Did you guys look at anything like that in the Time Box yesterday?"

"Heaps of it," Erica said, "but I don't remember reading anything about something that could destroy the crystals. I don't think there were any theories about destroying them; most people only want to understand them."

"Yeah, I know," I said, "but Lisa said the most plausible theory of magic she ever read suggested that magic could be a separate thing from the crystals themselves, and if they could be separated, the crystals would just be normal stones."

James's eyes widened and he said, "Oh my God. Erica, the particles!"

"What?" I said, glancing from him to her and back again. James looked excited, while Erica looked dismayed. "What is it, you two?"

They swapped looks and then Erica said, "Well, there was one document we read yesterday, but it was so long and complicated that we gave up trying to understand it. It seemed so ludicrous that we figured it couldn't possibly mean anything—just the crazy ramblings of an insane genius."

"It was a thesis," James explained. "Back in the '90s, a student at a major university—MIT, I think it was—did a doctoral dissertation on magic theory. He already had a Ph.D. in physics, and I guess he was trying to bring the two together. He was one of those magicologists Derick Castle spoke about, the ones who believe that magic is a higher order of physics, only the stuff this guy came out with to explain it— well, even I couldn't understand a lot of it. He basically suggested that magic was a new type of particle that we had yet to isolate, and if we were only able to find it, we could start to understand the way it behaves."

"Magic particles," I mused. "Does that sound like the sort of thing Lisa was talking about?"

"Possibly, yes," James said, "but in order for us to understand it, we're gonna have to understand all that crazy shit in the thesis, and that's even supposing it's true. There's no guarantee that Lisa was right about this stuff."

"No, and especially since we've learnt a lot more since she died," I agreed. "She did say that we should use magic to try to test the theory, and that does seem like a good idea, so that we can move on to some other theory if this one turns out to be false."

"Agreed," James said, getting to his feet and motioning to Erica to do the same. "Come on; we should get back in the Time Box and start trying to make sense of that gobbledygook. You're in charge here, John; just let the others know what we're doing when they start coming down."

"Okay," I agreed, and watched as they opened the 'time' door in the cabinet and squeezed inside.

* * *

People started showing up in dribs and drabs between seven and eight o'clock. Marc and Amelia were the first to arrive, looking fresh and ready to go, and I was glad to see them. I'd had a little time to think before they had turned up, and what had only been an idea the previous evening had evolved into a full plan by the time they came through the door. Moreover, the timing couldn't be more perfect: Lucien had been busy as I'd watched, first getting an update from Fewul (still in Stella's form) on the progress of the African and South American invasions, both of which were going well, particularly within certain countries (I hadn't really been paying attention). He had since scheduled a press conference, which he was getting ready to deliver right now. Meanwhile, the only person in Lucien's living quarters was Lena, and she was fast asleep in Lucien's bed.

"How'd you sleep?" I asked them, and they both shrugged.

"Fine," Marc said. "I was stuffed by the time we got back last night, but I used that sleep thing you made anyway, just to be sure. Did you do all this stuff?"

He was referring to the work James had done, and it was my turn to shrug. "James did it when he got up. He and Erica know everything; they're in the Time Box again."

"Continuing where they left off?" Amelia said, glancing over at the cabinet. "Fair enough, but after all the time they spent in there yesterday, it feels a bit like treading water now."

"Not exactly," I said, "I gave them something new to work on—tell you about that later. I've got something else I wanna try now, while Lucien's busy and no one else is around."

"What's that?" Marc asked; both of them looked ready to jump into action again.

I carefully explained my idea to them, and watched as their faces grew more excited. I was pleased to see it; I'd had a period of doubt, not knowing if Marc had already tried this before I'd returned from Rock Haulter, but the looks on their faces meant that this idea was new to them.

"Let's not get our hopes up too high," Marc said reasonably. "If I were Lucien, I probably would have thought of this. And if not specifically, then the magic he performed might cover this sort of thing anyway, but it's definitely worth a shot. It might be sneaky enough to work."

"I guess you're the best one for it," I said, grinning at Marc, glad that the job didn't fall to me. I could have done it with the magic enhancer, but that would have been extremely awkward to say the least.

"Okay, but be ready to pull me in," he said, getting up and heading over to the corner, gripping the Hero Crystal as he went. "There could be an alarm or some sort of trigger—you never know."

I didn't think there would be—Lucien would probably be so supremely confident in his spellwork that he wouldn't think it necessary to set up a magical alert for this—but it wasn't impossible. I therefore nodded and took the controls, pushing the button to let him out of the base and having my finger ready on the button to draw him back in. Amelia pulled her seat up to the control panel beside me and the two of us watched and listened as Marc emerged into Natalie's little prison, waking her up.

"Wha…" she said sleepily, cringing and looking up fearfully before seeing who it was. She relaxed a little, but still looked wary. "Oh great, I'm still here."

"Yeah, but hopefully for not much longer," he said, approaching and crouching down so that they were on the same level. "Lucien's busy right now, and there's no one else around so I'm going to take the opportunity to try to get you out of here. How are you feeling?"

"Like I could run a marathon," she said weakly, her voice so flat and croaky that she couldn't even generate the appropriately sarcastic tone to go with the comment. She certainly looked bad: pale and gaunt, her eyes sunken and her hair straggly.

"Can you stand up for me?" he asked.

"I'd rather not," she said, "and I'd rather you not try to make me feel better. There's no point stretching this out for me."

"Oh, I can think of reasons," Marc said with a little smirk on his face, "the main one being that we will definitely find a way through this, and it would be so much better for us if you were still alive when it happens. Now come on…"

He stood up and used his magic to raise Natalie onto her feet. The magic imprisoning her allowed this but it kept her against the wall, her feet planted firmly on the ground. She looked unsteady, though, and Marc had to use his magic to hold her up. He then began working her over, making her look a lot better, if not necessarily making her feel better on the inside. He then rehydrated her, and this time she accepted the water without a struggle or complaint. As he worked, he began to tell her a little of what had happened on the outside, but she cut him off, telling her that Lucien had come to her to brag about what he'd done before going to bed the previous night, making sure she knew all the horrible details so that her spirits would be totally flattened.

"I won't lie to you; it is pretty bad," Marc said as she drank, "but we haven't given up yet. We'll keep on keeping on, right until the very end if necessary. In the meantime, John came up with an idea to get you out of here that we haven't tried yet, and it's sneaky enough that it could possibly work. It's based a little on how James got you through Arnold

Hammerson's dome, except it doesn't use thicky prison—we already know that doesn't work. We'll get started with it when you're done drinking."

He then set to work creating a magical egg, large enough for a person to sit in, and performing several different spells on it to give it the properties it would need. It would be comfortable, self-sustaining, impenetrable except by magic, and would keep the person inside it immune to anything that happened outside it. He then waited patiently for Natalie to finish drinking, and when she did, she really looked a lot better. She still looked like she'd lost a little weight, but other than that, she looked as though she'd regained quite a bit of strength.

"Before we get started, I'm going to need to re-test your movements," Marc said to her. "Can you move away from the wall?"

She tried to take a step, but other than being able to move a short distance to either side, she was unable to remove herself from the wall. Marc then asked her to try lifting her feet, but although she could lift one at a time, it seemed that part of her was required to be touching the floor at all times. My heart sank as I watched this; I hadn't taken this part of Lucien's spellwork into account when I'd formulated my plan, and as it went on, it looked more and more likely that it wasn't going to work.

Marc, however, had thought ahead, and had an idea of his own to get around this little snag. I never would have had this idea myself, because I never would have dreamt of doing such a thing to Natalie—or anyone, for that matter.

"I'm going to knock you unconscious now," he told her, "because what's going to happen next may be a bit alarming for you, and I don't want you to panic."

She nodded, and then went perfectly still and limp. She didn't fall, though, Marc's magic continuing to hold her up. He took a couple of steps away from her and began using magic to manipulate her body into a strange position, with one leg off the floor and one foot stuck there. He was able to move her back away from the wall, but only so long as one hand remained touching it. I had no idea what on earth he could be doing until his next spell. No wonder he had wanted her unconscious: it wouldn't have just alarmed her, it would have made her scream in agony.

Something invisible cut through Natalie's wrist and ankle, cutting her hand and foot clean off her body. The dismembered hand fell to the floor beside the dismembered foot, blood pooling around them, while yet more blood pumped from the stumps of Natalie's leg and arm. Only for a moment, though: within a second, the two cut-off body parts had reappeared on Natalie's body, mending her instantly. The end result of all of this, apart from the blood on the floor, was that Natalie was hovering in the air, no longer attached to the wall or floor. I had a moment to think that perhaps it was enough, that we could take Natalie right now, but apparently that wasn't the case: Marc couldn't move her any further from the wall or floor than she already was, which meant that my original plan could now proceed.

Marc used his magic to open the egg, as if on a hinge, and shifted it below Natalie so that he could drop her into it. He shut her inside it and then began shrinking the egg until it was roughly the size of a pill. He caught it in his hand and tried to step back with it, but even now, the magic meant to imprison Natalie was preventing her from getting any further from the wall than she already was. I was unsurprised, though still dismayed, that it had come this far and still we were unable to remove her; there was a very real possibility that this wouldn't work under *any* circumstances.

Marc put the pill in his mouth and swallowed it. He had to step closer to the wall to do this, but do it he did. He then used his crystal to clean the mess he had made on the floor, and then just stood there, gripping his crystal, using magic to follow the progress of the pill in his own body. This was all part of the plan: the egg wouldn't dissolve in there, meaning that Natalie would be perfectly safe, but he had to wait until he was sure it was firmly a part of himself before he tested the magical barrier around him.

Two more people entered the control room while this was happening: Peter and Frederic. We explained to them what was happening out there and that James and Erica were back in the Time Box. then they too settled in to watch Marc. I knew the moment when he decided it was time to go; he put the hand gripping the crystal in his pocket, closed his eyes, and began walking forward. He took one step, then another, then another, then another, and on the one after that, hit the wall opposite where Natalie had been. I felt like I could jump with joy: finally, we had a checkmark in the 'win' column.

Marc put his hand up to be let back into the base, and I quickly obliged. As he reappeared in the corner, I began scanning the display screen as closely as I could, looking for any sign that the egg had somehow remained behind in the room, but couldn't see any sign of it anywhere. While I was distracted with this, Amelia pushed the button to release Marc from the corner so that he could come back and take his seat.

"Well done," Frederic said, patting him on the shoulder. "Do you think it worked?"

"I'm quite sure it did," Marc said, putting his hand back around the Hero Crystal and drawing it out. "The capsule is still inside me, at least. I can't track Natalie directly, because she's untraceable, but the anti-teleportation protection I put around the capsule should have prevented her from being left behind."

"So what's the plan now?" Peter asked. "Do we have to wait till you crap that thing out?"

"Nope, I'm going to puke it up," Marc said, "and if I do it right, I won't even be sick doing it."

And so he wasn't. After about a minute, he began gulping repeatedly until finally, he was able to spit the pill into his open palm. He quickly performed a spell on it, but not before I caught a tiny whiff of the thing. Puke may not have come out of him, but the smell of it had. He quickly remedied that situation before getting up and enlarging the egg back to its original size, setting it down near the door where there was a space free of chairs. He opened it up, and I was more relieved than I could say to see Natalie huddled inside it, still unconscious and totally uninjured. A part of me was still horrified by what Marc had had to do to her to get her away from that wall, but Natalie herself hadn't felt a thing, and there would be no lasting harm. It would certainly be a lot less traumatic for her compared to what she'd been through while being Lucien's prisoner, anyway.

Marc levitated her into the air, laid her flat on the floor, and then vanished the egg. We all gathered around her as he brought her around; her muscles spasmed very briefly, probably because she'd gone from standing to lying down without any noticeable movement, or so it would have seemed to her. She then relaxed and looked up, her face breaking into a huge smile of relief as she recognised where she was and who was around her.

"Welcome back, Hon," Amelia said, reaching down to help her up.

"Thanks," Natalie said, flushing and beginning to cry as she threw her arms around Amelia.

The rest of us backed off a step to give the two of them a bit of space, a little surprised in my case (I hadn't realised those two were so close), but Natalie wasn't having any of that. She quickly turned from Amelia and gave Marc a big hug, taking him by surprise, and then before he could hug her back, she turned from him and threw her arms around me next. I was completely taken aback by the intensity of her embrace, but not enough to stop me hugging her back. She only spent a couple more seconds hugging me than she had with Marc, before moving onto Peter and Frederic, but it was enough to answer a few questions I'd had about how she was going.

Firstly, she looked a little shocked to see me again, though not surprised. Marc had mentioned that I'd been the one to come up with the idea for her escape, but in the moment I'd gotten a look at her face as she turned her attention to me, I'd seen how my presence here had affected her. I didn't think she had necessarily gotten over what I'd done to her, but it had been put into perspective by the horrors that had taken place since—whether her own experiences, the fate that had befallen me, or both. I couldn't be sure how she would be going forward—all of this would take a long time to get over, assuming that time was to be had—

but I did feel sure that she and I would be okay, at least for the rest of my life.

"It really is good to have you back, Natalie," Frederic said fondly.

"Thanks," she sobbed, looking around the control room. "Er—is this all there is? Where's—"

The door opened at that very moment as if in response to her words, and a sad-looking Rebecca trudged in, looking as if she had struggled just to find the will to push open the door. She stopped short when she saw us all on our feet, and then let out a squeal as she recognised her sister amongst the small pack. The two girls launched themselves at each other and broke down, both of them sobbing against each other and clutching at each other. Once again, the rest of us took a step back from them, but this time they didn't break apart. I understood why well enough: Not only had they both probably thought that Natalie would be dead very soon, but they had also lost their parents into the bargain.

"How'd you do it?" Rebecca finally managed to ask, looking over her shoulder at the rest of us. "I thought you couldn't do it before."

"I—I don't know," Natalie faltered, and she too looked around at us. "How *did* you do it, anyway? Why'd you have to knock me out?"

"Er—well," Marc too faltered, glancing at me, "I basically put you inside a capsule and swallowed you. I had to wait until the magic could no longer detect your presence before I could get you out, and only when you were a part of me could it work."

"Well—thanks," she said for the third time. "I—I really need to eat something. What time is it?"

"After everything you've been through, it's bedtime," Marc said, going over to the cabinet, opening one of the drawers and pulling out a device.

"Oh no, not yet," she said quickly. "I wanna eat first, and I wanna catch up on what I've missed around here—the things that Lucien hasn't told me. Where are James and—"

That was when Marc shot her with the sleep inducer. She staggered slightly and had to be steadied by Rebecca.

"It's for your own good," he said, putting the device back in the drawer. "Just a few hours of sleep comes first, and then you can catch up on the rest of what's been going on around here after lunch. You can have a little something to eat before you sleep."

"And James is in there," I told her, pointing at the Time Box—or rather, the door that now concealed the Time Box. "He and Erica are busy doing research, so better not to disturb them."

"What research—"

"Again, we'll catch you up later," Marc said, walking up to her and taking her by the forearm. "Come on, upstairs with you. don't make me use my crystal to get you up there."

And with that, the two of them left the room. The moment the door had closed, Rebecca went to Peter and the two of them embraced, she once again dissolving into relieved tears, leaving me to swap looks with the two Woodwards.

"What research, John?" Frederic asked, and I shrugged.

"It's pretty complicated; I'll tell you guys when Marc gets back down here."

Marc took a little while to return, making me wonder exactly what he and Natalie were doing up there (probably just creating food for her to eat, but I couldn't stop my mind from wandering elsewhere). Before he got back, though, other people began showing up, after having had their breakfast. Among them were Felicity, Jessica, Harry, Simon, Liam, Siobhan, Underwood and even Tommy; and all of them wanted to participate in some meaningful way in whatever business we were doing today. After what Lucien had done the previous evening, everyone seemed to want to do all they could to help. I was glad to see it, although I couldn't think of any way to organise them all; and all I could do was swap dismayed looks with Amelia, Frederic and Peter as we all realised how in-over-our-heads we were.

Meanwhile, Lucien appeared to have finished his press conference and was getting started on more meetings. Shortly after I noticed this, Katie and Sophie entered the room and reported on all that Lucien had said during the press conference, which was basically a great big wad of nothing much. He would be returning to Melbourne later in the afternoon to rebuild the damaged infrastructure (an operation which would supposedly take no more than a couple of hours for such an experienced Sorcerer as himself).

Katie and Sophie also told us something that we hadn't been aware of: Apparently, mass rallies were being organised for around noon this very day, all of which were in support of Lucien. Supposedly, thousands upon thousands of people all across the country (and later the world) would be making their voices heard, standing firmly behind their leader and demanding that he do everything within his considerable power, whatever the cost may be, to put a stop to these acts of terrorism once and for all. I had no proof that Lucien was behind these rallies, not having seen him organise them (or even order someone else to organise them), but I knew that he would use them as an excuse to bring in more authoritarianism, making it look as though he were just doing what the people wanted.

Chapter 18: The Thesis

"Whoa, what's all this?" Marc asked as he pushed open the control room door, only to find it packed and noisy, with precious little controlling going on.

"Everyone wants to help in some way," Amelia told him as she, Peter, Frederic, Lillian and I joined him at the door, "and we can't figure out what jobs to give them."

"Mainly because we haven't quite figured out what jobs *we'll* be doing this morning," Frederic added, "but also because we're not sure if there's anything these people *can* do to help us."

"But they're all desperate to," I added, "after what Lucien did last night—mainly the nuke, but I think a little bit for Stella as well."

"Okay," Marc said to us, and then he projected his voice over the top of everyone else to get their attention. "Okay, everyone. Thanks for coming down here. I think it's great that you all want to help. We're not exactly sure what jobs you can all do, but given how much crap is going on out there—"

"Oi, language, Marcus," Harry chided him. "There are ladies in the room."

Marc shook his head. "Sorry, like, not at all, but we don't have time to muck around like that. And for the record, my name isn't Marcus—it's just Marc. As I was saying, given how much—er—stuff is going on out there, I'm sure we could use all your help to at least attempt to keep up with it. If anyone has any bright ideas about how we can do that, we're all ears over here."

"How about we try to knock Lucien over again?" Darcy suggested. "Like we did yesterday?"

"I honestly can't see Lucien falling for that trick again," Frederic told him. "We used all the tricks we have and now Lucien knows about most of them, even if he doesn't quite understand how we did what we did. If not for that, I would be on board with your idea."

"Not that we won't try that again at some stage," Marc added, "just…not right now. Anyone else?"

"If there's so much going on out there that you can't keep up with in here, why not send us all out to the corners of the globe to deal with it?" my dad suggested. "Make sure we're all magically armed and able to protect ourselves in case of trouble, like Freddy used to do, and let us loose."

Marc glanced at Frederic and said, "What do you think? Could that work?"

Frederic hesitated and then said, "Perhaps, but there's a major risk in doing that. Something like that would work under normal circumstances, given the untraceability we have; but the fact is, Lucien has ordered

Fewul to keep a watch over all the operations he has in progress at the moment. Even though Fewul won't be able to directly trace us, it will sense the presence of any magic we perform against any Hammerhearts over whom it's watching, and it's likely to attempt to flush us out. That kind of magic coming from the Beast of Magic is very hard to defend against, especially since you won't have your own magic to defend yourself with."

"In other words, it's too dangerous," Lillian concluded. "What about recalling Fewul, then?"

Marc shook his head. "He's right; that won't work either. Lucien's set up a magical alert to let him know the instant Fewul vanishes, and he proved yesterday that he can recall it just as quickly without even interrupting whatever he's doing at the time. That doesn't matter, though, because I've had another idea. What if we do exactly what Mr. Playman said, only we do it all from in here? I can make little workstations for everyone and they can use magic to browse whatever's going on outside, and perform bits and pieces of magic to make little differences here and there? If Lucien or Fewul tries to flush them out, nothing will happen, because there won't be anyone there."

That sounded like a pretty good idea, and I could tell by their faces that Amelia, Peter, and several others nearby agreed. Frederic gave it proper consideration before saying, "Yes, something like that could work, so long as you're very careful when placing protection around these workstations. You need to make sure nothing Fewul or Lucien do can trace the magic back to its source."

And so that would be the job for much of the army for that day. We got them all to back against the walls, leaving the centre of the room clear. Marc went around vanishing the chairs (except for a couple in front of the controls) and replacing them with small workstations, which he set up in a grid that resembled one of those old-fashioned classrooms where the desks folded up so that the students could store their books inside. Instead of a flat surface, these desks were tilted up at a thirty-degree angle and contained an LCD screen. The only other thing on them was a small pad on the bottom right-hand corner; I didn't need Marc to tell me that it was how the operator would perform the magic.

While all this was going on, I cast my eyes over to the control panel. The main display showed that we were still in Natalie's now-empty chamber, but the spyers James had put atop the panel showed a lot more going on. Lucien was still in a meeting, while Cornish appeared to be in another meeting. Hall was somewhere outdoors and appeared to be in the process of organising police officers (I didn't recognise where he was, but even though I couldn't hear anything, I could see urgency in his manner, and assumed that whatever he was doing had something to do with the pro-Lucien rallies taking place in just a few hours). Sebastian appeared to be sitting in his lounge room, watching something on TV, while Hignat and Wilwog senior were in their respective houses, doing equally boring things. Their sons, meanwhile, were wandering around the Big Room, which was now completely empty, and both of them looked pretty mad.

As for Lena, she had gotten out of bed and was having a shower. The spyer showed it all; I saw it in the brief moment before Harry and Simon's grandmother covered that particular screen with a handkerchief. I also saw when she was drying herself, the spyer again showing everything, because the handkerchief had either fallen off the screen, or because someone had accidentally-on-purpose knocked it off. It was one of those things which everyone in the room was aware of, but nobody spoke of directly; but all the same, it was a considerable relief when Lena got dressed and started focusing on her hair and make-up.

At last, Marc was done, and he called everyone to attention again.

"Okay, folks, we're ready to go. As you can see, I've made as many workstations as can fit in this room. If not all of you get a place, we can set up more around the base—or I suppose we can expand the size of this room. Is that something we can do, John?"

"I think so," I said thoughtfully. "I mean, as long as it only internally expands; it may knock the whole building down if you don't do it right."

"I'm not knocking any buildings down today," Marc said, smiling slightly. "Anyway, you guys, pick a spot and wait for assignment. I think the best way to do this is to give everyone a separate assignment so that you don't all get in each other's way with whatever you're doing. I'm sure there's enough mayhem going on out there to spread around."

"And how exactly do we use these things, Marc?" Katie called.

Marc looked over at her and Sophie, apparently surprised to see them. "Er—haven't you two been up all night?"

"Yes, sir," Sophie said, snapping him a crisp salute which made Harry and Simon laugh.

He shook his head. "You two don't need to do this. If you wanna help out, go on in there"—he nodded at the 'time' door in the cabinet— "and help James and Erica with their assignment. I think you'll find it's quite urgent."

And probably more important than anything going on out here, he didn't add, in order not to offend everyone else in the room, but I knew he was thinking it.

"The question is valid, though," asked a woman I didn't recognise, but I knew she had been brought in from the Big Room when Peter and Rebecca had emptied it. "How *do* we use these things?"

"Well, it may take a little practice, especially for those of you who have never performed magic yourselves—which as I say that, I realise is most of you," Marc added, flushing a little. "Basically, when you take your seat, you do everything by putting your thumb on the pad just there" —he demonstrated with the nearest workstation"—and think at it. When you need to move the view around, think at it and it will move. When you need to stun someone, knock someone out, wrap them in thicky prison or do something else to them—just think at it while putting your thumb on the pad, and the magic will happen. The magic isn't completely unrestricted, but it can do a lot of stuff—pretty much everything I can think of that you might need. It'll even let you capture Hammerhearts and teleport them into the workstation itself—although the teleportation will only work if there's no anti-teleportation protection around them, and if they're knocked out first—just in case."

"And the protection?" Frederic prompted.

"It's pretty good," Marc explained. "It uses totally non-magical nanobots to do the surveillance. Well, not totally non-magical; they have a magical link to each workstation, but the bots themselves are totally untraceable, and set up to make any magic pass directly through them—the same as the spells we were using yesterday. And if something does interfere with them they'll immediately self-destruct, and a new nanobot will be created in their place by the workstation. So even if the magic being performed is detected, I can't think of a single way they could trace it back here."

Everyone tried then to claim workstations for themselves. It became very quickly apparent that there weren't enough for everyone, and after a little debating, Marc decided not to expand the control room to create enough space for everyone. Instead, he vanished one row of the workstations, leaving a little more space around the control panel, saying that he didn't want it to get too noisy in here. He ordered everyone else to go upstairs to the games room and wait for him there; we were going to set that up as the 'other' operations room, since nobody had really made much use of it in the few days we'd been in this base.

Before we too went upstairs, though, the six of us (me, Marc, Amelia, Peter, Frederic and Lillian) went around the room, assigning jobs to the people who would be working from here. Felicity and Jessica would be tagging Hall, and they would work together to deal with him (we all agreed that Hall could be dangerous enough to require teamwork to deal with him). Harry and Simon would tag Hignat and Wilwog respectively, while their sisters Misty and Michelle would tag Hignat and Wilwog's fathers respectively. Liam and Siobhan would tag Cornish between them; Darcy would keep a close watch on Sebastian, and interfere with him if he got up to any trouble; and Jacob Underwood elected to spy on Lena, a job which we initially didn't think strictly, necessary but Underwood managed to justify it by pointing out that she could get herself into trouble, and given what she had been to us, we didn't want anything really bad to happen to her. (Of course, it was also the easiest job of anyone, and he knew that.) Other people were given jobs relating to the things Lucien was doing, such as trying to slow down his invasions of Africa and South America (which both appeared to be too far-gone to save by this point), setting up the criminal trial in Hong Kong, and just generally trying to stop Hammerhearts carrying out their casual abuse of the innocent.

The only person who flatly refused to do any of these jobs, however, was Tommy. He had taken a workstation and now claimed that the only job he wanted to do was tag Lucien himself, and cause as much trouble for the head honcho as possible. Marc had done a good job getting Tommy on our side, but it hadn't changed the fact that Tommy now possessed severe tunnel vision, and at the end of that tunnel, all he really saw was the Honnie to whom he was so desperate to return. Before that, however, was his personal score to settle with Lucien, the man who had put him in this position in the first place, and he had no interest in doing anything that didn't serve his immediate goal of taking down the leader of the Hammerhearts.

Our initial thoughts were that it would be better not to interfere with Lucien at this time—let him get complacent again, was our thought process. It was Peter who pointed out that he would know very quickly what we were doing, if Fewul told him, so the idea of making him complacent probably wasn't going to work. In the end, we ordered Tommy to follow Lucien everywhere he went, and to do everything he could to interrupt his meetings. To be sure that Tommy didn't get carried away, however, Marc put a spell on his workstation to prevent it from capturing Lucien, just in case Tommy tried to do that.

We then went upstairs to the games room, and Marc created a bunch more workstations there for the rest of the army to get involved in the rebellion. By the time he was done it was after ten o'clock, and we hadn't yet achieved anything with the morning except to organise ourselves. Almost everyone in the entire base was now involved, and the few who weren't appeared to be in the control room, watching television and keeping an eye on things there. The gym, dining room and computer lab were all empty, so if there was anyone else around the place, they were either still in their bedrooms (like Natalie), or out on the grounds, perhaps using one of the small chambers I had installed which simulated certain caves from Rock Haulter. Most of them had been put there with recreation in mind, but there had been precious little time for recreation while we had been in this base.

All of this left us with an interesting little problem that hadn't occurred to any of us until we left the games room: Where were we supposed to go now? We couldn't run our operation from the control room anymore because the place was packed and would be far too distracting. We couldn't go in the Time Box because we would disturb the crew in there, and they needed all the concentration they could get. In the end, the six of us went into the dining room and sat around a table that had only been designed for five (Frederic had to drag a chair over from another table).

"And what exactly is it that we're doing up here, anyway?" Peter asked. "And as long as we're here, does anyone want some morning tea?"

"Morning tea sounds like a good idea," Frederic agreed, smiling a little, "but the reason we're here is because we need to figure out what comes next. What's going on down there is only minor stuff that isn't going to make a great difference in the scheme of the war. We need to figure out how to use our position to deal with Lucien, before he has another chance to kill thousands more people."

"Then perhaps we should go and get James—he's pretty much crucial in this conversation," Amelia said. "Is he still carrying on that research from yesterday? I thought that didn't amount to anything?"

"Not exactly," I said, figuring now was as good a time as any to tell these five what was *really* going on. "I spoke to Lisa again last night before I went to sleep, and she gave me an idea of something we can try. What James and the girls are doing now is following up on that lead. It's difficult to explain, and the truth is, I don't understand all of it myself anyway—"

I faltered at the intense look they were all giving me. "You might as well do your best to explain it, then," Marc said. "Is it going to be that important?"

"Possibly," I said hesitantly. "Once they're done making as much sense of it as they can, you're going to need to do some experiments with your magic to figure out if we're on the right track. Basically, James thinks there's a chance that—well…" I faltered again, glancing at Frederic. "How much do you know about magic theory? Have you heard of magic particles?"

Frederic slowly shook his head. "I know a bit about magic theory, but to be honest with you, I never really had a lot of respect for the field of magicology. To me, it always felt like they were trying to explain something using methods that they didn't have the scope required to truly understand it. I was always happy to accept that magic was magic, and as long as it was there, and it did what I needed it to do, it didn't really matter to me how it may or may not be operating beneath the surface. To this day, I'm not at all convinced that there even *is* an underlying explanation for magic; it could just be that magic is, and that may be all there is to it."

I shrugged. "I'm quite sure that James would disagree with that, and for all our sakes, I hope he's right. If magic is as simple as that, then it's probably impossible to destroy the crystals, and that in turn means we're all screwed. To answer the question, though, James is following up on a theory that some aspiring magicologist had back in the '90s which, if true, could make it possible for us to separate magic from the crystals, turning them into ordinary rocks. If that's possible, then it's probably also possible to separate magic from Lucien and all the devices used by the Hammerhearts."

"A lot of *ifs*, by the sound of it," Peter said nervously.

"Well, yeah, that's why we'll need to find a way to test the theory," I said. "Fortunately, we will have James for that part, so long as it's even possible to make sense of whatever they're reading down there. They've been in that box now for a little over three hours, so that's thirty hours for them. The girls will probably crash after lunch, but we'll have to get James to re-energise himself so that we don't waste any time."

"These tests we'll be performing," Marc said slowly, "they had better not put the Hero Crystal at risk. I mean, the last thing we need—"

"Most definitely not," Frederic said at once, glancing at me. "Surely, any experiments we perform won't risk destroying the Hero Crystal— right, John?"

That thought made me feel a little nervous, but I shook my head decisively. "I hope not, but it seems unlikely. We still need to beat Lucien, and doing that without the Hero Crystal would be just about impossible, and James knows that. I imagine we'll perform the test on a magical device, like a bludginator or something, or perhaps even one of the other crystals. I can't see a particular use for the Darkness Crystal, for instance."

"Okay, good," Marc said, appearing to relax, but my nervous feeling didn't go away. I couldn't shake the feeling that Marc was completely reluctant to let go of the Hero Crystal, and yet if this theory was even close to accurate, a time would come—and hopefully not too far into the future—when he would have to do just that. Would he be able to?

"So what now, then?" Amelia asked. "We still need to figure out a path going forward, just in case this magic particles stuff turns out to be nothing useful. What do we do about Lucien?"

What followed was a lot of brainstorming, and none of the ideas on their own were very good. Everything from capturing Lucien to stealing the Sien-Leoard Crystal was brought up, along with dealing with Fewul (nobody had any good ideas there). Perhaps we ought to try attacking Lucien's Honnie mind, or perhaps find a way to disable the magical alert he'd set up to let him know when Fewul had been recalled. The trouble with all of these ideas, though, was that Lucien and Fewul looked after each other: Whenever the beast was recalled, Lucien immediately re-summoned him; and whenever any kind of disabling magic hit Lucien, Fewul wouldn't be too far away to fix him up.

"Maybe we can bring all this stuff together into something like a plan, though," Peter suggested, looking hopeful. "I mean, if we can succeed in cutting off the connection between Fewul and Lucien, and then we can recall Fewul, that'll give us a small window during which we can attack Lucien before he has a chance to call for reinforcements."

"Maybe, maybe," Lillian agreed, "but we would need to make sure he doesn't have the Sien-Leoard Crystal in his hand at the time, because the moment he comes under attack, the first thing he'll do is call Fewul to him, and the second thing he'll do is summon Fewul back to Earth if Fewul doesn't immediately respond. We have to make sure that wherever he is, whatever he's doing, he can only rely on the magic from his crystal chips to help him in battle."

"Then maybe we should nail him while he's nailing Lena," Peter suggested. "From what I saw the other day, he prefers to keep his hands free while he's doing that."

Most people around the table cringed at his wording, but nobody could deny that it was a pretty good idea. Marc said, "When we did that last time, I was standing right next to the Sien-Leoard Crystal and didn't realise it. I'm not even sure if there was a shield around it—probably, since there was one around the Villain Crystal in the brief time he had it, but I got through that one pretty easily."

"So, let me see if I've got this right," Amelia said, holding up a hand and beginning to tick things off. "Wait till Lucien's in bed with Lena; disable the magical alert he has to let him know that Fewul's been recalled; recall Fewul ourselves; then what? Do we attack him or do we steal the crystal first?"

"First, we try to find out if he has any alert to let him know if someone has stolen the Sien-Leoard Crystal," Frederic said. "We know he doesn't have an alert to let him know if someone else touches it, because if he did, it would have been triggered by that device John made that uses magic from the Sien-Leoard Crystal—but that doesn't mean he doesn't have an alert on the shield around the crystal. We'll need to determine if he does before deciding whether to try stealing the crystal or attacking him first."

"What if we can't locate the crystal exactly?" I asked. "Or what if we can't tell if there's an alert or not?"

"If we can't tell if there's an alert, we try to steal the crystal, and be ready in case Lucien responds," Frederic said, "something we should do even if there isn't an alert. As for not being able to locate the crystal, if that happens, I'm not quite sure—"

"I know of something we can do in that scenario," Marc suggested, grinning and holding up the Hero Crystal. "If he doesn't notice that Fewul's gone, that'll give me a chance to call it forth myself. Then, I can set up an alert to let me know the instant Lucien recalls it with the Sien-Leoard Crystal, because I'm sure that's the first thing he'll try when he figures out what we did, and I'll be able to call it back instantly—just like he keeps doing to us."

That made everyone around the table smile, but Peter was quick to spot a problem with that plan. "That's certainly worth doing, but there's no guarantee you'll be able to call Fewul forth as quickly as Lucien does. You don't have the Honnie mind he uses to multitask the way he does."

"Which brings us back to the Honnie mind," Frederic said, "and I would suggest that permanently disabling it is the perfect step to take the moment we have stolen Fewul from him, and it would be even better if we can also take the Sien-Leoard Crystal along the way. If we can do all that, all he will have are his crystal chips, and while that's still a lot of magic, we will be able to overpower any magic he performs just by sheer force."

"And what about the crystal chips?" Amelia asked. "As long as he still has those, he will still be dangerous. I would suggest those old Hammerheart devices that were able to disable the chips inside the body, but for one thing, they probably have devices that can just as easily fix that kind of magic. For another thing, I have no idea if they can work on more than one chip in the same body."

A pause followed this before I said, "I think this may bring us back to where we started, and whether it's possible to destroy the crystal chips, even if it means destroying the Sorcerous Crystals."

Marc was giving me a very dirty look as I said this, which I dutifully ignored, but before anyone could say anything to this, someone knocked on the doorframe and came into the dining room. It was Sophie, holding her phone in her hand and looking absolutely exhausted.

"Hey, you," Peter said, looking around at her. "How's the research going?"

"Could be better," she said, pulling out a chair at a nearby table and slumping down. "Could be a lot worse, though. James sent me to tell you guys what we've found so far; I wasn't sure where you were until I came up here."

We all swapped looks and then Frederic said, "And what have you found? Anything?"

"Well, it's very confusing," she said, holding her phone up and beginning to press buttons. "When Katie and I went in there, it sounded at first like James and Erica were talking another language, but we started to get the hang of it eventually. The thesis didn't make a lot of sense when we tried to read it, but James was able to isolate the important points, and we took a bunch of notes on them."

"And that's what you've got there," I clarified.

"Yeah," she said. "Okay, so basically, the theory is that magic exists in a state of particulate matter when it's not being used, and an energy state when it is being used, and that the use of magic is basically the shifting of these particles to and from energy forms. The thesis went on to talk about how this might happen, like if two particles have to join together to make the change, or split apart. It goes on to theorise what subatomic particles might exist in magic, if any, or if magic contains a previously unknown subatomic particle. James told me not to write any of that down because it probably doesn't matter, but I remembered it anyway."

"Okay," Frederic said slowly, "but I can already see a flaw in that theory. If it were true, then there would be a finite amount of magic in each of the crystals, and when it ran out, the crystals would be non-magical, but we know that isn't the case."

"Correct," Sophie said, "it's not the case. The theory suggests that magic particles are able to self-replicate, either on the conversion from matter to energy, or going back the other way. It's the only explanation this magicologist could come up with to explain how you could create a magical device using magic, and then that the newly-created device could also be capable of performing magic."

This was getting hard to follow, and I couldn't understand how Sophie was able to look so calm as she said all this. Maybe it was just her exhaustion catching up with her.

"Is that even possible?" Frederic said, looking uneasy. "I can understand how such a thing could be, of course, but coming from a magicologist, it surprises me. What does he say to explain how they could self-replicate?"

That made Sophie grin, taking me even more aback. "I'm glad you asked. This is where it gets really good. It's a bit of a stretch, but if this part of his theory is true, it means it really *will* be possible to destroy the crystals. This guy was a physicist as well, and in his mind, the only way that magic particles could be allowed to exist in the universe is if they had a counterweight, which he referred to as 'antimagic'."

Frederic's eyes widened. "Ah, I think I know where this is going. I've never heard of anything like it, and you're right: It *is* a stretch of the imagination. To be honest, I don't believe this theory is correct, but it *is* worth testing. If antimagic is real, then it can actually destroy magic altogether, and that would solve all our problems."

That made me feel hopeful, while around the table, Peter wore an expression that was probably similar to my own. Lillian and Amelia both looked startled, while Marc looked dismayed.

"Do you have any more in there, Sophie?" Lillian asked.

"Nope, that's pretty much it," she said, getting up and pocketing her phone. "Do I have to go back down there again? 'Cause I'm totally stuffed."

"Please do go back down there," Frederic said, "and tell James to come and join us up here. Then you, Katie and Erica can go and have a nap—I think you've earned it. Don't be surprised if we have to send you back into the Time Box later, though, after we've disproved this theory and we need more ideas."

"Thanks, I'm on it," she said, and she left the room.

"Why are you so sure that this theory's not right?" I asked him. "I mean, I get that it requires a bit of imagination to come up with something like this, but it actually sounds kind of plausible."

"I just haven't seen any evidence in all my life to back it up," he said earnestly. "I could be wrong, of course, and if we can find a way to prove or disprove it, I guess we'll know then."

"What if we can't prove or disprove it?" Amelia asked. "What if every single experiment we think of is inconclusive?"

"That wouldn't surprise me either," Frederic shrugged. "Magic is meant to be mysterious—it doesn't like to give up its secrets easily. I'm sure that James's scientific mind will come up with the best experiments to try, though, so if there's anything to find, I have no doubt that we'll find it."

James came into the dining room a few minutes later. As he did, I heard the sound of the elevator rising higher up into the base, no doubt delivering the three girls off to their bedrooms.

"Nice setup down there, Marc," he said, sitting in Sophie's vacated seat and stifling a yawn. "Everyone looks pretty happy with what they're doing."

"Did any of them mention if they'd achieved anything?" Marc asked.

"I didn't ask," James shrugged. "Sophie said you wanted me to come up here so we could talk about the theory."

"Mr. Woodward doesn't think it can be true," Marc shrugged.

James glanced at Frederic. "Well, it might not be. Remember, this magicologist had no access to any Sorcerers when he came up with this theory; he was just a student and not really recognised in his field. That meant that he had no way to test his theory and refine it. That's probably why his thesis was so long and convoluted; he was trying to pre-empt ways that he could be wrong, and adapt his theory to fit everything in."

"This 'antimagic' thing sounds interesting, though," Amelia said. "Do you really think we can use that to destroy the crystals?"

"I think we could, and that we should, if it turns out to be real," James said.

"Wait, hang on," Marc piped up, his objection surprising me not at all. "If antimagic will destroy magic the moment it comes into contact with it, how on earth are we supposed to control it? Won't it just destroy every spell or magical device we use to try to touch it?"

A brief silence followed this as we all realised that Marc was actually right. Finally, James said, "Then, we'll have to use magic to create a non-magical device to attempt to control it. I'm sure it's possible to do, but you're right: It is going to be tricky, and possibly dangerous. Still, it doesn't change my opinion that if we can find a way to control it, we should use it to destroy the crystals, as well as every other form of magic in the world. I know how extreme that sounds, but like we've already established, all of it can be turned bad if accessed by the wrong people."

"And then what'll we do?" Marc argued. "If we destroy magic, we won't have anything with which to fight—"

"Fight against what, Marc?" James asked calmly.

"Against the Hammerhearts!" Marc almost shouted, such was his frustration. "You said it yourself months ago: If we take away their magic, they'll just resort to non-magical fighting, and after what happened last night, we all know what that'll look like!"

"That's a fair point," Amelia said, putting a hand on Marc's arm in an attempt to calm him down. "That was why you thought having a Honnie would be a good idea in the first place: to calm that sort of thing down, should it ever come to that."

"On that score, I would suggest we keep some of our own magic while we destroy everything Lucien could touch," Lillian said, "and then only destroy ours when we are sure we'd put things as close to rights as we can, so long as we accept that nothing we do is going to make the world perfect. Any attempt to do so would ultimately make us no better than the Hammersons."

"That's probably the best we can do," Frederic said, "but in the meantime, let's not look that far ahead into the future. None of it will matter if this whole 'magic particles' theory is false, so for starters, let's figure out how to either prove or disprove that."

The rest of the time before noon was spent coming up with experiments we could try in the afternoon that could definitively determine, one way or another, if we were on the right track.

Chapter 19: Experimentation

One advantage of working in the dining room was that we were all able to have an early lunch as we talked (except for James, who had taken a food creating device into the Time Box with him so that he and Erica wouldn't starve, and was already satiated). It meant that we were able to get ourselves out of there well before anyone else came in for lunch, and in fact, meant that we were able to catch them all and debrief them on their progress for the morning before they could leave their workstations.

We went to the games room first and found that while everyone there had accomplished at least something this morning (such as saving a few lives, preventing a few women from being raped, and capturing a whole bunch of Hammerhearts from all over the world), none of them were ultimately able to slow the enemy's progress. We told them that they were free to go and have lunch if they liked, but that it would be good if some of them could stay back here and keep an eye on things. About half of them were good about staying, and the other half companionably agreed to bring back some lunch for the rest of them before getting back to work themselves.

We then went downstairs to see how things were going in the control room, and found that for many of them, the story was quite the same. There were a few exceptions, though, such as Darcy, who reported that Sebastian had done bugger all this morning, and that spying on him was the most boring movie ever. Felicity and Jessica had done a very good job of making Hall's business difficult through the morning, making him so mad in the process that he actually punched a brick wall in rage and hurt his hand. They had even considered capturing him but had decided against it for the time being, preferring to watch him run around out there getting madder and madder all the time. Marc said this was probably a good move—not that capturing Hall would be difficult, or even dangerous, but we couldn't be sure how Lucien would respond to such a provocation.

As for Lucien, he'd had a similarly frustrating morning as Hall. Tommy had kept him off-balance every step of the way, making it impossible for Lucien to get any business done, and ruining every single meeting along the way. He started off by performing magic around the people in the meetings, which distracted them for a while, and confused the hell out of Lucien when he couldn't figure out how it was happening. When the Hammerhearts figured out that ignoring it was the best strategy, Tommy began attacking them directly with bludginators, thicky prison and other similar things, using the magic light trick to pass through any shields Lucien put up to protect them. He even did this to Lucien himself, just for his own satisfaction. Finally, whenever he saw a sufficiently important Hammerheart, Tommy would invariably capture them, and then watch as Lucien's rage grew.

Harry and Simon had started out tagging Hignat and Wilwog, but their jobs had changed in the time since. As it turned out, out of necessity, they had been forced to capture the two boys who had once been nothing more than our old school rivals. The twins reported that after Hignat and Wilwog determined that there was no one in the Big Room for them to screw around with, they had become angry, and had decided to go up to Lucien's living quarters and ask him if they could rape Natalie again. There, they had found only Lena, so they had asked her for permission instead. Lena had told them that she didn't have the authority to make a call like that, but that she thought they'd done enough 'taking advantage of women'.

Naturally, they hadn't taken too kindly to that, and had turned their attention (and their lust) on her. Given Wilwog's size and strength, they would have easily succeeded in doing whatever they wanted to her, but before they could do more than lay hands on her, the twins sprang into action. Underwood had also watched all this, and kept an eye on Lena after it was over. He reported that she had been shaken by the ordeal, but didn't seem to have any curiosity about what had happened to the two boys or how they had just vanished like that (at least, he had no obvious evidence that she had wondered).

She may have even felt some remorse for her actions, for she had gone into Natalie's chamber shortly afterwards (Lucien must have made it possible for her to do so, for what reasons I couldn't guess), looking (according to Underwood) close to tears, and perhaps about to apologise, and maybe even try to help her escape. Only, Natalie hadn't been there, of course. Once again, we couldn't know what Lena thought of this (perhaps that Lucien had moved her), but whatever went through her head, she didn't speak it aloud. She had spent the time since arming herself with Hammerheart weapons and looking, in Underwood's opinion, thoughtful. That was enough to get my hopes up: Lucien had done a lot of damage to Lena's mind, but perhaps, if given enough time away from his Honnie mind and magical influence, she could find her way out of it.

"Do you think I should capture her?" Underwood asked us when he had finished his report.

Marc hesitated, glancing at Frederic. "What do you think? This experience may have changed her mind towards things a little, but surely she won't actually blame Lucien for what happened—will she?"

"She might, if she considers that it's his authority that is permitting people like Hignat and Wilwog to think it's okay to do this stuff," Amelia said reasonably. "Also, Lucien did leave her alone and vulnerable there —I imagine that thought would have crossed her mind."

"That *could* occur to her," Frederic said thoughtfully, "but that doesn't mean she'll automatically want to stay with us. Also, it's likely that when Lucien finds out what happened, he'll hit the roof and want to defend her with everything he has, which probably *will* be an appealing thought for her. I think the best thing to do, for now, is keep watching her and make sure nothing else really bad happens to her. We'll re-evaluate what to do for her as events unfold."

As this was happening, a few people, such as Felicity and Jessica, were watching the pro-Lucien rallies around Australia, which were now underway. It was disheartening to see thousands upon thousands of people walking through the streets, holding signs and waving flags, yelling and chanting about how much they loved Lucien, how much they wanted him to do everything in his power to save them, and how they were willing to do 'whatever it takes' to stand with him as he did so. Some of the people watching this had even figured out how to turn the sound up on their workstations, so we were able to hear exactly what they were saying. There was a police presence, of course (Hall was part of it), but it looked like there was no trouble—except, perhaps, for us.

I was relieved to get away from it all. After a quick debate, we decided that we might as well go into the Time Box for the next part of our operation. Marc, Amelia, Peter, Frederic, Lillian, James and I squeezed through the door, one after another, and before we had a chance to shut the door and begin warping time, we were joined by a fresh-looking Natalie. She'd had her few hours of sleep and was now ready to jump back into action (as ready as one could be after going through all she had over the last few days). She'd gone to the dining room to have a quick lunch (missing us by not much, I gathered), and then had come straight back down here, expecting us to be working out of the control room.

The eight of us shut ourselves away in the Time Box so that we could explain to Natalie, wasting as little time as possible, what was going on out there—and then what was going on in here. She hadn't known about the Time Box, of course, so that had taken some explaining. That had led to explaining about the other new inventions I had brought back from Rock Haulter, and that had led to explaining what I had found out from Lisa, and the dreaded prophecy about the last Sorcerer. She already knew about Stella, of course, thanks to Lucien's bragging, so all we had needed to do there was explain *why* she did what she did. Finally, though, we were able to reach the present, and explain to her about the theory of magic particles and the corresponding theory of antimagic.

"Magic particles," Natalie repeated, giving her head a little shake. She had digested most of what we had told her well enough (even handling the discussion about my presence in the in-between reasonably well), but this last bit appeared to have stumped her. "Do you guys all get this? I can't wrap my head around it."

"I get the basics," Peter said, shrugging. "don't ask me to expand on it, though; that's JSandwich's job."

"Just do the best you can to follow along for now, Nat," James smiled at her. "Hopefully, after you see what we're doing, it'll start to make a bit more sense to you. I guess now we have to figure out how to prove or disprove magic particles, right?"

"I think that's the plan," Amelia said. "Any ideas?"

James glanced at Marc, and then took a magical device out of his pocket. It was the re-energiser, the one he was using to keep himself going after already having spent thirty hours in here this morning. "I figure the best place to start would be to find a way to observe, as closely as possible, what changes one of these devices goes through when magic is used. Marc, can you create some sort of magical microscope that'll be able to observe this thing on the particle level? It'll need to be magical itself because we're going to need a way to filter our hands out of the equation."

Marc obliged, and James leaned forward to put the device under the microscope. What appeared on the digital display above it didn't look remotely like the device I was seeing with my bare eyes. James twisted the device around so that it was pointing at him, and gave it a click. I saw it work on him, but I didn't see anything on the display. After a few seconds, Peter said, "That proved nothing, dude. I'm no scientist, but I'm thinking you need some way to focus this experiment somehow."

James paused in thought for a few seconds and then said, "Marc, did you think specifically of magic particles when you created this?"

"Er—no," Marc said, his face falling, as he took the crystal back out of his pocket, "but that'll be easy to—"

"No, don't," James said quickly, making Marc jump. "For all we know, magic particles will resist any obvious attempt to observe them. We'll go like this for now, and if it doesn't work, we'll try being more specific."

"And if that doesn't work, then what?" Frederic asked.

"Then we be less specific, turn it into a completely non-magical microscope," James shrugged. "The thing about this kind of experimentation: you have to be wrong a hundred times or more before you're right. The trick is to not let it get you down. I'm gonna shift this thing so that the microscope is directly over the point where the magic comes out. Marc, can you put a red dot on the device to indicate where the microscope is focused?"

Marc obliged once again, the dot showing that it was focused on the centre of the device. James shifted it and then tried again, but the result was equally inconclusive. Marc worked his magic to make the microscope focus on magic particles, but once again, nothing happened. According to James, this could mean that magic particles didn't exist, but it could just as easily mean that they did exist, and the microscope just couldn't see them, which made it inconclusive for the third time. Taking James's advice, Marc turned it into an ordinary old microscope with no magical enchantments on it whatsoever, but for the fourth time, it showed nothing.

"The theory is looking less and less likely to me," Frederic said, but he didn't look altogether unhappy about it.

James, however, was unperturbed. "The truth is, on top of not knowing if they exist, we don't know what magic particles look like. We could be seeing them in the microscope right now and just not realising it. Or, they could be invisible, like the Sien-Leoard Crystal—that wouldn't surprise me either."

"Or they could be inside the device, not on the outside," I pointed out. "In fact, I'm sure that's *exactly* where they are if they exist. Do we have any devices where the magic could be on the outside?"

"Possibly this," Marc said, holding up the crystal, and then leaning forward and swapping it for the device under the microscope. The display showed a lot of rapid movement as this happened, but when it was focused on the Hero Crystal, there was still nothing remarkable to see—and certainly nothing that we could conclusively call a magic particle.

"Maybe we're going about this the wrong way," Natalie suggested, and we all looked at her. She blushed and then said, "Well, didn't you say that the act of performing magic causes the particles to turn into energy and then back again? Maybe you should be looking for magic energy rather than magic particles."

"Not a bad idea," Amelia agreed.

"Not bad? I think it's a great idea," James said, and he looked excited. "If we can find a way to catch magic while it's in motion, whatever results we get will be more definitive. Marc, I'm going to ask you to create a new device, but there's something I wanna try with this one first."

What he tried was positioning the reenergiser on one side of the device and himself on the other, so that when it was shot at him, the magic would pass beneath the microscope. It meant that the person sitting opposite him (Lillian, as it were) had to activate the device, but when she did, yet again nothing happened. Either the microscope had just missed the focus on the beam of magic, or there hadn't been anything to see anyway. Since we weren't sure which, Marc created a stunner (a device which shot visible light when activated) and tried the experiment with that. This too failed, which seemed conclusive to me, but James was unconvinced. He asked Marc to put a spell on the microscope to make it follow any light that passed through it, and Marc did so, but yet again, nothing happened.

I had now lost count of how many experiments had failed, but James seemed satisfied that magic energy, even if it came with a light which we could see, could not be observed in this way. He therefore asked Marc to vanish the microscope and create a new device, this one entirely magical. It took the shape of a small whiteboard, except that it was enchanted to catch whatever magic hit it and then reflect it in some way that would be visible. None of us, including James, were quite sure what to expect here, but as with every experiment before it, I felt my hopes rising.

"Before you do this," Amelia said, "maybe you should see if you can perform a spell that'll make it possible for you to sense how much magic is clinging to an object. Don't think of particles—just think of magic as you know it. I imagine something like that will work, and if it does, at least we'll have a way to track the magic's movements, even if we can't observe any particles."

Marc did so, and reported that this kind of spell was possible. At last, something had worked, and he proceeded to check how much magic already existed in the board, as well as in the reenergiser (roughly the same amount, and quite a small amount, according to him), before James performed the experiment. A second later, the board displayed text that showed it had been hit by magic which would boost the current energy level of a living being, but when Marc checked the magic levels of the two devices, they hadn't changed from how they had originally been.

"Huh?" James looked thoroughly confused by this turn of events. "How is that even possible?"

"It actually *does* make sense to me," Peter said, and we all looked at him. The idea that Peter could have understood something that James hadn't, was unheard of. "Well, those devices don't have a set number of times that they can work, so you wouldn't expect the magic level to change there. As for that thing"—he nodded at the board—"well, when you do that to a person, it doesn't leave traces of magic inside that person, does it?"

"No, it doesn't," Frederic agreed, "which means, the only way this can be possible, staying within the theory we're testing here, is if the magic hits the board, does its thing, and then returns to where it came from. Is there any way to test that, James?"

There was, but it involved Marc using his crystal to monitor the magic levels of the two devices as the experiment progressed. He reported that the magic level in the board spiked for an immeasurably short amount of time as the reenergising magic hit it, before returning to normal. He then reported the same phenomenon in reverse from the end of the reenergiser. James then tried the same experiment using the stunner, but this was where things got really strange: The spike in magic upon the board lasted slightly longer than the reenergiser, and furthermore, there was no dip in magic within the stunner at all.

This turn of events flummoxed everyone, including James. What could possibly explain this? Since we weren't sure, and nobody could come up with a hypothesis, the best idea any of us had was to repeat this experiment over and over again using different magical devices. Peter and I left the Time Box and gathered up copies of all the other devices in the cabinet (except for the crystals and the ones James had locked up), and carried them back into the box. For a long time after that (at least a couple of hours of box time), we tested them one after another against the board, while Marc created a new device to monitor the amount of magic throughout (one for the board and one for whichever device was being tested), just to make his job a bit easier.

It was dull work, but eventually, a pattern began to emerge, and when James spotted it, it was almost like a 'eureka' moment for him. In fact, once it became clear what was happening, I was a little surprised that none of us had figured it out after what the stunner had done. The devices which spiked the board for the shortest amount of time, and which lost a corresponding amount of magic from themselves at the same time, were the ones which didn't perform any ongoing magic after they had been used. Similar devices, such as the unboggler and the bludginator, as well as those that had been programmed to create things, behaved in the same way.

The ones that *did* perform ongoing magic, such as the stunner and agonator, caused the amount of magic on the board to increase for the duration that the device was used, while not losing any of their own magic in the process. When the stunner was released, the magic on the board would instantly return to its normal level, which drew us to the only possible conclusion: Magic that was not ongoing would always return to its original location after being performed, while magic that *was* ongoing would self-replicate as it was performed. It did still leave one strange question unanswered—where did the magic from the stunner go after it fell off the board?—but now that we had come this far, James reckoned we would soon be able to answer that question as well.

It was time to turn our attention back to magic particles, and our attempts to observe them. Marc first put a spell on the board to make it catch the magic that hit it, not allowing it to fall away the moment it was no longer active, and then James hit it with the stunner once again. We observed that the spell had worked—the magic level didn't drop when James released the stunner. Under James's instructions, Marc performed some more spells on the board, and I got a little lost trying to keep up with what it was that they were doing. So far as I could tell, Marc was separating the two forms of magic (the part that made the board work, and the part that had been added to it by the stunner), and he reported that even among the magic of the board, that too could be separated. James seemed to understand what this meant, though none of the rest of us did, and he advised Marc to go on separating the magic in any place it seemed logical to do so.

It didn't take long after that.

"I can't seem to do anything with it," Marc told James, "but it's pretty obvious how it's organising itself. There's only one section of magic that's inactive at the moment—the part which makes the board write what magic's being performed on it—but the rest of it is in motion, including the magic I'm performing to figure all this out."

"What about the stunner?" James asked.

"The same."

"Can you make it motionless?"

Marc tried, and then shook his head. James then advised him to create yet another magical device, and this one I understood: it would attempt to catch the residual magic as it fell away from the board. He then performed a spell on the board to undo what he'd done earlier, so that its magic level could return to normal, and as it did so, the magic level of the new device rose by that same amount. Marc was then able to confirm that the magic he had captured was motionless. Finally, he turned the new device into a microscope so that we could observe what was inside it, and after he re-jigged it a little, we were finally able to lay our eyes on magic particles.

"They can't be seen by anything normal," Marc said, "but if you put a spell on the microscope to focus on the magic—if you know what it is you're looking for—they'll just show up, right there."

"I don't believe this," Frederic said in a hushed voice, looking awed. "They really *do* exist."

"It would seem so," James agreed. "Part of me wonders if they are only showing up now because it's what we expect to see, but given how hard we had to work to get to this point, the evidence doesn't back that up."

"I certainly wasn't expecting to see this," Frederic pointed out.

"Neither was I," said Natalie. "I mean, not like this."

"Marc, can you create a device that can track magic particles?" James asked.

Marc did so, the new device being handheld and revealing how many magic particles it could detect within a radius of about ten centimetres. He then began going around the room, touching it to various things and observing the results. No matter where it went, it detected at least a few magic particles, and at first I thought this was from the Time Box itself until we figured out that it was picking up the magic in Marc's hand. It wasn't so much that he was the Seventh Sorcerer, but that he was four-dimensional, which explained the magic in his body. The rest of us had similar and slightly varying levels of magic in our bodies (though mine was by far the highest). Of course, the moment this new device went near the Hero Crystal, the number shot up so high that it could no longer fit on the small screen, and who knew how many digits had fallen off the side.

"This is a breakthrough for sure," James said happily, "but it's not yet a *useful* breakthrough. Observing magic particles isn't going to help

us defeat Lucien. We need to see if we can manipulate magic particles
—"

"I don't think I can," Marc said quickly. "I mean, maybe there are
some things I can do, if you can think of them, but I wasn't able to turn
magic energy back into particles earlier, not until I triggered the event
which was holding them in an energy state in the first place."

"Exactly, you *were* able to do that," James said, "which is a good
sign. See if you can turn those particles in the microscope into energy—
or even just one of them."

Marc looked dubious, and I didn't blame him—based on what he'd
just said, this experiment probably wouldn't work. And so it didn't.

"Never mind," James said, unperturbed. "Next, see if you can get the
crystal to tell you what those particles will do if they are converted into
energy."

Marc didn't argue but gripped the crystal in his hand. A few seconds
passed, and then he shook his head. "I'm getting nothing here."

"Which could mean that the magic didn't work," James said, "or it
could mean that the particles themselves don't know what they'll do if
they are converted into energy. It could be that they won't actually have a
magical function until they are converted into energy."

"Which is still utterly useless to us," Frederic pointed out.

"Agreed," James said. "Next, Marc, see if you are able to use the
crystals to move the particles around under the microscope."

Marc did as he was told yet again, though he looked as though he
was starting to get tired. I didn't blame him—he'd done a lot of magic in
the last few hours, for that was how long we'd been in here. Once again,
this experiment failed, leaving James looking a bit downhearted.

"Well, that doesn't surprise me," he said, sitting back in his seat, "but
it is still a bummer. We need to find some way to at least move them
from one place to another. If we can't do that, then we really won't be
able to use them at all."

"Well, performing magic directly on the particles doesn't appear to
work," Amelia said, "but they do respond to some other stimuli. Maybe
we should try to figure out what it is that causes them to go from particle
form to energy form instead?"

"That's not a bad idea," I agreed. "At least, magic seems a lot more
willing to move around when it's in energy form."

After a bit of playing around, Marc was eventually able to partially
succeed in this endeavour. By performing a spell specifically designed to
activate the particles (nothing about energy in there), he was able to get
them to produce a bright flash of light. As earlier, the particles returned
to where they had been before, but it was a hopeful sign.

James, however, had been thinking about something else while this
was happening, and now said, "Maybe the best way to do this is not with

magic at all. I could activate magic particles just by pushing a button on my stunner, which means it doesn't take magic to activate magic—"

"Unless there is magic energy inside the stunner as well as particles," Frederic suggested.

James hesitated then said, "Well, let's find out. Marc?"

Marc sighed and got to work examining the stunner with the crystal. He reported that no: as far as he could tell, there were only particles inside the stunner, and no energy. James grinned as he said this.

"So if it's not magic, then what is it?" Natalie asked. "Surely it isn't just the act of pushing the button."

"Maybe it responds to a certain type of vibration," Lillian said.

"Or an electrical current," I added.

"Both possible," James agreed. "I imagine, whatever it is, when we create these devices, the magic automatically does whatever it needs to do to make the devices work the way we want. We don't have to think too deeply about what's *really* going on beneath the surface, but I imagine that if we *were* to focus on that part of it, we could probably control it. Marc, see if you can create a device that can move magic particles; only when you do, make sure you specify that the device is to contain no magic of its own. Can you do that?"

"I'm sure I can," he said, gripping the Hero Crystal. "Whether or not it works is, of course, an entirely different question."

He created another handheld device, which he gripped and pointed at the microscope. He was able to get the particles within to vibrate in a way that they hadn't been doing before, but beyond that, nothing else happened.

"That's not really what I was trying to do," he said, his shoulders slumping.

"What *were* you trying to do?" Peter asked.

"I was trying to raise them into the air in there and make them spin around."

"Maybe that's a little *too* controlling," James suggested. "Maybe try drawing the particles to you. See if you can get them to enter that device you just created."

"But this device can't just do that. It's non-magical, remember?"

"Oh, yeah. Well, vanish it and create a new device designed to draw magic particles to itself, and remember, it can't contain any magic of its own."

Marc obliged, and this time, the result was quite remarkable and unexpected. The particles under the microscope slipped away and vanished, and Marc had to measure the amount of magic in the new device to confirm that they had moved there. Only, something else was happening: the level of magic in the particle drawing device was steadily growing. By the time it topped out, it was well above where we had expected it to be. James's expression became horrified as he watched this, and he scrambled out of his seat and snatched up the device Marc had earlier created to measure magic particles. His face relaxed when he confirmed that we hadn't all just had our own magic sucked out of us, nor had any of the devices we had brought into the room with us, and certainly nor had the Hero Crystal.

"So what on earth just happened?" Peter asked.

"My theory is that we just scooped up a whole load of residual magic," James suggested, staring at the particle drawing device. "Every time we performed a spell on that board that caused the magic to fall away, it had to go somewhere. The particles were probably floating around in here all along, and now we just collected them."

"You know," Natalie said, beginning to look excited. "There's probably a lot of that kind of loose magic floating around in the world. Do you think it would do us any good if we could draw it all in like that?"

James shrugged. "It probably wouldn't make a whole lot of difference. All of that magic couldn't do what the Hero Crystal can, but it might be good to have it all the same."

"Okay, so what now?" Marc asked, looking around at us. "Is this something we can use against Lucien?"

James hesitated and then said, "I think the next step is to try to confirm the existence of antimagic. As far as weapons go, that is going to be much more potent than anything we do with magic particles."

Marc's face fell as he spoke, and even I began to feel nervous. The idea of attracting a substance that could literally destroy magic was quite scary.

"I dunno if we should do that in here," Amelia said, her voice shaking a little. "If we draw antimagic into the Time Box, it could destroy us all, or trap us in a time loop or something."

"I don't even think we should do it in this base," Marc added. "I mean, look how much magic there is around this place. In fact, we probably shouldn't do it at all, given how much magic we all have inside us. What do you think would happen to us if antimagic got inside our bodies?"

"I imagine we'll turn into normal human beings, heaven forbid," James said, smiling a little. "But I tend to agree with Amelia—we probably should do this somewhere more open, and surrounded by as little magic as possible. Besides, I think we've spent enough time in the Time Box for one day."

That was definitely true. More than three hours of Time Box time had passed (which was only a little over twenty minutes on the outside), but I couldn't risk spending any more time in here than I already had. Doing this every day was bound to eat into what little time I had left.

Chapter 20: Radius of Destruction

Only eighteen minutes or so had passed on the outside since Peter and I had come out to raid the cabinet for devices to test, but it was immediately obvious that something big had happened in that eighteen minutes. As we began to emerge from the cupboard, one at a time and all carrying magical devices in our hands (though not those which Marc had created in there—those had been vanished, to be recreated later when the next phase of experimentation began), many in the packed control room looked around us and immediately began jabbering. All their faces were pale and their eyes wide and horrified.

"Hold on, hold on," Frederic said, raising a hand. "One at a time, please. What's going on?"

They all fell silent, looking at each other to see who was going to talk first. It was Jessica who took the initiative, telling us, "There's been another terrorist attack, at the Sydney protest. A couple of people started shooting at the protesters, and they got loads of them before the police could get to them. And then a truck exploded about a kilometre away. It's —it's mayhem."

A rush of blood went to my head and I actually swayed slightly, bumping shoulders with Marc before righting myself. I clenched my fists as I understood. That was meant to look like us, or people affiliated with us, killing indiscriminately for the purpose of standing against Lucien— just as people affiliated with us had done several times over, during the week. This was just going to keep on happening until Lucien got his way with us—and perhaps even a little after that, just so that he had even more of an excuse to take full control of the people.

"What should we do?" Rebecca asked imploringly. "Most of us were busy sorting out other messes when this happened, but Felicity and Jessica were there and even though they tried to help, they couldn't make much of a difference. There was a stampede and more people were injured and probably killed, and there was nothing we could do."

Marc went over to Jessica's workstation and looked at the screen, a few of us in step behind him. It showed Hall, and several other police officers, using magical devices to herd the panic-stricken crowd into columns, where they would be unable to run away or cause any further problems. More people were running between the columns—other police officers, by the look of it, as well as some paramedics.

"This is bad," Frederic said sadly, "but I don't think there's anything we can do. It looks like we missed the worst of it, and the police now have it under control. I don't think that they'll make things worse out there—not the way they're going about it."

"Is that really the right way to stop a riot?" James asked dubiously.

Frederic shrugged. "I suppose that depends what they do next. For now, though, it appears to be working, so we shouldn't consider it a bad thing."

Marc glanced at Frederic and said, "This is going to sound awful, but I don't think we should stop what we're doing to sort this out. Lucien probably meant this to be a punishment rather than a distraction, but that doesn't mean we should let it *be* a distraction. We still have important business to do."

That did sound awful, but it also sounded practical. Like Frederic had said, the worst had already happened, and the Hammerhearts (who would be on the same side as us, if we were to help them in this case) appeared to be in control of the situation. The eight of us swapped looks, and one by one, nodded our agreement.

"Did anything else happen while we were in there?" Lillian asked the room at large.

A few looks were swapped, and then Simon said, "You were only gone for like twenty minutes—not a lot is going to happen in that short time, apart from all that stuff in Sydney."

Lillian shrugged and grimaced. I didn't blame her—it was easy to forget, even though you knew about the time warp, that so little time had passed out here compared to what we had experienced in there.

"Yes, something did happen," Underwood chirped up suddenly, taking us all by surprise. He gestured at Tommy, who was sitting at the workstation next to his, and said, "It wasn't just Sydney. There were attacks on other rallies in other cities as well, probably at almost the exact same time too. Lucien was only just told about them a couple of minutes before you came out, and when the Hammerhearts left him alone, he said aloud that it was retribution for whoever was giving him so much trouble this morning."

We all hurried around to the other side of the control room so that we could look at Tommy and Underwood's workstations. The latter screen was still focused on Lena; she was alone in Lucien's living quarters, and not doing anything noteworthy. As for Lucien, he was alone in what was clearly the bomb-struck area of Melbourne, and appeared to be using the Sien-Leoard Crystal to reconstruct the destroyed infrastructure— returning it to how it had been prior to the nuke, minus the people who had been obliterated by it.

"What exactly did he say?" Marc asked them.

Underwood shrugged and looked at Tommy. "I basically just told you all I caught."

"Yeah, what he said," Tommy agreed, "but he did tell them to compile reports of the damage at all the rallies and to identify the terrorists, and that he would check them as soon as he was done with the reconstruction."

As he spoke, Tommy put his thumb on the magic pad of his workstation; a moment later, on the screen, one of the buildings Lucien had just recreated went crumbling to the ground.

"Wait, stop," Marc said, grabbing Tommy's wrist and lifting it off the workstation. "Sorry, but I think you should let up. This terrorist act only happened because of what you put Lucien through this morning. That doesn't make it your fault, but it does mean that we probably shouldn't do it anymore—"

"Strongly disagree with that, Marc," Frederic cut in. "Lucien may have *said* it was retribution, but remember, he doesn't need an excuse to do this stuff. If it hadn't been Tommy, it would have been something else that made him decide to do this. We cannot accommodate his behaviour, and that means Tommy should keep on doing exactly what he's doing."

"Good, because after what he took from me, I want him to suffer," Tommy said fervently.

"Okay, fine," Marc relented, "but at least wait until he's done fixing Melbourne; there's no good reason to make *that* harder for him."

"Why does he deserve a break?" Tommy asked indignantly.

"Actually, there is a good reason," James said. "He's going to get that stuff fixed eventually—his reputation depends on it—but the longer it takes him, the longer it'll be before he can turn his attention to other things; at least until he thinks to get Fewul onto it."

Marc shrugged. "That is a good point, but what if he gets so mad that he does another terrorist attack?"

"Then it'll be an excuse for him to do something he wants to do anyway, like Mr. Woodward said," James replied.

With that settled, the eight of us left the control room and crowded into the elevator, only realising that now that the control room had been reassigned, we once again had nowhere to go. The computer room was thrown up as a possible suggestion (it hadn't seen a lot of use by anyone, mainly because the base had no Internet access), but several people within the group wanted to go somewhere more private, and preferably as far from the magic that surrounded this place, as possible. After a few suggestions were thrown up and knocked down (including actually leaving the base, which would have necessitated putting loads of magical protection around ourselves, making us extremely vulnerable to antimagic should we find it), we eventually settled on converting Stella's bedroom into a secondary meeting room.

Not that a lot of converting took place. None of us really wanted to change the layout of the room (that felt like an insult to Stella), but the round table with chairs, and the circle of couches at the back, meant that it was already suitable for this purpose. All Marc needed to do was change the protection on the door, making it possible for the eight of us to enter without needing someone with magic to let us in. While he did this, Peter, James, Natalie, Frederic, Lillian and I made ourselves comfortable at the table, while Amelia went around the room, gathering up what few of Stella's possessions remained behind (most of them were either magical devices or things she had created for herself using magic devices, such as clothes), but when she was done, Amelia covertly slipped one of them into my hand before sitting at the table. I had glanced down to see that it was an envelope with my name pencilled on it. With curiosity and a little dread, I slipped it under my thigh on the seat so that it would be hidden from everyone else.

"Okay, so what?" Marc said as he too joined us at the table. "Are we going to ruin all our lives by bringing antimagic into it now? Is that how we're going to do this?"

James winced as Marc said this and said, "Well, why don't we start by recreating some of the things we were using in the Time Box? A device that is designed to draw and hold magic particles that are loose in the air, and one to measure the amount of magic particles nearby."

Marc did as he was told, and we all watched as the two devices combined to tell us that a small amount of magic had been gathered from the atmosphere. James observed this and then said, "Marc, that device that measures magic particles, does it contain any magic of its own?"

Marc hesitated then said, "I imagine it does, but there's no way to prove it because it filters out its own magic when it does the measuring."

"Okay, well, can you put a spell on that thing"—James indicated the particle drawing device—"to make it measure its own particles? Only make sure it uses some sort of non-magical method to measure them?"

"Is that even possible?" Amelia said nervously.

"Well if it's not possible, it won't work, so it's worth a try," James smiled.

Marc did as he was told, putting a display on the particle drawing device to show the amount of particles it contained as a sort of graph. James then told Marc to let a few particles out so that we could test it, at which point Marc had to put another spell on the device to make it capable of dropping particles back into the atmosphere—something it hadn't initially been designed to do—and when it did, the display showed the amount of magic contained within had dropped very slightly. Only for a moment, though, as the device quickly drew those same particles back in. Marc then finished that particular experiment by putting another spell on the particle drawing device so that it wouldn't automatically draw in any particles it detected.

"How exactly does that thing work, anyway?" Natalie asked. "If it's not using magic, what *is* it using?"

"It's partly electrical, partly mechanical," Marc said, leaning back in his seat. "If you check the bottom, you'll even see where the batteries go in—it takes two double-A's."

A few of us burst out laughing at that. It may have been a bit of nervous energy being let out, but there was something really funny about this incredibly sophisticated magic-manipulating device being run on double-A batteries.

"Well, that's good," James nodded. "However that thing is operating, it is using science to do so, and that means that we can create a similar device, equally non-magical, to manipulate antimagic."

Marc's face fell. "I just knew that would come up eventually."

"Come on, Marc—" James began.

"You know, we still haven't proven that antimagic even exists," Marc pointed out. "None of this"—he waved his hand at the two devices on the table—"or anything we did downstairs proves that magic particles mean antimagic is real."

James nodded again. "That's very true, which is why that's the first thing we need to do. I know you're nervous about antimagic, Marc—we all are—but the fact is, there is no better weapon to use against Lucien than something that will literally cancel out his power. I think the first place to start is to duplicate that device, Marc, and put a spell on it to draw antimagic instead of magic. Can you do that?"

Marc pursed his lips, staring around at us all. Everyone stared back at him, waiting for him to swallow whatever was holding him back and get on with it. Finally, he nodded stiffly and took his crystal out again. I never knew what pushed Marc over the edge—perhaps it was Amelia's encouraging smile that did it—but whatever it was, I knew that it wouldn't be the last time we would have to do this with Marc. I made a mental note to bring the magic enhancer up with me the next time we did anything that involved antimagic.

About twenty seconds later, an identical-looking magic drawing device sat next to the first. Marc used magic to move the two devices a safe distance apart (nobody objected to that) and then set it to begin drawing in antimagic. We all watched and waited to see what, if anything, would happen. If I'd had any money on me, I would have put it on nothing happening. Surely, after all we went through down in the Time Box, it wouldn't be this easy to get our mitts on antimagic particles. If I had put my money on it, though, I would have lost it.

"Wow," James breathed as the antimagic display slowly increased, first equalling and then surpassing the amount of particles in the other device. Before it got much further, though, Marc leaned over and flicked a switch on the device, causing it to stop.

"What did you do that for?" Peter asked.

"Because we already have proof of concept, I think," Marc said, shrugging. "We don't need any more than this—right?"

"Right," James agreed. "We really only have one experiment left, and we'll only need a very small amount of each type of particle to perform it. We need to see if bringing them together will cancel them out."

"I can think of another experiment that we should probably do before that one," Natalie said, getting up and heading over to Stella's bed where Amelia had placed all her possessions. After giving the bed a speculative look that I didn't miss (was she wondering if I'd been in that bed with Stella?), she selected a bludginator and came back to the table.

"And what are we to do with that?" James asked.

"See if you can literally take the magic out of it," Natalie said, placing it next to the particle drawing device. "If it works, theoretically that bludginator should turn into a normal knife, right? With a button on it that does absolutely nothing?"

"Yes, let's do that," Marc said quickly, snatching up the bludginator. "If we can do that, maybe we won't need antimagic at all. Maybe we can just suck all Lucien's magic out—"

"You mean, suck the magic out of the Sien-Leoard Crystal and the crystal chips?" James asked levelly. "Well, it might be possible, Marc, but what do you think is going to happen to all that magic if we do that?"

"Assuming nothing bad happens to the Hero Crystal if the chips are damaged," I added.

Marc glared at me and then said, "Would it matter what happens after that? If we had that magic, we could find a way to use it to fix Lucien's mess, and Lucien won't be able to do a damn thing to stop us."

"Unless he finds a way to steal it from us," Lillian said quietly.

Or one of us becomes the next Lucien. That was my thought, but I had no intention of saying such a thing aloud. Still, the thought of having all that power so easily at hand made me nervous. Even though I wouldn't be around to see what eventually happened, I dreaded to think what might....

Marc bit his lip and then said, "Let's just do this experiment first, shall we?"

It meant putting a spell on the particle drawing device so that it could capture magic particles that were contained within something else, so long as it was touching the device. That last restriction was necessary to make sure it didn't strip us all of our magic, or damage the Hero Crystal. He then put the bludginator against the particle drawing device, and we all watched as the display revealed the results of the experiment. The amount of magic within the particle drawing device had increased by a small amount, and when Marc picked up the bludginator, he was able to confirm (by swiping it at James) that it was no longer functional.

"Terrific," James said, grinning. "Okay, so I suggest later on we create that sort of functionality in the control room, so that we can strip away magic from things outside the base. We'll need to do it on a much wider scale, but at the same time, it'll need to be highly focused, so that we don't take it from places we want magic to stay. Does that—does that make any sense?"

We all nodded, and Peter said, "That's not going to stop Lucien, though, not unless we attack him directly. Remember, magic particles can self-replicate, so the only way we can defeat him is if we cut off his access to magic altogether."

"Which brings us back to antimagic—" James began.

"Or not," Marc interrupted. "I still think sucking the magic out of him is the best way to go. Remember all that stuff we talked about in the dining room before Sophie showed up? We actually had some good ideas to get at Lucien there; let's not forget all of that just because of this. If we can get Fewul and the Sien-Leoard Crystal away from him, what we have here actually *will* be useful in taking down the Hammerhearts."

James considered these words and then nodded. "Perhaps you're right. This may be the best place to start, assuming that your ideas are good, of course. You'll have to fill me in on those later. But if any part of that plan doesn't work out, or if magic once again falls into the wrong hands, we'll still need a backup. That's why I think we should still test the antimagic and see if it really does cancel out magic particles."

Marc swore under his breath. "Fine, fine, let's do this thing. What exactly do you want me to do this time?"

James thought it over then said, "We're going to need a new device. It needs to have two containers—one to store magic particles and one to store antimagic—and they obviously need to be separate from each other. It needs to be capable of drawing particles of both types in, though not at the same time, and it needs to be able to collect the particles from out of those two devices. Finally, it needs a third container between the first two, where the particles of both types can be merged together upon command. Most of all, it can't contain any of its own magic. Take your time over this one, Marc; there's a lot of detail in it, and we need you to get it right."

Marc did take his time over it—almost half an hour, in fact. The rest of us got a little impatient as he worked, a few people getting up and using Stella's bathroom while they waited. James even went downstairs to bring back some afternoon tea for us—for it had been a few hours since we'd had lunch, as far as our bodies knew, and we were starting to get a bit peckish. I didn't move from my seat, though, for I didn't want any of the others to see Stella's letter to me. As curious as I was to read it, I didn't want anyone else (other than Amelia) to know about it—I didn't want the questions that might follow. Whatever it was, I felt sure it was personal, and had probably been written sometime yesterday, between the time she had decided to go to Lucien and the time she had first told me of her plan.

Finally, though, after all of us (except Marc) had eaten a little something, the device was ready to go. Marc sat back in his seat, looking pretty drained, while James leaned over the table and began operating the devices, drawing the magic out of the magic drawing device and into the new thing, and then repeating the process for the antimagic. There was now a single display which measured both containers, and it showed that they held almost exactly the same amount (the antimagic had started out with more, but it had almost equalised since the bludginator's magic had been added).

"Is everyone ready?" James asked, his eyes alight with anticipation. "If this works, the two should cancel each other out, and we'll have only the tiniest bit of antimagic left in there. Marc, will this thing still measure the particles after they've been moved into the centre tank?"

Marc shook his head. "No, but it will sort through the particles and send them back to their rightful tanks when you push that button. Then you'll be able to measure what's left."

"Good enough," James grinned. "So here we go, on three…two… one…"

He pressed the button with a dramatic jab. I had enough time to see the numbers on the display drop as the particles slid out of their tanks and down towards the centre tank. I didn't see the particles themselves as they went, nor did I see anything in the centre tank, but I knew the instant that the collision had happened. The way James had talked about it, I'd been expecting it to be no more interesting than filling in a hole. Magic was like dirt that had been dug out of the ground and antimagic was like the hole that had been left behind by the dirt; putting the dirt in the hole would therefore leave neither the extra dirt nor the hole behind. That was how I pictured it, anyway.

I was therefore totally taken by surprise by what happened. Several people were knocked out of their seats, but I wasn't one of them, so I got a pretty good look at everything that happened. The first thing I saw was the blood that went flying from James as he was thrown backwards away from the device, over the back of his chair and onto the floor. The second thing I noticed was the circular table at which we were all sitting; it had turned into a giant chocolate biscuit. The devices which sat atop it were just a little too heavy to be supported by the biscuit, which crumbled and split down the middle.

Meanwhile, as people around me began to scream in alarm, I felt a weird sensation all over my body. I looked down at myself and let out a cry of dismay: my clothes were gone, and my skin had changed to an ugly greyish colour. I batted at it and flecks of it fell away, revealing—for a moment—that I had another layer of skin beneath it, which still looked normal. A little slow on the uptake, I realised that my skin itself hadn't changed at all, but my clothes had apparently been turned into something. I swept some of it off and caught a whiff of it: salt. Whatever that magic–antimagic collision had been, it had turned my clothes into salt.

Compared to most of the others, though, I was pretty lucky. James, Peter, Marc, Frederic and Lillian had all been knocked out of their seats;

I could no longer see James, as he had been across the table from me, but I could see all the others. Marc was on the floor behind his chair, and his legs were twitching and jerking so much that every time he tried to push up, he invariably fell over again. Peter had managed to get to his feet, only to bump his head on the roof and fall down again, as he appeared to have grown to no less than twelve feet tall. His clothes hadn't been torn away, as he was still as skinny as he'd always been, but now his shins were showing as was his very long belly. As for Frederic, he was just to my left, and he too was having trouble regaining his feet, owing to the fact that his feet were now roughly the size of surfboards. His shoes and socks lay in shreds around him as he tried to drag himself around the table towards James.

For the females at the table, it was less obvious what had happened to them. Lillian was on the floor, but she appeared, on the surface at least, to be unharmed. The reason she had been knocked out of her seat was obvious: Her seat had turned into cotton wool and collapsed on itself. Around the table to my right, past where Marc was still trying to get up, Amelia was in an almighty panic as she tried desperately to do something. Only when I looked more closely at her did I see what was happening to her: Her hair was growing at an alarming rate. It was already several feet long, and if it continued for any more than ten more seconds or so, it would be long enough to reach the door. And that was just the hair on her head: The rest of her body was sprouting hair too, though it wasn't growing quite as fast.

I scrambled out of my seat, completely forgetting about Stella's letter (which I found later hadn't been affected at all by the rogue magic), and ignoring the fact that I was, for all intents and purposes, naked. I couldn't decide where to go or who to help first: Peter and Frederic certainly needed it, but there was nothing I could do to help them. James was in the most dire need if the blood I'd seen was any indication, but without magic of my own, I couldn't do much for him either. I still had no idea what was wrong with Lillian or Natalie: Lillian had managed to pull herself up, though she hadn't said a thing or even made a sound through all of it. As for Natalie, she appeared to be frozen in her seat, face pale and eyes wide and horrified. I had a flashback to poor Graham and the end that had befallen him, but I didn't think that was what was happening to Natalie; she looked frozen in the metaphorical sense, not the literal sense.

I went to Lillian and tugged on her arm. "Are you okay?"

She shook her head and tapped her mouth. I took that to mean that she couldn't speak, so I said, "Go and see what you can do for James."

Without waiting for her to do so, I hurried around to where Marc lay flat on his back, his legs waving in the air and a shocked expression on his face.

"Are you okay?" I asked him.

"Do I look okay?" he snarled back.

"Marc, John, help me!" Amelia's strangled voice rose above the rest, which were beginning to quieten down as the initial shock of what had happened wore off. I looked up at Amelia where she sat in her seat, but I couldn't really see her face anymore; there was so much hair there that it looked like it might actually strangle her. I had an urge to jump up and try to wrench it off her, but not even a hundred pairs of scissors could keep up with what was going on with Amelia right now. I had only one choice to sort all this out.

"Marc, grab your crystal and fix yourself; the others need you."

"I can't, the crystal rolled away."

"What? Where?"

"Right there," he jerked his head roughly to where the Hero Crystal lay on the floor, next to one of the upright table legs and partially hidden from view by remnants of chocolate biscuit.

I scrambled for it, remembered that I couldn't touch it without it splitting into the six Sorcerous Crystals, and began gently swatting at it with a piece of biscuit until it was near enough to Marc's hand for him to grab. He fixed his legs up first, jumped to his feet, and quickly turned his attention to Amelia and Peter, who were nearest, before moving around to James. Suppressing irritation at Marc for not clothing me while he'd had a clear and present chance to do so, I hurried back around past my chair until I was beside Natalie.

"Are you okay?" I asked her.

She turned her eyes on me, and didn't even react to the fact that she was seeing me naked again—something she had no doubt planned to never let happen again. "No," she said in a small voice, "I'm—I'm—peeing."

"What?" I said blankly, looking more closely at her, and then down at her lap. Yes, she was urinating as I watched; her lap was soaked with it, her legs were dribbling with it, and a large puddle of it had gathered beneath her chair. Now that I knew what it was, I could even smell it, and it took all my focus not to gag. There was no way a person could piss that much and still have more in the tank, which could only mean that it was uncontrollable, and was a direct result of whatever magic had done all this (and not just Natalie's panicked reaction to it all).

Fortunately, that was when Marc came around the table to us, having just fixed up Lillian and Frederic. A second later, I was fully clothed again; and a few more seconds later, once he'd figured out what had happened to her, Natalie too had been returned to a normal state. With all eight of us taken care of, Marc was able to turn his attention to the furniture that had also been a victim of whatever had happened with the collision. As he did so, the rest of us re-took our seats and tried to get our nerves back under control.

"Are you sure you don't wanna keep some of that biscuit?" Amelia asked. "It might be nice for something tasty to come out of this."

"So John's naked body doesn't count, then?" Peter asked, grinning at me, and I felt myself blush.

"Well, something positive then," Amelia said, also blushing and shooting a reproving look at Peter.

"Hey, I got to be tall for a change," he shrugged. "I'll take whatever I can get."

"I don't think we should be making light of any of this," Frederic said seriously. "James, we need to know what happened just now."

James's expression was very white as he looked around at us all, and I didn't think it was just blood loss. It turned out that James had begun bleeding profusely from every orifice of his body when the magic hit him, and would have undoubtedly bled dry within minutes if Marc hadn't fixed him up.

"I have a theory, and I'm such an idiot for not thinking of it before," he said. "First, though, we need to check the device and see if the magic and antimagic really did cancel each other out after all that."

"Does it matter if they did or not?" Marc asked as he worked. "I mean, how can you possibly justify using antimagic after this?"

James shrugged. "I do hear what you're saying, believe me. Thanks to you, I'm not dead right now, and the rest of you are lucky to be alive as well. Whatever it was, it turned Lillian's chair into cotton wool; imagine if it had done that to her whole body?"

A shiver passed around the circle and then James went on, "But it doesn't change what we might have to do. We need to know, so…"

He leaned over the newly restored table and looked at the display on the device, which had miraculously not been affected by the explosion of magic, despite having contained all the particles that had caused it. It presently showed several zeroes, before he pushed the button to organise the particles in the centre tank and return them to their origins. We waited as this process took place, and when it was over, the numbers reflected what James had initially suggested they would: a tiny amount of antimagic, and no magic particles.

"Okay," James said, leaning back in his seat. "So what I believe just happened was a magic annihilation. The theory of physics goes that when matter and antimatter collide, they produce a massive amount of energy. It stands to reason that when magic and antimagic collide, they would do the same; only as you saw, it took the form of an uncontrolled burst of magic energy. It appears to have only been in a small radius from the point where the annihilation took place, though, which means that the amount of magic energy produced is directly proportional to the amount of particles in the annihilation."

I looked around the room and realised that he was right. Outside the circle of tables and chairs, nothing else in Stella's bedroom had been touched by magic.

"And the magic energy that was produced, what happened to it?" Natalie asked warily. "Did it turn back into magic particles somewhere?"

James shook his head. "That wouldn't make sense to me. I think it far more likely that it just disappeared altogether. The energy was released by the destruction of the particles and it dissipated on its own. That's my theory anyway, but maybe it couldn't hurt to draw any residual magic in the area back in—"

"No, enough of this," Marc said flatly, and taking the Hero Crystal from his pocket, he vanished all the devices on the table. We all stared at him in shock.

"What did you do that for?" Frederic asked.

"Have you guys all lost your minds?" Marc said loudly, looking around at us all. "Did you miss what just happened? That was a tiny amount of magic being cancelled out, and you're talking about doing that to the crystals and Lucien's crystal chips. What do you think is going to happen to the world if we do that?"

"It won't be good," James admitted, "but—"

"But it could destroy the whole world!" Marc shouted. "It could be *us* fulfilling the prophecy if we do that. It wouldn't even take all the magic in the world to destroy the whole thing—turn the Earth's core into peanut butter sandwiches or something!"

"That is a fair point," Amelia said, once again putting a wresting hand on Marc's arm to calm him down. "Is it really worth doing that to the world just to stop Lucien?"

James hesitated then said, "No, it's not worth destroying the world, not unless it looks like Lucien's about to destroy it in the process of doing whatever it is he plans on doing. If worst comes to worst, we can take the crystals away from Earth—far enough away so that if we have to destroy them, any magical explosion won't be able to take the whole planet out."

"Dooming us in the process," Marc said, folding his arms and glaring at James. "I'm on board if you go with the plan to suck the magic particles away from the Hammerhearts, but anything involving antimagic is a no-no. I'm not doing it, and I'm not doing any more magic to help you with it, and that's final."

He and James glared across the table at each other, the rest of us watching them warily. The tension in the room was thick enough to cut with a knife. Finally, James said, "Fine, if that's how you want it. But Marc, if that plan doesn't work, or if it makes things worse, you're going to have to seriously consider changing your mind. If you don't, then we'll have no choice but to push ahead without you. You may be our main source of magic now, but that doesn't mean we can't find a way to move forward without it."

Chapter 21: The Planner

The mood among the group was extremely uncomfortable as we all left Stella's bedroom and split off in several different directions. Marc and James were totally ignoring each other; Amelia followed after Marc, talking quietly to him (probably in an attempt to calm him down), while Peter did the same to James. If I had to pick sides, I tended to lean towards James, but I ignored the rest of the group for the time being. Peter, James and Natalie kept looking at me for reasons probably of their own, but my top priority, now that we were moving, was to stash Stella's note to me away in my bedroom, where I would read it later tonight before I went to sleep—that way whatever reaction it caused in me, I wouldn't have to clamp down in a hurry.

That only took all of a minute, though, and I had to stay in my room for a few more minutes longer so that it looked like I were in there for some other reason. It gave me time to think, and I had plenty to think (and worry) about. I could appreciate Marc's position, not just because he didn't want to lose his magic, but because his points were valid. Using antimagic would be extremely dangerous, and would probably do a lot of awful things to a lot of people. However, I also understood where James was coming from. If nothing else worked, antimagic would be our only option, and the last thing we needed was to be left with that one option and have Marc actively using his magic to prevent us from using it.

But right now, the most pressing issue was that after that meeting, the group had split apart with no united plan regarding what step we were to take next. Whatever we did, we all needed to be on the same page; and right now, none of us were quite sure what that page was going to be. Marc and James had their own ideas what the next step should be, and I reckoned I could guess what they were. James would want to create a device to gather as much antimagic as we could, and a second device that could shoot antimagic like a gun, or perhaps shoot it as a wave, destroying everything magical in its path. Even if he didn't plan to immediately use it, he would want it there, just in case we were left with no other choice.

As for Marc, he would probably want to skip that step and jump straight into sucking all the magic particles out of Lucien, and all the Hammerhearts and Hammerheart equipment around him. I could see the value in that, but I could also see the major drawback. Whatever magic we stripped from them, Lucien or Fewul could just re-create, and they would only need the tiniest bit of leftover magic to do so, given that magic particles could self-replicate. Unfortunately, the same drawback existed with James's probable plan, unless we could destroy all their magic at the same time, and that would result in a magical annihilation so massive that much of the world would be turned inside-out.

Alone in my room, away from the determination and pressure of the others, it was easy for me to think my way through this dilemma. I couldn't shake the fear—a fear that would almost certainly come to fruition—that this was all going to go badly wrong, no matter how we went about it. The best we could probably do was remain as understated as we could for as long as we could, and only resort to using antimagic, or even manipulating magic particles, when there was nothing else left— when we were forced to escalate to that level. And it *was* escalation, because if Lucien ever discovered what we had discovered today, we (and the rest of the world) would be doomed.

And remaining understated without actually doing nothing meant only one thing—fighting Lucien using magic he knew about, but in ways he hopefully wasn't anticipating. What Marc had said at one point back in Stella's bedroom was correct. We really should focus on the things we had brainstormed in the dining room that morning, before Sophie had showed up and explained magic particles to us. It didn't mean that we should put all our eggs in that basket—I tended to think we should set the wheels in motion for our other plans at the same time, so that we wouldn't waste time scrambling around later—but it did mean that our next direct move against Lucien should be…

…should be what, exactly? We hadn't actually come up with a real plan earlier; we had got as far as waiting until Lucien was busy with Lena and attempting to disable the magical alert Lucien had set up to let him know the instant Fewul was recalled, and then recalling Fewul ourselves. Then what? Do we attack Lucien, steal the Sien-Leoard Crystal, call Fewul ourselves, or a combination of all three? I tried to organise my thoughts into a straight line, but found that it was impossible; there were simply too many things that we couldn't anticipate happening in this plan.

I needed to sketch all this stuff out—seeing it laid out in front of me would hopefully make it easier to work through it. I didn't have any paper or pens in here, though, which meant either going down to the computer room and doing it there, or going down to the control room and using magic to create what I needed. If I was going to do that, I might as well skip over creating paper and pens, and create something electronic that would be specifically designed for this sort of planning. I spent a few minutes visualising what this device should look like and how it should work, then left my room and took the lift down to the control room.

It was as packed as it had been earlier. The shock of the terrorism appeared to have worn off and most people were back to work at their posts. Marc and Amelia were the only people from the group upstairs who had come down here; Marc was going around the room, checking in with people on how they were doing, while Amelia was out the front, apparently watching the spyers James had installed that morning. I glanced over at them and saw that Lucien appeared to be giving another press conference, and it looked like Cornish and Hall were also present. Furthermore, on either side of Lucien stood Fewul (in Stella's form) and Lena.

I shrugged when Marc and Amelia cast curious looks at me, and walked over to the cabinet to retrieve the magic enhancer. I shielded it from the rest of the room with my body as I used it to create the planner I had imagined upstairs, then put the magic enhancer back in the drawer. I was about to turn around and leave with my new device when Marc spoke behind me, making me jump.

"Whatcha doing?"

I turned and showed him the planner. "I just created it. I'm gonna use it to try to figure out a plan."

He pursed his lips. "Not one involving antimagic, I hope."

I frowned at him. In truth the plan probably *would* involve antimagic, even if it would be further down the line and after we'd tried a bunch of other stuff, but I had no desire at all to get into it with Marc now, especially in front of all these people. "No, it's about what we were talking about this morning. I'll talk about it with you guys later."

And without another word, I turned away from him and left the room without looking back, not even when I heard a girl's voice (most likely Amelia) saying my name. I took the elevator back up to my room and sat myself down at the round table in the centre, briefly visualising it turning into a giant chocolate biscuit before turning my attention to the planner. It was a pretty nifty device, and it wasn't just electronic either: It contained just a touch of its own magic that would help organise the plan into a workable structure once I'd thought of all the things that we should try, and all the things that could go wrong with each one.

By the time I'd finished with the planner, it was a quarter to six in the evening—forty-five minutes until dinner time. The afternoon had flown by, especially the two hours I'd spent at this table, working away on a plan. The good news was that the plan had taken shape as I went, with me adding to it simply by putting my finger on a pad on the device and magically transferring my idea into it, and then sliding my finger around on the display to shift things into an order that made sense. Finally, I pressed a button to convert the diagram I'd been working with into a list form, and as I read through it, I knew that what I'd just come up with was the best way to go.

Now, since we had time, I might as well go and show this to the others. I stood up and hesitated, my mind flicking back to Marc. He had been ready to be confrontational earlier on, and I knew that if he saw this plan, he would get confrontational again. The plan called, as I'd originally expected, for us to create devices to work with antimagic while we waited for the perfect time to put the rest of the plan into action, and Marc would oppose that idea straight away. How strenuously would he oppose it, though? Would he simply refuse to help us, or would he actively use his magic to prevent us from creating such devices? I didn't know, but either way it meant that I should probably show this to James first, rather than Marc.

I went back down to the control room, stepped inside and looked around. It was a little less packed now than it had been earlier, but Marc and Amelia were still the only ones from our group present. By the one glance I'd had, it looked as though Marc was setting up the army for the evening, in anticipation that most people would be sleeping through it and that very few would work through the night. On the plus side for him, Katie, Sophie and Erica were back in the frame, and they appeared to be in the process of learning how to use their newly assigned workstations.

I waved once at Amelia, who had just beckoned me to come over to her and Marc, before backing out of the room and heading back upstairs, this time to the ground level. There, I found a half-full lounge room focused on the television, and one look around the room showed me that Peter, James, Natalie, Frederic and Lillian were all there, and all sitting together, along with Rebecca. I went over to them and playfully shoved James to the side so that I could squeeze onto the long couch between him and Peter (Peter had Rebecca on his other side, and Natalie on her other side, so shoving him would have been more difficult).

"Where have you been?" Peter asked, rolling his eyes at me. "And what is that thing?"

"I've been indisposed," I said, "and this thing is a little something I created to help organise my thoughts."

James glanced at the planner (the display of which was blank at the moment, giving nothing away), and then back at my face. "Well, I know you weren't with Marc, because we've been keeping in touch with Amelia, who can't quite work out where she wants to be at the moment, and she kept saying that she didn't know where you were—"

"Except to create something in the control room," Frederic added, "and I'm assuming that's it?"

"Yeah."

"And what thoughts are these?" Peter asked, and I didn't miss the little sideways glance he threw at Rebecca—or more likely, past Rebecca and towards her sister.

I tapped the screen so that it once again showed the bullet-point list that was the end result of my labour, and handed the planner to James. "You read through this and see if it flies. I wanna know what's been going on down here. I thought I saw Lucien giving a press conference when I was in the control room earlier—is that right?"

"Yes, he did," Frederic confirmed, "and it was basically everything you would expect it to be. It finished a little while ago now, though, and it appears that Lucien's gone back to base to actually begin working on magic to suppress the population."

Peter gave me a little nudge with his elbow, and when I looked at him, I saw that his expression had turned more serious. "They don't have a final death toll from the attacks, but they figured out who the attackers were, and there were lots of them—"

"Not just in Sydney," Lillian said, "but there was one in Melbourne, Brisbane, Adelaide, Perth, Canberra, Auckland, and a bunch of other cities where smaller rallies were taking place. There were going to be even more in other cities around the world later on, but during the presser, Lucien ordered them all to be cancelled for the people's own safety."

"And they were relatives of ours," Peter went on, and my stomach lurched. "Since the Big Room is empty now, Lucien couldn't use anyone close to us, so he had to use magic to identify more distant friends and relatives of people in here, so that we would know he was going after us. The two shooters in Sydney—they were Uncle Dom and Aunt Sonya."

"Oh crap," I moaned. Uncle Dominic was Mum's brother, and Sonya was his wife. I had met them a few times but only when they occasionally came down to visit; they had lived in Sydney for years because Uncle Dom had gotten a well-paying job there. I would have wondered how Lucien had found them, for we had certainly never told him of them, and then I didn't—he had so much magic at his disposal that it wouldn't have taken a lot. I then would have wondered how he was able to take control of people across the country, and even in New Zealand, and force them to do things they otherwise wouldn't have done —or even known how to do—and then I didn't. Again, with his magical powers, none of this was outside Lucien's ability to manufacture.

"Also, two of our aunties and their husbands were behind the attacks in Adelaide," Rebecca said, looking tearful, "and James's Aunt Anne was driving the truck that blew up in Sydney, and a whole bunch of others like that."

"And a few people we knew from school," Peter added. "There was a rally in Melbourne, a safe distance from the bomb area, and it was attacked by Holly Smith, Anna Edgord and Ellie Dragon."

I swore under my breath. This was just getting worse and worse. I forced myself to say the words that needed to be said. "I assume they're all dead now, right?"

"Some of them committed suicide," Lillian said, "but most of them were eventually killed by the police. None of the attackers in any of the locations were taken alive."

"I like this, John," James said quietly, finally raising his head from the planner and looking at me. "This is really smart, and it covers everything I can think of. Here"—he leaned forward and handed the device to Frederic, who was sitting adjacent us along with his mother— "read through this and see what you think. Peter, can you go down to the control room and get the magic enhancer and its self-destructor, and bring them back up here?"

"What for?" Peter asked, surprised.

"It's in the plan," James said simply, and I nodded. Getting the magic enhancer somewhere safe was first on the list, just in case it occurred to Marc to activate the self-destruct, thereby making himself the only source of really usable magic in the base. Yes, we would have the other crystals as well, but they wouldn't be nearly as useful as the magic enhancer. Looking confused, Peter agreed and got up.

"And try to make it look like you're getting something else, if you can," I added before he could leave.

He shrugged. "Okeydokey. Anything else?"

James and I looked at each other. Was there anything else? Probably not, but the real question was, how much was all of this necessary? Finally, I said, "don't think so. Just be careful."

This time, Peter got it—I could tell by the look on his face. He nodded and slipped away, heading for the door and the elevator beyond.

I didn't have to wait long for a chance to see Lucien's press conference. The evening news came on a few minutes later, and there was so much crap to report that the terrorism during the week (the plane crashes and the fire in that apartment building, and a couple of others that had already slipped my mind) had been pushed right out of the picture. The first thing they did was provide an abbreviated version of the press conference, showing only what they considered to be the most important points, and telling their viewers that they could watch it in its entirety on their website.

Lucien spoke very briefly first, offering his condolences to all those innocents who had been hurt or killed that day, and saying that the time for lenience had passed, and that he would be doing anything and everything to make sure things like this couldn't possibly happen in the future. He had received the message from the public that they were willing to give up some of their freedoms in the interim if it meant an assurance of their safety, and he would be taking steps that very evening to meet their demands. Exactly what those steps were, he would cover later in the conference, but for now, it was over to the Police Commissioner to explain exactly what had happened that day.

While Lucien spoke, as his words weren't all that important to me, I had analysed what I was seeing on the screen. There were five people out the front, and they were all standing up (this seemed a little odd, given that in the previous press conferences I'd seen, both by Lucien and Arnold Hammerson, they were usually seated). It may have been meant to symbolise their willingness to get to work (not sitting on their butts and just talking about stuff, in other words), but I wondered if it served another purpose as well.

Four of them were dressed in suits (even Fewul, in Stella's form, was dressed in such a way that it was clear that she was just as important as Hall or Cornish), but Lena was wearing a dress. Even if I hadn't known what Lucien was doing it would have been very obvious to me, by the way she was standing just behind Lucien's shoulder and the way she had been made up, that that was his partner. By having her on her feet instead of sitting down, it showed her beauty off to maximum effect. Even after all I'd been through with Lena, a small part of me felt jealous that a girl that hot was no longer mine.

When Hall started speaking, though, I had to pay closer attention. He confirmed what Peter and Rebecca had said earlier about who was responsible for the attacks, and he detailed exactly how, to the police's best knowledge at this stage, they had gone about it. He also touched on the victims (not the attackers, who were also victims of Lucien's in my opinion), and said that investigators were working very hard to identify all of them, and were in the process of contacting their families to inform them of what had happened. Finally, he proposed that the evidence they had so far gathered suggested that these attacks were coordinated, but that they were probably planned at short notice and that hopefully, the masterminds behind them had been careless enough to leave traces of their identities behind. The expression on his face told everyone that he was quite sure he knew who the masterminds were, though, and given the number of times he dropped the word 'opposition' during his speech, everyone else was supposed to make that same connection.

The news broke in then, exploring other perspectives on the day's events—interviewing witnesses, talking to other police officers and investigators, and just generally lowering my spirits—as only a news program could. Peter returned a short way into this, telling us that he had succeeded, and that neither Marc nor Amelia had suspected him of doing anything strange. In fact, as he was leaving, Amelia had remarked that 'that' had been a good idea, before using the energy booster on herself. Having Peter be the one to retrieve the magic enhancer had been part of the plan because he was the one least likely to be suspected of being up to something, but I hadn't planned on Marc and Amelia assuming that he was running low on energy. It had worked out really well, though, because as it turned out, all of us were beginning to flag a bit—and no one more so than James, who'd been in the Time Box twice already today.

Not too long later, the news turned its attention to the nuke—still less than twenty-four hours earlier—and provided us with an update on that. They were still tallying the death toll, but they were pleased to report that Lucien had been through town and repaired all the damaged infrastructure, and that as of five o'clock that evening, people were allowed to return to it. One of their reporters was sent into the area with a camera, so that we could all marvel at Lucien's magical handiwork. The said reporter even remarked that it would now be safer because Lucien had fixed up all the broken and uneven footpaths. When they went back to the news anchors, they also said that Lucien had promised a memorial to be built somewhere in that location, which would contain the name of every single person who had been killed there.

Now they returned their attention to Lucien, and showed us another part of the press conference that had taken place earlier. Cornish had just spoken about something (that part had been cut out), but now the focus had been shifted back to Lucien, who began to speak about all the measures that were going to take place in the next couple of days.

"I understand that some of the things I will announce here today may be unpopular with some," he began, "but I am also in the way of believing that not only are they going to be popular with many, but that they are totally necessary. Bear in mind that eventually, such measures won't be necessary, once we have firmly defeated all opposition to our regime and ensured the safety of *all* our people in the process. Once that time comes, we can move away from such firm control and towards a system where magic will only need to be used to improve people's lives. I am looking forward to that time very much, which motivates me to do all I can to bring it forward.

"Firstly, all air travel within Hammersonia will be permanently grounded. It has been suspended since Wednesday, of course, but I can now say that it will not be returning. In fact, I would go further and criticise my predecessor, Arnold Hammerson, for reinstating it in the first place back in May. I had wondered at the time why he had done such a thing, but since I have gained access to his archives, I can tell you that with all that was going on at the time, he decided that allowing air travel within Hammersonia for the time being would be easier than rushing in a system of teleportation. He never dreamt that our enemies would resort to terrorism, I don't think, and maybe back then they wouldn't have, but our enemies have changed since then, and no longer include only the former Sorcerers and their minions.

"Now, I understand that making such a bold move as banning all air travel is going to cause problems for some. I've already had to refuse meetings with airlines all over the world who wish to complain that I'm taking away their business, but guess what; I couldn't care less. I *do* care, however, about the millions of people around the world whose plans I've ruined by taking this action. That is why bringing teleportation stations into operation is one of my top priorities. I already have some of my ministers working on a document that will outline how the rollout will take place, and how airlines can pivot their business models towards teleportation and still make a profit—potentially a much larger one, in fact, given that teleportation doesn't require fuel.

"But that is only one thing on my fairly large agenda. The most pressing issue, and I think the one which most of you out there want to know about, is how to locate and detain criminals before they have a chance to commit acts of terrorism and mass-murder. I have been grappling with this issue for days now, since one of my former allies blew himself up in a crowded supermarket and killed more than four hundred"—I gritted my teeth and clenched my fists at these words—"and with the understanding that we are really only limited by our imagination, I believe I have come up with a solution.

"By tomorrow morning, all police officers and security personnel around the country will be armed with specially-created magical devices. These devices will be designed to detect, by scanning a person's brain, whether they have the intent to commit a crime, or a desire to commit a crime; and will enable the person using the device to detain any potential criminals so that they can be questioned further. It will target only some crimes, however, as I wish to have these devices in circulation as quickly as possible, and I think it most important to focus on crimes that would result in loss of life, injury, assault, or dissidence. As far as the legal ramifications of these devices go, a person detained by one of them can only be held for forty-eight hours without charge, and they can only be charged if police are able to definitively prove exactly what crime they had thought of committing, and if they had made any concrete moves to prepare for such a crime. These protections are in place to ensure that these new powers cannot be abused."

He continued on in this manner, announcing some further measures that would be made:

restrictions on large gatherings of people;

stringent screening of people attending public events, such as sporting events and concerts;

facial recognition technology in public places, and a global database to monitor movements of anyone they consider suspicious;

an absolute ban on all firearms except for police and security personnel, complete with magical tools to round up such weapons from civilians;

similar restrictions on anything that could be used as an explosive;

armed officers on all public transport still in operation, including magical screening of people getting on or off in case they were thinking of committing a crime;

a magical web crawler which would attempt to locate potential criminals on the internet, based on the pages they visited, the emails they sent, and the content they posted to social media; and more things besides.

The longer it went on, the more obvious it became that these measures wouldn't have any impact on us, but would be plenty effective when it came to rounding up anyone who thought badly of Lucien and his rule and placing influential charms on them to bring them into line.

"He's moving too fast," Frederic said, sounding regretful but not really looking it. "He is very young and doesn't really have the background in sociology or knowledge of social engineering to understand the mistake he's making. All the things he's doing are things the Hammersons intended to do eventually—and in fact, a lot of governments prior to this happening would have liked to do such things, but just didn't have all the tools to do so—but Lucien's rushing it all. He probably thinks that he has enough magic to quell any opposition as it comes up, but if he worked it more gradually, people would get used to it, and quite often, find a way to live with it."

The news continued on after that. There was so much going on that it would probably continue all evening, but I had no intention of watching any more of it. At last, dinner time had arrived, and everyone was happy to get out of the lounge room and go and eat something. I sat at a table with Peter, James, Natalie and Rebecca, focusing on my food and trying to put Lucien's totalitarianism from my mind. It was easy enough to do given that Peter, Natalie and Rebecca kept pestering James and me about the plan I had developed, wanting to know what was going to happen next. Frederic had given the planner back to me as I had left the lounge room, quietly telling me that it was a pretty good one and that we should get started on it as soon as dinner was done. That sounded like a good idea to me, but I didn't say any of this at the table: It seemed like a good idea to keep it quiet for now.

Marc and Amelia had entered the dining room shortly after us and sat down at a table with Lillian and Frederic not too far away. Marc had given us a curious look on his way past (at least he had given Peter, Natalie and me a curious look—he had ignored James). Amelia had given us a more longing sort of look, as though seeing that there was no room left at our table made her feel left-out. I could see why she would be the most torn-up about the splinter that seemed to have taken place in our group. Marc was her boyfriend, and she wanted to support him as much as she could, but at the same time, part of her must have known that James was ultimately right.

As dinner wound down, it was time to put the next phase of the plan into operation, and given how close Marc was, it had to be done as quietly as possible. It required one of us to go upstairs and begin creating magic and antimagic manipulating devices, but nobody was really sure who should do it. Peter and Rebecca both refused, and given that neither of them had a lot of experience at creating things with magic, that was fair enough. James also begged off, saying that given what was about to go down, we would be better served with him in the control room, directing things from there. That left it between me and Natalie. I didn't want to do it because I also wanted to be in the control room, but also because I was getting tired enough that I could easily have messed up—

which is something that one definitely doesn't want to do when one is playing around with antimagic.

Natalie was the freshest out of all of us, having slept through the morning, and although she had been the last to know about magic particles, she had seen enough of the experiments through the day that she could probably do what needed to be done. However, there was a hitch: the person who went upstairs was required to keep in telepathic communication with someone down in the control room, so that they would know when it was a good time to return—or if they needed help in their work. The problem was, Natalie didn't have a telepathic communicator on her, nor did any of the rest of us as they were all downstairs in the control room. Peter therefore had to hurry down there to get one, under the pretence that he was retrieving a reenergiser for the rest of us—which he might as well actually do, since we were all pretty stuffed. It was also decided that I would be the person with whom Natalie kept in telepathic contact, since I could do it without needing to use a device, and would therefore be all but impossible to detect. That would be a little awkward, of course, but we both had to bite the bullet this time; it was necessary.

We were pretty lucky. Marc finished his dinner a little after us, and since he had his back to us as he ate, he probably hadn't noticed anything. He and the others at his table did go straight down to the control room after dinner though, arriving no more than a few minutes after the rest of us. When we had arrived, there were only a handful of people in the control room, still busy at their workstations. Katie, Sophie and Erica were among them, as was Tommy, who was still following Lucien around. When I looked over his shoulder at his display, I saw that Lucien appeared to be having dinner in the Dining Hall—or *trying* to, as the food on his plate kept bouncing up into his face.

"Nice one," I said, suppressing a smirk. "How come you didn't do stuff like that during his press conference?"

"I wanted to," Tommy told me, "but Marc said it was better for 'optics' if I didn't do that where the whole world would see. I don't get it myself."

I shrugged. I didn't really get it either. Lucien was already portraying us as the bad guys—what difference would it make if we made his suit pink while he was on TV? If anything, not attacking him would further the narrative that he was in control, and that all we really cared about was attacking innocent people. Marc probably had a rational motive for making Tommy back off—perhaps he was worried about how Lucien might spin it—but it seemed to me like it could have been a mistake.

"What's everyone doing down here?" Frederic asked as he entered the room, followed by Marc, Amelia and Lillian.

"Actually, I'm curious to know what the plan is for working these guys through the night," James said from where he was seated beside Erica. "*Is* there a plan?"

"Sort of," Marc said cagily, glancing warily at James, and I was pleased to see it. He didn't look happy, but maybe he was ready to at least try to mend fences. My guess was that the three Woodwards had had a word with him over dinner. "I basically told everyone who was in here earlier, and all the guys in the games room, to work as long as they could and then just go to bed and pick up in the morning. I know it's not perfect—it would have been better if we'd gotten some of them to sleep during the day so that they can take nightshift—but people do need to sleep at some stage."

"And in the meantime, we'll be taking the nightshift, since our sleeping patterns are already messed up from all that time in the Time Box," Sophie said without raising her head.

"Some people might use those energy boosters to keep going till the early hours of the morning, so until people start getting up," Amelia said. "I went around the dining room before and asked some people if they would do that. Felicity said she would, and so did Jacob Underwood, which surprised me a little. It's not much but it's better than nothing."

"Hey, we're sitting right here," Katie said indignantly.

"Good enough for me," Marc said, looking around the room, and then looking curiously at Rebecca. "Where's Natalie? You're not Natalie, are you?"

"I could pretend to be, but I don't think Peter would like that," Rebecca said, her tone playful but her eyes narrowing—she always hated it when people mistook her for her sister. "Natalie went upstairs to have a little rest, but she'll probably be back down later on."

"She does deserve a break, after all she's been through," Frederic said, glancing at me, and I knew what he was thinking. He had seen the plan—he remembered that someone had to separate from the group and begin working on the particle devices. He knew that Natalie wasn't really resting, but he was smart enough to play along.

Marc and Amelia swapped sympathetic looks before Marc said, "Okay, and what's going on out there?"

"Lucien's having dinner with Lena," Erica said, "and there are other Hammerhearts around them. Hignat and Wilwog's dads are going crazy because they can't find their sons. Sebastian's trying to get close to Lucien so that he can do more favours for him and get more rewards. Everything else is pretty much bullshit."

"Speaking of Hignat and Wilwog, what's the plan for all the Hammerhearts we've captured?" I asked, looking around at all the workstations. "Are we just gonna leave them in those things?"

"I've already removed them all and put them in the prison," Marc told me. "At least, the ones that we'd captured up until that point—I'll probably have to do it again tomorrow morning. don't worry; I vanished everything they had, right down to their clothes, and dressed them up in uniforms that say 'Prisoner of Woodwards'. They'll love that when they wake up."

"You didn't wake them up?" Lillian asked.

"I'll do that tomorrow morning—wake them all up at the same time," he shrugged.

"Has Lena told Lucien what happened to her earlier?" Peter asked, glancing at Tommy.

"Yeah, it was the first thing she said to him when he went to pick her up for the press conference," he said. "He was mad."

Marc nodded. "He didn't explode, though; it looks like he has more control over his rage now than he did before. He did say that for their sakes, Hignat and Wilwog had better hope we don't let them go, because when he sees them again, he's gonna introduce them to horrors they could never have imagined. Also, he *does* know about Natalie being gone now—Lena told him that too."

"And how did he react to that?" I asked.

"Much the same," Amelia said. "In fact, I think he may have even been a little relieved, because now he doesn't have to worry about her staying alive, and he knows that it'll take her a long time to recover from everything that happened to her. As for how we did it, I don't think he's too worried about it—or if he is, he hid it well from Lena."

A silence followed this before Marc hesitantly said, "So…what are we all doing now? What's the plan?"

He was looking at James as he spoke, and James smiled warily. "I think, according to John, the plan is to prepare to strike at Lucien."

Marc looked quickly around at me. "What? Strike how? Is that what you came up with on that planning thing you created earlier?"

"More or less," I said, taking the planner out of my pocket and glancing at the screen. It still showed the plan in list form, and I touched my finger to the top two items to indicate that they had already been accomplished. They vanished from the screen moments before Marc could get close enough to read them. It meant that although particles and antimagic came into the plan later, all the items on the screen at present regarded Lucien, and how we were to attack him and Fewul.

Marc reached me and looked down at the planner, reading his way down the screen. Everyone else in the room (who wasn't busy at a workstation) gathered around behind us so that they too could read the plan. Marc was first to finish and he looked up at me, smiling.

"I like how you've done this—it has all kinds of contingencies. I think the word Tommy would have used to describe a plan like this was 'robust'."

Tommy looked up at us at the mention of his name, shrugged, and got back to work.

"So it doesn't have any antimagic or any of that stuff in it?" Amelia asked hopefully.

I shook my head. "It actually does, but it's a last resort. The way I've figured it out, we should try the least dangerous things first, and only resort to getting down and dirty with particles if we absolutely have to."

Marc looked at me with raised eyebrows. "I still don't like that, but for the sake of everything, I'm gonna focus on the part of the plan that I can see. It looks good, and if it works, maybe we won't have to worry about that other crazy stuff."

I felt myself relax as he spoke. That was about the best outcome I could have hoped for. Now, at least for the time being, we were all on the same page. Marc didn't need to know that even now, Natalie was upstairs, preparing for a possible outcome that he absolutely wouldn't approve of.

Chapter 22: Mental Assault

The evening dragged on without much success, and for two reasons. Firstly, while Lucien set to work on what appeared to be creating magical devices to help him realise the promises he had made in his press conference, he seemed to have found a rather effective way of getting things done in spite of Tommy's attempts to throw him off his game. Every time something interfered with the magic he had just performed, it would immediately, and almost instantaneously, return to how it had been before. In other words, only magic performed by Lucien himself was sticking; everything Tommy did was undone in mere moments.

And that wasn't all. Lucien had also found an effective way of going about political business in spite of Tommy. I could never imagine how he was able to do this, but we saw it all on the spyers. Lucien duplicated himself, creating an identical clone of himself. The two bodies appeared to share a mental connection, for they both seemed to be following the same will without needing to speak of it. The clone then went off to have boring meetings with Hammerhearts while the real Lucien stayed here—we knew it was the real one because the spyers couldn't seem to follow the clone. I could only conclude that he was using magic (or perhaps his Honnie mind) to strengthen his powers of concentration and focus even further to handle all these different tasks at the same time, and that was definitely not a good thing for us.

Meanwhile, we had run into a hitch of our own. The plan I had concocted allowed for this to happen, but it was still really sucky that we were failing at our very first test. No matter how hard Marc tried, and with all of us suggesting ways he could go about it, we were unable to figure out exactly *how* Lucien was alerted the instant Fewul was recalled. As the clock ticked through eight o'clock, nine o'clock and towards ten o'clock, we had to resign ourselves to the probability that it wasn't going to happen for us this evening. As Natalie re-joined us at last after a far more successful evening of performing magic (which she told me of telepathically), and as Tommy finally grew weary and left his workstation to get some sleep, leaving Katie, Sophie and Erica as the only people at workstations, we were forced to move onto the next phase of the plan.

"Attack his Honnie mind," James read off the display of the planner. "Well, this could be a bit hit-and-miss, but it's something we would need to do anyway. The first thing we're supposed to try is filling his mind with a noise so loud that he can't think through it, then recall Fewul at the same time. Then we're supposed to call Fewul from in here so that Lucien can't. Marc, do you think you can do all that?"

Marc shrugged. "I guess so. Do I need to go outdoors to call Fewul?"

James started to say "Yes", but I interrupted him. "Lucien never goes anywhere when he calls Fewul back, so maybe you don't have to go outside so long as you think of Fewul reforming somewhere outdoors and then teleporting to you."

"What if Fewul can't teleport to Marc because he can't find him?" Peter asked.

"He will, he said so himself when Lucien asked that question," James said. "That's a good idea, John. So what do we do? Do we wait till Lucien goes to bed or do we prepare some more stuff?"

A brief silence, and then Marc said, "I'd suggest creating a device to perform the magic to use against his Honnie mind, but how would we focus something like that? At least when I use the crystal I can just think of Lucien, but with a device, it would need to be close to him at the very least in order to work—wouldn't it?"

"Not necessarily," Frederic said, and nodded to the row of spyers across the top of the control panel. "Those things are set to follow people far, far away, and I assume the magic used to focus on the person is set into the device, and not just a template that can be switched to another person at any time? Is that right, James?"

"Erm—I think so," James said, looking a bit confused, and I didn't blame him. I thought I understood what Frederic was trying to say, but it was a tricky thing to describe. "I basically thought of the person when I created each one. The magic focusing on each person is as much a part of the device as the ability to trace them, or to locate untraceable things."

Frederic nodded. "That's what I thought. Which means, Marc, all you need to do is think specifically of Lucien's Honnie mind when you create the device. Then, so long as the magic works at all, it should work at any time, no matter where the device is in relation to Lucien."

"Okay," Marc said. "That also means someone else can be in charge of activating it, which leaves me free to focus on calling Fewul using the crystal."

Marc set to work creating the device, and so far as he or anyone else could tell, it would work perfectly when the time came. Unfortunately, because it was created specifically to target Lucien, there was no way to test it until it actually came time to use it. We were ready before Lucien was; he was still in the main area of his living quarters, diligently working away, while at the same time no doubt having meetings around the world with his clone—or perhaps the clone was now doing media stuff. Who knew how much he would be able to do in this fashion, or how many clones he would be able to control at the same time. This *really* had to work.

While we waited, James browsed a little down the list to check the contingencies in case this part of the plan failed for whatever reason. The first one he covered was what to do if Lucien decided to go straight to sleep tonight, instead of having sex with Lena as we all assumed he would, and in that case we would wait until he was fast asleep, and then slowly and carefully attempt to put him into a much deeper sleep—unconscious, really—that could only be reversed by us, hopefully leaving us free to do what we needed to do without interference. It would also require recalling Fewul, just in case the beast could overpower us, but the timing of said recall would have to be perfect—too soon for Fewul to wake Lucien, but too late for Lucien to call it back.

The next contingency after that was what to do if Lucien decided not to go to bed at all, but continue working through the night. If he didn't go to bed by one o'clock in the morning (that was our cut-off time), we would firstly try to fill him with mental exhaustion, again targeting his Honnie mind; and if that failed, we would try to hit him with physical exhaustion. We would do it gradually so that he would hopefully not suspect that it was brought on by magic, but if he stubbornly refused to give in, or if he continued to use magic to keep himself going, we would be temporarily out of options. We would have to call it a night and set up an alert to let us know when he entered his bedroom (hopefully to go to sleep), and then return to the plan. If this too didn't happen by sometime tomorrow, there was another plan to attack him while he worked, but James didn't go that far down.

While we waited for Lucien to finish up for the night, Marc created the devices we would use to exhaust him and slowly put him into the deepest of sleeps, making sure to put all the intensity of the Hero Crystal into it so that if Lucien did think to fight it, he would require the Sien-Leoard Crystal or Fewul to do so, for his own crystal chips wouldn't be powerful enough. When he was finished with this and Lucien still hadn't called it a night, he set to work on the next devices we would use in the event that Lucien did go and have sex with Lena, and yet the sound device failed to take him out.

At last, though, Lucien started to show signs that he was flagging, and to our relief, he didn't bother trying to push through it. What he did do before finishing up, though, was create some sort of magical lock box to store the devices he had created this evening in. James suggested we also try to destroy his creations or steal them, but Frederic said that it wouldn't slow him down; he could just remember what he had done and re-create everything in an instant. That may have been true, but I didn't think Lucien would think to check if the devices had been tampered with come morning time. As long as they were there, and they looked the same, he would probably assume that the magic remained as he had set it, but we could probably alter them to do our bidding instead of his if we were clever enough. It was an idea that had never occurred to me while I'd been working on the plan that afternoon, but now, I stored it away for later use.

We hadn't paid any attention to Lena throughout the evening, so I had no idea what she had been doing for the last four hours, but when

Lucien entered his bedroom, she was in there, fast asleep. He cast her a satisfied glance as he crossed the room and then began to slip out of his clothes, but still she didn't stir. The eight of us in the control room at this time watched the main display as, now naked, Lucien pulled back the covers without any regard for his sleeping partner, and got inside. Lena did stir at this, but didn't really come fully awake—that was until Lucien lay down, grabbed her, and pulled her on top of him.

"Wha…" she said sleepily, her hair falling down around her face and obscuring his.

"I've been working hard all day," he told her, his voice now gruff, "and now it's play time."

"Right now?" she moaned. "But I was asleep. Can't it wait till—"

He sat up very suddenly then, lifting Lena up with him and throwing the bed covers almost right off the foot of the bed. He lifted her clean into the air, balancing her on his hands in such a way that he was obviously using magic to support her weight, spinning her around in a way that would have surely made her dizzy, and ultimately ripping her nightclothes off and tossing the torn shreds to either side of the bed. Without straining any of his muscles, without looking as if he exerted any real effort at all in doing all this, he brought her down across his bare lap so that her bottom was facing upwards. With one arm supporting her from beneath, the hand on the end of said arm doing something under there that we couldn't see, he began to spank her.

"No, my dear," he said, speaking calmly and silkily between each spank. "It can't wait till tomorrow, because I want it now, and it is your job to give me what I want, when I want it. You know that, don't you?"

"Oh yes," she said emphatically, and now she was fully awake. Furthermore, she was well and truly into this. Whether he was using his Honnie mind on her now to get her into it, or he had already done such a good job on her that he only needed to start to get the ball rolling with her, I knew not. All I knew was that however she had felt when he first woke her up, now she had put it clean aside and was completely focused on the pleasure he was giving her. He continued to spank her, forcing her to submit to him, making her say, in exactly as many words, that she would do whatever he wanted, whenever he wanted, and that she would love every bit of it.

When the spanking ended, the sex began, and given that the covers were almost off the bed, we had a clear view of the whole thing. We didn't stop to watch the X-rated show, though; this was what we had waited for, and it was now time to get to work. Marc had the Hero Crystal in hand and it would be his job to call Fewul forth at the first opportunity. I would recall Fewul mentally using one of the enchantments I had put on myself, while James had the device Marc had created a little earlier which would fill Lucien's Honnie mind with a sound so loud that he couldn't think through it. The three of us lined up ready to go, and Amelia counted down from three…two…one…

The three of us went at almost exactly the same time. I went first, making sure that Lucien would be thoroughly distracted in the moment when James activated his device, which he did so less than a second later. Marc jumped into action less than a second after him, and amazingly, the plan worked well enough up to this point that the beast actually began to take shape right there in the control room. We all noticed that this was happening, but other than Marc, we paid barely any attention to it, for the show outside the base was much more entertaining, and ultimately more important.

Lucien let out a great cry of agony, his whole body jerking with it. He threw his arms up to his head and basically clenched himself against it, moaning and rocking back and forth, gasping and sounding a bit like a gorilla, I thought. He was so sufficiently distracted that he never noticed how much he was bleeding, Lena having bitten down hard on him in that moment. Peter, James and I all clenched ourselves in sympathy as we saw this, too, distracted by this part of it to notice that the danger for us hadn't passed.

When it looked like Lucien was unable to use his Honnie mind to fight through what was happening to him, Lena took matters into her own hands in a way that none of us—not even my planner—had anticipated. Without waiting for Lucien to take control of her as he had done the other day (something he probably couldn't do this time), she reached out and took hold of the Sien-Leoard Crystal. Exactly how she had known where it was on the bedside drawers, given that she'd been asleep when Lucien put it there, I had no idea—perhaps she took a guess based on the last few days with him. She turned the crystal on him and probably tried to fix whatever was going on; but of course, she would have had very little understanding of the Honnie mind compared to us, and no idea how we were doing what we were doing; so naturally, it had no effect.

"Master," a deep voice said behind us, and looking over my shoulder, I saw that Fewul had taken its original form of a lethal-looking teddy bear right here in our control room, and it appeared to be in Marc's control.

"Now would be the perfect time to get the crys—" I began to say, turning my attention back to the main display, but we were already too late.

Lena may not have known what was really going on, but in light of all that she had become this week, it had been a mistake to discount her as someone who couldn't take her own initiative. She was still quite smart, and it hadn't taken her long to figure out a way through this. By putting the crystal in Lucien's hand and not letting go of it herself, she seemed to be able to lend him magical strength, or concentration, or something, through it. Whatever it was, Lucien was able to use it to either drown out, or somehow neutralise, the noise inside his mind. He took a moment to steady himself, and about five seconds later, called the Beast of Magic back to him.

"Crap! Crap!" Marc roared as Fewul began to reform before Lucien. With all that was going on, we had clean forgotten how easily Lucien could force Fewul back to Earth, and then recall it himself—exactly as easily as we could, in other words. The same way that he was unable to stop us from doing it, we were equally unable to stop him from doing it. Seeing how quickly this part of the plan was slipping out of control, James slammed on the button to fill his head with noise again, but it had no effect. Whatever Lucien had done, he would no longer be vulnerable to this kind of attack.

"Abort," James said sadly, watching the display screen. "We'll have to wait and see if he resumes having sex with Lena; but for now, he's too alert to attack again."

By the time Fewul had reformed before Lucien and he had ordered it to once again take Stella's shape, he had fully composed himself, healed his injury and cleaned the mess that had been left on the bed. "Get back to what you were doing before the interruption," he commanded the beast, and with a servile nod, she teleported away, leaving the naked couple alone in the bedroom.

"That was them, wasn't it?" Lena said quietly.

He sighed. "Yes, it was, and thank you for doing what you did there. That was an attack I never anticipated. I've made sure nothing like it will happen again, but still, it was a good one. It could have gotten the better of me."

"The crystal," Lena said, looking at Lucien's fist full of thin air, "I could touch it. Did you not have it shielded? What if they'd thought to try to steal it?"

"I'm sure that was their plan," he said, "but it wouldn't have worked. It *was* shielded, just not from you; and if they had tried to take it from you in that moment, that wouldn't have worked either. After what they did back on Tuesday, I anticipated that kind of attack."

"What did they do?" she asked, touching his bare chest and staring intently at him.

"They attacked my mind directly," he said, reaching out and stroking her, making her shiver, "but don't worry, I've put a spell on myself to protect my mind from any outside magic such as what they tried. Nothing like that will happen again."

They continued to touch each other, and that quickly led to more. At Lucien's last words, however, James and I swapped a gleeful look. Lucien was reacting as we had predicted he would, and now it would be possible to move straight onto the next contingency. This time, we deviated slightly from the plan and decided that a few of us should leave the base, so that we could attack them directly should the need arise. (If one of us had knocked Lena out while she was holding the crystal, even if it was shielded from us, we could have prevented her from coming to Lucien's aid.) We also memorised exactly where Lucien set the crystal down in the moment he'd decided that Lena's body required both of his hands, so that we would be able to steal that as well. After all, there was no point getting Fewul back on our side if Lucien could just as easily call it back to him with the crystal.

Marc, Peter, Amelia, Natalie and I left the control room and dropped into Lucien's bedroom, leaving James at the base controls, and watched on by Lillian and Frederic. All five of us were untraceable and under an invisibility veil, choosing for the time being not to enter our shadows, so that it would be easier to attack Lucien. Marc was armed with the Hero Crystal, and he had a specific job to do—namely, call the Beast of Magic the moment it looked as though the Sien-Leoard Crystal was out of Lucien's reach. Frederic was charged with calling Fewul back to Earth from inside the base, leaving me, Peter and Natalie free to attack Lucien and Lena should the need arise. All three of us were armed with devices that could punch through any shield Lucien thought to use by way of X-rays, and we took up strategic positions around the bedroom so that we could get at them from different angles without risking hitting each other.

As for Amelia, she was in charge of operating the magical device Marc had created for this part of the plan, and the only reason she wasn't in her shadow was that we didn't want to run the risk of it not working across dimensions. When it was activated, it would create a brand new Honnie mind, exactly the same shape and size as May's had been before Lucien had gotten to it, and it would happen slowly, so that when Lucien sensed it, he would think it was a legitimate Honnie approaching him, probably mistaking him for a fellow Honnie. This new Honnie mind wouldn't be controlled by any of our minds, as Lucien controlled his, but it would be controlled directly by the device, and if Lucien reacted to it as we anticipated that he would, it would give us a golden opening to attack him in a way that he couldn't predict. Of course, there were a couple of ways that the plan could go wrong (Lucien doesn't react as we expect, or our assumptions about the way Lucien's Honnie mind is linked to his human mind were incorrect), but if so, we wouldn't be any worse off than we were already.

Before we began, however, Marc crept over to the bedside table where we knew the Sien-Leoard Crystal to be, careful not to get too close lest he activate whatever shield Lucien had put around it, and put his own shield around the table. It wouldn't keep Lucien out altogether, but it would give him or Lena an electric shock if either of them touched it, enough to slow Lucien down if he had to go for the crystal in a hurry. It could give us a few crucial extra seconds, and our experiences over the last couple of days had taught us that a couple of seconds could make all the difference.

Then, we were ready to go. Lucien was still busy doing his thing with Lena—she looked like she was flagging, only able to pant and gasp and not move very much—but that little factoid was hardly slowing Lucien down. If anything, it only made him hungrier for her—to take advantage of her while she was unable to stop him, and not even needing to use magic or his Honnie mind to do it. I turned my mind away from them momentarily to telepathically coordinate the attack, with all the others using telepathic communicators to connect with me. It was tricky to separate all their thoughts, but part of the ability I had given myself was being able to manage all of this without it overwhelming me. I focused mainly on Amelia and Frederic, as they were the ones who would have to jump into action at almost the same time. As Amelia had counted us in verbally the last time, I now counted them in telepathically from three…two…one…

Frederic hit his button first, a fraction of a second before Amelia pressed the button to create the Honnie mind. I only had her mental assurance that it had worked, for Lucien showed no outward sign of noticing anything just yet, and none of us could sense anything. The device had functionality to control and monitor the mind it had just created, and Amelia now visualised it for me and Marc so that we could see what it was showing us. It had inflated to its full size and was now touching the outside of Lucien's mind. Amelia began to direct it to examine the size of Lucien's mind, as a normal Honnie would do, and then to swallow it if it were smaller than its own—something else a normal Honnie would do.

We all saw the moment when Lucien noticed the presence of the Honnie mind; he only paused for a moment before resuming what he was doing, but it was enough to put us all on high alert. Amelia then made the Honnie mind open up and attempt to swallow Lucien's, and this time, as though he had either half or fully expected it, Lucien reacted the same way he had when May had tried to do the same thing to him. He turned the mind inside out so that he could take control of it. Lucien probably didn't believe it was May he was dealing with; he was most likely going to destroy whatever Honnie had dared to approach him, merely for the purpose of removing a potential threat before it could do anything.

It wouldn't take Lucien long to figure out that the Honnie mind he had just ingested was not real, so Amelia had to act quickly. She pushed another button—the one which we had all agreed would be the best place to start when this moment came—and we all crossed our mental fingers in the next split-second. What happened next was very similar to what had happened a little earlier, though without the biting part. Lucien began to scream and thrash on the bed as his regular human mind was subjected to the power of the agonator—his regular human mind could not be protected from Amelia, now that she was literally inside his Honnie mind.

It couldn't have worked out any more perfectly, at least thus far. Being exhausted from her almost continual orgasms, Lena was slow to react, and being pinned down by an out-of-control Lucien didn't help. Still, there was no point taking a chance with her, and Peter and I attacked her at almost the same time. I knocked her out, while he hit her with a solid-outliner which quickly attached itself to Lucien and began spreading over him too. Meanwhile, now that she knew she had access to his mind, and he couldn't protect himself from her, Amelia pushed another button on the device in her hand, and Lucien collapsed on top of Lena, now knocked out cold.

The next part of the plan called for Marc to take possession of the Sien-Leoard Crystal, and then call the Beast of Magic to help him protect it. If that part of the plan had only worked, we probably could have defeated Lucien that very night. Sadly, though, we never got a chance to find out, thanks to the failsafe Lucien had installed at some point to activate in the unlikely event that he succumbed to a magical attack. Before we could so much as move, we were suddenly surrounded by things—maybe a dozen of them all up. I had no idea exactly what (or who) they were, but they took the shape of miniature humans, coming up to about our waistlines, and with ugly, pointy faces.

Whatever they were, they were clearly magical, and they immediately went on the attack. Untraceable though we were, it didn't stop them sending out a wave of magic in all directions. Most of it went right through us, given that we had also put that protection around ourselves in case Lucien *had* managed to attack us, but the same protection didn't exist for our invisibility veil, which was wrapped around the outside of all our individual selves. All five us quickly popped back into visibility, and the gnome-like creatures immediately began double-teaming us.

Lucien had clearly created these things for the express purpose of battling, because they were damn good at it. It took them no time at all to figure out that their spells were going right through us, and they quickly resorted to other means to attack us. The floor beneath Amelia's feet ignited, and since the fire itself was totally non-magical, Amelia went up with it, screaming. Marc was quickly able to put it out with his crystal, ducking beneath what looked like a metal pole which went swinging towards his head. Natalie had attempted to slip away into her shadow to escape the creatures, but ominously, two of them followed her. As for Peter, I only got a glimpse of his battle before I had to focus on my own: The creatures had him in a corner and appeared to be walling him off.

Meanwhile, I was being attacked by swords; I ducked under one and just managed to jump over another before a third one sliced into my left arm. It hurt like a son-of-a-bitch, but thanks to the regeneration magic I had given myself back on Rock Haulter, it barely slowed me down. Other than Marc, I was best able to fight these things, thanks to the expanded magical abilities I now possessed. I quickly sprang up a physical shield around myself and began trying to attack the creatures, but most of what I tried had no effect on them. Part of it may have been that they were shielding themselves too, but it seemed also to be their very nature; with my light device, I was able to land a hit on one of them, but it seemed to feel no pain as the power of the bludginator cut into it.

Across the room, Marc was attempting to protect Amelia while fighting four of the creatures himself. He actually managed to destroy one of them, by making it explode into fragments, but a moment later, a new creature appeared to take its place. That could only mean that they were not true living creatures, but quite possibly robots, or something like robots, and could be created on demand in countless numbers at any time when necessary. In other words, there was no point trying to fight them, because we had no chance of winning. Our only option was to return to base, and a moment later, that was exactly what Natalie did (at least, she vanished into thin air, so I had to assume), but if there was still a hope of snagging the Sien-Leoard Crystal and taking advantage of the score we had already made here…

"Aha!" Lucien roared, springing up from the bed and dismaying all of us. Apparently, part of the job description of these things was to bring Lucien back from the brink as well. He looked around the room at the four of us who remained, untraceable but clearly visible, and rage filled his face. Marc immediately engaged him so that he couldn't attack the rest of us, while behind him, Amelia vanished into thin air, hopefully dragged back into the base. I held off the gnomes for a few more seconds before I too was sucked back into the base, where everyone bar Marc was already waiting, shaken to the core.

"You gotta get Marc now," a white-faced Peter told James, who was rapidly pressing buttons and pulling levers. As I fell into a seat, however, I could see how difficult that was going to be. Lucien and Marc were having one almighty magical battle, neither of them able to do more than attack and defend, and the ways they were moving meant that catching Marc was going to be very hard indeed. Worse still, Lucien had already taken the Sien-Leoard Crystal, so if Marc lost his focus for so much as a split-second, it would be too much. On the plus side, now that Lucien was back in commission and the rest of us were gone, the gnomes had vanished back wherever they had come from.

"You really thought I didn't have backup plans in case you did something I hadn't thought of?" Lucien grunted as he did battle with Marc. "Honestly, you continue to underestimate me."

"And you continue to underestimate us," Marc snarled back. "We're never gonna give up, you know, no matter how many people you kill. Even the Hammersons knew where to cap their destruction."

"And look where it got them!" Lucien roared, looking more evil in that moment than anything I'd ever seen—his face was twisted in a way that looked almost demonic.

"What do we do?" Amelia squeaked. "How do we get Marc out of there?"

"If only he'd called Fewul when he had the chance," Lillian said sadly.

"Maybe he should use the fourth dimension to escape," Natalie suggested. "Should we contact him telepathically and suggest that?"

"A telepathic message could distract him sufficiently for Lucien to get a hit in," James pointed out, shaking his head sadly. "I'm sure there's a way to get a fix on him. John, did you design this thing so that it can track a person while they're on the outside, so that'll be easier to bring them in without lining them up?"

"No, but it wouldn't matter anyway, since Marc is our kind of untraceable," I said.

"Should we attack Lucien as well, then?" Frederic suggested. "I know he's prepared for it, but it might give Marc an opening to get away —"

"Except then we'll be stuck there instead of him, and he's way more equipped for it," Peter sighed.

It looked like our only option, unless Marc found his own way to get out, was to try to tag his every move, and snag him the moment he stood still long enough. In the end, that was what we managed to do. He was totally out of breath and sweating profusely when he appeared in the corner of the control room, but managed to smile weakly at us as he said, "Well—that went well."

Outside, Lucien was trying to flush Marc out, but within seconds seemed to accept that his brother had slipped away. He settled back on his bed, where he had been throughout the entire battle, and glanced down at Lena—who still lay unconscious beside him—completely naked and exposed for us all to see. Honestly, I had seen more of Lena's naked body in the last few days than I had the entire time I had known her, and that was even taking into account the two times I had been 'with' her.

"I'm sure you're still here, watching me," Lucien said, projecting his voice so that it filled the bedroom, "and if so, that means you're listening to me as well. Feel free to keep trying to do things like that, but as you now know, it isn't going to make any difference. I am going to keep doing what I'm doing, and though you may cause me some annoyance, you're really as insignificant as a fly that lands on my ear in the height of summer. Sooner or later, despite what you may think, you will come to accept this; but as you also know, the longer it takes you to do so, the more people will suffer in the interim. You may be prepared to sit back and allow me to kill by the thousands rather than surrender—I know now that such manoeuvres won't sway you—but I also know that they will eat away at your spirits every single time.

"Now, if you don't mind, I am going to go to sleep. Feel free to do what you will, while you will, but I *will* sleep through the night, and tomorrow is going to be a *very* significant day. How significant? Well, that remains to be seen, doesn't it? Since I spotted five of you in my room tonight, perverts as you are, I think there shall have to be five incidents tomorrow. Just a little something for you to look forward to."

With that, he pulled the covers up, finally hiding their naked bodies, and then began to recall Fewul to himself. He set her back to work and then appeared to settle into sleep, dropping off fairly quickly, and not even bothering to bring Lena out of unconsciousness. The eight of us in the control room didn't even wait for him to be completely gone before we began figuring out our next move.

Chapter 23: Let Sleeping Morans Lie

"Okay, he's going to sleep now," James said, "so are we gonna try the deep sleep thing?"

"Yes, but I think I'll have to modify the device first," Marc said. "It's designed to edge him slowly into what would probably be considered unconsciousness, for all intents and purposes, but now we know that if we do that, we'll get attacked by those pixies again."

"I thought they were more like goblins," Peter said.

"They reminded me more of gnomes," I added.

"Be serious, you two," Amelia said reprovingly, and Peter and I swapped abashed looks.

"What about Fewul?" Frederic asked. "We know now that while he's awake, he can't automatically call it back to himself the moment we recall it if he's distracted, but we don't know what system he has in place for when he's asleep—and at this point, we have to assume there's something."

"Perhaps we should wait until he's actually asleep, and then get rid of Fewul and see what happens," Peter suggested. "I mean, whether or not it wakes him up, or if he has some way of bringing Fewul back even while he's asleep."

"What if it *does* wake him up?" I asked.

Peter shrugged. "So what if it does? He already knows we have this capability—we won't be surprising him, or giving anything away."

"He's right," James agreed, stifling a yawn—he wasn't the only one getting seriously exhausted by this point. "At the very least, it'll give us a little more information about what we're up against without ruining the next part of our plan."

We all agreed that this was a good idea, but the level of enthusiasm was beginning to drop. It was hard to tell what the cause of this could be. We were all very tired by now, and however the next stage of the plan went, it would probably be a good idea for us to take advantage of Lucien's sleeping time by getting some rest ourselves—we would probably need it for whatever he had in store for us tomorrow. Then there had been the brief but intense battle with Lucien's little army of whatever-the-hell they were, thwarting us for the umpteenth time, when we had been so very close to scoring a major win over him.

Then, there was the fact that we were quickly coming to the last of the tactics covered by the planner which didn't require the use of the devices Natalie had spent the early part of the evening creating. By now, I fully expected that at the very least, we would need to use magic particles in some way to strip Lucien of his magic, and what we were doing now was basically shooting blindly in the hope that it wouldn't come to that. Only Marc, who had set to work modifying his deep sleep device, and still didn't know of everything else contained in the planner (but probably suspected), was treating this as though it were a make-or-break assault.

"I think he's asleep," Natalie told us—she had been watching Lucien on the display this whole time.

"Is there any way to be sure?" Lillian asked. "This little experiment depends on knowing that he's definitely asleep."

"As soon as I'm done with this, I'll create something else that can measure that when pointed at a person," Marc said vaguely as he worked.

"I have a better idea," Natalie said, getting up and heading over towards the cabinet containing all our magical devices. I had no idea what she was doing until she opened the one that had stored the magic enhancer, pretended to reach inside and take it out, and then put it in her pocket—where the *real* magic enhancer had been the whole time. It was a little act to fool those who didn't know what she had been doing upstairs, to explain why the device was in her pocket. She closed the cabinet and came back over to us, holding said device in one hand.

"Good idea," Amelia said approvingly. "We have more magic than just the Hero Crystal—we really shouldn't forget that."

Natalie created a device like the one Marc had described and then left the base, dropping back into Lucien's bedroom so that she could use it. She used her telepathic communicator to keep in touch with Amelia back here, letting her know that Lucien was in a light sleep, but was slowly sinking into a deeper and more refreshing sleep, and she would let us know when the best time to attack would be. By the time we got the message that now was as good a time as any, Marc had finished modifying the deep sleep device.

"Tell her to go into her shadow for this part," Frederic told his daughter as he held up the device that would recall Fewul, "in case he wakes up and does some quick magic."

The room went silent for a few seconds before Amelia told her father to push the button. We all fixed our eyes to the main display to watch what happened next. Whatever it was, it was totally unremarkable. Lucien didn't stir, nor was there any sign of magic being automatically performed in the air around him. Yet when Frederic looked down at the device in his hand, he sighed.

"Something did happen," he said grimly. "It worked briefly, but he was able to somehow call Fewul back to him. Given that this is the real Lucien and not a clone that we're watching, we have to assume he doesn't even need to be fully conscious to do it. He has obviously set this up in full anticipation that we would try that."

"And if he doesn't need to be conscious to do it," James said slowly, "then putting him into a deeper sleep won't stop it from happening. It might even work if he's fully unconscious, but like Marc said earlier, we'll immediately come under attack if we try that again."

"So this won't work," Marc sighed. "Any ideas for what we can try now?"

"Well, maybe," Frederic said, getting to his feet. "Let Natalie know that I'm coming out there; I have something I would like to try, and I think it best be done using the device she has, rather than the Hero Crystal or any of the magic we have in here."

"What are you doing?" Amelia asked warily.

"I'm going to see if I can figure out what magic is being triggered when he calls Fewul back to himself while he's asleep."

"Good luck," Marc muttered. "I couldn't figure it out earlier."

Frederic went over to the corner and James let him out of the base. He immediately joined Natalie; the two of them spoke for a moment before he took the magic enhancer from her and began to use it. In the silence that suddenly filled the control room, I looked around at all their faces; Marc and James looked the most exhausted, but Peter, Amelia and Lillian weren't too far behind. I was probably about the same as Peter: it had sure been a long, protracted day, and although it had been filled with discovery and new knowledge, we were still no closer to actually making any real ground against Lucien.

Minutes passed before Amelia, who was still holding her communicator said, "It looks like Dad can't figure it out either. In fact, by all the laws of magic he knows about, what Lucien's doing should be impossible. Calling Fewul is supposed to be a conscious act, and Lucien is somehow able to do it while he's asleep and without needing to hold the Sien-Leoard Crystal. It doesn't make any sense at all."

We let Natalie and Frederic back into the base where they both re-took their seats, looking unhappy.

"I suppose there are ways to do what he's doing," Frederic told us. "At the very least, he has been creative enough to find ways to do what ought to be impossible. Since I was unable to figure out how he is recalling Fewul, and none of us could figure out how he is keeping track or his magical alerts and where the magic to operate them is coming from, we'll have to accept the fact that we can't get rid of Fewul while he's asleep. What does the planner suggest we do next?"

Lillian checked it, tapping the screen a few times to eliminate a few items which were no longer possible.

"What is it?" Peter asked, leaning forward in his seat.

"Well, if we assume that trying to take the Sien-Leoard Crystal is also off the table at this point," she began.

"I don't see why we can't at least try that," Marc said. "I mean, even if Fewul does turn up, it might still be possible."

A silence fell and then Frederic, who was still holding the magic enhancer, heaved himself to his feet. "I'll see if I can't use this to get a hand on it. Marc, use that device of yours to make sure he stays asleep, won't you?"

"And if Fewul does turn up?" Amelia asked, looking anxiously at her father.

Frederic hesitated, and I thought I understood why. Even if the Beast of Magic was under orders not to wake Lucien, it could still do plenty of damage on its own. Would Frederic be able to fight it, even with the magic enhancer? If he were fully alert, perhaps, as Arnold Hammerson had been able to at least break even with Fewul when they had battled a couple of weeks earlier; but not tonight.

"Then we'll drag him in as quickly as possible," James said, "and if that fails, we'll recall Fewul with that device. Even if it only gives us a second of reprieve, it should be enough."

Frederic handed me the device to recall Fewul as he went back to the corner with the magic enhancer. James pushed a button on the control panel and once again, he dropped into Lucien's bedroom—the scene of so many recent struggles.

"Who's got the deep sleep device?" Peter asked suddenly, looking around at everyone in the room.

"Relax, I've got it," Marc said, withdrawing it from his pocket. He looked at it, then at the Hero Crystal in his other hand, and handed the deep sleep device over to Peter. Good move, I thought; each of us should only have one responsibility at a time. That reminded me of mine, and I readied myself to recall the beast at a moment's notice.

Frederic walked around Lucien's bed to his bedside table where we had seen him place the Sien-Leoard Crystal. Although it appeared bare to us, he stared down at it as though fascinated by the polished woodwork. The seconds continued to tick by, perhaps as long as a minute, but while Frederic's facial expression flickered rapidly, he never budged. I assumed he was using the magic of the enhancer to probe at the shield Lucien had put around the crystal. It went on long enough for me to start believing that nothing was going to happen, but to all of our surprise, something did happen.

Instead of being completely invisible, the shield around the crystal became translucent. It looked a bit like a hemisphere atop the table, but more accurately it took the shape of slightly more than a hemisphere, its one circular side curving inward slightly at the bottom. It was just large enough to fit the Sien-Leoard Crystal and not much else. As we watched, Lillian's eyes lit up and she turned to me.

"This might actually work, John, and mainly because of the way you designed that thing. Since he's using the magic of the Sien-Leoard Crystal, it's as if he is already inside the shield itself and it's highly doubtful that Lucien thought to protect it from the inside."

That was a good point, and Frederic must have been aware of it too. It was the only way to explain why he was able to make the shield visible, because Lucien certainly wouldn't have planned for that to be possible. In fact, anything that gave away the position of the Sien-Leoard

Crystal while he wasn't using it would have been a big no-no.
Meanwhile, Frederic appeared to be braced for something; a moment
later, the shield became invisible again. Nothing happened for a few
seconds, and then at last, Frederic moved. He reached out and plucked
something off the bedside drawers, and the shape his fingers took made it
obvious that he had finally laid a hand on the crystal—but we only saw it
for a fraction of a second, for that was when yet another of Lucien's
contingencies kicked into gear.

A flash of bright red light filled Lucien's room. It would have been
disorientating for anyone in the room at the time, but since we were only
looking at it through the display on the control panel, we had a clear
view of what actually happened. Frederic let out a cry of pain and fell
down backwards, dropping something at the foot of Lucien's bedside
drawers as he did. Even before I registered what had actually happened, I
activated my internal magic to recall Fewul—a move that had probably
saved Frederic's life, or at the very least prevented his capture, as in the
instant before it vanished, I saw that Fewul, still in Stella's form, had
materialised in the bedroom, looming over Frederic.

Amelia and Natalie both screamed then, while Marc and James let
out cries of horror. The rest of us weren't far behind as we realised what
had happened to Frederic. He was covered in blood, and it continued to
pump from the stump of his arm. The thing that he had dropped to the
foot of Lucien's bedside drawers was in fact his hand—the hand that had
dared to take hold of the Sien-Leoard Crystal. The shield itself couldn't
have done it; otherwise Frederic would have surely detected and disabled
that feature. I could only assume that Fewul had been ordered to detect
when someone unauthorised—someone other than Lucien or any of
Lucien's recognised minions—laid a hand on the crystal. Lucien,
meanwhile, went on sleeping through all of this, thanks to Peter who had
jammed on his button at the same moment I had.

"I'm going out there to get him," Marc said, jumping up and
hurrying to the corner. "John, be ready to recall it if it comes back
again."

James let him out of the base and he began tending to Frederic
immediately. I watched the display like a hawk, ready to recall Fewul at
the first sign of anything unusual happening. As the seconds stretched on,
however, it appeared that Fewul wasn't going to come back. I had a clear
but unexplainable sense that Fewul had indeed been called forth again,
but perhaps its previous orders had been voided? I didn't know the
reason; all I knew was that I had to be ready.

Marc had reattached Frederic's hand and cleaned up the mess of
blood. Now they were both on their feet and searching the floor around
the bedside drawers for the Sien-Leoard Crystal, while on the bed beside
them, Lucien continued to sleep. It turned out that the whole thing had
been for naught, however, because Frederic soon located the crystal—it

was back on the bedside drawers, back inside the shield he had just defeated. It would be simple enough to go through the process again, but what would be the point if at the end of it, the person who touched the crystal would lose a hand over it?

Marc and Frederic were speaking quietly—too quietly for us to hear. As they talked, a realisation slowly dawned on me that not all hope was yet lost. Now that we knew about the hand thing, the person who touched the crystal could put up their own protection to prevent it from happening again. Furthermore, if I were able to recall Fewul at just the right time, perhaps I could prevent the beast from taking any action at all. Of course, Lucien would have foreseen that if we did fall for the hand thing, we would most likely pick ourselves up, dust ourselves off, and try again. It was highly likely that he would have a backup plan of some sort, but as long as we were ready for anything…

"Are we gonna bring them in or what?" Peter asked into the silence.

"Hold on," James said slowly. He was ready on the controls, but like me, he had realised that the two of them out there were up to something. "I'll let them in if something else happens, or if they give us the signal, but I think they're gonna have another go."

And so they were. Marc faded back into his shadow, where hopefully he would be safe, but still close enough to jump into action should it be necessary. Frederic began to go through the process with the shield again, only more quickly this time, and skipping the step where it became visible to us. I focused my mind on Fewul throughout this procedure, and when I saw him reach for the crystal, I immediately activated the enchantment to recall it—not just once, but over and over again, just to be on the safe side. My instincts were telling me that as long as I kept doing this, with less than a second between recalls, Fewul would stay gone; but it would reappear the moment I stopped. That sucked, because not only was there no easy way to do this continually (it wasn't like a button in my mind I could hold down), it was much more mentally draining than I would have believed, and made it very hard to follow what was going on.

Outside the base, Frederic picked up the Sien-Leoard Crystal, then held his hands up to either side of his face—the signal to be let inside the base. James obliged, and the former Sorcerer appeared in the corner of the control room a moment later. Seeing what had just happened, Marc emerged from his shadow, already raising his hands in the same signal. That was when I made a monumental mistake. The moment Frederic had returned to base, holding up a hand which appeared to be gripping thin air, proving that he had succeeded in reclaiming the Sien-Leoard Crystal, I had allowed myself to relax for a moment. It was only a moment, but it was long enough

Before James was able to let Marc back into the base, Fewul pounced on him out of nowhere. Marc wasn't completely caught off guard—I supposed he and Frederic had both been prepared for Fewul to turn up at some stage, not knowing that I'd found a way to keep it away at least temporarily; but he wasn't ready for Fewul to come at him with all of its power. He never even got a chance to defend himself before the beast had completely immobilised and disarmed him of his crystal. In the same moment, despite Peter using the deep sleep device again, Lucien awoke with a start and quickly leapt out of bed when he saw what was going on.

Other than horrified gasps and a scream from Amelia, not a word was spoken in the control room. We all knew what needed to be done in this moment. In theory, the Sien-Leoard Crystal for the Hero Crystal would be a winning trade for us, but it wasn't a winning trade if we lost Marc at the same time. Frederic took a step backward, placing himself back in the corner of the base, and James immediately let him out. He emerged in the bedroom, completely visible for all to see, and immediately launched into battle against Fewul, disregarding a still-groggy and still-naked Lucien for now.

Peter Jammed on his device to bring sleep upon Lucien again, and at the same time, I once again recalled the beast. Fewul vanished again, giving Marc and Frederic a moment of reprieve, and I began doing it repeatedly once again so that they would have a better chance of getting out of there. Lucien, however, was not so easily overcome; now that he was awake, no doubt woken by Fewul in response to an emergency, the deep sleep device was having very little impact on him. It was supposed to slide him into deep sleep in a way that made it feel like he were just going to sleep; but if he wasn't already in a position where he could sleep, all it succeeded in doing was making him feel a bit weary. He shook it off as he stepped towards Frederic and engaged him in battle.

For once, it looked like we could actually win this one. Frederic was at least as skilful as Lucien, and probably more so; and to top it off, he had more raw power to throw into it. Yet for some reason, Lucien was at least able to keep pace with him, and my only guess at an explanation was that he had performed protective spells around himself while he had the Sien-Leoard Crystal which, although it wasn't in his possession anymore, still held. Neither of them had any spare attention to give Marc, who remained immobilised and separated from the Hero Crystal. If he were just able to get it, he could finish the battle off for good, and then we could get out of there with all five of the Magic Crystals, leaving Lucien with nothing but his crystal chips…

And of course, that was the answer. None of us had any devices which could, without any doubt, help Marc out of his predicament. Furthermore, if any of us left the base now, it would interrupt the battle out there with unpredictable results. If someone were to use the Villain Crystal, however, they could fix whatever had been done to Marc without even needing to leave the base. But I couldn't do it—I was using up all my focus on keeping Fewul out of the battle, my mind working so hard that I feared I may black out if I had to keep it up for long. I didn't dare speak my thought in case it interrupted my flow, giving Fewul enough of an opening to knock Frederic off his feet, so I could only hope that one of the others thought of it.

If only Frederic had thought to throw the Sien-Leoard Crystal aside the moment he had materialised inside the control room; he could have gone back out and fought Lucien with the magic enhancer and we could have assisted more effectively. It was yet another of those moments I would think back to later on, and wonder how different things might have been if we had made that one simple move. I couldn't blame Frederic, though, nor could I really blame any of us; seeing Marc overcome so effectively like that had pretty much driven all other considerations from our minds.

I had a dizzy spell. It was only a moment, but it was enough. A burst of magic, so fast that it could barely be seen, knocked Frederic off his feet, and he toppled over backwards. Lucien was on him immediately; mere moments later, Frederic was just as immobilised as Marc, and Lucien was holding what looked like a fistful of thin air. He was smiling in triumph as he glanced from Frederic to Marc, and the Hero Crystal lying nearby.

Amelia let out a scream. "What do we do?"

The brief silence in the control room was terrible as we all glanced, wide-eyed at each other. I opened my mouth, about to voice my idea about the Villain Crystal, but before I could, James took the controls. He focused in on the Hero Crystal just as Lucien moved toward it; a moment later it vanished from the floor, only to clatter to the floor in the corner of the control room. Lucien froze, his face twisting into a grimace, but before he was able to do anything else, James continued working the controls. Another moment later, a completely immobile Marc landed on his butt in the corner, quite possibly landing on top of the Hero Crystal; it rolled a little and then came to a stop next to his knee.

"What about Dad?" Amelia asked, her face pale.

"Well, first of all," Lucien said, as if he were responding to Amelia, but he was actually turning back to face Frederic, "this is quite impressive of you. I'm not surprised that you tried this, but I am a little surprised that you succeeded. It looks like I will have to put even more protection around this crystal; protection that you will have no chance whatsoever of overcoming. Hmm…"

He looked thoughtful as he glanced from Frederic to Lena, who I had forgotten about while all this was happening. She was presently sitting up in bed, looking bleary-eyed and not especially interested in the fight that had just happened all around her. She was also still naked, but on this occasion, she had pulled the covers up so that there was nothing to see.

"Do you have any ideas for how I can protect this crystal, my dear?" he asked her conversationally. "Anything that they won't be able to overcome?"

Lena didn't answer, but her face twitched as if she had thought of something. Lucien smiled as he took this in and then said, "Yes, I quite agree, and the vibe I'm getting right now is that I can do it too."

While this had been happening, Peter had been out of his seat. He had gone over to Marc and carefully nudged the Hero Crystal into one of Marc's hands. Now, Marc had used it to recover himself, and was getting rapidly to his feet. At the same time, James was in motion, moving the base over to where Frederic sat immobilised, forced to watch Lucien's next move. As for Lucien, if he had known of the extra bit of magic Frederic was carrying he would have surely paid him more mind, but his full attention was on the Sien-Leoard Crystal and the extra layer of protection he was about to put around it.

I knew what was about to happen almost right away. Lucien raised the Sien-Leoard Crystal up to his face and opened his mouth as wide as he could. As he put the invisible crystal against his mouth, it somehow opened even wider—wider than should be humanly possible. His whole face contorted as flesh and muscle stretched much further than they were designed to do. It could have been Lucien's own magic doing that, but more likely it was part of the magic of the crystal itself—that if the user of the crystal chose to take this action, the crystal would make it happen, as the Villain Crystal had done with Marc and Lucien's (and my) father.

He began to feed the solid air into his mouth. His cheeks bulged out, and then his neck as the crystal slid down his throat. Then it disappeared into his chest, which didn't bulge—I could only assume it had shrunk, or that some other magic was at work to make it fit in there. Lucien relaxed and closed his mouth, smiling comfortably as his face returned to its normal shape and size. Lena, who had watched all this without comment, also began to smile.

"How do I look?" he asked her, and then didn't wait for a response. "I think the important thing is that you now know that you won't be able to—"

He was turning back to Frederic as he spoke, but Frederic was no longer sitting on the floor, immobilised. James had drawn him back into the control room seconds before, leaving Lucien standing alone on his bedroom floor.

"I know you're still here," Lucien called as he climbed back into bed beside Lena. "I'm not going to repeat my speech from earlier; I think you got the idea. I would advise you not to keep trying to do this to me through the night. You can try, but you won't succeed. The Sien-Leoard Crystal is mine. Fewul is mine. The world is mine. And soon, you will be mine too. Take advantage of my sleeping time to get some rest yourself, because if you want to save yourselves, you're going to need to be fully alert for the day I have in store for you tomorrow."

"Yeah, yeah, whatever you say," Marc muttered bitterly as Lucien allowed himself to drop into a light sleep.

"What do we do now?" Natalie asked.

A few looks were exchanged, and then I spoke up. "I know this idea won't be very popular, but I think we should do what he said and get some sleep. If we use the sleep inducer, we can get four or five hours of good sleep and that will be enough for us to be well-rested tomorrow, and still probably wake up before he does. I don't think we'll be able to steal the Sien-Leoard Crystal from him now."

"Maybe resting is a good idea, but we can't give up on getting the crystal altogether," Marc said fiercely. "I mean, that's basically the same as giving up fighting."

"No it's not," Lillian said, swiping the planner to dismiss the next couple of items on the list. "It just means that we will have to resort to manipulating magic particles after all, and possibly antimagic."

Marc blanched, glancing around the group, but no one seemed surprised by this. "Those are my thoughts as well," James said, "but there's still hope that we can do this without it causing untold mayhem. I agree with John, all of us are very tired, especially me, so let's call it a night and regroup here at…what time would you guys suggest?"

"Maybe six o'clock," Frederic said, checking his watch. "That's about five hours from now. If Lucien's still asleep, we'll have time to have breakfast and shower and the usual morning stuff. If he's awake, we may have to jump straight into action, but the important thing is five hours of sleep. So let's all take a dose of the sleep inducer and get up to bed."

We all took turns zapping ourselves with the sleep inducer and then left the control room together, leaving Katie, Sophie and Erica as the only people holding down the fort. They had been present all along, but even through all the drama, had kept focused on their individual workstations. We took the elevator up to the first floor, and those of us whose bedrooms were on that level (everyone except Lillian and Frederic) got off. I said good night to the others and closed myself in my bedroom. Sleep was crashing in on me already—unsurprising, given how tired I had already been before zapping myself—but I still took the time to undress and get into my pyjamas before climbing into the blessed comfort of my bed.

It was only then that I noticed the letter on my bedside drawers, the letter that Stella had written for me before she had practically thrown her life away. I wanted to read it, but I was way too tired to do it tonight. I therefore settled down in bed and lay on my back, looking up at the dark ceiling, feeling the waves of sleep crashing over me. I was gone in seconds, sleeping dreamlessly and then waking in an almost equally dark bedroom. I sat up and looked around, feeling a little sleepy still but also feeling like I didn't necessarily need to go back to sleep. The sleep inducer had done its job; now it was the crack of dawn, and time to face the new day.

I looked around my dark bedroom as I got dressed, unable to shake the feeling that I were seeing it for the last time. Lucien had promised that today would be a big day, and the planner also promised a big day ahead. We would be using at least some of the magical instruments Natalie had created the night before, and even if we didn't have to resort to using antimagic as a weapon, tampering with magic particles still promised to mess things up royally. It was rational to think that if we weren't able to stay in control of the situation, we could unintentionally destroy our own base; and if not us, Lucien would sure like to do that if he could.

It was six o'clock. Time to go down and get on with it, I thought, wishing that I could take the time to have a shower—I felt pretty dirty after such a long day yesterday—but feeling dirty would be better than falling under Lucien's spell, or worse. But even with that pressure, I had no intention of leaving here without reading Stella's letter to me, especially if it really *did* happen that I wouldn't get another chance to come back up here and get it. I sat down on the side of my bed and took the note, sliding it out of the envelope and unfolding it.

Dear John,

I'm not sure when you'll read this, but I'm writing it on Friday, September 3rd. I can't predict what might have happened between now and then, but my guess is that you're not very happy with me, and that might be an understatement.

At least allow me to tell you that if I am dead, I meant to achieve something with it—something more for others than I could ever have for myself in life. I do hope that I succeeded, but if not, it was still the right thing for me personally, because as I tried to explain to you last night, without you there is nothing left for me in life.

To be honest with you, I'm not sure that there would have been anything left for me even if you weren't going to die in two weeks' time. You probably have some idea of how messed-up I am on the inside from being in my mind all those times, so surely you can understand how I'll never be able to be a normal person. No matter what happens to the world in the future, I would have always carried my past around with me.

I hope that you can forgive me for everything.

All my love,

Stella Lindsay Hammerson

Hmm, I thought.

Hmm, I thought some more.

I slowly slid the note back into the envelope and put it in the top drawer. Then I sat on the side of my bed, thinking about what I had just read. It hadn't really told me much that I hadn't already guessed had been going through Stella's mind, or that she had told me herself before she had died. She had written that not to enlighten me, per se, but to try to make me feel better. I did understand how she felt; I still didn't believe that justified doing what she had done, especially with the knowledge gifted to me by hindsight—that it had made no difference in the end— but I couldn't judge her for feeling the way she had. How could I, when I had no prospects of a long life waiting for me?

That thought brought on an interesting question. Given that I now had perhaps nine or ten days left to live, did it absolutely have to be nine or ten days? I knew for sure that I wouldn't live past that time, the exact time of which I still couldn't quite calculate, but what about before then? What about today, or this coming week? What would happen to my soul if I died today instead of when I was supposed to? My guess was that nothing would happen differently, that the two week period was only a maximum time I could spend here, and not a definite time that couldn't be cut short should something go wrong.

If that were the case, then I needed to take advantage of this moment of freedom to do something—something that really ought to be done sometime before I died, and preferably at a time when it might make a difference. Thankfully, as it had been when I had gone to talk to Lisa the night before last, I only needed an instant to do what I needed to do...

Third Interlude: Unholy Mary

I was back in the place again—that place of nothingness. I wasn't standing, sitting or lying; I was only existing. I wasn't alone in the place, for I could sense the presence of others around me, and I could reach out to them if I chose. This time it would be different; I knew what I was doing, sure, but unlike last time, my business would require me to look for someone totally unfamiliar. Would I have to wake every single soul from whatever sleep normally occupied them, or would I be able to identify them without having to disturb their peace?

As carefully as I could—grateful that I could take all the time I needed, time not existing in this place, of course—I began to reach out to those souls I could feel around me. It didn't take very many tries before I determined that unfortunately, it wouldn't be possible to find the one I was looking for without disturbing everyone else I found along the way. As long as they existed in their state of eternal sleep, no part of the personality they'd had in life could be sensed in any way; and even once awake and forced to interact with me, many of them were unwilling to give me any idea as to who they were.

After I'd done this a few times, and had started to feel terribly guilty for what I was doing to these souls, I gave up on this approach and tried to think of something else I could do. That probably required engaging with my brain, the one back in my body, existing at a specific point within the space-time continuum; and doing this probably actually cost me a moment, perhaps only a fraction of a second, in real time—though I was so busy with what I was doing that I hardly noticed.

When I had come to the place the last time I had found Lisa immediately, most likely because I recognised her from interacting with her in this form the first time. There was probably a chance I could repeat the process with my mother's soul, given that I had seen her as a ghost earlier in the year, so surely I would recognise her soul now if I happened to touch it. That would definitely be something worth trying, but it wasn't my business today. I needed to touch a soul with whom I had never interacted in any form, and the only fast way for me to find that soul would be if I could quickly find someone who *had* interacted with that soul; and luckily for me, Lisa could once again provide me with what I needed.

I reached out for Lisa, and just like last time, found her immediately. Just like last time, she recognised me immediately, and at the same time not quite immediately; and as she did, the place of no description once again shifted into the form of the cave.

"John Playman," she observed for the third time.

"Hi, Lisa," I said.

"You're here too," she said sadly. "I'm sorry."

"Me too," I said, noting that this conversation could go exactly as the previous one had if I let it. Lisa had no way of retaining her memories from visit to visit, so even though I already knew how this worked and wanted to get to the point of why I was here, I would have to walk her through all that she would need to know before she would be willing to help me.

She paused a moment that wasn't really a moment at all but could have been any length of time, before saying, "You are whole, unlike me."

"Yeah, I'm still alive. I came back four days ago."

"Then I guess you may have a week left, or a little more. What happened?"

"Er"—I hesitated. I really didn't want to have to go through all this, but I couldn't imagine her wanting to help me unless she understood, so —"there was an attack and I got caught in the middle of it while trying to save some people. The war against the Hammersons isn't going well; they have almost all the magic now, and James—do you remember James Thomas?"

"Yes," she said, and like last time, she pictured his face. It didn't happen as quickly as before, though, making me wonder if I could help her regain more lost memories the longer I talked to her and got her to try to remember things from her life. It might have been worth trying if I didn't have more pressing business, and if I didn't have the lurking worry that I would end up making her sadder by forcing her to remember more things.

"He has told us that the only thing we can do to make things better is destroy the Magic Crystals," I told her. "That's how bad it is, but we have some concerns. We think we know how we can destroy the crystals, but there may be other consequences we can't foresee."

Lisa took some time, which was no time at all, of course, to process this. Finally she said, "Okay, I understand. Losing magic would be a great loss, but if that is the only way to keep it out of the hands of those who would do evil, it makes sense."

"I need you to help me."

I felt her give me some sort of motionless shrug of sadness. "There is nothing I can do to help you with this."

If I got her to think harder, I could get her to remember the thesis she had read which had pointed us towards antimagic, but that wasn't the help I needed this time. "I need you to locate Mary Sien for me; she is the only one who might be able to tell me what I need to know."

Comprehension didn't come all at once, but as it dawned on her who I was referring to, I felt her cringe. "You don't want that. You *really* don't want that."

"I need it, though," I insisted. "Please help me. I can't find her on my own, and I believe you can."

I knew so, because her diary had said that she'd encountered Mary Sien right here in this cave, so unless Lisa herself had been mistaken, or I was mistaken about how this whole thing worked…but I wasn't going to tell Lisa any of this. She didn't need to know how much I'd figured out, given that she would forget it all as soon as I left; and she certainly didn't know that I, along with several others, had read her most private thoughts —not that she would likely care at this juncture, but still.

A struggle of wills began between Lisa and me, but it didn't last very long. Lisa had almost no will of her own, compared to my exceedingly strong will, fed to me by my humanity and the seriousness of the situation awaiting me back in my life. When she gave in, warning me that she herself wished not to have to interact with Sien if possible, it transpired that Lisa didn't actually have the ability to search Sien out on her own. Only with the little point of memory Lisa's soul possessed was I able to go forth and seek the soul of Mary Sien, quickly locating the one which had felt familiar to Lisa and bringing it forth to the cave. This cave had been Sien's memory originally, so it seemed only fitting that we should meet here.

What followed was unnerving in a way that I could never find words to accurately describe, although I was asked many times by the living to do so. Sien didn't know who I was, but she knew well enough what was happening; perhaps she was able to retain slightly more memory than other souls in this place. Communicating with her was odd because we didn't speak the same language, and yet we were able to understand each other as if we did. But the most apparent thing about her soul, which came through loud and clear the moment I dared to disturb her, was a terrible and malicious glee, as if she were pleased to note that someone else had dared to sacrifice part of their soul to continue living just a tiny bit longer.

It took some effort to face her, and given that I still had some part of my humanity about me, I wasn't above feeling fear and even a touch of disgust. Nevertheless I faced her, and I said to her, "I know who you are, creator of the crystals, and I seek your knowledge and wisdom."

That got her attention, but not all at once. She immediately understood that I was speaking the truth when I said I knew who she was, but she had to ponder over the rest of it before she understood my meaning. It was as though she had spent so long here in the timeless void that she had forgotten her life's work, and all she knew now was this eternal damnation. When she *did* remember the Magic Crystals, however, her glee changed to a more genuine joy, as well as considerable pride as she recalled what she and Leoard had done. I knew she was recalling it because she was sharing the memories with me, and I knew she was sharing the memories with me because I had sought her out in the knowledge that she had created the crystals and was responsible for much of the magic that existed in the world I knew. In short, she thought I was worshipping her, and was behaving accordingly.

It was a good thing I had experience with Honnies, because it prepared me for what I needed to do next. I tempered the story I was about to tell her by showing her some of the good things magic had brought to the world, such as the old Woodward living quarters, and backpacks whose insides could carry an almost infinite amount of content. It was a waste of effort, though, as Sien seemed to regard such trivial uses of magic as a waste of a precious resource. I had to remind myself that it had been Leoard who had preferred magic to be used for things like that, while Sien's visions had been much grander. She was much more likely to sympathise with what the Hammersons had tried to do, which would make this next part a little tricky, but I still thought I could get this little slideshow to where I needed it to go.

I showed her the Hammersons, both from fifty years ago and the present year, and all they had done to build up their army, including their global network of bases, the Hammerheart Highway, and the many magical devices they had created to arm their foot soldiers. This impressed her, until I showed her what the agonator did, and how much the Hammersons and their minions had enjoyed using that terrible curse. From there, I progressed to everything else the war had brought about, making sure to underline all throughout the point that magic was the one thing enabling all of this to happen.

Sien did not respond directly to this—at least not in any way I could sense—but I knew she was still there and still paying attention to me. I hadn't thought about exactly how I was going to order this story to get to the ultimate point, so I merely continued to emphasise the suffering that was taking place as a direct result of magic, and making the point that more and more of the magic in the world had fallen into the hands of those who would wield it to do harm. At this point, I finally got a response from Sien, and this time, rather than sharing distant memories or thoughts, she spoke to me directly.

"It is the nature of people you object to, not the presence of magic. People will always bring suffering on others, using whatever tools at their disposal, to achieve an advantage for themselves. Magic may increase suffering, but it also increases your ability to fight back."

It was so weird. She wasn't speaking or even thinking in English, and yet I understood that to be exactly her meaning. If I'd had a head to shake, I would have shaken it then, because her argument fell down the moment all the power was on one side, and no power was on the other. Instead, I confirmed that I was aware of the problem regarding human nature, but it wasn't enough to justify the role of magic in the present disaster, because magic wasn't just enabling the suffering of countless nameless numbers around the world: It was on the verge of destroying the world and wiping out humanity altogether.

That gave her food for thought, and she pondered over how to respond. Finally, she asked me a question which allowed me to hope: are you sure?

In response, I ran her through the decision tree, as I understood it, which James had used to arrive at the conclusion that destroying the Magic Crystals would be the only way to prevent their enormous power from doing irrevocable damage to the world. It was the only option because we had already tried to defeat one tyrant, only for another to rise up and fill the void. It was the only option because attempting to hide the crystals would only put off the destruction for a time, so that future generations would ultimately pay for our folly—and that was assuming we could even get our hands on all the crystals in the first place. And finally, it was the only option because if we didn't do something immediately, there would be no one left with any magic with which to fight anymore.

Sien understood. I could tell that she got the point. As great as magic was, it wasn't worth losing everything for. Her response, however, was much less encouraging: "If you are proposing to destroy the Magic Crystals, I don't know how, or even if, it can be done."

If she didn't know that, then she didn't know about antimagic. And if she didn't know about antimagic, then she almost certainly wouldn't know what would happen if we attempted to use it. That probably made this whole endeavour pointless, and I was almost about to thank her anyway and leave the place to return to my physical body before another idea occurred to me, and I paused.

"My friends and I *do* know how to destroy the Magic Crystals, but it will be incredibly dangerous. Just obtaining the knowledge we needed required me to sacrifice my life so that I could come here. We swore an oath that if we were willing to do what it took to get to this point, that we would have the full power of Sien and Leoard on our side; and we know that it worked because the oath was etched in our blood. Does any of this sound familiar to you? And if so, what do we need to do before we can count on your help?"

I waited for Sien's response, and she weighed my words. She didn't immediately know what I was talking about, so I showed her the stone tablet James had used. She recognised it almost immediately, and then comprehended what we must have done.

"Your goal in all of this is to end the power of the crystals," she observed, and I confirmed this. Then, I waited for her answer...

Part 4: Things Fall Apart

Chapter 24: Establishing the Beam

I went straight down to the control room, catching the elevator at the same time as Amelia, who didn't look tired, per se, but certainly she looked worried. Marc, Peter and James were already in the control room when we arrived, and they were the only ones present. I looked quickly across the various screens along the control panel and was relieved to see that Lucien was still asleep, where he had hopefully been since we had left him hours earlier.

The first words from James confirmed this, and then he added, "The three girls left a few minutes ago—I told them to get some sleep, just in case something happens later in the day that will require us to evacuate the base—but I didn't tell them that part. They've kept up the resistance through the night, but it still looks like the Hammerhearts and Fewul have pretty much quashed South America, and at their current rate of progress, they will have done Africa by this time tomorrow. Even if we can stop Lucien before that happens, he's destabilised that region so much that it's gonna be chaos no matter what happens."

Frederic Woodward entered the room just as James was finishing this update, so James began to repeat all that he had told us. As he was winding up, the door opened and Lillian shambled into the room, looking more tired than all the rest of us despite the best efforts of the sleep inducer—maybe she was just getting too old for this, I thought worriedly. James began to tell her everything he had told the rest of us, and then turned back to the screens to have a look at the still sleeping forms of Lucien and Lena.

"We're lucky, because we have a chance now to talk strategy before he wakes up, and we need to make the most of it."

That was when the door opened once again and Natalie entered, looking a little more put-together than the rest of us, and I suspected that she had taken a little extra time in her bedroom before coming down just so that she wouldn't look like she'd slept on a park bench. She needn't have bothered, of course, and it may have cost us about a minute as James quickly went over it for a fourth time, but at least now we were all here and we could get on with it.

"Okay, so the Sien-Leoard Crystal is now inside Lucien's body," Marc reminded us. "Can anyone think of a way we can get it out of him? Anything that he might not have already thought of himself?"

"You mean besides manipulating magic particles?" I said.

Marc shrugged, his expression unmoving, but I knew it was deliberate control. "Let's try to think of other options first."

"Well, this is more James's area of expertise," Peter said, "but let me see if I can break it down. We *could* cut the crystal out of Lucien's body, or try to burn it out the way that Hammerson did to your father, Marc, but that would require us to knock him unconscious for long enough to do that, and knocking him unconscious would require us to find a way through all the various protections he has around himself which anticipate that we will try to knock him out, plus it requires us to find a way to deal with Fewul such that Lucien himself is unaware that we are dealing with Fewul so that he can't just call it back—"

"Breathe, Pete," James said, suppressing a smile.

Peter took a deep breath and concluded, "And unless I'm mistaken, we've already tried most of that. Does anyone have anything to add?"

"Don't forget the pixies," Amelia pointed out. "Even if we do find a way to knock him out, we'll have to deal with them again, and I don't think there's any way to prepare for that."

"It's also worth reminding you that we have run through all the ideas on John's planner which *don't* involve magic particles," Lillian added.

"That means there probably *isn't* anything else we can do," James said flatly. "So, show of hands, who here thinks we should try something involving magic particles?"

Seven hands immediately went into the air. Marc looked around at us all, shrugged, and joined the club. "Fine, if this is how it's going then I won't object. But James, even if we *do* use magic particles, what do we do with them? I would have thought sucking the magic out of his crystal chips was the obvious first step, but that isn't going to accomplish anything now that he has the crystal inside his body."

"Perhaps we try to suck all his magic out, Sien-Leoard Crystal and all?" Peter suggested.

"Does anyone else feel like that would be extremely dangerous, trying to extract that much magic all at once?" I asked.

Frederic nodded. "I'm thinking we start by attempting to suck the magic out of Lucien himself. Not necessarily targeting his crystal chips or the Sien-Leoard Crystal, but by focusing on the enchantments he has placed upon himself. If we can do so in a way that he can't detect, we may be able to remove enough of his protections to make him more vulnerable to standard attacks."

That idea sounded good, and all the others seemed to agree, including Marc, but I could see a flaw. "But he could just replace his protections the instant that he detects something wrong, and even if he doesn't immediately notice all his protections gone, he's guaranteed to notice his Honnie mind disappearing. And I don't think there's any way to control which of his protections we take at a time; all the stuff we did yesterday made it look like manipulating magic particles would be pretty indiscriminate when it comes to what that magic actually does. Does—does any of that make sense?"

"It does," James said heavily, "and there's also Fewul, who might detect what we're doing and try to warn Lucien. With all that, though, I'm thinking it's probably a good place to start. Where's that planner of yours, John? Can you remember what was the next item on the list?"

"I think it was to attack his crystal chips," I said, "but it never accounted for him swallowing the Sien-Leoard Crystal. I'm not sure if that fact changes things now."

The planner had been put away inside the cabinet. James had gone to it as I was speaking and was presently returning with the device, reading the screen as he walked and not watching where he was going, such that his foot caught the leg of a vacant chair and he very nearly went down before regaining his balance and sitting heavily down in his seat.

"So, it looks like John's right," he said, scrolling down the list a short way, "and furthermore, there are no specific items in here that address the magical protections he put around himself directly. Did you not think of that, John?"

I hesitated. "Well…I thought of it in the early part," I said a little defensively, "but no—I guess it didn't occur to me to attack those magic particles, probably because I couldn't visualise exactly where those particles are—and to be honest, I still can't. I mean, I know some of them are probably placed on his person, but what about all those alerts that link him with Fewul, for example? Where would *those* magic particles be?"

"Most likely, they would still be on his person," Frederic said, "and even if part of the enchantment is placed somewhere else, it still needs to be able to link to his body, in the same way that the crystal chips link him to the Sorcerous Crystals. I think that attacking his person is still the best thing to try. What you said earlier about him detecting it is a risk, but I don't think there is a single thing he could do to actually stop us, save place further enchantments on himself which would only give us more magic to suck up."

"That has to be an acceptable risk, so long as he remains ignorant of magic particles," Lillian said. "Before we do that, though, can anyone here anticipate how he might block his magic particles escaping his body, should he somehow figure out that's what we're doing?"

No less than five people opened their mouths, about to speak the obvious answer, and then everyone faltered. He couldn't use magic to effectively stop us using this tactic for the reason Frederic had already pointed out. Furthermore, magic particles, so far as we had observed them, didn't necessarily have to be constrained by physical barriers. Theoretically, if Lucien locked himself away in a steel box with no air hole and we were on the outside with no way of getting in, we could still attack his magic particles, so long as we had a device strong enough to suck particles from that distance. Admittedly, the flaw of such a device was that it would probably suck up a lot more of the magic in the air before it touched Lucien, but it would eventually get to him.

Finally, James said, "He wouldn't be able to block it altogether. His only strategy that could work would be to go immediately on the offensive, but if he couldn't land a hit on us, there would be nothing at all that he could do."

Amelia shook her head. "In that scenario, there is one thing that he could use to bring us down, and it's the same thing we would use to bring him down if he *did* figure out magic particles. I don't know how scientific Lucien's mind is, but if he is capable of understanding that magic can exist in a particle form, then he may be able to make the jump to antimagic. We all know he would use antimagic against us if he could figure out how, and that would leave us having to use antimagic ourselves, because there is literally no other weapon that could stand up to it. And we all know what would happen then, right?"

"Apocalypse," Marc breathed, his eyes very wide.

A silence followed before Peter said, "Let's not forget that magic particles are beyond the ability of magic to manipulate. That probably means that it would be very difficult for Lucien to come by the information. Unless he is somehow inspired to read the same thesis we did, the thought wouldn't naturally occur to him, and as for Fewul"—he hesitated—"well, I guess it is technically possible that Fewul could tell him how magic works on the base level, but only if Lucien asked the right question. Amelia's right about how badly things will go if Lucien learns the truth, but let's remember that we basically have no other choice at this point—unless you consider surrender to still be a valid option."

I didn't, of course, but I was surprised at how many people paused for a moment to consider Peter's words. Of course, if it were a choice between a dystopian paradise with Lucien ruling and controlling everyone and everything, and a wasteland where magic had destroyed all life and perhaps the foundations of the planet itself…when you looked at it like that, the prospect of taking the risk was a lot more daunting.

It was Frederic who spoke. "It is a big risk, but Peter's words make me think that we have a good shot at making it work for the better, so long as we are able to attack him from a position which he cannot strike back. I vote in favour of attacking the magic particles in his body. All those in favour?"

The vote wasn't very enthusiastic this time, but it was a clean sweep all the same. I checked my watch and saw that it was 6:50 AM; I glanced at the control panel and incredibly, Lucien and Lena were still asleep. Good.

"In that case, Natalie, you had better go and get your stuff—just the relevant ones," James told her, and those of us in the know knew he meant the particle devices, and not the antimagic devices.

"What?" Marc said, looking around at Natalie, and then at James. "What stuff?"

"Natalie already created some devices that could deal with magic particles last night," James said, meeting Marc's eyes unflinchingly, "so you won't have to worry about doing it now. We always hoped that we wouldn't need to use them, but the plan called for having them on standby, just in case a tough decision needed to be made in a hurry, and we couldn't afford to use the complexity of the devices as an excuse not to do it."

Marc considered this, his eyes narrowing. "And would I be right in thinking that you went out of your way to *not* tell me this earlier?"

"You would be right," James said evenly, "and I make no apologies for that. It needed to be done, Marc, and it's time for you to get with the game. If we can't unite behind this plan of action, we're doomed."

Marc took a moment to weigh his words before saying, "Fine, I won't say another word about it, and I've already agreed this morning that we should try to take Lucien's magic particles, so that should be enough."

James relaxed visibly, and I noticed Amelia and Frederic also exhaling, as though they had been holding their breath through that conversation. I felt a little better myself, but not entirely. I didn't miss the calculating look on Marc's face, nor did I miss the fact that he completely neglected to mention antimagic. That could have been because James also hadn't mentioned antimagic, but I had a feeling that if we had to resort to using antimagic, Marc would put up a much greater resistance, and that might include using his own magic to prevent us from taking that course.

A few minutes passed before Natalie returned to the control room, carrying a few different devices in her arms. Before that happened, though, we were able to observe Lucien emerging from sleep and getting out of bed. He rose quickly, shaking off all remnants of sleep and coming fully awake and alert in seconds. Perhaps on some other day he would stay in bed and enjoy the company of the woman beside him, but he had big plans for this day, and I dreaded to think what they might be. Lena came awake too, and when Lucien went into the bathroom to have a shower, she followed. Once again, we were treated to a full and unobstructed view of both of their naked bodies, but that was when Natalie returned, so we all had an excuse to turn away from the screen— save Peter, who took the job of keeping an eye on Lucien, just in case.

On the whole, I had now reached a stage in my thinking where Lena had no power over me; I'd seen so much of her body in recent days that it somehow didn't seem attractive to me anymore, even though her body itself was the same as it had always been. It could have been because of how she was behaving toward us; it could have been how she was behaving toward Lucien; it could have been the fact that I'd been with her, and as good as it had been in its own way, I didn't have to wonder about what I was missing; it could have been the fact that I was going to die in nine or ten days, and desire for a girl paled into insignificance compared to that; it could even have been, though it probably wasn't, that I was just starting to grow up after all. Most likely, it was a combination of some, or all, of the above. Whatever; it didn't matter anymore, except that I was able to focus on the issue at hand without my eyes wanting to go back to the display screen.

Meanwhile, Natalie was laying out the devices she had brought down and was explaining how they worked. They all essentially had the same functionality: They would suck the magic particles out of the surroundings and store those particles inside a crystal contained inside it. The smallest of the devices was specifically designed to target a person or a device; the vacuum would only affect a narrow beam and a distance of no more than seven or eight feet, though it would work more effectively for the particles closer than the ones further away.

The second device was a fair bit larger and took the shape of some sort of megaphone rather than a typical magical device. Natalie explained that it had the same functionality as the smaller device, but a much larger beam which would spread out as it got further away from the device, and a much greater target distance—up to a hundred feet. The third device was actually slightly smaller than the megaphone; it wouldn't have been entirely inaccurate to say that it was shaped like a penis, but it would have been more accurate to say that it was shaped like a microphone. It was the most powerful of the devices she had created: it was omni-directional and it would affect a distance of kilometres rather than feet or metres.

"In other words, it's a last resort," Natalie said. "If we have to use this then we have to expect to lose some of our own magic as well, since the only way to get out of its beam is to get a long way away from it. I've created a remote control that can activate it from a distance, but since I don't dare activate it using magic, we have to rely on radio waves, and there's no guarantee that the signal will properly reach the device, or that it won't be triggered by a signal coming from someone else entirely. I did my best to work around that, but there's no way to be absolutely sure, without using magic on the device itself, that it will work."

"Yeah, definitely a last resort," James said. "Also, I'm not sure if anyone else has thought of this but it's a major pickle: We can't put any magical protections around any of these devices to stop Lucien from finding them, without the devices eating through the protection. How on earth are we gonna stop *that* from happening?"

A silence filled the room as several people opened their mouths, and then closed them again as they realised their ideas wouldn't work. Sure, there was nothing to be done about the microphone of doom, as I now found myself thinking of it, but the other two had the advantage that you would be safe from them if you stayed behind them. Was there any way to use that fact in our favour? I couldn't see how, because any shields, invisibility or untraceability spells would have to wrap around the whole device for them to work at all—wouldn't they?

Well, it didn't have to be so, apparently, not when you had a skilled Sorcerer in your midst. After some experimentation, Frederic was able to use the magic enhancer to create a special wrapping spell which he put around the two devices, whereby the magic, though it would affect the whole device it was touching, would only be stored at the back of it. We were then able to toggle the visibility and untraceability of the device from behind it. Doing so threw up another flaw that Natalie hadn't thought of: There was no way to make the devices invisible without making them invisible to ourselves. The person using the device to attack Lucien would be able to do it by touch, but they wouldn't be able to see what they were doing; it wouldn't be safe to put any magic around the device and a person at the same time.

By the time we had prepared as much as we could, Lucien was in the dining hall eating his breakfast. Lena wasn't with him; she had stayed upstairs and was presently having her own shower. While Frederic had been working, I had eavesdropped on some of their conversation. Lena had been trying to get him to pay attention to her in the shower, and he'd told her that he had a very busy day ahead of him and that he would be able to give her all the attention she craved once things settled down. She was pretty peeved by this, but almost immediately complied with grace, making me think he had used his Honnie mind on her again. Now, as he ate, he looked deep in thought, and the way his expression ticked made me think, though obviously I couldn't be sure, that he was thinking about us, and how he would go about punishing us for all the trouble we had caused him last night.

"Okay, so someone's going to have to go out there," Amelia was saying, "and whoever it is has to feel confident in their ability to use this thing by touch alone, and absolutely cannot put any part of their body, not so much as a fingernail, in a place where the device might affect it. Any volunteers?"

In fact, everyone other than James and Lillian put their hand up for the job. Smiling a little, Marc said, "If this weren't such a serious job, I would suggest a game of rock-paper-scissors, but I think we should do this as quickly as possible, so I'll count myself out. Anyone wanna join me?"

Peter put his hand down at once, and then said, "Actually, if the person is going to have to handle that device with care the whole time, then just in case there is some sort of danger, it should probably be someone who will be able to act quickly with his own magic. That's you, John."

"What?" I said in surprise, then understood. "Oh—yeah."

"It's a good idea," Amelia said, putting her hand down as well. "Are you up for it, John? You did put your hand up for it."

I shrugged. "I wasn't expecting to get it for that reason, but yeah, I'm willing to do it. I *do* have a question, though. If someone fires a magic spell at me from in front, how will the device behave?"

"Honestly, I'm not quite sure," Natalie said slowly. "I would think that if you can catch the spell in the beam of the device, the magic would just get sucked up and not touch you at all, but I'm not sure how it would behave if the spell contains more magic than the device can handle all at once."

"That makes it sound like it could work as something of a shield," James said, "but it's a pretty small shield, and the beam of the smaller device is just too narrow. In that case, it would actually be a lucky hit if Lucien managed to hit it; more likely the spell would zoom past the device and hit you, John, so I would advise getting the hell out of their instead."

"Well, I see no reason why we can't test it first, as long as we do it quickly," Amelia suggested.

We did so, me standing with the smallest of the magic sucking devices, and Peter standing opposite me with a solid-outliner, a nice safe distance away. The space between us was completely devoid of all magical devices, anything that could be considered a magical device, and all people—they'd all gathered behind me. Natalie stood just behind me where she could look over my shoulder and see the device as she showed me how it worked.

"It's pretty straightforward," she said, and as important as this was, I couldn't help wondering if she was as aware of how close we were standing together as I was. If so, she made no sign of it, and I did my level best to follow her lead. "The red switch just near your thumb there will turn it on and off. The one above it toggles the intensity of the magic vacuum by increasing or decreasing power to it; it's set to medium at the moment, and that's probably the best setting if you want to keep it targeted on Lucien without it taking too long, but you might want to put it on high if you come under attack because that'll make it cope with weapon fire better. The drawback of the high setting is that it makes the device less targeted and increases the range."

I took all this in, glancing down at the switch she was speaking of. Putting it on the high setting would require me to flick it to the right, judging by the tiny 'H' to the right of the switch. I closed my eyes and felt it with my thumb, committing the feel of it to memory. The device was small enough that the best way to use it was just to do everything with the thumb of the hand holding it.

"And the display," she went on, "will only show anything when the device is turned on, so that it saves battery power. When it's on, there'll be two numbers: one to gauge how much magic it has inside it, and one to say how much, if anything, is currently being sucked into the device. I guess it'll be pretty useless once the device is invisible, though."

I shrugged. "Are we ready to try this thing?"

"I am," Peter said from across the room. "Let's hurry up here before Lucien finishes his breakfast already."

Natalie took a step to the side so that she would be directly behind me, and not in Peter's line of fire should he miss me. I flicked the device on and nervously waited to see if anything would happen. The display jumped for a moment, as if it had found a loose magic particle in the air, but then it settled down. Anxiety increasing, I flicked the power to high and watched again. Nothing.

I nodded to Peter, who took careful aim with his solid-outliner and fired; it just missed the device and hit my wrist, the white stuff beginning to spread over it immediately. He quickly fired again, probably to undo what he'd just done, but this time his aim was perfect. The magic vacuum caught the white line in mid-air and it hung there, as if linking the two devices. I glanced down at the display, and yes: both numbers had changed. The incoming magic level was constant, but the magic stored inside the device was rising rapidly as the particles continued to stream from Peter's hand into mine.

Then we ran into a problem we hadn't anticipated at all. Peter couldn't turn the solid-outliner off. Normally once it had hit its target, the solid-outliner switched itself off, but that wasn't happening this time, and it had no setting within itself to allow a manual override. All Peter could do was continue pressing the button, which caused the device to try to renew its attack, but it couldn't do that either. The device had malfunctioned in a way which its designers, the Hammersons, couldn't possibly have predicted. By the time we realised this, it was too late for me to turn my device off, as the thicky prison had entirely wrapped up my hand and was now spreading down my arm.

Marc and James came to the rescue. Marc used the Hero Crystal to vanish the device in Peter's hand, and once the device disappeared, so did the white line linking it to my hand. At the same time, James shot a solid-outliner at my arm—nowhere near the device in my hand—and the thicky prison disappeared, freeing both me and the device. I looked down at the display and saw that it was no longer sucking magic, but that it hadn't lost any of what it had already obtained.

"Well, it worked in a sense," James said, pocketing his solid-outliner, "but if it's gonna behave like that when you get attacked, I still say you're better off dodging. Besides, if you can get close enough to your attackers, you might be able to suck the magic out of their weapons before they get a chance to use them anyway."

"Okay," I said, and took a deep breath. I was probably as ready as I could be. "Let's go."

I switched off the magic vacuum, put the usual protections around myself (untraceability, invisibility, soundproofing), allowed Frederic to put those protections on the device using his special wrapper, and went to stand in the corner to be let out of the room. The rest of the group arranged themselves in the usual positions around the control panel, with James once again at the controls.

"You ready to go, John?" he called to me.

"Remember, we'll contact you telepathically if we think of something in here we think you should know," Amelia told me, "and we'll only draw you back in if it looks like you're in danger, or if the job gets done."

"Sure, yeah, no problem," I said, and then James pushed a button in front of him.

Well, this is certainly one of the stupider things we've done in recent times, I thought to myself, and suppressed a smile. I'd been expecting to emerge in the dining hall, a few paces from where Lucien was eating breakfast, but I had instead been dropped in Lucien's bedroom, the scene of the previous night's battles. We had been watching Lucien's movements on one of the spyers, completely forgetting that we actually had to follow him manually in our base when he moved around. It would have been funny if it hadn't wasted however much time it took me to get down there, and indeed I did have to fight down the urge to laugh. I couldn't see Lena from here but I could hear her moving around in the bathroom, either drying herself or doing her hair or putting on makeup or whatever, and that meant she would hear me if I made any sound. And then I remembered that I had a soundproof barrier around me, and the thought occurred to me—I must have *really* gotten up on the stupid side of the bed this morning.

I didn't dare teleport inside the Hammerheart base, nor did I want to waste time figuring how to quietly and covertly get from here to the dining room, so I slid into my shadow and then dived through the floor, using the flying skills I had acquired to ignore everything my brain was telling me about how gravity and solid floors were supposed to work. I had to judge my location as best I could because the things I was seeing made no sense—that was, until I dropped through the high ceiling of the Worship Hall. I flew through the open doors and around the corner into the dining room, looking around and spotting Lucien immediately; he was sitting alone at the small table which had, once upon a time, been reserved for the Hammersons only, on a raised platform so that if he cared to, he could look down on the rest of his minions.

I landed behind him and then left my shadow, no more than a few paces from him, well within range of the magic vacuum, but also within range of Lucien himself if he pulled back his chair and turned around more quickly than I could get out of his way. I would have to be ready for that but in the meantime, I took a moment to contact Amelia, who had implied that she would be in charge of the telepathy, to let her know that I was with Lucien, and that they had better bring the base down here as quickly as they could because I couldn't afford to wait for them.

I did get a response from Amelia, but by then, I had already flicked the power switch back to medium and turned the magic vacuum on. It took seconds for something to happen, but it wasn't what I'd been expecting. Loud running footsteps sounded to my right, and looking in that direction, my stomach did a backflip of nerves. Stella was hurrying as fast as she could through the dining room, those bright eyes of hers fixed on Lucien and a look of urgency on her face. Whatever had happened, it was serious enough that Fewul felt it required Lucien's immediate attention, but not quite urgent enough for her to break her cover as Stella and simply appear beside Lucien.

Lucien had also heard the footsteps; he turned, the bit of his expression I could see ready to scold whoever was disturbing the peace of breakfast, and then froze in place as he realised who it was running towards him. By the time Stella had practically bounded up the stairs to the highest platform where Lucien sat, he had composed himself. I, meanwhile, was caught in a terrible mental struggle of what to do now. I felt pretty sure I would be safe from Fewul's attacks, if Fewul *did* attack, but the question was, what could Fewul know? How much awareness did Fewul have of magic particles? If magic couldn't manipulate magic particles, did that put them outside Fewul's ability to comprehend? Or, was Fewul above the usual restrictions of magic? Could she perhaps reverse what I had just started doing to Lucien in such a way that I would lose my magic instead of him?

"What's happening?" Lucien asked her without preamble when she stopped beside him.

I held my breath as Stella appeared to lean down, as though to whisper something conspiratorial to him, and said, "Something is attacking you, Master."

Lucien hesitated, and although I could no longer see any of his face, I could feel his irritation. Finally, he said, "Of course I'm being attacked; it comes with the position. Either be specific or let me finish my breakfast in peace."

"I can't be specific, Master. It is something I cannot identify. It is stranger than anything I have ever known."

Lucien heaved a sigh. "Okay, fine. At least tell me what little you are observing that makes you think I am under attack."

"There are fluctuations in the power emitted by your crystal chips," she said. "They are behaving unstably, and their connection to the Sorcerous Crystals seems to be fraying, though they haven't broken altogether. The magic you have put on your body is behaving similarly."

A silence followed this, unless you counted the frantic beating of my heart which was pounding through my head; I was amazed that neither of them could hear it. It felt like it ought to be loud enough to pass through the soundproof barrier around me.

"Can you think of any way that they could do what they are doing?" he asked in a hiss.

"There is no way they could be behind this," she said, "not unless they have found a source of magic even greater than me. I don't have the power to break the crystal chips, nor does the Sien-Leoard Crystal, or any of the other crystals."

"Well if not them, who?" Lucien hissed frantically.

Fewul hesitated then, and somehow, I had a feeling I knew what was coming—not the true explanation of magic particles, but something else I would prefer Lucien not to know. If there is a God up there, I thought, looking up towards the ceiling, please don't let Fewul say what I think she's about to say. Sadly, God didn't hear me.

"A power may be gathering around you," she said quietly, "a power that commands all magic, including my own, and if what I suspect is true, it may have aligned itself with your enemies. There was a certain ritual created by Sien and Leoard just prior to their deaths, which can bring their power forth if certain conditions are met. It does not give them full control of all the magic in the world, but it will give them a power much greater than anything we can stand up to."

"And what power is that?" Lucien hissed back, and the fury in his voice was unmistakable.

"The power to bend fate to their will," she told him, "the power to dictate the final outcome, if not all the details along the way. It will put fate in their hands."

A stunned silence followed as Lucien took this in. I could see only two ways he might react to this news: either jump up and send his magic forth in such a blast of fury that the whole Chopville base might disintegrate around him, or decide to be patient and wait to see if Fewul was right, and to not allow himself to worry about something that may or may not be actually happening. Thankfully, he chose the second option.

"I can't feel anything unusual happening inside my body," Lucien told her. "Are you absolutely sure that something is happening to my magic?"

"Certain, Master. I can feel it happening even as we speak."

"But how?" he breathed. "I mean, even if they *can* control fate, you said yourself that they can't control the details along the way. That means that in order for them to get the outcome they want, they still have to stay inside the boundaries of what is actually *possible*."

"That is true, Master, which means that what they're doing *must* be possible," Fewul said, "and simply outside of our ability to comprehend it."

"Which also means that we still don't have any proof that they're actually controlling fate, when they could just as easily have gotten lucky and stumbled over a technique I haven't thought of yet," he said smoothly, appearing to relax. "Please continue to monitor my magic, and if anything else unusual happens, besides what is happening now, let me know. Otherwise, I'd like to be left alone now and for you to go back to your previous orders."

"As you wish, Master," she said subserviently, and turned to leave. As she descended the steps and headed for the door, running just as fast as when she had arrived, I exhaled, unaware that I had been holding my breath up till that point. That had been a close call, but for now, Lucien continued to be unaware of what we were doing here.

I planted my feet, ready in case Lucien decided to get up, and trained my device on him, continuing to suck the magic out of him.

Chapter 25: Maintaining the Beam

You would be forgiven for thinking that standing behind Lucien, as still as a statue, in full readiness for the moment when he stood up from the table, would be boring. It was anything but, however, on the contrary, it was so stressful that I thought I could feel a headache coming on. I was invisible, but that didn't mean I couldn't disturb a speck of dust that might be seen by someone. I had a soundproof barrier around me, but that didn't mean that shifting my weight in anyway wouldn't cause any kind of vibrations through the floor. I didn't have to worry about my breathing being heard, but I did have to worry about it being felt if I got too close or exhaled too hard.

I had something else to worry about too: I had no idea what the magic vacuum in my hand was doing at this time, if it was still working, or if it had run into a barrier of some sort. I couldn't think what that would be, but Lucien had remained silent and almost unmoving since Fewul had left, save for finishing his breakfast. He was deep in thought, and he could have still been thinking about how he was going to punish us for last night, or perhaps he was now thinking about all the political stuff he would have to do today, and whether or not he should duplicate himself again—but surely at least some part of his mind was concerned by what Fewul had told him.

Not that he could do anything about it, of course. As we'd established, if he tried to stop magic from leaving his body, he would probably only think to use magic to do it, and that magic would just get sucked into the device in my hand along with the rest of it. If he was smart enough to try something more physical and non-magical—an intellectual leap I didn't expect him to make without the knowledge we had discovered the day before—but if he did, it would matter little anyway, as the magic particles would just go through it. That made me wonder how magic particles stayed inside a device once they were put there; didn't that mean that there *were* barriers which could keep them in place? Or was it just that they would stay wherever they were programmed to stay?

No, none of that really mattered at this point. I couldn't afford to let my mind wander off the job. My concern was the device in my hand, and what it was doing right now. If it was still drawing on the magic in and around Lucien, what magic was it touching now? Had it eaten through the protection around him, or were those particles still inside his body? How much longer would it take to deal with the crystal chips? Had it had any effect on the Sien-Leoard Crystal yet? The only information I had to go on was that Lucien continued to behave as if he felt nothing, which may or may not mean that he continued to feel nothing; and Fewul had not reappeared to update him on anything as yet, which could mean that the drawing of magic had stopped—or it could just as easily mean that the rate of magic leaving his body hadn't changed.

In other words, I had bugger all to go on, and I absolutely did not dare make the device visible long enough to look at the screen. If I'd had the magic enhancer with me I might have considered attempting to place an enchantment on the device so that only I could see it—and then I remembered that the device would just suck that magic away. Shut up and stop thinking about it, John; you have a job to do. Maybe so, but it was increasingly difficult to stop my mind from straying to other areas.

Then something else distracted me altogether—a telepathic message reached me from Amelia. In all my thoughts, I'd forgotten that back in the base, those in the control room would have been discussing what was going on, perhaps asking the same questions I was asking and attempting to come up with a solution. One of them had succeeded in using the magic enhancer to connect back to the Sien-Leoard Crystal and check on its magic levels. She tried to explain to me how it worked—something about combining magic and non-magic tools—but it was so thoroughly confusing that when she concluded by telling me that the Sien-Leoard Crystal was so far unaffected, I didn't know if I should believe her.

A minute later, Lucien finally stood up from his table and vanished his plate and the remains of his breakfast. At the same time, I took a step back from him, keeping the beam of the vacuum trained on him as he pushed his chair in and walked towards the steps down from the platform. I followed close behind him, grateful that he wasn't running; if he broke into a sprint, I'd have trouble keeping him within range without also running and then risk colliding with someone or something. As it was, even though we weren't going especially fast, there was something exhausting about keeping a distance of six feet behind him, give or take, and keeping the device pointed at him, when walking normally at the same speed would have been hardly exhausting at all.

A very unpleasant surprise waited for me when we left the dining hall and turned towards the elevators—Stella was standing there waiting for him. I very quickly backed back into the dining room and to the side so that I wouldn't be smack-bang in the middle of the doorway. I didn't dare get into any position where I would risk putting Fewul in the beam of my magic vacuum; there was no telling at all how she might react, but she would definitely notice if she lost so much as a single particle, and it might be enough to give away what we were actually doing here. It meant that I had to remain side-on to Lucien as he paused, frowning at her.

"I'm sure I ordered you to get back out in the world and get on with your job," he said conversationally. "That did happen, didn't it?"

"It did," she conceded, "but this is more important. I must talk to you in private, right now."

"Is it about what you were telling me before?" he asked, continuing towards the elevators and temporarily leaving my range. I had to scramble out of the dining hall, pointing my device off to the side where there weren't any Hammerhearts standing around, before I was able to line Lucien up again from behind.

"Yes, it is," she said, and my heart rate quickened again.

They stepped into the elevator, and I had an instant of indecision. If I stepped in there with them, I would be running an enormous risk to myself, and having the vacuum active while I was in such an enclosed space with them would make it much worse. The only way I'd be able to keep Lucien in the beam without also getting Fewul would be to actually put myself closer to the Beast of Magic. My options were to turn the device off and get in the elevator with them, or not get in the elevator at all; either way, I would have to resume the attack as soon as Lucien got out of the elevator.

I chose the second option, but made a compromise. I flicked the switch on the device to turn it off, sent a rapid telepathic message to Amelia to tell her what I was doing and that she and the others should follow (which they were probably doing anyway), quickly drifted into my shadow, and then darted straight through the elevator's closing doors (not between them, but actually through them). As the elevator began to rise, I made myself rise with it so that I could now listen to the private conversation between Lucien and Fewul.

"What is this emergency now?" he asked sharply. "Have you got anything definite to tell me this time?"

"Only that you have definitely lost all your magic," she replied, and Lucien blanched.

"You're kidding," he said, and a moment later, the elevator lights dimmed and then brightened, and his face flushed. "No, you're wrong; I am still able to do things with magic. What are you on about?"

"That was the Sien-Leoard Crystal," she told him. "It was also being affected by whatever was happening to you, but it only started just as you were leaving the dining hall. Prior to that, whatever was happening was only affecting your own magic—both the crystal chips and the magic you have put around yourself. That magic is all gone now, so you will need to recast your shields before you are attacked, because right now you are completely vulnerable."

Lucien let out a cry of dismay. "*Aaaaaargh*! You're right! My shields are gone!" He paused a moment, and I knew he was taking a moment to protect himself again. Then he said, "How is this possible? You're making it sound like they're actually taking the magic itself, and not just using magic to get inside my shields or overpower them or something."

"That is indeed what they are doing, Master," she said. "The crystal chips are no longer connected to their Sorcerous Crystals, but I am not able to detect where their magic has gone. If it weren't for the Sien-

Leoard Crystal inside you right now, you would have no magic at your disposal."

Lucien's face had gone very pale now. "But—but—I've never heard of this. I didn't know this was possible. What can I do to stop it?"

Fewul hesitated, and Lucien said, "If you know or suspect anything, I demand you speak openly."

That was when the elevator stopped at the top floor and the doors opened onto the empty hallway beyond. Lucien checked to make sure it was empty before stepping out, followed by Fewul, and in turn followed by me. I considered resuming the attack, and then didn't. Better to wait until Fewul had left, or until they started talking about something else. It might be that there wouldn't be another safe chance to resume the attack, but I would worry about that later. For now, I just wanted to know how much Fewul could guess about what we were doing.

"My guess," she finally said, speaking in such a way that if she were human, I would have said that she were very carefully weighing her words to make sure they were entirely accurate, "is that they have found a way to manipulate magic itself. I don't mean using magic the way you and I do, or the way the Seventh Sorcerer does; I mean actually moving the substance of magic around to their will."

Lucien's face lit up with hope, and I knew what he was probably thinking. "You can do that? How come you never mentioned this before? Can it be done over great distances?"

"Don't get your hopes up, Master," she said quickly. "You *can't* do that. *They* can't do that. They shouldn't be *able* to do that, and I have no idea how they could, which is why it makes no sense to me. Magic is designed in such a way that you cannot use it to peer into its own nature; any attempt to control it at the most basic level will fail."

That was all true, but would either of them take the next step along the path of logic? It could have been my own prior knowledge of the subject, but I could just imagine one or both of them thinking that if it couldn't be done with magic then it had to be something non-magical doing it. I held my breath…

"If that's all true," Lucien said slowly, "then as bad as this is, there's no way that my enemies could be behind it. It must be something else entirely causing this. Is there anything else that could be destabilising magic? Should I reconsider having all six crystal chips in my body? Have I kept you in the world too long? Maybe I'm using magic too liberally and it's starting to get out of control."

My heart leapt with hope. I couldn't believe such a smart man was making such a stupid logic error, but if he continued on that line of thinking, it would be fantastic for us. Well, unless he did something totally stupid in an attempt to rectify it, but…

"Number one, you can't move the crystal chips around without the Sorcerous Crystals, which you don't have," Fewul pointed out. "Number two, it wouldn't matter where the crystal chips were, because they no longer have any magic in them. And number three, the rest of that stuff you mentioned shouldn't have any effect on the balance of magic. You're not using magic any more liberally than the Hammersons used it, and in fact there was much more magic around during the Great Sorcerous War than there is today."

"So what then?" Lucien snapped. "don't just stand there pointing out the problems; help me come up with solutions. What should I do about this?"

"Unless you are able to figure out how to do whatever it is that they have figured out how to do, there *is* no solution," Fewul said firmly.

"And you're not going to help me with that?" he enquired.

"I can try, but I am restricted within the constraints of magic," she said, "and yet they were able to find a way around that using only their own intelligence. If they can do it, there is no reason why you can't follow the same thought processes as them. You *do* know how they think, remember."

Lucien shrugged. "You know, I notice that I still have my Honnie mind. How is that possible if they are, as you say, stripping me of my magic?"

"Because your Honnie mind isn't a magical thing," she said, as though this was obvious, but it nevertheless took me by surprise. "You used magic to create it, but the mind itself has never been magical. Honnies are extraordinary beings, but they are not magical—or if they are, it is a type of magic completely different and alien to the type you and I use."

"Okay," he said, appearing to come to a decision as he sat down. They had been walking this whole time, and they had now arrived in the living room of Lucien's living quarters. "I want you to continue monitoring the situation, but if you have anything to tell me, do so telepathically instead of just dropping what you're doing and interrupting me. I'm going to be around people most of the day, so I can't afford that."

"Okay, but Master, it *isn't* an imbalance of magic; someone *is* attacking your magic."

Lucien waved her away, and she vanished into thin air. It was the moment I'd been waiting for; I stepped out of my shadow, trained my device back on Lucien, and flicked it back on, wondering how long it would take to drain the Sien-Leoard Crystal—probably longer than I would have before Lucien left this base, judging by how long it had taken just to attack the crystal chips, and considering the deep reservoir of magic contained in the Sien-Leoard Crystal.

"Ah, good morning, again," Lucien said, and for a heart-stopping moment, I thought he was talking to me. Then I saw where he was looking and turned my head in that direction; Lena had emerged and was standing just outside the hallway leading to the bedrooms, and I wondered how much of the conversation between Lucien and Fewul she had overheard. However much it was, she acted as if she knew (or cared) very little.

"Good morning, my king," she said in a very seductive tone.

"You're looking rather stunning this morning," he observed. "Attending any fashion shows I haven't heard about?"

He wasn't kidding; for reasons I couldn't imagine, Lena had chosen to really dress herself up this morning. She looked good in pretty much anything, of course, but she would normally wear pretty chill outfits that were made up of pants, jeans, shorts, a skirt, a T-shirt or a blouse, and all of them tight enough to show off the irresistible shape of her body. Only occasionally had I seen her actually dress up for something, and in a long, sleeveless dress with a split, a plunging neckline and more than a little cleavage, she was certainly doing that today. She'd even done her hair and makeup, though not in a way that suggested she'd spent hours on it.

In response to his question, she shrugged and looked a little sad. "No, I just thought I'd dress up. It's nice to occasionally put in a real effort to look good, even if no one's there to see it."

That was so obviously meant as a rebuke to Lucien for brushing her off that morning. I knew it, and so did Lucien, but once again, he wasn't affected. "Good for you. Do yourself up however you want. Take plenty of pictures. Recruit a few Hammerhearts to film you if you like, just not any male ones because I don't want them seeing you looking that good, and I *will* find out if any do see you like that. You can trust me on that."

"You don't want to take me out and show me off?" she asked, batting her eyelids at him. "I would really make you stand out, you know."

"I stand out plenty as it is," he said, smirking, "but no, probably not today. I wouldn't mind you on my arm looking like that if I were attending some public function, a high-profile dinner or something, but not if it's just a press conference or something that calls for a bit more modesty—and I will come and get you if I want you for anything like that."

He checked his watch and added, "And I'll be heading out of here pretty soon anyway; I have a meeting at nine o'clock in Hong Kong regarding the trials starting tomorrow. I would have liked to have it earlier, but they're two hours behind us, so it wouldn't have been feasible for anyone else there."

Lena didn't seem to be paying any attention to the last part of what he said, and as soon as he was finished talking, she zeroed in on the only part of what he'd said that really mattered to her. "So you don't want me to do anything then, except just hang around here waiting for you to be ready for me to do something?"

Lucien looked up at her then, his expression a little surprised but not angry. Although I couldn't be sure, I had the distinct impression that this kind of backchat *would* be the sort of thing that made him mad now, but only if it came from someone he actually respected. Apparently, whatever feelings he had for Lena, he didn't actually respect her opinion on things that really mattered.

"Well, yes," he said patiently. "What did you think you were here for? I am way too important to bend my schedule around your whims, Lena. Your job is to be my arm candy in public, but only when I want you to be; and then to entertain me in private. That's what you're here for."

Unsurprisingly, she looked stricken by that, but whatever she'd been about to fire back at him died before it reached her lips. He was using his Honnie mind to make sure she didn't flip out on him, but he wasn't using it to take total control of the situation as he easily could have. If he weren't so evil now, I'd have said he wanted to give her at least a little independence of thought, just so that he wouldn't feel as though he were talking to himself, but now my first guess was that he found the whole thing amusing. I felt bad for Lena and what he had reduced her to, compared to how intelligent and independent she had been before, but right now, my chief emotion was gladness at the fact that he was staying in one spot long enough for me to keep sucking up his magic without interruption.

"You know, the partners of prime ministers and presidents typically do more than just be arm candy," she said sullenly. "They often have their own projects on the side—charitable things that would really help your public image, if you would just let me."

He smiled indulgently at her. "Well, that is certainly something to look at when the war is over. Of course, at that time I would prefer for both of us to finish school first, and that will be a few more years for you, but after that, you'll have your whole life ahead of you to make lunch for homeless people or whatever you think you can do to help humanity. For now, though, you will remain here, where I know you'll be safe."

"Do I need to point out that we've both been attacked right here in these living quarters more than once?"

"No one's going to attack you when I'm not here; it's me they're after, not you."

"They abducted me once already, remember?"

"And they haven't tried to get you back after you escaped, which means they probably won't bother trying it again."

Lucien sighed, and I could tell that he was finding this whole thing with Lena less amusing now. He stood up and slowly walked towards her; to her credit, she kept her feet planted just outside the hallway. I had a good view of her as I shadowed close behind Lucien.

"No one's going to hurt you, my dear," he said, stopping in front of her and stroking her neck; she shivered very visibly with pleasure at his touch. "Yes, I know that you're bored here, and believe me, I am sorry about that. I tell you what," he said, seeming to be struck suddenly by an idea, "how would you feel if I got a tutor in here to work with you, so that you'll be able to finish year-ten this year in spite of all the interruptions caused by the war? Not only will you get through school more quickly, but you won't be bored while you're here, and you'll be able to fit in with my schedule when you need to. I think it's a more than reasonable offer."

There was never a question of her saying no, and whether it was an organic emotion or not, Lena did look happy about the suggestion. I supposed it was possible that she really *was* happy about it; although she had never been as bookish as Lisa, she had been somewhat bookish when I had first met her.

"I would love that," she said, "but it would need to be someone who's smart enough to do all my subjects at a higher level than I do, otherwise I won't learn much."

"There's no reason why I can't recruit a whole staff of them," he said softly, continuing to touch her, his fingers now trailing down the bare top of her left breast, "and don't worry— I'll make sure they're all very friendly, very smart, and very much able to teach you well."

"You'll use magic to make them comply, won't you," she said, phrasing it as a question, but her tone made it sound more like a statement.

"Well, naturally," he said as his hand disappeared very slightly beneath the top of her dress. "I imagine there would be plenty willing to serve me without extra persuasion, of course, but I'm not going to settle for the best of that specific bunch when I could settle for the best the whole world has to offer. And"—he checked his watch again—"I'm sure I could do it all in the next seventy minutes before my meeting in Hong Kong is due to start. Come to think of it, there are a few junior Hammerhearts who might also benefit from this, if you don't mind sharing, do you?"

"Sure, no problem," she said happily, and threw her arms around him. He responded in kind before stepping back from her slightly, and placing both hands on her bare shoulders.

"Come to think of it," he said in a very soft voice, "I probably only need sixty minutes."

He gently but firmly turned her and backed her against the wall just inside the hallway. He then took hold of her dress in both hands, and the air was rent with an almighty ripping sound. It fell away from her, leaving her not completely naked but not far off it. Not for the first time, I was forced to watch as he had his way with her, this time against the hallway wall, this time not in the non-privacy of his bedroom, but where

Hall, Cornish, or a number of other Hammerhearts could come along and observe him. I wished I could close my eyes, but I had to make sure, through all the thrusting and thrashing, that Lucien stayed within the beam of the device in my hand.

Rather later than I would have expected, I got a telepathic message from Amelia asking me what I wanted to do. While all this had been going on, a discussion had taken place within the control room regarding what they would do next. I'd kept the attack up long enough that his shields were probably gone again; meaning that if we could do it quickly enough, a direct attack against him could be successful. However, doing so would interrupt the attack I had going now. It would also run the risk of bringing Fewul back in a hurry, and there wasn't a damn thing we could do about that; if Lucien had given Fewul an order to come when he was attacked, Fewul would come whether we liked it or not...or would she?

Maybe we actually *could* do this in a way that would work. If someone in our base were to recall Fewul, would Lucien be able to call it back instantly as he had done in the past? What if the beast were recalled, and the magic that Lucien had set up to alert him to such an event was no longer in his control? How long would it take him to wonder what was going on? Would it be long enough for us to launch an attack on him that would subdue him? What about those gnome creatures; would they come back? There were a lot of unknowns, and I mulled over them as I watched the X-rated show in front of me.

I sent back to Amelia to wait until he was done with Lena before acting, and when her response came, it was tinged with amusement as if she (and perhaps the others) thought I just wanted to continue watching them. The truth was that I wanted to give myself as much time as I could afford to make this decision, and I could pretty much count on Lucien to stay put as long as he was doing what he was currently doing. And once I acknowledged that thought, the decision came pretty easily. I knew for a fact that Lucien would be moving around a lot throughout the day, going into various Hammerheart bases around the world to conduct his various meetings, plus whatever else he had to do, and all that moving around would make it very difficult to keep up the attack against him.

I took the allotted time, but in the end, the decision was as easy as that. Attacking him now was no more risky than attacking him last night had been, and although there had been more than one very close call then, it hadn't stopped us from trying again, and it wouldn't stop us from trying again today. As Lucien withdrew from Lena and stepped back so that he could lean against the wall opposite her, and as she sank to the floor, her knees too weak to hold her up, I sent back to Amelia that we should try attacking him right now, before he had a chance to leave the base.

Amelia's response was quick, but contained a lot of detail that I had to take a moment to process. She herself would coordinate the attack telepathically, since although the others were all under a single invisibility veil—I had been extracted from it just in case it was affected by the device I was using. It meant that the other attackers could see each other, but they couldn't see me and I couldn't see them. Marc, Peter, Natalie and Frederic would leave the base to perform the attack, while Lillian would be responsible for making sure that Fewul was gone, James would be responsible for controlling the base, and I would be responsible for turning the magic vacuum off and getting the hell out of the way so that I didn't get caught up in the attack.

I hurriedly flicked the device off and stepped sideways towards the other door, the one that led out of the living quarters and towards the rest of the base. My shoulder bumped into one of the other invisible people but neither of us acknowledged the other; I had no idea who it had been. As I stepped firmly out of the way, another message came from Amelia, telling me what to expect. The moment the signal was given, Natalie would try to knock him out directly, and if that somehow failed, she'd try to attack him with a solid-outliner. If both attacks failed, Peter would attack using the device I'd created which used light signals to get through shields, and that would hopefully knock him out. Marc and Frederic, the latter of whom was using the magic enhancer, were the backup, just in case Lucien survived our attacks and was able to fight back, or something else happened that we couldn't anticipate.

Amelia counted us all in telepathically, and then the attack came. I'd gotten my hopes up that with Lucien's shields most likely gone, he would go down in a single shot; but of course, that was far too optimistic. He started in surprise and then spun around, tripping over one of Lena's outstretched legs and falling over backwards. I saw a jet of white light that had to be from a solid-outliner (not invisible as the device itself was, which surprised me), fly high and wide over his head. A second one came a moment later, hitting him squarely in the face, but once again, it had no effect.

"*Aha!*" he roared, jumping back to his feet and leaping over Lena towards us, seeming to know exactly where the attack had come from. "I *knew* something like that was coming! Did you think I would just knowingly let my shields deteriorate? I've been redoubling them every ten seconds just to be sure."

Only his magical shields, I thought to myself, as physical shields would have stopped him from doing what he had been doing to Lena just before. The same thought must have occurred to either Marc or Frederic, because a moment later, a fist-sized stone appeared out of nowhere and flew towards Lucien, hitting him squarely in the head. He went down like a sack of shit, not completely knocked out but thoroughly stunned. He didn't have time to rise before Peter attacked, and this time, he was knocked out cold. A second held suspended while we all waited for something to happen in response, but when the response came, it wasn't anything magical.

Lena screamed, leapt to her feet and bolted over Lucien's unconscious body, swinging her arms aggressively. Even though we were all invisible to her, we were all so thoroughly taken by surprise by this new attack that no one responded with magic in time before she gave someone a hard wack, and then collided with someone else—probably Natalie and Peter, given where I thought their positions to be. There were words in her screams; at first they were incoherent but as I took aim at her with my own magic, I began to understand them.

"You can't do this! You can't do this! You can't do this! Lucien, wake up! Revive, Lucien!"

As if she thought saying it would make it so, I thought, as I sent a jet of thicky prison at her, which hit her squarely in the chest—the only part of her body that was still covered by some sort of clothing, unless you counted her feet which were incredibly still in high-heeled shoes. She noticed what had happened to her and spun back to one of the people she had bumped into earlier, and by a bad stroke of luck, managed to grab onto said person and pressed said person's head against her chest so that the thicky prison began taking said person as well. I thought it was probably Peter, and I later found out that my guess had been correct, but there was never a chance to react to what had happened for the unexpected and utterly impossible thing which happened next.

Lucien had woken up and bounced back to his feet, as if Lena's words really *had* revived him. Waves of magic went crashing throughout the living room; I felt them pass harmlessly through me but it was still a scary thing to stand there and wait for it to pass. Lena was knocked down by the magic, pulling Peter down on top of her, while Peter himself, along with the others, were all protected by the same magic as me. Marc and Frederic launched a coordinated attack against Lucien; he didn't go down, but having them both attacking him at the same time meant that he was forced to give them all his attention.

An alarmed thought from Amelia distracted me then: I had to release Lena and Peter from the thicky prison so that he could be drawn back into the base. I did so, and then waited to find out what was to happen next. Amelia was kind enough to give me a running commentary of the things I couldn't see in front of me. Peter and Natalie had both been retrieved, and seconds later, they took Marc as well. Frederic only had to maintain the attack for a few more seconds on his own, which thanks to the magic enhancer being as strong as the Sien-Leoard Crystal, along with his many years of magical experience, he was able to do. When the fight suddenly stopped, Lucien seemed to be unsure if he had won or if his attackers had fled, so he tried sending out more magic to flush us out.

"I know you're still here," he called to us, looking satisfied to have survived yet another attack. "I don't know how many times I have to tell you this, but I'm going to tell you anyway: Quit wasting your time by trying to attack me. No matter what you try, it won't work. I have contingencies stacked on top of contingencies, and even if it's true that you are somehow stealing my magic, it isn't going to help you in the long run because the magic to protect me isn't just set on my body but in the very walls themselves, and that applies to anywhere and everywhere I go. You can't win by doing this, and I will find a way to punish you for continuing to try—a way which you will *not* be able to ignore."

He then revived Lena, used his magic to raise her to her feet, and with a wave of his hand, he picked up the torn remains of her dress and fixed them back onto her body as if they had never been torn in the first place.

"What—what happened?" she asked.

Lucien began to explain that they had been attacked, which she seemed to be aware of, and then told her how her words had activated a magic set into the walls which had revived him. He also told her that there were other commands she could speak to activate different types of magic in his defence, but he didn't speak what those were aloud—I assumed he had just placed them in her head. Only part of my mind was on this whole conversation, though, because Amelia had contacted me again, asking me if I wanted to come back into the base and let someone else take over the magic sucking job for a while. I initially said no, until she reminded me that I hadn't had anything to eat since dinner last night, and as soon as she pointed it out, my stomach growled so loudly that I thought surely Lucien and Lena must hear it.

A few seconds later, I disappeared from the living room and appeared in the corner of the control room. I sighed and made myself visible again before looking at the others; none of them looked entirely displeased, even though the attack hadn't worked.

"You did great, John," Peter said, grinning at me.

"But—but the attack didn't work—"

"And now we know why," Marc said, grinning, "and we've already figured out what we're gonna do about it."

"Really?" I said, taking a seat and glancing at Natalie and Amelia before switching my gaze back to Marc, but it was Frederic who spoke.

"We do need someone to follow Lucien wherever he goes to keep up the attack, because it does look like we'll have to drain him of all his magic after all. You would be ideal for the job, John, but you don't have to do it all yourself; someone else can take over from time to time, and use the magic enhancer to keep up with Lucien if he uses magic to get around quickly. If we are unable to take all his magic by the time he gets back here, whenever he chooses to return, we'll have a surprise waiting for him."

"We're gonna suck all the magic out of the living quarters," Peter told me, "using that thing"—he indicated the megaphone-shaped device —"and someone is going to have to stand behind it at all times, making sure it does what we need it to do, and be ready to protect it in case it gets found by someone."

"Which obviously also means that you'll have to stay away from the upper levels of the base going forward," James added, "or at least go into your shadow when you do, because these devices are all three-dimensional, so you'll be safe at any other point along the fourth dimension."

"Guys, I've had an idea," Marc said, and his grin had broadened even more. "Instead of getting someone from in here to do that job, how about we use an influential charm to get a Hammerheart to do it instead?"

Everyone stared at him in surprise. I took the chance to glance at the display screen, only to see that Lucien had recalled Fewul and was in the process of sending her back out to do his bidding.

"Is there any particular reason why that would be an advantage?" Lillian asked.

"They won't have to be invisible," Marc said, "they'll be able to actually watch the display screens to see how the magic is going, and if they get caught—which they almost certainly will—they'll be the one in trouble with Lucien. We should get someone we really can't stand to do it; that'll make him completely nuts."

I shook my head. "And then Lucien will have access to the device. If he shows it to Fewul, she might be able to tell him what it does, given that the device itself isn't magical. That'll make him aware of magic particles, and that'll ruin everything and risk bringing antimagic into the equation."

"Not if we can find a way to vanish the device the moment Lucien is on the verge of seeing it," James said, and he too was smiling, "and that shouldn't be too difficult to do. I imagine that Lucien would take the Hammerheart's mind in his own and force it to tell him everything, but if we don't tell the Hammerheart what the device does, he wouldn't learn anything of value except that we're using some sort of device to do what we're doing. As long as he doesn't know how it works, he won't be able to make one of his own or try to think of a way to stop it."

Frederic shook his head this time. "No, it would be far too easy for him to just recreate whatever the Hammerheart is thinking of, and then he will have one of his own no matter what we do. A better thing to do would be to wipe the Hammerheart's memory the moment Lucien arrives, and that means that someone would have to stay with the Hammerheart after all so that all this can be managed."

"This idea is nice to think about," I said, "but it's sounding not really practical. If someone has to stay behind anyway, that person might as well do the job himself, right? The only reason to drag a Hammerheart into it is if we want to focus on getting that Hammerheart in trouble, and that shouldn't be our main priority here. At least, I don't think it should."

"Maybe not, but I don't have a problem putting Hall on the wrong side of Lucien if we can manage it," Peter said, grinning, "or Hignat."

"I vote to recruit Hignat and Wilwog for this job," Natalie said at once, which Amelia immediately seconded. Marc, Frederic and Lillian also agreed to recruit Hignat and Wilwog for the job, and I understood why: It was payback for their raping of Natalie and Amelia. I couldn't blame any of them for that, so even though I had misgivings about this job, I agreed to go along with it.

"If we're going to do this, though," I said, "then we're going to have to let Hignat and Wilwog back out of the base—I'm pretty sure they're still locked up in here. Before even that, though, I think there's something else we should do as well."

I began to explain what I was thinking, and everyone other than James and Natalie blanched as my ideas took shape in their minds. Those two knew about this part of the plan already—James because he had read far enough ahead in the plan and Natalie because she had created the devices which could do this—but even they were surprised that I was ready to jump this far ahead. Normally I wouldn't have, but I could easily foresee how this could backfire on us and force us to resort to the use of antimagic. The vote to proceed with my idea went seven to one, with only Marc voting against, and he made it clear that although he couldn't stop us from doing this, he wanted it on the record that he strongly disagreed with it.

Chapter 26: Four Points of the Compass

We agreed not to attack Lucien for the next hour as he went about rounding up tutors for Lena, in the hopes that it would be long enough for him to let his guard down. It gave us a chance to have breakfast and go back to our rooms to shower, as long as we did both things quickly. It still needed someone to be in the control room at all times, though, just to keep an eye on things, and just in case something happened that required an immediate response. Marc, Amelia, Natalie and Frederic selected themselves to stay first, while Peter, James, Lillian and I went upstairs for our breakfast.

By the time I'd finished eating, gone upstairs for one of the quickest showers of my life (I probably hadn't been thorough at all) and returned to the control room, Natalie had finished altering the devices we would need for the next part of the plan. At some point while I'd been away, she'd gone up to her room and retrieved two more devices (leaving only two behind, so far as I knew). One of them was an antimagic version of the great microphone device, which she had altered using the magic enhancer to make it so powerful that it could suck up antimagic particles from thousands of kilometres away, and duplicated it so that we now had four of them. If we placed those four devices at strategic locations around the world, we could probably gather almost all the antimagic in the world—certainly we would get the vast majority of it, which ought to be enough. The other device was basically a storage unit where we could transfer the magic particles to from the four devices once they had gotten all they could.

As Natalie, Amelia, Marc and Frederic left the room to have their own breakfast and so on, the rest of us were free to watch what was happening on the various screens on the control panel and talk about what came next. Lena remained in the living quarters where Lucien had left her, and she was indeed using what looked like a mobile phone rather than a camera to take pictures of herself by holding the phone as far out from her body as she could and then angling it in different ways to get different sorts of shots. Surely it would have been much simpler to get someone else to take the photos, I thought, unaware of how trendy such photography would eventually become.

"Does anyone know how antimagic devices respond to magic particles?" Peter asked suddenly.

A brief silence, and then James said, "Probably not well, Pete, if you're thinking what I think you're thinking. If you try to put magic around the device to make it untraceable, for example, the magic won't get sucked up by the device, but it will get annihilated by the antimagic that's getting sucked in. It'll have the same end result, only much more spectacularly."

Peter shrugged. "Well, there's no question stupider than the one not asked, except maybe 'why did the chicken cross the road'."

James gave Peter a very serious look. "You shouldn't joke about stuff like that. The chicken could have all sorts of reasons for wanting to cross the road. You can't presume to know a chicken's mind, especially when you haven't even met it."

I opened my mouth, hardly knowing what smart-mouth comment I wanted to make, and then shut it again. This would have been a bad time to compete on Harry and Simon's turf, where I would have probably crashed and burned anyway if I tried. Instead, I said, "I've been thinking about that myself, actually—not the chicken thing, the antimagic thing. My hunch is that we might be able to do this completely undetected; surely if Fewul can't talk directly about magic particles, and certainly can't manipulate them, then it'll be even more blind to antimagic. The Beast of Magic is made up of pure magic; it couldn't even come into contact with antimagic without it ending in disaster."

"That's a good point," James agreed, "but still, I feel almost naked just leaving those things lying around where anyone could pick them up. Should we consider recruiting some more Hammerhearts to stand guard over them and say that they're on official business which is so top-secret that anyone who doesn't know about it is obligated to just shut up and forget about it?"

"We should hold off on making that decision until we're all here," Lillian said, "but it's not a bad idea. You'll have to pick four Hammerhearts you know can defend the devices, but who you feel comfortable possibly sacrificing, given that if they are forced to use magic too close to the device, they could get turned inside-out."

"I've been thinking about that too," I said, "and if we really wanna do this whole 'recruiting Hammerhearts' thing, then for this job, I suggest Hignat and Wilwog's fathers, along with the Hammerhearts coded 3P69 and 3E57. I've seen them all in action and they're pretty decent fighters, and they're all bloody criminals so I don't feel bad at all about sacrificing them."

"Can we swap one of them out for the big guy who killed Kylie with his bludginator?" Peter suggested. "I think his name was Eric but I don't know if we ever found out his code."

"Or 3A93," James added. "I think he ran the security system in the Chopville base—at least I vaguely remember someone telling me that. Then there's 3K17, but she's not as evil as the others, so maybe we should spare her from this."

"3A93 might be a good candidate for sucking the magic out of Lucien's living quarters," I said, "if we can't get one of those guys to do it for whatever reason."

I was referring to Hignat and Wilwog, glancing at the spyers set to track those two as I spoke. Marc had released them from the prison while

I had been having breakfast and planted some false memories in their minds so that they would have no idea that they'd been captured. He hadn't put any influential charms on them yet, though—that would wait until we actually recruited them, so that we would know exactly how best to use them. Right now, there wasn't a lot interesting to show. Hignat was standing in his bathroom, shaving, while Wilwog appeared to be finishing his breakfast. I could easily foresee how we mightn't be able to use either of them for the job though. If Lucien had been thinking of those two when he spoke of junior Hammerhearts who could also benefit from the tutors, he might call on them to attend school today, even though it was Sunday. If he did that then they would both be accounted for, and using them would tip Lucien off to trouble well before we were ready for him.

"So we can't fit Eric in anywhere?" Peter asked, a little sadly. "Or Hall, for that matter?"

We all glanced at the spyer that was following the police commissioner. He was already on duty, in a location I recognised from the previous day as the scene of one of the riots, and he appeared to be directing a clean-up operation. It might be possible to recruit Hall for something, I thought, but his absence would certainly be remarked upon, so it mightn't be worth it until later on. Also, there was the fact that we didn't really need to do much to get Hall in trouble; he was already on the outs with Lucien, judging by what had happened to him in the room where Natalie had been prisoner half the week.

"We might be able to fit those men in somewhere," Lillian said, "and Cornish too, for that matter, but let's not try to find jobs for them right now; I'm sure jobs will come up throughout the day, even if this operation goes well, but especially if it doesn't."

We continued to wait for the rest of the main group to return to the control room, keeping a close eye on Lucien's activities as we did. He was teleporting from location to location, obviously using his magic to quickly find the most ideal people for the job. Each time, he spent no more than three minutes speaking to the person, wherever they happened to be (most were at home, though one was going for a run outdoors, two of them were driving somewhere, and one young man happened to be fast asleep in the bed of a strange woman he'd just spent the night with, and neither of them particularly appreciated being woken up by the ruler of the world—at least not for the first few seconds before Lucien dealt with them. Each time they agreed to go with him, which they all did, of course, they seemed to disappear into his pocket, so he was obviously using some sort of magic to store them all in there in a way that wouldn't be uncomfortable. Good thing we weren't attacking him now, I thought, for if we were, those people would be stuck in there.

As nine o'clock ticked nearer, people began coming down to the control room to resume working at the workstations as they had done the previous day—except, of course, that we had cleared away all the workstations. Each time, we sent them up to the games room; and when Natalie returned to the room, the first of the four to do so, we sent her back upstairs with the magic enhancer to make sure there were enough workstations for everyone who wanted to help. I had misgivings about having them throwing magic around throughout the day with everything else we were doing here, but I kept them to myself—it probably wouldn't make much of a difference.

By the time we were ready to jump back into action, there were now ten of us. Rebecca and Erica had decided to re-join the main group, even though neither of them were in the loop about what we were doing, and Rebecca didn't even know about magic particles or antimagic. Katie and Sophie were sent back upstairs to join the attack along with their boyfriends, but no one suggested sending James and Peter's girlfriends up with them. Who could say that having two extra people down here wouldn't be an advantage? After all, in the last attack we'd launched against Lucien, all eight of us had had some sort of job.

"I thought you, Katie and Sophie would be sleeping all day," I said to Erica as she took a seat on the other side of James.

"Oh, I forgot to mention, they were sleeping in the Time Box all along," James said, grinning at Erica. "They got a good long sleep and hardly missed anything. They came out when we were upstairs, I suppose."

"Yeah, Marc was sitting where you are now when we came out," she said.

"Okay, you guys," Marc said loudly, and silence fell. "I'd like to be able to explain to you both how much we've done and how much we've learned in the last twenty-four hours, but there really isn't time for that. You're both just going to have to go along with what we're doing as best you can, and contribute when you feel ready. Now, Nat, are we definitely ready to go with these things?"

"Yeah, they're as ready as they can be," she said, "at least without us having taken them out and tested them."

"We were talking about some things while you guys were upstairs," James told them, and he repeated my observation about Fewul, and our suggestions about who should stand guard over the antimagic vacuums.

"I quite like those suggestions," Marc said, and Natalie and Amelia nodded enthusiastically along with him.

"I'm afraid we may have to reconsider Hignat and Wilwog, though," I said, indicating the spyers following those two. "It looks like they're being called in, and my guess is that Lucien is going to try to put them into school with Lena."

At this stage, Hignat and Wilwog were just arriving on the fifth floor of the Chopville base, having come separately and now meeting up just outside the dining hall. They weren't the only ones either. Glancing to my left, I saw that Sebastian was also approaching the fifth level, meaning that he was most likely a part of all this. Lucien hadn't yet returned to the base, but I had a feeling he was dealing with the last tutor, and he only had less than ten minutes before he was due in a meeting in Hong Kong, apparently.

"Can't we still take them?" Amelia asked hopefully.

"Yeah, surely we can put the whole lot of them out of action once Lucien's left," Natalie added.

James slowly shook his head. "I wish we could get those two in trouble too, but the fact is, Lucien could check in to see how Lena's doing at any time, and we don't want to throw up any red flags that might make him consider coming back before we're ready for him. We need that living area to be completely devoid of magic if we are to attack him successfully."

"John suggested we get 3A93 for that job," Peter said, "though I'd rather get the guy who killed Kylie myself."

"Wasn't 3A93 the one who first noticed when we escaped from the Basement that time?" Amelia asked.

"Yeah, he's in the security department, we think," James said, "so it shouldn't be all that suspicious if he's there. We'll have opportunities to get Hammerhearts in trouble later, if we want, but this operation is too important to try to use it to achieve some other end at the same time. If we're going to get any Hammerheart to do this, it should be one who isn't going to raise eyebrows by being there, at least until his cover gets blown, and 3A93 should fit that description."

A brief silence, and then Marc said, "Before we start any of these operations, we need to figure out where *we're* going to go so that we'll be safe. Am I right in thinking we should take the whole base into the fourth dimension?"

"I think that would be best," Frederic said, "even if it means we won't be able to use magic from the crystals inside the base without emerging. But that means one or more of us should leave the base so that we can round up those five Hammerhearts, put influential charms on them, and set them to work. Who's going to do that?"

We all looked at Marc, who hesitantly said, "I guess I could do it, although I'm not all that happy about it."

"No, someone else," I said quickly, my stomach falling as I realised what might happen if we left this job to Marc. He was so set against using antimagic that he would be highly motivated to sabotage the devices. "I'd offer to do it myself, except of all the powers I gave myself, the ability to perform influential charms wasn't one of them. We do have unbogglers, but they wouldn't be specific enough for this, I guess."

"I guess I'll do it," Frederic said, and heaved a sigh. "It's not the first time I've done something like this, although I've never done anything *quite* like this, but I know it is within my skillset."

He stood up, took the magic enhancer from Natalie, and then gathered the five devices in his arms. It was so hard for him to hold them all that he had to put them down and then use the magic enhancer to create a bag in which to carry them. While he did so, Lillian and Amelia went about collecting the devices with which they would protect him in the usual ways while he was out there, and once he was invisible and so on, he was ready to go. James let him out of the base, where he promptly dropped into Lucien's living quarters only feet away from an utterly oblivious Lena. A moment later, he disappeared into his teleportation.

"Someone please tell me he remembered to take a communicator with him," I said into the silence which followed.

"I'm pretty sure he has one in his pocket," Amelia said, "but if not, he can do telepathy with the magic enhancer, so he'll be fine. What should we do while we're waiting for him?"

"Let's watch what happens here before we do anything else," James said, referring to the spyers, and we all fell silent. Most of them were muted so that we wouldn't have to put up with the constant chatter of multiple locations at all times, but James now turned the volume up on one of them.

Lucien had returned to the Chopville base and had just let the tutors out of his pocket. I now saw that there were an even ten of them. Three of them were girls, who all looked quite young, while the other seven were men. Of the men, six of them were youngish, perhaps in their early twenties, while one of them was middle-aged. This one I recognised—it was Mr. Hall, the other Mr. Hall, not the public enemy we had spent so much time fighting but the one who had betrayed us to the public enemy. Obviously he was still a Hammerheart, but apparently he hadn't faked being a teacher as part of the job.

"Thank you all for doing this," Lucien told them as they gathered in front of the elevator, still on the level of the Hammerheart Highway. "I know you are taking time away from your regular lives to do this, but I assure you that you'll all be well compensated for it. How does…five hundred dollars a day sound, along with a promise that your regular jobs will be waiting for you when you return? And you three"—he addressed the girls—"won't fall behind in your own studies."

They all looked appreciative of this, except for one of the young men —not the one who'd had a one-night stand the previous night, but one of the others. "You run the whole world now," he pointed out. "Surely if you're going to do this, and you want us in particular, you can afford to pay us more than five hundred a day."

Lucien gave him a dangerous look. "You're not expendable, you know. Five hundred a day is a damn good deal for what you'll be doing, but if you'd like a revised deal, here's one just for you. Two hundred a day, and a promise that if you backchat me again, the lives of your family may be in jeopardy."

"I'll take whatever you want," he said immediately, and Lucien smiled.

"Okay, so it's two hundred a day for Mr. Grant, five hundred for the rest of you. Now, there are only going to be four students to start with, but there may be more in time once I learn of other junior Hammerhearts who have fallen behind in their studies. I promise, though, that there'll never be more than ten; I want the student-to-teacher ratio to be favourable here."

"May I ask a question, Sir?" Hall asked respectfully, and Lucien nodded. "What about yourself? I'm given to understand that you're supposed to be doing year twelve this year. Are you intending to finish your studies?"

"Oh, yes, eventually," he said, "but not this year; there's just too much else to do. If you all do a good job here, you may even have the honour of tutoring me down the track; I can promise your careers will be fast-tracked if that happens."

The elevator doors opened then, and the eleven of them stepped inside. As they did so, Lucien said, "We're just going to pick up three of the students before we go up to the study area, which I haven't actually set up yet, but I'll do that before I go. I should tell you now that the fourth student is my woman, and I expect not only propriety from all of you where she is concerned, but the best teaching you are able to give her. The quickest way to lose this opportunity is to treat her badly, or to give her less attention than she deserves."

It was a rather intimidating speech, and none of them dared do more than nod in response to it. A moment later, the doors opened onto the fifth floor and Lucien told one of the tutors, "Hold the door open while I'm out there—this might take a minute, but I want you all to stay in here. If any other Hammerhearts try to get in, point to me and tell them that I've ordered you to let no one else in, and that they can take it up with me if they have an issue."

The moment Lucien stepped out of the elevator, before he could get anywhere near where Hignat, Wilwog and Sebastian were waiting for him and looking dubiously into the elevator, he was waylaid by Hank Cornish. Arnold Hammerson's former right-hand man had a list of things he wished to speak to Lucien about, but Lucien was having none of it. Since the spyer was still following Lucien, we quite clearly heard him tell Cornish that his schedule for the morning was full but that he might have time for him in three or four hours' time, depending on what happened between now and then. He then shook the man off and strode over to the three teenage boys.

"You three are to come with me," he told them. "I've set something up for you that is not only going to keep you busy today, but probably for the next three months or so."

"Is it an important job, sir?" Sebastian asked hopefully, his eyes gleaming.

"Only the most important thing in the world," Lucien said, smiling at them, but it was impossible to miss the wickedness in his expression. He knew they were going to be disappointed by what he was about to tell them, and he relished every second of it. "It's time for the three of you to catch up on all the school you've missed this year. I've arranged some very special tutors for you, and you will spend every day between now and December doing the work you should have been doing for the last few months."

The expressions on all three of their faces were priceless, and in that moment, I couldn't blame Lucien for enjoying it.

"But Sir, surely we can be more useful than being stuck in some stupid classroom," Hignat protested.

"On the contrary, there are few things more useless than stupid Hammerhearts, and I don't want you three to be stupid Hammerhearts," he said. "Besides, I'm making my girlfriend do this as well, so it's not like I'm punishing you or anything. It's for your own good, and when your parents find out about it, I'm sure they'll agree. Come on, the bell's about to ring."

"Seriously, a bell?" Sebastian said, trying to keep the scorn out of his voice and not doing a very good job of it.

"No, not literally," Lucien amended, "but it is almost nine o'clock, and I have somewhere else I need to be, so quit wasting my time and follow me."

"But it's Sunday, sir," Wilwog almost howled. "I have a bunch of TV shows I was planning to catch up on today."

"That's terrible grammar there, Mr. Wilwog," Hall called from the elevator as the four of them walked towards it, "but don't worry, we'll fix that up quickly enough."

"Oh, you've gotta be kidding me," Hignat grumbled as he scurried along in Lucien's wake.

They crowded into the elevator, and as the doors closed, the introductions began. I didn't listen to all of them—those poor people Lucien had spelled into doing this didn't matter all that much to me—but I did notice one interesting thing, which surely had to be by design, and I couldn't decide if I ought to feel glad about it or not.

"Dad just contacted me," Amelia said suddenly, startling several people. "He's got all five of them with him now and he's about to start teleporting around to the points where we agreed to put the antimagic devices. I just told him to tell them to synchronise their watches so that they start at the same time, and that'll give us all time to get into our shadow and out of the way."

"Oh shit, should we do that now?" James asked, actually putting his hands on the control panel, but Amelia shook her head hard.

"No, that'll cut off the telepathy if you do that. We need to stay out here, at least until the job's ready to go."

That was a good point, but I hardly registered it as I was wrapped up in what was happening on the screens—now a full four of them. The elevator had reached the top floor and the group began to walk along the corridor towards the living quarters where Lena continued to wait, and looks and smiles were being exchanged between several of them. Lucien may have claimed that he'd gotten the best tutors for the job, but he hadn't specifically ruled out that there were more criteria than intelligence and teaching ability. He had chosen three girls, the same as the number of boys whom they would be teaching. All three of them were young, and he had indicated in passing earlier that they were still students themselves. Now, each of those three girls was eyeing one of the three boys, and the boys were returning their looks of interest.

Hignat, Wilwog and Sebastian didn't deserve to be set up with these girls in this manner—it was way too good for them, especially given how good looking all three of these girls were. The ones who seemed to have been paired up with Hignat and Sebastian were quite petite, although in Sebastian's case, she was pretty busty. The one who'd been matched with Wilwog was tall and statuesque, model material for sure—wonders will never cease, I thought to myself. All the same, I thought I understood why Lucien was taking this opportunity to set them up. It was probably less of a reward and more of a desire to get them off his case. Perhaps he had become sick of them wanting to stick their dicks wherever they could, especially after they'd tried to do that with Lena just the previous morning.

When they reached the living quarters, Lucien introduced Lena to each of the tutors and then told her to go and change into something appropriate for the day. (Before she left, however, he took the opportunity to kiss her and squeeze one of her breasts.) Once she was gone, he apologised to all who remained, saying that he didn't have time to set up a study area for them this morning so they would just have to do it here in the living room for today, and he would have something ready for them tomorrow. He explained to the tutors that he'd selected them not just because they were all intelligent, but because they possessed knowledge across a wide range of subjects. They were to spend the day testing the students to determine their levels, and then come up with a curriculum to suit each of them for the remainder of the year.

"I have to jet now," he said, hurrying to the door, and then looking back over his shoulder. "Oh, and Hall, you're in charge here. Make sure they all do what they're supposed to, students and tutors alike, and make sure no one goes anywhere else in the base besides this room. There's plenty to eat and drink here, so there's no reason why any of you should leave before four o'clock this afternoon at the very earliest."

He vanished through the door, and I tracked his progress along the corridor downstairs before switching my attention back to the disorganised classroom in front of me. This was going to be pretty dull to watch, but at present, it was all I had to look at (unless I wanted to glance over to the screen showing Lena changing her outfit, but I'd honestly seen enough of that). Hignat, Wilwog and Sebastian would have been quite content to exchange coy looks with the three girls with whom they'd been matched, but Hall wasn't having any of that; he called everyone to order and began trying to organise the whole thing with what little tools he had at his disposal.

"How's your dad doing, Amelia?" Peter asked then.

"I assume he's doing okay, but he hasn't contacted me yet," she said, checking her watch.

"Did he say he was going to take your suggestion and tell them to synchronise their watches?" I asked.

"I got the impression that he thought it was a good idea, so I assume so," she said anxiously, looking across the row of spyers before us. "I wish we had some way of tracking him."

"We do, sort of," James said, pointing at one of the screens, and then another. Those spyers were set to follow Hignat and Wilwog senior, and they were indeed doing so, but those two were no longer with Frederic. We had agreed to place the antimagic vacuums in Panama City, Israel, Hong Kong, and right here in Chopville, but we hadn't decided who would go to which location. That decision had been left up to Frederic, but all we could tell thus far was that neither Hignat nor Wilwog were in Chopville—I would have recognised it if they were.

"Can you tell where they are?" Peter asked James.

"Not for sure," he said, "except that neither of them are Chopville, and I don't think either of them are Hong Kong—we can ask Mr. Woodward when he gets back. Since he's already done two of them, and they're doing just what they're told and waiting for the right time, I don't think he'll be much longer."

And he wasn't. He contacted Amelia again within a few minutes, by which time Lena had returned to the living room in a 'more appropriate' outfit per Lucien's instructions. It was her typical style of tight clothing to show off every delicious curve of her, and it certainly had an effect. Everyone in the room ogled her as her breasts bounced perkily in their faces, some of the men trying harder than others to cover it up; but incredibly, Hignat, Wilwog and Sebastian were the quickest to turn away, seemingly more interested in the other girls than in Lena. Yep, I thought, as attractive as those other girls were, it wouldn't be possible to turn that quickly from Lena if all things were normal. This was Lucien's work, pure and simple.

As Hall recovered himself enough to begin asking Lena questions about the living area and what tools they had available to them (paper, pens, computers, etc.), Frederic Woodward suddenly materialised in front of us, and he wasn't alone: 3A93 was with him. The small Hammerheart was standing obediently by his side, contrite as if he had realised the error of his ways all this time and was all too eager to begin making up for his mistakes right here and now. They didn't stay put but moved off, out of the living quarters and around the corner into the other hallway.

That was also part of the plan. Though there were a few places where it might have made strategic sense to place the magic vacuum, the best of them was close to the end of that particular hallway. The beam would broaden as it travelled, meaning that it would capture most, if not all, of the living quarters. The risk was that Lucien's bedroom might be too far away, but if Natalie had made this thing the way she'd intended to make it, it should be within range. It wouldn't make any sense to put the device too close to Lucien's bedroom, for there the beam would be too narrow, and would probably allow a blind spot where some magic might survive our attack.

We waited with some anxiety for Frederic to return, and soon enough, he did so at a light-footed run. James didn't even wait for him to get into position in front of us, not wanting someone in the room to feel vibrations through the floor from his footsteps. A moment later Frederic disappeared from all the display screens, and Lillian pointed a device at the corner of the control room and gave it a click; he appeared there instantly.

"Okay, I think we're good to go," he said, panting as he came to sit back down, and I noticed a light sheen of sweat on his forehead. "It's probably a good idea to move along to the fourth dimension now, wouldn't you say?"

"Yeah, we'd better do that," James said, taking the controls and doing so just a small amount. We were still able to see the living room outside now, but not very well; it had darkened and blurred a little, as if the base itself was suffering from cataracts, but we all knew it was because we were now in our shadow.

Fortunately, the spyers still worked, designed as they were to track people wherever they went, including other points along the fourth dimension. It looked like we would have to use those to keep an eye on things outside going forward. I had another look across the row and was pleased with what I saw—we would have no less than four viewpoints of the classroom, should we choose to watch it. We could also watch Lucien —he was in what looked like quite an important meeting, and to my surprise, 3K17 was sitting beside him. Didn't he say more than once that it was in Hong Kong? We could also watch Hall (the police commissioner) and Cornish, and once I recognised what I was seeing, I realised that we were, in fact, tracking 3E57, 3P69 and 3A93 after all. (For the record, 3P69 was stationed in Chopville. The others were less obvious: 3E57 appeared to be in a forest, Hignat in a desert, and Wilwog in a dark alley in a city.)

"Any second now, and they will all begin their work," Frederic said, checking his watch.

"Any ideas what we should do in the meantime?" Marc asked.

"Yeah, just one thing," I said. "We need to wait and see if anyone notices what we're doing. The big one is Fewul; I don't think she'll notice anything about the antimagic, but we still need to make sure that's right before we can settle down. Also, she might have put some kind of spell to activate if the magic in Lucien's living quarters changes, so we need to be ready for anything there too."

"But wouldn't that spell just get sucked away like all the others?" Peter asked.

"Not if it triggers an alarm before those particles are disturbed," James said. "I think John's right: We're going to have to wait and be ready for some sort of response. But, I think we all knew it couldn't be this easy."

"It never is," Natalie agreed, and Amelia and Frederic nodded.

The seconds continued to tick away, and all fifteen of us were checking our watches repeatedly—even the Hammerhearts were following our lead at this point. At last, the moment came, and all five of them turned their devices on within two seconds of each other. I was expecting something major to happen to at least one of them, if not all of them, but there was nothing of the sort. On the contrary, nothing whatsoever happened to any of them, but it didn't let us relax. If anything, the tension in the room increased.

I glanced at the five spyers following the five Hammerhearts, and when nothing noteworthy happened to any of them, I switched my gaze to Lucien. If he or Fewul noticed anything out of the ordinary, the evidence of it would show up on that screen, but the meeting was still going—it didn't look as though it had been interrupted at all. I supposed Fewul could have contacted Lucien telepathically, and he was responding to it in kind without letting it draw him away from what he was doing, but even if that were the case, he would have surely commanded Fewul to return to base and see what was going on there. But no, nothing whatsoever was happening anywhere.

"This is weird as," Peter finally said. "Did one of you guys recall Fewul and forget to mention it?"

"No, but maybe we should do that," Marc suggested. "I mean, if Fewul's not around, it's less likely to come into antimagic and accidentally blow up the world or something."

"Fewul and antimagic have coexisted all this time without blowing up the world," James pointed out. "I think we're safe in that regard. I'd say the idea to recall it might be good, except that it might tip Lucien off that we're attacking him, and even if he just calls it back within a second, do we really wanna let him know that we're thinking about him?"

"James, I'm pretty sure he's going to guess that we're thinking about him," Marc pointed out, "and if he doesn't hear anything from us all day, he's going to wonder what we're doing. He might assume that we're planning something big, and he'll raise his readiness accordingly. It might actually work better to recall Fewul, and keep recalling it every couple of minutes, just so that he goes on thinking that we can't think of anything better. Reverse psychology, you know?"

James's eyes had lit up as Marc was speaking. When Marc was done, he said, "That's actually a *really* good idea, Marc. We *should* be thinking about what Lucien might think we're up to, and that'll work as well as anything to lower his guard. He might be smart enough to think we could be doing more than one thing at a time, but I doubt he'd think that we're deliberately misleading him."

Rebecca was closest to the cabinet; she jumped up and retrieved the device to recall Fewul. She looked around the group for a volunteer to use it, and Natalie said, "No reason why you can't do it, Bec. You only have to push that button once every couple of minutes. Easiest job you can imagine."

"Well, okay," she said, sitting back down, "but I *am* capable of doing more than this."

"And I bet you'll get the chance to do *way* more before the day is done," Peter said, putting his arm around her and planting a kiss on her lips.

"You know, I'd like to think I'm a fairly open-minded fellow," Frederic observed, "but if you do that again right in front of me, young Playman, I *will* have to tell your mother about it."

Chapter 27: Disaster

Not much happened for a while after that. It actually got so dull in the control room that I found myself feeling a little bored, though I wasn't foolish enough to wish for more action. This was the eye of the storm, we all knew it; we had gone through a lot of drama to get here, and there would yet be more drama—probably much worse drama—before we got out again. All we could do was sit and watch the various screens in front of us, turning the volumes on different spyers up and down depending on who we wanted to hear speak. For the most part, that was only the classroom scene before us, Lucien in his various doings throughout the morning, and occasionally Hall as he went about his business in the wider world.

At about nine thirty, when it looked like nothing was going to happen anytime soon, Frederic told us that he had something he wanted to do while there was still a chance, and asked to be let out of the base. None of us really wanted to let him go out, and even Lillian asked him if it was really a good idea to be out there on his own at this time. He assured her that he knew what he was doing, that he would have the magic enhancer with him anyway, and he would be ready for anything in case someone came to investigate—whatever that meant. Marc offered to go with him, but both Amelia and Frederic asked him to stay behind. I could guess why Amelia didn't want him to possibly put himself in danger again, but why wouldn't Frederic want help with whatever it was he was doing? In the end, though none of us liked it, we didn't feel like we really had a right to hold him against his will, and once he had been protected in the usual ways again, James reluctantly let him out in Lucien's living room.

"Why was he so cagy?" Peter asked as Frederic left his shadow and teleported away a moment later, without anyone else in the room noticing a thing.

"Something he doesn't want me to know, I imagine," Marc said grumpily, "like all those devices Natalie made."

James slowly shook his head. "I don't think so. I guess it's possible, but I don't think so. My guess is that this is something private that may possibly have nothing to do with the fight against Lucien. If it was something that would concern us in any way, I'm sure he would let us know what it was. Can you think of anything, Amelia?"

"None at all," she said. "I guess it's something he wants to do with magic if he thinks there mightn't be a chance later, but I can't think of what it could be."

A couple of minutes later, Frederic sent a telepathic message to Amelia, telling her that he was safe and not to worry, and that he would teleport back to the Hammersons' living room when he was done, which would probably be in half an hour or so. She asked him once again what he was doing but he chose not to respond to that message, which put Amelia in quite a bad mood. The rest of us weren't too happy about it either: Now we had to wait thirty minutes for him to appear or to not appear, without knowing if something had happened to him in the meantime. I supposed the reason why he wouldn't keep us updated constantly was that he needed his full concentration for whatever he was doing, but still, it didn't make any of us feel better.

So with no other options and one extra thing to worry about, the nine of us sat in silence and continued to watch the spyers and listen to some of their conversations. One of the most important screens, though by far the most boring, was the one showing 3A93; he was sitting silently, watching the numbers on the screen before him continue to climb and climb as the device sucked up the magic particles around the top floor of the Chopville base. I kept glancing at it repeatedly, but it was showing no signs of slowing as of yet. The screens showing the four Hammerhearts with the antimagic devices were almost as boring, except that they were in public, and occasionally (or frequently), people would walk past them. Only 3P69 had to contend with some people coming up to him and asking him how he was doing; nobody bothered Hignat or 3E57, and in Wilwog's case, for the few people who saw him, it was obvious that he was a Hammerheart, and that was enough to discourage the locals from getting too close lest there be retribution.

Meanwhile, in the living quarters, the four students had been taken into different rooms by four of the teachers—Lena into Lucien's bedroom by none other than Hall, Sebastian into Tankom's old room, Hignat into Stella's old room (a place he would have liked to be under entirely different circumstances at an earlier time), and Wilwog into the private dining room on the other side of the main area. The other six teachers had remained in the main area, where they were tasked with coming up with written tests to determine where the students were at in their particular subjects (the subjects having been assigned earlier on), while the students did verbal tests in four other subjects. That was what was supposed to be happening, and indeed Lena seemed to be doing very well in the verbal English test Hall was giving her. The three boys, however, were doing no such thing; the three girls had volunteered to test them, and all three pairs were in the process of making out in their respective locations.

Elsewhere, Lucien appeared to have finished up in Hong Kong, leaving 3K17 in charge of what was going on there for the rest of the morning. It transpired that he had made her the lead judge in the trials; he wanted a Hammerheart to run it, to show the world that the Hammerhearts really were responsible people; but at the same time, he wanted one who could appear to be fair, and that narrowed down the field quite a bit. She would be assisted by a few other Hammerhearts from different parts of the world, as well as a few judges from Hong Kong, but the final decision in all cases would be hers.

Well, in truth, the final decision would be Lucien's, because he had already given her a formula to follow: the death penalty for those who are found guilty and refuse to denounce their actions; life-long prison sentences for those who plead guilty and show genuine remorse; and should they come across someone who really *is* innocent, that person would be set free, just to prove that the trials weren't fixed. As it was, the trials really *were* fixed, given that Lucien himself had supervised the collection of all these dissidents with Fewul, and he had already used influential charms on some of them so that they would play by the scripts come trial time. He told all this to 3K17 so that she wouldn't be caught by surprise, because the whole point of this trial was how it appeared on the outside. The world needed to know that Lucien was fair, but firm as well.

Lucien was now in another part of the world entirely, most likely South America. It was obvious enough that it was somewhere in Latin America because Lucien had put a spell on himself to make him speak fluent and flawless Spanish, and the people he was speaking to, all had brown skin. What made me think it was South America rather than Mexico or Costa Rica, for example, was that he appeared to be getting ready for a public appearance, and if James had been right about the Hammerhearts having almost conquered the continent, it would be almost time for him to publicly announce the annexation of those territories by Hammersonia. I wondered if he would go back and get Lena and put her by his side when the cameras turned on, but he was showing no signs of doing so. Rather, he appeared to want the most important of the local Hammerhearts to appear beside him, perhaps to show the region that for the most part, he would be the ultimate head of state, but they would still be governed by their own people.

At about ten to ten in the morning, which would have been evening in South America, Lucien was preparing to make the first public appearance, and he had chosen to do Colombia first. I wouldn't have known it was that country if not for Lillian, who had recognised the flag, which had been set up in such a way that it was now partially obscured by the much larger Hammersonian flag. The message from Lucien to the people of Colombia was clear: don't get too comfortable. These regents may be your own kind, but you still come under my rule, and don't you forget it.

As the final preparations were being made, however, we were distracted by another telepathic message from Frederic. He had just contacted Amelia to let her know that he was finished and would be back in the Hammersons' living quarters in mere moments. Sure enough, when I looked back at the main display screen, there he was, ready to be let back into the base. James took the controls and did the honours, and a few seconds later, he reappeared in the corner of the control room as he lifted his protective enchantments.

"All done," he said cheerfully, "and nothing went wrong for me. Has anything interesting happened here?"

"Are you gonna tell us what you were doing out there?" Marc asked sharply.

Frederic shrugged and smiled. "Probably nothing that matters, and if I were to tell you, I know you'll tell me that I just wasted half an hour of my life and that I'm a fool. But I'm also a father, and these things matter to me."

"What on earth are you talking about, Dad?" Amelia asked, her eyes wide.

"Yes, what *are* you talking about, Frederic?" Lillian added.

He just smiled and shook his head. "I notice that none of you answered my question."

"Nothing's happened here," James told him, "except that those three are not doing the work they're supposed to be doing, and Lucien's about to annex Colombia and he'll probably do the rest of South America in the next few hours."

"Colombia?" he said, his eyes widening. "That's awfully close to one of our antimagic stations. You haven't noticed anything unusual going on there?"

"If you mean explosions that might turn his microphone into a candy cane, no, nothing like that's happened," Natalie said. "But then again, I haven't actually seen him use much magic while he's been there—just little things."

"And Fewul hasn't appeared at all," James said. "I don't think he's noticed a single thing, and for something this big, I can't imagine him pretending not to notice it if he had."

"Oh, was I supposed to stop calling Fewul back?" Rebecca asked suddenly, and until she spoke, I'd forgotten the job she'd been given. "I've just been doing it every couple of minutes, like you said."

"Well, you keep on doing that," Frederic said, smiling at her. "Most likely he's calling the beast back almost instantly and setting it to work so quickly that nobody around him could notice a thing, but there is a chance he is unaware that Fewul has been recalled. If that's the case, his attacks over in Africa may well have stalled, and that can only be a good thing for us."

"Even better that Fewul can't tell him what's going on with the magic in his bedroom," Peter added.

There was no more to say for the time being, so we continued to watch things progress on the outside. Sebastian and Wilwog hadn't come to their senses, but Hignat seemed to have realised that he and his new girlfriend should probably do at least a little studying, or Hall might report to Lucien that she was a bad distraction and should be fired. Hall himself was just about done with Lena; his commentary suggested that there wouldn't be very much about the language itself to teach her, but he could think of a couple of pieces of literature she could benefit from studying.

Lucien, meanwhile, made his announcement in Colombia, not taking a lot of time over it before moving on—perhaps they would have one of those television programs like Australia had a few months ago where the Hammerhearts would tell each region specifically the way it would work going forward. He then pressed on to make the same sorts of announcements in Venezuela, Brazil, and a smaller one in Uruguay. Each time he arrived, the stage was already set up for him and ready to go; obviously the Hammerhearts in each location had been aware of exactly when he would be arriving and had made the arrangements without needing him to be there to direct them. Or perhaps he had used magic to make sure everything was set up for him, who knew.

It was as Lucien was finishing up in Uruguay that something finally happened. It was Erica who first noticed that 3A93's device seemed to have finished its work; he was sitting there, watching the screen, which showed the enormous amount of magic the device had collected, and a zero to indicate that no more magic was coming into it. He observed this for a few seconds, and then as per Frederic Woodward's instructions, he turned the device off for now. We had all agreed on that earlier. Though it would have been interesting, it would have definitely been noticed if we turned the direction of the beam to face downward instead of outward, sucking the magic out of the whole Chopville base instead of just the top of it.

"What now?" Marc asked, looking at Frederic. "Did you give him any further instructions?"

"Only to stay there and wait until Lucien came back, and then to turn the device on again," he said. "Yes, I know Lucien will probably be alerted instantly the moment he starts losing magic again, but we can't give him a chance to put the protections back up before we have a chance to try attacking him again."

"What's the plan for attacking him if you can't use your own magic without it being stripped away?" Erica asked. "That is how this whole thing works, isn't it?"

A brief silence followed this and Erica looked quite nervous, thinking that perhaps she'd interrupted only to say something stupid. In actual fact, it was a good question, and it deserved some consideration. Finally, James said, "Well, unless we attack him with non-magic weapons, I guess we will have to turn the device off just before we attack him. It shouldn't be too hard to make that happen, right?"

"Well, I know 3A93 will listen to me," Frederic said, "but I'm not sure if he'll respond the same way if a teenager tells him what to do.

Maybe you can be in charge of giving him instructions to coordinate with our attack?" he asked his mother.

"I imagine I could," Lillian said. "At least, I'd hope that he recognises me as your mother and a Woodward."

"I'm sure he will," Frederic said. "In that case, the device goes off the moment we're ready to leave our shadows and attack, which we have to be prepared to do almost instantaneously. We should probably have someone ready to knock Lena out at the same time, in case she gets in the way again; and the same for any other Hammerhearts who might be present, if there are any. We can't take any chances."

"Does that cover everything?" Marc asked, his face screwing up as he tried to think. "Lucien will still have his own magic, but if we keep the device on him long enough, he mightn't have any shields. We can account for that if we use those light devices first I suppose; then he won't have a chance to respond. Then, if there's no magic in the walls to come to his aid, we might be able to—er, guys?"

"Yeah?" several people said.

"What's the plan once we get him down?" Marc asked. "Obviously we keep him knocked out, but do we try to get the Sien-Leoard Crystal out of him? Or should we try to suck all the magic out of it instead?"

"I'd think that getting the crystal out would be a lot quicker," James said, "but before even that, maybe an influential charm should be put on him. Maybe if we can turn him into a good guy again, he'll be able to go out there and fix some of the damage he's done."

"There are a couple of problems with that," Frederic said. "Firstly, the evil we saw consume Lucien has infested his very spirit. That evil came from Arnold Hammerson, and I think it is probably beyond the reach of any mind-altering magic to change. Secondly, the ability to operate from inside the body comes from the Villain Crystal, and my research has told me that if it can, the Villain Crystal will attempt to defend its host if it detects that someone is trying to extract it. The only way to stop that from happening is if the host is beyond help, as Moran was; or if the crystal is overpowered, like it was when Fewul extracted it from inside Hall."

"So you're saying that if we try to cut Lucien open to get the crystal, it'll wake him up and give him enough strength to fight us off," Peter summarised.

"That's basically it," Frederic said, and he gave Marc a very level look. "We may have no choice but to kill him before we can take the crystal; it may be the only way."

Marc sighed. "I've already resigned myself that we'll have to do that. That man out there isn't really my brother; he's just occupying my brother's body. But, if we do that right away, what's going to happen out there?"

"Chaos, no doubt," Frederic said, "but that's inevitable too. It would be the same sort of chaos which would have followed the defeat of Arnold Hammerson if not for Lucien, or for the fact that we had a Honnie on our side when that happened. This time, though, there won't be another Lucien to take charge; there'll probably be a bunch of mini-Luciens who will fight for control and cause all sorts of untold destruction."

"Do you think we should proceed with our antimagic plan even then?" James asked. "I mean, maybe we won't have to destroy the crystals, at least not then and there, but it might be a good idea to destroy the rest of the magic that's floating around out there. All those agonators and bludginators and all the rest of it—the world would be so much better off without them."

"That's not a bad idea, but let's not make that call until we know what's going to happen to Lucien," Frederic said firmly. "Right now, wresting him of his magic is our top priority; nothing else matters until we've done that much."

And so the morning continued, now approaching midday. The four Hammerhearts continued to stand guard over their antimagic devices, which were steadily gathering up all the antimagic they could find—the flow was still coming in thick and fast in all four locations. In Lucien's living quarters, 3A93 remained hidden away at the far end of the corridor with his device, while in the main area, the students and teachers had once again gathered, where they would have lunch before the students would spend the afternoon on the written tests—something which would be way more boring than the morning had been. Towards the end, even Sebastian had realised that he'd better at least be tested a little so that he would have something to report, but no such realisation had come to Wilwog. His tutor-turned-girlfriend reported that his geography was very rusty and she would have to work hard on him, though she omitted the part where he was perfectly good at nailing her on top of the Hammersons' expensive-looking dining table.

Lucien had moved on through Argentina, Paraguay and Bolivia, and was now addressing the former nation, now Hammersonian territory, of Ecuador. He was all business this morning, but he had been on the move and constantly active for four hours now, if you stretched his day back to the moment when he'd had Lena against the hallway wall; surely that meant that he would be flagging a little, or at least be ready to sit down to a good lunch. I wondered what he would do at lunchtime—if he would return to the Chopville base and check in on Lena and the others, perhaps even make that study area he had promised them; or if he would stay out and have a more formal lunch with officials from Japan or Korea or something. Whatever he chose to do then, he wasn't showing any signs of slowing down, and my knowledge of South American geography was so terrible that I had no idea how many more countries he had left to annex.

We ourselves were starting to get hungry by the time Lucien finished in Ecuador and moved onto Guyana, so much so that we decided we might as well take advantage of the lull in activity and have a quick lunch before Lucien decided to do something different. As we had at breakfast time, half the group went and had lunch while the other stayed in the control room. I was part of the first group along with Peter, James, Rebecca and Erica, and the five of us spoke hardly a word to each other, nor answered any questions from the other lunch-goers who were curious to know what we had been up to.

When we returned, Lucien was still hard at work, but Marc told us, "He's in Peru now, and we think he only has one country left after this, so anything might be about to happen. We'll get back as quick as we can, but you guys had better be ready for anything."

As if we needed to be told that, I thought, but we all agreed and settled ourselves back in front of the controls as Marc, Amelia, Natalie, Frederic and Lillian left to have their lunches. Nothing much happened for a short time after that, except that Lucien finished up in Peru and moved onto Chile, possibly the last country he had left to do this morning (or this afternoon, as it now was for us). The rest of the spyers didn't have much to show either. In the living quarters, they were finishing their lunches and getting ready to start the first of the written tests which would be in mathematics. Elsewhere, the police commissioner too, was settling down to a nice lunch after a hard morning's work.

To my relief, the five returned to the control room just a couple of minutes before Lucien finished up in Chile, so we were all ready when he teleported from there to Hamster's Stretch Reserve, and then entered the Chopville base through the guest entrance. It looked like he would be going to check in on Lena and the others after all, and that presented us with a dilemma which we had barely a minute to solve: what do we do now? We probably could spring an attack on Lucien and get away with it, but what if those other people got caught in the crossfire? Or worse, what if Hignat or Wilwog were able to intervene in some way? I had no doubt at all that they would want to. I had no such concerns regarding Sebastian, of course; he was a coward and would probably scurry into a corner at the first sign of trouble.

"I say we go for it," Marc said as Lucien stepped out of the elevator and began walking along the corridor below his hidden quarters. "Those people out there aren't armed, and even if Hignat or Wilwog are carrying something, it won't work now—those magic particles are all gone. We can wipe their memories of the whole thing once we're done—those tutors don't even need to remember that they were ever there, really."

"Okay, that sounds reasonable," Frederic said, "but let's not go out there just yet. Give 3A93 time to attack Lucien a little first, just in case he's put up some new protections around himself which are different from any we've experienced so far."

"And if he notices?" Marc enquired.

"It won't be worse than this morning," Frederic shrugged, "but just in case, Rebecca, please press that button more rapidly for a little while —like twice a second instead of once every two minutes. That should keep Fewul away."

We watched silently and alertly as Lucien passed through the wall into the living quarters and began climbing the stairs. The people in the living room heard someone coming and stopped what they were doing, most of them looking nervous—Hall looking ready for trouble—and only Lena looking relaxed, as if she had come to recognise what Lucien's footsteps sounded like compared to those of other people.

Down the other end of the living quarters, 3A93 hadn't heard the footsteps, but he did seem to have heard something; perhaps he had been listening to the sound of the distant voices, and noticed when they had suddenly cut off. He picked up the magic vacuum and began creeping forward with it so that he could hear what was going on, and only when he had drawn level with the den did he recognise the voice of Lucien, at which point he dutifully switched the device back on and pointed it in Lucien's general direction. Good little Hammerheart, I thought to myself.

"How's everything going here?" Lucien asked the group at large. "Have they been productive this morning?"

"We have proceeded as you instructed us, sir," Hall told him. "They've already had lunch, and they're about to start some written tests which will take them through the next four hours at least."

"Ah, very good," Lucien said. "I'm not stopping in for very long—I mainly came back here for lunch, and to check on them—but I guess I do have time to set up a proper learning facility for them. So, while I'm eating, and they're doing their tests, you all brainstorm things you think you'll need to do your jobs as efficiently and effectively as possible. I suggest you go in there"—he nodded at the dining room where Wilwog had been with his girlfriend earlier—"so that your talking won't disturb the kids. I'll come back when I'm done eating, which will probably be in no more than fifteen minutes."

They all agreed and trooped off to the dining room, while Lucien created four small desks for the students, each with its own seat, which he placed far apart from each other so that they couldn't look at each other's work. Then, when they each sat down, he placed a further enchantment on them which would hold them in their seats so that they couldn't get up and spy on each other, unaware that the magic holding them in place would probably be gone within thirty seconds.

"I know it's a bit inconvenient," he said as they squirmed. Or rather, three of them squirmed; only Lena looked comfortable. "But I'm sure you all understand that it must be done. We can't have any cheating going on here, and I know you boys—you in particular"—he glanced at Wilwog—"will be tempted to take a shortcut here and there, but I'm afraid I can't allow it. It's for your own good."

"Then how come *she* isn't held in her seat?" Sebastian asked, glaring at Lena, who smirked back at him.

"Because she knows better than to try to look at any of your answers," Lucien responded. "She knows that if she does, she'll get lower marks than if she just does the work herself; we all know it's true."

"But sir, what if we need to go to the—" Hignat started, and then stopped very suddenly, his eyes widening. My heartbeat quickened as I realised why: the enchantment holding him in place had just lifted, without Lucien even being aware of it.

"Go to the…" Lucien enquired, raising his eyebrows at Hignat.

"To the toilet," Hignat finished meekly.

Lucien shrugged. "The enchantment will lift on its own if it gets really uncomfortable, but otherwise, hold it in until your tutors get back. Once they're here, they can keep an eye on you all, and there won't be any need for this."

Lena was totally unaware of the significance of this, but the three boys swapped surprised looks, mixed with a dawning comprehension. They understood now that something had happened; an enchantment had been lifted from them, and Lucien hadn't done it. There were so many ways this situation could have gone wrong—and indeed, if any one of them had any common sense, they would have spoken up and told Lucien that something was wrong—but none of them did so, perhaps because they were all so relieved to be able to move their bottoms, and they didn't want to give Lucien a reason to put the spell back on them again. I exhaled slowly—that had been *way* too close.

"If that's how fast the magic is being sucked up," Marc whispered, as though he thought Lucien or the others might hear him if he spoke in a normal voice, "then his shields are probably gone now. We should attack now before something else happens to blow our cover."

"I agree," James said, not bothering to whisper himself. "Who's got the magic enhancer now?"

"I have it," Frederic said.

"Okay, so you and Marc go out with your magic, and Peter, you go out with the light device you used earlier. I imagine that's all we should need this time, since the tutors are out of the way and those guys—oh shit!"

The time we had taken to discuss the attack, though it had only really been seconds, had cost us dearly. Lucien had left the living room and had gone around to the other side of the top floor; 3A93 had heard him coming and without any time to hide properly, had darted into the den so that he wouldn't be seen when Lucien came around the corner. Unfortunately, the den happened to be Lucien's destination—probably he'd been intending to have his lunch in there—but he was brought up short when he came face-to-face with 3A93, holding that ridiculous megaphone thing before him like a shield (which I supposed it was, in a way), and looking utterly horrified.

"Er—what's going on here?" Lucien asked into the startled silence, but no response was coming from 3A93. The man looked paralysed with fear, and I couldn't blame him; Frederic wouldn't have planned for this, and he probably hadn't given the man any lines to say.

"We gotta get out there, *right* now. *Right now!*" Marc shouted, jumping to his feet and dashing into the corner.

"Marc, wait! You have to be protected!" Amelia screamed in alarm as Peter and Frederic also jumped up and hurried to the corner.

In the time it took us to gather up the devices to make the three of them invisible, untraceable, and in separate soundproof barriers, the worst of the damage had already been done. The unfortunate Hammerheart had recovered himself to do one thing before Lucien dealt with him, and that was to withdraw a single magical device from his pocket—one which had survived the magic vacuum by virtue of being behind it the whole time—and gave it a single click. It was a vanisher, I saw, and it sent the magic vacuum to a place where Lucien would never be able to reach it. The vanishers Amelia and I had created, of which this was one, were designed in such a way that something that had just been vanished could be brought back if the same device was used. That meant that the magic to bring it back would be possible if Lucien tried it quickly enough, or if he had access to the device in question, but that wasn't something that occurred to him.

In fact, in the beginning, at least, Lucien paid no mind at all to the thing that had just been vanished in front of him. His focus was one hundred percent on the Hammerheart before him, and as we watched, Lucien took his mind within his own and began sifting through it. By the time Marc and Frederic were on the outside, and James was letting Peter out, Lucien would have learnt everything the Hammerheart had known—which wouldn't have been all the details, but it would have been enough to cause him great concern.

"So, you have betrayed me," Lucien said, his voice cold, his eyes colder. "There is only one ending befitting of people like you, but I'm going to give you one chance to repent. Tell me *how* that device worked. Tell me *how* they were able to come up with a way to actually steal the very substance of magic."

A silence followed. The man opened and closed his mouth a few times, but no sound was forthcoming. Lucien gave him a few seconds, and then said, "I see—you really don't know. Of course, they wouldn't tell you something like that. They only told you enough to get you to do what they wanted, and they knew that if you got caught, you would be dispensable to them. That is a little surprising that they would stoop to such a depth, but oh well—it matters naught to me, as do you, my friend."

Lucien blinked and the Hammerheart instantly fell over, dead. I'd known that was coming, and I knew it would be quick and utterly unremarkable so far as Lucien was concerned, but it was still a shock all the same. The attack against Lucien came an instant later, and unfortunately, in the time since the magic vacuum had been vanished, Lucien had thought to recast his shields. He spun around, attacked, dodged, attacked again, and it was well underway. I had no idea if it was Marc or Frederic with whom he was engaged, but I knew it was only one, because the other was doing something else. From one of the pockets of the dead Hammerheart, unnoticed by Lucien, the vanisher rose into the air, and then disappeared as it too was vanished, thereby putting the magic vacuum out of any possible reach for Lucien.

The fight continued then, with bright lights flying in every direction, several loud bangs filling every second, and Lucien moving around so quickly that Peter was never able to land a hit on him using his light device. At one point, Hignat, Wilwog, Sebastian and Lena all came around to see what was going on, and all four of them were knocked unconscious as remnants of the battle spilled over in their direction. Smarter than that, the ten tutors didn't come to investigate the noise, though they surely would have heard something going on.

"You keep pressing that button, Bec," Natalie said to her sister, her voice a higher pitch than usual. "We've actually got a chance to win this if we can keep Fewul away."

"Yes, we really do," James said through clenched teeth. "If they could just land a hit on him—one single hit. He won't have time to cast protections on the base, so if they knock him out, that'll be the end of it."

It should have been a simple equation. Lucien only had the Sien-Leoard Crystal, while Marc and Frederic had the Hero Crystal and the magic enhancer, and both of them were more experienced with magic than Lucien. The Sien-Leoard Crystal had been weakened at least a little bit by the magic vacuums it had been subjected to, but then the magic enhancer was getting its power directly from the Sien-Leoard Crystal, so that didn't count as an advantage for either side. What did count as an advantage for Lucien was his Honnie mind, and the increased powers of concentration had to be the only reason why he was able to take them both on and remain standing. It did explain why he had to dodge so much, as for once he had less raw power than his opponents.

"Should any of us help?" I asked into the terrified silence of the control room.

"I don't think we can do anything without putting them in danger," Amelia said, and there were tears in her eyes.

There was a massive explosion then, one which shattered almost everything in the den and caused the walls to begin to crack. There was no sign of Lucien after that, which meant they'd either gotten him or he'd gotten them and then teleported away. I quickly checked the spyer set to follow Lucien to see which it was, and my heart sank: he was standing alone in the living room, still within earshot of where the fight had been, and as I watched, he began placing more spells upon himself, including that of invisibility. When the spyer started moving again, it was to reveal that he was on the verge of ambushing Marc and Frederic from behind.

There was no time to warn them of the attack coming. They were caught off-guard, but Frederic was at least able to turn and respond in kind. The two of them began to battle with nothing but the unconscious bodies of the four students lying between them. Lucien seemed to notice that the attack wasn't as fierce as it had been before, and the reason for that was that Marc was no longer participating. The ambush had caught him off-guard sufficiently enough that he had been knocked out cold. Peter stood hesitantly to one side, but he no longer dared to use his device to attack—whether because he couldn't see Lucien or because he couldn't see Frederic and didn't want to risk hitting him now that the orientation of the battle had shifted, I didn't know. All I knew was that, for the time being, all our hopes rested with the former Sorcerer.

"What can we do? What can we do?" Rebecca squeaked.

"You can just keep pressing that button," Erica said harshly. "As for the rest of us, is there any way we can revive Marc? Or should we bring him and Peter back in?"

"We have to keep Lucien busy," James said, "so that he doesn't have a chance to think about what he might have gotten out of that guy's head. We have to press this attack as best we can, and anything we do could upset things. Even Marc could cause problems if he jumps in now. I'm going to bring him and Peter back in, and if anything goes wrong with Frederic, we'll send Marc straight back out again to pick up where he left off."

So it was in that spirit that we drew Marc and Peter back into the base, but then we hit a small snag. Marc couldn't be revived by any magic we had readily available to us. Whatever Lucien had done had been a little different from the normal knock-out magic we normally used. It meant that when Frederic flagged in exhaustion and was on the verge of being overcome, Marc wasn't ready to take his place. We were forced to bring Frederic back into the base earlier than we would have liked, leaving Lucien without an opponent, but there was nothing else for it. Even in our advantageous position, we couldn't risk losing any of our number, and especially not Frederic Woodward.

Lucien didn't waste any time speaking to us this time, as he normally would after we failed an attack against him. He only took a moment to revive the four people on the floor before teleporting away, and the spyer showed him reappearing in a strange, snow-covered place I didn't recognise at all—but for the moment, there was nothing we could do about that. Marc was still unconscious, and we needed to solve that problem before we could give chase.

Chapter 28: Covering Tracks

Natalie and I were the first two to scramble out of our seats to help Frederic stagger into one of his own when he reappeared in the corner of the control room. He had seen Marc's unconscious body where it lay a short distance from the corner, with Amelia crouched beside him, trying desperately to wake him up. Frederic passed the magic enhancer to Natalie, it still being in his hand from the battle, and she hurried over to Amelia's side to attempt to rouse Marc. As precious second after precious second ticked by and Marc still didn't wake up, I began to worry that this was more serious than just being knocked out. What if Lucien had done something far more damaging and possibly permanent to him?

There certainly were plenty of options if Lucien had wanted to do permanent damage to Marc—he was really only limited by his imagination, and he'd had enough time, as he ran back around from the living room, to come up with something truly awful. The worst thing he could have done was wipe Marc's memory, as Hall had once done to Amelia (without a Honnie on our side, that would be a permanent loss now), but I didn't think that was what this was. For one thing, Amelia hadn't been knocked out by that, and whatever this was, it was keeping Marc unconscious.

Erica too scrambled out of her seat, heading for the cabinet and retrieving something else from it. The sudden glare which filled the room a moment later revealed it to be the Light Crystal, and my heart leapt with hope—if nothing else worked, the Light Crystal might. Erica ran around the chairs and passed the crystal to Amelia, who gripped it tightly and screwed up her face, her tears now falling freely. It didn't happen all at once but I did see a twitch in Marc's body, and then a low groan came from his throat.

"Marc?"

"What's so bright?" he muttered, opening his eyes, and then trying to raise his hands to cover them.

He's gonna be okay, I thought, as Amelia wept and Erica hurriedly took back the Light Crystal and returned it to the cabinet. I let out a relieved sigh and looked back at the control panel…and then my breath stopped as suddenly as if a giant rock had suddenly appeared in my throat. Sheer horror filled me as I realised what I was seeing—Lucien was standing in the snow in a place I didn't recognise, with nothing around him but more snow. The wind was blowing his clothes around him as he stood there in the midst of what looked like a very serious conversation with the Beast of Magic, who remained in Stella's form. Everyone else in the control room had been so thoroughly distracted by

Marc's plight that nobody had kept an eye on what he was doing, and Rebecca had forgotten to keep pressing the button…

"*Shit*! *Shit*! *Shit*!" I finally managed to say, and the alarm in my voice caught everyone's attention at once. James saw where I was looking and his face went as white as a sheet.

"*Rebecca*! The *button*!"

She gasped in horror and pressed it, causing Fewul to vanish from Lucien's side in a flash of bright light. More flashes of bright light followed as Lucien continued to attempt to call on the beast, and Rebecca struggled with him to keep it at bay. Both of their faces were screwed up in concentration; Lucien looking determined, Rebecca looking desperate and scared.

"Hang in there, Bec," Natalie said as she and Amelia helped Marc into his seat.

"Pass the thing to someone else if you need to give your finger a rest," I told her, remembering how it had only taken me a moment of fatigue for everything to go wrong the previous night.

She was beginning to pant now, her face gleaming with sweat and her eyes ready to shed tears. "I'm so sorry!" she squeaked. "I forgot to keep pushing the button."

"Let me do it for a bit," Erica offered, and Rebecca gratefully handed it over to her before sinking back in her seat and burying her face in her hands. Natalie went to her and the two of them clung to each other, both of them looking pale and scared.

Erica began pressing the button in earnest, but the handover had been enough time for Lucien to achieve a small victory. I'd had one eye on the spyer the whole time so I saw how he did it. Though Fewul hadn't been given enough time to truly take shape, it had been enough time for Lucien to give the beast a single order, and for the beast to comply before disappearing again. There was now a piece of paper in Lucien's hand, and his eyes moved rapidly as he quickly read and digested what it said. A slow smile began to dawn on his face as he did so, and there was what looked like hope lighting in his eyes.

"What's he doing?" Peter asked very nervously. "Is there any way to angle this thing so that we can see what he's reading?"

"You don't have to," Amelia said, and a moment later, she was proven right by the display swinging around to look over Lucien's shoulder at the words Fewul had written to him. "It will angle the display automatically depending on what it thinks we need to see most. That usually means a front-on view, but occasionally it will be something like this."

Nobody responded to her words. I heard them, and I supposed the others did too, but none of us were really paying attention. All our focus was on the piece of paper in Lucien's hands, and I managed to read the whole thing once before the display swung back around to its original position. James may have created the device which was now watching Lucien, but its design had been based on the original magic performed by Amelia back on Rock Haulter; and whatever intelligence she had given it, it wasn't smart enough to understand that we might think the piece of paper a bit more important than the knowledge that Lucien was trying to call Fewul again. For when the display settled, that was all it showed: bright flashes of light around Lucien as he resumed the struggle with Erica.

I didn't really need a second read of the paper, though. The message hadn't been long, but it had been enough:

> *There is no doubt at all that your enemies are manipulating the substance of magic. Your living area is now devoid of all the protective spells you placed on it, and the crystal inside you has been weakened considerably. If given much more time, you will no longer be able to call on me safely.*
>
> *You ask me what path you can take to learn what they now know. I can only advise you to research magic theory, specifically those theories which explore what magic may be made of. Most of what you read will be wrong, but it is your only chance to learn what they have learnt.*

Shit! *Shit*! *Shit*! I didn't say it aloud this time, but I certainly thought it. Fewul had just pointed Lucien straight at the thesis we had read the day before. The beast couldn't tell him which one was correct—maybe because the beast itself didn't know which one was correct—but it knew enough to know that someone had found the correct solution, and it was far more likely to be a magicologist than an original discovery by us.

"We need to go out there before he learns anything else," Marc said, looking at the main display and then realising that the base was still in the now shattered Hammerson den, where James had moved us the moment Lucien had run into poor 3A93, whose usefulness to us had now ended.

"We're gonna have to teleport to him," James said. "You guys ready?"

We all were, so James concentrated on Lucien and the base disappeared into the nothingness of teleportation. It wasn't the longest teleportation I'd ever experienced, but it was sure up there with them. Eventually, we reappeared just feet away from where Lucien stood, but we all realised immediately that teleporting the whole base had been a mistake. Erica hadn't been able to keep up her side of the battle while we had all been frozen in place during the teleportation, and it had been enough for Fewul to give Lucien another piece of paper. This time,

James flew us around behind Lucien so that we could read it over his shoulder:

> *There does exist an encyclopedia of magic, some of it you have seen before. It was compiled by the Woodwards and they update it regularly with new research and resources. It is stored on an Internet server and is protected by magic as well as cyber security, but you can access it from anywhere with the credentials below. I can tell you also that the entire program was downloaded by someone from the Chopville Public Library three days ago, which is strong evidence that your enemies used it to learn what they now know.*

Sometimes, there just weren't any words bad enough to cover it.

"Someone needs to get out there and vanish any more pieces of paper that come along before he gets a chance to read them," Frederic said firmly, his face very pale, and not just from his previous battle, "but I fear it may already be too late. Those are the same credentials we used."

"It took us yonks to find the right theory," James said, "and we were smart enough to manipulate time to do it. We're better off going straight to the server and destroying it before Lucien can download anything from it."

"If we're going to teleport, we need to leave someone behind who can make sure Fewul doesn't come back," I pointed out. It was bad enough to make such a mistake once; doing it again would be unforgivable.

"I hate that I'm the first one to say this," Peter said, "but I think it's time to say it. It may be time to use the gun."

"We can't use the gun right now," Natalie snapped, "not without any ammo, and the time it'll take us to get some will be too long."

They were referring to the last and worst of the devices Natalie had created, one which hadn't been brought downstairs yet. I hadn't seen it except in Natalie's mind when she had been communicating with me telepathically the night before, and she did think of it as a gun, whether it looked like one or not. It was a non-magical device like all the others, but it was the only one that was meant as a weapon. The plan called for us to resort to this device only when all other options had failed, and we were forced to destabilise all the magic around Lucien (and now that he had swallowed the Sien-Leoard Crystal, that would make him even more vulnerable to this kind of weapon if we could hit it directly).

It stored small amounts of antimagic inside it, and when the trigger was pulled, it would release a tiny burst of antimagic in the shape of a bullet. If we understood magic and antimagic particles the way we thought we did, the bullet would continue at speed and with no deviation until it hit magic, at which point it would annihilate. If there was more antimagic than magic, the remainder of the bullet would just keep going; if the other way around, as would usually be the case, then some magic would be left over after the explosion, and more bullets would be required. The gun could store enough antimagic for over a thousand bullets, though Natalie hadn't been sure of the exact amount. Reloading the guns would be impossible in battle because it had to be a careful procedure where the gun was connected to the antimagic storage unit, so if we had to use them, we had to shoot well and do as much damage as possible the first time. We would also have to be as far from the target as we could reasonably be.

Meanwhile, leaving us with no choice, Lucien teleported away again. James swore loudly and nobody bothered to tell him off.

"We have to go after him," he said, "and I know this will give him a chance to call Fewul again, but we have to teleport the base. I'm going to take us back to the Chopville Hammerheart base and then we can get out and teleport after him in person, but we can't just leave the whole base here."

I wanted to argue with him—this really did feel like it fell under the category of 'making the same mistake more than once'—but I could think of a good reason why we should follow his advice. If magic started going bonkers, we would all need to make a quick getaway from the base —not just us, but everyone else in here. If that happened, we would need to be somewhere reasonably familiar—somewhere where we wouldn't be trapped and killed, by starvation or cold weather or anything. Anywhere inside the Hammerheart network would be equally bad given that it was all shrunken, but at least we would have time to fly out if necessary.

Nobody else objected to James's suggestion, so he wasted no time in taking the controls, concentrating for a moment, and then executing the teleportation. We all froze in place as we were sucked into nothingness for a time, reappearing shortly in the living room of Lucien's living quarters. Very little time had passed since the battle, and though the four teenagers were awake, they were all pretty shaken—Lena less so than the others, given how many of these types of episodes she had witnessed in the last few days, but even she was a little rattled. Only one of the tutors, Hall, had emerged from the dining room to see what had happened; the others were probably still sheltering in there in terror.

"So who's going out there and who's staying here?" James asked.

People began getting out of their seats at once. Marc, Frederic and I all hurried into the corner while Natalie and Amelia went for the cabinet, returning with the Villain and Light Crystals respectfully. Peter also joined us in the corner, after he'd collected a number of devices from the cabinet to go along with the light device he already had. That would leave James, Rebecca, Erica and Lillian here to monitor things as best they could.

There was no time to fiddle-fart around with protections that would make it possible for us to communicate with each other once we were out, except by telepathy which was confusing at the best of times. James therefore dropped Marc out of the base with only two types of protection around him: untraceability (our kind) and the spell which would make magic pass through him. That meant that the people in the living room were aware of him immediately, but none of them had a chance to do or say anything before he dropped all five of them, one after another. Then as the rest of us were let out of the base one at a time, Marc went to drop the rest of the tutors in the dining room. There was a single shout and a couple of terrified screams, and then silence as Marc hurried back to us. He hadn't killed them—I could see that Sebastian was breathing, at least —but at least we could operate without having to worry about them sneaking up on us.

Lucien wasn't here, of course, but now that we were out, it wasn't going to be easy to find him. Too late, I remembered that he was untraceable, which meant that we wouldn't be able to just teleport to him. It was easy to forget that little factoid back in the control room, where James had set up the spyer so that it could keep track of his particular hole in reality.

As Marc re-joined us and began casting an invisibility veil around us along with a soundproof barrier, however, my problem was solved. Rebecca contacted me telepathically then, choosing me over Natalie because I was guaranteed to receive it thanks to the spells I had put on myself. She was visualising Lucien's current location, according to the spyer, which was showing him alone in a large warehouse, surrounded by rows and rows, and columns and columns, of computer servers. He was presently walking slowly up and down the aisles, examining each server with his magic, and we had no time at all to waste. I told Rebecca to send that message to Marc so that he could teleport us all at once, and then watched his eyes widen as he received the message.

"We're teleporting now, you guys, hold onto yourselves," he said, and a moment later we did.

Teleporting in person was different to teleporting in the base. When we had been in the control room it had been the base which was hurtling through the void, so although everything outside the base had appeared as nothing, I could still see the control room and the people around me. We were all frozen in place, not a single part of us able to move, except perhaps neurons. This time, however, as it was ourselves being teleported, even though the teleportation was being applied to the whole group rather than each of us individually, there was nothing at all for us to perceive between locations. There was nothing at all until we materialised in the server warehouse, Marc standing no more than a few paces away from Lucien as he walked away from us.

"John, let James know we're here," Marc hissed at me, and then in a more normal voice, added, "Oh—we're in a soundproof barrier, so we should be fine to speak. Now, how are we gonna find the right server before he does?"

Frederic started to say something but I wasn't listening, wrapped up in the telepathy as I was. I let James know where we were, and he let us know that we hadn't shown up on the spyer following Lucien, and I let him know that the spyer didn't carry that same enchantment which made it possible to see invisible people—that only applied to the main display. I then told him to tell Erica to keep pressing that button as much as possible; we absolutely could not risk Fewul appearing here at the same time as us, not even with all the magic we had on our side.

That included the small magic vacuum I had used earlier, which was still in my pocket, and for a moment, I considered using it—surely it couldn't hurt to make Lucien a little weaker while we had a chance. Then I rejected the idea. The first thing that device would do, the instant I turned it on, would be to eat up all the protection around us. It might work if I made myself invisible and soundproof, and then Marc released me from the group protections, but there was no time to walk him through that now.

"Great," Marc said sourly in response to Frederic's words. "Okay, here's what I'm going to suggest. You, me and Natalie should split up and search the servers just like Lucien is, and if one of us finds the server that has the encyclopedia on it, we should use our magic to extract the relevant hard drive. You three"—he looked at Peter, Amelia and me— "follow Lucien, and if he looks like he's found one that interests him, do whatever you have to do to stop him from getting it. Vanish the whole server if you have to."

"This crystal mightn't like what I'm trying to do with it," Natalie said hesitantly. "What if it thinks I'm doing good by trying to stop Lucien?"

"You're stealing a hard drive from a server farm; that's about as illegal as you can get," Marc pointed out. "I think you'll be fine. Come on, let's go."

We set off in different directions; Marc, Natalie and Frederic heading one way, no doubt intending to split up at the earliest chance; and the rest of us heading the other way. We had to scramble to catch up with Lucien, me leading the way and the other two following close behind. I didn't dare look over my shoulder at either of them, but I had seen them both before I had passed them: Amelia had her hand in her pocket around the Light Crystal, and her other hand had been holding a communicator— whether she would be using it or not, I didn't know. Peter had several devices in his pockets, so he could have been holding any of them right now. I hoped one of them was the light device, because I was sure that Lucien must have a shield around himself at this moment.

"Pete," I hissed out of the side of my mouth, once again forgetting that Lucien wouldn't be able to hear our words, "maybe you should try shooting him now. He won't be able to revive himself if you get a hit in now, and he's probably not expecting it."

"That's a good idea," Peter said, and a second later, I heard the tiny click of the device in Peter's hand.

It missed. I don't know how, but it missed. Almost the very moment when it should have hit him directly between the shoulders, Lucien swayed slightly, and it flew past him probably by mere centimetres, zooming down the remainder of the aisle and whacking harmlessly into a set of drawers at the far end. Without turning or even breaking stride, Lucien flicked a spell over his shoulder in Peter's direction; it went straight through Peter and onwards up the aisle, whacking just as harmlessly into whatever had been at the end of it. Lucien appeared unconcerned by any of this; he just kept doing what he was doing, looking for the right server, though now he was aware that we were here. Damn it, I thought, and the sentiment was echoed aloud by Peter behind me.

How had he done that? How had he known that something was coming that he would have to dodge, and then known exactly when and how to dodge so that it missed him? That shouldn't have been possible, not even with his level of magic. He certainly didn't have Fewul to help him, not only because Erica should have been still pressing the button to keep Fewul away (unless the job had been passed back to Rebecca now), but also because I hadn't seen any of the bright flashes of light, or the smoke, which would have indicated the return of the Beast of Magic.

"The crystal isn't helping me," Amelia said sadly behind me. "I'm trying to get it to help us find the server before Lucien, but it won't go warm. Why won't it go warm?"

"Maybe it knows that you're asking it something that's impossible," Peter suggested.

"Or it's too specific a request," I added, though I didn't think that would be it. Didn't the Light Crystal realise that if Lucien found the server before us and was able to learn the truth about magic from it, it could very well be the end of magic? No, of course not, because if that were to happen, it would be our doing which brought about the end of magic in response to Lucien, not the other way around. Understanding why the Light Crystal responded to some things and not others really was a tricky business.

"Maybe ask it to help us get through this without anything really bad happening to any of us," Peter said.

A brief silence, and then Amelia sighed. "Okay, I think that worked —I *hope* that worked. I hope the crystal interpreted it the way I meant it. I guess we'll have to wait and see."

Lucien had reached the end of the aisle; he turned and began traversing the next one, slowly looking to either side as he went. The three of us crept along behind, trying to make our footsteps as light as possible so that nothing could be felt through the ground. That probably wasn't much of a risk given that the ground was made of stone, and the constant whirring of spinning hard drives, not to mention the deep rumbling of industrial air conditioning, would have covered up any sound we might have inadvertently made, so long as we were careful.

Then without warning, Lucien stopped, staring at one of the servers to our right. It was on the third row and looked no different to its cousins all around it, and yet it had captured Lucien's attention. We all stopped as well, and I knew the others were holding their breath just as I was, waiting to see if this was the moment to jump into action. I stared at the server, ready to vanish the whole thing if necessary, never mind who might have been storing their baby pictures on there or whatever.

Lucien raised his hand, extending one of the fingers towards the server. The finger continued to extend past its regular dimensions, lengthening and changing colour. I had no idea of its exact function, but it was clear enough that he had attached something electronic to himself; and although it didn't seem to have any adaptor that I could see, I could guess what it would do. He had come up with a quick and easy way of downloading information directly into his brain, so that he could use his Honnie mind to rapidly sort through it and reject anything that wasn't relevant. Later, I would wish that I'd come up with the idea to put a virus in there or something, but there was never a chance for that.

I knew what I had to do, and didn't waste any more time asking questions. I focused on the server (it would have to be the whole thing after all, since Lucien hadn't made any effort to remove the hard drive), and caused the whole thing to vanish. There was a brief spark from the hole it had left behind, and peering in there, I saw a few dangling wires —the only sign that there had ever been a server there. Lucien started in surprise, but it didn't look right to me, somehow. I couldn't have explained how it didn't look right, but it only took me a few seconds to recall why it wasn't right. Lucien knew we were here, so he *would* have been expecting us to try to stop him from downloading the information.

He appeared to steady himself, and then said in a quiet voice that nevertheless reached all our ears, "Nice try, but you really think I'm that dumb? Something that valuable, I'm sure there are backups. I just have to look for the ones that are protected by magic."

He began moving again, resuming his search to either side of him, now holding the electronic thing attached to his finger in the air, as if ready to use it at a moment's notice. My heart rose in surprise and gladness—I knew for a fact that there wasn't a backup. Frederic had said himself that there was only one copy, and if that had been it, the rest of Lucien's search would be fruitless. He would figure that out for himself soon enough, but in the meantime…

"If that's it, then I'm gonna let Marc and the others know what just happened," I told Peter and Amelia, and then lapsed into the telepathy. Marc, Frederic and Natalie began teleporting in behind us moments later, but while Marc and Natalie joined us in our slow pursuit of Lucien, Frederic hung back by the hole where the server had been.

"So what now?" Marc asked. "Should we try attacking him again?"

"We can try, but he's figured out a way to know exactly when and how to dodge our attacks," Peter said, holding up the light device, "including this one."

"Maybe we should send so many at him that he can't dodge them all at the same time," Natalie suggested, smiling a little.

"Stay with him," Frederic said, catching up to us, and the tone in his voice made me turn in further surprise—he sounded much more alert and alarmed than I felt.

"What's up?" Amelia asked.

"That wasn't the server we used," he said grimly. "I don't know why he thought that it was, but it was never the right one. I'm not sure exactly where the right server is—they do get moved around sometimes, and I already checked where I thought it was—but I would recognise the traces of magical protection around it anywhere. Even if Lucien found a way to neutralise the protection, he wouldn't be able to get rid of all the traces, and he probably wouldn't even bother trying anyway."

And that could only mean… "Then the server's still out there, and he could still find it," I said. "Come on."

The pursuit continued, all six of us now following Lucien and quite likely all of us considering ways we could attack him. If Marc, Frederic and Natalie all laid into him at the same time, with Amelia standing back and wishing for their safety the whole time, he would have so much magic stacked against him that he couldn't possibly win, and might even end up losing. Would it be enough to halt his search? Perhaps, but then it would be down to Peter and me to find the right server, and neither of us had any tools at our disposal that would tell us which server contained the encyclopedia.

Then Lucien stopped again, and we all stopped with him. He was once again looking at a particular server, this one on the left and on the second row. I immediately vanished it, not hesitating for a second, but a moment later, Frederic said, "Again, wrong one."

A slow and truly evil smile began to spread across Lucien's face. "Thanks for giving away your position to me, you fools," he said in a soft, dangerous voice. "Did you really think I had to be standing in front of the right server in order to access its contents? The moment I knew you were here, I started checking them all with my mind and my magic. I've already got everything I need, and you're *too late!*"

He ended his little speech in a roar, and sent a huge blast of magic at us a moment later. It passed through us all, but the air rose in temperature around us as it did. Two things happened almost simultaneously then: Lucien vanishing into thin air, teleporting out of the warehouse now that he had gotten everything he needed; and all around us, though mostly behind us where the magic had been directed, servers beginning to explode into fireballs. The enormous room filled with the sound of explosions and bright lights as flames burst up all around us, then overriding all of that came a blaring security alarm.

"Let's get out of here!" I shouted as the columns of servers on either side of us swayed, and things began to topple off their shelves.

The six of us tried to gather close together, which wasn't easy as a large server crashed to the floor right between us, spouting flames in all directions and causing us all to jump back. Marc could have still operated the teleportation, if it hadn't been for a tangle of wires coming down and draping itself over him. They weren't live wires, but they were still sparking, and one of them set his hair on fire. Still, he managed to teleport us a little; we rematerialised a few paces from where we had been, and I let out a gasp of pain as my leg came up against something that was on fire.

Frederic took charge. Unlike me and Marc (and Natalie and Amelia, I would learn shortly), he wasn't on fire, and he was able to use his magic without distraction. A cool head in a crisis was our Frederic Woodward. He started by putting a protective bubble around the six of us, forcing all the wreckage of the servers in our area to fall a safe distance away from us. It included the very odd sight of one such server sliding along thin air over our heads, as if there were a glass slope there and it was sliding down towards the floor.

The next thing Frederic did was put out all the fires within the bubble, so that the six of us were able to straighten up. Marc's hair looked blackened and burnt, as did part of Amelia's long hair. Natalie's hair had been spared, but her clothes hadn't been; her top was singed, but at least it wasn't falling off her. My right pant-leg was in a similar shape, but Peter, the lucky bugger, looked totally unhurt. I never got a chance to ask any questions, though, for that was when Marc teleported us away from the now ruined warehouse, well before any of its staff found us. We reappeared in Lucien's living room, where everything was just as we had left it, but there was no sign of Lucien here.

"We have to find him, before he has a chance to really look at what he's found," Marc spoke rapidly. "I'm gonna ask James."

As he lapsed into telepathy, Frederic went around the group, fixing up those of us who had been burnt in some way by the disaster of the server warehouse. Seconds later, Marc spoke again, and it was in some confusion.

"According to James, Lucien's appeared in a desert of some sort, except it's nowhere near here because it looks like sunrise there."

"He is covering all points of the compass just to try to throw us off," Frederic said grimly. "The server farm where we just were was located in Alaska, and though I'm not completely sure, I think prior to that, Lucien teleported to Antarctica. If he's now in a desert and it's sunrise, he's probably in the Middle East or eastern Africa."

"I'm teleporting us now," Marc said, and a moment later, he did so. It was another long transportation, but we soon enough reappeared a few paces away from Lucien. Yes, we were most definitely in a desert; the air was cool and fresh, and the sun was only just appearing in the east. Lucien was standing stock-still, his expression focused, flickering rapidly as his mind worked at a frenetic pace.

"Spread out, encircle him, and we'll start attacking," Frederic said. "Peter, give me that device of yours."

"What? Why?" Peter asked, his eyes wide as Frederic snatched the light device from him.

"I'm altering it so that it'll remove his shields from the inside if it hits," Frederic said, performing a spell on it and giving it back to him. "You might as well try something different, if you think he'll be able to dodge what you were doing before."

It was less a circle than a square in the end, for Amelia had no weapons with which to fight and therefore stepped back out of the way, gripping the Light Crystal in both hands. I also didn't join the circle, though in my case it was because I was doing something I'd thought briefly of doing two days earlier, when we had encircled Lucien back in the old school grounds: I raised myself up into the air and hovered over him, ready to rain spells down on him from above. Marc did a quick lap of the circle, enclosing us all inside an anti-teleportation ring to prevent Lucien from escaping (if the rest of us needed to escape, we could do so by slipping into our shadows).

As soon as Marc took his place in the circle, directly opposite Natalie and with Frederic to his left and Peter to his right, he counted us all in from three. All five of us attacked at exactly the same time; Lucien anticipated an attack again, but not all of it this time. He was able to sway out of the way of the attacks from Peter and Frederic, forcing both of them to quickly dodge out of the way so that they wouldn't get hit by each other's spells. My attack also missed, hitting the ground where he had been standing a fraction of a second earlier, but Marc and Natalie both scored direct hits. Both spells bounced harmlessly off his shield (perhaps they could have overpowered him if they'd hit in the same place instead of on different sides, but maybe not even then).

Marc and Frederic quickly moved a little closer to each other, so that the four of them could attack in straight lines without having to worry about hitting each other, and then the attack resumed. Lucien didn't even bother to fight back this time but just kept ducking and weaving in and out of the spells, looking rather fluid as he did so. It didn't seem to be troubling him at all to be doing this, and he was even able to keep that look of concentration on his face, as if he were able to fight all of us and read his encyclopedia at the same time.

On the contrary, I was getting rather tired up here. It wasn't so much the hovering that was doing it (that was fairly easy, actually), but the constant use of magic. This approach wasn't having any effect at all—I didn't have any magic that could penetrate Lucien's shield, nor did Marc or Natalie. Frederic technically had the same level of magic as Lucien, so if he landed a hit, it *might* work, but then again, it might not. Peter's attacks *would* work if they could just hit, but no matter how hard he tried, he wasn't able to land a single shot on Lucien. How? How could this be possible?

We need a new approach, I thought to myself, pausing in my own attack so that I could catch my breath and think. What else can we try that might work? For a moment, nothing came to me, and then something did. The only thing that could be making it possible for Lucien to do all these things at the same time was his Honnie mind, so that was what we needed to attack—and fortunately, we had ways of doing that. True, Lucien knew about those techniques now, and may have protected himself against them since we had attacked his magic that morning—but then again, maybe he had focused on the shields and the untraceability, and had forgotten to protect his mind…

"Attack his Honnie mind," I told the others—those who would be able to perform that kind of magic. "Fill it with noise like we did last night—he may not be protected against that anymore."

"Good idea," Marc panted, easing up on his attack so that he could concentrate. "I'll have to duplicate the device I made that did that—"

It was a mistake. I knew it as soon as Marc started talking, but it was too late to do anything about it. Lucien immediately noticed that the attack had slowed on one side, and he sent a huge blast of power out in that direction. It overpowered all of the protections Marc had put around himself, including the magic that would cause other magic to pass right through him. He was blasted backwards, crying out in pain and dropping his crystal; and even from my position, I saw a smile light up Lucien's face as he looked around. He had successfully neutralised all our protections, overwhelmed them by sheer power, and now he could see and sense us all.

Peter and Natalie immediately did the smart thing and vanished into their shadows. Lucien probably assumed they had teleported away and turned his attention to Frederic. The two of them began to battle, and I quickly flew out of the way lest I get caught in the line of fire. I dropped to the ground a short distance away, scooped up the Hero Crystal, had to juggle the crystals as they split into the six Sorcerous Crystals, and then scrambled over to where Marc lay in a pool of blood. I pressed the crystals into his hand and watched them slowly reform (far too slowly) into the Hero Crystal again.

"Fix yourself up, now, quickly," I panted into his face, and then stood up, ready to defend him if necessary.

Ahead of me, I had a clear view of the battle between Lucien and Frederic. It was a good battle, but as experienced as he was with magic, Frederic couldn't win it. Lucien was too fast and far too focused. I could see where Natalie and Peter, still in their shadows and appearing like ghosts in my vision, had positioned themselves too. Natalie had taken up position behind Lucien, not quite in direct line with Frederic, while Peter had stationed himself almost directly in front of me. As I watched, he emerged from his shadow, took a single shot at Lucien, and then disappeared again. It was a nice tactic, but Lucien dodged this spell as easily as he had dodged all the others.

"You're too late, again," Lucien snarled at Frederic as the two of them continued to dance around each other, "and as per usual, you're no match for me. How many times do I have to crush you before you understand that, you fool?"

"You're nowhere near as invincible as you think you are," Frederic snarled back. Unlike Lucien, he appeared on his last legs, and it was taking all his concentration and sheer will power to keep going.

"Oh really?" Lucien actually looked amused, appearing to consider this statement seriously in the midst of the fight. "Well, let's see. I know you've figured out a way to make spells pass right through you without touching you. Oh yes, I know about that now," he added, grinning at the look of shock on Frederic's face. "Not just because of the way you gave it away just now, but I knew it anyway. It was the only thing that could explain why most of my attacks against you failed, unless I directed the full power of the Sien-Leoard Crystal at you. Only then could I overpower your magic, including that annoying little spell of yours."

My heart sank. Now that he knew how to beat that particular protection, we could no longer rely on it. Actually, we never really could rely on it; Lucien could have beaten it at any time if he'd really tried.

"What I don't understand," Lucien went on, now looking thoughtful, even as he fired spell after spell at Frederic, "is how you're able to keep up with me, old man. I know you're not a Sorcerer anymore. I know you're not using the Hero Crystal, because you couldn't. I know you're not using the Villain or Darkness Crystals, because they aren't powerful enough to match me. How are you doing this, I wonder? I'm sure I could figure it out if I really…tried."

On the last word, the ground beneath Frederic's feet buckled and shifted. A loud crack rent the air, and Frederic went down in a cry of pain. I couldn't see the damage through his trousers, but I knew he had broken one of his legs. Lucien advanced on him, but that was when Natalie launched an attack on him from behind. It was a good effort, but he didn't even have to turn around to defeat her. A powerful blast of magic came out through Lucien's back, slamming into Natalie and sending her flying. Lucien reached Frederic and bent over him, but that was when his concentration, so focused on the former Sorcerer and the device he held in his hand, wavered. It was enough for Peter to take another shot at him, and this time, Lucien didn't get out of the way in time.

That was my cue to jump into the battle. I fired several spells at him in quick succession; the one intended to knock him out missed and hit Frederic (well on the bright side, at least he was out of pain for the time being), but the jet of thicky prison hit Lucien's hip and began wrapping itself around him. He cried out and tried to vanish it, but his efforts had no effect. He pulled a face then, and I knew instinctively that he had just realised that he was surrounded by an anti-teleportation ring. He growled angrily in my general direction. A moment later, a huge flash of light filled the morning sky, making me think that he'd managed to call Fewul back to his side, but in fact, he had simply overpowered and blasted apart Marc's anti-teleportation ring from the inside.

"You're all too late!" he shouted at us, his voice echoing and bouncing all over the empty landscape. "I know your secret now. I know how that weird-looking magic sucking device works, and the next time you see me, I'll have an even more powerful one, and it'll be the end of all of you!"

Then he teleported away, the thicky prison continuing to wrap itself around him at a rapid rate. He would probably only have another twenty seconds before it would have him completely enveloped, but that would only be a minor hiccup for him. Once he'd found a way out of it, he would start setting up magic vacuums of his own, assuming he hadn't been bluffing, and the battle would be on in earnest. Whether or not he had made the leap of logic to antimagic as of yet, we couldn't be sure, but it looked inevitable now that we would have to destroy all the magic particles we could find, just so that he couldn't use them.

Chapter 29: Bring It

"Great, what now?" Peter asked, looking around at the rest of us.

"Back in your shadow," Marc said, "we're all totally vulnerable out here."

That was a good point, so Peter and I quickly withdrew into our shadows where we could watch what was happening without being sitting ducks. Lucien did know about the fourth dimension, but for whatever reason, other than the gnomes from last night, he'd never tried to follow us along it. It meant that we were probably safe here, at least until Marc was ready to put some fresh protections around us...or maybe Frederic should do it next time, since Lucien had managed to blast right through Marc's spells once he threw all his might into it.

By the time Lucien had teleported away, Marc had recovered himself and was on his feet. He hurried to Natalie to fix her up, while Amelia rushed over to her father with the Light Crystal. Natalie was on her feet in no more than five seconds, and she immediately withdrew into her shadow and came over to join me and Peter. Frederic took a little longer to get to his feet, but Amelia had managed to both revive him and heal his leg. As the six of us gathered close together, those of us in our shadows emerged so that Frederic could walk around us and put the protective spells back in place—all except Marc's special untraceability which only he had a clear idea of how to perform, which he put around us on the inside of Frederic's shields so that they wouldn't be vulnerable if Lucien attacked us again.

"So...what now?" Peter repeated.

"That depends," I said—I'd had a chance to think, and now I voiced some of the thoughts that had occurred to me. "Do we wait and see if he really *does* know about magic particles, or do we assume that he does and resort to antimagic?"

"Do we have to resort to antimagic if Lucien knows about magic particles?" Marc asked.

"I think we do, Marc," Amelia said quietly. "You know what he's going to do if he can figure out how to manipulate them. He's going to come at us with a device of his own and he won't be careful about how he uses it. He won't care how much he destabilises everything because he'll know that doing anything else would be worse for him."

"But shouldn't we at least try to come up with a device to suck all his magic out at once first?" Marc asked. "I mean, surely whatever damage that ends up doing won't be as bad as what antimagic will do."

A brief silence, and then Natalie said, "That might be true, Marc, but what if he figures out how to work with antimagic himself? It was mentioned in the same thesis as the whole particle theory, so he might figure that if he can't beat us by taking our magic, the next best thing will be to neutralise it altogether, and he won't know about the dangers of it because the thesis never mentioned the annihilation; we only found out about that the hard way."

"I think we'd better get back to our base," Frederic said, "so that we can see for ourselves what move Lucien makes next, and to retrieve those devices you made, Natalie. We're going to have to keep them on us at all times now, I think."

Without waiting for any of us to respond (mine would have been along the lines of, 'Shouldn't we at least ask James where Lucien ended up before we go back to base?'), Frederic teleported us back to Lucien's living room. It was almost exactly the same as it had been when we had left (which had actually been less than twenty minutes ago, though a lot sure had happened in that twenty minutes). The unconscious bodies of Hall, Hignat, Wilwog and Sebastian lay exactly where Marc had dropped them, and the same would probably be true of the rest of the tutors in the dining room.

What had changed was Lena—she was no longer unconscious. In fact, she was no longer there at all. Almost exactly where she had been, though, lay a Lucien-shaped figure, completely enveloped in thicky prison and completely immobile. All six of us gaped at this, hardly able to believe our luck. The one time we *weren't* trying to chase him, we track him exactly. I wracked my brain, trying to think of anything we could do to take advantage of this situation while there was still a chance...

"Just knocked him out," Marc said into the silence. "I'm pretty sure he was awake in there before, but now he's not. What should we do with him?"

"Make sure he doesn't wake up, for a start," Frederic said. "Can you think of any way we can put him in a state where only our magic can rouse him?"

Before Marc could respond, the sound of hurrying footsteps reached our ears. We all paused, waiting to see who it was (my guess was Lena), and as we did so, a second set of footsteps reached our ears, this one coming from the stairs outside the living quarters. My initial guess had been correct: Lena burst into the room from the hallway leading to the bedrooms, took aim at Lucien with two devices in her hands, and fired them both almost at the same time. Marc or Frederic dropped her quickly but not before both shots struck Lucien's body. The first came from a solid-outliner, and it released him from his prison of immobility; and the second one woke him up.

It all happened too quickly for any of us to stop it, and when Marc tried to knock him out again, Lucien had already raised his shields.

"Shadow," I said at once, and thankfully, they all obeyed me without so much as a pause. The blast of magic Lucien sent in Marc's direction, one that probably would have been powerful enough to overwhelm the

Hero Crystal, passed through the empty air where we had been. I waited to see if Lucien would try to attack again, but he seemed satisfied that he'd either gotten us or we had fled. I then stepped out long enough to send a telepathic message to all four who were still in the control room, unsure which of them would receive it first, telling them that we were in our shadow now and they should pick us up. I then dropped back in my shadow to watch what Lucien did next.

He took a moment to wake Lena again, and another moment to do the same for Hall, but he didn't bother to wake any of the others. Without waiting for the two of them to come to their senses and sit up, he turned his attention to the person who had just paused in the doorway of the living quarters, brought up short at the sight of the bodies on the floor.

"What brings you here, Hank?" Lucien asked wearily.

"I—er—still have some issues that require your attention, sir," Cornish said warily.

Lucien gave his head a little shake. "Well, no issue you have to tell me about is as important as the one I have going on. I'm glad you're here because I have a job for you."

"Er—but sir, I already have—" Cornish began.

"You need to execute a mass evacuation of the entire Hammerheart network," Lucien told him, and Cornish froze in horror. "You know how to do this, don't you?"

"Well—yes, I do, but—"

"I would do it myself except that I have a much more pressing issue I need to deal with," Lucien went on. "don't ask questions, just make it happen—and do it as quickly as you can. Anyone who stays in here longer than necessary is putting their lives at risk."

"Are you serious?"

"*That's* a question," Lucien snapped. "Just make it happen. And *you*"—he rounded on Hall—"are responsible for Lena's wellbeing. I don't know what's going to happen in the next twenty-four hours, but if anything happens to her—anything at all—I'll be holding you accountable. Wake all these people up and get them all out of the base immediately."

"Yes, sir," Hall said at once, and then paused. "Er—how exactly do I —"

Lena was on her feet now, and she took charge of the wake-up operation with the same device she had used to rouse Lucien. As she woke the three unconscious forms nearby, and then headed for the dining room, Lucien turned and hurried out of the room, beckoning for Cornish to follow. Out in the corridor beyond, I heard Lucien saying something about granting permission for Hammerhearts to take refuge in any and all government facilities which they found convenient, but I didn't hear all the words as they faded beyond the security wall outside.

Then all sounds of the living room cut off as, without warning that it was going to happen, I was sucked into our base. Peter and Amelia had already been sucked in before me, and I had to scramble out of the way so that James could retrieve the other three.

"You heard what Lucien just said, didn't you?" I asked them as I took a seat.

"Something about Hammerhearts being allowed to stay in government buildings if they had nowhere outside the network to go," James said absent-mindedly as he worked the controls, now picking up Natalie.

"Not that, the mass evacuation," I said impatiently. "You know what that means, don't you?"

All six of them looked expectantly at me. Well, all except James, who was now picking up Marc.

"It means that he's expecting a showdown," Lillian finally said solemnly, "and he's anticipating that the network could have all its magic stripped from it, which would trap all the Hammerhearts inside it."

"It's more than that," I said. "It means that he *knows*. He wouldn't be taking such drastic action if he only *thought* it could happen. He knows that it's going to, which probably means that he himself intends to suck up all the magic he can find so that he can fight us. And if that's what he intends to do—"

"Then it means that he wasn't bluffing," Amelia said in a small voice, her face very pale. "He was serious. He thinks he knows how we did what we did, and he's going to do it bigger."

A silence filled the room now. James had just retrieved Frederic, so now all ten of us were here, and although Marc and Frederic hadn't heard the whole conversation, they'd heard Amelia's last words and that was enough.

"Natalie, go upstairs and get the rest of the devices you made," Frederic said at once. "We may need to make some alterations to them, but we're definitely going to need to use them, and probably as weapons directly against Lucien now. James, how are our antimagic collectors going?"

"Nothing's happened there," he said, checking each of the four spyers in turn. "Nope, they're still where we left them, although Wilwog looks hungry—we might want to take him some food so that he's not tempted to leave his station. As far as the devices go, though, they're still sucking up antimagic. There's still a lot of it out there, so I sure as hell hope Lucien doesn't think to try getting some of his own."

"You know, if he does figure out how to use antimagic, and creates a weapon like ours that can use it as a weapon," Amelia said slowly, "then all of us would be much safer if we weren't magical. We should consider having a device that can lift all the magic we have on and around our bodies, just in case he fires antimagic at us. You know what would happen to us if it hits, don't you?"

"The much more frightening thing about that is, we *don't* know what would happen," I said, "except that it could be anything from getting a loose bladder to being turned into a chocolate biscuit. The trouble is, if we make ourselves totally unprotected, we'll be totally vulnerable to Lucien. Even if he is smart enough to follow our lead and lower his protections so that he won't be hit by antimagic, he won't hesitate to take advantage of that."

"Maybe we can come up with a protection that stores the magic in a different place," Marc suggested, "like what we did this morning when you were standing behind him, John."

"That's not the worst idea," Peter said, "but don't you think we're taking a huge risk just taking the Hero Crystal out there at all?"

"Then how are we supposed to defend ourselves?" Marc retorted. "We can't go out there with no magic at all. And don't forget, he still has his Honnie mind, and according to Fewul, no amount of magic or antimagic manipulation can take that away from him. If we go out there without protection, he'll grab our minds and that'll be the end of it."

That, unfortunately, was a very good point. I tried to wrap my mind around the magnitude of this disaster, and I kept coming back to the same thought. We had to take him out before he had a chance to attack us using his new-found knowledge. I glanced at the spyers again: Lucien was now alone in the elevator in the Chopville base, while Cornish was returning to the living quarters. My guess was that the resources he needed to organise a mass evacuation of the entire network were located back there somewhere, intended by the Hammersons to be used only by themselves or their closest subordinates. But Lucien, what was he doing? If he was on his way out of the base, why wasn't he just teleporting out?

James spoke then, and he voiced what I was thinking. "We only have one choice now: we have to bring the fight to Lucien before he can bring it to us, and we can't hold back anymore, no matter what the consequences for the wider world may be. I don't wanna sound dramatic, but this is a matter of all of our survival. Lucien would believe that if he can just defeat us, no matter how much damage he has to do to the world in the process, he can fix it up later and then re-write history so that no one ever knows the truth."

"I agree," Frederic said grimly, "so I'm going to try to create a device that quickly strips us of all our magic at the push of a button, so that we won't actually have to go unprotected unless it becomes absolutely necessary. We'll optimise Natalie's works if we can, but if worse comes to worse, we may need something else."

"What else?" Amelia asked, eyes wide and scared.

"I think I can guess what else," James said quietly. "You think we should arm ourselves with non-magical weapons—guns and grenades and so on, right?"

Frederic nodded. "It will be all we have left."

"No, that can't possibly work," Marc said at once. "How on earth are guns going to stand up to magic if Lucien's prepared to use it against us?"

"We wouldn't use guns in a fight against magic," James said, "in the same way that you wouldn't use a knife in a fight with an opponent who was using a gun. But we do have to have something to fall back on, in case he is able to neutralise our magic before we can neutralise his."

"Shouldn't we have something that can protect us from his Honnie mind?" Erica said. "If his mind isn't magic, then don't you think there would be a non-magic response to it?"

"If Lucien encounters another Honnie mind, he can turn it inside out and take control of it, which is something no real Honnie could do," Peter pointed out. "It wouldn't protect us, but it might make us a more obvious target."

"Not necessarily," I said thoughtfully. "I mean, what you say is true, Pete, but that one part of his mind *could* be magical, for all we know. We haven't tested it since we took his magic, and if Lucien himself believes that—well—" I broke off, trying to organise my thoughts so that I could explain it properly. Before I could, James comprehended where I was going, and took the initiative.

"Lucien hasn't come across another Honnie mind since last night, and prior to that, he probably hasn't met a single one since May," he said, beginning to look hopeful. "He believes that it hasn't changed, but if that ability you spoke of really was enabled by magic, then he wouldn't be aware that he's lost it. It may just be a normal Honnie mind now, and if that's true, then a larger and stronger mind *would* protect us, and—maybe —be able to take control of his."

"Er—I hate to be a party pooper, but does anyone here have any idea how to control a Honnie mind without using magic?" Amelia asked.

That brought us all up short. I opened my mouth a couple of times, but couldn't think of any affirmative response that would be the truth. My belief was that if I were to create a Honnie mind for myself, then once I had it, the ability to use it would come instinctively; but the cold hard fact was that I didn't actually know if this would be the case. Lucien had learnt to control his Honnie mind well enough, but he had two advantages over us—he may have used magic to speed up the learning curve, and he had taken three days between obtaining the Sien-Leoard Crystal and using his mind for the first time, so far as I knew anyway.

Marc was the first to recover from this setback. "It would be simpler if we could just destroy his Honnie mind so that he doesn't have that advantage anymore. I know he's been using his magic to protect it up until this point, but surely there is a way to get rid of it if we can just remove the magic he has around it?"

"That might be possible," Frederic conceded, "but it might also be possible that the Honnie mind is an actual part of his person now, and it would be impossible to just get rid of it and return his mind to what it used to be. We had better proceed with both plans, just in case one of them doesn't work, so Marc, you create a device that should be able to get rid of his mind. As for making one of our own..."

He trailed off in hesitation, looking around at us all. Finally, he said, "I have a bit of an understanding of how Honnie minds work, but not a very clear one. I never had a chance to sit down with May and probe her about it; I was only able to determine what she could and couldn't do regarding the job we had at the time. I don't think I can perform the magic to create a Honnie mind, so who here does?"

Everyone's eyes shifted to me then, and I shrugged. "My understanding is not much different from the rest of you guys—"

"Except that you were able to connect with May in a way that the rest of us couldn't," Peter pointed out, "and though I could be wrong, I think part of it had to be an instinctive understanding of how her mind-reading worked, and how you could use it to communicate with her."

"I'm pretty sure James came up with the idea to communicate within May's mind like that," I reminded them, glancing at James.

He shook his head. "That may be true, but I don't have the magical experience that you do, John. You're the best one for this job."

"Let me think on it for a moment," I conceded. "You guys get started on your magic and I'll let you know."

A few of them looked like they wanted to argue but I held up a hand to forestall them, and then settled back, wracking my brain as hard as I could. The two main issues were the magic I would need to perform to make this happen, and then what else I would need to do to prepare for Lucien's most likely responses to it. Actually making it happen probably wouldn't be too difficult; I would only really need to make it copy whatever Lucien had done, and to remember as much of May's mind as I could if necessary. If I did that while holding the magic enhancer, I would know very quickly if it had worked, and would probably also know very quickly what I needed to do if it didn't.

I imagined that once I had a Honnie mind of my own, it would probably be like having a whole new sense added to my body that my brain wouldn't know how to interpret. I would surely have to use magic just to cope with that, but based on what I'd seen from Lucien, once I'd come to terms with it, the rest ought to come naturally to me. It would be the 'coming to terms' part that would be most difficult, because I didn't have any Honnie instincts to draw on, and there was little in my humanity that could prepare me for what I would have to deal with, so it would have to be done using magic.

And then what? Assuming that I was able to create such a Honnie mind, I would have to figure out how to take possession of the minds of everyone in the base in order to protect them from Lucien, and I had to be able to do it in a way that didn't do any damage to them—that could be a tricky operation. By the time this became necessary, all the rest of our magical protection would be gone out of necessity, which meant that I would also lose any ability to use magic to control the Honnie mind, so I would have to be able to do all that needed to be done—which would mostly be simply keeping everyone else's minds safe—without magic.

And then what? If we got to this point, we would be facing Lucien with nothing but a Honnie mind and a bunch of non-magical creations, which Frederic was in the process of creating at this very moment. Lucien may or may not have magic on his side; if he didn't, then as long as my Honnie mind was bigger than his, he wouldn't be able to…oh, wait. My brain ground to a halt as I realised what Lucien would do if he came face-to-face with a Honnie mind. He would assume, correctly, that we had nothing else with which to defend ourselves, and he would do whatever it took to take possession of all our minds. If he had magic, he would simply enlarge his mind so that it was big enough to swallow mine, exposing everyone inside. If he didn't have magic, he would enlarge his mind the same way May had done: He would destroy however many human minds were necessary to strengthen his own.

The end result, however, would be the same either way. Peter had been partially right—having a Honnie mind would make us a target, and even without magic, it wouldn't be difficult for Lucien to turn the situation to his advantage. If it were possible to destroy his Honnie mind, this would be the far better plan of attack, but the best way forward was to prevent it from getting to such a point in the first place. If we ended up in a situation where Lucien had magic on his side and we didn't, the war would already be lost.

I opened my eyes again and looked around. Unnoticed by me, Natalie had returned to the control room while I had been in contemplation; she had taken the magic enhancer from Frederic and was now using it to make modifications to some of the magic particle and antimagic devices she had created the night before. Frederic was continuing his work, now using the Villain Crystal, and Marc was deep in thought holding the Hero Crystal, but he hadn't yet created any devices that I could see. Everyone else was watching me, having waited patiently for me to come to my decision. I took a deep breath.

"No, we can't do it," I said. "Even if we expose our minds to Lucien's Honnie mind, there's a chance he won't think to take advantage of it, not if he's totally focused on the magic side of things. If we *do* have a Honnie mind, he will definitely try to take advantage of it, and he won't even need to use magic to make his own mind larger if he needs to —he'll just do what May did and kill loads of people to make it happen."

A short silence followed, and then James turned to Marc. "How are you going there, Marc?"

"I dunno if I can do this," he said, opening his eyes and looking at us. "I mean, I'm sure I *could* destroy a Honnie mind, but I'm also sure that Lucien will have thought of that, and he will have put magic around it to stop me from doing exactly this. It would work if we could get rid of that magic, but this device will have to depend on magic—I can't find any non-magical way to do it—which means that if both sides lose magic, he'll still have the advantage. This will only work if we can nullify his magic without losing our own, which I guess could happen."

"Go ahead and create the device," James suggested. "If we don't get a chance to use it, so be it, but we might as well have it just in case. This leaves the rest of us with a big decision to make."

I was sure I knew what was coming, and sure enough...

"What do we do if Lucien succeeds in creating devices that can divest us of our magic?" James asked. "How far are we willing to go to resist him? I know the instinct at this point is to not give up until we have absolutely no options left, but now there's a genuine chance that this fight could actually wreck the entire world. You have to think that even surrender would be better than doing so much damage that the world can never recover, or that the human race is wiped off the map altogether."

"That's chiefly what I'm afraid of when it comes to antimagic," Marc admitted. "It's like Amelia said earlier, he's not going to care how much he destabilises the world in the process, and that means he won't hesitate to escalate. Us *not* escalating may be the only thing that saves the world if he discovers antimagic, and even if the future looks bleak with Lucien in control of pretty much everything without opposition, at least there will still *be* a future."

"But what if there's still a chance of beating him?" Peter asked. "I mean, what if, even if it does a lot of damage, we can still defeat him with antimagic after he has discovered it for himself? Yeah, the aftermath would be bad, and there would probably be a clean-up operation and all —"

"Also, what if Lucien decides that antimagic could be a useful weapon, even after he's beaten us?" Erica asked. "I don't see how, but people that power-hungry would love it anyway."

James shrugged. "I think you guys are pretty much echoing my thoughts. The future really would be terrible with Lucien in control of all the magic in the world, so if we need to escalate a bit, just to see if he really will escalate with us, then we may have to take that chance. But I also agree with Marc that there has to be a breaking point, and now I'm thinking that we mightn't know what that breaking point is until it arrives."

"Which means that the best way to deal with it is to prevent it altogether, if possible," Frederic said, raising his head from what he was doing to look around at us. "Now, I'm finished here, so what's the next plan of attack?"

"How are you going, Natalie?" James asked.

"Well," she said, and held up one of the magic particle vacuums. It was of the same type as the one I had used when following Lucien around that morning. "I've made this a bit more powerful and focused it as much as I could. It should be able to quickly suck magic out of anything it's pointed directly at, but not over a very long distance, and with no expanding beam. It would be best to use this either on anything Lucien creates that might have magic in it, or Lucien himself.

"And this," she held up another device, "is the antimagic gun. Each one can't store a whole heap of antimagic in it, but they can all store enough for several thousand rounds, since even the tiniest bit of antimagic is pretty destructive. The thing is you have to aim well with this thing; if you miss your target, the antimagic bullet will just keep going without ever losing momentum, until it hits something with enough magic particles to annihilate all of it.

"And this," she showed us a third device, which looked a bit like a handheld canon, "is for shooting larger balls of antimagic. I honestly can't see a situation where using it would be a good idea, but it's better to have it and not need it than to need it and not have it. Now, these antimagic devices don't have any antimagic in them at the moment, so we're going to have to load them up before we can use them."

"We can do that with one of those things," Frederic said, nodding at the spyers showing the four former-Hammerhearts who were collecting antimagic for us, "but this is going to be time-consuming. You can duplicate those antimagic weapons now while they're empty, but once they're loaded, no magic will work on them without causing a magical explosion, and that includes teleporting to wherever Lucien might be. How many weapons like that should we have?"

"I would say no more than half a dozen," said James. "We do need more than a few, in case Lucien manages to take some of them out, but we can't have loads of people shooting off antimagic at will. I'm far more concerned about what you say about teleporting, because you're right: No magic will be able to touch them, which means whoever goes and gets the antimagic will have to join us without using any magic, and that'll be a huge disadvantage for us."

"It's not great, but at least Lucien would have the same problem if he tries to move around," Lillian said, "so once the next battle starts, I don't think there will be any more running away this time."

Natalie duplicated the three devices in her hands, passing the two antimagic weapons around to me, Peter, James, Amelia, Frederic, Erica and Rebecca, and keeping one for herself. The magic vacuum devices she gave to everyone, and the antimagic canon, as I thought of it, went to Peter.

"This device," Frederic said, holding it up to show us—it was no more interesting than a thumb-sided panel with a small button set into it, "is connected to all our magical protections—not just those of us in the control room, but everyone who is currently in the base. If it is pushed, all that magic will simply vanish from us, and it should only be pushed the moment we learn that Lucien has discovered how to use antimagic—no earlier, but especially no later."

"What about all that stuff?" Peter asked, looking at the piles of weaponry on the floor beside Frederic's chair.

"Ah, well, these are for all of us," he said, picking up what looked a bit like an automatic rifle. "These guns are as easy-to-use as I could make them, without putting any magic in them, but I still hope we don't have to resort to using them, given that I'm guessing most of you have little or no experience with guns. Each of us should have one of these strapped to our backs, but I'm not going to bother handing out ammunition other than what's already in them. Teaching you all how to reload and then having to do it in battle without any preparation—well, there's no way that could work.

"I've also got some grenades here, and I'm going to hand a few out to each of you," he went on. "Now, these are newly made and very powerful. When you pull the tab, you have exactly seven seconds to throw them, and given how polished they are, I'm sure it will be exactly seven seconds. You'll have to make sure the explosion is at least ten metres away from you, though; any closer and I can't guarantee your safety.

"I've also made a number of plastic-explosive time-bombs, which are already set up and only need to be activated by pushing a button—the allowed times are one minute, five minutes, thirty minutes and one hour. We've also got one rocket launcher, which is probably overkill, and a number of devices which will emit toxic gases when they are set off—not lethal, but enough to render a person unconscious very quickly, and possibly permanently disabled if no magic is available to cure them. So if we have to use those, we'd better have a plan for making sure we're not anywhere near them when they go off, because no face mask will protect us."

"I *so* wish we had more time to train with these," James said regretfully, "but I don't think we have any more time to even talk about it, let alone practice with them. Duplicate them and start handing them around. Now, who's going to go and get the antimagic supply? I think getting the one in Chopville is the most sensible, since by the looks of it, 3P69 is only about a five-minute sprint away from where Lucien is now."

The former-Hammerheart was located in the Chopville Town Central, while it appeared that Lucien was now hidden just near the forest area of Hamster's Stretch Reserve. As far as I could tell, he had enclosed himself inside some sort of solid dome which looked silver and metallic on the outside. Obviously that dome possessed some sort of magical protection to keep us out, and whatever it was had to be pretty clever. Lucien knew about magic particles now, which meant that he knew we would probably try to suck them out of any protection he put around himself. If he'd thought of a way to prevent that, it would be part of that dome.

The real question was, why the dome at all? What was he doing in there that required him to hide himself so completely? I had a bad feeling it was rather scientific—rather experimental—and very similar to what we had done in the Time Box the day before. If so, then the quicker we put a stop to it, the better.

"I'm probably going to have to be the one to deal with him," Frederic said, referring to 3P69, "since he knows he's on my side, but I don't think he'll respond quite as well to any of the rest of you. In fact, some of you he won't even recognise as being on my side."

"There's just one more thing before we start," Amelia said quietly. "If Lucien thinks it's a good idea for all the Hammerhearts to abandon their network, then it's probably a good idea for everyone to evacuate this base as well. It's surrounded by magic, and if antimagic does get let loose, anyone left inside will be torn to pieces."

"That's all well and good, but where are all those people going to go?" James asked. "We don't have any government facilities to send them to, nor do we have any homes out there. We're all a bunch of outcasts and have been for some time, remember?"

"I actually do have an idea for somewhere to send them," Frederic told us, "and it's close enough that none of us will need to worry about them having trouble getting there. I think that some of them would be willing to join in the battle, though. Do you think we should let them?"

I opened my mouth to say yes—any increased numbers had to be a good thing for us—and then hesitated. None of the others, save Katie and Sophie who had been involved in the research, knew what magic particles and antimagic were. They wouldn't understand the true stakes of the battle, and they wouldn't be able to behave accordingly...

"I don't see why not," James said, undercutting my train of thought completely, "as long as they understand that this could be a battle to the death, and that they must follow our orders at all times."

"Then if we're gonna prevent Lucien from discovering antimagic," Marc said solemnly, "we'd better get moving."

Everything, from then to the end, happened very quickly after that....

Chapter 30: Battle Stations

Frederic used the public address system to order a complete evacuation of the base, but he instructed everyone to evacuate through the control room rather than the emergency exits in their bedrooms. They had been intended for use if we were invaded, but it wouldn't work in this case because we needed to outfit and equip every single person before they left. Frederic then gave the magic enhancer to Lillian before taking possession of the Darkness Crystal for himself.

While we waited for people to arrive, Marc created belts and straps for us to carry our various weaponries, which were customised for each of us based on what we would be using. Lillian was also using magic, in her case to create the entirely non-magical bags Frederic and those who chose to accompany him would use to carry their tools in, the ones which would transport the guns and canon to the antimagic hub in Chopville, and then transport the deadly non-substance to the battlefield.

The rest of us quickly discussed roles, and were thankfully able to persuade most people, when they got down to the control room, to go along with our ideas. Harry and Simon were at first disappointed when they discovered that a battle to death was about to take place and that they would be on the sidelines, at least at first, until Frederic told them that the job they would be doing with him, although not as dangerous in the beginning, was all the more important. When he heard these words, Jacob Underwood volunteered himself to join them, and so there were four people who would be dealing with the antimagic.

An equally important job was to keep Fewul away, which would involve the continual, unrelenting pressing of a button on a device. Peter and James volunteered their mothers for this role, a sentiment with which I agreed, and thankfully they were happy enough to play a part that was important, but not directly involved in the fighting. They were far less happy about the three of us being in the thick of the fighting, but as Dad and Charlie rightly pointed out, it was far too late in the game to stop us from fighting now.

Some relief came for the Thomases, though, when Jessica accepted her assigned role; and Felicity, who we had expected would join the battle, chose to go with her instead. Their responsibility could end up being dangerous, but only if the rest of us failed entirely—and if that happened, nobody would be safe anyway. They, along with Darcy, Liam and Siobhan (the latter three volunteering to join them) would be the armed protection force for those, including Mum and Marge, who wouldn't be fighting.

However, there was one unenviable role which someone would need to fill, but which no one who knew anything about what was going on wanted. Someone would need to stay in the base, just in case it became necessary to retreat here (though under what circumstances that would be wise, I couldn't imagine). It was incredibly dangerous given that if anything happened to strip this place of magic, the person would be trapped here, and there wouldn't be any way to get them out.

We had thought that no one would take this role, but surprising most people (though not quite all), Alice Fletcher volunteered herself. Natalie and Rebecca protested, of course, but Alice was old and fairly broken since the murder of her son, and she was willing to take the hit. I reckoned that if Stella were still here, she would have been willing too; but if Stella were still here, she would be on the front line with me, using her magical experience for good. I had to quickly force my mind away from this melancholy train of thought; there was just too much going on for that.

Then, it was time to go. Frederic, Underwood and the twins left first, quickly setting off to where 3P69 stood waiting. They went visibly but with untraceability spells on them; this seemed incredibly risky to me given what they were transporting, but Frederic believed (strongly enough that he was willing to risk their lives on it) that so long as they didn't actually touch the antimagic with their bodies, there ought not to be a problem. I supposed it made sense; for magic and antimagic to exist together in the world without having blown the place to the stars hundreds of years ago already, there must be some sort of magnetic force repelling them from each other, perhaps like two magnets being pushed together. They would go together if the issue was forced, but not on their own. That thought gave me a moment of anxiety as I wondered if the antimagic guns or even the canon would work on that basis, and then I disregarded it; it was far too late to do anything about it if that were so.

It was time for the fighting force to leave the base. Natalie quickly showed Alice how to use the control panel, and explained to her (in a whisper) how and why to take the base into the fourth dimension at the first sign that antimagic was going to start flying. While she did this, Marc gathered the entire fighting force (there were about forty of us, and half of them were people I only knew by sight as old Woodward soldiers) and wrapped us in an invisibility veil and soundproof barrier. Other than the individual untraceability spells we would all have on us, this would be our only protection. There wasn't a lot of point wasting time with more, as Lucien only had to figure out how to manipulate magic particles to strip it all away from us.

One by one, Alice dropped us all out of the base and into the park. As soon as I landed on the grass, knowing that I would never see the inside of that base again, I followed the lead of those who had gone before me and took up a position around (but still several metres away from) Lucien's dome. James was a short distance to my right, and Peter took up a position to my left just seconds later. It felt good to have those two with me for what was probably going to be our last stand, for better or worse, but I still felt horribly exposed.

Part of that feeling was most likely what we were up against, compared to what I had on me. The only weapons I carried were a rifle over my back (which I thought I'd have trouble just pulling out of its strap, and I'd probably fall over when I fired it), six grenades on my belt, and some plastic explosives which could be used as a time bomb. I would also have some antimagic weapons, but only when Frederic and his crew returned with them. The only actual magic I had was the magic I'd given myself back on Rock Haulter, which was useful, but how useful would it be today?

Mind you, most of the army was probably worse off than me. Peter and James were carrying most of the same weapons, although they both carried magic vacuums, and James was also carrying a small device which, when triggered, would instantly dispel all the magical protections we had around ourselves (to be used only if Lucien discovered antimagic). Other soldiers carried similar weapons, but there were exceptions. Marc had the Hero Crystal, a device which could, if it worked, destroy Lucien's Honnie mind, and a small rocket launcher on his hip instead of plastic explosives. Amelia had the Light Crystal and a device to initiate a chemical attack, Natalie also had a chemical weapon along with the Villain Crystal, Frederic had the Darkness Crystal, Lillian had the magic enhancer, and the rest of the army were fitted with the light devices in place of magical weaponry. We were as armed as we could be for such a fight, and yet it still felt like the man concealed by the dome of doom before us would be more than a match.

"Okay guys," Marc called when the entire fighting force had taken up position, and Alice had taken the base away to the secret location Frederic had set up as the safe zone where she would drop the rest of the army, "Margaret and Marge have sent Fewul away and they're keeping it away. How are we gonna do this?"

That seemed a strange question. Wasn't it obvious what we were going to do now? Then I realised: I had no idea what came next either. Our only plan was to stop Lucien before he could discover how to manipulate magic particles, but beyond that, we hadn't actually discussed how we were going to do it.

"We should probably start with you guys," James called to Marc, nodding also to Amelia, Natalie and Lillian, "using magic to destroy that thing. I imagine he's set it up with the Sien-Leoard Crystal and made it magically strong enough that a weaker source of magic won't be able to remove it, but maybe the magic enhancer can anyway."

"Maybe we should use these things then," Peter said, waving his magic vacuum, "just to give you guys an even better chance."

That seemed like a good idea, but James shook his head.

"Why the hell not?" Marc asked, echoing my thoughts.

"Because he'll be expecting that," James said calmly. "Plus, it won't be fast enough; it'll give him time to react because it'll be obvious that we're around him. We're better off blasting the thing apart if we can."

Marc nodded. "That makes sense, but if it doesn't work then we have to suck the magic out of the thing, right?"

James shrugged. "I guess so."

"It'll be great if this thing works," Natalie called, "but if not, we should still keep trying magic stuff until the guys get back with the antimagic. If he figures out how to strip us of our magic, we really need them to be here."

That made sense to me, and Amelia nodded (while a full three-quarters of the fighting force looked on in confusion), but Marc looked unimpressed. "Let's try not to let it come to that, okay? You go first," he said to Lillian.

She tried a few things, but of course, none of them worked. Marc, Natalie and even Amelia joined her, all forcing their combined magic on to a simple point of impact, and still they weren't able to make any change to the dome. This perplexed me: Surely with that much magic all focused on the same point, they could overpower literally any magic Lucien could have performed without Fewul...

"Do we still have magic?" Marc asked, and to answer his own question, he changed the colour of his sweater. "Okay, fine, so then why didn't it work?"

"Lucien's used brain rather than brawn on this one, I suppose," James said, and he didn't look entirely disapproving. "It doesn't mean you can't get rid of it; it just means that you can't do that type of magic. What were you trying?"

All four of them answered at once, and naturally, they all said slightly different things. James shrugged, calmly told them to pick one and work together on it. They took up a more organised attack after that, but had just as little success. Vanishing the dome didn't work. Vanishing part of the dome didn't work. Turning part of the dome into air didn't work. Turning part of the dome into a window didn't work. Setting the dome on fire didn't work. Making it explode didn't work. Striking it with lightning (real lightning from the sky, which was utterly terrifying to be so close to) didn't work. Even trying to dig under it didn't work—it seemed to go down as well as up.

"Okay, so the obvious tricks aren't working," James said, gingerly running his hand along the barrel of the gun on his back, "and I'm thinking that non-magic force won't work either, based on what just happened there. Come on guys, get creative; think of every spell you've ever performed and ask yourself if it could work here."

They kept at it. Moving the dome didn't work. Shrinking it didn't work. Enlarging it (which made no sense anyway) didn't work. Filling the inside of it with water may have worked, but there was no way to prove it. All around me, those of us without magic we could use to help watched on in growing anxiety. I kept running over all the spells I possessed, but none of them would be any good in this case, except maybe…

I shot a jet of thicky prison at the dome from my fingers, startling Peter, James and those nearest me. Nobody was close enough to the dome to be in danger of getting wrapped up in it, though. Marc, Lillian, Natalie and Amelia stopped what they were doing and watched as the white stuff slowly covered the dome, stopping when it reached the ground. Once it was covered, the group of four began trying to manipulate the dome, but it proved to be just as impenetrable as before. Sighing, I shot more thicky prison at it, cancelling out the first.

"It was worth a try," I sighed dispiritedly.

"Can we use these yet?" Peter asked, waving his magic vacuum again.

"What do you think, Marc?" James asked him.

Marc hesitated then said, "I tend to think we should attack him that way, but those devices won't be fast enough. We need something to disable him quickly and efficiently, and I think I have an idea for that. We need to create a dome around his dome and make it a magic vacuum that will suck all the magic from inside it into itself, if that makes sense?"

"If Lucien figures out what you're doing and it's not instantaneous, he could just teleport out of it," James pointed out. "You know that, right?"

"Not if Lillian puts an anti-teleportation ring around the outside of my dome," Marc told him.

A brief silence fell as we all looked at each other, each of us trying to poke holes in that theory. Admittedly, most people looked confused, although Sophie, who stood three places to my left, looked as though she was following proceedings—perhaps based on the stuff she, Katie, James and Erica had been doing in the Time Box the previous morning. Not only did I think it could work, but I could think of something that might make it work even better, if it were possible.

"See if you can use the magic particles you get from him to strengthen the anti-teleportation ring," I suggested.

Marc looked dubious. "In that case, maybe you'd better do it," he looked at Lillian who nodded, "you know, just to make sure they work together properly."

"They're back!" a voice called from around the other side of the dome. It was a woman's voice but I didn't recognise it, so it was probably one of the old Woodward soldiers.

I leaned sideways so that I could see around the dome, and yes, Frederic and his crew were returning. They were sprinting towards us and would probably reach us in about thirty seconds, but although we could see them, all they could see was the dome. We were under an invisibility veil and soundproof barrier, and because they needed to communicate with 3P69, they hadn't been put under it. If Lucien was on the ball and had set something up so that he could visually see what was happening outside the dome, he would know they were coming, and that would alert him to our assault—if the magic we'd done hadn't already.

"Marc, go put them under our protective spells," James said, having been on the same wavelength. "Lillian, you do what Marc just suggested."

Marc turned and sprinted around behind the dome and out of my sight, while Lillian stood stock-still with a look of intense concentration on her face. It made me nervous to see it—I really hoped she had a complete understanding of the idea Marc had come up with, and my idea to strengthen it. I swapped a look with Peter, who I saw had also been watching this process anxiously, but James appeared to be more concerned with the dome. I turned my gaze back to it and felt my own anxiety ratchet up another notch. If Lucien hadn't yet worked out that we were out here, it would only be a matter of time…

"Okay, it's done," Lillian said suddenly, looking over at James.

"It is?" he said incredulously. "Where is it?"

"It's invisible," she told him—and by extension, the rest of us. "An invisible dome that will prevent his magic passing through, and on the outside of it, an anti-teleportation ring powered by the Sien-Leoard Crystal, plus any magic the outer dome sucks into itself. Have I missed anything?"

"Your dome is a magic particle vacuum?" James said, and she nodded. "The whole dome, not just on one side?" Another nod, and he shrugged. "Thought so, but the only stupid question is the one not asked."

"Are we good?" Marc asked as he re-took his original position. We all nodded, and he said, "Well, as Lucien used to like to say, 'no time like the present'. Turn her on, Lillian."

She counted down from three and then did so, with me and several others holding our breath in anticipation. Nothing happened immediately, which made me both more and less nervous; it gave me time to wonder what came next, and the longer it went on, the worse the feeling got. Lucien was still in there—this thing wasn't going to be able to strip him of all his magic all at once, no matter how powerful it was. He was going to respond with something at some point; it was only a matter of time before he tried something to bust through Lillian's dome. What would happen when he realised it was more powerful than his own magic, as he surely would before too long?

If I'd had more time, I would have gotten to the same conclusion Lucien did, and maybe in time to realise what would be coming next. Sadly, Lucien was still quick on his feet, and may have already been probing at Lillian's dome before she had even turned the vacuum on, for all I knew. Even if he could have destroyed the dome with his magic (before it started leaching off his), he couldn't have broken through the anti-teleportation ring, which meant that his only option was to quickly and decisively swing the battle back in his favour.

"His untraceability's gone!" Marc shouted. "He's—what's he—"

I glanced over at Marc and noticed his face rapidly draining of colour. It was as though the next second or so happened in slow motion. I saw Marc's mouth beginning to open, even as I shifted my centre of gravity forward and allowed my knees to unhinge. By the time I heard his shout to "get", I could no longer see him, as I was flat on the ground. The intended call to the group was to "get down!" but it was cut off by an almighty explosion of sound all around us. Within it, there were two identifiable sounds: the disintegration of Lillian's dome and the rapid fire of the machine guns Lucien had just teleported from inside his dome to outside it, but still within our dome, to launch his own non-magical attack.

Exactly what became of the wreckage of Lillian's dome, I never found out. How many bullets flew through the space I had occupied moments earlier, I also never found out, although I did feel one of them tug at my right sleeve as it came within a whisker of winging me. It went on for an eternity that was probably five–ten seconds before it suddenly stopped, and although my ears were ringing, I was then able to distinguish the sound of people screaming and crying out in horror—and in at least one case, agony.

My instinct was to stay down until I knew the danger had passed, but both my curiosity and my sense of the occasion overrode it. If Marc, Lillian, Natalie or someone else had found a way to stop the attack, it wouldn't take Lucien long to either restart it or do something else devilish. I quickly scrambled back to my feet and looked at the scene around me. Peter and James looked fine; Peter had dived like me and was now clambering up, while James appeared to have fallen over backwards, perhaps blown off his feet by the attack, although he was now pulling himself up and he wasn't bleeding—I took this for a good sign.

Before us, the dome looked just as it had before—no sign of a change in Lucien's dome and no sign of Lillian's invisible dome at all. Around to my right, everyone who had been there appeared to be miraculously okay—in fact, in Marc's case, he appeared not to have even lost his feet through the whole ordeal.

The same could not be said for the people to my left. A girl was spread-eagled on the ground not too far from Peter, a bit further back from the rest of the circle, as though the bullet which had hit her squarely in the face had blown her all the way back there. I knew it was a girl from the shape of her body, but I couldn't be entirely sure who it was because her face was completely gone. She was dead, of course, and beyond anyone's help. There was also blood on the ground further around to the left, and by moving back a bit, I was able to see who it belonged to. Greg Pont was also on the ground, curled up into a foetal position, injured but clearly not dead. Dad and Charlie were on either side of him, and as I watched, Amelia was hurrying over to him with the Light Crystal. I quickly scanned to either side of me for the girls I knew: Amelia, Natalie, Rebecca, Katie and Erica were all on their feet and appeared to be unhurt, making me think that it was probably poor Sophie who had been killed; she had been standing around that spot after all.

As I turned my attention back to Marc and James, registering that Lillian was moving as quickly as she could around the dome, past me to where Sophie lay; I felt a strange tingling sensation all over my body. It didn't last long, and it wasn't entirely unpleasant, but when it ceased, I realised what it was and what it meant. All the magic I'd given myself had just been stripped from me. I quickly went for my solid-outliner, pointed it at the dome and gave it a click: nothing whatsoever happened. All my magic was gone, which probably meant that everyone else was in the same position; and the only magic left to us was the four magic crystals, which even now were probably being depleted by the same magic vacuum Lucien was using against us. It had to be the same idea we'd had, only in reverse—his dome wasn't just protecting him; it was attacking us.

James may or may not have felt his own magic being stripped—at the very least, he was no longer four-dimensional—but he certainly saw what I'd done with the solid-outliner and understood what it meant. Even in the face of total disaster, his brain didn't stop moving. He yelled at the top of his voice, "Everyone with Magic Crystals, shadows now! Everyone else, non-magic weapons!"

Marc, Natalie and Amelia all dipped their hands to their pockets and vanished a moment later, hopefully using the magic from the crystals— the only magic they had left to them—to do what James had just said. Also hopefully, though I couldn't see him as he was around the other side of the dome, Frederic had done the same with the Darkness Crystal. Losing those four with their magic was an enormous pang, but it was our only option—the only way we could continue to make some sort of stand against Lucien. Hopefully they could figure out a way to launch an attack against him from their new positions, but in the meantime, the rest of us were alone, facing a foe infinitely more powerful than us, and who was about to use another weapon in his arsenal which I had once again forgotten all about.

There was enough time for someone on the other side of the dome to fire a shot at it—a shot which had no effect, of course—before I felt the soft, smooth glove of Lucien's Honnie mind wrap around my own and take it into his possession. For a moment, I felt my will to resist him give a little; and then for some reason, it strengthened again. Enough freedom remained to me to look to either side, and see from the faces of all the others that they too had been taken in by the Honnie mind. And yet, while he had the power to achieve so much of what he wanted in this very moment—removing almost all his opposition in a single stroke, bringing me and James firmly over to his side—he chose not to immediately take it.

"The fight ends here," Lucien spoke to us then, and his voice was inside all our minds. At least, it was inside my mind, and I had no reason to think he was only speaking to me and not all the others. "You are all in my power. I have all your minds within my own and I can make you all do literally anything I want. I could make you kill yourselves, or kill each other. Hell, I could make you all fornicate with each other, believing that you're fornicating with your own parents and loving every second of it. I can even make it happen in the physical world if I choose, as I have all the magic and you don't. Except, of course, for those you enabled to get away. I am very unhappy with that, James; I adore your brain and I am pleased that it will now be working for me, but you still need to be punished for the difficulties you have caused me. I have special punishments waiting for the four who escaped me, of course, and John has quite a bit coming his way as well, but I see no reason why you can't receive your punishment first. Everyone, gather around James so that you can see."

My heart was racing by this point, but there seemed no reason not to do as he said. I went and stood close to James, and Peter gathered in close to us as well. One by one, everyone left came to stand close to James, and I was pleased to note that no, Frederic wasn't among them. He and the other four would be in their shadows right now, watching all this in their own kind of horror. Or maybe they would have moved on somewhere else, knowing that Lucien knew about the fourth dimension and might try to go in himself and flush them out. I didn't think he would do that, though; he hadn't up till this point, for what reason I didn't know but could possibly guess at—maybe he was worried about how his magic would work in there. Anything that levelled the playing field was worth avoiding, I supposed.

"Good. Very good," he spoke to us again. "That kind of instant obedience is exactly what I expect from all of you from this day forward. Now, make sure you can all see clearly what is in store for James, because I'm afraid he won't see it for himself, and he will want someone to describe it to him later."

For a moment, nothing did happen, and then someone behind me began to move around the outside of the pack. It was Erica, moving around to stand in front of James. At first, I thought she was just going to be close to him through whatever Lucien was going to do; and then, for just a moment, I thought she was going to try to stand in front of him and shield him with her body. That wouldn't have worked, of course, and not just because she was far too petite to cover him thoroughly enough. It was only when she took up her position about a foot from him, facing him, that I realised Lucien was putting her there as part of whatever he was planning to do.

"You know, a possibly fitting punishment would be for you to kill your own girlfriend," Lucien spoke to us, and I had to agree that would certainly be a major punishment—the sort of thing that would break him. "It would be bad, but it isn't really what I'm after. I want you to be focused on my work, and that may not happen if you're losing your sanity. I'll let you keep your beloved for now, James, but I'm going to have to take something else from you; and since Erica needs to be punished as well, I will give her the tools to perform the—extraction."

We all watched raptly, with fascination no doubt provided by Lucien, as Erica held her hands up before her face, palms facing James. She curled the tips of her fingers a little, and as we watched, they elongated and turned into claws, exactly like the ones Lucien had used to ravage Stella's body just a couple of days ago. Surely he wasn't going to get Erica to do that to James, although it would fit the profile of what he seemed to want—not to break James's mind, which then had to mean breaking his body in some way.

Nobody moved. I couldn't speak for anyone else but I just had no thought of moving. If I had thought of it, I might have tried to put a stop to it; certainly I felt the appropriate amount of repulsion at what was happening. James himself was completely motionless, and in his case, Lucien may have actually been using magic to hold him in place, as mind power alone probably wouldn't be enough to override the flight instinct. He looked utterly terrified as his girlfriend stood before him, claws outstretched, ready to practically pull his face off.

What happened next wasn't quite as bad as that, but it was bad. Erica twisted her wrists so that her claws were pointing upwards, and then raised them to James's wide, terrified eyes. The pointer claw of each hand slid into each of his eyes, beneath the eyeballs, and dug them out quickly and fairly cleanly, making a soft squishing noise as they were extracted from their sockets. They rolled neatly into Erica's palms with an unpleasant squelchy sound, her fingers quickly returning to their normal shape and size, and leaving two wide and bloody holes where they had been. Lucien was quick to stop the blood pouring out of James's eyes, and he may have cleaned up any wounds within them, but he didn't do anything to replace them. And that wasn't even the end of the ordeal. To top it off, Erica, her own eyes gleaming and with a big, happy smile on her face, ate first one eyeball and then the other, chewing them up and swallowing them as if they were as tasty as meatballs.

"Good. Very good," Lucien spoke to us in our minds, his tone full of nasty satisfaction.

Two things happened simultaneously then: James sank to his knees and threw his hands up to his face, his expression shifting to devastation and anguish; and Erica, equally anguished, burst into tears, also dropping to her knees and throwing her arms around him, babbling useless apologies to him. I realised that I no longer had any will keeping me in place, and now understood that of course, Lucien had actively prevented all of us from interfering in his spectacle. Thank God none of James's family are here to see this, I thought, wondering if they would ever even find out about the humiliations Lucien would put us all through before bringing us officially over to his side.

"Would you all like a little of that?" Lucien's voice asked us in our heads. "I can fill your minds with James's memory of his eyes being taken out, or Erica's memory of how it felt to be eating those eyes—only unlike her, I won't make you enjoy it. If not those, I have many other thoughts or memories I can put in your minds, specific to each of you, that I know would bother you immensely. For example, Peter, I know you would particularly hate this thought."

We all looked at Peter, who was trembling with what looked, judging by his twisting facial expressions, like despair and fury.

"Or John, I know you won't like this one, especially because you know, for a fact, that it really happened."

I was gone from the park. In fact, I was gone from John. I had become Lucien, and I was standing inside the room off his bedroom where he had kept Natalie locked up for three days. There was something happening on Lucien's left but he was paying no attention to it, and I already knew what it had to be so I didn't give it any notice either. It was Natalie, and what Hignat, Wilwog and Sebastian were doing to her which was occupying his attention, and therefore mine.

From Lucien's vantage, I watched the terrible things the three boys did to her, and the way Lucien himself chose to assert his own dominance in the process—not by rape, which I knew would happen later that night anyway, but by other means. The scene shifted and I was back in the park, where only a fraction of a second had passed. I only then became aware that, like Peter, I too was trembling with rage and despair. For me, it was hopelessness at our situation, and rage at now knowing at least some of what he had done to Natalie—some of the details which Marc, James, Peter and others had seen and chosen not to tell me because they knew how much it would hurt me to know. I was also concerned for Natalie; how could she have bounced back so quickly from that? Had Marc or Frederic done a little magic of their own to help her move on from it?

Lucien, meanwhile, did this routine with a few more people, either providing them with true memories like mine, or made-up ones like what he had probably given Peter, before addressing the group in our heads again.

"Would you like some more of that?" he asked, his voice full of malice. "I imagine you don't, and as much as I would enjoy putting you through it, I would even more enjoy for it to just be over, and for us to all be able to push forward together. Sadly, that can't happen until Marc, Amelia, Natalie and Frederic Woodward also re-join us, and bring their crystals with them. So what do you say?"

"You guys," James called, raising his voice and cupping his hands around his mouth, "Marc, Amelia, Natalie, Frederic Woodward, come out now."

"Come out now."

"Come out now."

"Come out now."

The chant went up from everyone, me included. I don't recall making a decision to chant along with everyone else, and supposed they hadn't made a decision to chant either. Nevertheless the chant went up, and once it did, it was impossible to stop.

"Very good, very good," Lucien spoke in our heads, and he sounded pleased. "Keep at it, guys. Keep at it. I know they will think you're under my control, but keep it up anyway. This war will be over very soon."

Chapter 31: When the War is Over…

I came awake slowly at the sound of the alarm, as usual. Although it was now well into spring, the weather was still behaving in very winter-like ways, and it took a considerable effort to struggle out of bed each morning. I rolled onto my back, flung my left arm out sideways, aiming for the button to shut off the alarm; instead knocking the clock off the bedside table and onto the floor, spilling its batteries, and achieving the right outcome all the same. I then rolled back to face Natalie, who lay in the bed beside me, and who appeared to have woken at the sound of the clock clattering to the floor rather than the alarm itself.

"Morning," I said blearily, resting my forehead against hers and reminding myself, as I had every morning for close to a year now, how lucky I had been since the end of the war. Either by Lucien's spellwork or as a result of having the magic sucked out of me that day in the park, I had lived well beyond the two-week timeline I'd been expecting since cheating death. Everyone who had survived the war was now living in prosperity—admittedly some more than others, but naturally the ones in greater favour with Lucien were the ones afforded more opportunities. And to top it off, when the dust had settled and we were all figuring out how we were going to fit into this new world, Natalie had come back to me and offered me the proverbial reset button, on the one condition that I be completely honest with her about everything that I'd done. With nothing left to lose, I'd taken her up on it, and we had been closer than ever since.

"Hey you," she now said, rubbing her nose against mine. "Happy birthday."

My heart skipped a beat. Oh yeah, it was September 17; I was sixteen years old at last. On top of that, it was Saturday, which meant that although it wouldn't be a completely free day, it would be a lazier day than week days. Week days these days consisted of a schooling program which Lucien had commissioned after the war, and which was scheduled to run from February this year until December. It was designed to combine two years of high school into one in such a way that no important material was left out, and meant that once we were done with it, we could return to regular school next year without having lost any time. I was in the nine–ten program along with Peter, James, Harry, Simon, Katie, Erica and Liam. Lucien himself was taking the program so that he could finish year twelve, albeit a year late, but with enough free time along the way that he could still rule the world with the crystals, all five of which he now possessed—although I doubted he kept them all on his person.

I was distracted from this thought by the feel of Natalie's lips on mine, and I happily returned the kiss. "Thanks," I now said, putting my right arm over her and squeezing her body full-length against mine in a way that made every inch of me wake up.

Natalie moaned and said, "We don't have to get up right away, do we? I kinda wanna stay in bed and enjoy a little of this," she said, and I felt one of her hands feeling around between my legs.

I did too, but we had a regular Saturday morning appointment with Lucien in just a couple of hours, and if we stayed in bed, we would have to skip breakfast, or Natalie would have to skip doing her hair, or something else equally disastrous. The alternative—being late for Lucien —was not an option. I decided to handle it in a way that I'd done before, and which gave me a lot of enjoyment in the process.

"You know I do too," I said, giving her but a squeeze, and kissing her lips, before sitting up and raising her up with me. "Unfortunately, we can't do that."

She continued to lean on me as we sat there together. Not looking at me, she said, "Do you think Lucien will ever be done with us?"

I hesitated before answering. The truth was, I liked the work we did for Lucien, and for a couple of reasons. It gave me a sense of purpose beyond anything I could get from school, and it paid super well. We would probably have enough for me to retire by the age of thirty and live very comfortable lives for a hundred years. Without it, we would still be reasonably well off, for the inheritance Natalie and Rebecca had gotten equally between them after the rest of their line had been practically wiped out was quite substantial; but this would last a lot longer and would set us up for what would come once we were finished with school —whatever careers we each chose, and then, hopefully, a family.

But Natalie didn't share my enthusiasm for the work. The money was no novelty to her, and she didn't feel the same sense of purpose I did. She had explained to me once that it was because she couldn't see herself having anything to do with politics for the rest of her life, and she had always dreamt of making a difference in people's lives through something artistic.

"I think he will eventually," I said after a moment. "I think he thinks he's rewarding us by giving us what he considers more important than anything else: power. I don't think we've repaid him enough to ask for more freedom to do our own thing, but I imagine that he'll be more willing to give it to us once he gets used to his role."

Although to be fair, Lucien was a lot better at being ruler of the world now than he had been in the beginning. Even in the aftermath of the war, he still tried to do too much too fast, with the usual result of him feeling overwhelmed and like everything was slipping out of his control. It was the counsel of me, Marc, James and Frederic which had given him the confidence to move more slowly, yet more sure-footedly. Since then, he had been able to more methodically bring in better thought-out magical solutions to problems around the world, and some of those solutions were paying off in ways that were actually lightening Lucien's overall workload. This made me think that eventually, he would only need us every now-and-then, instead of practically every day as he did now.

"I hope you're right," she said, resting her hand quite high up on one of my legs. "Are you sure you don't wanna spend a little more time here before getting ready?"

I smiled, scooped her up into my lap, and then swung my legs out of bed and put my feet on the floor. As I stood up, pulling her to her feet along with me, I stroked her neck and trailed my fingers down her chest, between her breasts, down her belly and over the gentle bulge of her crotch.

"I can't," I sighed. "If I do, we'll lose a few hours before we even know it."

"You talk big, Mr. Playman," she teased, bumping her crotch against mine, "and yet here we are, standing *beside* the bed."

She was turning it around on me by taking a shot at my sense of manhood. It was a good tactic, and might have made me instantly change my mind and prove myself to her—if it weren't so obvious that she was doing exactly that. I was in love with Natalie, but that didn't change the fact that this little dance of ours was a game, and I couldn't win it unless I played it properly. And the number one rule in this little game of ours was, 'make sure you're the one setting the terms.'

"Are you questioning my follow-through, Ms. Fletcher?" I teased back, taking her by the shoulders and holding her at arm's length, not gripping her hard but hard enough that she couldn't have shrugged away from me if she'd tried.

She arched her eyebrows at me. "What if I am?"

"Well, I feel that the only appropriate response would be for me to go and take a shower and get ready for the day," I said, and before she could react, I picked her up and rushed off to the bathroom with her in my arms. Naturally, a shower together followed, and since one shower was quicker than two, there was time for a bit of action after all…

* * *

As we had been doing through much of the war, we were residing in a contained environment. This one had been built by Lucien in the aftermath of the war, and had been done primarily because thanks mainly to the effectiveness of Lucien's propaganda machine, many of us—particularly the Woodwards, Fletchers, Tommy and me—could not safely go out into the wide world without being beset upon by people who thought they would be doing Lucien a favour by hurting—or possibly killing—us. This had since been expanded to include our schooling area as well as an area for us to meet with Lucien, and sometimes other advisors of his, where we would usually discuss either magic, the issues of the wider world, or both.

Even though we had been worried about being late, Natalie and I were the second couple to arrive after Marc and Amelia, who lived on the other side of the installation in the custody of Frederic. For a very brief couple of months, Marc had been Frederic's adopted son, but when Lucien had turned eighteen, he immediately made himself Marc's legal guardian—although the living arrangement stayed the same. On our side, Natalie and Rebecca were in the custody of Alice, who we'd had to trick into letting us back into the old base in order to capture her and bring her to Lucien; she'd ended up being the very last person to be brought over to the right side. Peter and I still lived with Mum, Dad and Hilda, but the dynamic of the family had changed. All of them, even Mum, now accepted that we had been through enough to be treated like adults, even to the point that there was no shame in us sleeping in the same beds as our girlfriends—not even for the fifteen-year-old Rebecca.

The Thomases were not so liberated. They appreciated Erica's presence, for she spent just about every free moment she had helping James with things, but they didn't let them share a bed, and they didn't let James do anything that might be remotely dangerous to him. They also refused to let Jessica date Darcy, although they couldn't stop her from seeing him. Baby Ivy was about six months old now, and although Jessica spent as much time as she could with her daughter, it was Marge and Charlie who did the bulk of the raising. Tommy, who had also been adopted by Frederic, often came around and attempted to spend time with his daughter, but the Thomases didn't trust him and wouldn't let him in; that situation threatened to get nasty in not too much time, but it still hardly compared to the nastiness of the war.

Frederic and his mother were the next two to arrive. Lillian was older than ever, but since the war had ended, she appeared to have regained some of her vitality. That had been discussed at school, and the common consensus was that Lucien had been merciful on her and used his magic, as were equally sure he had done with Alice, to keep them going a bit longer. If it were true, it was likely out of his own need for their knowledge than compassion, but it at least proved that he still had some compassion for us after all the trouble we had caused him.

About five minutes late, the door opened and Erica entered, with James close behind her, clutching at one of her arms with one hand and holding his cane in the other. Lucien hadn't been as merciful on James; he'd made prosthetic eyes which looked like normal eyes, but he had not used his magic to restore James's sight, which I was quite sure he could have done if he chose. I could only assume he had bookmarked that as a reward for further down the track, as a way to let us know that he really didn't need our assistance anymore and was using it on James to keep him loyal. I'd spoken to James about this multiple times and knew that such measures weren't necessary—James was all in on the mission of bringing peace and prosperity to the world—but perhaps Lucien didn't trust that he would feel the same way if he could see again.

Lucien himself came in just as James and Erica were taking their seats, and he was followed by Lena. We all stood up to greet them, shaking hands with Lucien and speaking to Lena, although for the most part, she didn't permit anyone to touch her. The exception was me, who she embraced—and for some reason, Amelia—those two also sharing an embrace. Lucien was as jealous as ever where his girlfriend was concerned, but for some strange reason, he permitted her to do that with me. I detected no desire for me in her when she was near—he had snuffed that out of her entirely—but he had not done so with me, meaning that whenever she was close to me, I couldn't help but desire her, and it took a conscious effort to remind myself that it could never happen, and wouldn't be worth it even if it could; I had things too good with Natalie right now to screw up.

Not that I had to worry about this very often, because we rarely saw Lena these days. Unlike the rest of us, Lena was already back attending regular school, and this was thanks to the tutoring program Lucien had set up for her on the last day of the war, which he had allowed to continue after the dust had settled. She had taken a test in December which had placed her at such an advanced level that she could probably have graduated on the spot, but she chose to go back and do the last two years of school anyway. Lucien was happy enough for her to do this; he had told me once, on an occasion just a couple of weeks back when it had been just the two of us working on a project on a Saturday morning not unlike this one (where the others had been sent off on specific errands), that he expected her to do her own projects down the track, but for the time being, he thought she would benefit from completing her education.

Lucien also told me something even more confidential about Lena in that same conversation, this time regarding her pregnancy. The fact that Lucien's presently unwed partner was carrying his child and the next ruler had been announced late last year and was publicly known—and despite the unwed situation, the world celebrated them. What I'd always found strange was that other than the announcement, there was no evidence at all that she was carrying a child; she certainly didn't look pregnant. She did have a healthy glow about her which could have been associated with pregnancy, but I could just as easily put that down to regular awesome sex. I assumed Lucien had some magic going on, either to make it more comfortable for her, more exciting for him (so that he could continue having sex with her throughout), or both.

In that same conversation a couple of weeks back, Lucien told me what said magic was.

"There were a couple of parts to it," he had said. "I want my children —all of them, if I have more than one—to be the best possible versions of themselves that they can be. Back before the crystal chips were wrecked, I knew—based on being around Amelia and Stella—that they would only be willing to use their own magic to a certain extent to achieve the best for themselves, so I gave them a leg-up—and in hindsight, I'm so glad I did. I don't wanna be continually using magic on them either, because they may not feel like my progeny anymore, so I did a bit of magic on myself to alter my sperm. Now, even without magic, they'll be almost like a perfectly evolved form of human being, and any imperfections they'll have—and there'll be some, given that they'll still be human—will come from Lena's genes rather than my own. Hers I didn't alter, because let's face it, she's got great genes as it is."

"Okay," I said patiently, knowing he was still to get to the point, "but that doesn't explain why she doesn't look pregnant at all—unless you made it so that they won't start growing until they're born or something. I suppose that'd make the birth a hell of a lot easier."

What I hadn't added, although he surely read it in my mind, was that even though she didn't look like she was carrying a child, one part of her body—or two parts, if you will—had adjusted as if they thought there were a child in there. Her breasts, which had already been large and firm before, had swelled even more, and although it couldn't be seen, I had felt them pressing against me on the handful of occasions when Lena had embraced me. They felt as though they were carrying fluid—quite a lot of it, I reckoned—and said fluid, whatever Lucien said about not altering Lena's genes, was bound to be more nurturing than regular breast milk.

"Nah," he had shrugged. "I suppose I could have done it, but to be honest, it wasn't the first thing I thought of, and I'm not sure if it can be done without using ongoing magic. Plus, who knows if that'll be safe for the baby. Nah—I just put a spell on her uterus to make it like an extender-case so that the baby can grow in there without it requiring the uterus to grow. Theoretically, it could grow to adult size in there without needing to be born, but obviously we're not gonna do that. Except—well —I made a little oversight when I did the spell."

"What oversight?" I asked, because the way he'd phrased it had made it feel like I was supposed to ask.

He had shifted uncomfortably in his seat. "Well, because of the spell, her fallopian tubes never got the memo that there was a baby in there. I should have twigged a lot sooner, because all the regular hormonal behaviour we were told to expect never happened. If she'd had a period in any of this time, we would have known something was off, but—well —that never happened either."

He had broken himself off and stared down at the table before us, which was littered with notepads and computer tablets. My mind had taken about three seconds to make the obvious connection.

"So, how many babies are in there now?" I had asked.

He had shrugged. "Eleven at this stage, of all different ages, and there aren't gonna be any more than that. We're gonna induce the first birth in a few weeks, and then one more every month or so after that. They ought to be slightly more developed than regular children because they'll be in the womb a few months longer, and everything they get after that will only be the best, of course."

That meant that Lena was only a week or so away from having her first child, if Lucien sticks to that plan. His words had made me wonder how Lena's breasts had been so obviously aware of her pregnancy when the rest of her body apparently hadn't, but I thought I could come up with an answer for that. Based on when I had first noticed it, I supposed they had only started to react after Lucien had done that bit of magic to stop any more babies from being conceived.

"Okay, guys," Lucien said presently, "we've come a long way in the last twelve months. I wanna recap some of it so that we're all on the same page and know where we are before we discuss where to go next. For a bit of context, Lena and I have a day jam-packed with meetings all across the world. Because of the whole time zone thing, it's gonna be almost thirty hours nonstop, and all these meetings are related to setting the medium-term agenda for the world. I'll be wanting your input before I speak to them, which is a big responsibility, but if it makes you feel any better, I'm not promising to take all of your ideas under advisement."

"Cheers," Marc smirked, and Lucien grinned back at him. The brotherly relationship between those two had been a bit awkward in the immediate aftermath of the war, but it had slowly returned to something very similar to how it had been before any of this had started—back in the days when Marc and Lucien lived at home with their (our) madman of a father, who may or may not have been secretly plotting against the Hammersons even back then.

Bit by bit, we went over everything we had achieved so far. Officially, the war had been declared over a few days after the Young Army's defeat; that had been when every single country in the world was either directly or indirectly under the control of Hammersonia. Since then, they had all been incorporated as territories of the global state, still occasionally referred to as Hammersonia, although the name, as Hammerson had intended, was now less important given that there was no place on Earth outside Hammersonia. Some former countries, such as the United States, China, Brazil and India, had been split into multiple territories to even out their populations, the divisions usually taking place along either language or cultural lines. Other territories had been merged together, usually due to a shared language or cultural construct. Most of the plans for these mergers and divisions had been put together by the Hammerhearts before Lucien's time; but as we had come to learn in the last twelve months, while the Hammersons had been horrendous in the way they had gone about their plans, the basis of their ideas appeared to be pretty sound.

The plan for rebuilding the world after the war and setting up the magical utopia envisioned by Lucien and the Hammersons before him had been, for the most part, put together by our core group of Lucien himself, Marc, Amelia, James, Natalie, Frederic, Lillian and me. Although she had brought James into the room, Erica was only permitted to enter so far as she was required to assist James to his seat, and then to come and get him when he was done; for the rest of the time, she did not have the authority to remain in the meetings. Peter and Rebecca, although they had been so deeply involved in the final stages of the war, were also not permitted in the meetings. Several of us had felt indignant at this, but Lucien had politely explained that other than Peter being my brother and Rebecca being Natalie's sister, neither of them had any special knowledge or skills to make them valuable in this company.

Those three—Erica, Peter and Rebecca—had since taken up a project of their own, which all of us—including Lucien himself—had contributed to in small form. They were opening a brand new war memorial in Chopville to recognise and commemorate all those from the area, on both sides, whose lives had been lost in the battle. Many of us had objected to Hammerhearts being included, but Lucien had stated that he wouldn't approve the project unless it was done that way, saying that for the most part, Hammerhearts had been led to their own doom by the carelessness and heartlessness of Arnold Hammerson and Tankom. He was at least willing to put them on opposite sides of the memorial, however, and that provided a middle ground on which we all felt comfortable.

The memorial was almost ready to be opened, but we had decided to hold off on the unveiling until February 1 next year, as that would be the two-year anniversary of the Chopville High magic display which we had all come to agree marked the beginning of the second Sorcerous War. Other ceremonies would take place throughout the year at the memorial, all of them being annual ceremonies and all commemorating important events of the war. Besides February 1, these included February 25 (the first Chopville High battle), May 6 (the third Chopville High battle), June 29 (the destruction of the original Woodward base), August 23 (Arnold Hammerson's death and Lucien's rise to head of Hammersonia, which was also a public holiday across all of Hammersonia and would be the most celebrated day in the world), and of course, September 5, the end of all serious resistance against Lucien's rule.

Meanwhile, the plan we had put together had three central pillars: union, innovation and forecast. The union pillar concerned bringing the world together under a single banner (which had been achieved for the most part already) and, for lack of better terminology, crushing any and all opposition against Lucien's rule across the world. After some debate, we had settled on the Hammersons' original idea of mind maintenance (regular influential charms) to eventually bring respect for Lucien into societal norm. The main opposition to this had surprisingly come from Lucien himself, who had hoped to bring about a society which allowed greater room for free thought based on self-interest, which he believed would encourage people to be the best versions of themselves without help from a central government. Eventually, though, thanks mainly to James's gentle words of wisdom, he realised that peace would always be just out of reach if he took this approach. Besides, it was working well enough that nobody was complaining about the results.

The innovation pillar was the one I found most exciting because it basically allowed us to speculate on the best ways to solve the world's problems using magic. Lucien permitted us to debate any ideas we had on this subject with himself as the moderator, given that up to this point, he was the one using the magic. We had already made enormous strides in this area: air and water pollution was a thing of the past, unless it came from natural sources such as volcanos (and even then, we had ways to deal with it quickly); sickness and hunger were no longer issues, as entirely new industries had sprung up around the concept of using magic to feed the world; and millions of people were being lifted out of poverty every month across the world—however this still had the furthest to go. The tricky point was that Lucien wished to preserve the unique culture and character of regions across the world, and he feared that using magic too liberally in this regard would result in every place in the world looking too much the same, which he told us would be a tragic loss which future generations could never forgive.

The forecast pillar, as its name suggested, concerned using what we knew and observed about the present to make medium and long-term plans for the direction of the world. I paid attention and contributed where I could to this part of the plan, but it didn't interest me as much as the others did because we didn't spend as much time talking about magic; too much of it seemed to revolve around politics and sociology, which was fine for people like Marc, James and Frederic (and even Amelia, occasionally), but Natalie and I just couldn't find a way to be too worried about the medium and long-term future of the world. It seemed to be in pretty good hands, after all.

And it seemed that after about an hour going over everything we had done in terms of union and innervation, the rest of this meeting was related to what would be coming next. Marc, James, Frederic and Lillian, for the most part, contributed their ideas for moving forward. Marc was very interested in developing a space program and using magic to branch out and colonise the solar system, and beyond, in due course. James focused mainly on the specifics of mind maintenance and how it could be used to increase people's overall self-sufficiency, as Lucien desired, while making sure they continued to respect the ruling regime. Frederic agreed with this concept and added that he would like to see territories granted small levels of autonomy, under the condition that they could not go directly against Hammersonian law.

Lillian was quite interested in the economic side of things and had put together a lot of thoughts on how a global economy could be properly managed; Lucien was interested in this project, mainly because it seemed like an easy way for him to prop up the struggling territories of the world using capital generated by the more prosperous territories. Amelia's main focus was on education, and as important as it was to educate children in line with the regime, she wanted to see education return, for the most part, to the basics—reading, writing and arithmetic— to which James added that he would like to see critical thinking taught from the earliest possible age to children across the entire world. Theoretically, if it were done properly, people may not always need mind maintenance; they would be smart enough to understand Lucien was doing the best they could ever hope for in their lives as it was.

Lucien took all this in, along with Lena who said nothing during the meeting itself, but who was clearly paying attention to everything. They then left to begin their worldwide day of meetings. We were all dismissed and had the rest of the weekend to ourselves. I wasn't sure about the others, but I would be expected back in the Playman living quarters very shortly, where Mum would make sure I got all my homework done before I could spend any time with Natalie, or Peter, or James, or the twins, or anyone else.

I felt pretty good about things over all as we got up and left the room, except for one thing. All this time, since the defeat of the Young Army, something had been nagging at me. I'd been carrying this distinct feeling that I was forgetting something, something potentially important. I'd brought it up with pretty much everyone, including Lucien himself, and to a man, they had all responded that they hadn't noticed anything obvious that had been forgotten. I'd even spent some long nights discussing it with Natalie, and she had wondered if it had something to do with me dying and the expected passage of death not eventuating the way it was meant to. She had encouraged me to try to forget it, as had Peter and James, but while I agreed with the idea that dwelling on it probably wasn't going to help anything, I just couldn't help myself.

As I walked past James, who was being assisted by Erica again, Marc had caught up with me and caught my arm.

"You're still thinking about it, aren't you?"

He was talking about the thing hovering on the edge of my memory —a thing that may or may not be real. I shrugged and said, "How'd you know?"

"I didn't," he also shrugged, "but you did have a distracted look on your face in there. Any closer to knowing if you've really forgotten something?"

I shook my head. "If there really is something there, I doubt I'll ever nail it. I do feel like it's got something to do with that day in the park—you know, when Lucien took all our magic and forced us to surrender."

Marc looked cautiously around, then looking back at me, he said, "All that could be true, which is why I tend to think that if you really have forgotten something, it's something Lucien is using his magic or his Honnie mind to make sure stays forgotten. That means it'd probably be painful to remember, so maybe you'd be better off not pushing it."

That did make sense, when he put it like that. May had once done the same thing to me in the aftermath of the battle in which we had defeated Arnold Hammerson, to help me forget something terrible that I'd done in self-defence which had ended up taking the lives of several Hammerhearts. Had I done something similar that day in the park? Perhaps something that had taken the lives of friends, rather than enemies? I couldn't think of anyone missing who shouldn't have been, but then Lucien could have made me forget all about them in an attempt to close any loopholes in a plan to make me forget. If that were true, though, why had he permitted me to go on wondering about this for a whole year now when he could have just wiped my mind of the question entirely? And perhaps the most important question of all; could I go on much longer with this nagging question in my mind? Would I ever be able to put it to bed entirely without knowing the answer, one way or another?

I turned a corner and saw Natalie in the hall ahead, heading back towards our living quarters (the Fletchers lived not far from the Playmans). I quickened my step to catch up to her, and was maybe half a dozen paces behind when pain suddenly filled my head. Along with it came a curious sensation that I couldn't have described at the time due to the all-consuming nature of it, but as soon as it let up, I was able to liken it to having my brains squeezed tightly in an iron fist. With it came complete disorientation, and a powerful wave of vertigo which knocked me for a loop and caused me to topple to the ground.

The first thing I registered was that I had just been either released, or partially released, from the hold of a Honnie mind; the feeling was the same as how it had been when May had been under assault and had almost lost her mental grip on us. The second thing I noticed was that I was surrounded by equally disorientated people, at least one of whom I'd fallen on top of, and at least one of whom had fallen on top of me. The third thing I noticed was that the ground beneath us was trembling and shifting, and the fourth thing I registered was that it was indeed the ground: I was no longer inside an installation built by Lucien, but was in fact outdoors. My first thought was that I'd been hit in the head somehow and was now having a dream or hallucination before I'd wake up in a hospital bed somewhere, but my senses were telling me to disregard that thought; everything was far too vivid for that...

I scrambled to my feet and looked around. To my astonishment, I was in Hamster's Stretch Reserve, surrounded by what had once been the Young Army. Everyone, including me, appeared to be clad exactly as we had been on that fateful day when we had been defeated by Lucien. Judging by our positions, I had returned exactly to that moment when we had been defeated, that moment shortly after Lucien had forced Erica to gouge out James's eyes; except it didn't look anything like I remembered it now. Why had my brain chosen to return me to this moment?

Part of the answer to that question may have been in the biggest change to history of all. The dome Lucien had enclosed himself in seemed to have vanished, and in reality, that hadn't happened until after he had wrested the Magic Crystals from Marc, Amelia, Natalie and Frederic. Where it had been was now a great big hole in the ground from which strange colours and noises were emerging. It was clearly the source of the rumbling and tremoring in the Earth, but what was it?

As I stood there, and other people clambered to their feet around me, all looking as confused as I felt, an enormous voice filled the air. Unlike how Lucien had spoken to us back on this day, the voice was in the air rather than in our heads. It was Lucien's voice, and yet not Lucien's voice as I had ever heard it. It was mutilated and distorted by levels of fury that a human voice had never been designed to carry, making it sound monstrous and even demonic.

"*How dare you defy me!*" it roared, and as it did, my brain rapidly made connections—forged understandings—and finally, was able to answer the question that had—in truth—never actually plagued me at all. "You will *pay* for this! You will *all* pay for this! There will be *no* happy ending for *any* of you now! You had your chance! Now, you will all *die*! *Every last one* of you!"

So, the last twelve months had never happened. Everything that had supposedly happened—getting back with Natalie, joining Lucien, the three pillars, living beyond my fifteenth birthday—none of it had been real. Lucien had constructed all of it and had delivered it using his Honnie mind, and judging by those around me, he had delivered the same thing to them. Whether it had been exactly the same—if we had all lived the same vision from our own perspectives, or there had been subtle differences—I had no way of knowing at this time. Exactly why he'd done it, I would never know for certain, but I would later come up with a theory. In case those with the Magic Crystals found a way to defy him, they would have a hard time getting us back on their side if he showed us how good things could be—*would be*—if we surrendered to him.

But his plan had backfired, because now that I knew what he'd done, I was more resolved than ever not to surrender to him. What we had just seen was how Lucien wanted things to be if he won, not how they would actually be if he had a chance to enact his vision of a magical utopia.

Based on the expressions on the faces of Peter, Katie, Erica, and some others I could see from where I stood, they were coming to the same conclusion.

As for what had happened to break the vision, now that I could see the whole scene before me, it was obvious. The only person who did not look disorientated, as if Lucien had completely forgotten to include him in the mental simulation, was Jacob Underwood. After watching whatever we had been forced to do in the short time that had elapsed since Lucien had taken our minds (and it really was only a few minutes at most, not the full twelve months we had been forced to believe), he had decided to take matters into his own hands, and he had been smart enough—or fortunate enough—to use the one tool Lucien had not expected, and had therefore had not been able to completely erase from my memory, not having known that he should: antimagic. The radius of destruction suggested he had only used a single bullet, but if it hadn't hit Lucien directly, it had hit a magic particle close enough to catch him a solid wallop anyway.

"You guys okay?" I asked, and Peter, Katie and Erica nodded. Even James nodded, the sockets where his eyes had been pointing straight at where the dome had been.

"Marc, if you're anywhere around here," Peter said quietly, "now would be a good time to attack."

Chapter 32: Darkness

We all stood (and those of us not on our feet were in the process of getting there), staring transfixed at the spot where Lucien's dome had been—the hole from which that terrible voice had issued. Exactly what had happened to Lucien in there, there was no way of knowing, but the single bullet fired on him would not have done much damage to his magic. He would still have plenty of it, and we still had none. A fight was about to take place—a fight we had no chance of winning—but one we had to at least try to win before we were all wiped out.

As the moment stretched into seconds, and Lucien did not immediately reappear, I took the opportunity to take stock of my arms. I had no magical weaponry and no magic to fight with, now that it had all been sucked out of me. I did have a magic vacuum device, but it was so small that it couldn't have done a lot of damage to Lucien on its own. Moreover, the magic it collected couldn't be turned into a form of magical energy capable of carrying a spell, making it useless in the heat of battle. I also had an antimagic gun, but as it contained no antimagic at this time, it would also be useless. That just left my non-magical devices: an automatic rifle, six grenades, and a plastic explosive which I almost certainly wouldn't have time to set up properly anyway.

Yep, on the whole, it looked pretty hopeless.

And that was when he emerged, rising vertically out of the hole and then hovering there, levitating a few feet above where the ground had been, staring at us all huddled together. My first thought was that whatever had happened to him in there must have destroyed his body, and without the magic of the crystal chips protecting him, it could only have been the Sien-Leoard Crystal inside him which had enabled him to reform. He was definitely still Lucien, but he was very pale. He was completely naked and his body, other than his head, completely hairless (I knew for a fact that it hadn't been hairless before). His eyes were black with an evil intent unlike anything I'd ever seen before, and I understood that he wasn't going to torture us anymore. No, he was just going to kill the lot of us and be done with it.

Not everyone was paralysed by fear, it seemed. Away to my right, I saw Harry and Simon pointing their rifles at Lucien. They unloaded on him in an explosion of sound, but the bullets hit a shield about a foot from his body, ricocheting away at angles (some went over our heads but none hit any of us). Rebecca threw a grenade at Lucien, but it missed him and dropped into the hole, where it may or may not have exploded. Then either Rob or Bob, I couldn't see clearly enough which it was, fired a rocket at Lucien; it fizzled in the air before Lucien's gaze and then turned and came back at us. We all had to scramble out of the way, Peter grabbing an oblivious James and pulling him roughly to the side just in time.

Yep; utterly, utterly hopeless.

I raised my head to look at Lucien, trying to think if there was anything at all that we could do. If not, then I at least wanted to be looking at him when I died. It meant that I was in time to see the four of them suddenly reappear behind Lucien, popping out of their shadows all at once and immediately bombarding him with magic from their crystals. I couldn't tell if they were able to penetrate his shields, but they certainly turned his attention away from us.

I took the chance to get back to my feet and help Peter and James to theirs, thinking that if I needed proof that I was no longer magical in any way, there it was. Before today, I would have seen the four of them in their shadows, appearing as ghosts. Apparently, I had been stripped of that ability along with everything else. It wasn't something I really needed, but it sure made a point.

"Guys, come on," Underwood hissed at us, distracting us from the magical battle which had begun, "load up on this stuff."

He was referring to antimagic; specifically, the large supply of it they had brought back to the battlefield. I was under the impression that they were going to just load the antimagic into all the devices, but I now saw that they had in fact brought the entire supply of it collected by 3P69. As it was, though, the only people who had antimagic guns, besides Underwood, Harry and Simon (who had all loaded up), were Peter, James and me. Peter immediately led James to the store (as I thought of it), connected his antimagic gun to it, and pressed the button to begin a transfer of ammunition. I hesitated for a moment, not wanting to resort to antimagic again unless there was no other way, but one look at the magical battle left me with no choice. Lucien was still stronger than the four of them combined, and perhaps even more so, if the magical vacuum he had used earlier had even slightly depleted the four Magic Crystals he was fighting against.

I skirted the outside of the group, who were for the most part watching the battle in terror as first Natalie, then Amelia, were blasted out of the fight. I reached them just as James had finished loading up his antimagic gun; he detached it and quickly gave it to Peter, who hurried away, perhaps to find someone else to operate it now that James wouldn't be able to aim. I attached my gun to the store as James's had been, then hesitated for a moment. I had no idea how to work this thing, and I hadn't seen how Peter had done it earlier. Fortunately Underwood was close by, and he leaned around me to press the button to begin the transfer of ammunition.

The process was a lot quicker than I had expected; within fifteen seconds, a light began to flash on the store, which had to mean that it was done. Underwood pressed the button again and indicated that I should do the same. By this time, Peter had returned to our side and was nudging James, perhaps with the intention of moving him out of the way. This didn't eventuate, however, due to a couple of things happening at that very moment. Firstly, with an enormous explosion, Marc was sent flying through the air, high over the park in the direction of the town centre.

At almost the same moment, Tommy, who I hadn't even noticed until that moment, but who had apparently been close by the entire time, watching the whole process raptly, suddenly lunged at Peter, tackling him to the ground and almost knocking James off balance as well. All of us cried out in surprise but everyone, me included, was too shocked to do anything. Within a few seconds, Tommy was rolling away from Peter and springing to his feet, holding something in his hands that hadn't been there before. Then, shocking me almost as much as the original assault had, he bounded straight at me, hitting me with his shoulder and sending me reeling to the ground.

Beneath the cussing of Peter, Underwood and a few others in the area, as well as the desperate enquiries from James as to what was happening, I was able to scramble onto hands and knees to see what was going on. Only then, when it was too late to do anything about it, did I realise what Tommy was doing. The realisation crashed home, bringing with it a wave of nausea as I expected death within seconds. Tommy may not have understood what antimagic was, but he had clearly made enough connections just from his observations. Underwood had used a single shot and done more damage to Lucien than any magic; he, Harry and Simon had brought back a huge supply of the stuff; half a dozen of us had guns capable of firing more rounds of the stuff at Lucien; and although it hadn't been used yet, he had seen a certain device poking out of Peter's belt—a device which could fire a much more powerful round of antimagic.

"*Tommy! Stop!*"

He didn't listen, of course. I'm not sure he would have listened even if he understood exactly what antimagic was and what it did. Jacob Underwood, who may or may not have been in the know (Frederic might have explained it to him and the twins while they were collecting it), made a half-hearted attempt to impede Tommy, to which Tommy responded by punching him in the face. Underwood was a big guy, tall and reasonably fit, but he didn't seem to be up for a physical scuffle. It was a pity, because unbeknownst to everyone, Tommy was about to do something of which nobody could have predicted the result. He connected the antimagic canon to the store, pressed the button to begin an ammunition transfer, and then without waiting, aimed the canon at the battle between Lucien and Frederic, the last one standing.

He fired the canon in the middle of the ammunition transfer. He only fired it once, but the connection between the canon and the antimagic store was open. It was maybe an oversight on Frederic's part when he created the antimagic store, or perhaps it was an oversight on Natalie's part when she created these devices, but more likely it was the former. Either way, the result was that the canon discharged the entire store of antimagic in a single shot—an entire quarter of the global supply of antimagic—enough to destroy two regular Magic Crystals (or half the Sien-Leoard Crystal) in a single shot.

And his aim was perfect.

The annihilation was so vast that it was impossible to track all that happened in the single instant of it, and yet all that I did notice made it feel like it happened in slow motion. I saw the sky go black, though strangely the sun was still shining, meaning that although the sky was black, I could still see clearly. I heard a thunderclap of noise, and other noises beneath it which could have been the roaring of monsters. But it was what I felt that demanded most of my attention. The first thing was being slapped in the face by what felt like a cool wind, and then the next thing I knew, my body had changed. My head felt the same, with the possible exception of having a strangely large tongue, but everything below my longer-than-usual neck had taken on the shape of a horse. The colour of my hide resembled the clothing I'd been wearing, and I was wearing horseshoes which, although they were definitely horse shoes, looked a lot like the runners I had been wearing seconds earlier.

Hmm, what an interesting development, I thought, swivelling my neck around to take in as much of my strange new body as I could. And then the sights, sounds and even smells of the world around returned to me, and I realised all that was going on.

For one thing, Hamster's Stretch Reserve had certainly changed for the worse. The grass had disappeared, to be replaced by jagged rocks which were really quite uncomfortable underfoot. The Jade River looked similar enough, but even though I was quite some distance from it, I could sense that although it was still liquefied, the temperature had dropped considerably. The trees still stood where they had always been, but now they were swaying ominously, and I could hear strange voices coming from that direction. They seemed to be whispering things to the effect of, "We resent you for being able to walk around. Come over here and we'll show you who's really tough."

Oh, and I was surrounded by a variety of animals, beasts, and other such things that had previously been my friends. I knew who they all were because like me, their bodies had taken on the appearance of their clothing; and also like me, quite a few of them had only partially changed. Peter still had his face, but the rest of him had turned into a very woolly sheep—and the wool was all black. James had turned into some sort of bird but he seemed unable to do more than flap around and stomp a bit. Tommy had become a snake, Underwood had transformed into a very cuddly-looking pussycat, and Rebecca a beautiful bluebird— and unlike James, she actually could take to the sky.

I would have taken some more time to analyse what had happened to everyone if not for a roar of fury which seemed to tear the air apart. Snapping my neck up, I beheld a dragon. No, I beheld two dragons, both of them towering over the rest of us. They looked every bit as terrifying as every dragon which had been imagined in fantasy fiction: thick scaly hides, iron claws, long leathery wings presently folded against their bodies, and massive jaws, already smoking and ready to belch fire. Neither of them had their original heads or faces, and yet I knew who they both were. The one further from me was Frederic, based on the colour of his hide. And the one closer to me—the one that looked naked and much more scaly—had to be Lucien himself.

And he looked super pissed indeed.

With a roar and a jet of flame, he took off into the air. Frederic went after him immediately, continually putting himself between us and Lucien at every possible moment. Every time Lucien attempted to spray us all with fire, Frederic was there to take the hit—and thankfully, the hits didn't seem to bother him. The airborne battle was nevertheless quite destructive; it set the trees in the Stretch ablaze and at one point, one of their powerful tails smashed into the Main Street Bridge, shattering it and sending the fragments into the river below.

And yet from the beginning, there could only be one winner. It wasn't immediately obvious why, but it soon became apparent that we had the same problem as before. Lucien had magic and we didn't. Frederic fought hard but bit by bit, Lucien was able to disable him. It even seemed that the more Lucien got on top, the bigger he looked (compared to Frederic anyway). I dismissed as a trick of the light until Lucien opened his jaws wide, not to spray fire but apparently to swallow a now defenceless Frederic whole. My brain jammed as I watched this, once again in slow motion, because surely Lucien couldn't actually fit Frederic inside his body even now…but then, he *did* have magic, so did it matter what the laws of physics said?

It didn't matter, because that was when Amelia, Natalie and Marc returned to the fight. After having been knocked out of it by Lucien before, they were once again ready to fight. They were the only three of us still in human form, perhaps protected by their crystals (which probably hadn't been affected by the antimagic, given that Tommy hadn't pointed the canon in their direction). Now they launched an attack against Lucien, taking him by surprise and making him forget about Frederic, who fell back to Earth with a crash, landing where the town centre had been and smashing several buildings flat—or more accurately, smashing flat whatever those buildings had been transformed into by the annihilation.

"I still have more magic than you!" Lucien roared, and his voice was strange—definitely the inhuman voice of an inhuman monster, and yet still perfectly coherent.

Maybe he did have more magic than them, I was no longer sure, but either way, he wasn't quick enough to recover from the attack before it was too late. With a combined effort, the three of them pushed him down towards the Jade River. Their intent may have been to put out his fire, if that was how it worked (scientists had never had a chance to study a dragon before, so who could say). Sensing this, Lucien had pointed himself skyward, probably intending to soar high into the air before anyone could stop him, and then rain fire down upon the lot of us. In this motion, the very tip of his tail touched the surface of the water, and immediately, his entire body froze solid, proving that the antimagic blast had done a little more to the river than what met the eye. Completely immobile, and seemingly in slow motion, the dragon dropped into the river and disappeared from sight.

"Is everyone okay?" Marc called, turning his attention to the rest of us. He and Natalie hurried toward us while Amelia sprinted towards the injured dragon that was Frederic.

"What the hell just happened?" asked either Harry or Simon; they had both been transformed into large dogs, the breed of which I was unsure, and it was no longer possible to tell which was which. Their voices were no longer human but somehow still able to speak in human speech; and as it turned out, the rest of us were the same.

"That was antimagic, wasn't it?" Peter said, looking first at James, then up at me, and then over to where Marc and Natalie had just reached us. As they did, the rest of what had formally been an army, and which now resembled a barnyard, gathered around to listen.

"Yes, it must have been," James said, "but I still can't see. How bad is it? And is anyone missing? And what on earth happened to me?"

"You've turned into a dodo," Underwood told him, "and—er—it looks pretty bad, wouldn't you say?"

"It's way bigger than we predicted," I said, casting my eyes over the rest of the animals, trying to take stock of who was still with us. James had raised a valid point: There was no guarantee that every single person had been turned into an animal capable of surviving in these conditions. If anyone had turned into a fish of some kind, they could be in real trouble. I couldn't see any from here, but that didn't mean much. We would need to do a headcount to be certain, and did we have time for that? How long could we count on Lucien being out of action anyway?

"Everyone stay still," Marc called, "we need to figure out everything that happened just now. I'm guessing someone fired an antimagic gun at Lucien?"

"No, Tommy stole my antimagic canon and fired that at Lucien," Peter called back.

James swore. "Tommy, you idiot!"

"How was I supposed to know this would happen?" Tommy retorted in something of a hiss. "All I knew was that this stuff was more effective against Lucien than anything else; I didn't know it would make the whole world go nuts."

"That's because you don't know what it is," Marc said, reaching us and examining the antimagic store, "and it's never wise to go using magic you don't understand. Oh shit," he said, looking up at me and then at Peter. "Guys, all the antimagic is gone—he discharged all of it."

That was when it hit home to me what had really happened: A quarter of the global supply of antimagic had been discharged in a single shot. Either it had all collided with Lucien, neutralising about half of the Sien-Leoard Crystal, or some of it had collided with Lucien and the rest had gone on to hit Frederic, neutralising a quarter of the Sien-Leoard Crystal and all of the Darkness Crystal. As it turned out, when Amelia and Frederic returned to the group, Frederic confirmed that it was the latter and he no longer had any magic.

"Well, that means Lucien does still have magic," Marc said, "about the same as me, Natalie and Amelia combined. It's not great, but it's not entirely hopeless. First things first, let's get you guys fixed up while we still can."

That turned out to be easier said than done. Normalising charms didn't work, nor did any easy spells to return us to what we had been before. Focussing on Lillian in the form of a cute little rabbit, Marc was eventually able to turn her into a human being, but he had to put a lot of focus into making sure she exactly resembled what she had been before. While he worked, Natalie went around the group, taking note of everyone present and comparing it with her best memory of who had been with us in the beginning. Fortunately, apart from poor Sophie, whose body seemed to have vanished for all I could tell, everyone was alive and accounted for.

"We don't have time to do this for everyone," Marc said, coming back to me, Peter and James. He looked exhausted and more frightened than I had ever seen him. "I can still use magic, and it doesn't seem to be any less powerful, but magic itself feels less stable now. That antimagic blast may have done more damage than we can see, even though we can see a lot."

This would have been a perfect moment for Marc to say, 'I told you so,' though for whatever reason, he said no such thing. I suppose James could have easily said that if it hadn't been for Underwood using antimagic on Lucien in the first place, we would have already lost. Maybe both of them knew that there was no point having such a discussion now; for better or worse, we had opened Pandora's Box, and now we had to deal with the consequences.

"So what now?" Amelia asked, coming over to join us. "If Lucien still has magic, he won't stay away forever."

"Also, where's Fewul in all this?" I added.

"Fewul would also have been weakened by this," Frederic's loud voice added to the conversation. He was on the far side of the pack of animals, and yet his hearing must have been sharp enough to hear our quieter voices even from there. There was no question of his voice not reaching us. "If magic really has been destabilised, it may not even be possible for Fewul to exist in this world until it has settled down."

"But we can't count on that," James said. "The best case scenario is that Lucien returns to the battle with an equal amount of magic to us; and the worst case is that he is able to bring Fewul with him, and we can't compete with that."

"So what do we do?" Natalie asked, but I could already see where this was most likely going…

"Firstly, are anyone's magical devices still working?" Marc said, looking around at us, only realising after he'd spoken that none of us any longer had opposable thumbs with which to operate the devices with which we had started the battle. "Never mind, I'll check."

He hunted around on the ground until he found one of the light devices I had created, infused with whatever spell. He pointed it safely away from everyone and pressed the button; nothing at all happened. He tried a few more times with the same result before chucking the device away despondently.

"Did it work?" James asked.

Marc shook his head, then remembering that James still couldn't see, said, "No, and you know that probably means the magic enhancer doesn't work either, which means we've lost even more magic than we originally thought."

"It's worse even than that," Peter said suddenly. He had one of his front feet on top of another device, and looking down at it, I saw that it was an antimagic gun. "All the antimagic we took out of the supply before this happened is gone. It must have been annihilated along with the rest of it."

"That's no loss—" Marc began.

"Actually, it might be," James interrupted. "I've been thinking about what we can do about this, and if Lucien is intent on putting up a fight, then unless we wish to surrender to him our only option, really, is to use the rest of the antimagic we've collected in the other three locations."

Marc opened his mouth in horror, but no sound came out.

"I was thinking the same thing," Frederic rumbled. "I'm not going to say that it's worth the risk because things can't possibly get any worse, because I'm sure they can. All I know is that if we can't put things back to rights using magic, then we have to do something, because look around, we can't leave things the way they are."

With that, I had to agree.

"In that case, we should try to annihilate the Light Crystal," James suggested. "It's a bit of a long-shot, I know, but if there's any chance of undoing the damage done by annihilating the Darkness Crystal, releasing the magic of the Light Crystal is the way to do it."

"We'd be better off just trying to annihilate Lucien again," said Erica, who appeared to have turned into a chicken. "If we do that, his crystal will mathematically be only as strong as each of ours; it would give us the best chance of overpowering him."

"Unless he uses his Honnie mind again," Peter said. "Hey, do you think he still has that?"

"If he does, he didn't use it at all during our fight," Frederic said.

Marc was looking around at us as this conversation played out. Now he said, "Well, out of a bunch of bad options, James's idea to annihilate the Light Crystal is probably the least bad, so maybe we'll try that. This assumes we're able to teleport to one of the other antimagic stations in these conditions; I guess we'd better find out."

He put his hand on the Hero Crystal and began casting his gaze around the group, apparently using his mind to encircle us in a binding spell without physically going around the group like he normally would. In my experience with magic, doing it physically gave you more control over the exact boundaries of the spell, but apparently Marc had decided that this time, speed was more important than detail.

"Any luck, Marc?" James asked.

"So far, but we won't know for sure until we go—"

His words were drowned by a tremendous roar from a short distance to the west, filling the air and causing me to actually whinny before I could stop myself. A lot of the others also let out similarly involuntary cries of horror and dismay. Far away, on the other side of Chopville, where the Jade River left the town and disappeared into the western woods, a large shape was rising into the air. Big, black, scaly, deadly. Lucien had finally found a way to free himself from the freezing river, and as we watched, he angled his body towards us and began to arrow through the sky. He would be upon us in seconds, and none of us—not even Frederic, who looked totally exhausted—could stand up to him.

"What have you done to me!" he roared, sending jets of flame down into the town centre, starting more fires just for the hell of it. "I have magic, and yet I cannot change my body! Well, maybe it's for the best. How many of you enjoy a good…barbecue?"

He opened his jaws wide and sprayed fire upon us. Amelia threw her hands up just in time to put a shield over the group, which was enough to stop the flames in their tracks (although it had the effect of making the sky itself look like fire over our heads). She had to keep it up continuously, however, for Lucien was also using his magic to blast through it, and he had far more power than Amelia alone. Even when Natalie joined her in the defence, they were unable to prevent the air around us from rising in temperature. Hotter and hotter it got, until I felt like I was going to be suffocated by the heat alone…

And then it all disappeared as Marc finally activated the teleportation, and just in the nick of time. We swirled through the nothingness until we came to land in an unfamiliar countryside. We appeared to be high up on the side of a mountain, and surrounded by a lot of very tall trees. Other than that, there wasn't much else to see; the sky was just as black as it had been in Chopville, and although the sun was in a slightly different position in the sky, that meant very little; I could have just been facing in a different direction.

There was no time for more. At that moment a great wind kicked up around us, and I thought it had to be Lucien following us, but it turned out to be nothing of the sort. The trees above us were all swaying ominously, stretching their branches further and further with every motion. A few seconds later, Frederic let out a great roar, chilling my blood. Swivelling my neck around, I was horrified to see that he had been seized by several trees. They hadn't just wrapped their branches around him; they had wrapped their entire trunks around him, as if they were gigantic woody snakes. They appeared to be trying to wrestle him to the ground, for what purpose I couldn't imagine, but as I watched, mesmerised and temporarily forgetting my own danger, I noticed that though the trees had certainly come to life, none of them had pulled up roots. When Frederic was able to send one tree flying through the air away from all of us by whipping it with his tail, it went completely limp the moment its roots left the ground.

"Help me!" Frederic bellowed, spraying fire out in all directions. It set several trees ablaze, which then set other trees around them ablaze, and the whole thing had just become even more dangerous than it already was.

"This way," Marc called to all of us. "Amelia, you help your dad, and Natalie, you put out those fires and make sure the trees don't get anyone. Everyone else, come with me."

Marc took off at a run; I cantered along after him, along with most of the group, with Natalie shadowing us, putting up invisible barriers which seemed to arch over us. At least she had managed to create a tunnel of sorts which none of the trees around us could penetrate. At the end of this tunnel, holding a firearm of his own and watching our approach dispassionately, apparently unbothered by the trees or the fires, stood 3E57. Marc came to a skidding halt before him and began speaking rapidly, but I only managed to hear the man's reply.

"Yes, I know who you are, Moran. I don't know why you're here instead of Frederic Woodward, and I don't understand what any of this means, but I am intent on making up for my sins of the past and that means I will not be taking your word for anything. I will only take my orders from Frederic Woodward, or if absolutely necessary, one of his subordinates who can prove to me that he has authorised them to speak to me."

"Mr. Woodward is right there," Marc shouted, pointing over his shoulder at where the dragon was being liberated by its human daughter, "and in case you can't tell, he's a little busy to back me up here."

"You expect me to believe that Frederic Woodward would use magic to turn himself into a dragon, and then not use magic to free himself from whatever that is?"

Marc swore. "And that's Amelia, his daughter—you know who she is, right?"

"I do," 3E57 conceded, "but she's only a teenager; she cannot be directing matters of such importance as Frederic Woodward assured me this is."

"Enough of this," Lillian cut in before Marc could fire something back—or just use magic to get the former Hammerheart out of the way. "Gilbert Elliton, do you know who I am?"

Thankfully, Lillian was the one person Marc had transformed back into her former self, so as 3E57 turned his gaze on her, he took a step backward in alarm. "You're—you're Lillian Woodward, aren't you?"

"Yes," she said firmly, taking a few steps forward so that she stood beside Marc. "Do as he says, and step away from the store; we need to use what's inside it to fix the crazy things going on. Surely you've observed from here that magic has become utterly unstable?"

"Well—"

"Sorry, but we don't have time to stand around talking about it," Marc said, stepping forward and waving 3E57 aside. At last, the man moved away from the antimagic store, looking around himself now with some confusion and concern.

The situation had stabilised somewhat since we had arrived. The trees around our area had decided to behave more like regular trees, the fires were out, and Frederic had managed to get back in the air and was hovering larger than life over the scene, his nostrils smoking slightly. Natalie and Amelia were both hurrying back along the path towards us and Marc had positioned himself behind the antimagic store, disconnecting it from the device which had been used to gather the non-substance and connecting it to the antimagic canon, the same one which had been used back in Chopville and which Marc had been carrying in his pocket since we got here.

"So how are we doing this again?" I asked loudly. "Which crystals are we pointing that thing at?"

"The Light Crystal," Marc said. "Who's got it now?"

"I do," Amelia said, holding it up; amidst the overshadowing trees and the black sky above, even though the sun was out, the Light Crystal was like a precious beacon of light. The idea that we would have to destroy it just to have a chance of getting the world back to normal was devastating to think of.

"That thing is probably going to fire the whole lot at once, right?" Erica the chicken asked. "If it does, then only half of it will destroy the Light Crystal. Where will the rest of it go?"

That brought everyone up short for a moment, but it was James who recovered first. "The best thing to do is aim it so that the Light Crystal is between you and Lucien, and the rest of it goes on to hit him. I don't imagine we would have to wait long before he shows up here; in fact, I'm rather surprised that he hasn't already."

There was half a second then, in which I had time to expect a terrifying roar of sound to fill the air as Lucien teleported into our midst. Then, a terrifying roar of sound filled the air as Lucien teleported into our midst, coming in high over the forest—higher even than Frederic— and immediately spraying fire down upon all our heads. Amelia quickly put up a shield to protect us all, as she had done back in Chopville. At almost the same time, Marc and Natalie launched themselves into the air with their magic, passing through the shield and the fire unhurt to do battle with Lucien. Frederic, now without magic of his own, but with a physical form far more capable than any of ours, also joined the fight.

That left Amelia and Lillian as the only two humans to organise the antimagic canon. Well, there was also 3E57, but seriously, he wasn't really part of this. Marc had already done most of the work now; all Amelia had to do was cast a spell using the Light Crystal that would hold the crystal in a fixed position in the air, and then find the best angle from which to fire the antimagic canon so that it passed through both the Light Crystal and Lucien. This last part was the trickiest, for getting a clear shot at Lucien through the battle without risking hitting Marc and/or Natalie was just about impossible. Those two were going to cop the blast pretty badly anyway; I could only hope that like the last time, their magic would protect them.

"Amelia, hurry!" Peter called to her. "I don't know how much longer they'll be able to hold him off."

It was true; Lucien was still more magically powerful than Marc and Natalie, even combined, and he was getting closer to breaking through their defences. His eyes were fixed on us and it was clear that his primary goal was to destroy all of us, something that no magic could undo once it was done. Seeing the urgency for herself, Amelia hurriedly waved us to get behind her where we would then be out of the aim of the antimagic canon. Although none of us any longer had our own magic, and the annihilation would hit us no matter where we went, it still felt more prudent, and so we all obeyed as quickly as we could.

Amelia had picked up the antimagic canon and the antimagic store, neither of which were too large or heavy for her to carry in her arms, and was shifting her position from side to side as she attempted to take aim at the larger of the two dragons. Between the jets of flame flying off in all directions and the lights of their spellwork, it was difficult to see anything, except that Frederic was now contributing very little to the fight, and as I saw a moment later, most of Marc's efforts were going into defending him rather than fighting Lucien. I knew this was so when Lucien succeeded in sending them both flying away from the battle; neither of them were badly hurt and both were already angling back towards Lucien, but it was already too late.

Natalie had been left to fight the great dragon alone, and the power of the Villain Crystal was not enough to stand up to even three quarters of what the Sien-Leoard Crystal had been. Within seconds, she would be overwhelmed, and there would be a second or two when nothing stood between Lucien and the rest of us. It was now or never, and Amelia understood it as well as the rest of us. She took aim at Lucien, narrowed her eyes, and fired the antimagic gun straight at the Light Crystal. There was nothing else to be done, even though Natalie had indeed placed herself protectively between us and Lucien—even if it was the only way she could defend us—even if it put her at far greater risk of being in Amelia's line of fire—there was still nothing else to be done.

And like Tommy's aim back in Chopville, Amelia's aim was dead-set perfect.

Chapter 33: Villain and Light

The first thing was a brilliant flash of light, so bright that it blinded not just my eyes but all my senses for the instant it lasted, and even had me dazzled for some time after. The second thing I felt was a shift in the Earth, as though the planet itself was groaning at the injustice of what was being done to it, having been blasted for the second time in what— probably less than half an hour. I couldn't know something like that, and yet I somehow knew it instinctively.

At the same time, I felt my own form shift again into something that definitely only had two legs (because I almost fell over when my front legs disappeared), but before I could topple, I was caught by a fierce wind. It seemed to sweep up from the ground, taking everything that wasn't fixed with it. Along with everyone else, their screams echoing in the still-black daylight before they faded as my friends were sent off in different directions, I was hurled into the air.

I seemed paralysed as I went up and up, and soon enough out. It was a bit similar to how it had been just days earlier when I had flown over the waters around Rock Haulter, only now I had no control over it. My limbs were stuck to my sides by the aerodynamics of my flight, not that I could have done anything useful with them anyway. I didn't dare move my neck in case the wind snapped it. All I could tell was that I was no longer within hearing or seeing range of anyone else, and I was flying over an ocean which looked more like a gigantic body of slime than water. My momentum seemed to be carrying me more forward than up now, but quite soon I would start to drop towards that slime, and that would be where my battle ended.

Strangely, I had a little time to reflect as I arrowed through the sky, beginning to dip toward my doom. I had been closer to the Light Crystal than the battle when the annihilation had happened, so I had probably been hit with more good magic than bad or neutral. It had apparently restored my human form, though it clearly hadn't done anything to protect me from any of the other consequences of the blast. The others had probably fared similarly, unless one or more of them had been given wings…

That was when I was teleported away from there, landing in a heap on soft earthy ground a moment later. There was a lot of chatter wherever I was—a lot of very human chatter—and so I knew it had to be a good sign. I quickly sprang to my feet and looked around. It seemed to be the same forest where we had been before, only now there were more trees and they were all much, much taller. The spaces between them were almost non-existent, and even now, when I looked down, I saw that I was standing on a root.

As for how I got here, that was obvious. Marc still had his crystal, the only one not seriously close to the annihilation, and he also still had his human form. He was busily running around between the trees with such speed and balance that it had to be magical, teleporting people back to him and, most likely, binding them within another spell that would make it easy for him to teleport us all to wherever the next antimagic store was—assuming that we went down that path. Given that Lucien still had to have magic of his own, I couldn't see how we could end this thing without at least one more annihilation.

I cast my eyes around, spotted Peter and James, who had come down pretty close to each other, and made for them, looking around for everyone else I knew as I went. There were plenty of adults around, all in human form, including Dad, Charlie, Greg Pont, and even 3E57. Lillian Woodward was steadying herself against an enormous tree not too far away, but I couldn't see any sign of Frederic anywhere. Natalie and Amelia too were missing, as was Lucien (thankfully), but Harry, Simon, Katie, Erica, Rebecca, Tommy and even Underwood were all present and back in human forms.

It was only when I reached Peter and James that I noticed the first bad sign. James still had hollow sockets where his eyes had been. The blast of good magic from the Light Crystal had undone the damage done from the previous blast, but it hadn't undone the damage done by Lucien's cruelty. Seeing where I was looking, Peter said, "I guess Marc was too worried about making sure no one else died to spend a couple of seconds fixing his eyes."

"Which is perfectly reasonable," James added, guessing what we were talking about, "but all the same, I hope I don't turn out to be a burden."

"What is that?" Peter asked, looking over my shoulder. I turned to see what he was looking at—and my mouth fell open in amazement, or astonishment, or pleasure, or maybe even horror—I honestly wasn't sure which.

"What? What is it?" James asked in frustration.

It was Amelia; that was what. Yes, she had retained a human form, but not a normal one. She was walking toward us through the trees, so light of foot that she barely disturbed the ground at all. She had a glow about her which actually illuminated those things closest to her. Her eyes were a brighter blue than they had ever been before, and her hair was waving about behind her even though there was no breeze to move it (the previous wind apparently having spent itself when it carried us away). Yes, she had been closest to the Light Crystal when its existence had come to an end, so she would have been given the greatest dosage of good, which explained why she now looked like the very embodiment of good.

Even the two figures on either side of her couldn't detract from her goodness, although they looked as far from good as it were possible to look. The one on the left was Frederic for sure, but if Amelia looked like the embodiment of good, he now looked like the embodiment of evil. Well, maybe evil was a strong word for how he looked—perhaps he looked like the embodiment of mischief. He had a humanoid shape now but his steps were slinky, as though he were creeping up on someone even when he was walking normally.

As for the creature on Amelia's other side, I honestly wasn't sure who (or what) it was. It was large and had a shape that was difficult to describe, though it seemed to have a lot of scales, claws and even horns. It too moved like it was creeping up on someone, though in this case I didn't think it was a natural gate. My guess was that person was deeply ashamed to look the way they did now, which led me to the logical conclusion.

Natalie had been holding the Villain Crystal, and if *that* crystal had been annihilated, the magic it sent out would have been pretty bad, though not as fundamentally evil as the Darkness Crystal had been in its final throes. That had to mean that Natalie had been transformed into that thing over there, Frederic had also been transformed into a Villain of sorts, Marc had been protected by his crystal, and who knew what would have become of Lucien. Except, of course, that we now only had Marc's magic, while Lucien still had three quarters of the Sien-Leoard Crystal. I had been wrong earlier, we would be needing no fewer than two magic annihilations to end Lucien now.

"Wow, Amelia," Rebecca said, making me jump. I'd been so focussed on the odd trio that I hadn't noticed her come up behind us and link her arm with Peter's.

"Is she okay?" James asked the group at large.

"Amelia's fine," I said, "Frederic's fine—I think—and if that's Natalie, I guess she's fine too, but all the same, we've gotta get our shit together and get moving before Lucien comes back."

"A bit late for that, oh brother of mine," said an awful voice from a distance behind me.

We all spun around to look. Yes, Lucien was standing there, back in human form and dressed impeccably in a dark grey suit, white shirt and dark purple tie. His trousers were perfectly creased and his shoes spotlessly clean. How on earth had he done that? And why? I was so distracted by his attire that I didn't immediately notice what else he'd done. Imprisoned in a cage of light behind him floated Marc. He was still holding the Hero Crystal and struggling for all he was worth, but every bit of magic he threw at his older brother was absorbed by the cage.

"Let him go, Lucien," Lillian said, pushing herself away from her tree and straightening up to face him. By some coincidence, other than Marc, she was the closest to his position.

He raised his eyebrows, looking at her with cold amusement. "don't think I don't know what you fools are trying to do, and have already done to some degree here. You've found a way to actually destroy magic, and you think that by doing that, you will somehow defeat me. Well, I won't say that you haven't shocked me, but sadly for you, you've overplayed your hand. I know that Marc is the only one of you who still has magic, and yet he cannot stand up to me. Meanwhile, I have full control over my magic again, unlike before, and I will be able to fix all the damage you have done to this world—probably in no more than a couple of hours. As for you—" he broke off, considering.

"If your next words are going to be something like, 'you all must die', please, just spare us the unoriginality," Lillian shot back, and I had to admit I was impressed with her cheek. Overall, though I could feel nothing but hollow emptiness. Lucien had overpowered Marc's magic, which meant that we had no way of teleporting away or standing up to Lucien, which meant that after everything, the fight would end here.

"Ah, yes, you all must die," Lucien smiled cruelly, "but I'm not going to make any mistakes this time. I shall dispense with the greatest risks first, which means that perhaps, it's about time we had a new Seventh Sorcerer in the world, don't you think?"

He turned away from us so that he could face Marc. As we watched in horror, the cage of light began to tighten and twist around him, contorting him at angles a human body had never been meant to endure. The Hero Crystal held him together, but it wouldn't be long before Lucien's magic ended it…and then an apple hit Lucien in the back of the head. It happened so quickly and unexpectedly that all anyone could do was gape. I could see who had done it though. Coming in rapidly behind the projectile were Amelia, Natalie and Frederic, the latter of whom was holding a second apple.

It was Natalie who went for Lucien, moving at such speed that by the time he had turned around to see what was happening, she was already on him. Somehow, she had swelled to a being more than twice Lucien's height—at least thirteen or fourteen feet—and her various claws and horns were perfectly placed to attack a human being. Before he could do anything to stop her, Lucien was picked up cleanly off the ground, decapitated, disembowelled, and his heart was extracted neatly from his chest. Claws cracked his scull open at two points to extract his brains, while elsewhere, still held up by her massive horns, she went to work removing other vital organs from what had been Lucien's body. I didn't see what became of them (although I suspected she had eaten them), but I did keep a close eye on his remains.

Just last night, Lucien had consumed the Sien-Leoard Crystal so that he could operate its magic as a part of himself. Bernard Moran and Hall had both done the same thing with the Villain Crystal. In Moran's case, Arnold Hammerson had been able to remove it from him simply by utterly destroying his body, and maybe that meant that we could obtain the Sien-Leoard Crystal the same way. If so, then this would all be over here and now, all thanks to the monster that Natalie had become. Yes, the crystal had been invisible, and even if it still was, that didn't mean we couldn't still find it. If its form had changed as a result of having a quarter of its magic destroyed, well, so much the better if it was now visible...

"Nice try!" Lucien roared, his voice sounding strange as it blasted out of what had been his head. Two flashes of light followed: the first one sent the beast that was Natalie flying backwards into a tree, and the second caused the parts of his body to reform, complete with dark grey suit, perfectly-creased pants and spotlessly-clean shoes. (What was it with Lucien and his clothes?) He was back on his feet and turning back to Marc, who had been freed from his cage by Amelia and who now stood resolutely between her and Frederic.

"You think you won't pay for this?" Lucien said, his voice getting louder and louder until it was an ear-splitting howl. "You think you won't pay!"

The ground beneath Marc's feet vanished. It wasn't as if it had split apart, or a sinkhole had opened up—it just vanished. I had time to see his eyes widen in horror and his mouth open in a scream before he disappeared. With a sinking heart, I realised that he must be either overpowered by Lucien's magic still, or perhaps he'd dropped his crystal, because he didn't teleport back to the ground as he surely would have if he could. Frederic managed not to fall in after him by pin-wheeling his arms and Amelia ought to have been able to do that too, but somehow she still slipped and dropped beneath the ground after him.

Lucien then turned his attention on the rest of us. There was a loud crack, and then for the second time, a fierce wind lifted us all into the air. This was different from the previous wind though. This one was stronger and more controlled, and it was taking us straight up, rather than up and out in all directions. I could no longer breathe, due to the speed at which I was rising, and my eyes had been reduced to slits, but I was still able to see the others around me. Peter and James were closest, and I could see that Peter's arm had been broken, but other than that, they both looked exactly as I felt—unable to breathe, unable to move, overwhelmed, and aware that Lucien was going to do what the magical annihilation hadn't: end us. In this case, it seemed like he was actually going to send us out of the planet's atmosphere altogether, which may not have been the quickest way to end us but would certainly be one of the most awful.

And then the teleportation happened, this one a fair bit longer than the previous had been, meaning we were being transported a greater distance. I came down on a hard, rocky surface, immediately lost my balance and toppled over. People were doing the same all around me, many of them crying out in pain, and lifting my head, I saw that Peter wasn't the only person with a broken limb. It was Marc, of course, who had saved us for a second time, and he was presently running around making sure that everyone who should have come with us *had* come with us. Amelia walked along behind him, glowing with goodness, touching people as she went. Every person she laid her hand on let out a sigh of relief as their wounds instantly healed, and I had to wonder. What on earth had Amelia become? Was she some sort of angel or something?

Well, whatever it was, she wouldn't be in that form for too much longer. Now that I had registered that we all seemed to be okay, I took the chance to look at our surroundings. Yes, we were standing on a hard, rocky surface, although exactly what it was made of, I couldn't tell—it was a kind of yellowish colour, a bit like gold, but that couldn't be right. When I had seen it on the display screens of the spyers back in the control room, it had been more of a rocky, sandy surface. As for the antimagic store, Tom Hignat was standing before it a short distance away from our group, watching us coolly and ready to fire on the lot of us with his massive machine gun at the slightest provocation.

"We need to use this," Marc said, hurrying past me and addressing Hignat.

Hignat took a moment to respond, during which he appraised Marc disdainfully. "I think not, young man. I answer to only one, and you are not that one."

"Just do as he says, Tom," a voice called from behind me. I turned and was surprised to see 3E57 walking forward—I hadn't expected Marc to teleport him here as well. Marc had also looked over his shoulder at the sound of the voice, and judging by the expression on his face, I wasn't sure he had actually made a conscious decision to bring 3E57 with us.

Hignat, on the other hand, didn't relax his stance. "You'd better explain why you're here, Gilbert, and do it fast."

In a flash of realisation, I knew what Hignat was thinking. He didn't know that Frederic had also brought 3E57 to our side, and in fact he didn't know for certain that we were on the same side as Frederic—we could have been under Lucien's mind control for all he knew, which also explained 3E57's hesitation back in the forest. Of course, there was the possibility that Frederic himself was under the control of Lucien, and Lillian may or may not have known that, and that Lucien had put a spell on Frederic so that he would put a spell on Hignat and/or 3E57 so that they would follow him, Frederic, seemingly against Lucien, though unknowingly still on Lucien's orders…I quickly stopped my thoughts at this point. That way lay madness.

"He's with us," Marc cut in before 3E57 could say anything, "and we're with the Woodwards, and we know you're on their side now, so quit wasting our time and let us take that thing before we have to use magic to get it."

Hignat didn't give him a chance to use magic though—he fired his weapon. Perhaps expecting it, Marc had put a physical shield around himself, causing the bullet to deflect off to the side where, thankfully, nobody was standing. Barely flinching, Marc jabbed over his shoulder. "Look behind me, you fool! All three Woodwards are there."

I looked back and yes, Frederic and Lillian were coming forward to prevent this scene slipping any further out of control. Amelia didn't join them; she was still busy healing people's injuries.

Hignat observed the two Woodwards, who had just drawn level with Marc, with not a little confusion. "Lillian Woodward, yes, I see you have brought me someone who has the appearance of Lillian Woodward, but this? This is a poor imitation of Frederic Woodward. You expect me to take you seriously, boy? Get out of here before I call on the *real* Frederic Woodward so that he can deal with you properly."

Frederic took a step ahead of Marc and Lillian and said to Hignat, "The labrador is taking up all the foot space."

Obviously that was some sort of code. Hignat's eyes widened in surprise, and perhaps guilt, and he opened his mouth to give whatever response Frederic was looking for. He never got a chance, though, because that was when Lucien teleported into our midst. Once again, we had run out of time to properly set up before he caught up with us. He looked just as unruffled as he had back in the forest, dressed as if he were about to attend an important meeting with some of the most important people in the world, and not about to wage magical war in a desert that may or may not be made of gold.

Lucien took a quick look around at the group, then headed towards Tom Hignat. He walked straight past me as he went without giving me a look. He didn't even acknowledge Marc or the Woodwards as he passed them.

"3H42, isn't it?"

Hignat hesitated, then said, "Yes, that is my code."

"Is it?" Lucien said mildly. "Or...*was* it?"

"I have no way of responding to that," Hignat replied, his sneer identical to that of his son, although I had to give him credit for being able to produce it in this scenario. Ahead of me, though I could see neither of their faces, I saw Frederic put his hand on Marc's shoulder, and knew Marc had been about to attack Lucien before he could do anything to Hignat. Why had he done that? I didn't like the guy but surely we couldn't just stand here and let Lucien kill him, right?

"Oh, don't worry, I understand," Lucien said, and even though he was facing away from me, I could hear the smile in his voice. "After all, I would know if I or any of my subordinates had instructed you to come out here. You have chosen to side against me with the Woodwards, just as 3A93 did. You know he is dead, now, don't you?"

"I…did not know that," Hignat said mildly, but as much as he tried to conceal it, I could tell that he was rocked by the news. I then heard a slight disturbance behind me, and looking over my shoulder, I saw 3E57 moving slowly forward towards Lucien, looking devastated.

"Well, yes," Lucien sighed. "The Hammersons have long had a policy of ending the lives of anyone who betrays them. It's nothing personal, you understand, but there must be a consequence for betrayal. Without it, we have anarchy. That is why, for Hammerhearts who have served for a long time, the policy must remain in place."

"So, you're going to kill me," Hignat said, and his sneer was even more pronounced now. "How very original. You know the Hammersons had the same problem, don't you? They used death and torture with an agonator so much that they got lazy and had to actually make an effort to think of more fitting punishments on the occasions they dished them out."

"I assume you're referring to the way they killed my mother to punish my father, which I believe you witnessed, didn't you?" Lucien said, his voice a bit colder now. "In fact, unless I'm much mistaken, weren't you the one who followed Arnold Hammerson's orders to activate the device which took her life? That makes you directly responsible for quite a lot of things, you know. I guess I should thank you, for who knows if I would be what I am today without your misguided intervention."

"You're welcome?" Hignat said, but Lucien's words had put him off balance. They had rather unbalanced me too. Was Lucien actually upset about our mother's death or was he simply making a point? Given how evil he was, I honestly didn't know.

"What say you, 3E57?" Lucien said, turning to look at the other former Hammerheart. He had been creeping up behind Lucien, looking ready to strike him, but apparently Lucien had been aware of him all along. "Do you have any opinions on all of this?"

I couldn't see 3E57's face, but now that he had turned I could see Lucien's; it was utterly empty of all emotion. One look made me think he fully intended to kill both of them before turning on the rest of us. As for 3E57, he seemed to hesitate before speaking, and when he did, I thought it had taken all his courage to do so.

"I think it only makes sense to gravitate towards the most suitable ruler, and you, Lucien, have done nothing to prove that you are capable of ruling the world. Look at everything that has happened on your watch —such things would never have happened under Arnold Hammerson's rule, and they won't happen under Frederic Woodward's either."

Lucien laughed coldly. "Oh, if Arnold Hammerson had been in my position, it would have been exactly the same. I know this for a fact, but I see no need to explain it to either of you. But come; I wasn't speaking of your motivations for turning against me, but what consequences would be appropriate for you both. Given the active role you have had in today's events, they must be as severe as possible, I'm sure you'll agree."

That was when Marc decided enough was enough, and he launched a magical attack against Lucien. Lucien must have been expecting it because he barely reacted, but allowed Marc's attack to fizzle against his magical shields, reinforced with more magical strength than the Hero Crystal alone could generate. Acting as if nothing had just happened, Lucien continued to speak, turning slightly so that he could include Tom Hignat in his monologue.

"I could kill your son, 3H42. I know that would be a devastating punishment for you. He is your pride and joy, after all, and the only thing you truly value, given that his mother has been gone for a full decade now. Yes, I could kill him in the most painful way imaginable, and you would have to live with the knowledge that you had failed as a father, not just because you could do nothing to stop me, but because it was your own actions which made it happen in the first place. Yes, that would be a fairly fitting punishment for you.

"As for you, 3E57, you have no children, no life partner, and as far as I know, no living family. Your family hated you, didn't they? They despised you and disowned you as quickly as they could. Being a Hammerheart is the only good thing you've had in your life since you were a teenager, I believe, and yet in a day of nothing but foolish decisions, you have thrown it all away. I can think of nothing valuable to take from you, unless it be your eyes, like I did to James—or perhaps your ears, or your feet, to make you a pretty useless soldier for whatever army you choose to fight for. Or maybe, I'll just strip you of some of your brain functionality so that you will know nothing but misery and despair for the rest of your days. I am limited only by my imagination, I think.

"There's really only one problem with all of this, I don't have time for any of it. I have too much to do today, and neither of you are important enough to me to waste any time on you. With that in mind…"

It all happened in less than a few heartbeats. Hignat and 3E57—Gilbert Elliton, Lillian had called him—were lifted about fifteen feet into the air and brought together so that they were side-by-side, hovering over a patch of ground where nobody was standing. A moment later, all their clothes vanished so that the two of them were completely naked. Another moment later, a large bowl appeared beneath them, large enough for me to stand in and have the rim come up to my shoulder. It was full of a completely clear liquid which looked like water, but couldn't possibly be water because it was radiating more heat than water should have been able to, and no steam was issuing from the bowl.

I expected Lucien to just drop the two men into the bowl, which would probably boil them to death within minutes—or seconds—but that wasn't what he did. Instead, he lowered them slowly into it. They both screamed horribly when their feet first touched the liquid, both managing to pull their legs up a bit so they weren't touching it, but I got a good look at what had happened to their feet in that instant. Some of the skin had already been burnt off, revealing yucky burnt flesh beneath, while the skin that remained was red-raw.

I had no desire to watch the rest of this show, especially as they began to scream again, worse now, as they were lowered even more. I instead looked wildly around for anything else to look at, and noticed two things. Lucien was completely engrossed in what he was doing, and nobody was standing guard over the antimagic store. I knew what needed to be done. I turned, scanned the crowd for Amelia, located her quickly thanks to the light of complete goodness she was still producing, and hurried over to her.

"The canon, where is it?" I asked her urgently.

She didn't respond immediately, still watching the Lucien show in horror—which sounded like it was getting worse and worse—so I had to shake her shoulder to get her attention.

"Oh, what? Oh, yeah, here."

Exactly where she had been keeping it, I wasn't sure, but suddenly she was holding it. She handed it to me and I took off, giving Lucien and the bowl of doom a wide birth as I sprinted around them and to the antimagic store. Seeing what I was doing, Frederic and Lillian had both positioned themselves between me and Lucien so that he wouldn't see what I was about to do. Whether he understood yet that we were using antimagic to destroy the crystals I wasn't sure, but at the very least, he would have guessed by now that this thing which Hignat had been standing over had something to do with all of it.

I was able to connect the canon to the antimagic store, open the link between the two and take aim at Lucien, all without interruption. It was going to be the easiest shot ever, much easier than the previous two had been. Lucien was standing apart from everyone, and not only was Marc well outside my aim, he was on Lucien's other side. I would have to shoot the antimagic right through Frederic, but given that he no longer possessed any magic (magic had been done to him, but he himself wasn't magical), I didn't think it would hurt him.

Of course, that was when Lucien noticed what I was doing. In an instant, he abandoned Hignat and 3E57, letting them drop into the bowl (thankfully that ended the terrible agonised screaming), and whirled on me. The attack that would have blasted me and the Woodwards apart crashed into a shield which Marc had managed to put between Lucien and ourselves, although it forced us all back a step. Undaunted, Lucien stared coldly at us, and I knew he was focussing his energy so that he could throw all his magical force at us in an attack which Marc wouldn't be able to block. I probably could have still shot him but Marc had come to the same conclusion as me, and immediately threw himself into an attack which Lucien couldn't ignore.

Then, it was all bright lights and ear-splitting bangs as the two of them engaged each other in magical battle. Lucien was stationary for the most part, knowing that he only needed to have a shield at least as strong as the Hero Crystal to block anything Marc threw at him. Marc himself was always on the move, dodging hither and thither in the knowledge that he couldn't produce a shield strong enough to block Lucien's curses. Yet there was a flaw in Marc's strategy, and Lucien was already looking to exploit it: The rest of the army were presently unprotected, and Lucien was able to force Marc to send his magical defences in other directions to protect the rest of us, sacrificing his ability to attack at the same time.

At one point, Marc was able to put a spell on the golden ground, causing Lucien to slip over and land on his arse (one of my favourite battle tactics in recent days), after which, Lucien took to the air to make sure it wouldn't happen again. Marc had to follow him up so that he wouldn't have a completely unobstructed shot at the rest of us, but this now made it impossible for me to get a clear shot at Lucien; the two of them were moving around too much up there, and Marc kept getting between me and him.

I assessed the situation, thinking of earlier when it had been Marc and Natalie battling a dragon, and thought I knew what would need to happen for this to work. It couldn't be exactly like that had been because that would sacrifice Marc's magic, leaving us with no way of fighting Lucien when he eventually followed us to the last antimagic station—or rather, not following us, because we wouldn't have any way to get to the last antimagic station, meaning that the war would end here on this golden field (or whatever it turned into after the next annihilation).

This situation was different in another way too. Although Lucien would certainly end up killing us if he had his way, some of his arrogance had returned since he had regained his human form. It had been enough for him to torture Tom Hignat and 3E57 to death rather than just killing them, and it would probably be enough to give us a few seconds if he turned his attention our way. At the moment, he was only feinting attacks on us as a tactic against Marc; if Marc got out of the way and gave me a clear shot at Lucien, Lucien would immediately attack the rest of us as a way to re-engage Marc, so that was out. If Lucien thought he had defeated Marc, however, he may let his guard down just enough to give me the chance I needed.

That was what I had to wait for, then, and I had to hope that Marc wouldn't come out of it too badly as we still needed him. The question was, how to convey all this to Marc without also giving it away to Lucien? Without our own magic, there was frankly no way to do it, unless…we did sort-of have our own magic. I called to Frederic to get his attention, and told him my plan in as few words as possible. To my relief, he didn't argue (though he looked like he wanted to), turned and hurried over to his daughter. After a quick word with her, she floated up into the air to be by Marc's side.

What happened next went better than I could have hoped, bar one small detail. Marc's concentration wavered slightly when Amelia appeared beside him, while Lucien's focus sharpened even further. He sent out a huge blast of energy, directed primarily at Amelia but wide enough to include Marc as well. Marc tried desperately to block it but he never had a chance; it blasted him backwards and out of the fight. Unfortunately, it also caused him to drop his crystal (silly boy), which was one thing I hadn't accounted for in my plan, but if I acted quickly enough, it wouldn't be an issue.

As I had hoped, the blast of magic which should have disintegrated Amelia passed right through her without harming her in the slightest. This took Lucien by such utter surprise that he didn't even bother looking to see what had happened to Marc, or notice that the Hero Crystal had hit the ground and was rolling slowly away. All he could do was stare at Amelia, a clear question mark on his face. Nothing non-magical could have stood up to what he had done, and we didn't possess enough magic to do it, so how had Amelia been protected from his curse? My own guess was that the annihilation of antimagic had twisted magic in some way that made the results of the blast different from regular magic. It explained why Lucien hadn't been able to change his form when he had been a dragon, and if my guess was right, he would be just as incapable of changing his form now.

And none of that mattered because Amelia was already getting on with the next part of the plan, floating back to the ground a safe distance from anyone else so that Lucien wouldn't think to take his confusion out on them instead of her. This unfortunately put her close to the Hero Crystal, which Lucien finally noticed, but he never got a chance to do anything about it because that was when I pulled the trigger. It was another perfect aim, and so perfectly timed that nobody else was within at least twenty metres of Lucien when he was caught in the epicentre of the third global annihilation.

Chapter 34: Hero

Not that the rest of us weren't also caught in the reaction as the world exploded for the third time that afternoon. It happened with a sharp cracking sound which echoed off in all directions as it died down to a thunderous roar—and yes, the thunderous roar wasn't as loud as the initial crack. It also came with a quick blast of air, as the other annihilations had, though this one was slightly warmer than the others. It also came with the transformation of pretty much everything around, as the others had, and I once again felt my body changing into an unfamiliar shape.

At first, I had no idea what I was. It felt as though my feet were the only part of my body that could move, though the longer I examined my senses, the more moving parts I found. The trouble was, I had no idea how to move any of them—my brain hadn't been wired to use whatever body this was. Only two clues did I have. As I looked out over a strange surface, even more strange than a ground of gold or whatever it had been before, I could see that the others had been transformed into all manner of things. No animals among them this time, but there did seem to be a theme. They had all transformed into human inventions of some kind. There was a refrigerator off to one side next to what appeared to be an elevator car; a comfortable-looking sofa was very close to being squashed beneath the front wheels of a truck; and furthest away from me was a helicopter next to a train resembling Thomas the Tank Engine, including the face on the front which was clearly the face of Peter.

The second clue was the ground. It was still a completely flat, smooth surface, but now it more closely resembled glass than metal. I could see unsettling movement beneath it—movement which looked a lot like rivers of lava slowly rising to the surface—but I could also see reflections of those things sitting on top of it. I did have eyes, yes, but they were the only part of my face which still remained; the rest of it had been replaced by a grill. By flexing every other part of my body that I could, and then rolling forward a little, I came to the conclusion that I had been transformed into a car of some kind.

Those who could began to try to move around. Jacob Underwood's face appeared on a TV screen, asking for help because he couldn't seem to do anything other than sit where he was and talk to us, and a similar sentiment was coming from a boom box, shouting out in James's desperate voice. Amelia was the only person who had retained her form; perhaps being an angel had protected her from the magical blast as well as Lucien's magic, but only so far as it allowed her to keep her shape. She no longer looked extraordinary or like she radiated light and goodness, but she was at least able to scramble over to where the Hero Crystal still lay abandoned, and then hurry over to where Marc had come to rest. Marc had been transformed into a kettle, but by opening him up and placing the six Sorcerous Crystals inside him, Marc was able to activate the magic of the Seventh Sorcerer. He wasn't able to change his own form due to whatever imbalance of magic was going on, but he was able to project a hologram of himself so that we could see him and he could communicate with us.

As for Lucien, I scanned the ground where he should have come down, but there was nothing there. Perhaps he had been blown off in one direction or another, but if so, who could guess what he had been transformed into. The Sien-Leoard Crystal could have protected him—at least, a quarter of it could have protected him—but I expected that he would have come out of the annihilation pretty badly. Perhaps he was now invisible, or perhaps he was one of those manmade inventions over there, mixed in with the rest of us, but as a good many of us couldn't communicate, who would know?

"Is everyone here?" Marc called as he and Amelia hurried over to us, Amelia carrying the kettle and Marc's hologram following her. "Is everyone okay?"

"Do I look okay?" James retorted. "I can't move at all, there are no radio stations out here, and nobody has any CDs they can put in me. All I can do is talk."

"That's never been a problem for you," Peter the train called. "I have no rails to run on, so I'm totally useless."

"Guys, seriously, not the time for joking around," Amelia said sharply. "Everyone who can, tell us who you are so we can do a headcount."

James and Peter declared themselves, as did Underwood. The truck almost about to run over a sofa turned out to be Tommy, as he told us by blasting out his own stereo system. I examined my parts and found that I also had an in-car stereo system, so I rolled my windows down and blasted out my name so that they could all hear.

"Also, where's Lucien?" I asked. "He should have been about there and he still has a quarter of the Sien-Leoard Crystal left, so we have to be mindful."

"And that's about the same level of magic as Marc," James added.

"I'm here," a ghostly voice came from the spot where I had been looking earlier—the spot where I had expected Lucien to land. "What have you people done to me?"

It was a very strange voice indeed, and yet, I understood what it meant. Lucien was more than just invisible; he no longer had any body at all. All he had was a voice and when he used it, he sounded low and haunting, like a draught blowing around the eaves of an old wooden house. It was a despairing sound, and yet it was somehow a befitting end for such evil. Except it wasn't really the end, because like I had just said, he still had the same level of magic as Marc; and even if he couldn't restore his body, he could still attack and even kill us…

…which raised an interesting thought. *Would* Lucien attack us now? Certainly he *could*, but if he killed us now—or more specifically, if he killed Marc now—there would be no way for him to regain his body. He would be stuck like this, and what would be the point of ruling in this form?

"Lucien?" Marc now said nervously. "Where are you? Show yourself."

"I can't," the voice mourned. "I have no body. I can't move away from this position at all. You have robbed me of everything I ever had."

"You brought this on yourself, Lucien," Marc said sharply. "You have no sympathy from me. Maybe you would have, once, but you have gone too far down the path of evil now to be saved, so I am not going to try. We are going to finish what we started, and if you can't move or do anything else, then you can stay there and watch."

"No," the voice moaned, and he put his magic into action, proving that evil really didn't know what was good for it. Marc's hologram turned towards the source of the magic and parried Lucien's moves, then cast a spell which caused the magic to stop.

"What was that you did there, Marc?" the voice of Frederic Woodward asked. I looked towards it and saw that it was coming from a speaker inside the elevator car.

"Put a shield around him so that he can't cast magic outside it," Marc said, "except it won't hold for long. Lucien took some power from the Hero Crystal back in Chopville earlier, so his magic is probably still a bit stronger than mine. Quickly, now—"

Several seconds of silence followed as the hologram of Marc looked slowly around the group, most likely casting a binding spell so that he could perform the next teleportation. When he was done, he activated the teleportation, and off we went into nothingness as we were transported away from that desert, eventually reappearing in the midst of a devastated city. Buildings had collapsed, others were on fire, and one appeared to have grown in such a way that it had knocked two other buildings beside it to the ground. The streets were cracking and full of mud issuing from several holes that had been ripped in the concrete. People were running everywhere, screaming and crying, all except for one man, who stood firmly over something and ignored everything else going on around him. He gave off the impression that he would have continued to stand there, even if the ground beneath him tore apart. It was Vincent Wilwog, of course, standing protectively over the final store of antimagic, and he took just as little notice of us as we appeared on the street as he took of everything else.

Without pausing for a moment, Marc cast another spell of some kind before sending his hologram flitting around the group (while the kettle sat abandoned on the ground), making sure that everyone was okay. Anyone who was small enough was levitated into the air and loaded into Tommy the Truck, meaning that those of us left (me, Frederic, Peter, Tommy, and a few others, including a helicopter who turned out to be Simon) were big enough not to be too concerned about being squashed or damaged. Once this was done, Marc started working very quickly on some magical device; I could see that part of it included an antimagic canon, and only then did I realise that the antimagic canon I had used earlier was gone—it had probably been turned into something by the blast, or maybe it had become part of my being. Either way, it was gone, and Marc—who appeared to be following a plan of his own—had already thought of a replacement.

While this was happening, Amelia had hurried over to Vincent Wilwog and was explaining that we needed to take the thing he was guarding. Unlike Hignat and Elliton, Wilwog seemed quite happy to take her word for it that her father had ordered her to come in his place, as he was too busy dealing with the global destruction which any idiot could observe. I supposed that made him less cunning than the other two, but in this case, it made him a hell of a lot smarter than both of them. Amelia was therefore able to take the last store of antimagic and place it down in front of Marc.

"That's not the same as the stuff Natalie made," she observed. "What is that?"

Marc paused and looked up at her, and there was a cagy look in his face. "Well," he said slowly, "it's enough to destroy Lucien, but will still leave us with a way to fix the damage and get back to Chopville. It wouldn't be smart to blow up all the magic in the world and leave it like this."

"I have a question," Peter called—I couldn't see him from where I was as he was on the other side of Tommy. "Where is Lucien now? I assume he didn't come with us, but why hasn't he followed us like he did the other times?"

"I'm not sure he can," Marc said, "but even if he can, he won't be able to find us unless he's really smart. I've made us untraceable just until I'm done here, and then I'll try to teleport him here so that we can finish this."

A silence fell—or rather, a relative silence fell around us, as none of us spoke and Marc continued to bend his concentration toward his work. There was still a lot of noise around us, and at one point Marc had to quickly break his concentration and cast a shield over us as another building toppled in our direction; it instead slid down to the side, causing more devastation and almost certainly killing a lot of people. Amelia was in tears as she watched it and she looked ready to yell at Marc, who had barely glanced to see what he had caused in his attempt to save us, but she held back. I knew the logic Marc would use to justify his actions, but the fact that it would be right didn't make it any more painful.

At last, Marc looked up from his work. "Okay, I'm ready. Let's get started."

"What are we getting started with?" Amelia asked nervously.

"Moving the antimagic into my thing," he said as his newly-created device connected itself to the antimagic store, and some buttons pressed themselves of their own accord. "It's completely non-magical, of course, so it'll be safe. It has two chambers and a canon attached to one of them, and it can move the antimagic between them according to a set amount of magic it can neutralise. Once Lucien gets here, I'll try to nail exactly how much magic he has so that I can shoot off exactly the right amount to finish him off."

"Wait! Wait!" Frederic called, and the alarm in his voice caused Marc to pause.

"What?"

"Is that device of yours still under the protection you put around us? The untraceability and all that? If so, trying to put antimagic into that device could set it off."

"Way ahead of you on that. I'm still under the protection but the device isn't, so it's perfectly safe to put antimagic in there. It's even safe for me to handle it since my magic is only touching the buttons on the device and not what's inside it."

"Okay, just making sure," Frederic said, allowing his doors to slide halfway shut in relief.

"What if the blast also activates some of the other antimagic because it's close?" Peter asked. "Remember what happened back in Chopville? Our antimagic guns weren't in the blast and yet after it was over, all our ammo was gone."

"I don't know if that will happen," Marc admitted, "but even if it does, I doubt we'll lose much extra. I'm more concerned about either leaving Lucien with the tiniest bit of magic that he can fight with, or having leftover antimagic continuing forward after it's cleaned up Lucien and causing another annihilation when it eventually comes into contact with magic. Either way, I can't see this being as big and bad as the other three were, but I guess we'll find out."

"Looks like it's done," Amelia observed.

So it was. I couldn't see what numbers may or may not be visible on Marc's new device, but I could see the display screen for the antimagic store, which was the same as the others had been, and it appeared to be empty. Marc disconnected it and examined his work.

"Yep, it's all here. Amelia, you might wanna take cover somewhere. You might also wanna take cover, Wilwog," he added, calling over to where the former Hammerheart hadn't moved from since we had arrived.

"Negative, I was told not to leave my post unless it was Frederic Woodward who told me to do so," he called back.

"You can leave your post," Frederic called. Wilwog gave the elevator car a dubious look, shrugged, and hurried off, climbing into Simon the Helicopter and hunkering down so that he couldn't be seen. Amelia, too, took up the kettle containing the Hero Crystal and got out of sight, at first trying to get in the back of the truck, but when it became clear that Tommy was full, she took shelter inside Peter instead.

The hologram of Marc had been sitting on the ground through all this. Now he took up a standing position, vanished the empty antimagic store, and appeared to stand firmly on the unsteady ground with his legs slightly apart. The device he had just created lay at his feet, the canon pointing ahead of him at nothing in particular as he stared at a spot roughly where Wilwog had been earlier. I didn't think he was really seeing in front of him, though; he was reaching out to Lucien, finding a way to wrap his magic around him so that he could yank his disembodied presence away from that desert and bring him before us. Little did I know, though I would have been very happy if I had, that he had also placed some extra protection around us. Before removing the outer layer of untraceability he had also placed separate protections around the rest of us, including another ring of untraceability as well as an invisibility veil, soundproof barrier, and the same enchantment that would cause spells to go straight through us if they came our way. Not knowing of this, though, I was very concerned about what trouble Lucien might cause when he finally arrived.

And sure enough, arrive he did. I knew the moment he was in our midst for a cold breeze kicked up, cold in a way that weather alone couldn't do. He began speaking at once, though his voice was very difficult to hear over the sounds around us.

"You will pay for what you have done to me, and to all I have made. Even if I die, my last great act will be to ensure that you never taste victory."

"I'm sorry you feel that way," Marc said coldly, "but I guess it proves the selfishness of evil. You don't care about making the world great in your image. You don't care about anything except your own power, and you don't care what you have to destroy in order to hold on to it. And the last thing you have to say is this: if you go down, you will take the whole world with you. At the very least, you've made my decision very easy. There is nothing left of my brother, and there is no humanity left in you. Whatever you are, you must be destroyed."

"And just how are you going to do that?" the ghostly voice retorted. "I don't have a body you can aim your weapons at. All I have is my magic, impossible for you to pin down to a single point. No matter what you try, I can and will evade. What is left of the Sien-Leoard Crystal is no longer a physical form; it is pure magic, and all of it is my very being."

"Yeah, whatever," Marc shrugged, looking supremely unconcerned. "You seem to forget that I was able to teleport you here, so body or not, I do have a way of targeting you with my magic, and that makes you vulnerable to me, whatever lies you tell yourself."

Lucien began saying something else defiant, but that was when I became aware of the game Marc was playing. As far as Lucien was aware, Marc was concentrating his magic in readiness for a fight, which was probably true, but Marc was also taking the opportunity to scope out Lucien's magic. The hologram never so much as glanced down, drawing no attention to the device at his feet, and yet, as I watched, a previously unnoticed slider on the device slowly moved a little to one side, and I knew it had to be Marc's doing, adjusting the amount of antimagic that would be fired off when the time was right.

"That could be the case," Marc said in response to whatever Lucien had said, "and yet you haven't opened fire on me yet. Perhaps you aren't actually able to use the magic that is keeping you alive—"

"You know I can," the ghostly voice retorted, and with a loud rumbling, the ground beneath Marc's feet opened up in a small fissure. Untroubled, Marc stood there, his feet planted firmly on nothing at all, the hologram naturally unaffected by any physical magic Lucien cast at it.

"Fair enough," Marc conceded, "but I've been checking you out, Lucien. You no longer have control over the exact nature of the magic you possess. You can use some of it, certainly, but a good amount of it is reserved for keeping you alive. If you try to use all of it, it will be the last thing you do, and then you will cease to exist. The crystal is telling me this is so, and if you search your magic, you will find it tells you the same thing."

No response from Lucien for several seconds. He was most likely doing as Marc suggested, and based on his next response, I guessed that he had come to the same conclusion.

"A person with a greater amount of magic can be beaten by someone who knows how to use it better. Do you, Marc, have enough wits about you to outwit me?"

"I have enough wits not to answer that question," Marc said, "except to say that a few hours ago our positions were reversed, and yet, here we are. When you look at it like that, who outwitted who?"

"We both know you had help, and speaking of which, where have you hidden them? I cannot sense any of them around here, and yet I feel certain that they are close."

"Oh yes, they are around here somewhere," Marc said, startling me —that seemed an unnecessary giveaway, "but you won't find them. You could never find us even with all the power on your side, and all because

I discovered a new spell—a second layer to the untraceability spell. Only I know how to cast it, and when everything else seemed to fail, that was the one trick of ours you could never rumble. So yes, Lucien, it was *I* who outwitted you."

Marc, stop, I thought to myself as my alarm began to rise. This was a totally unnecessary dick-measuring contest; the longer this went on, the more opportunity Lucien would have to find a way out of his predicament.

"You bluff," Lucien said, and the breeze grew even colder, "but it matters not. There is always a way for someone willing to look at other options."

A red light appeared in the air from the place where Lucien's ghostly voice seemed to be sounding, taking the shape of a star with more points than I could count. From each point, a jet of flame shot forth, a couple of which passed right through me without harming me, while others passed through Tommy, Peter, Simon, Frederic, and a few others. Everything else that got hit immediately burst into flames. The air filled with explosions and more agonised screaming of the locals. Smoke began to rise from every point and the temperature rose rapidly.

The jets of flame may have been magical but the flames engulfing the surrounding structures were not, and as they spread, I understood Lucien's plan. He could trace Marc's presence but he could not trace us; that had to mean that Marc was outside the protection he had put around us, which would make it very difficult to put protection around us without giving our position away. The alternative would be to let us burn, which would also be a win for Lucien. I had to admit, he was very good at putting us in situations where every option was bad.

At least, every option Lucien (and I, for that matter) knew of, but Marc was a step ahead of him. I would find out later that in order to release us from the protection after the danger was over, he had built into it a way for him to pass in and out of the spells he had created without having to open them up and risk Lucien following. In this case, it also made it possible for him to slip in beneath the untraceability spell and cast a shield around each of us, immediately cooling us and protecting us from the physical danger of the flames. The hologram never actually moved while he did any of this, so Lucien wasn't able to pin down our exact positions, but he was able to learn something new from this moment.

"So that's how it is," he said mournfully. "Your new untraceability spell is quite clever, Marc. I'm guessing that it was inspired by the tracing devices Arnold Hammerson invented to track down untraceable people?"

Marc looked surprised by this, but he nodded. "I guess you saw me go in and out of untraceability there and now recognise the difference. Well, I guess there's little harm in it now, but tell me—if you had learnt of this a couple of days ago, how would you have gone about countering it?"

"That, I do not know," Lucien conceded, "and it is a credit to you that I cannot immediately think of a way to detect that magic without observing it directly each time. But I imagine, given enough time, and the resources of the Beast of Magic, I would have found a solution."

Marc nodded again. "Well, we will never know. Let us be satisfied that you never found out until it was too late and the knowledge quite useless to you. Now, any last words?"

'Any last words.' The words echoed in my mind in a moment of déjà vu. Those were among the final words Marc had spoken to Arnold Hammerson before ending his life. Whether Marc had done that on purpose, I didn't know, but it signalled that he was finally ready to finish this. Several seconds went by before Lucien responded, but respond he eventually did.

"Only to say that I never wanted it to end like this," he said softly, and I had to strain whatever part of me still had the sense of sound in order to hear him. "It is clear that you have the ability to destroy me, and I no longer have enough power to defend myself. I know that you and I have been on different sides in this war a few times, but even in my darkest hour, I would not have imagined that it would be you who ended my life. Arnold or Dorothy Hammerson, or Frederic Woodward or one of his henchmen, certainly, but not my own brother. All I would ask, when you do whatever it is you will do, is to remember me as I was before all this happened—remember what I was without an influential charm, or guided by the cold intelligence of Arnold Hammerson. Perhaps I could have found my way back to that, but I guess we will never know now."

More silence then. That was evidently how Lucien intended to leave it between himself and Marc, but Marc didn't move. His hologram merely stood there, looking in the direction of Lucien's disembodied voice, and apparently hesitating. Lucien's little speech had certainly been touching, and if I didn't know better, I might think that he was actually remorseful for the things he had done in the last couple of weeks. Except, I did know better: I had seen him battling against that lump of evil inside him, losing the battle, and seen the evil consume him thereafter. A man who could look up after that struggle with such a dark and terrible face couldn't possibly be redeemed.

"Marc, what are you doing?" Peter cried as Marc continued to hesitate. "Just finish him off. Can't you see he's bullshitting you?"

Surprisingly, given that Marc was outside the magical protections around us, he seemed to hear Peter's words. I would eventually learn it had been because while the hologram was outside the magical protections, the kettle Marc had actually become was sitting in Amelia's lap, and Amelia was sitting in Peter's driver's seat. This actually put

Marc himself under our protections while the hologram was not, something I wouldn't have thought was even possible.

"You don't have to worry," Marc finally said, his voice more gentle than it had been all afternoon. "I've already come to terms with the fact that you're not the Lucien I knew, and nothing you've done, or could possibly do now, can tarnish my memory of him. I consider you to be Arnold Hammerson's last gasp—his insurance policy in case he failed, and I am just as willing to end you as I was willing to end him."

On its own, the antimagic canon Marc had created began to rise up so that the canon was pointing in the direction of Lucien's voice. I was very relieved to see it, and not at all surprised when Lucien sent a burst of magic at it. Thankfully, Marc had also been expecting it, and whatever Lucien had been trying to do dissolved against an invisible shield set a good foot away from the device.

"You *fool*!" Marc shouted. "You didn't mean any of that, did you? Well unfortunately for you, I meant *every word*!"

Marc fired the antimagic canon at Lucien. Whether he lowered the shield before it as he spoke or immediately before activating the trigger, I knew not. I only knew that he had gotten rid of the shield, for the annihilation was far too great to be just a simple shield being neutralised. Supposedly it was half as grand as the previous three, but when they were that big, the perspective was pretty difficult to grasp. It came with another thunderclap of sound, a cold blast of air, and once again, everything seemed to shift and change form.

The sky had turned a bright white colour—not due to clouds, but the sky itself had become white. The street had become a shallow pool of yucky slime. The fires around us immediately went out as the buildings turned into sludge. A brief bubbling noise hit our ears as they settled, and then silence fell. There didn't seem to be any people around anymore—at least, I could no longer hear any screaming or crying. Either they had all been buried in whatever yuckiness the world had become, or they had been killed outright. Or, most likely, they had all been transformed into objects which couldn't move or talk, as I had. I was no longer a car, but I wasn't a person either. I couldn't move at all, nor could I feel anything. The only senses I still had were sight and sound, and a fat lot of good they were doing me at the moment.

This was the worst result of an antimagic blast so far, I thought. It seemed to have destroyed everything and rendered every one of us utterly unable to do anything about it. The only small hope I had was Marc, who would have still possessed the Hero Crystal within the kettle. The crystal ought to have protected him from the blast, keeping him as a kettle, but also giving him the ability to project himself out, as he had been doing since the previous blast…unless, something had gone wrong, and he had destroyed the Hero Crystal as well, leaving us with no magic at all—except possibly for Lucien, who may or may not still be over there somewhere.

I didn't think that had happened, though. A third sense, one I couldn't identify but I supposed had to be instinct, was telling me that the Hero Crystal couldn't possibly have been destroyed. If it had, then a bit like the Light, Darkness and Villain Crystals, the blast would have let loose a certain kind of magic. When the Darkness Crystal had been destroyed, it had turned the world into a terribly dark place, and those closest to the blast had been turned into dragons. Lucien had only come out the stronger of the two dragons because the Sien-Leoard Crystal had also been caught up in the blast, and while Frederic had lost all his magic, Lucien still had three quarters of what he had started with.

When the Light and Villain Crystals had been destroyed, the results had been mixed. Natalie and Frederic had been closest to the Villain Crystal, and they had copped a thick dose of malicious but not altogether dark magic. The rest of us had been washed with the magic of the Light Crystal, turning us back to our normal forms, but Amelia, who had been closest, had been turned into an angel, imbued with more goodness than a normal human could possibly possess. I could have philosophised about how Amelia may have also gotten that because even without the magical intervention she was likely one of the 'goodest' people around, making her a suitable fit for such magic, but who could say if that was actually how it worked?

All of this led me to conclude that the Hero Crystal had to still be around, because surely its last gasp would have had a more positive impact than this. That didn't necessarily mean that Lucien wasn't still around though. Marc had obviously taken the time to make sure that he got the amount of antimagic fired off exactly right, and he had used magic to aim the device, so I doubted that any of the shot had gone astray. If Lucien were still here, surely he would wish to take advantage of this situation to deal with us, as I also felt sure that the protection Marc had put around us prior to the blast had been stripped away—or turned into something unrecognisable.

If Lucien (and with him, Arnold Hammerson's ultimate plot) had finally been ended, this seemed a rather anticlimactic way for it to have happened, and yet I couldn't help believing that Lucien was really gone. For all the nastiness of the world around me, it didn't feel particularly evil, just uncaring. That was good, not only because it meant that the war could finally be over, but because it meant that Lucien was finally free. For most of the time I had known him, he had been a tormented soul, unwilling to stand up to his (our) madman father most of the time, cursed by Dorothy Hammerson, fearing for his life after running out on the Hammersons but equally fearing for his safety if he joined the Woodwards, and having to live with the knowledge of the things he had done while cursed after he finally came back to our side—all the while, without even knowing it, living under the shadow of the time bomb curse Arnold Hammerson had placed upon him as a four-year-old—and worst of all, being imprisoned and forced into evil ways by the very soul of Arnold Hammerson. Now, if I was right in my feeling, he could finally rest and have nothing left to torment him.

But what now, then? How long was I to wait here to learn which way the final battle had gone? Would I ever know, or would the rest of my life be doomed to wait here, thinking the slow thoughts of a veritable vegetable? Well, if so, it would only last about a week and a half before I was due to die anyway, but then what about all the others? They had to be nearby, whether they were immobile like me or had actually been killed altogether…my mind scuttled away from that thought. In some desperation I strained my mind, looking for anything at all that might be useful, and in the end, decided to reach out with the one sense over which I still had any control.

Final Interlude: Closing the Loop

I was back in the place again—that place of nothingness. I wasn't standing, sitting or lying; I was only existing. I wasn't alone in the place, for I could sense the presence of others around me, and I could reach out to them if I chose. For a time that was no time at all, however, I did nothing, mainly because I didn't really have a specific purpose in being here. I had simply come here because there was nowhere else to be, and yet because time didn't pass here, being here wouldn't subtract from the time I spent waiting for whatever fate awaited me in the real world.

My main concern right now was my blood brothers, Marc and Lucien. What had happened to them? Had one succeeded in destroying the other, or had one been destroyed by his own weapon—or both? I felt a great sadness for both of them, not to mention my biological parents— and of course, myself. Was I the last one left, doomed to perish in a little over a week myself? Or was Marc the last one standing, now in possession of literally all the magic in the world? Or, was it Lucien, though not really Lucien, as Marc had pointed out?

Yes, the family that could have been had been utterly torn apart by the works of Arnold Hammerson. Regardless of how today turned out, it was too late to change that. Why was I thinking of that now, though? Was it simply that I was here in the in-between now, knowing I would be spending eternity here starting from a little over a week from now, which was causing me to reflect on all that had been lost? Or maybe it was due to the fact that the war was likely over now; at least as it had been, and maybe that was the cause of me thinking back to what had been lost. I didn't really think so. My biggest personal losses during the war had been the deaths of Nicole and Stella, and neither of them were at the forefront of my thoughts right now.

No, it was becoming increasingly clear why I was thinking what I was thinking. I was here because I really had nowhere else to be; and the only thing to do here, besides think long thoughts which could just as easily be thought in my brain rather than my soul or whatever this was, was to interact with the other damaged souls here. I could go to Lisa and tell her how it had all turned out, or I could go to Mary Sien and tell her that the last of the crystals standing was the Hero Crystal—no, that was out of the question. She would have no memory of our previous interaction, and she would probably consider what we had done to her precious crystals a terrible affront.

There was only one other notable person here: my biological mother. At least, I assumed that she was here, based on all I knew of this place. She had been brought back as a ghost by my father, which was probably what had caused her to end up here rather than passing on to a far more peaceful ending, but had she been recalled? That, I didn't know. My guess was that since she had been called by my father, she would have come back here after he died, having no purpose to exist as a ghost. I had done a school project on ghosts back in year seven, and although I believed much of what I'd read back then had been wrong (it had never mentioned this place, for one thing), that part of it still fit in with all I knew.

So thinking of the ghost woman as I knew her, I reached out and felt for that presence. She wasn't difficult to find; even by the standards of being in a place where there was no time, it took no time at all for me to find her. I recognised her immediately, and she recognised me almost as quickly. Her joy was palpable, and yet so was her sadness, for her first thought was that I must be dead to be here at all.

"I'm not dead," I assured her. "Well, I did die, but I was brought back, and I still live today, but I can come here if I need to."

Her sadness was not lessened by these words, but I felt her give me a small smile all the same. "It is difficult for me to imagine," she said, "a situation where we could communicate and for all to be well. I know you are my youngest son, and yet my memories of you are mostly after my death. I have almost no memories of the brief time I got to have with you as a child, but I understand that you were brought up in a loving family all the same. I hope they did good by you."

"They really did," I assured her, hoping she could feel the honesty in those words. "I—well—I never felt deprived as a child, even when I was told about being adopted. It was only when I found out about you and my biological father that I wondered what had been taken away from us. I'd like to say that it would have been good, but I don't know. He should never have gotten involved with the Hammersons."

"Yes, he shouldn't have," she agreed, "but he did, and walking out on them would have been a death sentence for him. I would not let him do that. I would have preferred to take the hit myself than deprive you boys of your father. What I wanted was for you boys not to be exposed to any of it, and if I had lived, I would have done all I could to make sure you weren't. I am so sorry that I was not there for you."

I disregarded this; she had nothing to be sorry for, in my opinion. Instead, I said, "So—so Moran—I mean, my father—he told you what happened to me when he brought you back as a ghost?"

"He told me lots of things," she said, "some of which made me happy, some not so much. He told me what he knew about you, which wasn't very much, but he told me more about Marc and Lucien. He was quite proud of them, especially Marc, but he was never able to connect with him. Even as a young child, Marc was mine, while Lucien had always been his little boy."

Moran was more proud of Marc than Lucien? He certainly hadn't acted like it, but then again, maybe I was basing that on what Marc had felt rather than what Moran had felt. It wasn't like I had ever spoken to him about it—in fact, only this ghostly woman had, so I supposed I had to take her word for it.

"Was it because Marc is the Seventh Sorcerer?" I asked her.

I felt her give some sort of shrug. "That meant little to him. The way he said it, the fact that he was the Seventh Sorcerer was less important than what made him suitable to be the Seventh Sorcerer in the first place; that being his courage to do what needed to be done without hesitation. He sensed that Lucien had a lot of potential, but he had only seen Marc actually reaching his potential."

I hesitated for a moment that was not a moment at all, then told her, "I don't know if you remember this from when you lived, or if my father ever remembered it either, but Arnold Hammerson put a curse on Lucien to set up his future. It activated when Marc killed Hammerson, and it—"

"Marc killed Arnold Hammerson?" she cut me off, her emotions suddenly becoming much sharper.

"Well, yeah, he had to."

"That is good," she said, and I only realised then that her emotions were positive. "After what that man did to our family, it is fitting that Marc was the one to finish him. I hope his mother met an equally suitable ending."

"Oh, I killed her months ago," I told her. "I was pissed at her for torturing my friends."

Her joy was radiant. "I would not normally be happy about people dying, even if they were aligned with the Hammersons, but those two—those two deserved all they got, and the fact that my sons made it happen—I couldn't be more proud."

I would have liked to let her go on feeling this good, but I needed to tell her the rest. "Arnold Hammerson left a parting gift. His soul took possession of Lucien and made him evil. He took over the Hammerhearts after Hammerson's death and became just as cruel and deadly as Arnold was."

"What?" she said slowly, and I waited while she absorbed this, letting her feel the truth of it. "But why? Why Lucien?"

"I don't think Hammerson ever believed it would really happen, but he liked the look of Lucien as a child, and he thought that he might be a suitable leader if anything should wipe the Hammerson line out. Lucien *was* good at it too, because he knew all the secrets we had found out and used against the Hammersons. It's over now though. Marc had to kill him as well, because it wasn't really Lucien we were fighting anymore. Whatever became of the *real* Lucien, he's free now—at least, I'm pretty sure he is."

"What do you mean by that?" she asked me.

"I mean," I said slowly, "I don't know what actually happened at the end. Lucien may or may not have survived. Marc may or may not have survived. If Lucien lives and Marc doesn't, the world will be a terrible place, but it'll be even worse if they both died because—well, it's too hard to explain, but it'll be worse. If Marc lives, he can fix everything up, even if Lucien survived, because Marc has far more power than Lucien now. Does that—does that make any sense?"

"Not really," she admitted, "but I can feel that you believe it, and I don't believe you are insane. Bernard said you seemed quite smart to him, very brave and very capable of operating magic when you had it. Am I right in thinking that you are here, talking to me, because you are afraid to find out which of your brothers yet lives?"

"Maybe," I hedged.

She gave me another sad smile. "I think you need to go now, John, and find out what is going to happen next. If you can come here any time, then you can let me know how it turned out."

"You will lose your memory of this conversation if I do that," I told her.

She just went on smiling. "Then, since time is nothing here, we can repeat it all again—as many times as you want to."

"Okay," I said, and would have sighed if I'd had a body with which to do so. "Er—can I ask a question before I go?"

"Anything, my son."

"You called me 'John' just before, and I suppose you know that's my name because my father told you. Was that my original name *before* I was adopted?"

It was a question I had been wondering about for a very long time, and to which I had never known how to find the answer. Neither Marc nor Lucien knew that they'd had another brother until I found out that I was a Moran. Smiley hadn't known anything, and neither of my biological parents had mentioned my name in the memory I had seen of them handing me to him. I was always told by the Playmans that John was my great-grandfather's name (on my mother's side, as Peter was named after our great grandfather on our father's side), and that was where it had come from, so what was I called prior to becoming a Playman?

"I'm afraid I don't know your birth name," she said sadly. "I have thought of you as John because that is what Bernard said they called you these days. He did not tell me your birth name—he did not mention it because thinking of that time always made him sad. I am sure you could find out for yourself what it was, though; you would only need to find a copy of your birth certificate and there it would be."

"I probably won't get a chance to do that," I said, thinking of how much time I had left, "so I guess it'll be one of those things I'll never know. Thanks, Mum; I'll come back if I can."

Part 5: The New Normal

Chapter 35: Glimmer

"Is everyone okay?"

The voice startled me so much that any and all other thoughts I'd been lost in were cut off abruptly. That had been Marc's voice, coming from the direction where he had been before—not his hologram, but the kettle he had become after the third annihilation. It was a perfectly normal voice—a perfectly human voice—and I wondered at it. He had clearly survived, then, but why had it taken him a full five minutes to do anything? In response to his words, however, there was no answer—not from me, as I had no mouth with which to speak—and not from anyone else either. Hopefully they were like me, turned into something incapable of speech. Hopefully they were not like…like…

Things were shifting around out of my line of sight. I waited for something to happen—something to move me, or something to come across my vision. Eventually, I was moved, levitated into the air, turned around and then lowered onto a large, square block of what looked like wood. Once I was lying flat on my back, looking up at the empty, white sky, I couldn't see anything at all; however, I had seen a bit while I had been in motion. Marc was standing on the block of wood, back in human form and holding the Hero Crystal. He had used magic, firstly to put himself back together (I would learn later that because of their proximity to the Hero Crystal, he, Peter and Amelia had all kept their shapes). Now, he was using magic to locate the rest of our party and lay them on this block of wood so that he could work on turning us all back into humans. I had also seen Amelia, sitting in the driver's seat of Peter the train, both of them watching proceedings.

Nothing much happened for a while as Marc worked. Eventually, though, he believed he had found everyone, and set to work transforming a handful of people back into their human forms. Peter was first, followed by James, and then me. I felt nothing as my form slowly shifted; I could still see and hear, but Marc didn't allow the rest of my senses to return to me until he was finished. That was probably good— maybe it would have hurt a bit if I could feel it—or a lot. Once he was done with me, he proceeded to work on Natalie, Frederic and Lillian, taking about five minutes over each so that he could get them right.

Not that we all turned out exactly as we had before. Only Natalie, Amelia and Marc himself came out looking exactly as they had before. Peter and I were mostly the same, though perhaps a little taller; Lillian and Frederic, and especially Lillian, had come out looking a little younger and more vital; and James had been slimmed a bit, though he was still on the tubby side, and his eyes were back where they belonged —in their sockets. I took two things from all of this: Marc was doing us all a kindness at a moment when it seemed convenient to do so; and Marc had to use his magic very specifically just to achieve what he had.

This last was ominous because it meant that even though the fight seemed to be over, magic was still very much unbalanced in the world. In any other time, Marc should have been able to use a single spell on each of us—or even all of us at once—to return us to how we had been at a certain time, not including our brains (wouldn't want to lose all our memories), and that would have been sufficient. It was especially ominous because my hope, unacknowledged up until now, was that the last annihilation would have transformed the world back to how it had been before Underwood and Tommy had opened the antimagic can of worms in the first place. Now, though, it looked like Marc, the only person left with any magic, would have to do a world tour, fixing everything that had been busted up—and he would have to do it all alone —and he would have to do it with impaired magic.

Only when there were eight of us standing together on the block of wood did Marc take a break from doing magic and come to consult us.

"Okay," he said to us, wiping sweat from his brow. "So, as far as I can tell, Lucien is truly gone—I can't trace him anywhere on the entire planet, and I can't imagine that he would be untraceable now. Everyone who was with us before the last blast is alive and trapped in the body of a doll or figurine."

I looked down, and sure enough, there were what looked like toy dolls littering the block of wood. In the instant before I saw them, I was imagining the Lego women that Erica, Kylie and Serena had been turned into by Moran so very long ago. Not the case though—the dolls all looked different from each other, there was nothing whatsoever about them which resembled who they had once been. At least when the three girls had been Lego, they had still looked like themselves, but now, only Marc's magic would be able to identify which doll was which person.

"You can change them back, though, right?" James asked nervously. "You were able to change us, so why not them?"

"I will change them, but we need to figure out what comes next," Marc said. "At the very least, it seems like we should try to get back to Chopville, and start whatever comes next from there. I may have to do this for every single person in the world, and I don't think I'll even be alive that long. That's why I want to ask you three"—he eyeballed the three Woodwards—"how you did it after my dad went nuts at the start of the year. You cleaned the whole world up in like three days, so have you got any tips?"

The three of them hesitated, the two women glancing at Frederic as if only he could say whatever had to be said. Finally, he did. "Marc, most of what we did was using magic to return things to how they had been before the weather had changed. The spells we had to use did have some parameters, and there were times when we had to stop and do more specific magics depending on the situation, but most of the time, the only real task we had was to fly around and make sure we covered the entire globe's surface. Only the fact that there were four of us doing it meant that we able to get it done as quickly as we did. Do you feel that your magic is functionally capable right now of doing any of that?"

It was Marc's turn to hesitate, but finally he shook his head. "Okay, if I can't do that, then I have to do it some other way. I'm sure you'll agree that I can't *not* do it. I'm the only one who can, for one thing; and I'm at least partially responsible for it, for another."

"I think Lucien is a lot more responsible than anyone, Marc—" I began.

Marc shook his head, then reconsidered. "Well, yes, but I have to answer for his crimes now, since he can't. Also, he only became what he did because Arnold Hammerson died, and I did that."

"Arguing over who is responsible is pointless," Lillian said firmly. "It is done, as you say, and we have to deal with it. Let us not forget that we wouldn't have defeated Lucien without antimagic—"

She cut herself off then, and I was sure I knew why. She was probably about to say something like, 'so it was worth it', but was it? Was this future—the one where the world had become a swamp and it would take Marc lifetimes of men and beasts to fix it—better than the one Lucien had manufactured in all our minds before Underwood had fired on him? Most definitely not, and the faces of Lillian, Peter and James—the others who had experienced the mental simulation—confirmed that they felt the same way. I had to remind myself that Lucien's real intentions for us wouldn't have been anything as utopian, given that he had been consumed by that lump of evil. Having that running the world, in the long run, *would* have been worse than this—once we got to work fixing up the damage, anyway.

"Okay, okay," Marc said after a few seconds of awkward silence, "point taken. Still, it doesn't change the fact that I have to fix it, but I need your help. I don't—I don't even know how to start."

My heart went out to Marc in that moment. He was putting on a brave face, but it was brittle. It reminded me a bit of how I had felt the night Stella had died, and I understood how it must be for him. He had come so far and achieved so much, but right now, he was just a teenage boy with the fate of the world in his hands. He looked imploringly at the Woodwards for help, but it was James who answered.

"I think you're right about needing to go to Chopville and starting from there, since it is home. Let's not forget that we've got a bunch of our friends there waiting for us—at least, I really, *really* hope they are still there and still okay. Do you think you can teleport us, Marc?"

Marc nodded. "It worked to get us here, and magic was already unstable then, so if I put my mind to it, I'm sure I can get us back that way. Then what?"

Another silence as everyone wracked their brains. I was the one who spoke up next. "We need to find out what the exact limitations on your magic are. It would be a mistake to assume there aren't any efficient ways of fixing this without at least looking for them. You said you used a spell that returned something to a state it had been in at a previous time," I addressed Frederic, "plus or minus a few variables. Can we try to see if that kind of spell would still work?"

Marc looked incredibly dubious, and I found myself wishing that I was in his position. Sure, it must have been overwhelming for him, but I would at least be willing to try stuff.

"It can't hurt to try it," Frederic said, looking at Marc. "You can do it on a small scale to test it, and if it works the way we need it to, we'll figure out how to expand it. We'll walk you through what you need to do to make sure it comes out the way you intend."

Marc shrugged. "Well, we do have to start somewhere. What should I test it on?"

He gazed hopelessly around the swamp that this city had become, but that wasn't where Frederic was looking. I followed his gaze and understood what was going to happen.

"Here," he said, picking up one of the dolls and handing it to Marc, "you can do it on this. You'll need to encase it in a binding spell so that the magic doesn't touch anything other than the figurine, and then you'll need to identify its brain so that it doesn't lose any of its memories. Finally, you need to carefully select the correct time to return it so that it will be in its human form and won't be hurt. You should probably also make it unconscious for the transformation, though."

"Does it matter who it is?" Marc asked.

"Make it so that it doesn't matter who it is," Frederic told him, "otherwise you will be placing a limitation on yourself which you really don't need."

Marc shrugged and got to work, holding the crystal in one hand and the doll in the other. For a couple of minutes he just stood there, and we all just stood there, watching him. He then turned from us and placed the doll on an empty spot of wood, took a step back from it, and then activated the magic. A moment later, Tommy was lying there, looking the same as he always had. He was even wearing the same clothes he had been wearing at the start of the battle, and as far as I could tell, he looked unhurt. In spite of everything, I felt a glimmer of hope: Maybe we could repair all this damage after all.

Marc shrugged again and let out a great sigh. "Okay, it was exhausting, and really no quicker than the way I recovered you guys, but

I guess it can be done on a larger scale. Do I do that for all the others then?"

Frederic, James and I all spoke at the same time, and all of us said entirely different things. Frederic said, "Yes," James said, "No," but as I said more than a single word, it was my question which was noticed.

"Are you going to wake Tommy up?"

"Yeah, sure," Marc said distractedly, and then turned his attention to James, "but why not the others?"

"Because I was already thinking ahead to the most efficient way of expanding the reach of that spell," James told him, "and unless you guys have a better idea, I think you should create some sort of flying machine, Marc; something in which we can fly above all this stuff and cast the magic down at it from. Once that's done, you should certainly fix the rest of these guys up, but if you fix them first, there isn't going to be enough room on this thing for all of us to stand."

That was hardly an issue, I thought; it would be the simplest thing for Marc to make the block of wood larger, but I saw another logical reason to wait. They would all be standing around doing nothing, waiting for Marc, and frankly, it was just easier to keep them as they were until we were ready. Also by that logic, we might as well let Tommy sleep for a little.

Marc, however, was thinking of something else entirely. "Cast the magic down at it? I assume you mean program it into the machine itself?"

"If you can," James said, "but if you have to perform that spellwork yourself, at least you'll be doing it from a safe position."

Marc shrugged once again and got to work. What he ended up creating took the shape of a jumbo jet, and it was certainly as big as one. It hovered about ten feet above us, blotting out the sky completely, but it was obviously powered by magic and wouldn't be relying on such mundane concepts as aerodynamics. It had no landing gear, no engines, and as far as I could tell, none of the flight controls a regular plane would have on its tail or wings. To complete the strangeness, a hatch opened in the belly of the fuselage, and as we watched, a set of stairs lowered so that their foot came to rest right beside Amelia.

"You guys wait here for a few minutes," Marc told us, edging past his girlfriend and beginning to head up the stairs. "I'll just go up and make it a bit more comfortable."

"Is that really important, Marc?" Lillian called.

"Actually, it might be," James said. "He's probably thinking of the water vessel we used to get to Rock Haulter back in May that he and John created, but we could end up having to fly around in that thing for days—or longer. Who knows."

The seven of us stood there in silence for a while. It felt like hours but was probably no more than thirty minutes, before Marc came back down the stairs and told us that we could go up. In single file, we did so, with Marc bringing up the rear, levitating an unconscious Tommy before him. He was also levitating the rest of the dolls but I wasn't aware of this until a bit later.

As James had suspected, the inside of what I could only think of as 'the jet' looked quite similar to the inside of the water vessel Marc and I had created to get to Rock Haulter back in May. We emerged into a rectangular room with a long hole in the middle of the floor from which the steps had risen, and I supposed would fold up as a sort of trap door when it was time for us to fly off. The room was lushly carpeted and softly illuminated from three large light bulbs placed above the hole. There was enough floor space on all four sides of the hole for two people to walk around it comfortably. On either side of the room were what looked like luggage compartments (though none of us had any luggage) and above them, windows looking out on the swamp that had once been a vibrant city. At either end of the room, the walls sharply drew together to form a doorway, leading to what looked like corridors with rooms off to either side.

"A few days indeed," Natalie said as she looked around her. "I would have preferred to do this from inside our base, but I guess that isn't an option, is it?"

"I don't think so," Marc said as he reached the top of the stairs and began raising them, closing the hole behind him. "It's hard to imagine that the base survived after everything that's happened today, and if it did, by some miracle, then it would be untraceable and I won't be able to find it anyway."

Natalie bit her lip, looking upset, and I could guess why. Her grandmother had been in that base, responsible for making sure that everyone got out safely, but with no one left to let her out, she had no way of escaping herself. If the base had been destroyed (or more accurately, had all its magic stripped away), Alice would be stuck in there forever—or more accurately, she would die almost straightaway without any life support systems in there, as they had all relied on magic. If the base did still function, though, it would presently be in Chopville, and we would only be able to get back into it if Alice let us back in.

"So now what?" Peter asked into the silence which had stretched after Marc's words.

"Well, I'm going to start trying to fix the world," Marc said, depositing the dolls into one of the luggage compartments and then starting to head down one of the corridors, Tommy floating along after him. "The rest of you, I guess, can make yourselves comfortable, look around, or come and help me—whatever you like."

"What about them?" Amelia called after him. "Are you just gonna leave them in there?"

"They'll be more comfortable than if I return them to their normal forms now," he called back. "There isn't enough room in this thing for thirty or however many it will be."

"Logical," James said, but he looked uneasy.

With nothing better to do, I decided to take a tour of the jet, starting by going the way Marc had gone. This corridor had doors on either side, and I found, by looking through a few of them, that they were small bedrooms. Tommy had been deposited in one of them, lying on the bed in what was probably a magical coma. Perhaps Marc reasoned that Tommy might cause trouble if he was woken up, and it was just easier to do things this way, but this made me uneasy. That, along with leaving a large portion of our army in a luggage compartment, made me wonder a bit about Marc's priorities. I couldn't exactly say they were scrambled, since he was putting the world ahead of us, but then what was it? I couldn't shake the feeling that it wasn't right and I couldn't put it into words, not even in my own head. I was glad that some of the others wore expressions suggesting they were feeling the same way.

At the end of the corridor, at what turned out to be the front of the jet, was a spiral staircase. I climbed it up and emerged onto the upper deck. This level was more open than the lower level had been. Most of the front of the jet was taken up by a large dining room. There were two doors leading off it; the one at the front of the room led to the cockpit, where Marc was presently at the controls, while the other led into the other room on the top deck, this one turning out to be a large lounge room filled with comfortable-looking sofas, seats and beanbags.

At the back of this room was another spiral staircase, this one leading back to the lower level. Down I went at the back of the jet, emerging in another corridor with small rooms off to either side. This turned out to be bedrooms like those at the front of the jet, with the exception of the back two, which turned out to be lavatories. I followed the corridor until, as I expected, I was back in the luggage room, coming from the door opposite the one I had originally gone through, thus completing the tour of the jet.

Very little time had passed since we had gotten on this thing, and I still had nothing to do. With no other ideas, I went to find James and Peter, eventually locating them—and everyone else—crowded around the entrance to the cockpit. There wasn't enough room for more than three people in the cockpit, and the three seats were currently taken up by Marc, Frederic and Lillian. My initial thought was that everyone wanted to help in some way with what they were doing, and probably they did, but since it was apparent that they couldn't, an argument had sprung up between Marc, Peter and James.

"You're not being reasonable," James told Marc sternly.

"What he means is, you're being a power-crazy prat," Peter snapped.

Marc glared back at both of them. "If that's how you feel, Peter, then screw you."

"Hey, no!" Natalie snapped, jumping suddenly into the fray. "They're not asking for much, and you have no good reason for saying no."

Marc shook his head. "I had very specific reasons for recovering the people I recovered first. I'm sorry that it didn't include your girlfriends, but I hope you understand if my top concern right now isn't making sure that you guys aren't bored."

"One of them happens to be my sister," Natalie shot back.

"It would only take you a couple of minutes for each of them," James insisted, "and besides, if you'd just done it to begin with, you would have already started your real work, so your point about not wanting to waste time is pretty much moot."

"Oh, fine then," Marc snapped, standing up, "but if the rest of them are pissed off with you guys because you only care about recovering Erica and Rebecca and not the rest of them, you can explain to them all that until they start having sex with you two, you're not going to look out for them."

"That's enough, Marc," Frederic said, also standing up. "I see the point you're trying to make, but there's no need to be uncouth about it."

Marc sighed deeply. "Fine, whatever, but if I do this, you guys had better not bug me for anything else. I've got enough on my plate as it is."

So that was what he did, after which Peter and James disappeared into a couple of the bedrooms with their girlfriends. Natalie and Amelia also disappeared, I wasn't entirely sure where to, as did Lillian. In her case, I knew it to be because she was exhausted and needed to rest. That left me, Marc and Frederic as the ones to occupy the cockpit and get down to the business of saving the world.

"So how does all this work, Marc?" I asked him, indicating the control panel.

"Well, I select the area to fix using the controls," he said, as if I couldn't figure that part out for myself, "then I activate the magic. It is supposed to return all the substance within the selected area to exactly the form and shape it had been before it was affected by antimagic. Most of it should be fine, but in case there are surprises, I'll jump in with the crystal to fix those up."

"And what's the plan for knowing if it's fine or not?" I asked.

He gave me a queer look. "What do you mean? It'll be pretty obvious if it's not fine."

"Possibly not," Frederic said. "I think I might know what John's getting at. It may look fine on the outside, but could be completely hollow on the inside—like a paper town, if you get my drift."

"Paper town?" Marc now looked dubious.

"It just mightn't be obvious if it's actually back to how it should be or not," I said. "The crystal might be able to tell you if it is, but if you use the crystal to fix it then I imagine the crystal will think it worked, whatever you did with it. Er—maybe it would be better to start this back in Chopville instead of somewhere totally unfamiliar, just so that we'll be able to use our own knowledge to check."

Marc nodded. "That actually would make it easier, and then once I've got a better idea how this thing is likely to go, we'll be able to move on to less familiar areas. This means we'll have to teleport there."

"Can you do that with this thing, or will you just use the crystal?" I asked.

"I programmed the ability into the jet," he said, "but I programmed it to require input from the crystal to specify a location. I did try to program it to take the information from my mind, but no matter what I did, it wouldn't work."

Frederic and I exchanged a worried look. That kind of magic was no more difficult than the kind we had used to program the conveyer belt to produce food for us in the first Young Army base, not to mention both Woodward bases. The base we had evacuated just hours ago didn't have that same ability because the magic on Rock Haulter hadn't been powerful enough to create it, but the Hero Crystal, even if it had somehow been damaged by Lucien at some point today, still should have been able to do it.

This led me to the only logical conclusion: magic itself had been damaged by the events of the day, and would likely never be the same again. This eliminated the glimmer of hope I'd been feeling that we could actually recover from this, and what it left was a hollow feeling. There was something else as well that I couldn't quite put my finger on. It was a sense of something being off, something being not quite right. It was easy enough to rationalise (of course, nothing was quite right at the moment) but I couldn't shake the feeling that it was something else— something else I was presently missing, but would be able to find if I just tried…

…which I was terribly afraid to do. The more I thought about it, the more it seemed that there was a truth hidden deep in my mind and I would be able to reveal it if I wanted to, but once I did, it would change me forever. I cringed away from the thought and chose to focus on Marc and Frederic, the latter of whom was speaking.

"don't be alarmed by what we see when we reappear. You have to expect that Chopville would have been damaged to a similar degree to what we're seeing here, certainly more so than what we left behind earlier. It could look something like this, or it could look like—well— just about anything. Remember, whatever it is, it's up to you to return it to how it was before."

"No problem," he said. "I'm not even going to try to picture the worst case scenario because I already know that it will probably be worse even than that."

"Wait, wait," I burst out in alarm, and both of them looked at me. "Hold on, I just thought of something. Marc, what did you do with the leftover antimagic?"

"I've kept it with me," he said, and a moment later, he went very pale. "Er—what would have happened to us just now if we had tried to teleport antimagic?"

"At the very least, it would have thrown us for a loop, and probably would have left us right here," Frederic sighed. "Good catch, John. I guess that means we have to fly to Chopville rather than teleport. Marc, how fast can this jet go?"

"Way faster than a plane, even a supersonic one," Marc said. "We're in Panama right now, but even at top speed, we can't hope to reach Chopville in less than four or five hours."

"What do we do then?" I asked. "I mean, I guess we can wait a few hours before getting started, but—I dunno. Do either of you feel like time may be against us?"

They both nodded, but Marc then said, "I do feel that, but I also feel like there is no way I can do this quickly. I have to do it as quickly as I can, but I also have to do it right."

"Then we should find out what it's going to be like as soon as we can," Frederic said, "which means we should start right here. If things go poorly here and we can't figure out what to do about it, then we'll have to fly to Chopville and restart from there."

Both Marc and I agreed to that, though in my case, it was because I had no better alternative. In fact, unless Marc could find a way to increase his magical abilities without more raw magic, I couldn't see how this could possibly work. Did we have several days to do this before ninety percent of the world's population would be dead? I somehow doubted it, and yet earlier in the year when the world had been rocked by those two global climatic events, caused by our father, it had taken four Sorcerers three full days to fix it—and this was going to be a far bigger job.

Yep, the hollow feeling inside me was growing ever more.

A silence fell in the small control room as Marc gripped the crystal, and Frederic and I let him do what he needed to do. For what seemed like a long time, though was probably no more than two minutes, nothing happened. Finally, Marc let out a noise of frustration.

"Problem?" I asked, unsurprised.

"There doesn't seem to be any way for me to return it to how it was before," he said, looking at the two of us with wide eyes. "I can't normalise this because there isn't any lingering magic in it, nor can I set it to how it was before all this happened, because I just don't know enough about how it was before it happened. The crystal can transform it into whatever I imagine it to be, but I can't make it determine what it should be on its own."

"That kind of magic is normally fairly simple," Frederic said. "Indeed, it should be simpler than imagining it yourself, as long as your mind is focussed in the right way. Are you sure you're focussing, Marc?"

"Hey, I'm not the problem here," Marc shot back. "It's the same as earlier when I couldn't just fix up any of your appearances—I had to practically remake your mother in the image I remembered."

"Well then, Marc," I said slowly, trying to wrap my mind around the enormity of the situation, "I guess the only option is for you to remake the world from scratch. If you're going to do that, I suggest you find some creative ways to optimise your productivity, like Lucien started to do. Do you reckon you could pull off duplicating yourself like he did?"

"The way magic is behaving right now, I'm not brave enough to try," he shrugged, his face screwing up as he fought to keep his emotions in check.

"That's fair enough, but still, John is right," Frederic insisted. "It will take you an age to remake the world, so you must find ways to do it more quickly, using spells which seem safe to you. I'm sure there are ways to do it, and you have me, John, my mother, Amelia and even Natalie here to bounce suggestions off—not to mention James who, although he hasn't used a lot of magic in his time, would probably be very good at coming up with ideas which might actually work."

Marc took a deep breath, steadied himself, and then said, "Okay. Since I'm not sure where to start, I'm going to do something about the still-living first. How's this for an idea. I create something to store all those who still live in, something that will remember who they are and exactly where they are at this moment in time, and it will keep them alive until I release some or all of them into the areas that are stable enough to support life."

Another silence as Frederic and I thought about this. It seemed like a good idea to me, at least to get those who may still be alive (as I had been before Marc had transformed me back into a human being) out of the swamp, or whatever else the surface of the world may have turned into. Would it damage them in some unforeseen way to keep them in some sort of magical stasis for an indefinite period? Who could say, but it couldn't be worse than what was happening to them right now.

And yet, it would not be enough. I felt that deep in my gut—deep in what remained of my soul.

"Are you able to draw in every living thing in the world from a single point?" Frederic finally asked. When Marc only gave him a questioning look, he went on, "The antimagic stores were designed to suck up all the antimagic substance in the world. Are you able to do something similar to attract all the living things in the world?"

Stephen Hayes

"I don't see why not," Marc said, "although it will be a little different from the antimagic stores because it will be sucking up physical things, not just the essence of their selves or whatever you wanna call it."

"Then make sure it doesn't suck us up as well, or that'll be the end of life as we know it," I said, getting to my feet. "Do you guys mind if I go lie down? I'm not feeling great."

They both gave me startled looks. "What's wrong, John?" Frederic asked.

'What *isn't* wrong,' is what I would have liked to say. What I actually said was, "I suppose, but I'm really tired, and I need to think. I only have one suggestion before I go."

"If it's as good as the one to make sure we don't get sucked up, ending life as we know it, go right ahead," Marc said.

"Fly us back to Chopville. If we need to settle down somewhere for a period of time to do this, it might as well be at home."

I left then, but not before I heard Frederic saying to Marc, "Since you should take your time creating this device, leave me to fly the jet."

I descended to the lower level of the jet and walked up the hallway. Four of the bedrooms were shut and I could hear no noises coming from any of them. In one of the open ones, I could see Tommy lying on the bed as if asleep, and I felt a wave of sickness. I had forgotten about him while I had been in the control room, and I imagined that Marc had too. Was it healthy to keep him in this state for such a prolonged period? Should he not be put with the rest of the army, stored safely away in a place which would, if nothing else, require nothing to keep him alive? In his human form, he required food, drink and oxygen at the very least…

Doom, that's what this felt like. Doom and the end of life as I knew it; and that would be the best case scenario. The far more likely scenario was that this would be the end of life. It even fit, when I brought it back to that awful prophecy Lisa had led me to: it wasn't the end of either life or magic, but the end of both. And yet, as I thought this, the feeling I'd had upstairs returned to me; this was not right. I was still missing something, but where before I had cringed away from the thought, now I clung to it in desperation. If I could just make sense of these feelings I was having, maybe I would find another alternative—one that actually felt *right*.

I shut myself in one of the empty bedrooms and lay down on the bed, wondering if I would sleep. For a time, I almost did, but though my body was ready to shut down for a while, my mind was not. At first, it flittered over the prophecy, understanding it much more than I originally had—or rather, almost understanding it. There was one word in the prophecy which almost, but didn't quite, fit with what had actually happened. I kept trying to tell myself that I was wrong, and that everything fit as perfectly as a prophecy could be expected to fit, but the gnawing feeling wouldn't go away.

At last, when I could bear it no more, I allowed my mind to go down a new path and ask the question I had been avoiding up until now: what would need to have happened for the prophecy to have fit properly? No, that was *still* not the right question. I chastised myself and forced my mind to ask the question: what needs to happen for the prophecy to fit properly? I finally allowed myself to think of the question, and of course the answer came to me immediately. It had all the rightness of the correct answer to a riddle the moment it is spoken.

My mind tried to cringe away again, but now that I was here, facing my worst fears, I refused to let it. Another word came to me, one that was not in the prophecy but had come from my own mind in response to all these thoughts. I almost disregarded it, not wanting to admit a connection, but before I could, it brought up another memory—that of the promise I had made along with Marc, Amelia, James and Peter, to come back from the dead to find the required information, should one of us be killed. Five desperate teenagers, with the vast majority of the magic in the world turned against them, looking for anything that might turn the tide back in their favour, unsealing powers which should have been left alone…

No, that wasn't quite right either. Even if we had somehow found our way here without ever having made that promise, we would be in no better a position. Could we have beaten Lucien by some other means? Not that I could think of, and the very existence of the prophecy argued against that idea anyway. And it was a moot point anyway because we had finished with that spell: Lucien had been destroyed, and we could…

No, again, that wasn't quite right. This was like being stuck in a maze: No matter which way my mind went, there was a dead-end. I cast my mind back to the night less than a week ago when we had made the promise, trying to find what I was missing. What I recalled were the words James had spoken after the spell had been completed: 'through the will of Sien and Leoard, we will succeed in our endeavour, provided we live up to our promise.'

No. Once again, that wasn't quite right. What wasn't quite right? I thought about it for a moment, but this time, the answer came more easily: The spell hadn't been truly completed when James said that. The spell required the promise to activate it, belief to carry it, and the sacrifice to complete it, and the sacrifice didn't happen until the following day when I had died and then been brought back…

No. No. No. I had lost count of how many times I had tried to think something that didn't feel right, but the more it happened, the better I was becoming at recognising it. This time, it took longer to find my way back onto the right road, but when I did, it was the last time I would need to try. This time, my mind found its way straight to where I needed it to go. It was Mary Sien I thought of, and the thing she had told me when I had visited her in the in-between less than twenty-four hours earlier. I hadn't had a chance to tell anyone about that encounter, what with all that had happened on this day, which meant that I alone had all the pieces of the puzzle to understand the terrible truth of the matter.

What needs to happen for the prophecy to fit properly? What is needed to truly complete the spell? And above all, what sacrifice is required to provide the power equivalent to the endeavour we wished to achieve? The answer to all three questions was the same, and now that I knew what the answer was, there was no escaping it. I let out a moan of despair and rolled over, burying my face in the pillow as tears filled my eyes.

Chapter 36: The True Sacrifice

Exactly how long I lay there, curled up in a foetal position, I never knew. I may have even drifted into a doze for a bit. At last, though, I knew that I couldn't stay there any longer. Soon, Marc was going to start doing stuff with the crystal, and I now knew that anything he tried would ultimately make things worse rather than better. I had only one option, and that was to gather the others and tell them what I now knew. It was going to be a terrible conversation, and yet it had to be done. I expected that they would all understand as well as I did, once the truth was laid bare to them. I also knew that some of them would not want to understand, and may resist the truth of it even when it was staring them in the face. I could do nothing to prevent that, but I had to get started.

I left my room and began knocking on the closed doors, waking Lillian, Peter and Rebecca from sleep, and disturbing James and Erica from whatever discussion they had been having. Natalie and Amelia were in a room together as well; they emerged looking as if they had been sleeping, and yet neither of them looked bleary-eyed as Peter and Rebecca did. Finally, I asked Marc and Frederic, who were still in the control room, to come to the lounge room at the back of the jet for a meeting.

It was well timed. We were now in Chopville, having flown while I had been asleep, but Marc hadn't put any magic into action. Looking through the front window, I saw that Chopville had been transformed into something I had trouble describing, even in my own mind. Its surface was craggy and jagged with rocky towers rising dozens, and in some cases hundreds of feet into the air, while below were ditches and muddy pools full of yucky, brown and green stuff. It wasn't pretty, and yet it was better than the scene we had left behind—at least there would be places to stand out there, should it be necessary to do so.

"What's all this about?" Marc asked, looking grumpy as he sat himself down near the door to the dining room.

"John, you look like you've aged about ten years since I saw you earlier," James observed, scrutinising me.

That didn't surprise me, but since I hadn't seen my own reflection since Marc had remade my body, I only shrugged. "Guys, we need to talk about something. None of you are going to like what I have to say, but this is one of those things that you'll know is right when you hear it—or at least, you'll know it's right when you hear all of it, even though you probably won't want to admit it."

"You're scaring me here, John," Peter said nervously.

Good, I thought, gazing around at them. Half of them did look scared; James appeared nervous but also curious, Frederic and Lillian wore level expressions, and Marc looked like he was ready to get his back up, even before he had heard anything.

I took a moment to organise my thoughts. This had to be done in the right order, otherwise they would shut me down before I could present all the facts to them, and then they would never understand what I needed them to understand. Making up my mind, I turned my attention to James.

"I need you to think back for me. The spell we performed earlier in the week, the one to get Sien and Leoard on our side, you said that we would succeed in our endeavour so long as we kept our promise. What did you mean by that?"

James looked taken aback, but he took the question seriously. "I meant that as long as one of us came back from the dead so that we could speak to Lisa—"

I was already shaking my head. "Not that part—I already know that part. I mean, what did you mean by 'endeavour'? What *exactly* was our endeavour that night?"

"Er—to beat Lucien, obviously," James shrugged.

"Was that all it was?" I pressed him. "Think back—think really hard about what was going through your mind when you were casting that spell. What was the ultimate goal? Was it to just overthrow Lucien or was it something more specific?"

Silence in the room then, a very loud silence as everyone watched James, all of us seeming to hold our breath. He considered for a good long while before saying, "I think my main concern when I was casting the spell was getting the wording right. It was in ancient Greek, and I was really scared that if I mucked it up, I would screw things up royally for us."

I nodded. "I guess that makes sense. Remember what Fewul said about the spell earlier today? It was something like, *we would have the ability to dictate the final outcome, if not all the details along the way.* Do you get why I'm asking these questions now? I need to know if the spell is still active or if the final outcome you asked for has already been achieved, because that's going to determine what happens next."

The last part was true, but it wasn't the whole truth. I already knew that the spell was still active, but they weren't ready to hear that yet. James, meanwhile, looked like he was catching up to me. "Actually, John, I don't think it was me who determined that. Remember—all five of us were connected during that spell, and all five of us had to believe in it for it to have worked at all. What were you guys thinking about during the casting?"

"I was just thinking about Lisa and the Enlightener," I said, realising that in order for the spell to be still active, I must have contributed very little to it. Rather, I may have contributed the part that had originally cost me my life, but not the part that had kept Sien and Leoard on our side all the way through the battle against Lucien.

"I was thinking that I didn't feel anywhere near brave enough to be doing any of this," Peter said in a quiet voice, blushing a little and meeting nobody's eyes, "but that if it was the difference between succeeding and failing, I would do what I had to do."

"I was thinking about Lucien," Marc said quietly, "and that although I didn't like the idea of sacrificing my soul, I would do it if that's what it took to stop him from doing any more evil. Also, I think I was thinking that I still wanted to save him from the influence of Arnold Hammerson, but I guess Sien and Leoard didn't hear that part."

"On the contrary, I think they must have heard you loud and clear," Frederic said gently. "If it is true that we could only dictate the final outcome and not all the details along the way, then it may have been that the only way to liberate Lucien from Arnold Hammerson was to kill him."

"I hope you're right," Marc said, "but I hate to think that even in death, Hammerson's soul could still be latched onto Lucien's."

A silence then as everyone looked at Amelia, waiting to hear what she had to say. She seemed not to notice at first, but when she became aware of everyone's eyes on her, she said, "Um—well—I wasn't actually thinking about Lucien at all, or Lisa. I was thinking about—well—you guys."

A stunned silence, and then James said, "Can you be more specific?"

"I mean, I was thinking about all the people I cared about," Amelia said, blushing a little, "and I guess I was saying to Sien and Leoard something like, I'll keep my promise, and what I need in return is for the people I care about to be able to go back to a good and prosperous life. I'm not wording it the way I was thinking it at the time—I'm not sure how to explain how I was thinking it. Does—does that make sense?"

It made enough sense to me. Out of all of us, it was Amelia's will that had kept the spell going as long as it had. Marc's endeavour would have kept it active long enough to defeat Lucien, and something would have had to happen in the final battle that would have completed it. As it was, the final outcome of the spell would be for all of us to go back to happy lives, by which I understood Amelia to have meant that we should be able to go back to lives somewhat like what we had before all this had started.

"So..." James said slowly, letting the word trail off.

"Is that the answer you were looking for, John?" Erica asked.

I shrugged. "I wasn't looking for any specific answer, only one that would fit with what I already know to be true, and I believe it was Amelia's thoughts during the casting that contributed the most to the spell. Now, I need to tell you all something else about the spell, something that none of you would know, except maybe you," I glanced at James, "but I don't think so."

"And how would you know something about the spell that I don't?" James asked, looking curious but not at all offended.

"Because this morning, I went back into the in-between and had a conversation with Mary Sien herself about it," I told them, and then took a moment to enjoy the startled looks on all their faces.

"Why on earth didn't you tell us that earlier?" Marc breathed.

"There was really no opportunity to tell you guys about it," I admitted, "but also, it didn't seem all that important until Lucien found out about magic particles, and things moved way too quickly after that."

I told them in brief what Sien and I had said to each other, and then said, "When I told her of the spell, I framed it a little differently, though I don't think I realised it at the time. I told her that our goal was to end the power of the crystals, because at the time, I was thinking in terms of probably needing to use antimagic to destroy Lucien's power—which was, of course, how it ended up playing out."

"Hang on," Marc sat up straighter in his seat. "Did you tell Sien about needing to use antimagic against Lucien? If so, no wonder that was how it played out. For the love of God, if it was their will we needed to bend fate, no wonder things turned out the way they did."

I felt stung. "Marc, I didn't tell her about antimagic. All I said was that our goal was to end the power of the crystals."

"Also, Marc, that isn't how that spell works," James cut in. "John couldn't possibly have influenced Sien's will by telling her something in the in-between. For one thing, she would have forgotten about it the moment he left, because as he told us yesterday, Lisa didn't retain any of her memories from the first time he spoke to her there."

"Hey, yeah," I said, having forgotten that minor detail.

Marc wasn't convinced. "That was Lisa; this is Sien. Sien is a whole different beast and you know it."

"For another thing," James went on, "when the spell refers to Sien and Leoard's will, it isn't referring to a sentient thing. Neither of them are conscious enough to have their own will in this matter; all they have is the power they once held as the first Sorcerers, survived and contained within that stone tablet we used to unlock it. I suppose they unlocked a greater power beyond their own magic when they died—I'm not sure how that part works—but it's not really relevant, is it?"

"How do we know what's relevant and what isn't?" Marc shot back.

"Marc, try to think," Frederic said gently. "The point John is trying to make, I think, is that the spell must still be active, which means the final outcome hasn't yet occurred. If that is the case, the use of antimagic was just one detail along the way, and as we know, the spell only dictates the final outcome—not the details along the way. Is that about right, John?"

"Yeah, more or less," I said, giving Marc a reproving look, but for the time being, he seemed satisfied with Frederic's words.

"So what of it, John?" Peter asked. "What did Sien say when you told her that?"

I took a deep breath and said, "She told me that the sacrifice needed to complete the spell had to take place at the end of the spell and not earlier. She also told me that it had to be something that, under any other circumstances, we would not be willing to part with. The sacrifice had to be something with value equivalent to the value of the final outcome we were trying to achieve. Do you see the significance of this?"

For a few seconds, nobody did, until Natalie suddenly glared at James. "Hey, you told me that John's death was the sacrifice, but if what he just said is true then it couldn't *possibly* have been the sacrifice, could it?"

James went as white as a sheet. "Oh shit!"

"What?" Peter asked, looking scared.

"Oh crap," Amelia said, her eyes widening in comprehension. One by one, Marc, Frederic, Lillian and even Erica understood what I was saying.

Marc was the one who finally spoke. "So John's death and resurrection was never the sacrifice. We promised to do it, and that was what opened the spell, and because it was promised, it couldn't possibly count as the sacrifice. *That's* why the spell is still going, and that means that another sacrifice is required."

"But we've already sacrificed so much," Rebecca said, tears beginning to roll down her face.

"That is true," Frederic said slowly. "We have sacrificed quite a lot—seven eighths of the magic contained in the Magic Crystals is a gigantic sacrifice, not to mention the fact that we have probably lost the Sorcerous Crystals forever as well. If we're required to make a sacrifice equal in value to the value of the outcome we wish to achieve, how could that *not* be sufficient?"

I had been expecting someone to say something like that, for that rationality had occurred to me as well during the time I had tried desperately to *not* understand the truth of the matter. "Well, maybe it would have been, or could have been," I said, "but maybe it didn't happen that way because we were only thinking in terms of defeating Lucien when we made those sacrifices. In terms of the spell, that may have been equal in value to defeating Lucien alone, but not equal to the final outcome of returning us to a stable world."

"But you're only theorising when you say that," James observed.

I nodded. "Yes, that's my theory of why it didn't work, because it's obvious that it didn't work. If it had, we wouldn't be here now."

"Er—stupid question, maybe," Peter said, "but how do we know it didn't work?"

"Because out of all of us who made that promise, Pete, Amelia's final outcome still hasn't been achieved," James told him. "The rest of ours *have* been, so we have to assume that the spell worked based on that alone. Logic dictates that the spell can't be truly complete until the *real* final outcome has been achieved, and that means we have to be able to go back to normal lives for it to be completed."

"Then what next?" Natalie asked. "What else do we have to sacrifice that's even more valuable than seven eighths of the world's magic?"

Marc's face lit up hopefully then. "It may not *have* to be more valuable than seven eighths of the world's magic. I'm not sure how to explain this…" he hesitated for a moment as he organised his thoughts. "Okay, this is going to sound a bit weird, but the sacrifice to defeat Lucien would have needed to be bigger than the sacrifice to go back to normal lives, just because if we hadn't defeated him, we probably could have gone back to relatively normal lives in the end, albeit under the heel of a ruthless dictator. Think of it this way: Once the spell *has* been completed and we've reached the final outcome Amelia desired, then the sacrifice needed to get there would have included seven eighths of the world's magic, in addition to whatever else we need to sacrifice now."

There was a silence as everyone considered these words. I, well ahead of everyone in my understanding, given that I knew what the sacrifice would need to be, nodded in agreement. "You're not wrong— well, I'm not sure I agree with the idea that we could have had relatively normal lives under Lucien's rule, especially with the way he was behaving in the last few days—but your main point is valid."

"In that case, I may know what the sacrifice needs to be," Marc said heavily, and we all looked at him in surprise, and none more so than me. Marc was the person I'd expected to have the most difficulty with here, but when he spoke again, I could have slapped myself. "It's me—I'm the sacrifice. If I'm the only one who can use magic, then I'm the one who has to give myself over to fixing the world, even if it means there is literally nothing else in my life."

Yet another silence followed as we all tried to wrap our minds around this. James finally said, "I'm not sure I'm understanding the logic in that. What you're describing sounds like an extremely gradual sacrifice that is unlikely to be completed for days—months—years, even, and one which you could choose to turn back from at any moment. The way I understood the spell, the sacrifice has to be made in a single moment in such a way that it can't be reversed, and the only way you could sacrifice yourself in such a way would be to kill yourself. That can't possibly achieve anything in terms of fixing the world: It would only make it impossible for us to do anything at all, since there would be a new Seventh Sorcerer somewhere in the world, and we wouldn't know who it is."

"Not necessarily," Peter piped up. "I mean, the way magic is now, maybe there won't be another Seventh Sorcerer. In fact, I'm pretty sure that first prophecy we saw said that there would only ever be one

Seventh Sorcerer who would work out how to use his powers. If Marc *does* sacrifice himself, maybe that would set off some sort of magical reaction that would cause the world to be fixed."

James shook his head. "That is disturbingly tortured logic, Pete, and not worth sacrificing Marc's life just to find out if it's correct. Whatever sacrifice we *do* make, we need to know that it's the right one, and that just doesn't feel right to me."

"It isn't," I spoke up, deciding that I had let this go on long enough. "James, you say it doesn't feel right to you—I'm glad to hear that, because I *do* know what the sacrifice is, and it *does* feel right to me. I'm hoping that it will feel right to you when I tell you—to *all* of you," I added, looking around at them all.

I certainly had all their attention now, and every single one of them looked scared of whatever came next. Peter said, "Are we all gonna age ten years when you tell us like you apparently did?"

I shrugged and made no response to that. What I did was consider my words carefully. My gut feeling was telling me that they still weren't quite ready to hear it, and there was one more puzzle piece that needed to be shown to them. "It comes back to the prophecy," I told them, "not the one Pete mentioned, but the most recent one. Can anyone remember exactly how it went?"

A brief silence, and then James recited it. "When end times come, the world fades to black. He rises above, as the world around him falls. Chaos unrivalled, he revels, he cares not his folly. The box is open, there is no turning back. And magic reigning, raining, changing, arranging, pouring, roaring, searing, disappearing. The last Sorcerer will take it all."

"Geez, it sounds different in the context of all that's happened today," Erica observed.

"And no less unclear," Marc said, "in fact, possibly even more unclear. Was Lucien the last Sorcerer, or am *I* the last Sorcerer now? If that's true, then maybe we really *are* stuck here. We opened the box by using antimagic and now there's no turning back."

I hadn't actually considered that, and tried to parse Marc's words in light of what I already understood. Unfortunately, there was an awful plausibility in them, and that was when I understood the perilous position we were in. If we chose not to make the last sacrifice, Marc would be the last Sorcerer, and life on Earth would basically be dictated by his will and his magical abilities; but if we did make the sacrifice, either one of them—Marc or Lucien—could have been considered the last Sorcerer, but the end result would still be far better.

James was thinking in similar terms. "That could be the case, but if so, what is the sacrifice? The only thing that comes to mind—"

He broke off, his face going pale as he glanced at me. "Disappearing?" he said to me, and I knew that at last, one of them understood completely. I nodded, and he sank back in his seat and covered his eyes. "Oh Jesus Christ," he moaned.

"What? What?" asked several people in alarm.

I looked at James, willing him to speak, but he was far too rocked by the revelation. Sighing, I said, "It goes back to what Lisa said. We have a choice here—we can let this be the end of the world, or the end of magic. Either way, the prophecy is mostly right, but if we let things stand as they are, then there's part of it that isn't quite right, and that is the use of the word 'disappearing'. The second last line—or maybe it was two lines, I never actually saw it in writing—spoke of the transformations that magic would go through, and the last word was 'disappearing'. At the moment, most of the magic *has* disappeared, but not all of it."

"No, no," Marc said quickly, his eyes widening in alarm. "Are you trying to tell us that we have to sacrifice the Hero Crystal? The one thing that actually gives us a chance to put things back to rights? Are you saying that we should just throw it away and hope that the last antimagic blast will just return everything back to normal? You've gotta be kidding me!"

I didn't have to respond. The rightness in it was impossible to deny, and as I looked around the room, one by one, I saw all the others come to realise the truth in the matter. Marc looked around at them all in dismay. "Why are you guys listening to this madness? James, you said that it wasn't worth sacrificing my life to find out if the sacrifice is correct— this is far worse. If we sacrifice the Hero Crystal only to find things no better than they are now, or possibly worse, what are we supposed to do?"

"They won't be worse," Amelia said gently. "It'll work—it'll put things back the way they were, if you want it to."

"Huh?" Marc gaped at her. "What does that mean?"

"Okay, everyone calm down," Frederic said loudly, and silence descended. Everyone looked shocked, and as I had earlier, many of them were crying. Even James, who I wasn't sure I had ever seen shed a tear, looked close to it now. Only Marc and Frederic (and I) were dry-eyed now.

"Okay," Frederic said again, more quietly now. "John, I think you're right about the feeling—this *does* feel right to me. If we make this sacrifice, we have to trust that the will of Sien and Leoard will allow the end result to be what we want. It certainly fits the conditions: the sacrifice is at the end of the spell, it is something that we wouldn't part with under any other circumstances, and we have to consider it at least as valuable as the value in having a stable world again. We know that the spell is still active, and we know that magic is no longer functioning properly. Doing this will cause the end of magic, but at least it will fix the destabilisation caused by magic. Finally, it is the only thing I know of that will be powerful enough to actually *fix* the world."

Nobody spoke for a time after this. Most of them were dealing with things in their own ways: Amelia, Natalie and Lillian seemed to be the most emotionally affected by it, while the others looked much the way I felt about it. Even Marc struggled with the truth of it; he was the first to speak, and when he did, I felt hope beginning to kindle in my heart.

"This would be a sacrifice for all of us," he said, "but especially for me. I—do I really have to do this? Is this what it has come to?"

"I'm not sure I can offer any words of advice that will help you with this, Marc," Frederic said, "but what I can say is that while it is always difficult to choose to relinquish power, magic is one of those things which nobody has any right to lay a claim on. That includes us, even though we have had it for the vast majority of our lives. We only had magic because we were born into a family that had it. The Hammersons only ever had it for the same reason. Natalie only had it because someone had to have it instead of the Hammersons, and we thought the Fletchers would be the most suitable. You only had it because you happened to be born at exactly the right moment. Ironically, the only person who earned their magic was Lucien, but even he never actually *owned* it.

"The other thing that should be pointed out is that the Seventh Sorcerer isn't chosen solely based on the moment in which they were born. Granted, that is the most determining factor, but there would never be only a single candidate for it. Sien and Leoard may have assumed it would be based on the moment of birth, but we know a bit more about life now, and modern magicologists are sure that it would actually happen sometime in utero, and probably within a range of days or even months, depending on how quickly the foetus develops. The point I'm making is that the Seventh Sorcerer could be any of these babies, but it isn't: It is the one who would be most suitable to be the Seventh Sorcerer, should he or she come into their powers.

"As far as what makes a person *suitable*, the information we have is that firstly, they have to be capable of controlling the magic, which we know you are. They also need to be good, humble and noble, and not driven mad by power. I believe you possess all these attributes, for even before Lucien took our powers, you had more raw magic at your disposal than we did and yet you never chose to subvert our will with your own at any time. Well—maybe once or twice," he amended with a wry smile, and I knew he was recalling the night when, against the wishes of the adults, Marc had led a raiding party of the Young Army to rescue Tommy from Tankom in the Berlin Hammerheart Base.

"What's your point?" Marc asked hollowly.

"My point is that the Seventh Sorcerer is ultimately a hero," Frederic said. "The Hero Crystal isn't given its name for no reason: It can only be wielded by the Seventh Sorcerer, who must ultimately be a hero to do so. You have done numerous deeds this year which could be considered heroic, Marc, including a major one this very day. I would venture to say that there have been times when you would have been willing to sacrifice your life if it meant saving the lives of others, would that be right?"

Marc shrugged. "Off the top of my head, I can't remember ever being faced with that dilemma, thank God. I'm not sure I would be willing to sacrifice my life, though—not because my life is more valuable than other people's lives, but because, like James said earlier, you guys wouldn't have a Seventh Sorcerer anymore if I did that."

"Perhaps, but when Peter made the suggestion, be honest with yourself: Would you have been willing to try it?"

A brief silence as everyone stared at Marc. Finally he said, "If it—if it had felt right, and James hadn't said what he said, then…yes, probably."

"Then, you have what it takes within you to make the sacrifice," Frederic said gently. "Your evolutionary instincts ought to make it more difficult to sacrifice your life than anything else, and yet you would be willing to do that if it meant returning the world to a state of balance. You have what it takes to sacrifice your ability to use magic; you just have to come to terms with it."

Marc heaved a sigh. "But how do we know that it'll work? It's all well and good to say that Sien and Leoard's will is enough, but then what? People will still have been hurt and killed by all of this. So much stuff was wrecked by Lucien before we ever started using antimagic. If we sacrifice magic, we won't have any ability to put things back to rights."

"And that is the full gravity of the sacrifice," Frederic said, now looking around at all of us. "By doing this, we not only relinquish the power, but we also relinquish the responsibility that goes with it. After all, who are we to decide what is right for the world? The Hammersons thought it was their job, as did Lucien, but our philosophy for fifty years has been that of self-determination, which is the reason why our goal was always to use magic to make sure that it couldn't be used against those who didn't have it. Let the masses go about putting things to rights in the way that seems best to them, and we will do the same for ourselves. After all, we are no smarter or more qualified to make those kinds of decisions than anyone else."

"The thought of an enormous power vacuum is pretty terrifying to me," James said hesitantly, "but I see your point. If we don't like something, we should do our best to fix it in the same way that anyone else would. That's going to be the new normal, isn't it: a normal that'll be the same for us as it is for everyone else."

A long silence followed these words. Nobody spoke for maybe a full minute or longer, and as before, it was Marc who finally broke it, speaking words I had been thinking before I had come into the lounge room to have this meeting. "If we're going to do this then we should probably go outside, because I don't know what is going to happen to this jet—or frankly, anything that has had magic done to it since antimagic made the world go crazy. You said before that doing this will put things back to the way they were, if I wanted it to," he said to Amelia. "What did you mean by that?"

"Well, the results of the antimagic blasts seemed to be sort of based on the crystals that were being blown up," she said. "The Light Crystal did good magic, the Villain Crystal did mischievous magic, and the Darkness Crystal did frankly dark and evil magic."

"I'm not sure turning me into a horse was all that dark and evil," I pointed out.

Amelia shot me an exasperated look. "Part of the Sien-Leoard Crystal was also blown up in that moment, and it would have been closer to where you were standing, given that Dad was on Lucien's other side. I imagine the results of the Sien-Leoard Crystal would have been neutral, but there's another possibility. It could have been based on what Lucien was trying to do in that moment, and he was trying to disable us. He obviously couldn't control the final result of the blast, but if in each case he had been trying to disable us from fighting him, it would explain the results: animals the first time, machines of various types the second time, and dolls the last time, none of them able to fight in any meaningful way."

"Okay, okay," Marc said, raising his hand. "So you're saying that if I put the right intentions into the crystal before we blow it up, I can *will* it to fix the world? Maybe not the finer points, but the ultimate outcome?"

She nodded, and Marc reluctantly stood up. "Well, if we're going to do this, then let's go and do it. Everyone get anything you brought with you—if you brought anything with you—and meet up downstairs by the hatch."

As we all got to our feet, I felt a swell of affection for Marc. He had been so firmly set against the use of antimagic all along, and a big part of the reason for it was the possibility that he would ultimately have to give up the Hero Crystal. Now it had come to it, and he was doing the most selfless thing he could possibly do. I could see on his face how difficult this was for him—the eyes that had been dry earlier were no longer so— but however he felt on the inside, he wasn't letting it stop him or even slow him down.

On the bottom level, Marc lowered the stairs and we all descended to the rocky ground below. I could tell that we were in Chopville, but I wasn't sure how I could tell it. I had lost track of time since we had left our old base but it was obviously night time now, and given how much we had done and the hours it would have taken to get back here, it had to have been a good twelve hours ago. We had to stand some distance apart as there were no stones big enough for us all to stand upon. All we could do was stand there and wait for Marc to come down and do what needed to be done. As I stood there, my heart was racing, not just because we were in for another magical annihilation—the very last one that would ever be—but because now that it had come to it, I was nervous. What if the rightness we had all felt had deceived us? What if it didn't work? I didn't believe that would be the case, but the doubt was impossible to quell entirely.

Marc finally came down the stairs, levitating some things behind him. Tommy was first, still unconscious as he floated along behind Marc; the storage locker was second, in which the rest of our friends were still being stored; and finally, the antimagic device he had created, the one holding all the remaining antimagic in the world. He stepped off the stairs, then made the entire jet vanish into thin air. He lowered Tommy and the storage locker onto nearby rocks, and then sat himself down on his rock, holding the Hero Crystal in one hand and the antimagic store in the other.

"Do you know what you're doing, Marc?" James called to him from where he stood.

"Yeah," Marc called back, "at least, I think so. Do you guys think I should be holding the Hero Crystal when I blast it or not?"

"Yeah, hold it," Amelia called back. "You ought to have greater control over the will of it if you do. The blast should do more or less what you're thinking about when you pull the trigger. Just focus on fixing the world, and nobody else distract him while he does it."

"Okay, in that case, give me a few minutes to organise my thoughts before I do it," he said. "I'll let you know when I'm about to, okay?"

"Okay," we all replied.

Then silence and stillness fell among the group. I tried not to make a sound as I shifted my weight from foot to foot, full of anxiety for what was about to happen. After a minute of it, I reminded myself that there was a slim chance that my own thoughts might have an impact on what happened, given how close I was to the epicentre of the blast when it happened. That probably wasn't the case, but I thought I had better fill my mind with positive things, just in case.

I therefore focussed on what I imagined the best possible outcome of this to be: everything back to how it had been prior to the very first antimagic annihilation, the one that had taken place within our base the previous day. That had been tiny, and it wouldn't make much of a difference now if that hadn't happened, but it seemed simplest to go back to the earliest possible moment before magic became destabilised. I then revised it to slightly earlier: the moment before we had gone in the Time Box and begun to experiment with magic particles. Reset the world to that moment, like a system restore on a computer, but with a few exceptions: we should still remember all the things that had happened in the intervening time—Lucien needed to remain dead, and magic needed to remain gone from the world.

"Okay, I'm ready," Marc called. "I'm not going to count down, but I'm going to do it in about ten seconds, so prepare yourselves and don't say or do anything."

Nobody answered—good, I thought. Then I quickly recalled the things I had been thinking a moment earlier, and waited. Seconds ticked by, and then came the annihilation. It was as the others had been, complete with the thunderclap and the feeling of the world shifting beneath, around and even through me. A moment later, it had ended, and I blinked in surprise. I was still human and felt pretty much normal, which was a good start. In fact, I felt *too* normal…what was that about? I did feel like I had somehow moved since a moment ago, but I couldn't have said why that was. Then I noticed the lights, and blinked again…

I knew where I was—*exactly* where I was. The grass beneath my feet told me that I was standing in Hamster's Stretch Reserve. It was still night time, so there wasn't a lot to see, except for the street lights in the distance which illuminated the Main Street Bridge and the Jade River beneath it. The last time I had seen it, the Main Street Bridge had been smashed into the river by a rogue dragon's tail, but it looked perfectly fine now. The air was chilly, but I was wearing the same clothes I had been wearing when I first left the base so I wasn't too cold.

I looked around me, and they were all there: Peter and James on either side of me, and the full circle of the army that had taken on Lucien in the positions they had been in at the start of the battle. Sophie was missing and I was disappointed that the blast hadn't brought her back to life, but not altogether surprised. Then came the final kicker: The dome that Lucien had hidden himself within at the beginning of the battle was still there, dark and ominous.

"Did you guys just turn back time or something?" Harry called from a way around the circle. "What's going on?"

"Why is the dome still there?" Peter asked. "Marc, what's this about? Where are you?"

"I'm here," Marc called from the other side of the circle, "and it's fine. I'm pretty sure the dome is empty. It wouldn't have brought anyone back to life, not even Lucien. You guys can probably shoot at that thing to destroy it."

"Guys, I get that it's night time, but how can you see anything when it's so dark out here?" James called, staring around himself but apparently seeing nothing.

My heart sank when I realised what that could mean. "Er—James, can you see the street lights on Main Street?" I asked him.

"What street lights?"

"Oh crap," Peter said as he and I hurried over to James. He turned his head to face us, and there was just enough light for me to see the empty sockets where his eyes had been. Of course; Marc had repaired his eyes after magic had gone crazy, while Lucien had damaged them beforehand. James had clearly made a sacrifice of his own, without meaning to, and he hadn't even realised it yet. What were the words he had used earlier? This would be *his* new normal.

But I couldn't be too unhappy about it. It was too early to be completely certain, but it felt right to me—everything felt right to me. Marc had succeeded in repairing the world. He had made the sacrifice, and now we would all be able to go on living normal lives. Normal…the word made me recall what I had been thinking earlier, and now I understood why I felt *too* normal. I had lost the ability to sense the in-between. In less than two weeks I was going to die, but now I could no longer be sure that I would get stuck in the in-between. What was going to happen to me now?

Chapter 37: Last Days

So once again, as it had been before the Sorcerers had come to town, Chopville had become just another insignificant grain of sand on the beach of life. Granted, there had been so much chaos going on all over the world in the days following Lucien's downfall. In some places, like Australia, the Hammerhearts had managed to cling to power in a rather unusual way: by re-establishing the form of government that had existed prior to the global coup, though with themselves remaining in positions of power. The same struggle was happening all over the world with varying results, but I made no effort to keep up with it. We were all resigned to the fact that the world map was going to look very different by the end of the year, and even more so by the end of next year, and there would probably be further wars before it all settled down.

The end result of all of this was that it had become a case of every man, woman and teenager for himself. Nobody was coming to help us. Nobody knew nor cared, what was going on here in Chopville except for those of us who were stuck here. And what was going on was that many of the town's residents had been rendered homeless; and that included, but was not limited to, the entire Woodward Army. Since we had returned to town, we had been directed to the only space capable of holding the many homeless: Chopville Secondary School. It was amazing how often in this war we had found ourselves returning to this place.

The mystery of what Frederic had been doing on the morning before the universe went toes-up was solved when we realised we were all totally exhausted and had nowhere to go. Anticipating the possibility that we may defeat Lucien, and that there may be no magic left in the world when it happened, he had taken the opportunity to use it while we still had it and had rebuilt both the primary and secondary schools from scratch. If I'd known what he was doing at the time, I would have said that he had his priorities scrambled up, but now I understood why he had done it. Life was going to have to return to normal eventually, or as close to normal as possible in light of all that had happened, and a good place to start that normalisation was the place where we should have been spending most of the year.

And he'd done a really good job of it as well. Not one to put in a half-arsed job, he had rebuilt it as it had been before the Hammerhearts had used it as a battle zone on numerous occasions, only he had made it brand-new, putting in all the repairs it had needed and even redoing the materials and furnishings in such a way that it now felt like a rich kids' school. He confided in us that before we had returned, he had feared that the battle with Lucien might have ended up destroying his good work anyway, but his worries had turned out to be needless. He probably hadn't intended that the school would be used as a sort of refugee centre in the aftermath of the war, but as there was nowhere else in town that could do it as well as the school, this was where we had lived for the last few days.

It hadn't been used just as a refugee centre either. When we got there, we found that the rest of our army, those who hadn't been in the fight against Lucien, had been based there throughout. They had all gone through the rollercoaster of magic in their own way, not having a clue what any of it meant, but thankfully not doing anything stupid in response to it. They had their own stories to tell of their experiences, and in the days since the battle, there had been plenty of opportunities to listen to them as well as to tell them about how the battle had gone down.

It had been fine enough, but none of us wanted this to be a long-term solution; and as it became increasingly clear that there was no point waiting for the authorities to step in and fix things for us (ha ha, what authorities?), we decided it was time to take matters into our own hands. So early on the morning of Saturday, September 11, a large group of us left the school grounds, armed with every useable weapon we could find and dearly hoping that we wouldn't need to use them.

Although some of us still carried a few formerly magical weapons for sentimental reasons, most of those devices had been discarded as the useless pieces of junk they now were. The group was an alliance of five families, and it was led by those old-time soldiers themselves—Dad and Charlie. Greg Pont, who had thankfully been healed of his battle injuries by Amelia prior to the use of antimagic, would be third in command, and they were backed up by me, Peter, Felicity, Harry, Simon, Misty, Michelle, Natalie and Rebecca. The aim of this morning's mission: take back our houses from the Hammerhearts who had been squatting in them for the last three months or so.

We had the makings of a plan: to get the Hammerhearts out, and contact Frederic on a walky-talky to let him know that we had cleared the house; he would then escort someone to the house, who would then guard it while we moved on to the next house—and if all went well, by the time the sun came up on that morning, the four houses in question would be in the hands of their rightful owners. I say four houses, even though there were five families, because there was no question of Natalie and Rebecca living alone in their big house. The Fletchers and Ponts had done a deal where the Ponts would take the two Fletcher girls in, and in return, they would all live in that large house on Greenly Street where the Fletchers had lived prior to becoming Sorcerers.

None of us were expecting the whole thing to go as smoothly as that. We were armed and ready to fight, but none of us actually wanted to, because any fight was likely to do major damage to the houses we were going to such lengths to reclaim. Then there was the very real threat of the Hammerhearts employing a scorched-earth policy if we actually *did* manage to force them from the properties, which in this case would not be a metaphor.

First on the list were the Playman and Thomas houses, which we would do at the same time because we weren't sure if the Hammerhearts occupying them had kept the underground tunnel hidden in the cupboards under the stairs in each house or not. Hilda and Violet would occupy them after we had won them back, and they would be assisted by Jessica, who would have the job of patrolling in both houses until we got back. Then we would head down to Flint Street, behind the school grounds, and evict whoever was in the Maivis residence, and Harry and Simon's grandparents would hold the place until the two sets of twins returned from the Fletcher house.

"Is everyone ready?" Dad hissed to all of us, following along Lopher Lane in a disorganised straggle. "Ready for anything?"

There were various noises of ascent from the group, which gave me no comfort at all. There was so little strategy going on here—so little discipline to speak of—that it was hard to see us getting out of this morning in one piece. If I were watching other people do this, I would fully expect them to walk right into an ambush and get cut down to the very last man. That probably wouldn't happen today, though, for the same reason that we were doing this in the first place: there was no law enforcement to intervene. The Hammerhearts out here were just as alone as we were; the only difference was, they may or may not have figured that out yet.

Fortunately, when we actually reached the houses, Dad and Charlie began organising us in such a way that showed they must have given thought to it earlier. The two sets of twins, along with Peter and Rebecca, jumped the fences and covered the two back yards, all of them keeping hidden and only required to take action if the residents attempted to escape that way. The rest of us were out the front and would provide the main thrust of the assault, but the plan first called for us to attempt the eviction without violence altogether.

While Charlie led Greg and Felicity against the Thomas residence, Natalie and I followed Dad up to the door of the old Playman house and rang the doorbell before taking a step back, waiting for someone to answer. The three of us didn't look very threatening on the face of it, but that would change very quickly once someone noticed that we all had rifles strapped over our backs, not to mention the grenades we all held. The aim was to appear non-threatening unless or until it became necessary to be threatening, in which case we shouldn't hesitate to reveal the full extent of our arms.

Dad had to ring the bell a second time and then knock loudly on the door, but finally, someone opened it. The man looked about forty and had clearly been asleep; he blinked a few times, trying to focus on Dad, and apparently not seeing either me or Natalie further back on the porch.

"What's this?" he said blearily. "Who are you?"

"Sorry to wake you so early," Dad said in a business-like tone, "but this is an eviction. You were given access to live in this house by an authority which no longer exists. It is my duty this morning to clear this property so that it can be reclaimed by its legal owners. You will need to pack your things and leave immediately. Do you understand this?"

"Immediately?" the man repeated, alarmed. He had roused himself quickly as Dad spoke, but now he looked shocked. "I expected this and was planning to move out soon, but I can't just go right now. What about all my stuff? My furniture?"

That took me by surprise. He had been planning to move out? Maybe it hadn't been necessary to do this after all; maybe these Hammerhearts were less confrontational than we assumed them to be. Dad, however, didn't miss a beat.

"The local high school is offering their facilities to anyone made homeless by recent events. You will be able to stay there while you look for alternative accommodation, and this includes storage for your furniture. You will be able to organise for it to be picked up soon, but in the meantime, you have ten minutes to pack anything majorly important to you before you must leave the premises."

Wow—even I thought that was pretty harsh. Now that I was looking at the man, I had to make an effort to remind myself that he was a Hammerheart, and had been an enemy during the war. Granted, the war was now over, but for us, it wasn't really over until this guy was out of our house. Still, we had dragged him out of bed and were now about to drag him out of the house where he had been living for three months. He was still in his pyjamas and his hair was all messed up; were we going to give him a chance to get dressed or anything?

Echoing my thoughts, the man licked his lips and said, "Well—I don't want any trouble, so okay, but can I at least get dressed and get my family ready before we're turned out?"

Dad's expression didn't soften; I understood why it was necessary for him to act like a hard-arse, but it was still a little shocking to see. "You may," he said, "but that'll only give you an extra five minutes. Now, you need to open the door so that one of us can supervise you while you pack. It's just a precautionary measure and not meant to be an invasion of your privacy, but it could be dangerous for others if you think of calling in help."

The man just shrugged. "Help? There's no help to be had, as far as I know, but if you need me to open the door for you…"

He left the sentence hanging, but Dad merely shrugged as well. "That would be your choice. Not a very smart one, of course; we're perfectly capable of entering the house without you unlocking the door, but it would be better for all of us if it didn't come to that. You wouldn't want to frighten your family, would you?"

The Hammerheart blanched at those words. He looked more closely at Dad, finally noticing that he had a weapon on his back, poking over his shoulder. He hurriedly unlocked and pushed open the screen door, and Dad caught it and stepped in after him. The two of them disappeared into the darkness, leaving Natalie and me there alone.

As far as I could recall, it was the first time the two of us had been alone since I had brought her back into the base. So much had happened since then, but I was suddenly hyper-aware of all that had happened between us prior to my death and resurrection. That thought reminded me that I probably only had four days left to live, and any discomfort I had regarding Natalie evaporated instantly. I glanced sideways at her, but she was (deliberately, I thought) avoiding looking at me. I sighed internally; closure was going to be much more important for her than it was for me, but I couldn't help her get it unless she was willing to talk to me.

Redirecting my attention elsewhere, I looked to my other side. Over on the neighbouring lawn, Greg and Felicity had taken up much the same positions as Natalie and me, and Charlie had disappeared into the house. Apparently, they hadn't had any trouble either, and I supposed I shouldn't have been surprised. We were armed with non-magical weapons—the same weapons which Frederic had created prior to our battle with Lucien—because although they had been created by magic, they didn't require any magic to function, which meant we could still use them. The idea that any Hammerhearts would have any non-magical weapons was laughable—most of them had become so complacent that the most dangerous non-magical thing they were likely to have would be a kitchen knife. Even if these ones had possession of those guns with the formerly magical bullets, they would know—the moment they initiated a confrontation—that we had the superior firepower.

About fifteen minutes later, I saw movement beyond the screen door. Natalie and I faded off to either side of the door, me stepping into the garden and Natalie stepping in front of the window, to make way as Dad led the Hammerheart, his wife and two children from the house. All of them were dressed now and the kids, both of whom looked under ten, looked a bit scared, while the wife looked surly and the man resigned. When they were on the porch, Dad remained in the doorway and looked out at them.

"Do the four of you know where the school is?" he asked them.

The man nodded and said, "Mate, I moved to this town to work at that shithole before it was levelled by those Sorcerers."

"Good," Dad said, not reacting at all to the bitterness in the Hammerheart's voice when he uttered the word 'Sorcerers'. "Go there and one of those Sorcerers, Frederic Woodward, will see that you're made comfortable and you will be able to look for alternative accommodation. The rest of your belongings will be sent over there in the next few days."

"Come on, everyone," the Hammerheart said, turning his back on Dad, and ignoring me and Natalie completely, "time to go for a bit of a walk. After we get there, we can go into town to get some breakfast. How does that sound?"

And off the four of them went, out onto the sidewalk and down towards Main Street. Dad waited till they were out of earshot before speaking to us.

"Natalie, can you go over and check how they're doing next door? John, can you come inside and check what—if anything—they have done with the tunnel under the stairs?"

We both did as we were told, while he busied himself making radio contact with Frederic Woodward to let him know that the first stage of the operation was complete. It felt so strange walking through this house now—my childhood abode, and yet not my childhood abode. Most of the personal effects seemed to have been taken away with the family but the unfamiliar furniture was honestly jarring; it just didn't seem right in this house.

Trying to ignore the wrongness of it all, I went to the cupboard and had a look inside. It wasn't how I remembered it: coats were hanging above and a shoe rack lay empty on the floor. Where the tunnel had begun was completely blocked off by a wall which, when I tapped on it, was revealed to be quite thin and would probably be easy enough to remove once we got around to it.

I went back to report this to Dad, by which time, the family that had been living next door were walking away down the street as well; and Greg, Felicity and Charlie were holding down the Thomas residence. Dad told me to go around the back and advise all those stationed around the two houses that the first part of the job was done, and that until Jessica arrived with Hilda and Violet, their job would be to look outward rather than inward just in case any Hammerhearts tried to take the houses back.

That didn't happen, but what *did* happen was that the police came roaring up the street to confront us, taking us all rather by surprise. The general disorder of the place had made us honestly believe that the police were either utterly overwhelmed to help us or that there simply weren't any police in town. The Hammerhearts reported that they had been evicted by someone with a gun, but there were no guns to be found on any of us when the police arrived—Dad had made me give them all to the folks around the back, which hadn't made sense to me at the time, but which had turned out to be a stroke of brilliance. To top it off, Dad and Charlie had promptly shown the cops the deeds to each of the houses, which they had brought along in case it was necessary to prove to the Hammerhearts that they weren't the lawful owners of the property. The end result was that the police left in the firm belief that the Hammerhearts had been squatters, and we were free to live here again.

And yet, I had noticed something strange about the call to the police which none of the others apparently had. When we met up with the rest of the crew again, ready to head back over the river to the Maivis residence, Felicity had told us that the tunnel had been blocked in at their end as well—much the same way it had been blocked in at our end. That suggested that the two families were each concerned enough for their privacy to go to the effort, and yet the similar way in which they had done it suggested a bit of coordination in the effort.

Finally, even though they had left within a few minutes of each other, the police were called to come to both houses—not one squad for each house, but one squad for both houses. I didn't think the police could have coordinated that quickly, which meant that the Hammerhearts must have done it. All this led me to one conclusion: There was something in the houses that both of them wanted, but didn't dare remove in front of Dad and Charlie. I was rather interested to know what we might find when we knocked out those boards blocking off the tunnel...

When Jessica finally arrived, she was followed by not just Hilda and Violet, but by Mum and Marge as well. I had thought those two were going into town to do some shopping, as we were returning to our home with barely more than the clothes on our backs. The vast majority of our possessions had been removed from these houses months earlier when we had moved full-time to the Woodward Base, and there they had remained when Hall had infiltrated and destroyed the place. When I had time to think about it, though, I supposed it made sense: For at least a few days, we would be living on what the Hammerhearts had left behind, so we might as well prioritise those things which we didn't already have.

We left them to it, gathering up our army and heading off to perform the same procedure at the Maivis house. However, it turned out not to be necessary at all there. The house was locked up and abandoned, and when we got inside (thanks to a spare key which in all the months since hadn't been found by anyone), we found it to be empty. There was a fine layer of dust on some of the surfaces, but not as if it had stood empty for a long time. Felicity, the only one of us to have come within viewing distance of the Maivis house during the assault on the school three weeks ago, despite my group having been further up on Flint Street, told us that there had been a car in the driveway on that day. The most likely conclusion we drew was that unlike the Hammerhearts on Lopher Lane, these ones *had* already moved out when their jobs at the school became redundant.

Things went much less smoothly at the Fletcher residence. This was one of the grand estates of Chopville, and it had been gifted to a Hammerheart of high importance—not a Level 2, I felt sure, but one who must be close to promotion, and who was basically responsible for

managing the on-ground operations in the area. He had not become
redundant when the school base had been shut down, nor did he believe
he was redundant now, as he was employed by the Shire Council rather
than the Hammerhearts themselves. He spoke to us through the intercom
but refused to show himself, preferring to call the police rather than give
us a chance to force entry.

The police who came out were locals, and at least one of them
recognised Natalie and Rebecca as Brian Fletcher's daughters, and
everyone who had been in Chopville for at least a year knew that Brian
Fletcher lived in one of the big houses on Greenly Street. Unfortunately,
that was where the good luck ended, for Brian wasn't here as part of the
raiding party. When Dad told them that Brian and his wife were killed a
week and a half ago by Lucien, he earned some sympathy from the
police, but it ended up backfiring on us. We were told that we couldn't be
let into the house until the Fletchers' estate was dispersed according to
the wishes laid out in Brian's last will and testament, and until then, the
house would have to remain shut. The only good thing was that at least
they kicked the Hammerhearts out of the house as well before locking it
up.

* * *

The rest of that weekend was spent assisting other displaced peoples
to either reclaim their old homes or find new ones. The Woodwards had
taken Marc's old house, with his blessing, and he had gone to live there
as well. It meant that Amelia had to share a bedroom with her
grandmother, but that was a small price to pay. (I might have suggested
she and Marc share his room, as they had done numerous times without
the parental supervision, but Frederic obviously wasn't having that.) That
house had become a lot smaller somehow, now that the hidden quarters
were no longer possible to open, but it would do for the time being.

Tommy and his parents were able to reclaim their old place on Rail
Street as well, as were Katie, Erica, Liam and Darcy. The families of
Serena, Kylie, Sophie and several others who had died, who had been
taken into the Woodward Army at the same time, were also assisted to
find homes, though in the case of Serena's parents, they made it quite
clear they would be moving away from Chopville at their earliest
convenience. They weren't the only ones either: Underwood and
Siobhan, neither of whom had any particular reason to stay, had left
Chopville less than twenty-four hours after the battle against Lucien had
concluded. Their aim had been to get back to England, and I received a
text message from Underwood on Sunday night saying that after a few
days stuck in Melbourne due to there being almost no flights out of the
airport (they had been suspended for several days prior to the battle, and
it took a while to get them going again), they had finally touched down

in London. Siobhan sent us no messages, and I doubted that we would be hearing from her ever again.

The Ponts and Fletchers turned out to be the last ones from the Woodward Army left at the school, and now that they were surrounded by an albeit dwindling number of Hammerhearts as they too sought out alternate arrangements, they were desperate for somewhere to go. None of us had any room for them, though, and it was only after pleas to Frederic that he was able to persuade Kylie's family—who incidentally lived next door to the old Fletcher place—to take them in. The house wasn't quite as grand as the Fletchers' house, but the Cunkourds were well-off in their own right and they had the room, even if it meant Natalie, Rebecca and Jason all had to share the bedroom that had once belonged to Kylie. None of them were particularly happy about that for several reasons, but for the time being, they had to lump it.

Meanwhile, in the Playman and Thomas residence, Peter and I found ourselves sharing a room again. I had expected that one of us would have moved into Nicole's old room (not me, of course, since unlike Peter, I had seen her die there), but before we could lay any claim to it, the Thomases sprang into action. Felicity and Jessica no longer wished to share a room, especially since six months from now there would be a baby in there as well. Marge and Charlie didn't want her moving next door, so it was Felicity who ended up in Nicole's old room. James got his old room back; he had requested to move to Nicole's room as well, so that the three of us could be closer, but Marge and Charlie wanted him to stay close to them so they could keep an eye on him—not because they thought he would get up to trouble, but because they were worried about what trouble he may do to himself as he adjusted to his new blindness.

The parentals in both families were consumed with getting the Hammerheart property out of the houses and replacing it with new (or at least newish) stuff that we could call our own. Fortunately, money wasn't a problem for two reasons, both of them highly unexpected. It turned out that under Arnold Hammerson, Hall had confiscated all assets belonging to the Playmans and Thomases, including bank accounts, shares, superannuation, and of course, the houses themselves. This deed was reversed by Lucien when he had put influential charms on the parentals to join him, wanting them to be self-sufficient when he released them from the Big Room—and apparently, he hadn't thought to rereverse it when they had defected again.

The second reason was the loot which, as I had anticipated, we found when we reopened the tunnel between the two houses. It was full almost to bursting with boxes upon boxes, and Peter, James, Felicity and I were tasked with sorting through them and categorising what we found. The main things we found were fine art, fine wine, jewellery, a handful of bars of gold bullion, and piles and piles of cash in both Australian and American dollars. The parentals reckoned that the two families that had lived here had been doing a bit of embezzling, as it seemed unlikely that the Hammerhearts would have asked them to store such treasures here when their network contained countless locations far more suitable.

After a discussion between the adults, some of it heated, and all comments made by anyone under eighteen dutifully ignored, it was agreed that we would have to notify the police of the discovery. The practical truth was that some of this stuff was worth nothing to us unless we could sell it, and the moment we tried to sell it, the police would be all over us as criminals. This was particularly true of the art. So on the Monday, we were set to the task of going through the boxes again, sorting those we would present to the police from those which we would keep for ourselves. Naturally we would be keeping some of the treasure for ourselves—we never professed to be saints.

We were instructed to pack the boxes up as close to how we had found them as possible, and then it was time to get some outside assistance. Out of all our friends, Tommy was the least well-off, so he was the one we called. His parents agreed to the deal whereby if they stored the treasure we intended to keep while we dealt with the police (who would probably do a search of the house to see if there was anything else hidden somewhere), they would get to keep one of the boxes stuffed with cash and another of the boxes stuffed with jewellery.

The whole thing went off as close to perfectly as possible. The police were impressed that we had done the honest thing, confirming that some of the artwork had indeed been reported as stolen; and as expected, they performed a sweep of the two houses, finding nothing else that had been reported stolen, save for the furnishings which we had still not yet returned to the squatters. The part we hadn't anticipated was that over the following days, the police would perform searches of all the other properties which had housed Hammerhearts in the last few months. By the time they got around to searching Tommy's place, however, we had already returned the treasures back to our houses, and Tommy's parents had put their share into storage for safekeeping.

By the time all this had been taken care of, at least as far as it concerned the Playmans, it was already Tuesday, the fourteenth of September, 2010. Two weeks ago today, I had been blown to pieces in an ill-fated attempt to save hundreds of lives from a bra bomb. Two weeks was the expected time period I would have to live my second chance. As James reminded me, I had actually been resurrected twenty-four hours later, so I probably still had another full day; but as I reminded him, I had spent time in the Time Box since then, and who could say if that would shorten my life expectancy.

The whole thing was quite depressing, and as the day turned out to be the finest we'd had in quite some time, Peter and James decided to take me out for a bit of fun around town. It had started with James asking me over breakfast that morning, in such a way that the adults in the room weren't able to gage the true context, "Hey John, if there was one thing you wish you could do before you die, what do you think it would be?"

Across the table, Peter had just about had a choking fit, while I took the question as seriously as I could. The first answer that had sprung to my mind, knowing how close my death was, was 'have sex one more time', but I wasn't about to say that in front of Mum and Hilda—even Dad wasn't quite ready to hear that. Then, as I took a few more seconds to think about it, I found that in actual fact, sex wasn't on my to-do list at all. My last six months had been highly sexually active for a fourteen-year old, so I couldn't say that I had really gone without. On top of that, since my last time had been with Stella shortly before she had died, it felt appropriate that it should go on being my last time.

Instead, I had looked out the window and said, "Jump in the river like we used to do."

Peter and James grinned at each other, but to my right, Dad frowned. "I imagine there were times when you would have wondered if you'd get to do that again, John, but it's not like you're gonna drop dead tomorrow or anything."

To say the moment was uncomfortable would be a major understatement. I had shrugged as nonchalantly as possible and taken a mouthful of toast, and then fortunately, Jessica—who had dropped in to have breakfast with us along with James after having had some sort of argument with Marge over something or other—had come to the rescue with a typically inappropriate remark about death. Hilda had then piled on with an even more inappropriate remark about her own death, leaving me to reflect on what a close shave that had been.

I'd had more than one practically sleepless night since my resurrection regarding how I was going to handle my last days with those who didn't know what I had sacrificed along the way to victory. If I told them that I was going to die, I would spend my final days with them surrounded by their grief, but at least they would have a chance to say goodbye. If I didn't tell them ahead of my death, they would have to go through the grief without ever having had a chance to say goodbye, but at least I would be gone for it. I had chosen the coward's way out, not wanting to have to deal with it, wanting my last days to be enjoyable (as much as possible, anyway) and not surrounded by whatever grief there would be.

I still didn't know if I was making the right decision. Their grief may seem worse to them given that we had just survived the war, only for me to go and die of whatever was going to happen to me. On the other hand, it would also seem worse to them if they were to learn that it wasn't just my life that I had lost but a portion of my soul as well. Finally, there was a small chance that further down the track, they would cop the double whammy. Say Peter or James, or one of the other handful of people who knew the truth, let something slip to someone, who let it slip to someone else…and then before you knew it, everyone knew. My family would cop a second round of grief after they had already come to terms with the first; and quite possibly some betrayal as well, if it were learnt that Peter and James were in on the secret and hadn't confided it to anyone else.

While I had been processing all this internally, Peter had been hatching a plan, and when breakfast was over, he took James and me aside. "It's a pretty good day outside, wouldn't you agree, John?"

"Yeah," I said, glancing out the window, and then back at Peter. What it was outside was spring; it had been a long and seemingly endless winter, but finally it looked like it was behind us.

"Good Jade River conditions, wouldn't you say?" he went on, winking at me.

"I—er—maybe," I hedged.

James frowned. "I'm not sure if there was ever any truth in the rumours that the Jade River was enchanted to feel warmer than it should have, but if so, it'd be pretty bloody cold today. It would need to be ten degrees warmer for you to get me in there."

"That sounds like a challenge, JSandwich," Peter grinned at James, making me feel very nervous.

While most of us were just about ready to wrap James in cotton wool so that he wouldn't bump into or trip over something, Peter seemed to be going out of his way to be as insensitive as possible. James made no secret of the fact that he appreciated what Peter was doing, but pushing him off one of those bridges in the park had to be taking it too far. Even if James could guess when he was about to hit the water, how was he going to know which way to swim to get back to the bank? The whole thing seemed ridiculously and unnecessarily dangerous to me, which was probably why, at Peter's last words, James quickly changed his tune.

"Maybe it is a challenge, grasshopper. If I recall correctly, it is usually we who, quote unquote, 'get' you in there."

"You guys are nuts," I laughed in spite of myself. "don't be too surprised if you're the only one walking home today, Pete."

So the three of us did the dumbest thing possible on a day when I was due to die sometime in the next thirty-six hours, give or take. We headed off to Hamster's Stretch Reserve with our swimming gear to jump off bridges into the river. Of the three of us who left the house that morning, five would return later in the day, due to Peter calling Harry and Simon and asking them if they wanted to come out, and them being happy to do so. They were in the dark about my impending doom of course, but it didn't matter—just having them here, the five of us together, the old crew, was good enough for me. As far as they were concerned, we were just doing what we could to get back to normal, and to help James feel as normal as possible. Between the four of us, it turned out that there was no serious danger for James; and whatever perceived danger there was, he seemed to relish.

The only thing that got me down that day, as it had done over the last week or so, was the comparatively little time I was spending with other people I cared about—namely Marc, Natalie and Amelia. They weren't the only ones I missed, but they were the ones I missed the most, mainly because they three knew what would soon be happening to me. I had seen a bit of Natalie in the two days leading up to the raids on our houses, but I'd heard nothing from her since Saturday, and as neither Felicity nor Jessica had wanted to come out today, she too had begged off. Amelia had also begged off, claiming to be busy with her father, while Marc's phone had been turned off altogether. Marc had spoken very little to any of us since the battle with Lucien, and as far as I knew, hadn't been around anyone other than those he had now lived with since Saturday. I supposed he was struggling with his own issues after having surrendered the Hero Crystal, but it still hurt that he couldn't be with me at the end.

I went to bed that night feeling satisfied, because I now knew it was going to be either tonight or tomorrow that something would happen to take me. As I lay in bed, however, a new thought hit me. What if whatever it was, took out others around me? Daniel had once said, of this kind of death, that it could be anything to cause it, even something as unlikely as a car falling out of the sky. That wasn't going to happen now that there was no magic in the world, of course, but that meant that unless it was something targeted at me, it could put others around me in danger. If I walked across the Main Street Bridge tomorrow and it collapsed beneath me, I had better hope there was no one else on the bridge at the time or we would all be riding the rollercoaster together.

It took some time to get to sleep that night, and it was a fitful sleep when it came, full of half-forgotten dreams that I felt sure had included my mother in some form, but which I couldn't remember when I woke up. If that was her telling me that it was time for me to join her, I got the point. As a result, I was very groggy the next day at breakfast, which wasn't going to serve me well. Blissfully unaware of what was really going on in the world, Mum was organising some make-up schoolwork for us to do today, as we had apparently been on holidays quite long enough. She and Marge would also be making phone calls through the day to hopefully organise getting Chopville High back up and running.

It quickly became apparent that whatever was going to happen to me, it was going to happen here at home. The weather had turned overnight and it was raining outside, and Hilda and Violet were tasked with supervising us while we worked on exercises which I felt sure were left over from a few months ago when we had been locked in the Woodward Base. Even James had to study, because apparently having your eyes ripped out less than two weeks ago was no excuse. Charlie had bought a new computer for James specifically so that he could study (no doubt

Marge's nagging had been behind it), and Peter and I had figured out how to get a basic text-to-speech program running on it.

The day was a total drag, and torturously so for us boys, knowing what was coming and not knowing when or in what form. It was especially so after lunch, for that was when we officially passed the two-week mark, in minute-by-minute terms anyway. I knew that William, Carl and Lisa had met their final ends earlier than this point, but Daniel had met his roughly twelve hours later, so I wasn't about to start thinking that this was going to be different. And yet, as dinner time approached, James and Peter's dispositions seemed to be improving. In spite of all we knew about the in-between, those two idiots were getting their hopes up. It was going to devastate them when they came crashing down again, so after all the others had gone downstairs, I stopped the two of them.

"You guys do realise it's going to happen tonight," I hissed at them, "and if not tonight, very early tomorrow morning. It can't possibly be any later than midday tomorrow."

"That's true, but John," James said earnestly, "it's starting to occur to me that this really *might* be different."

I rolled my eyes at him, and then remembering that he couldn't see the gesture, said, "Okay, I know there's no magic in the world, so it's easy to think things have changed—"

"Like the fact that you can't get into the in-between anymore," Peter finished the sentence for me, though not the way I'd been planning to end it.

"It doesn't change the fact that part of my soul is gone. In fact, it dooms me even more. Who knows; maybe I *will* go on to whatever afterlife most people get, only I'll end up looking like Voldemort did in King's Cross."

"Oh John, that's not going to happen to you until Harry figures out where your horcruxes are," Peter quipped. "Look, you must have already come to terms with all of this yourself, right? You know where you're going, even if you don't know how you're getting there, so you worry about that and leave me and James to get our hopes up. That's just our way of dealing, and when whatever happens, happens, and we'll deal with that too."

"He's right," James agreed. "I'm no philosopher or anything, but I imagine it's just part of the human condition to get our hopes up. I don't see how it'll make things worse later, but it sure helps us in the present. Come on; let's get down to dinner before they think I've gotten lost in the bathroom again."

"What do you mean 'again'?"

Nothing happened to me over dinner. I didn't drown in my glass of coke. I didn't have a heart attack from Mum's over-salted chips. I didn't fall backwards off my chair and hit my head on the wall behind me. Afterwards, Peter, James and I had a four-way chess match with Dad, with Charlie carefully describing the board to James so that he could participate; and although my king got killed pretty badly, I certainly didn't. When it was over and Dad had wiped the board with us, we went upstairs and coached James through a racing game on his new computer. It was an unmitigated disaster for him, and I saw cars wrecked in ways I would never have visualised before, but the death and destruction remained confined to the inside of the computer. At the end of it all, I made it to my bed without anything bad or even remotely painful happening to me all day.

And the good luck continued when miraculously, I woke up the following morning. It was now the sixteenth of September, and I had been brought back to life fifteen days ago. The window of misfortune was rapidly closing, but as breakfast wore on and we listened to what Mum and Dad were telling us about what was going to be happening today, I found my own hopes beginning to rise in spite of myself. I reasoned that my death might not happen unless I started getting my hopes up, and then it would hit me when it would hurt the most, just so that the universe could give me the finger on my way out. And yet that couldn't actually be a thing, for Lisa had sensed her death approaching, and she had even chosen when it would happen to some extent—she could have stayed still for those Hammerhearts and been killed by them in a prison cell later that day.

I had to admit, James had been right. Hope clearly was part of the human condition, for as we went upstairs to continue studying, while Dad and Charlie busied themselves with moving a whole lot of Hammerheart furniture to the moving van that had just rocked up outside, I found hope beginning to rise unbidden inside me. If I did last the day, I may just wake up tomorrow morning, and if I did, I would make it to my fifteenth birthday after all.

"Hey John," Jessica said to me as I reached the top of the stairs, "this may sound a bit strange, but you may need to make some phone calls later today."

"Okay," I said, feeling my spirits lift as I thought I knew what she was going to say. "Er—who would I be calling? And why?"

"I'm not sure why," she said, "but Marc, Natalie, Amelia and Rebecca; they've all contacted me this morning and last night asking after you."

"That's strange, Erica sent me a message asking after you as well, John," James said in a far-too-innocent voice.

"What have you been up to, John?" Peter asked, winking at me.

I sighed. "I guess I'll call them all tonight and ask what's up. I doubt I'll get a chance sooner than that."

Not that I really expected I would be around by then, but just in case…

"Your doubt is justified, young man," Mum said, entering the room and having heard my last words. "You kids have a lot to do today, and the only chance you have of getting through it all is if you get cracking."

"If we don't get through it, we'll have to finish it tomorrow," Peter said, "but if we *do* finish it, you'll have more for us tomorrow. Is my scornful tone *also* justified, Mum?"

"It is," she said sweetly.

And so it was. The hours dragged on, through lunch and all the way to dinner, and nothing whatsoever happened to me. At last, I had to resign myself to the fact that my death seemed to be postponed. It was a very strange feeling. On the one hand, my second chance seemed to have been turned into a third chance, and I had even more time than I had bargained for. On the other hand, I had already come to terms with my death, and if it were to happen in the next few days, it was going to be even more disappointing than it would have been otherwise. As I ate dinner that night, thinking about the phone calls I would have to make shortly, I made up my mind how I was going to deal with it. Firstly, it didn't matter how disappointing or not my death was going to be—I would be dead, so why should I care? Secondly, as I had done two days earlier, I should treat every day as though it may be my last. If anything was going to give me a feeling of freedom going forward, that would be it.

Chapter 38: Looking to the Future

It turned out that there was some method in the madness of Mum and Marge. Apparently their true intent through all of this was to prevent us from having to repeat grades nine and ten next year, something that all of us would have found intolerable. If all went well, they would get their wish, thanks to the generosity of the powers that be at Chopville High. The newly reinstated state government of Victoria forbade any schools from skipping students ahead without having said students complete some sort of exam to determine that they were ready for the next grade; and in early December of that fateful year, that was what many of us in the Young Army would be doing.

That wasn't all the school had done for us either. Partly in deference to Frederic Woodward after he had rebuilt the place, and partly in appreciation of us, as it was no secret that we had pretty much saved the world, they had done all they could to prepare us for the upcoming exam. This included both group and private tutoring in areas we needed it most, as well as counselling for those of us that needed it after all we had been through during the war—which turned out to be all of us.

We were all suffering from varying degrees of post-traumatic stress disorder as a result of the things we had seen and done. Of those closest to me, James, Natalie and Tommy were struggling the most. In Natalie's case, it was mainly the things that had happened to her in Lucien's torture chamber that she was unable to get over, particularly the guilt of her parents being killed trying to come to her rescue. That was certainly bad, although I rather thought that the things that had been done to her in there would have to be causing her problems as well.

As for James, although he had initially coped well with the loss of his eyes, things only got more difficult for him as time went on and he came across more and more things he would need to do differently, re-learn how to do, or simply never be able to do again. He had become very moody as a result, and in more recent weeks, would spend a lot of time lying on his bed, staring at nothing, thinking about whatever it was that James thought about. All of us were worried about him but Erica was perhaps the most affected, as she was also coming to terms with her own guilt over having done it to him in the first place. The fact that Lucien had been controlling her, which everyone including Erica knew and accepted, didn't change the fact that she remembered how it had been to perform that act, and how she had enjoyed doing so until a few seconds after it was over.

And Tommy? Well, he still yearned to return to Ingi in the Honnie world, something that was now next to impossible unless a Honnie came to our world and somehow found him. Tommy had enough of his own mind to understand the situation for what it was. With our victory against

Lucien, we had sacrificed all the magic in the world, so even though Marc had promised to find a way to return him to the Honnie world after Lucien was defeated, it was no longer possible for him to keep this promise. For Tommy, his torment was going to be lifelong, and none of us could think of a single thing to do to help him through it.

Still, aside from school consisting more of tutoring than traditional classes, life was returning to something resembling normality. The school was presently open only to those of us who had been preapproved to do tutoring there in preparation for the exams; it wouldn't be fully reopening again until January. This was because they had been out of action for more than six months now and the staff that had been previously employed there had moved on. The ranks of teachers, which had already been depleted through the battles that had taken place on the grounds earlier in the year, had pretty much scattered after the school had shut down.

They had managed to persuade some of the teachers to return for the following school year, and they had embarked on a campaign to hire teachers from the surrounding district and even from down in Melbourne. They had done this, incredibly, by promoting all the things that had happened to the school throughout the year, emphasising that Chopville High was now a historically important location and it would be a feather in one's cap to be able to say that one had taught there. Unfortunately, it was during this process that, less than one week before the exams were due to start, they had done something utterly unforgivable.

To explain the chain of events leading to the school's betrayal of us, one had to go back to the governmental reforms that had taken place in Australia in the aftermath of Lucien's downfall. Most countries around the world had come under the rule of tin-pot dictators in recent weeks, but few of them were stable and there were a lot of scuffles going on. Countries that had stabilised were taking advantage of the disorder to initiate border squabbles with other countries, in a lot of cases reigniting disagreements which were almost as old as God and which had previously thought to be settled.

Australia was more fortunate than many for two reasons. We didn't have any land borders to worry about, and thanks to Lucien having put forth more effort to exert control here than anywhere else, the transition back to a democratic system had been so smooth that it was just about impossible to believe that it was real. None of us had been able to explain it, until about three weeks ago when the topic had come up over dinner at the Playmans.

"Freddy has a theory," Dad had told us. "He thinks it comes down to the bogglers that the Hammersons were using. Those things were designed to make someone persuadable to the ideology that we should be ruled by those who had magic, and who weren't afraid to use it to better society. This would have been the most nonspecific way of getting people to support the Hammersons and not the Woodwards, because the Woodwards were always in favour of magic *not* being used to rule over people. It also explains why the general public would have switched so easily over to Lucien when it became obvious that he had taken the power from Hammerson.

"Anyway, now that magic is gone, for anyone following that ideology to its logical conclusion, nobody in the world is more qualified than anyone else to rule anything. It seems to explain why Hammerhearts who were boggled have mostly become libertarians, while the majority of those who chose to join the Hammerhearts before the influential charms have become socialists."

It was difficult to know how much of that extended to the general public. Public opinion, once it had settled down and the world knew what had really happened, had turned decidedly antimagic (and yes, the irony was not lost on any of us). Public opinion wasn't uniform, of course, especially as there were plenty of people who had survived the war by laying low and going with the flow, and so avoiding being subjected to any mind-altering magic. The general consensus, however, was that magic itself had been the problem, and although the Hammersons had been irresponsible with their power when they had it, Lucien had simply been a victim of it—destroyed by a power too great for one man to manage. It seemed likely that history was going to remember him as a hero, which was bittersweet for us. He wasn't a hero for the reasons they knew, but he wasn't the real villain in the piece either.

You would think that with this mindset, people would appreciate that the Woodwards had done the right thing by trying to suppress magic and prevent people from going nuts with it, but you would be wrong. On the contrary, the Woodwards and Fletchers (mainly the Woodwards) seemed to be copping the blame for what had gone down. It may not have been a foregone conclusion that this would happen, but those unboggled Hammerhearts who were presently running the government had certainly done what they could to steer public opinion in that direction, rather than have the focus put on themselves. The only good thing that could be said was that we, the Young Army, and especially Marc, seemed to be credited by most people for having ended the madness of magic, so other than a few outliers, we had escaped the worst of the crucifixion.

As for those unboggled Hammerhearts presently running the government, they were led by none other than Hank Cornish. From what I had heard, as soon as the fight with Lucien was over and Cornish had discovered that magic no longer worked at all, he had gotten in his car and driven straight to Canberra so that he could be the first to claim power, claiming it by the authority given to him by Arnold Hammerson earlier in the year. In this way, he became prime minister again, and two of the first things he did when he had consolidated his position were to permanently ban all previously registered political parties from operating in the country, and then reinstating the exact legislative and executive bodies which had existed in Canberra prior to the coup in April.

This led to a result which would, if Cornish had anticipated it, have made it highly doubtful that he would have done what he did in those first few weeks. The federal politicians scrambled to form three new political parties, one of which Cornish tried to ban, but this time, he found that he was unable to do so due to constraints he had unfortunately placed upon himself. The Australian Unity Society (AUS) was the party in power, led by Hank Cornish, which was predominantly left-wing, and was proposing policies to return Australia to greatness by way of strict control over most aspects of life. The right-wing counterpart, the one Cornish tried to ban, was the Australian Values Party (AVP) who wanted to return the country to traditional values, but which wished to do so by suppressing the rights of those who outwardly opposed traditional values.

The third party was the one created by those politicians who had been boggled during the coup. It was called the Australian Individuals Union (AIU), and although they claimed to be centrist, they were actually libertarian in policy. They opposed both of the other parties in efforts they were putting forth to control people, while agreeing with one party or the other on some specific issues. The thing which Cornish should have seen coming was that once all the politicians had joined one of these three parties, the AIU had by far the most sitting members of parliament, well over fifty percent, and more than enough to prevent Cornish from passing any new legislation.

As a result of this, Cornish was forced to call an election, one of the first post-Hammersonian elections to take place anywhere in the world. The election would take place on the 11th of December, the day after the exams would finish, and we were all quite nervous about the result. We hoped very much that the AIU would win, because out of the three, they appeared to be the most likely party to leave us alone and let us get on with our lives. Because public opinion was so decidedly antimagic, the three parties were forced to take positions on what they would do to satisfy the voters regarding this issue, and what the AUS and AVP were proposing to do was punish the Woodwards and even some of the particularly bad Hammerhearts for war crimes. The AIU didn't dare come out in favour of magic, but their position was that any retaliation against the Woodwards should be left to the police and the existing legislature, for even the Woodwards were entitled to a fair trial.

Hank Cornish was unable to hide the fact, through all this, that he himself had been a close ally of Arnold Hammerson prior to the coup. In fact, his links to the Hammerhearts stretched all the way back to 1980, mid-way through the Great Sorcerous War. This meant that he needed to do something to demonstrate that he was going to go after anyone who had been guilty of using magic recklessly against people, and the target with the highest profile he could go after, besides the Woodwards and Fletchers, was none other than Dermott Hall—former Police Commissioner, former English teacher, present nothing.

In October, Hall was arrested and charged with numerous war crimes. Whether doing that had been enough for Cornish remained unclear—he was doing okay in the polls, at least—but getting him put on trial was all he was able to do. The rest had been up to the legal system, and that was where, as far as we were concerned, the ball had been dropped. To the fury of so many of the public, including us, Hall was cleared of all charges, save one: dereliction of duty. In other words, he was completely cleared of all the really terrible things he had done, and the only thing he was actually charged for was failing to capture the most wanted criminals at the time: the Woodwards and those associated with them. Then the sentence came down, and it was even worse: Hall was to face no jail time at all, nor was he to pay any sort of fine or do any community service. His only punishment was that he was permanently banned from taking any kind of political office in Australia, serving as part of any law enforcement, or participating in the judicial system in any form.

In other words, the career path Arnold Hammerson had set him on as a reward for being such a faithful Hammerheart way back in February had been cut off at the knees. And this is where we circle back to Chopville High and their betrayal of us. With no other options, Hall returned to Chopville to reapply for his old job as an English teacher. Not only did he get the job, but he managed to swing it so that Devin Hall, his relative who had most recently been tutoring Lena on Lucien's instructions, was also given a job, and the two of them would be pretty much running the English program at Chopville High.

What had happened to Devin Hall during and immediately after the battle against Lucien, not to mention Lena, Hignat, Wilwog, Sebastian, and all those other tutors, was an interesting story in itself, and it was one we learnt about from—of all people—Sebastian. He wrote it in a series of blog posts, covering the escape from the Hammerheart network, taking shelter in some government installation, the horrors of the global annihilations (not that he or anyone else truly understood what those had been), and finally to their safe return to Chopville. The conclusion of the series had detailed how he and Lena had tracked down their families, how Ather had been adopted by Vincent Wilwog (who had found himself in Panama when the dust settled, and who took a while to get back to Australia), and how Sebastian, Ather and Ugine were all happily engaged to be married now.

It was interesting how such bad people could end up with such happy endings; and none more so than Hall. The idea of him teaching us again was beyond the pale for all of us. Even Mum and Marge, who considered our education more important than just about everything, thought it inappropriate that we should have to be around Hall every day, after all he had done to us. The thought of being in a classroom with him, where he could slap us with detentions for whatever he liked, was sickening. It was for that reason that all who had been in the Young Army would not be returning to Chopville High the following year, despite all they had done for us in the last two months. Most of us would be going to schools in surrounding towns, while Natalie and Rebecca would be attending a private school up in Shepparton.

It was the four Maivis children, however, who would be going the furthest. Fed up with Chopville, their grandparents had already sold their house, and shortly after New Year, the whole family would be moving to Echuca. Learning of this had been devastating for us Playmans at first, as Harry and Simon had been in our lives for as long as we could remember. Naturally, we would be keeping in touch with them, but the reality was we would probably see them very rarely. With that in mind, Peter, James and I did the best we could to spend as much time with Harry and Simon as we could while we could—and whenever it was possible to get a free moment from studying.

Not that there were any such free moments in the lead-up to 'exam week', as we were calling it. Despite the weather being flawlessly beautiful all throughout that first weekend of December, the Playman and Thomas children were confined to the studies in each of the houses. Peter, James and I were set up in the Playman study, where we were going through practice test after practice test in all ten of the subjects in which we would be sitting exams throughout the week. Over in the Thomas study, Felicity and Jessica, who were doing year-ten exams in not all the same subjects as us, had a similar setup going, and in the last week or so, had been joined by Natalie. In his wisdom, Greg Pont had decided that the study environment Mum and Marge had set up for us would be far more effective than anything he could do for her, so he was bringing Natalie over each morning and picking her up at the end of each day so that Marge could keep her under guard during the intervening hours.

I firmly believed that Mum and Marge were going *way* over the top with all this exam preparation. As we all constantly reminded them, the exams wouldn't be too difficult at our level, and although the stakes were reasonably high (being held back a year certainly would suck), they weren't high enough to justify this. It wasn't like the results would determine whether or not we got into university, or whether or not we would survive the week, as some of the other tests we had undergone during the year had.

After the first day, however, all of us had changed our tunes completely. The first day of 'exam week' had only covered two out of the ten exams, and yet it was the most intense and exhausting day I could remember having been through since the war—and easily the most exhausting day I had ever experienced at school. It went from nine in the morning till four in the afternoon, consisting of the first exam from 9:00 till 12:00, the second exam from 1:00 till 4:00, and a one-hour lunch break. Each of the exams also had a ten minute intermission, at 10:25–10:35 and 2:25–2:35 respectively, during which time we were allowed to sit and rest, and regroup our thoughts if necessary; however these were optional, and if we were on a roll, we could choose to work through them. By the time we were allowed to leave at the end of the day, my brain felt like a wrung sponge, and the thought that the next four days were going to be just as difficult was enough to bring several people to tears.

On the Monday, the exam subjects for us year-nines were Maths and Science. For Peter and me, it was Intermediate Maths, while for James, it was Advanced. Harry and Simon had been put in the Elementary Maths class, but I privately thought they were actually smarter than that and that they simply chose to fudge a lot of their tests to make their lives easier. Even though the exam papers were different, we were all still put in the same classroom, and where possible, put nearest to people who were not doing the same paper as us—this was supposed to minimise the risk of copying off other people. This was irrelevant for the afternoon exam, however, as there had only ever been one Science curriculum, and so it was the same exam paper for all of us. I thought I did okay on the Maths exam without knocking it out of the park, but I had really struggled with Science; I could only hope it wouldn't affect me too badly.

The second day came, and the exams were English and LOTE—which for us year-nines meant French. I probably flunked both of them for entirely separate reasons: of all the subjects Mum and Marge had made us study, French was one of the ones we had paid little attention to. The war had certainly not required us to speak any French, so all of us were rather out of practice. As for English, that was because the exam was being supervised by none other than Dermott Hall; and although he was on his best behaviour and didn't say so much as a word to any of us, or even look at any of us so far as I noticed, his mere presence was a total distraction for me. It turned out that Peter had been distracted by the same thing, as had Katie, Erica and Liam when I got a chance to catch up with them later; but James had survived by virtue of the fact that he had no idea Hall was even there until he heard him speak at the end of the exam, while Harry and Simon had somehow been able to ignore him completely and get on with their work.

"Well, maybe ignore is the incorrect word," Harry said when we caught up with them over lunch break, "and I'm sure Hall himself would agree, being the English teacher that he is. It might be more accurate to say that Simon and I consider him to be beneath our notice. After all, we won and he lost."

We were all thoroughly wrecked by the time we got home that afternoon, but Mum and Marge insisted that we squeeze in an hour of study before dinner and another hour after, before we let our minds rest and regather strength for the following day's exams. For day three, it was Commerce in the morning and Health in the afternoon. I thought I actually did okay for these two, especially Commerce, and part of that had to be due to the nine hours of dreamless sleep I got the night before. Even Health, which had never been one of my stronger subjects, seemed not to be too bad, as the questions were, for the most part, things that had come up during the many recent hours of study.

The same held for the exams on the Thursday—Geography and Information Processing. At least, I felt sure I did well on Geography, despite the fact that we hadn't even been studying Geography at the beginning of the year. The way it would have gone if the school year had been completed properly was History in the first semester, and then Geography in the second. Because both subjects were required by the state to be passed, it was necessary to complete exams on both of them in order to progress to year-ten. As for Information Processing, that had been a first semester elective, which was why it was one of the subjects included in the exams. Like all the other exams, it was theoretical; but unlike the rest of them, it was done on the computers instead of on paper. The computer room was warm and stuffy, and although I did okay on the exam, more of my energy probably went towards trying to stay awake than answering questions.

It had been determined that due to the amount of school we had missed over the year, we were only required to complete exams for two electives instead of the full four—which was nothing short of a miracle for us, as it would have necessitated doing a sixth day of exams. In our case, it was Information Processing on the Thursday afternoon and Media on the Friday afternoon. We were told before the Media exam began that it would be the least important and count the least towards determining our overall score, which would then be used to determine if we would progress to year-ten or be forced to repeat. I was glad that it counted for very little because I could barely remember any of the subject material, and probably did even worse on this exam than I had on French or Science. The History exam on the Friday morning hadn't gone great either, but at least that was one of the subjects that Mum and Marge had hammered into us, so some of the content was fresh in my mind.

The feeling at four o'clock on Friday afternoon when we were finally allowed to leave the school grounds, only required to return a week from today to get our results and find out if we would be progressing or repeating, was one of incredible relief. The general consensus was that if this was what school is going to be like going forward, none of us were going to live to see year-twelve. All of us wanted to celebrate our freedom, as unlike victory in the war, this was a purer form of freedom.

Now, for the next almost-two months, we could do just about anything we wanted. Even Mum and Marge were ready to let us celebrate that night by letting us order in a bunch of pizzas. Trouble was, we were all so buggered that once dinner was done, we pretty much trudged upstairs and fell unconscious in our beds.

That was okay, because there was a real party booked for the following night. Election Day had finally come around, and it was the first time most of us had taken any interest in politics, mainly because we were likely to be directly affected by the result. The parentals took the grandparentals off to vote in the morning, and then when evening came around, we all headed over to the Fletcher-Pont residence for the party. The idea was that we would all gather together to celebrate a number of good things at the same time: the end of exams; the Ponts and Fletchers finally getting back into Natalie and Rebecca's old house as of a few weeks ago; the end of the most difficult year any of us had ever experienced; and, with a bit of luck, the removal of Hank Cornish as Australia's Head of State.

It had taken longer than expected for Natalie and Rebecca to reclaim their old house due to nobody knowing quite where Brian Fletcher's last will and testament was. It turned out that it had been made way back in February, at a time when the war was just getting started and Brian had found out that he was about to become a Sorcerer. The will had been made under the assumption that if Brian was to die, it would have meant that the Fletchers had lost their magic, which probably meant that the war was going very badly. The reason it took so long to find was that Brian's copy had been lost, not in the destruction of the first Woodward Base, but rather in the destruction of the second. Another copy had supposedly been left with his solicitor, but nobody quite knew where the solicitor was or if he was still alive. When he had eventually been located and learnt that Brian, his wife and his mother had all perished, he presented Frederic Woodward with a key to a certain lockbox at a certain bank, where at last, the documents had been found.

The will had distributed Brian's assets amongst his relatives, with clauses upon clauses to cover those relatives predeceasing him. Natalie and Rebecca were each left with substantial fortunes, though the will stipulated that trust funds should be set up for them, and access to them only given when they turned eighteen, which the solicitor—whom Brian had nominated as the trustee—had already begun to set up. As for the house, a list of names had been given in order of priority, with his wife Minny first and his mother Alice second. Minny was known to be dead, of course, so she was automatically skipped over. Nobody knew for certain that Alice was dead, but that was the assumption on which we were basing our decisions. Even if she had somehow lived through the battle against Lucien from inside the base, she couldn't possibly have lived after it, for all its life support systems had been magical.

This was one of the many things I had to deal with in my regular counselling sessions, for the decision to set the control room up in such a way had been mine and mine alone. I had deliberately made it so that it would not be possible for the last person in the base to release himself or herself through the control room; the intention had been that the protection needed to be strong enough to keep anyone unauthorised out, and that meant that we too would be kept out if it came to a point where there was no one on the inside to let us back in. Of course, there was another way Alice could have escaped if the conditions had been correct —the bedrooms had emergency escapes in them—but they wouldn't have been triggered because the base had no indication that there was an emergency. For that to have worked, Lucien would have had to bring the fight directly to us, not the other way around. The only consolation I had, which the counsellor had provided to me and which I shared with no one, was that Alice had volunteered for the job—and after all, she was quite old, so the decision had probably only shaved a few years off her life at most. It sounded pretty heartless, hence why I told no one about it, and yet it was all I had to keep me going.

Anyway, back to the house. The third name on the list was Natalie, and it was stipulated in the will that ownership should pass directly to her if she was eighteen or over. Since she would not be eighteen for another nineteen months, a convoluted setup emerged to manage the property. The house would go into the trust fund and be legally managed by the solicitor, but its practical usage was to be determined by what the will termed as a 'Property Manager'. This person was to be the next name on the list who was qualified for the role, who turned out to be Frederic Woodward at number five. (Rebecca was fourth on the list, and the property would have gone to her only if Natalie had died in the war. For whatever reason, though Rebecca's trust fund was hefty in its own right, Natalie would be getting a fair bit more than her younger sister.)

Since the reading of the will, Frederic and the solicitor had worked together to arrange a setup where the Ponts would move into the house, and though they wouldn't own it, they would not be obliged to pay for rent or any other bills. Those bills would be taken directly from Natalie's trust fund until she turned eighteen, and only then would the Ponts be required to pay rent, assuming Natalie would want them to continue living in her house. The whole thing was a goodwill arrangement in which the Fletchers would be rewarding the Ponts for taking Natalie and Rebecca in the first place, something that they had never been obliged to do, and Natalie and Rebecca themselves were quite happy with it all— once they understood it, anyway.

The first function the Ponts were to have at the old Fletcher place was set to be a big one. Besides Greg, his wife, Natalie, Rebecca and Jason all being there, all of us Playmans and Thomases were invited (including Hilda and Violet), Harry, Simon, Misty, Michelle, Frederic,

Lillian, Amelia, Marc, Erica and her parents, and Katie and her parents. Harry and Simon's grandparents were invited, but they chose to stay home and watch the election coverage on their own TV. Tommy and his parents also begged off; so far as I knew, Tommy's Australian parents didn't speak English, and Tommy himself showed little interest in anything anymore.

The party took place in the largest room in the Fletcher-Pont residence, which was normally a sort of rec room but could be transformed into a large dining room if necessary. On this night, there was a big table in the centre of the room around which we all sat for dinner, and numerous couches and sofas around the edges of the room. When the meal finished, the dishes were all removed and new dishes brought out, laden with party food and drink. People were then free to move about and socialise, or sit on the sofas and be comfortable. Music played throughout the evening, but turned down low so that it was firmly in the background. What was also on in the background was a large television at one end of the room; it was on silent, but it displayed ongoing coverage of the election results as they came in throughout the evening.

For many of us, the party began to seem less enjoyable after eight o'clock or so, and over the course of the following two hours, it got more and more gloomy. One by one, people began to realise that the results weren't stacking up in a way that was going to be good for us. By eleven o'clock, the result was beyond doubt. The AUS had taken enough house seats to form an outright majority government, and it would turn out that by the time the dust settled, the other two parties each had less than twenty percent of the house seats. Things were more balanced in the Senate, where the AUS would need to work with at least one of the other parties to pass laws, but none of that mattered to us. What mattered was that Hank Cornish had been voted in as our next Prime Minister, and our only hope now was that he turned out to be as prone to breaking campaign promises as a typical politician—but my hopes of that were low.

* * *

Four days later, Frederic, Lillian, Amelia and Natalie were all arrested by the Australian Federal Police and charged with what seemed an endless list of war crimes. Large squads were sent to both houses early in the morning of Wednesday, December 15, breaking down both doors and dragging the four former Sorcerers out of bed. Though I hadn't seen either of the early-morning raids, I would hear about them both from Marc and Rebecca, who had witnessed them. In both cases, the police were so heavily armed that it was almost as if they expected magic to be used against them. All the former Sorcerers had gone quietly, but Greg Pont certainly hadn't; he too was arrested for getting in the way, but he was held in a cell here in Chopville and ultimately released later in the day.

When the police publicly announced what they had done that afternoon, they proceeded to read the charges against each of the Sorcerers, and the group of Sorcerers as a whole. The staggering detail that had gone into it made me firmly believe that this had been in the works for quite a while, but that Cornish had held off pulling the trigger till after the election to give it legitimacy. Even Natalie and Amelia had charges against them, though very few attributed to them directly; their greatest crime seemed to be that they had used magic in the first place.

The media coverage, not to mention the social media coverage, was ruthless towards the former Sorcerers. People wanted to see them executed—they actually advocated for bringing the death penalty back specifically for the Woodwards and then outlawing it again. Cornish had already ruled out doing that, but there was one thing he hadn't ruled out: extradition. Shortly after the arrest, more than seventy other countries around the world put out warrants against the four former Sorcerers, and some of them *did* have the death penalty.

All we knew so far was that a trial would take place here in Australia before anywhere else. It would be a group trial, dealing mainly with the group charges, and what came next would depend on the results of that trial. In the meantime, Frederic, Lillian, Amelia and Natalie were all taken away and imprisoned somewhere, and it would be several months before I would see any of them again—or receive confirmation that they were even still alive.

Chapter 39: Trial of the Sorcerers

"Hey, how you doing?" I said in surprise, taking a seat.

Marc started and looked up from the magazine he was reading, equally surprised. "Hey, what are you—oh," he faltered, and then grinned. "Are you here for the same reason I'm here?"

"Are you here to receive the results of a certain test?" I asked.

"You could say that," he said. "Er—is your appointment with Dr. Ling?"

"Yep," I nodded, beginning to understand a question that had puzzled me for a good few weeks now.

All this took place in the waiting room of a clinic in Melbourne in late June, 2011. It was the first time I had seen Marc in six months, and it was certainly good to see that he appeared to be doing well for himself. After the Woodwards had been arrested, he had been left without any legal guardian and, according to my parents, had most likely become a ward of the state. He had left Chopville within days and none of us had seen or heard from him since.

As for why I was in the waiting room of a clinic in Melbourne on the first day of the winter school holidays, it was the end result of a struggle that had been going on almost since the start of the year. A number of people who had previously been in Chopville had scattered since the war, and we Playmans and Thomases had done our best to keep track of them through social media. It had taken until January for any of us to locate Lena Tuck, but locate her we eventually did. Her silence made it quite clear that she had no intention of keeping in touch with any of us, save one person: For whatever reason, she accepted Jessica's friend request on Facebook, perhaps not recognising her, or simply not caring what Jessica knew about her doings.

Or maybe it was another reason entirely. Jessica was entering the third trimester of her pregnancy at this stage, and Lena would have known that, for it was through Jessica that we learnt that Lena, too, was expecting. We didn't know right away how far along she was, but a clue came up in a post about a month later, indicating that she was due in early–mid June. In other words, the timing was just close enough that the father could have been me. That had left me with a big decision to make: Do I, or don't I, follow this up? Following it up meant telling Mum and Dad about having been with Lena, but not following it up meant never knowing if I had a child out there.

I had eventually decided that I needed to know, after having talked it over with Peter and James. It had felt like an Earth-shattering scandal for me, but James assured me that Marge and Charlie had come down harder on Jessica than anything I copped from my parentals. Still, it had probably changed my relationship with my parents, no matter that I assured them that it had only happened once and that it had been the end result of a curse put on me by Lucien. They still only knew a small fraction of the things I had done with girls during the war, and it looked like there wouldn't be any need for them to find out more.

The next step had been to get a paternity test done to determine if I really *was* the father, for the odds were much higher that it was either Marc or Lucien—they had been with her far more often than I had. Dad had come to my rescue, attempting to make a deal with Lena's parents to arrange it, but he had been met with resistance at every step—until just a couple of weeks ago. Quite suddenly, the Tucks changed their minds, and now I knew why: Marc had come to them with the same request.

"Well, I'm not really expecting anything to come of this," Marc said now, "but it still seems like the responsible thing to do to find out."

I hesitated, then said, "Wouldn't the chances of it being you be higher than Lucien? I mean, he was only with her for—what—a week?"

"It was a very active week, remember?" he said, suppressing a smirk. "Also, if Lucien was thinking the way I imagine he was, Lena would not have fallen pregnant unless he intended for her to; and if he did, then it wouldn't have been with one of our children."

That made me remember something Lucien had once said to me, not in reality, but in the fictional universe he had created when he had taken all our minds during the last battle. He had told me that he had performed magic on his sperm to make sure his progeny would be the best possible versions of themselves, and although his telling me hadn't been real, it didn't mean that he hadn't actually done something like that prior to the battle. What he had shown us had been how he envisioned the future panning out at that moment, and it would have had to take into account things that he had known at the time—things that he had done, or planned to do, in the week leading up to the battle. If it were true, then his sperm would have roared through Lena's womb like a freight train, making sure that no other lingering sperm could possibly survive. It was even possible that the sperm had continued to live inside her until the next egg had come down to be fertilised, which could very well have been after Lucien himself was gone. This was all too complicated to explain to Marc, so I simply nodded.

Changing the subject, I asked Marc what he had been up to lately.

"Busy pretty much all the time," he told me. "I live on my own here in Melbourne now, I'm still in school, I work—in fact, I have to go to work after this today."

"Work? What do you do?" I asked. "And—and who do you live with? And why Melbourne?"

"I'm a server in a restaurant in the city," he said. "I'm here because it's way easier to get work here than it would be in Chopville, and well— I don't wanna go back there anyway. Other than you guys, I don't have any good memories there, and even my memories of you guys are basically all about fighting the Hammersons and watching my big brother go insane."

I shrugged, unable to deny any of that. "Do you—like—live in a foster home or something?"

He laughed. "No, I live on my own. I was able to get myself partially emancipated, probably because I'm almost seventeen anyway, but also because when the Woodwards were taken, the state came in and took possession of the house. They were about to start selling everything off when they found Dad's will, which stated that everything was to be left to me. I couldn't believe it when I found out, because this was made when Lucien was alive, and yet he got skipped over except for some things which had been his anyway. By the time this all got processed, I had been living rough down here for a couple of months, but I'd gotten work and enrolled in school, so I guess they thought I was responsible enough to take care of myself."

"Is that why they're digging up your house on Hag Crescent?" I asked, having assumed that Marc probably knew nothing about that.

He shrugged. "Probably, but I don't care what happens to that place. The land wasn't hugely valuable but I still got over a hundred grand after the dust settled, so I'm doing okay."

That was when Dad came over and sat on my other side. He had been filling out some paperwork on my behalf up at the desk, and he looked as surprised as I felt when he saw Marc sitting there.

"What are you doing here?" he asked.

"Hey Mr. Playman. I'm here to receive the results of a paternity test," Marc said, and he took a moment to enjoy the look of dismay on my father's face.

"John," Dad said slowly, "you didn't mention that Marc had been with the same girl."

Marc raised his eyebrows at me and said, "Well, yeah—she was my girlfriend for a few months, but she was always more into John than she was me. He was never really into her though—I doubt he would even be here if Lucien hadn't put that curse on him."

"Did John just tell you about that too?" Dad asked, frowning at me.

"Huh?" Marc looked at us in confusion. "Tell me about what? I was there when all that stuff happened."

That was when I realised that Dad had doubted all along the truth in my story about having been cursed. He knew I'd had plenty of time to cook up a story with Peter and James, so their backup had apparently meant very little. The only time I'd had to tip Marc off had been while we had been sitting here, as it was well documented in both families that none of us had been able to contact him for many months. The obvious sincerity on Marc's face made it all too clear that he was telling the truth.

"Okay," Dad said slowly, then pulled himself together. "Well anyway, this is what's happening. As you know, the Tucks have lived in

Perth since late last year, and none of them thought it appropriate or necessary to come all the way over here. Furthermore, Lena is adamant that neither of you are the father, and she doesn't want to see either of you. So what is going to happen is there will be a video link between us and Lena's parents, who are with their doctor in Perth. This Dr. Ling, is she your doctor, Marc?"

"No," Marc shrugged, "I only got referred to her for this test."

"I don't see how Lena can know which of us is the father," I said, "because she was with all three of us in quite a short window—"

"All *three* of you?" Dad repeated, looking very stern indeed.

"Oh, by the way, Dad, thanks for driving me all the way down here," I said quickly. "I'd hate to think how loud this place would be if we were having this conversation with Mum."

Mumzilla all over again, I thought.

"Oh, your mother will be hearing all about this, young man."

"Mr. Playman, Lena had a curse put on her too," Marc said quickly, "right after she was with John, in fact. I don't know if you've seen a picture of her, but she's like really, *really* attractive, and Lucien thought to make her his arm candy. I vaguely remember her even being on TV with him one time during one of his press conferences; it probably wouldn't even be hard to find the pictures."

"Hey, yeah, she did," I said, remembering. "I think Cornish might have been in that picture as well. We'll have to track it down later."

"And you wonder why people are happy that there isn't any magic anymore," Dad muttered.

"*I'm* not happy about it," Marc said, a little defensively. "I mean, I know why it was necessary to do what we did, but just look at all the stuff Cornish and his cronies are getting away with now, and there's nothing we can do to stop them. The Woodwards are gonna be crucified no matter what happens next week, and anyone with half a brain knows they don't deserve it."

"Most people have less than half a brain," I sighed. "I can't believe how easy it's been for them to practically rewrite history."

They were doing a damn good job of it too, and by 'they', I mean the antimagic crowd. Cornish probably had played a major role in it, of course, but he couldn't have done it alone. From the news to the entertainment industry, and right down to the education system, everyone was speaking of the Woodwards as if all the trouble had been caused by them using their magic to resist in the first place. Nobody was calling the Hammersons saints, of course, but the belief was that if the Woodwards had simply rolled over and refused to use their magic to fight, countless lives would have been saved. The fact that doing so would have meant submitting to magical tyranny seemed to be lost on such people.

That was as far as our conversation got as we were then called into Dr. Ling's office. The three of us went in and took up seats around the doctor's desk. She came in after us, went to the desk, and pressed some buttons on her computer to set up the video link. Introductions were then done between us, the doctor at the other end, and Lena's parents, both of whom I knew by sight but hadn't seen in about a year, before the first Woodward Base had been destroyed. They greeted us with barely veiled hostility, which I could understand. Here were two boys who had been off taking advantage of their daughter while she had run off with them to try to stop the war.

They also looked like they had both aged somewhat since then, and I understood that as well. They had been separated from both of their children for two months, only to have Lucien put them under influential charms, kill their son, and turn their daughter into a willing sex slave. Then when they got her back and attempted to escape it all by moving to the other side of the country, they found that Lena was pregnant, carrying the son of one of the three boys she had been with during the war. Lena may have been denying her involvement with me and Marc but her parents couldn't be stupid enough to think we would go to the trouble of having these paternity tests if there had never been sex between us.

Fortunately, we didn't have to look at them for long, as Dr. Ling changed the display on our side so that she could read the results of the tests, while sharing her screen with the doctor at the other end.

"Firstly, Mr. Playman," she said, addressing Dad, "I must ask, is Marc a relative of yours? A nephew or second cousin, perhaps?"

"No," Dad said politely, "but he and John are biological brothers, and John is my adopted son. We only found out last year who his blood relatives are."

"That makes sense," Dr. Ling said, and then turned her attention to Marc. Apparently, I was the only person in the room with no authority to speak in this setting. "Now, to confirm, you also have another brother who is older than you, and was also with Ms. Tuck around the time of conception?"

"Yeah, Lucien," Marc said distastefully. "Everyone knows who he is."

"Okay," she said, turning back to her screen. "If we had some of his DNA to test, we would be able to give you a result with one hundred percent accuracy. As it is, we found that the two of you share many DNA markers, while Lucas shares some with you, but fewer. He also shares some markers with each of you that you don't share with each other. This means that of the two of you, Marc is slightly more likely to be the father; but in reality, neither of you are likely enough for our satisfaction."

"So you think it's Lucien, then," Lena's father said, his voice coming distortedly through the computer speakers.

"Like I said, we can't be sure of that without his DNA," she said. "It is true that in most circumstances, if we tested all three brothers, we could determine with one hundred percent accuracy which of them was the father. However, there is a small chance that Lucien would have fewer matching DNA markers than either Marc or John. There is also a chance that the child would share more DNA markers with an uncle rather than the father, but this is extremely rare."

"What are we supposed to do with this information, then?" Dad asked.

"Well, I will print out reports for each of you," Dr. Ling said, "but essentially, the decision with how to proceed is going to rest with Ms. Tuck and her parents. They could move forward under the assumption that either Marc or Lucien is the father, but I should tell you, Marc, if they decide that you are *not* the father, your paternity test results are not going to be enough to give you any legal standing if you choose to fight it."

"And what if they decide that I *am* the father?" Marc asked warily.

The doctor hesitated for only a moment before saying, "Well, that would be between you and them to figure out how to move forward—"

"I think he's asking to make sure they can't take him for a ride," I chipped in, causing both Dad and Marc to glare at me.

"Not a chance; we want nothing to do with either of them, and neither does Lena," her father said through the speakers.

An uncomfortable silence followed before the doctor on the other end of the video link—a male—said, "Well, that seems to settle things. As far as we're concerned here, Lucien is the most likely father."

"Technically, that still makes us uncles," I said, causing more glares, but I couldn't help myself.

It was fine enough that Lena wanted us out of her life—I didn't really want anything to do with her either—but the fact remained that Lucien had been our brother, and that meant that Lucas—wait, she named him *Lucas*? Nothing wrong with the name on its own, I supposed, but I had no illusions about where the inspiration for *that* name had come from. The influential charms put on most people had been made redundant by the destruction of all the world's magic, but the destruction of the world's magic hadn't had any impact on the damage Lucien had done to Lena using his Honnie mind. It now made sense that she would want nothing to do with me or Marc, but it also made me pity her immensely. She was going to be loyal to Lucien for the rest of her life, and while her torment most likely wouldn't be as great as what Tommy was going through in his longing for Ingi, it would be comparable. Based on what Jessica had told us regarding her Facebook posts, Lena was devoting her life to her son, the only piece of Lucien she had left.

"I think we're done here too," Dad said firmly, shutting down any further discussion and getting to his feet. "We've heard enough, but I will take a copy of that report, if you don't mind."

"Me too," Marc said, also getting to his feet.

* * *

Getting the results of the paternity test wasn't the only reason I was in Melbourne, nor was I the only one who had made the drive down. This was just a short stop on our way to the airport, where we would be catching a flight to Canberra for the trial of the Sorcerers. In addition to the legal team, each of the four accused had been allowed to have three people at the trial for emotional support. Whether that was something normally permitted or if it was a special arrangement made for this trial, or if it was in fact a restriction not normally in place for such trials, I didn't know.

I was one of the three chosen by Amelia to attend, while Dad was one of Frederic's three. In addition to us, all the Ponts (save Jason), Rebecca, Peter, Felicity and Charlie would also be going. Natalie had actually requested Jessica rather than Felicity, but Jessica didn't want to leave baby Giselle at home, and everyone agreed it would be too complicated to bring her along, so Felicity was going instead. Natalie had also requested Rebecca and Lisa's mother, who she had become quite close to in the months they had lived together. This meant that Jason Pont would be home alone, so he had been sent to stay at the Playmans' until we got back. Frederic had requested Dad, Charlie and Greg, while Lillian requested nobody—maybe she didn't know anyone to ask, or maybe she didn't think they would come.

Amelia had requested me, Peter and Marc, but nobody had been able to find Marc in the lead-up to the trial; and when I told him of this on the way out of the clinic, offering him a chance to come with us, he declined, saying that he was needed at work, but he wished us and the Woodwards all the best. He got on a bus and headed off, and that was the last time I saw him. He remained off social media and he made no effort to reach out to any of us. I would later figure that sacrificing the Hero Crystal had been much more difficult for him than he had shown at the time, and his only way of coping with the loss was to distance himself from all things reminding him of the power he used to have—and sadly, that included his only living blood relative.

Still, it was a relief that we were requested, because until the requests reached us, we had no proof that the four former Sorcerers still lived. It would have been easy to imagine such a corrupt government arranging for there to be an 'accident', causing them all to be killed out of hand, but the fact that Amelia had requested me was reassuring. It didn't sound like the sort of thing that someone pretending to be Amelia would do, and what would be the point of that anyway?

The trial was set to start on June 29, which was the day after tomorrow. Tomorrow, we would get to see the Woodwards and sit in on their final meeting with their legal team. We would also get to celebrate Natalie's seventeenth birthday, which happened to be on that very day, and given that the whole thing was going to be under police guard, it was apt to be quite as cheery as Natalie's previous birthday, which had been crashed by Hall in spectral form.

As far as I knew, Natalie and Amelia had been isolated from the world for more than six months, having been only allowed to speak to each other and their legal team in all that time, so seeing us tomorrow was going to be big for them. The reason it had taken so long to get from arrest to trial? Well, I didn't know the specifics, but a lot of it had been due to politics, and the Australian government having to deal with other countries which had their own ideas about what sort of punishments should be in store for the former Sorcerers. Several of them were threatening sanctions and a couple even threatening war, but although sanctions seemed possible, war was regarded by most as highly unlikely, even if the Woodwards were let off scot-free.

Another part of the delay had been for legal reasons. It transpired that at the time of their arrest, the Woodwards had almost no assets to their name. Even before the war, the only thing they had actually owned was the block of land on Morelle Street where their house had been, the one which had contained the hidden entrance to their true residence in the first Woodward Base. That block of land had been confiscated at the same time as ours, but unlike ours, Lucien hadn't bothered to return it to them. This meant that the Woodwards had very little money and no way to get more, which in turn meant that they couldn't afford their own legal representation. They were entitled to a public defender, but every public lawyer they met with was advising them to plead guilty to everything. The Woodwards had good reason to believe the fix was in, and so they had turned to Natalie for help.

Because he was her legal guardian, Greg Pont was permitted to make decisions on her behalf when it came to legal representation. It turned out, though, that he hadn't been able to do so until very recently due to the state taking much longer than usual to process Natalie and Rebecca's adoptions. This had only added to the speculation that there had been an 'accident' of sorts, or at the very least that the government were doing all they could to deny the former Sorcerers a fair trial. At last, though, Greg was able to make himself heard, and he and the solicitor who had set up Natalie's trust fund agreed that it should be used for her representation. Furthermore, since so many charges were against the four of them as a group, the Woodwards could be represented by the same team.

From there, though, their troubles had only continued. Most lawyers they approached wouldn't touch the case, believing that even if they were paid for it, there could be no benefit to arguing in favour of the Woodwards. They all believed, as we did, that the government were doing all they could to make sure the case went a certain way, and none of them wanted the reputational damage that would come from having lost such a high-profile case. The ones who believed their reputations could survive such a loss didn't want the reputational damage that would come from representing the former Sorcerers in the first place; the stigma that now surrounded magic was such that anyone found to be associating with the Woodwards was going to lose far more than they could gain.

Things had become quite desperate for them until just a few weeks ago, when one of the lawyers Greg contacted was finally interested in taking on the case. So far, only Lillian, Frederic and Greg had spoken with this lawyer, but from what I understood, she was not advising them to plead guilty, and she even had some strategies in mind that may get them off some of the charges. Best of all, at least as far as Natalie and Amelia were concerned, she had an idea that might be able to clear the two girls entirely, but doing so was likely to make it more difficult for Lillian and Frederic to clear their own names.

This was as much information I was able to get out of Dad during the drive to Melbourne, and then Greg on the plane to Canberra, but it was enough to give me hope—slim though my hopes were. None of it changed the fact that the vast majority of the world wanted to see the four former Sorcerers subjected to all kinds of torment. Some of the things I'd read on social media, and even seen on TV, made me sick and furious in equal measure. I just hoped that this lawyer they had found, and the team she had put together for them, would be able to swing a miracle in the court room.

My hopes were dashed the moment I set foot in the room where we would finally get to catch up with the Woodwards, when I saw exactly who this mystery lawyer was. The feeling was short-lived, though, for when she went over the strategy she was planning to use with the adults, it actually sounded quite strong, and any reasonable jury would find it difficult to see otherwise. Still, it was very difficult to fathom the idea that the Woodwards' best chance of surviving this trial was a former Hammerheart, for the lawyer was none other than 3K17—or Laura Kollerie, as she was now known.

I would have liked to ask her why she was interested in helping the Woodwards, having been so firmly against them all along, and had even been prepared to be the main judge in Lucien's show trials. I never got close enough to speak to her, though, and other than Natalie and Amelia, she ignored the rest of the teenagers in the room as if we weren't there. Thankfully, Charlie also knew who she was and was thinking along the same lines as me, for on the way out of the room, I overheard him pose that very question to her.

"Self-interest," she told him, utterly unabashed. "I think that other lawyers missed a golden opportunity by not taking this case. I'm fully aware that our chances of winning aren't great, but I still think I can make a name for myself by being such a big part of a trial that the whole world will be watching."

"Ahuh," Charlie said, not looking impressed, "but then how can we be sure that you'll fight as hard as you can for us?"

"Because it's my job," she said simply. "I'm being paid to do a job and I'm going to do it. Besides, it won't be in my best interest if I'm seen to be throwing my clients overboard."

"And the fact that you were on the other side in the war?" Charlie pressed her.

This should have caused her some discomfort, but she simply shrugged. "If you're trying to gauge my personal opinion on the subject, I don't believe that they should be punished for the crime of having magic. Beyond that, any opinions I have regarding my clients shall remain my own."

After the legal team left, we were allowed to spend a short time with the former Sorcerers, and it was a mostly happy reunion. I received hugs from both Natalie and Amelia, and this was a great relief to me. Even before she was arrested, I hadn't had much to do with Natalie. She didn't say much to me today either, but I got a feeling from her that she had moved passed my betrayal of her. She and Amelia both looked very tired and thin, though, as if they hadn't been eating or sleeping well for a long time. Lillian looked even worse; in fact, I thought she had aged rapidly since the arrest, and the thought hit me that if this trial were prolonged, she could actually pass away before it concluded.

The trial began promptly at nine o'clock the following morning, and although Laura had warned us about the tactics the prosecution were planning to use, some of it still came as a nasty shock to me. For hours that day, and the next two days, I had to sit there, listening to some of the most outrageous allegations I had ever heard levelled against the Woodwards. As the trial focussed on the group charges rather than those against the individuals, they all tended to focus on the magic itself, and nobody was quite sure who it was who had performed it.

Over and over, Laura pointed out that if the crime had been caused by magic, then the caster could have been invisible, which meant that it could just as easily have been one of the Hammersons behind it. She also pointed out that for much of the war, save late May and June, Marc Moran also had magic, and could have been behind some of it. On the occasions when she brought Marc into it, she promptly followed it up with an alibi, and every one of them sounded true to my ears. For more than half of them, I was quite sure I knew exactly where Marc had been at the time, and for those that had happened while I had been in the Honnie world, the idea that Marc could have been behind them was laughable. I was thankful that for the charges from late-February to mid-May, I was left out of the reckoning. I'd had possession of the Sien-Leoard Crystal during that time, and while I hadn't used it to kill anyone, it still would have been bad for the spotlight to fall on me while I sat there in the second row.

The point of the exercise was to cast so much doubt over each of the charges that it wouldn't be possible for the jury to determine anything beyond all reasonable doubt, and I had to admit, the woman formerly known as 3K17 was doing a damn good job of it. The expression on the judge's face didn't give me any hope that he was going to see reason, but the expressions on the faces of the jury certainly did: They didn't look angry, but they did look nervous, as if they had come in expecting one thing and were getting quite another.

It was on the third and final day of the trial, right before the prosecution were preparing to rest, when Laura threw the grenade. I had almost forgotten about it, and had been beginning to wonder if she had changed her mind about it, but in the end I was glad that she had done so. She faced the prosecution and argued that Natalie and Amelia had no legal responsibility for anything that had happened during the war, even if it had resulted from magic which they had cast. She cited a number of existing laws and precedents which put the responsibility squarely back on the parents—which in this case meant Frederic, as none of the other parents were alive.

Finally, she argued that neither girl was responsible for anything because all decisions in the war had been made by their parents: Amelia had been brought up by the Woodwards to think of magic in a certain way, while Natalie had never decided to receive her magic, but that it had simply been given to her when the Woodwards decided that the Fletchers were the most suitable line to possess it—and this, at least, was basically the truth. It was these arguments which, if successful, would set the girls free, but may make Frederic and Lillian look guiltier. I only hoped that the jury would remember everything that had happened up to this point during the trial.

From there, the closing arguments were delivered and both sides rested. The jury adjourned and were apparently sequestered all weekend. I would find out later that they'd had a lot of trouble coming to a consensus. When they finally did, though, it turned out to be better than I had been expecting: Natalie and Amelia were cleared of all group charges, while Lillian was only found guilty of a couple of them. Frederic was found guilty of only one more than his mother, but the third was a big one: In the eyes of the jury, he was responsible for the events that had taken place on September 5, 2010, in which Lucien and magic had come to an end and hundreds of millions of people had been killed by the blasts of magic that had rocked the world. The judge still gave the jury a fair blast for, in his eyes, 'letting them off lightly', and then closed by stating that sentencing for Frederic and Lillian would take place the following day, while separate trials would be set for each of the four to face their individual charges.

We stayed long enough to attend the sentencing, in which Lillian received two years while Frederic received twenty without parole; but after that, it was time for us Playmans to get back to Chopville. Only a few days of the school holidays remained, and Peter and I had a couple of projects for school that we hadn't even started. The day before we were to go back to school, however, we found out that Laura had successfully argued that the nature of the charges against Natalie and Amelia weren't serious enough to warrant trials in the High Court of Australia, as they were unrelated to the group charges, and so those trials would take place in Melbourne. As for Frederic and Lillian, as they were still imprisoned in Canberra, their trials would have to take place there, and Laura would just have to do a lot of flying between them so that she could be present for both.

The individual charges against Amelia had all been related to the things she had done to impede the Hammerhearts during May and June of the previous year, before the Young Army had split from the Woodward Army. Laura was able to get them all dismissed quite easily on the grounds that if she couldn't be held responsible for the group charges, she couldn't be responsible for these. She wasted no time trying to convince anyone that Amelia hadn't done the things she was accused of doing, as in these cases, there were witnesses who had seen her performing magic; but as far as the law was concerned, Amelia wasn't responsible for having decided to go there and do those things, which sadly meant that Laura would have to revisit the charges in Frederic's trial.

As for Natalie's trial, the charges were more interesting. Some of them were similar to Amelia's, but there were a couple that were very specific, and in both cases, the witness was none other than Ather Hignat. The first of these charges was related to the beginning of the final Chopville High battle, in which several Hammerhearts were killed when some of the primary school play equipment was ignited. In actual fact, I had been responsible for that and not Natalie at all, but thankfully, neither Natalie nor her legal team threw me under the bus. Instead, they threw everyone else under the bus, claiming that the Hammerhearts could have done it in an attempt to roast us before we could get away. They pointed out that Natalie had been hit with a weapon which neutralised her magic for a time, meaning that she could be no more likely to have done it than anyone else. They even raised the possibility that it had been done by Stella, who was seen entering the school grounds immediately before the fire started. None of these things were very convincing, though, and for one reason: Natalie was the only person in this picture who had useable magic, whether it had been neutralised or not. She did get off the charge, though, not because of any legal tricks, but because of her own sworn and rather tearful statement, in which she described seeing the flames take hold, and her first thought being for her sister, who was very nearly killed along with the Hammerhearts.

The other charge had been assault, and for this one, Ugine Wilwog popped up as an additional witness to the moment when Natalie had kicked Hignat in the nuts. This was where I came in, for I had been the only other witness to that event. The defence Laura put forward for this charge, entirely truthfully, was that Hignat had been attempting to rape her. It showed how dumb Hignat and Wilwog were that they even showed up to make a statement regarding this charge, for Natalie and I had no trouble sticking to the true story when we were questioned on the stand. Once Laura started cross-examining Hignat and Wilwog, however, their story fell apart so quickly that even the prosecution probably wanted to crawl out of the room by the end of it. They weren't prepared to admit to the sexual assault, which meant that they were forced to lie about what had led to the ball-kicking in the first place. Laura tore them to shreds so that in the end, there was no chance of that charge standing up.

In the end, Natalie and Amelia were cleared of all charges against them. Natalie was able to return to Chopville and go back to live with her sister and the Ponts in the house that would, very soon, be hers. The only downside for Natalie was that she had missed more than half a year of school, and this time, there was no opportunity for her to take an exam to catch up. By the time she was settled back in Chopville, it was already September, and the decision was made that she would have to start year-eleven afresh the following year, putting her in the same school year as me.

As for Amelia, like Marc, she became a ward of the state; but unlike Marc, she was never emancipated, partially or otherwise. She didn't return to Chopville, at least not until she was a bit older, but I was able to keep in touch with her through social media. She clung to her old friendships like lifelines, for life as a Woodward and former Sorcerer was not an easy one. It reminded me of something Stella had said to me shortly before her death: 'What kind of life can you really expect a Hammerson to have? Even if I changed my name, I'll always be Arnold Hammerson's daughter to the rest of the world.' It now appeared that what Stella had predicted for her own future, Amelia was living in reality.

Chapter 40: 2020

"Wow, this looks different," I observed as we pulled up and Peter switched off the car.

We had parked in one of the empty spots at the back of the Chopville Town Hall, which I supposed were usually meant for people who had some sort of business at the town hall. We didn't, but these happened to be the nearest parking spots to the Chopville War Memorial, which had always been located at the back of the town hall and was accessible by a long driveway from Main Street. When we had been young, the war memorial had been quite small, and few people bothered to go there often besides those tasked with keeping it clean. Dad and Charlie had made us come every now and then, though, to see where William and Carl's names were carved in stone and to remind us that someday, we too may be required to fight for our freedom.

That was then, but on the 5th of September, 2020, it had been expanded significantly. The original memorial was still there, of course, but now a new building had been resurrected behind it; and although this was the first time I had seen it in person, I knew it to be dedicated to what was now referred to as the 'War of the Crystals', distinguishing it from the 'Great Sorcerous War' of thirty years earlier. Dad and Charlie had been the driving forces behind the new building, pouring much of the wealth they had come by as a result of the Hammerheart loot in the tunnel into building it. That was fine, but the thing that the four of us in the car had come to see was the Young Army exhibit which Jessica, one of the only people in the Young Army who had remained in Chopville, had made happen.

"It doesn't look like much on the outside," Natalie said as we got out of the car and headed up to the building, "but Jessica sent me some pictures of the inside; you'll be surprised."

She wasn't wrong. When Peter opened the door and held it for us to walk through, I saw that the inside of the building looked bright and cheerful, not at all like the shabby look of the exterior, and in stark contrast to the sombre feel of the rest of the memorial. The carpet was a lush blue colour, the walls a dark red and padded with what looked like velvet. This was only the foyer, but there were five rooms beyond: one was an admin room, while the other four were dedications to the Woodward and Fletcher soldiers, the Hammerheart soldiers, the Young Army, and innocent civilians—the latter of which would contain a lot of names and pictures of staff from Chopville High in 2010. Even the Hammerhearts were appreciated here, for the general consensus—one with which we didn't agree—was that they were as much victims of the Hammersons as anyone else.

We had a brief look at the rooms for the Woodward Army and civilians, Natalie and Rebecca taking a bit more time to honour their parents and grandmother, before turning our attention to Jessica's labours. The centrepiece of the Young Army exhibit was the wall dedicated to those who had perished, which displayed their pictures and inscriptions of their names and a brief quote or motto, each chosen by their living relatives. There were twenty people up there, and it rocked me to recall that twenty of our own had lost their lives in the fight that year. They were arranged in four rows of five, from left to right: Jane, Nicole, Lisa, Daniel and Serena on the top row; Tulip, Justin, Craig, David and Della on the second row; Robyn, Candice, Kylie, Dean and Joanne on the third row; and George, Belinda, Sophie, Stella and Lucien on the bottom row.

Lucien was dedicated twice in this memorial, once in the Hammerheart room and once here. In our case, it was because he *had* been on our side for the part of the war that had included defeating Arnold Hammerson. He had been a victim of Hammerson as much as anyone, and more than most. I had known he would be there because it had been up to me to come up with the inscription for him, as Marc couldn't be found, and his son—Lucas Tuck—had never met him. The inscription below Lucien's picture read: 'Lucien Moran, a tortured soul now free'.

There were two other features of the Young Army room which we took a moment to look at. One was a dedication to the soldiers who had lived and who had freed the world of magic, and that list included the four of us. There was also a large digital display and a control panel from which it could be programmed to run a number of video displays. Each of these videos was dedicated either to a specific person or a specific moment during the war that deserved recognition. Included in it was the sacrifice of Lisa, the sacrifice of Tommy (both in Germany and in the Honnie world), the loss of Amelia's memory, a dedication to May and what she had done for us, a dedication to Stella and the awful life she had lived in 2010, a reenactment of what Arnold Hammerson had done to Lucien, and many more things besides.

We didn't stay to watch any of the videos, though. It was already quite late in the morning and the idea had been to drive up early in the morning from Melbourne, where we all now lived, take in the new war memorial, head over to Hamster's Stretch Reserve where the reunion would be taking place through the afternoon, and then head over to the Playman house on Lopher Lane where we would all be spending the night with the folks before driving back the following afternoon. Given that we saw nobody else at the memorial, this meant that most of them were probably already at the park, and we would end up being fashionably late.

"Okay, now remember the deal, you guys," Natalie said as we pulled up on the nature strip not far from the entrance to the park, "no work talk today. Work talk is banned. If I hear any, the person who dared speak it will be in serious trouble."

"You're terrifying, Nat," Peter observed, winking at me in the rear view mirror.

Rebecca, who was sitting in the passenger's seat, gave him an elbow. "You haven't seen anything yet."

Work talk probably was going to come up, though, because a whole bunch of us who would be coming today happened to work for the same company. Young Army Limited had been dreamt up by Harry, and with capital provided by Natalie, they had done well to get it off the ground. Harry's road to becoming a businessman had included getting engaged to Katie in 2013, even though their relationship was primarily online as she still lived in Chopville and he was in Echuca; marrying Katie in January 2014 and moving with her to Geelong, where they had both attended university; graduating in 2016 with a Bachelor of Information Technology specialising in game development; and then in early 2017, moving to Melbourne where he got the company off the ground as the Chief Operating Officer. Katie wasn't involved with the company; she had become a dietician.

As for Natalie, after graduating from high school in Shepparton in 2013, she had moved to Brisbane to study business administration, where she knew nobody and could leave her past behind her for a time. When Harry proposed his idea to her, she decided to move to Melbourne to help him get started. She was now the Chief Executive Officer and probably responsible for the good fortune that had come on all of us. She had come a very long way personally too, having not dated anyone since me until she was in university. There, she was briefly engaged to a man named Douglas, but he had turned out to be physically abusive and had alcohol issues.

Since April of 2017, though, she and I were an item, brought about by the two of us working late one night and getting into a frank and open discussion about everything that had happened between us during the war. She had been twenty-two and I twenty-one, and the pain was far enough in the past that we could look at it without flinching. She had pressed me for details of all I had done, including exactly how it had felt when I had been cursed, and I had hidden nothing from her. Amazingly, she had trusted me a lot more since, though I supposed it helped that although I'd dated some girls in the years since the war, I had never two-timed anyone ever again.

As for me, after graduating high school, I had started studying information technology in Melbourne, moving in with Peter, who also made the move. Rebecca, a year behind Peter, joined us a year later; they got engaged during that time (they married in November 2016, right after they both graduated from university).

Now, we all worked for Young Army Limited; I was in charge of interface and graphics, Peter was in charge of market research, and Rebecca, who had studied music, was responsible for producing soundtracks. The business of the company, if you haven't guessed it, was to produce video games with a military bent to them. Some of the games were straight-up shooting or fighting games, but most revolved around tactics and using strategy. Most of our games had small followings, but a few were so popular that they brought in more than seventy-five percent of the company's revenue.

We weren't the first ones to arrive at the Stretch, but we weren't the last either. When we reached the clearing through which the Jade River ran, we found a number of people we knew. Peter and I made a beeline for our parents, of course, before quickly kissing Hilda on the cheek and then going to find the Thomases. Hilda was very old now, and the only one of the grannies left, as Violet had passed in 2015. She was confined to a wheelchair full-time and was suffering from dementia, but she seemed in good spirits for all that.

"Hello, boys," Charlie said, clapping Peter and me on the back and then quickly hugging Natalie and Rebecca, who had followed us. "I hope you two are taking good care of our boys here, 'cause you know they can't take care of themselves."

Rebecca snorted, while Natalie grinned and said, "Nah, we just bring in the money so that these two can stay home and pump out our babies."

It was my turn to snort.

"I heard that," Mum said, catching up with us and giving Peter a hard look. "Now, young man, you've been married for almost four years, and yet all I see here is this," she gave Rebecca a poke in her slender waist. "Why haven't you put anything in this yet?"

"Mum!" Peter cried, looking mortified, while Natalie and I shared a nervous look. Both of us knew that this lay in our future as well, once we got married, which we were planning to do next year. Of course, I was only the adopted child, so although it wasn't spoken of openly, there was less pressure on me to reproduce than poor old Peter.

"Mrs. Playman, you really want me to give up this?" Rebecca said, also indicating her waist. "These are the best years of my life; I'm not ready to give this up for kids. Besides, I'm only twenty-four; there's plenty of time for that, if we decide to have them anyway."

"Don't give me that," Mum fumed, turning her glare on Rebecca. "These *are* the best years of your life, and nobody deserves them more than your children. I didn't go through all that trouble to push him out of a birth canal just so that I could *not* have grandbabies."

I burst out laughing in spite of myself; perhaps not very wise, and I did earn myself a few glares, but we were saved from further discussion of this uncomfortable topic by the arrival of Jessica.

"How's everyone doing here?" she asked.

"Couldn't be better," I grinned, still on a bit of a high after watching Peter's embarrassment.

"I love what you did at the memorial," Natalie said, giving Jessica a hug.

Jessica shrugged, looking awkward. "It was nothing, really. I couldn't have lived with myself if it wasn't done."

She turned her head and called to her daughter, "Giselle, come over here and say hello to your uncles."

The nine-year old girl looked up from the phone she had apparently taken from Jessica's bag. She was very pretty, with long, black hair, caramel-coloured skin, a clear complexion and perfectly symmetrical face (that she'd inherited from Jessica). Five years from now, she is going to begin leaving a trail of broken hearts in her wake, I thought to myself. Right now, though, her pretty face was marred by the fact that she looked grumpy as all get-out to have been interrupted from whatever she was doing on the phone.

"They're not my uncles," she said in a clear, clipped voice. "We learned about this in school last week. Uncle James is my uncle, but they are not your brothers and they are not married to your sisters, so they are not my uncles."

"She's so mouthy lately," Jessica muttered.

"We love you too, honey," Peter called to her, and that caused her face to soften.

She relented and came over to give us each a hug, then as she was about to turn back to her phone, she let out a squeal of delight. "Aunty Felicity!"

Off she ran, practically jumping at Felicity, who had to quickly throw her arms out to catch the young girl. It appeared that Felicity had only just arrived—had probably been not far behind us on the drive up, as she had also lived in Melbourne since 2017. Prior to that, she had lived here in Chopville, choosing to stay and help out Jessica as a new mother. They had both started studying in 2013 in Shepparton, which was close enough that they could drive there each day. This was after Felicity had graduated high school and Jessica had dropped out a short way into year eleven. Felicity had studied marketing for three years and then got a job at the Chopville Luxury Inn where she ran the entire publicity operation for them. A year later, Harry asked her to come on board and lead Young Army Limited's promotional operations, which she had been doing ever since. As for Jessica, she had decided to be a primary school teacher, and after studying for four years, she had done just that, getting a job at

Chopville Primary. She was close enough to Giselle every day for Giselle to find it annoying, and yet she hadn't actually taught her daughter.

Felicity wasn't the only person who had just arrived. It appeared that in addition to Alison, her girlfriend of two years, she had carpooled with James and Erica—two more people who worked at Young Army Limited. Not only that, but James and Erica had brought their two-year old son Oliver with them, so it was just as well that Felicity drove a four-wheel drive. James and Erica had come close to breaking up after the war, but once James had begun to find himself again, they were able to get their relationship back on track. After they had graduated from high school, they quickly got engaged and moved to Melbourne together, where he studied computer science and she studied economics. They married in April 2015 and became parents in May 2018. They had come on board with Young Army Limited at the same time as the rest of us; James had specialised in cryptography in university, so he was in charge of security, while Erica was the Chief Financial Officer.

"Hey guys," Erica said as they joined us, "hope you're good, catch you later, bye."

She left James with us and hurried off after Oliver, who had just made a dash towards the river.

"Good to see you again, James," Peter said. "What has it been, eighteen whole hours now?"

"Nineteen, grasshopper," James smirked. "John, I'm glad I caught you before this thing really gets going. I was looking over some of the code you sent me last night and I think we may have an issue with—"

"James," Natalie said in a very fierce voice, "I know you can't see me glaring at you, but trust me, I'm glaring at you."

"No work talk today," I muttered, "under penalty of castration."

"Castration?" James said, putting his hands in his pockets and looking amused. "Surely your fiancé isn't going to do that to you; it wouldn't be in her best interests, would it?"

"Maybe not," Natalie admitted, "but I won't be at all affected if it were you, James. You have a child, so you won't be needing them anymore."

"No work talk today," James said in an overly cheerful voice.

Natalie and I moved off to give James some time with his family. Other than the few who had arrived after us, most of those already here so far were people who currently lived in Chopville. This included Liam, who had gone to Sydney to study for a few years, but who had come back to Chopville after his arts degree had failed to net him a job. Since then, he had been working in the admin building of Chopville High, and just last year, had accomplished something enormous. After some two years of effort, he was able to array an alliance of school staff and parents against the two Halls, causing them both to be fired in disgrace. Exactly what they had been fired for, I still didn't know, but Liam claimed that a lot of students and even some parents still didn't like either of them. They had both left Chopville in a hurry and hadn't been seen or heard from since.

We also came across Misty and Michelle Maivis, who had returned to Chopville in 2014, after having studied at the Victoria Police Academy in Melbourne. They had both served on the Chopville Police Force for six and a half years, and although neither of them had children, they were both happily married. Then there was Jason Pont, who unlike the rest of us, had chosen not to go to university right out of high school, but had taken a year off to work. He had since become an electrician, one of the only electricians in Chopville, and that meant that he had a good business going.

Of course, there were a couple of people who lived in Chopville who I definitely did *not* want to see today. Ather Hignat and Ugine Wilwog had gone to Melbourne in the aftermath of the war, both of them marrying the girlfriends Lucien had set them up with in late 2013. Hignat had then studied politics and joined the AIU, while Wilwog had taken a job as a security guard. Eventually, Hignat had hired Wilwog as his personal bodyguard, something he had been doing unpaid for a long time anyway, and in 2019, they had both moved to Chopville so that Hignat could run for federal office in the newly-created division of Nicholls, which included Chopville and much of the surrounding area. Sebastian, who I tended to lump in with Hignat and Wilwog in my thoughts, had not come with them. I knew of his movements due to the blog he still ran in his spare time, which was most of the time. After completing an arts degree in Melbourne, he had become a stay-at-home father, while his wife—the same one Lucien had set him up with—provided for the family. They had four kids together, but unlike Wilwog, Sebastian made it clear in his blog that they were finished reproducing.

As for Hignat and Wilwog, though, it was the move to Chopville that had brought them to our attention, as we had lost track of them for many years between, but now we knew all of this, along with the fact that Hignat had two children with his wife and Wilwog had four, with a fifth on the way. Tragically, Hignat had won the seat for the AIU; tragically because he surely didn't believe any of the policies for which he was advocating. The AIU, after losing horribly in 2010, had worked on its image, and although they were still libertarian in nature, they now had a coalition with the AVP which had been in power since 2013, combining to edge out Cornish and his government—which other than their arresting Natalie and the Woodwards, had turned out to be little worse than any prewar government had been.

The next person to arrive was Darcy, who we quickly greeted and then moved on. Darcy had drifted apart from the rest of us after his relationship with Jessica had ended in 2014. He had stayed in the area for her, choosing to study in Shepparton, but when she had turned down his marriage proposal, he had flipped his lid and blamed her for dictating his life. She refused to take responsibility for what she called 'his choice to revolve his life around me', after which Darcy had moved to Melbourne, finished his degree, and then gotten a job as a call centre operator at a bank, as he was unable to find anything better.

We drifted through the crowd, greeting people here and there, all the while waiting for the last few people to turn up whom we really wanted to see. At last, though, Harry and Katie arrived with their two daughters, the three-year old Claire and the one-year old Astrid. Not far behind them came someone we had wanted even more to see, as unlike Harry and Katie, we hadn't seen her in quite a while. Amelia's life had been really tough since being freed of the charges laid against her, much tougher than it had been for Natalie, but she had done amazingly well to keep it on track. She had finished school in Melbourne before going to Canberra, so that she could be close to her still-imprisoned father, where she had studied medicine. She was now a cardiologist at a hospital in Canberra and doing very well for herself—not just from the money she made there, but also from a book she had published a few years earlier.

The world had softened on the Woodwards in the years since the trial, and for several reasons. Part of it was surely just the passing of time, and part of it would have been sympathy for Lillian, who had led the defence of the world in the Great Sorcerous War and who had died in prison in early 2012. Then there were Amelia and Natalie, who had been let off the charges, and whom the world eventually came to realise ought not be held accountable for what had happened. Natalie had chosen to leave her magic legacy in the past, but Amelia was unable to do so, so at the request of so much of the public, she had written a book about her life as a Sorcerer, and it had been a monster best-seller all over the world.

Then there was Frederic: the world had softened a lot on him too, and all because of something that Laura had brought up during one of his individual trials, but which hadn't been brought up in the more public group trial. It had been utterly disregarded at the time as inconsequential to the things he had done with his magic, but on the morning of the final battle against Lucien, Frederic had left the base with the magic enhancer to perform magic unknown. Part of that had been the rebuilding of Chopville High, but that hadn't been all of it, or even most of it. It turned out that he had also gone all over the world, vanishing every single nuclear weapon in existence at the time. He had anticipated perfectly what the aftermath of the war might look like if magic were ended, and by doing what he did, he had prevented the world from being plunged into an even worse war in the years since. It had taken governments years to admit that this had happened, but the truth couldn't be buried forever. It was odds-on that the technology would be reinvented by some rogue nation, but so far as anyone knew, that hadn't happened yet.

"How is everything?" I asked Amelia after we had both given her a hug. She certainly looked like she was doing well; she had been a pretty and frankly sexy teenager, but she had since matured into a very attractive and stylish woman.

"Things are good," she said. "Things are really moving along with my dad. I doubt it'll happen this year, and maybe not even before the next election, but there's a lot of backing for him to be pardoned now."

"That is so awesome," I grinned at her, genuinely happy for not only her, but for Frederic too. He had lost a lot of time while in prison, and although his daughter was allowed to see him, he couldn't be with her to enjoy her successes. He was closing in on sixty years old now, so I hoped that if he were let out soon, he would be able to enjoy his final decades with her. The only thing he would still be missing out on, at least the way things stood, was grandchildren, for as far as I knew, Amelia had been single ever since she and Marc had drifted apart, and I wasn't sure if she had any intention of dating again. I even wondered if that were my fault, for in an attempt to take Amelia off my own case, I had asked May to mentally intervene to put her and Marc back together. Did that mean she would not, or perhaps could not, date anyone else? And if so, why did such dedication only go one way, for Marc had made no attempt to reach out to Amelia in the years since, and it would have been easy for him to find her if he wanted to.

The three of us moved through the park together so that Amelia could say hello to the rest of the attendees. Among them, we found, was Laura Kollerie. I wasn't sure if she had been invited, or had simply seen the ad in the paper and decided to come, but nobody really begrudged her being there. She had become good friends with quite a few of us since defending the Woodwards, and none more so than the Ponts. She and I got on okay, and the main reason why we had to was because Natalie insisted that I be nice to her after what Laura had done for her.

At around two o'clock, a loud whistle blew from somewhere near the barbecue that had been set up. Rob, Bob and Grillion appeared to be in charge of the bulk of the cooking (at least where the meat, fish and potatoes were concerned), while Mum and Marge had brought along numerous fruits and salads to dish up. It appeared that it was time to get down to some serious eating. A long row of tables had been set up and we all took our seats, trying to get close to those we wished to talk to—I ended up between Natalie and James.

Dad and Charlie stood at the head of the table together, as it had been they who had organised for this reunion to go ahead, on the ten-year anniversary of the battle against Lucien, marking the final end of the War of the Crystals. As people began to sit down, they looked up the table, and I heard Charlie saying, "I guess this is it, hey—no one else coming?"

I knew what he meant. There were some people we knew not to be coming, and some whom we hoped would come after seeing the ad in the paper, but doubted that they really would. Among the latter was Marc, who hadn't been issued an invitation because nobody knew where he was, while among the former were Lena and Jacob Underwood. Lena's decline had been a polite but distant-sounding letter, while Jacob had taken the time to call; and although I hadn't been on the receiving end of the call, Dad told me that he had sounded genuinely regretful that he was too busy to come. He still lived in London, and like Hignat, he had become a politician; and also like Hignat, it (hopefully) kept him too busy to show up.

Then there was Tommy. There was no chance at all of him showing up today. He and his folks had moved back to Sydney in January 2011, almost a year to the day since they moved from Sydney to Chopville in the first place—a move which his parents probably regretted bitterly. None of us had seen or spoken to Tommy since, but we had certainly heard about all that happened to him. In 2013, at the age of nineteen, he was arrested and charged with raping an indigenous teenage girl. He never attempted to deny the charge, instead saying that he mistook her for someone else, and then pleading insanity. I didn't have to wonder what that was likely about: The girl had probably looked a lot like Ingi, and he had instinctively thought she could handle whatever he did to her. Tommy had then been institutionalised for a couple of years, and then let out again for reasons unknown—perhaps they thought he had recovered. He hadn't, of course, and in 2017, he was found dead of a drug overdose after having been on the streets for two years. The fate that had befallen Tommy was a tragedy in every sense of the word.

Just as I was thinking these gloomy thoughts, though, a loud horn sounded from the direction of Main Street, and what appeared to be an armoured truck came into view through the entrance. It wasn't there long, but before it drove off, a man in military uniform jumped out of the passenger's seat and came striding through the entrance towards us. I swapped a grin with Natalie as we all got to our feet and prepared to salute.

"Ladies, gentlemen," he boomed when he was within earshot.

"You're very late, Captain Maivis," Harry called. "Is that the kind of tardiness they teach you guys at ADFA?"

"Hey, go easy on Simon," Peter shot back. "He was probably just getting ready. It must take a lot of time and effort to shampoo and condition one's own back hair."

"Bite me, Playman," Simon grinned, joining his brother. "You know, he may be insulting both of us there, old chap."

"You may be right, old chap," Harry agreed. "We may have to teach him a lesson; Maivis style, I'm thinking. Tell me, what's the temperature of the Jade River like at this time of year?"

Those of us near enough to hear this exchange laughed as we got down to our lunches. Simon had become interested in the military shortly after moving to Echuca, and his grandparents' steadfast opposition to the idea probably only made him even more enthusiastic. He had joined the Royal Australian Air Force straight out of high school and gone to study at the Australian Defence Force Academy in Canberra, studying information technology and specialising in automation and robotics. He was now based in the Northern Territory where he was involved in top-secret projects, and just last year, he had been promoted to the rank of Captain. He was unmarried and seemed to go through a new woman every few months or so, but he had chosen not to bring anyone with him today.

The atmosphere around the table was very cheerful, because this was a celebration. We were celebrating now for the same reason that Dad and Charlie had chosen the new building in the war memorial to be bright and cheerful rather than dull and solemn. It wasn't about forgetting the trials of the past, nor was it about taking the sacrifices of those who had died in the war for granted. It was about appreciating all that had been done to get here, for the victory against the Hammersons would be pointless if we weren't allowed to enjoy it.

Epilogue

It was no more than a few years later that subtle signs of magic began to reappear in the world....

The Magic Crystals Series

Book 1 - The Seventh Sorcerer
Book 2 - Rock Haulter
Book 3 - Hunt and Power
Book 4 - Corridors
Book 5 - The Cloak of Steel
Book 6 - On the String
Book 7 - Antimagic

www.TheMagicCrystals.com